THE SPIRIT OF...

A NOVEL

BRYAN CARON

phoenix
Design & Publishing

PUBLISHING.PHOENIXMOIRAI.COM

The Spirit Of...
1st Edition
Published by Phoenix Moirai
©2016 Phoenix Moirai
publishing.phoenixmoirai.com

Text Copyright ©2016 Bryan Caron

Original Cover Art
Designed by Bryan Caron
©2016 Bryan Caron

The creation of this book has been ten years in the making.

Thank you to my family (especially my mom and dad) who have supported me throughout the years in all of my creative endeavors and helping them to become a reality.

I also want to thank Fr. Isaiah Mary Molano, Kristen Aiello and Andrea Allen for beta reading this book, keeping my writing honest and giving me the feedback necessary to make *The Spirit Of…* what it is today.

And to God — the truth, the inspiration and the gracious hands that help guide us all through life.

Amen Dello Keli.

Previous
Publications

Year of the Songbird

Jaxxa Rakala: The Search

In the Light of the Eclipse

Memoirs of Keladrayia: Jaxxa Rakala

Short Stories
(published on chaosbreedschaos.com)

A Story With No Beginning

The Traveler and His Guide

I Whisper

Films

My Necklace, Myself

12

Secrets of the Desert Nymph

When all perception is stripped away, all that's left is the madness of truth; it is whether one accepts the truth that reveals the pure beauty of one's soul.

The light of the heart can only be found by embracing the darkest depths of the mind.

THE SPIRIT OF...

PROLOGUE

The water pressed against my face. Soft and smooth, it caressed my cheek like my mother's hand used to do when I fell off my bike and scraped my knee, or when my Shih Tzu puppy, Cuddles (named after her mother, from what I was told, by the strange guy behind the desk of the shelter with all the marks on his arms) was hit by a car. I didn't see it happen, but the image of Cuddles running out into the street, scared to death — frozen — as the tires squealed across the blacktop, burned itself into my mind for weeks after my mother told me. I pretended to be him; I felt the fear and the lack of strength, the dry bumper shoving me under the weight of that thousand pound Chevrolet. (It was always a Chevrolet; that's what my mom drove and that's all I knew.) But every time I cried to mourn the death of Cuddles, my mother brought me to her lap, held me tight against her chest and sang me my favorite song. She sang to me as I fell asleep for as long as I can remember and then some. From the moment I

was first brought home, that song was a part of my life. And as she sang, she would caress my cheek.

I was her little kitty.

The song was so clear; my mother's voice rippled through the water that no longer felt like water. I knew I was sinking deeper and deeper, but no — I was flying. I was being protected. But by whom? In my life there have only been two people that I've ever felt safe with. My mother, of course, who up until a week ago, I hadn't seen in three years; and my father, who wasn't around as much as I would've liked, but was honest and faithful. Whenever he promised he'd help me with something — anything — I knew he'd follow through on that promise. He never lied to me, though, occasionally, I lied to him. It never sat right with me, and more often than not, the guilt would push me to fess up. They were the only two I let into my heart — until now.

My father was above me. My mother was above me. My life was above me. But all I could feel was the grace of the water's love. My mother's arms, my father's trust — none of it compared to the freedom the water gave me. Soothing, soft, calming — no thoughts clouded my mind from the tranquility. I was drugged; I was dead;

I was kissed —

BOOK ONE
DISCOVERY

Connecticut – Friday, 3:16 pm

Kaleena rode her bike past the registrar's building heading toward the science labs. If she didn't speed things up, she'd be late, but she knew better than to ride faster than she was already. Campus police were brutal about giving out speeding tickets to kids that blasted their way through the school. She didn't understand it, either. "If you're in that much of a hurry, you might as well just not go," she'd always tell her friends. "Besides. That's what I love about college. No one cares if you're late for class."

As she locked her bike into the rack outside the science building, "Who Are You" started playing from her pocket, cleverly signifying an unknown caller. Even though she never answered calls from unknown numbers — not after having been harassed for years by doctors, pathologists and would-be writers who all wanted to use her to make themselves famous — she pulled the old iPhone 4 from her

pocket out of habit. She hit ignore, knowing full well if they left a message she'd have a record of it in the off-chance she ever had to prove to the authorities that some psycho stalker (like the young drug addict whose message led police to confiscate eight kilos of heroin from his teenage whore house) should be in prison.

A message was left. But it wasn't from who she expected. She dialed the number back as she headed up the stairs into the building.

"Hey, it's me," Kaleena hummed into the receiver. "Where are you calling from?"

Kyla, whom Kaleena would claim as her only friend, said, "Got a new phone, bitch."

"What happened this time?"

"Long story. Tell you later." Kyla giggled a little. "Look, where you at right now, girl?"

Kaleena rolled her eyes. Kyla always had a knack for trying to sound hip.

"I'm late for class," Kaleena responded quickly as she yanked open the door. She only had two flights of stairs to tackle before heading down two hallways to get to class. The conversation would have to be short.

"Where's your dad these days?"

Asking about her father always meant Kyla had something up her sleeve. It being Friday, it most likely meant: party.

"Bermuda."

"Hot new fling?"

Annoyance was starting to get the best of Kaleena. "He's trying to find some artifact that'll lead him to another dead end of whatever wild theory he's addicted to this week or some shit. Why?"

"I have a favor to ask."

Why didn't Kaleena feel good about this? "What?" she asked sternly. Her class was just a few doors away.

"You've got the most rockin' apartment, Kal," Kyla said. Kaleena could see the gleeful sparkle in her friend's eyes.

"No." Kaleena stopped outside the door. Her hand stayed glued to the handle as she rushed to finish the conversation.

"Come on, why not?"

"I don't need a bunch of drunk high school kids trashing my apartment."

"But I've got some of the hottest hound dogs hooked up for a party tonight."

"I don't care. Find some other place to have it."

"Kaleena —!"

"I'm late." Kaleena pressed the "End" button and switched the phone to vibrate before entering the room. There were only a little over a dozen students in the class, every one of whom looked at her with a slight pierce of resentment. She ignored them all as if she had just walked into a lecture hall with five-hundred students, where anyone could — and usually did — go unnoticed, and took her usual seat near the far back corner.

The professor had been rattling on about something as he scratched his thoughts onto the chalkboard. When he finished, he turned to the class and set his sights directly on Kaleena.

So much for going unnoticed.

"Miss Stevens," he said, putting her on the spot as punishment for her tardiness. "Could you please reiterate the importance of relativity?"

Kaleena examined the board for a moment, confused as to why he would ask such a basic question, then realized it was because the test they took last week proved to Kaleena what she already knew — the majority of the class was on the verge of failure. This would not do well for her already insufferable reputation. "The theory of relativity states," she started, her eyes averted downward, "that an object begins to travel at a rate faster than another object the way in which objects outside of the moving object appear to be moving faster than the moving object. It's important to understand, though, that when an object is moving fast enough, it doesn't appear to moving at all to the object, but to a viewer outside of the object, standing still, would see the object moving at great speeds." Kaleena scanned the group to emphasize her last thought. "The point

is, not all things are true to the eye and what one person sees is not always what another person sees."

The professor quickly shot back, "Nice try. But you didn't answer my question."

"I did too."

"No. I asked for the importance. You gave me a theory."

Kaleena drew in a breath to contain her scorn, then fired off a tirade with heightened flair. "Fine. Let me give you an example. You, Professor, just assumed that I didn't answer the question you posed to me. I, myself, feel I answered the question very thoroughly and with great complexity. That is the point of relativity. We see the answer to your question very differently, and though most of the students in this room would agree with you, that may have more to do with their resentment for me, rather than an actual understanding of what I just said. They hate me because I'm so young. You are against me because I was late. Of course, to each his own, and each one of these people in here might see things quite different than I do. But most average people follow the crowd, the trends. It's in our nature to do so, you know, to keep from standing out. But because I do stand out, I can't just follow along like a lamb to the slaughter. Because of the nature for which these fine, smart adults in this room grew up, they all agree with you, for no other reason than that. I don't, because my view is different than all of the people in this room, which is going to be different than your own. To that end, each person sees this situation a little bit different as well, depending on his or her age, class, race or gender. And though I'm not a moving object, the entire situation is relative to the upbringing to which each individual was accustomed. That, Professor, is the importance of relativity. Every single person on this planet sees everything in a different way. But because we don't want to feel different or out of place, we ignore that in favor of becoming one giant perspective."

For the next twenty seconds (which felt more like an hour in the dead silence), Kaleena stared at the professor. When he finally cracked a smile and chuckled, Kaleena realized he was toying with her.

"Does anyone agree with Miss Stevens's assessment?"

No one raised their hand. They all instead chose to shift in their seats with uneasiness.

"And does anyone agree with my assessment," the professor continued, "that our fourteen-year-old genius is full of shit?"

"Professor —" Kaleena blurted out, rising to her feet. The professor raised his hand to stop her objection. With no more than the gleam in his eye, she could tell he was simply trying to sell his point. As Kaleena sheepishly sat back down, every student raised their hand.

"And because of that," he said with a slight wink to his voice, "it turns out Kaleena is absolutely correct."

Kaleena fought a smile as the professor continued his lecture. The antipathy bore into her, but her pride kept her from absorbing any of it.

Bermuda – Friday, 6:18 pm

Having lost all sense of time, Matthew Stevens, in his rustic, Indiana Jones fedora, dusted the dirt from the small bone-like artifact that had recently been uncovered about ten feet underground. How Matthew had found it could be classified as a miracle. He normally stopped digging after about five feet, but something inside him urged him to continue. For the last ten hours, he'd been down in that hole. Food had been scarce and his canteen was almost dry, but his concentration never waned, as if this artifact meant more than anything he'd ever discovered — even if he still had yet to figure out what it was.

Lifting the small, soft brush, Matthew spent the next eight minutes watching it as if it would move. It was curved like a bowl, though the material was far from clay. To the touch, it felt smooth, like wet metal. The fading sunlight gleaned against the curvature, giving it a brilliant spark. The closest thing he could relate it to was the shimmer of candlelight in his ex-wife's eyes on the night of their honeymoon; beautiful and gentle — those faded blues melted his instincts.

"You gonna sit there all day?"

Matthew looked up, unaware. Henry Green, Matthew's very conservative, quiet associate, hovered over him. They'd met a few years earlier during the freshman arrival banquet at Yale, where Matthew worked as a professor of Archaeology. Henry was an eager young kid with hair past his shoulders and a skull hanging from his ear, yet despite his appearance, Matthew embraced Henry's keen interest in the thesis he'd done as a graduate student at the University of Cambridge, which soon after publication was lambasted throughout the archaeological community as pure blasphemy.

To know a Pharaoh was to know a witch, Matthew had written. *The Pharaoh was not only rich, with idols of gold laced upon their walls, but very fluent in the art of witchcraft. Stories are told in the Bible of men parting seas and changing water into wine. Though these attributes were linked to the God of Abraham's almighty power, there is concrete evidence that these 'Acts of God' are in fact acts produced by the sorcery of the Pharaoh, who, upon death, would use this power to haunt the realms for which they slept. Disturbing their realm, though it makes the soul angry, does not cause the supernatural to occur. It goes much deeper than the act of entry, and in fact draws its power from the mind of the man that enters the realm. The 'curse' left behind by a Pharaoh was not one of disdain or hatred or pain or evil. It is an attribute to the heart of a man and the purity for which that man enters the realm of the sleeping God.*

"You know my work," Matthew said, shaking Henry's hand tightly.

"Do you thrive on the controversy, Professor?" Henry said in a slow, quiet tone, not sure what Matthew's reaction would be. It wasn't the first time someone had approached Matthew with that exact statement.

"Would you forgo expressing your thoughts and opinions solely because there might be a good chance someone would disagree with you?"

"Disagreement is one thing, sir," Henry said. "But the reaction you got…"

Matthew smiled. "What is life without argument? Without a healthy breath of debate? If there's any one thing you take away from your time here at Harvard, let it be that pursuing the road less traveled is usually the road worth risking your

life for. Or in the case of your studies, your career. In the case of your love life; your heart."

"A sheep is always slaughtered," Henry said in return. "The hungry survive past the attack."

Matthew winked before turning his attention to others who, like him, had also been forced to come to this tired affair.

Henry pulled lightly on Matthew's arm. "Professor, wait." Matthew looked back to him, partially annoyed, but attentive nonetheless. For a moment, Henry had lost his thought, which seemed to annoy Matthew even further.

"Did you need something else?" Matthew asked.

"I just wanted to say that, unlike most other sheep, I thought your piece was extraordinary." (Matthew was intrigued now.) "Your distinction of Pharaohs and Egyptian kings being the true gods written about in the Bible was a masterful theory. It answered a lot of questions I've had about the discrepancy between what was written as religion and what was known as fact."

"The piece was not about the connection between history and the Bible," Matthew corrected. "It was about the power that the Pharaohs possessed."

"Yes, I know." The kid seemed to feel a little awkward, as if he'd offended Matthew on a deeper level. "I didn't mean to insult you."

"No insult taken. I'm just curious about why you would read it that way."

Henry took a breath (*of relief?*) before beginning his explanation.

"Well, you continually refer to the Pharaohs as gods, and continually refer back to Biblical events. I've read the paper a couple dozen times, Professor, and I must say that a lot of your theories and expeditions into the pyramids seemed to have led you to the conclusions of discovery rather than need. So I read some passages in the Bible that refer to the acts of God and what He believed to be the act of true love and that of which was an act of genuine shame. The similarities to your belief that Pharaohs only curse or harm those that enter with greed and leave those that enter with purity of heart alone links the Pharaohs to how God felt about those He created. Eve betrayed him in favor of greed and because of

that, was cursed with the knowledge of shame and pushed from a world of purity."

Matthew wasn't sure why Henry stopped, but he was eager to know more. "Go on."

Henry smiled. It was the first time his listener wasn't bordering on slumber.

"Okay, well, with that in mind, I researched a few historical documents of that period and linked them back to several different figures of the Bible. I then created a small timeline between the events of the Bible and that of history and came to the conclusion that the Bible, though starting from the beginning, doesn't actually start from the true beginning of the world, but with the first hieroglyphs found on tablets in southern Egypt and Israel. It seems some of those writings tell of a story for which men and their families were sent to the desert to die after stealing fruit and grains from sacred properties. Most of these men were poor, but the main focus was of a man named Adamus, who was banished with his wife Evestylyn. They were rich by the standards of the time, but were without the sacred fruit for which they stole because they felt they were entitled to it."

One of the most celebrated journeys Matthew had taken after becoming a professor was when he spent a year in Egypt researching the pyramids and writing about their connection to supernatural occurrences and rumors, and not once had he ever considered such a hypothesis. "And you have accurate, historical documents that prove this theory?" Matthew said.

"I do."

Matthew remained skeptical, but sensed a real passion from the young boy. He nodded.

"I've spent three years on this, Professor. I even wrote a paper on it my senior year for a course I took at the local CC. I'd love for you to read it."

"I'd like that very much..." Matthew paused, his hand extended.

"Henry, sir. Henry Green." Henry took his hand.

"Henry," Matthew repeated back, burning the name into his mind. "Drop by my office on Monday and we'll take a look at it together."

"Yes, sir," Henry said, his excitement pouring through his handshake.

"Please. Professor will do just fine."

"Of course," Henry said. He wouldn't let go of Matthew's hand.

"I better get to hobnobbing a bit," Matthew finally said, urging Henry to let go with a slight blush of embarrassment. Matthew smiled, a little dismayed about having to do his professorial duty. He had to inch away from the banquet in order to jet off to an upcoming expedition, but Henry's theory had infected his mind. When he returned, he kept his promise of reading Henry's paper, even going as far as to say it had the potential for publication. He spent the next couple of months helping Henry hone the writing and added support to a few of his weaker theories. Henry couldn't have been more excited when it did get published in a small magazine that would go defunct a year later. But it was published nonetheless, which was a great accomplishment for any undergraduate student. It only took a year of one-to-one lectures during off hours (and occasionally over a home-cooked dinner) for Matthew to assign Henry a spot on his team. And looking up at him now, from ten feet within the earth, Matthew could still see that eager young kid — a little wiser, a little stronger, yet just as determined — who would abandon his family for the rest of his life if it meant proving something he believed in. It would never come to that, of course.

Matthew stretched his shoulders. "Just a few more minutes, Henry."

"Professor. You haven't eaten in twenty-six hours. We're all going to the festival. Join us."

"No, you guys go. I'm gonna go a little deeper."

"It's almost dark, Professor. We can finish this in the morning."

Matthew just wanted to be left alone with the earth and history surrounding him. It engulfed his mind and kept him at peace. But Henry was just as stubborn; it's probably why he liked him so much. He knew Henry wouldn't give up until he agreed to go. "You're divorced, not dead," Henry would always say when he tried to get Matthew to clear his mind. "You have to dust off that second head of yours every once in a while or else you're liable to get Alzheimer's." It was a bit vulgar to be sure, but he knew that's exactly what Henry was thinking at that very moment.

"Come on, Matthew." It was Lauren Mead, Matthew's best friend since that first expedition to Egypt. Her shape was that of a petite statue, towering over him like a guardian angel, her greasy blonde hair glowing against the orange sun. He couldn't see any of her features, though he could see those dirty brown eyes drilling into his with gentle amour. "You need to have a little fun."

Matthew thought a moment, looking over the artifact. Its brilliance had faded with the setting sun. Maybe he did need to get away for a couple of hours — clear his head. And not the one Henry was thinking about.

He nodded acceptance. "All right. But tomorrow morning, we dig until this thing is completely uncovered."

"Yes, sir," Henry said with a wink. He smiled at Lauren, hoping she'd catch the small glint in his eye. She just walked away.

Matthew sat for another few seconds studying the artifact before finally climbing the ladder to the surface and restraining Henry from ogling Lauren's tight, beautiful ass.

Connecticut – Friday, 4:19 pm

The class seemed to take forever. Five minutes after schooling everyone on relativity, Kaleena felt everyone's eyes boring into her skull. She refrained from looking away from the board or her notebook, knowing full well if she caught someone else's gaze, she'd absorb the hatred these adults held toward her natural abilities. That is if you could call them "adults". She once wrote in a sixth grade paper that:

Adults are humans who have reached a certain maturity. They understand the concept of accountability and will refrain from anything that would jeopardize that responsibility. In other words, grown-ups that are lazy, inconsiderate, jealous, and or greedy, are not adults, but oversized children that have yet to understand that they need to open their eyes to themselves and accept accountability.

Even though they were, on average, eight years older than her, Kaleena knew she was far more adult than anyone in the class. As far as she could tell, their immature disgust stemmed from jealousy. But what was there to be jealous about? Just because she had an innate ability to learn quickly and grasp higher levels of knowledge didn't mean she was smart enough to navigate life, or communicate well with others. She was a freak that way, and the guilt over being gifted with these natural abilities ate at her enough without having everyone else in the world picking at the leftovers.

When the clock finally hit 4:20, the children gathered up their belongings, even though the professor was still mid-sentence.

Inconsiderate mindless sheep, she thought.

Kaleena continued to take notes she'd probably never look at again until the professor finally stopped lecturing, giving in to the demand of his classroom — an act Kaleena felt was extremely lazy on his part. It was his classroom; make them stay.

Mob rules.

Keeping her mouth shut was hard, trading her verbal animosity for a low growl that no one heard, or cared to hear. She refused to stand until the last student had left the room. The professor, diligently wiping the board clean as she made her way to the door, caught sight of her in the corner of his eye.

"Kaleena."

She looked directly into his comfortable hazel eyes. There was something about him that made her heart beat a little faster whenever she was alone with him. Perhaps it was the odd hand-made sweaters and khaki slacks he wore year-round. Regardless, she knew it wasn't love; that would constitute a reciprocal attraction that was impossible on his part. He was nearly twenty years older than her (as far as she could tell; he could have been older, what with the silver trim lining his ears) and married… with children. She may never have known that fact had she not had dinner with him to discuss a theory she abandoned recently, feeling it was just too complicated to prove. But she could tell they were his life, despite never talking about them as if they were all Pulitzer prize

winners, like most doting parents. "Yeah?" she said, making sure she hid her child-like attraction.

"I'm sorry for putting you on the spot."

"No big deal," she lied.

"I knew you'd have the right answer. You always do." Kaleena could tell he was trying to defend himself, even though she didn't really need it — or want it. "I realize it can be a grind trying to fit in with people this much older than you."

Why does everyone always think they know how you feel? she thought. *No one will ever know how anyone else feels. Unless they're psychic, which is utterly absurd.* "I manage," was all she was willing to say aloud.

"Hang in there. Half of these kids won't make it out of their mom's house. You're much more than that. Believe me, you're on the road to great things."

Kaleena smiled and nodded to make the professor feel as if she were listening. Did he really think she'd never heard this speech before? Even her pediatrician had given her this speech; she didn't need to hear it again from him. She indulged him just the same.

"Thanks. I'll be okay."

The professor smiled his cute, dimpled smile. "I'll see you tomorrow."

Kaleena nodded, gifted him with a half-smile of her own and turned back to the door. She could feel him watching her —

Lusting over her?

— and felt oddly uncomfortable, causing her to rush out faster than she should have. As she rounded the corner into the hall, she tripped and fell to the ground. Those walking the halls to get to their classes made sure she became the center of attention. Some of them laughed in snickered bursts, others recorded her embarrassment on their damn iPhones that sucked up the majority of their pathetic lives. She would soon become the flavor of the week on the Internet, and there was nothing she wanted more than to be able to cloak herself and disappear from the world at large.

She did her best to ignore the grade-school ridicule as she trotted outside, where

she was able to talk herself into feeling better. So what if she had a million .gifs scouring the web with some fancy YouTube mashups that had her crash and burn to the tune of a couple million hits. The world was a fickle community and her humiliation would quickly collect pixel dust. But why did they have to laugh at her?

Immature children.

Then she got to the bike rack and her skin turned flame red.

"GODDAMN IT!"

Kaleena screamed so loud, there was a small echo in the open wind. People stared at her in confusion and fright. She looked back at them, grinding her teeth over the destruction she had just encountered. Her bike — her only mode of transportation — had been stripped. And not just a few parts here and there. Except for the front tire and the frame, the whole thing had been pilfered. To top it all off, an envelope with the word "Freak" written in bold, blood-red letters was taped to the frame. Tears clouded her eyes as she opened it. Inside was a piece of paper and what appeared to be a chunk of her leather seat, which she let fall to the ground in order to open the tri-folded letter.

Enjoy the walk home, preemie.

Kaleena carefully studied the words for what had to be minutes. Was it a threat or harmless jealously? She wondered if the jackass had stuck around to get a good laugh at her when she saw the vandalism. Everyone seemed to be ignoring her, though, cluelessly walking to their next class, their next lab, their next make-out session. No one was even remotely interested in her or her dilemma. Then she saw him (or her — Kaleena couldn't be sure) standing near a tree about a hundred yards away. All she could make out were maybe half of "its" features. The eyes squinted in the sunlight and the mouth sat sterile under a shaded nose. A prominent cheekbone glinted above a slightly thinner than normal frame and wispy shoulder-length hair. For a moment, it appeared Alan Cushing had just stepped off the Death Star for a breath of fresh air. Kaleena felt almost lost in the stature and mystery of the unknown watcher.

Suddenly, someone slid up to the bike rack with a small squeak of cold brakes on hot tires. In the brief moment Kaleena took to avoid being run over, the watcher disappeared, and no amount of scanning the grounds would help her catch sight of him again.

"Wow. Sucks to be you," the speedster blurted out.

Kaleena pierced him with annoyed anger. "Fuck off."

The kid, who couldn't have been more than eighteen going on fifteen, ran away like the little mouse he was destined to remain. Kaleena kept her eyes on him with a hint of guilt. It wasn't his fault. She had no right to take her animosity out on him. Too late to apologize now.

Returning to her dilemma after one last check for the mysterious watcher, Kaleena tossed the note away and rubbed her mouth tightly. Without her bike, she had a long three-mile trek back home. It would be dark before she got there, which was not something she wanted to think about. But what else could she do? The only person she could call for a ride was Kyla, and even if she wasn't already at the mall hunting for her next fuck buddy, her license had been suspended a month back, so the point was already moot.

For the first time in a long time, Kaleena truly felt alone.

She shook the feeling off and headed for the security building, figuring she'd at least try to hitch a ride from one of the rent-a-cops before making her way home. At the very least, she could report the heinous crime.

Bermuda – Friday, 9:32 pm

"Come on, Matthew," Henry said, already a little drunk. The heavy aroma of alcohol floated past Matthew, whose own drink grew warmer as it sat against his palm. He didn't want it but Henry had insisted. "Are you gonna have fun or just sit there like an ass on a canyon?" Henry's bottom lip curled out into a contorted frown, exposing the tip of the blister forming on the inside of his gums.

Matthew cracked a feigned smile and turned away without an answer. He

set his eyes on Lauren, who'd been sitting next to him since they arrived at the outdoor bar that was a bit too crowded for Matthew's taste. "I thought you'd be more excited," Matthew said, continuing the discussion they had been having before Henry interrupted.

"I am," Lauren said, more defensive than she needed to be. "Believe me, if this is what you think it is, I am overly excited. But I'm not about to get my hopes up again. We've been down this road so many times already and every time…" Lauren took a swig from some Caribbean drink Matthew had never heard of before, but knew was a virgin. Lauren had sworn off alcohol a few years ago after being hospitalized for alcohol poisoning, which led to a broken kneecap after falling over the balcony of her second story apartment. She spent three months in the hospital and another six in rehab to regain strength in her reconstructed knee. *If I ever see a beer again I'll puke*, was what she told Matthew just days after the accident. He spent a lot of time watching over her since then — a little out of a respectful love toward her, but mostly because of his need to forget.

"Not every time," Matthew said. "You remember southern Florida."

Lauren looked away, sucking her lower lip. "We got lucky."

"Florida?" It turns out Henry was still sitting on the other side of Matthew. "What are you talking about?"

"I never told you about Florida?"

Henry shook his head as he took a drink from his vodka martini. His eyes stayed fixed on Lauren.

Matthew collected his thoughts. He could swear to God that he had told everyone this story — especially those that worked with him. It could very well be alcoholic amnesia. "A few years ago, about a year before I met you, in fact, we'd found some evidence that led us down to Florida near the Keys. During our dig, we started running into some money problems."

"We were spending money out of pocket," Lauren interjected, smiling slightly as a fresh drink came to her.

"On him, ma'am," the bartender said, pointing at Henry.

"No, thank you," she told the bartender quietly. "I'll pay myself." She peered back to Henry, who gave her a slight wink in recognition.

"That's not true," Matthew said.

"It was, too. You barely had enough on your credit card to pay for that last meal."

"Suffice it to say," Matthew said through a cracked smile, "the team decided —"

"You decided," Lauren cut in again. "Get the story straight." She took a sip from her drink. She tasted a slight hint of alcohol but thought maybe it was just her mind playing tricks. The thought passed quickly.

"*I* decided," Matthew continued, making Lauren happy, "that we should get as much work done before we ate anything. I knew something was there; I could feel it. If we could just find it, we'd have enough to take back to the college to continue the expedition. So we spent the next twelve hours working our fingers to the bare minimum with nothing but a canteen of water between the four of us. As the sun started to set, Lauren finally found it." Matthew turned to her, thinking she might want to pick up the story from there.

"Go on," she conceded, the small straw pinched between her fingers and her lips.

He nodded graciously. "It was this small piece of wood no bigger than your index finger. At first we weren't sure what to make of it. Then we found a tiny inscription written in a language that we'd never seen before. It turned out to be a slight mix of Aramaic and Latin. Carbon dating placed the wood back at least three thousand years. I swear it could have been older."

"What did it say?" Henry asked out of feigned curiosity.

"To the day of spring comes waves of darkness," Lauren said, almost as a sweet song.

"What the hell does that mean?"

"That's what I wondered," Matthew continued. "My guess? It was a warning of some kind. A prophesy, if you will."

"I thought it was a poem," Lauren quickly added.

"So what happened?" Henry finished his drink.

"We took it to the financier of the Palace and he agreed we might be onto something," Lauren said. "They gave us funding for three more years."

"Exactly. And here we are on the brink of a new discovery and all you guys seem to want to do is sit around and talk about it."

"I'm not," Henry said. He walked to Lauren and held out his hand like a would-be gentleman. "Would you care for a dance, me'lady?"

Lauren's eyes lit-up like a little schoolgirl getting asked to a party by her second grade crush. She finished her drink and gently took his hand. They skipped out into the crowd to join the other members of their team: Kara Reisen, a professor in anthropological linguistics at Brown University, and Thomas Demeut, a freelance archaeologist who was being financed by a highly religious curator at Topkapi Palace looking to co-mingle the Islamic holy relics with Biblical artifacts. Though they were both pushing forty (and showing it), the two of them had been dancing all night like a couple of teenagers at their first homecoming.

But Matthew kept his attention on Lauren. He hadn't seen her quite like this since the accident and was glad she was having fun again. There was a time when he thought she would never find it again. The four of them danced a few numbers together: one fast and pretty comical, as Lauren tried to turn on some old dance moves that went out with disco; another one slow and a bit disheartening. He could only watch the two of them hold one another for so long. Eventually, the sight of their bodies flowing across the ground together as if it were the music itself dancing became too much and Matthew had to leave. He had no need to stay. Everyone was having fun, as they should, but the only fun he knew he would have would be finding the treasure he so longed to get his hands on. For the past three years, work had become his own guilty mistress and he needed to return to her before his mind burst.

He dropped a hundred-dollar bill on the bar. "That's for everyone," he said. "Keep the change."

Connecticut – Friday, 6:45 pm

It was a quarter to seven when Kaleena was close enough to hear the music oozing through the night air. She'd spent almost an hour with college security, giving them her statement, the description of the bike and the whereabouts of the crime. And it wasn't just one; she told probably six security guards (which was actually only four, but it felt like six) the exact same thing. It got so mind-numbing, she actually asked why they couldn't have waited for all of them to be there before telling her tale.

Around five-thirty, they finally said she could go. It was nearing sunset, so she tried to talk one of them into giving her a ride home. The only excuse she got in return — they were all too busy.

"Too busy?" she said, muffling the scream she so desperately wanted to let loose, choosing to keep her composure instead. "Doing what? Jacking off?" That didn't sit well with them. The lead guard, a larger, portlier man with a bit of a stubble, asked her politely to leave. When she wouldn't, the smaller, skinnier guard who looked as if he'd just stepped out of the eighth grade, took her by the arm.

"This is physical abuse," she cried as she was pulled toward the door. "I will see to it you all lose your jobs." The threat was baseless, as she could very well have taken that skinny ass down without any effort. Before she knew it, Kaleena was outside, the cold sun fading behind her with no way of getting home except her own two feet.

It was a three-mile walk back to her apartment where she lived (some days) with her father. Part of the road she had to take was covered in a thick brush of oaks. It was a great tranquil spot to travel through during the day, but she absolutely loathed having to walk through them at night, and not because of the visual Poltergeist had imprinted on her mind —

Damn you, Spielberg!

A few years ago, Kaleena had been at a friend's house when her dad was on an expedition in Morocco. They thought spending a couple of weeks together

(sisters to the end) would be awesome, but after a week, they had a major falling out, mostly due to her friend's immature boyfriend. Her friend's parents had been away on a business trip so the only way out of her self-inflicted predicament was to walk home.

The only light she had was the moon, and the soft cloud cover above faded even that. She was only about halfway there when she heard soft howls in the distance. *Wolves*, she kept thinking, somehow believing it would make her feel safer. The louder they got, the faster she went, praying they wouldn't smell her fear.

She was relieved when she could finally see the lights on the outskirts of the city. The smell of chicken from the KFC helped ease her heart rate even though it also turned her stomach. It was once one of her favorite places to go. She would always get the chicken strips and a biscuit; her dad would usually order a three-piece meal with coleslaw and a corncob. One night, she asked if she could taste the coleslaw. The smell was never that enticing, but Matthew had always urged her to try new things, so she went for it. Once the coleslaw touched her tongue, she couldn't help but regurgitate the chicken she'd already eaten. Matthew laughed as one of the other three customers ran for the bathroom. It had to have been Kaleena's most embarrassing moment — fused to her personality forever — and she wouldn't ever step inside that KFC again.

A howl made her freeze for a moment and look around. Somehow, she felt the animal closing in on her. She had to hurry. The moon had now been washed completely from the sky, but she was smart enough to use the town lights as her guide. As she swiftly traversed the brush, another howl (this one even closer) led her to wonder if anyone would miss her if she were to suddenly run directly into the mouth of the wolf. Her father would eventually, as he usually called every night to check up on her — unless, of course, he got into an artifact and lost track of time. But was that all?

The closer she got to the town border, the quicker her pace became. The growing buildings — the assurance of protection — became her motivation. Another howl; every step pushed her faster. Her heart pounded; her breath was

non-existent. She burst through the door of the nearest building, a mom & pop ice-cream shop that was about ready to close. It felt as if the door was against her as she tried to push it closed. When it finally gave way to her strength, Kaleena held it shut with her back, finally able to take a breath.

"Are you all right?" the elderly woman asked from behind the counter.

Kaleena had to catch her breath. She held her head against the cool glass of the door until she no longer felt like throwing up.

"Excuse me?" The elderly woman had gotten closer to Kaleena. Her eyes were warm and friendly. Kaleena smiled, but that didn't last long. Tears rolled from her eyes. She tried her best to hold them back, to show strength in the shadow of adversity, but they fell — and she fell, her body succumbed to the weight of her fear.

The woman, with her thick, round eyeglasses dangling from her neck by a small chain, reached out to Kaleena. "Honey?"

Kaleena kept her eyes away, hoping the woman would leave her alone. She didn't want to be comforted; she wanted her mother. She was the only one who could protect her right now. No one else.

"Is there anyone I can call, dear?" the woman asked.

The child never answered. Her tears continued in short bursts for a half hour. Every time she thought she was bringing them under control, Kaleena felt the wolf driving her, the absence of help from her mother (and to a lesser extent, her father) and the lack of strength she would have after her escape, and the tears returned in force. She couldn't talk, she couldn't breathe, and all the while the elderly store owner sat with her, waiting for her to finally open up.

Ever since that night, Kaleena forbade herself from walking through those woods at night. And now, because a couple of lazy security guards (*Yeah, that's what they are*, she thought. *Real secure.*) forced her to break that vow. The fear hit her like a knife to the scrotum as she pondered whether she should even try. It took several minutes to muster up the courage. This was the only way home; she had to take it. Her pace would be swift, her mind on things other than the sounds of the night.

The first step was slow and labored, but the longer she walked, the better she felt. She hoped the wolves she remembered so vividly had been vanquished, but their cries were undeniable. They were softer than she remembered. Were they farther off than before, or had her fear heightened her level of perception? The thought —

The logic! —

made her more comfortable. That is until another series of howls erupted eerily close-by. Her heart fluttered as her legs froze solid. She looked around the woods for the predator with just her eyes. Every shift flushed her mind with a deeper sense of disassociation. Was she imagining things? Was she so afraid, so childish, that she couldn't distinguish between her mind's eye and what was truly real?

You fucking pussy. Get the fuck out of your head and get moving. Kaleena felt the strength return to her legs and moved quickly down the path. Whether it was her imagination or not, she didn't really want to find out. It was a little past six when she came to the conclusion it had been her imagination all along and that she'd let her fear get the best of her. She was more than halfway home now and slowed her pace, succumbing to her body's need to rest.

The rustling came like a bolt of lightning to her gut. Her stomach turned as she looked to see where the noise had come from. Once again, her feet had turned to stone in the wake of petrifying fear. She couldn't see anything but the trees, which absorbed the bright moonlight and excreted a ray of shadow that made them all seem ominously like several hundred strangers haunting her — stalking her every move. Kaleena's instincts said run, but the magnitude of the crackling in the trees locked her down tight. The wolves had gone silent (or at least Kaleena was no longer paying attention to them) as she focused on what she could swear was something — someone — watching her. It was hard to make out, but a dark shadow seemed to be floating against the brush, hollowed out by the shape of the trees. Two small bright green lights, which Kaleena assumed to be a pair of eyes even though she couldn't make out any pupils, much less a head, danced among it. Was her imagination playing tricks with her again? Would she live past this moment? Could she fend off the shadow? Would anyone care?

A howl brought the still night to life and the green lights disappeared as they flew to the right. That was Kaleena's moment of relief. Her instincts kicked her adrenaline into overdrive. As she raced down the path, the urge to look back was overwhelming. The lights continued to stare at her, but thankfully stayed put. For a moment, Kaleena felt the shadow wasn't stalking her so much as protecting her, making sure no harm came to her as she traced her way home.

Kaleena didn't stop running until she could see the small mom & pop ice-cream shop (or at least where it once was). The sign was still up, but the entire row of buildings was vacant. Like many independently-owned businesses, they had to close when the economy shit the bed a few years back. The addition of the Baskin-Robbins and a Dairy Queen a few months after didn't help either.

There's just no sense of community anymore.

Kaleena went to the store's closing with Matthew and bought four ice-cream cones. They were both sick for the whole day after, but it was worth it. The elderly woman, who claimed she was closing due to arthritis, didn't remember her when she came in, and Kaleena didn't feel the need to remind her. The entire incident was better left in the past.

As she stared into the blackened window, Kaleena picked up the faint sound of pop music rocking through the air. She couldn't immediately pinpoint the where-abouts of its origin so she ignored it, believing it was coming from the karaoke bar a few blocks down the street. She looked at her phone. It was a quarter to seven. Matthew would be calling soon.

Bermuda – Friday, 11:02 pm

The ocean roared, highlighted by the moon and resonate light coming from the bar, which was still partly visible in the distance. Lauren and Henry walked nearly shoulder-to-shoulder a few yards from the shoreline, which was unusually high for this time of year. Lauren had insisted Henry come with her when she decided to abandon the party to take a stroll, and though he wasn't exactly sure why, who

was he to tell a beautiful girl no to a quiet, personal walk along the beach? If anything, it would give him the chance to finally make his move, something he'd been hoping to do since the first time they met.

After having worked all day on some translations Matthew had tasked her with deciphering, Lauren decided to head out to the pool for a quick swim and tan — something she took very seriously; tan lines were not in her agenda. The splash was the first thing Henry heard as he stepped through the front door with Matthew. Eager to meet his new co-worker — or partner, as he considered it — he asked Matthew to lead him to the pool. Lauren's naked back glistened in the bright sunlight, leaving Henry spellbound. As the water flowed over her tanned, smooth skin, he wished the water were his own hands, giving Lauren the massage she was no doubt eager to receive.

"Lauren," Matthew whistled, knocking Henry from his infatuated stare. He was surprised (and a little concerned) that Matthew didn't seem to be affected by Lauren's nudity in the slightest. His first thought — the dude's as gay as San Francisco — swiftly changed to the utter disgust that the two were involved. Lauren turned to them before he could raise the question. Henry's first glimpse of that radiant smile was infectious. It didn't last, as Lauren quickly covered herself as soon as she caught sight of him.

"What the hell, Matthew?" she said, staring at Henry with sharp eyes.

"This is Henry," Matthew said nonchalantly. When Lauren didn't register the name, he continued. "My new assistant. I told you I was bringing him by today."

Lauren kept her eyes on Henry as she ran her hand through her wet hair, making sure her other arm did its job to cover her nipples. "Can you get him out of here?"

Henry felt Matthew's embarrassment. "Right. Sorry."

Matthew escorted Henry back into the house and Lauren swam slowly to the edge of the pool. Henry hoped to sneak a peek of Lauren as she got out but Matthew was intent on moving him to the kitchen as quickly as possible, making sure his line of sight was blocked the entire way.

"So, what is it with you two?" Henry finally choked out as they reached the kitchen.

"What? Me and Lauren?" Matthew chuffed slightly. "Nothing. Why?"

"I don't know. She just seemed very relaxed out there until she saw me." Henry sat down on one of the four stools lining the counter that separated the kitchen from the family room.

"We've known each other for nine years. We're comfortable together." Matthew pulled a couple of beers from the refrigerator and handed one to Henry.

"No sexual tension whatsoever?" Henry was hoping for the answer that eventually filled the room.

"We're just good friends."

Henry wasn't sure why he asked the next question, but it escaped his lips nonetheless. "Have you ever had sex?"

"Now I don't know where that concerns you," Lauren answered.

Henry lowered his head in deep regret as those words hung in the air like a rotting corpse. He watched as Lauren walked to the kitchen and grabbed a fresh peach from the refrigerator. Her clothes stuck to her body, forming a very sensual shape that moved with a soft fluidity.

"I'm sorry. I didn't mean to pry."

Lauren leaned against the door of the fridge and took a bite. "So why did you?"

Henry was caught in a corner he needed to get out of as soon as possible. He thought about his next words carefully as he watched Lauren sensually take another bite of that damned peach. "It was stupid. I apologize."

Lauren accepted the answer, but Henry knew it was going to be long, arduous road to gain her respect. In fact, it was months before Lauren and Henry would see each other again, and Henry believed it was because she was avoiding him. When Matthew secured funding for the expedition to Bermuda, he knew she'd have to at least pretend to get along with him. She did a pretty good job, and Henry was happy with her most recent attempt to warm up to him by telling jokes during their walk along the beach, each one lamer than the next. He wasn't sure if his

excitement was because the alcohol was catching up to him or because he was finally alone with Lauren; or it could have simply been the infectious whispered laughter of Lauren's amusement, gentle enough to keep others from hearing her, yet able to light up her thin face with a flushed red that highlighted her high cheekbones. Henry wanted nothing more than to slip his tongue between her undeniably thin, yet perky lips and leave it there for eternity. But he couldn't bring himself to do it; something like that would more than likely bring an abrupt end to the laughter.

"Wallabies," Lauren spit out after about five minutes of trying to find the word. "It was a wallaby. Silly little creatures."

A cold gust of ocean breeze whipped Lauren's hair across her eyes as she giggled copiously. Henry started to regret the three or four margaritas he coaxed Lauren to slurp down after getting her to dance, but it did allow him to remain hip-to-hip without her noticing. At times, they appeared to be Siamese twins, and Henry remained relatively hard the whole time. He'd be able to forgive himself for his *minor* deception.

"Have you ever seen one? I didn't think I'd ever see one. I came close, I guess you can say, with my first boyfriend. His name was Wally. Wally, ha. Funny name, too. He was the first person I ever had sex with. Did you know that? It was back in high school. I was seventeen, he had just turned eighteen and it was prom night. All of the magic was there and I was in love. Well, I thought I was in love. No, wait. I think I was in love. I mean, I had to be. I don't just have sex with anyone. Or, I wouldn't have back then, anyway, I mean I had never had it before, and I wasn't even sure if I would like it, to tell you the truth. We had talked about it for a while beforehand, whether or not we should do the *big deed* that night or wait. I guess I should have waited, but I don't think waiting would have helped me any. That night was the only night I would have real passionate sex with anyone. It would be the only night I would actually have a real orgasm, come to think of it, that is, if it *was* a real orgasm. I can't even remember now. It doesn't really matter, I guess, since the bastard left me that next Monday for Cheryl… Cheryl, that whore. Have you ever known a girl that pretends to be perfect because she knows she is? That was Cheryl, with her glorious green eyes and that perfect soft hair that flowed like it was in a constant wind. That perfect thirty-two, twenty-six, twenty-eight body. She had everything a man could want and Wally wanted it bad. He was just using me for practice, you know. He wanted to make sure he did everything right before going after Cheryl, the bitch. I was shattered when he broke up with me. I didn't know what to do after that. I couldn't help myself. I thought I was the ugliest person in the world and needed something. Someone, anyone, really, and that anyone turned into my husband. That son-of-a-bitch was the worst person I could have possibly been interested in, but, alas, because of Wally and my so-called *love for him*, I was a pathetic, self-deprecating bride without any self-confidence. Wally ended up knocking that bitch up that summer, you know. That was hilarious when I heard that! It was the first genuine laugh I had after the break-up, and even then, I don't know if it was out of hate or self-pity. I don't really care now, really. I used to dream they got married, popped out a couple more kids and are living in some trailer park outside of New Jersey, living week-to-week on barely-there paychecks, eating food out of a can, and wearing a hundred extra pounds each. Ah, who am I kidding? That would never happen, not to me — not *for* me. How come in this life, the people that hurt you the most, you know, those ones that you want to see hanged for their crimes, end up being perfect and you just end up a perfect wreck?"

Lauren stopped — not just talking; completely stopped. She stared off into the distance, her eyes glazed over with confusion and pain. Henry placed his hand to her cheek. "Lauren?"

Upon his touch, Lauren screamed and kneed Henry in the balls as hard as she could. Henry fell to his knees with his hands between his legs, unable to breathe. His teeth dug deep into his gums.

"Oh, shit," Lauren said after realizing what she'd done. "Shit, Henry, I'm sorry." She knelt down next to him. "I thought... I'm sorry, my ex-husband used to touch me like that before he'd beat the shit out of me. It was a defense reaction. I'm so sorry."

Henry tried to smile, but the only movement he could muster was a slight twitch of pain.

"Come on. We're almost home." Lauren slowly helped Henry to his feet. Every step was cautious and painful — at least that was what he made her believe. He didn't want Lauren to let him go (the smell of her perfume mixed with the slight aroma of alcohol was just heaven), so for the majority of the fifteen minutes it took to get back to the apartment, he faked his pain, hoping her guilt would lead to what he had been praying for since seeing her in that pool.

Connecticut – Friday, 7:02 pm

Kaleena was almost at a soft jog when she reached her apartment. She couldn't hear anything except for the raucous blast of music. Not even covering her ears helped. They were red hot as the music rolled on as if it were the only sound in the world. She could swear her eardrums were dying and she couldn't help but check her palms, believing her ears might actually be bleeding. This had to stop. It had to stop.

She bounded up the steps ready to burst in and throw the stereo through the wall, but when she reached the door, she was apprehensive as hell. If the music was this loud out here, she couldn't fathom how loud it would be inside. On top of that, there had to have been a noise disturbance reported by now. What if the cops arrived just as she entered the apartment? Would they believe she had just gotten there herself? It probably wouldn't matter. It was her apartment, so she'd be the first one arrested for serving alcohol to minors. What scared her more than getting her ass thrown in lockup for the night (and the hell she'd get from Matthew for making him come home early), was how the music had suddenly gotten softer. And she knew right away it wasn't because the music had been lowered; it was because her hearing had gotten worse. If she didn't turn that music off now, she'd be deaf in a matter of minutes.

Inside was like looking directly into chaos. Kids she hardly knew hung with other kids she didn't know. A sea of red solo cups flashed about the apartment and Kaleena's eyes watered from the hovering stench she couldn't quite place. She dropped her backpack at the foot of the door and scanned the room. Missy Perkins was making out with Donald Fether, half de-clothed, completely unaware of anyone else's presence; another couple French-kissed near the fireplace, looking as if they would eventually get their nose-rings caught together; and a few girls hung out by the television, laughing and pointing around the room. She couldn't hear what they were saying (at this point, she could hardly hear her own thoughts) but she recognized their condescending stares — ridicule most definitely the subject of their pretentious conversation. One of them, Paula Sherry, she knew quite well. Paula was one of the first people to loath Kaleena's intelligence and truly attack her for it. She was in a few of her eighth grade advanced classes, and being only nine at the time, Kaleena was an instant target for Paula's bullish fuckery, which included the first fist-fight Kaleena would be involved in.

"Hey smart-ass," Paula had called out, walking toward her in the lunchroom. Kaleena sat alone near the back of the building having had a hard time making any friends. Paula led the pack of extreme rebellion, wearing a mini-skirt and a tank top that was just short enough to reveal the brand new belly-button ring. Her hair was tied back in a ponytail and her bangs hung over her forehead like sprouts from a weed. Flanking her were two other girls, one shorter and a bit stocky, wearing what appeared to Kaleena as clothes that were way too small for the girl's figure; the other looked like Paula's clone, right down to the small Gucci handbag and light rouge lipstick.

Kaleena kept her eyes diverted, which she knew would turn out to be a mistake as Paula stepped up next to her.

"Hey. I'm talking to you, shit-bitch." Paula's goons took a seat on either side of Kaleena and picked at her warmed-over cafeteria lunch. The laugh was on them; she wasn't hungry for it anymore anyway.

Paula placed her long, fake nail under Kaleena's chin and pushed up. Kaleena swatted her hand away, which turned Paula's face red with anger.

"Who the hell do you think you are?"

Kaleena stayed silent. Her eyes burned with water. She tried to hide the fear tickling the pit of her stomach, but it steadily grew harder to control.

"Why are you here?" Paula asked. "Go back to the third grade where you belong."

"I can't do that," Kaleena whispered.

"You can't what?" Paula antagonized.

"I said I can't do that," Kaleena yelled. Some of the other kids turned to her. The room was still overwhelmed by other conversations, but those closest to her started to pay attention.

"You're not welcome here, you fucking baby. Go home."

Paula's two cohorts were smiling gleefully as they continued to enjoy her lunch, her tears, her discomfort. Kaleena wanted to run home, jump in her mother's arms and cry until she fell asleep.

I think you should shut the hell up and leave me alone, shitface, Kaleena thought. She wanted to yell it at the top of her lungs, but her mother had taught her not to swear or be rude in public (or, to fit the situation a bit better, be mean to others, even if they were mean to her). So all that left her lips was: "I think you should leave me alone."

Paula shook her body and waved her hands in the air sarcastically — as if a child four years younger than her could really frighten her. "What will you do if I don't?" she said with a grin so wide, her braces glinted in the lights.

"I'll tell the principal," Kaleena squeaked.

"Would you listen to her," Paula said to her goons. "She's going to narc on us."

The other two girls laughed and poked Kaleena, who finally started to cry. She was unable to wipe her tears away, not that she wanted to.

You should never be embarrassed with tears, her mother's voice reminded her. *They're nature's way of cleansing one's fear. When you stop crying, you'll no longer be afraid because your body will be washed of all the pain.*

Kaleena wanted to become fearless.

"Look at the baby, crying for her mommy," the two girls chanted. Paula laughed with them and took the roll from Kaleena's lunch tray.

"You don't think that scares us, do you?" She took a bite of the roll.

Kaleena let her tears fall into her dry spaghetti. Her mother was smart — the smartest person she knew — but no matter how many words she might bestow upon her, Kaleena was too fed up with the derision to hear them. It was clear her tears weren't because of fear of these jackals. They were born from anger over how they were treating her. Lunch would last for another twenty minutes, but even if she survived, what about tomorrow? Or the next day? Or the next? She had to prove to them (or maybe, to herself) that she could stand up for herself, that she was more than just a scared little child.

"Hey, cry-baby. I've got your diaper in my bag. You want it back?"

With that, Kaleena shoved her lunch tray into Paula's ugly face. The spaghetti instantly stained her tank top from neck to belly ring. Paula backed away; her friends could only look on in shock.

Kaleena hoped that would be a big enough diversion to escape, but as she stepped away from the table, the stocky girl grabbed her arm and pulled her close. She could smell that fat chick's awful tuna breath as she held Kaleena's face to hers. Paula walked up to them, everything about her screaming, "DEATH!"

"That was not smart, ya' little bitch." Paula punched Kaleena in the stomach without so much as a warning. Her knees buckled; she would have fallen to her knees had the stocky girl hadn't been holding her up like a Raggedy-Ann doll. Before Kaleena could find her breath, Paula took another shot to her gut, this one not quite as bad, but still extremely painful.

By now the entire lunch room had gathered around, catcalls of "Fight! Fight! Fight!" echoing across the building. Kaleena could hardly hear them, as her attention was solely on regaining oxygen. When she was finally able to pull in a breath, Kaleena was held upright and forced to look at Paula.

"Stay out of my face and keep your smart ass out of my classrooms." Kaleena wasn't sure what happened next. At one moment a thick teenager had her arms

locked around hers, the next she was lying on the cold porcelain floor, her eye and mouth bulging with pain. Through drying tears, she saw a blurry group of kids laughing and walking past her as if she were a piece of road kill on the highway. As she fought to continue breathing, she was afraid the pain would never go away.

Kaleena's left eye twitched upon seeing Paula for the first time since jumping two more grades. The urge to fly across the room and beat the living shit out of the flaming whore boiled deep within. Lucky for Paula, Kaleena had more pressing issues on her mind.

Locating the radio was easy. As she turned it off, finding her so-called best friend would end up being even easier.

Bermuda – Friday, 11:02 pm

Matthew sat on the edge of the hole, gazing in on the artifact that had been buried by the night's shadow. He hadn't turned on the work lights, not yet; he just wanted to sit still in the twilight and believe everything he'd done over the last three years was right here, waiting for him to help dig itself out of extinction. The real question still sat at the forefront of his mind: Was this the beginning or the end of his journey? The end would lead him back home where he would take care of his daughter, go back to teaching archaeology at the closest community college, watch TLC or the History Channel every night while munching on chips in his slightly old, uncomfortable recliner that squeaked every time he leaned back, wishing he could just have one last expedition — one last moment of glory — but know that his time had come and gone, that his last years on earth would be wasted away, alone, his daughter taking care of him until old age forced her to move him into a care facility so she could get married, have a son and daughter of her own with a man who would love her and cherish her and live with her until they both passed on and became part of the mystery of death. The thought frightened him with a chill that overpowered the cold wind blowing past his reddened cheeks. His life was worth more to him than that.

This was not his end.

Matthew dusted off the dirt from his jeans as he stood and then walked down the ladder into the hole. When he hit the ground, he knelt down and caressed the tip of his iceberg. "What do you have underneath you?" he whispered. "What answers are waiting to be uncovered?" He took a deep breath, inhaling the smell of the dew, the earth — his future. It smelled fresh, salty; it smelled copious. He knew what he had to do. In his mind he felt reluctant; in his gut, he felt assured that his next step would give him what he needed. It took a moment to grab hold of the shovel, but once he held it in the frozen sweat of his palm, he stood up and swung the shovel over his shoulder. He brought it back down against the artifact with brute force, revealing a cold, black underbelly beneath the tiny shatter of pieces.

Connecticut – Friday, 7:06 pm

Kyla clawed her way from the bathroom to find out what idiot had turned the music off. Her face was dowsed in thick rouge and eye shadow and her lipstick was partially smeared onto her chin, making it clear the only reason her red-striped hair was drawn back in what looked like a black-laced napkin was to keep it from interfering with whatever boy might be taking advantage of her tongue. As she maneuvered through the group of irate children throwing a flurry of insults ("What the hell?" and "Crazy bitch" being the most prominent) in one particular direction, she sloppily buttoned up her leather skirt that didn't hide her black-lace underwear any more than her tank-top covered her nearly see-through bra. Looking at this horrible mess of a young woman, Kaleena couldn't help but feel the tears of Kyla's regret as the thought of her transition from the sweet, church-going innocent to this licentious sex-addicted hooker lingered on her mind.

It was three in the morning. Kaleena was awake, busy writing. She couldn't help herself. When she wrote, she got lost in the subject matter; she got lost in the exhilaration of her own mind. Thoughts poured onto the laptop she had gotten

for Christmas, the glow of the screen the only light in the room. She was alone with her thoughts, inebriated by her insights. Sleep was never as gratifying as this.

The first ring sliced through the silent tapping of the keys, which sent chills of gooseflesh across Kaleena's body as she jumped. She wasn't quite sure what it was at first, but then it became clear as the second ring filled the quiet house and eased her adrenaline.

She set the laptop down and shifted her legs over the edge of the bed, expecting a third ring to trill through the darkness. Silence was all she got. What happened? Probably a wrong number, some drunk dialing for a cab, accidentally presses two numbers at once and gets a connection before he can press the last number. It freaks him out and he hangs up, scared to death that he just called Satan's personal line. Maybe it was crank caller, ready to ask his recipient if her refrigerator was running and to hurry up and catch it, amusing his friends over the inanity of the joke and caught by his mother, tired as hell, hearing squawks of laughter from the bedroom down the hall of her son and his friends who were supposed to be in bed five hours ago. Or it could have been a pedophile, calling Kaleena after seeing her around town, hoping to jack off to her voice; his wife eking up next to him asking what he was doing and his scared, sweaty eyes filling with guilty honesty that doesn't come out in words but can be heard for dozens of miles. The drunk would have chosen to walk, getting struck by a driver who fell asleep at the wheel; the kid would have been scolded by his mother and his friends separated into other rooms, too late (or early as you'd like to see it) to be taken home; the pedophile would have been yelled at for a couple of hours before his wife started packing her things to leave. But Kaleena would never find out which was true, or if any were true, as the cursor on the computer beckoned her back to work.

Sliding onto the bed to try and reclaim a comfortable position, the third ring finally burst into the room. Kaleena didn't hesitate; she hurried to her desk in the opposite corner and swiped her phone up. To her surprise, it wasn't the guy that was so depressed with his life, alcohol was the only thing that could calm

his stress; or the kid with the small mind to think it was hilarious to wake people up for no good reason; or the man that had a good wife — a loving wife — but couldn't find his joy without thinking of that girl down the street, her innocence still held deep within her.

It was Kyla. *What the hell is she calling for at three in the morning?*

"Hello," Kaleena whispered into the receiver after hitting the 'Accept' button. It didn't matter she was alone in the house. Her father was in Florida on another expedition and probably wouldn't be back in a few days. But she didn't want Kyla (or whoever might have Kyla's phone) to think she was alone. It was good she did, as heavy breathing was all Kaleena heard. At first she thought Kyla may have been kidnapped and some sick piece of scum was jerking himself off in front of her, waiting for the right time to let loose into her mouth. The thought wasn't completely ridiculous, not when Kaleena heard tears hidden under the erratic breaths. Yet, she couldn't be sure.

"Who is this?" she asked. The answer that came was a loud cry from someone who had been holding it all back until this very moment.

"Kyla?" she asked instinctively. "Kyla. What's wrong?" The answer was several more minutes of deep and uncontrollable crying. Kaleena pictured Kyla holding the phone tightly, her hand turning bright red as she huddled herself in the corner of her dark bedroom. Kaleena knew exactly how she felt.

"Kyla, are you at home?" Waiting for an answer was blistering. But one finally came, hidden under a runny, red nose and salted tears. It was soft, quiet and shaky. It was frightening.

"Yes."

"I'm coming over," Kaleena said quickly. She was only wearing a pair of cotton shorts and a light white t-shirt, but she didn't have time to do anything but slip her sandals onto her cold feet. Kaleena grabbed her bike (keeping it under lock and key inside was the best way to keep it from being stolen) and shot from the apartment. Her body shook as it snapped against the cool night air.

"Just stay calm," Kaleena said as the rear tire hit the pavement. "I'm not going

to leave you." Kaleena rode strong and hard, her heart pumping harder and harder with each stride. Thankfully, Kyla seemed to have calmed down, her tears having grown stale. *I hope to hell she's falling asleep.*

Thirty minutes later, her hand frozen to the handlebar, Kaleena saw Kyla's apartment complex from a nearby stoplight. She had moved there after her parents split. It had always been rumored that he left because her mother slept with one of her friend's husbands, but Kyla never liked to talk about her family and Kaleena respected her privacy. After her own parents split, the best thing she could do was be there; two friends with something in common — an unspoken bond.

By now the crying had completely stopped. Kaleena still disobeyed the law and flew past all the red lights and stop signs as if death was following her. Every few minutes she'd ask Kyla if she was still there. Kyla's answer was always a hoarse "yeah," which continued to give Kaleena hope. When she reached the apartment, she dropped her bike and pounded her fist on Kyla's door.

"Kyla, open the door," she yelled into the phone. It clicked off. "Kyla?"

A few heartbeats later, Kaleena heard the lock on the inside of the apartment and Kyla opened the door. Her eyes were puffy and pink, her cheeks a rosy red. She was wearing nothing but a robe. Kaleena immediately grabbed hold of her for no other reason than to relax her. Kyla didn't hug back. Her arms remained dead to her sides. Kaleena didn't care. She'd been waiting thirty minutes to hug her. The moment wouldn't be wasted by pettiness.

"What happened?" Kaleena whispered, holding on for dear life.

When Kyla refused to answer, Kaleena finally let go. Kyla kept her head down, most likely to keep herself from having to look into Kaleena's worried eyes. Kaleena wrote a paper once on the power of the eyes; how anyone could know any story, know the truth, know the pain from merely looking past the glassy exterior to witness the conversation that went on deep within. She had looked into her father's eyes after her mother left and saw his pain — how he never wanted her to leave; how he knew he screwed up and would do anything to get her back; the fear of being single, without her companionship. They never spoke a word to each

other about the breakup, but Kaleena knew his sorrow and how that suffering has yet to leave him, just by the way he continues to look at her. She desperately needed to know Kyla's story, but knew she wasn't going to give it to her verbally. Kaleena needed to get a glimpse into the eyes of the victim; find the story herself. She rested her icy hand gently to Kyla's chin, but as she allowed her head to shift upwards at Kaleena's touch, Kyla kept her eyelids closed tight, refusing to reveal the horror underneath.

"Kyla, look at me." Kaleena waited, then, "Please. Look at me."

The moment Kyla's flushed eyelids fluttered open, and those dark brown eyes laced with red lightning found their way to Kaleena's softened gaze, she knew Kyla had seen something she didn't want to see; had been part of a moment she became lost in and was still trying to find her way back from. She was dark and haunted, scared cold.

Kyla had lost her innocence.

Kaleena shook her head, fright for her friend mixed with anger at the assailant. Who was it? Who had done this to her?

As Kyla again burst into tears, Kaleena pulled her into her arms. This time, Kyla reciprocated. A few minutes later, Kaleena walked Kyla back to her room and lied her down in bed. She sat on the floor and watched over her the rest of the night. Kyla finally found slumber around six in the morning. It infuriated Kaleena that she never found out who abused her friend. She had her ideas, but it was something she was never brave enough to bring up to Kyla in conversation. So it simply drifted into the past, leaving behind a bad taste in Kaleena's soul as the silent bond between them slowly degraded until neither really knew who the other was anymore. Kaleena went off to college when Kyla entered high school, and the experiences of these two very different levels of maturity crept its way into their friendship. They each tried to ignore the problem as much as possible. Kaleena took on several additional courses each semester to keep her mind embedded in scholastics (and coincidentally locked in her room). During the summer months, or when she got too far ahead in her coursework, she'd find an extracurricular

project, usually writing an article for the university newspaper, heading out to do some freelance field work or just hanging out in the park or a library and watching people live their lives.

Kyla, meanwhile, met some new friends, most of whom liked to crash parties, skip school and hang out outside liquor stores hoping to score some smokes or a six-pack. It was during a homecoming party when she was first introduced to ecstasy. She never dove deep enough to try cocaine, but as alcohol started to sweat from her veins on a daily basis, her grades dropped dramatically, as did her academic prospects. She claimed to be happy, but the more she fell, the more depressed she became. Whenever both girls found a free moment they'd hang out together, but the friendship, the kindness, the love they had for one another was gone. Kyla spent most of their time together trying to persuade Kaleena to smoke a joint or swill a Saki bomb. She'd always refuse, and though Kyla would get upset with her for being "Such a child", Kyla always called to apologize, offering to make up for her stupidity with a cup of coffee or a new outfit. Kaleena would always accept, each and every time hoping — wishing — it wouldn't take a (near) fatal accident to learn from her mistakes. More to the point, she accepted in order to stay as close as possible, to keep an eye on her, ignoring the fact that Kyla would never be able to climb out of the hole she had dug. That ignorance kept Kaleena from truly helping Kyla from what would end up scarring her even more than that first night.

But it wasn't until Kaleena saw her friend storming toward her at the party that she finally understood that night had completely taken over Kyla's soul.

"What are you doing?" Kyla yelled over the yapping crowd. Kaleena could barely hear her over the throbbing that continued to pound her eardrums and pinch her temples to the point they felt ready to crush her skull.

"What am I doing?" Kaleena said. Her voice hovered around her as if it was coming from behind her. "I thought I said you couldn't have a party."

"You were serious about that?"

There was nothing left of her old friend. "Yes, I — I can't believe you."

"Come one Kal," Kyla said, calming. "Don't do this."

Kaleena's attention was suddenly on a boy — tall and lean with a heavily built in six-pack. He took hold of Kyla's shoulders. She kissed his hand as he pressed up against her.

"Party's over, Kyla." Sound was becoming clear again, though the pain in her forehead remained steady.

Kyla's eyes lit up in disappointment. "You can't do that, Kal."

"It's my apartment. I just did." Kaleena saw the hidden anger and frustration pierce Kyla's aura. What did she expect? She was disrupting her friend's popularity and lustful desire to return to acts of indecency.

"Kal. Please. Turn the music back on."

"Why?"

"Because," Kyla said, her eyes darting repeatedly to the boy behind her.

Kaleena looked at him. His dusty brown hair covered his eyes slightly, and his chest beamed with a soft coat of sweat. "No. Not gonna happen."

"Hey, you're Kaleena Stevens, aren't you?" the boy said, tilting his head up in an inane attempt to say, *Hey, you're hot. Let me see your tits.*

"Yeah," Kaleena answered slowly, unsure if she wanted to associate herself with this mannequin overflowing with masculine immaturity.

"Hey, cool," he said, his eyes lingering on her longer than she would have liked. "I read your book."

Kaleena was bewildered. "You read my book?"

"Yeah. Totally righteous stuff." The boy's smile held perfectly white teeth to match his bleached mind.

"Is that so?" Kaleena said, completely unsure of where this was going.

"Yeah. All that stuff about how ghosts are manifestations of the cerebral cortex and the mind's eye trying to convince a person there's something there. But in reality, it's only because they have a need for something that they can't fill in everyday life." He smiled and ended with, "Awesome."

Kaleena stood shocked. She looked back to Kyla, who smiled a sheepish grin of satisfaction. "Why don't you guys talk a little," she said, knowing full well when

Kaleena got started on her book, it would be hard for her to stop.

The boy walked out from behind Kyla. "Sweet, yeah. I'd love to hear what you think about aliens." The boy held out his hand. "I'm Dave."

Kaleena shook it, her eyes holding on Kyla, hoping to get an answer for a question no one knew was being asked.

"So what do you think? Real life beings or ways to get some attention?" Dave leaned up against the table, his eyes filled with curiosity.

"I'm not sure," Kaleena answered slowly. "Their existence has been long documented. I mean, do I think that all of those UFO sightings are real? No. There aren't enough solar systems in the universe to hold life, much less have them be so advanced as to have acquired space travel technology. It takes a complex system of molecules and natural fusion reactions to develop even the simplest of life forms. To actually believe that beings from another planet, should they exist at all, would come and visit us is a bit conceited."

As Kaleena rattled on about supposed alien sightings, how all of them come from some hick down in the bayous of Louisiana who most likely just wanted some attention because they're not smart enough to get a life, Kyla snuck in behind her and turned the music back on, steadily raising the volume just enough to keep the party going, but low enough that Kaleena wouldn't notice.

"I'll be dancing," Kyla said, giving Dave a thank you kiss on the cheek. As she disappeared into the growling crowd, who all seemed more willing to stay angry than to get back into party mode, Kaleena kept talking. It's not every day someone showed interest in her work and her thoughts just came pouring out — a stream of ideas being soaked up and admired by the fan she never knew she had.

Bermuda – Friday, 11:06 pm

Lauren fell to the ground after flopping Henry on the bed. He laughed right along with her steady schoolgirl giggles, which made her seem so innocent, so serene. Looking over her, Henry imagined himself lying on top of her, their naked bodies

held together with the sweat of their lust. He wanted to be inside her, loving her… being loved by her.

"What are you thinking about?" Lauren asked, staring at the outlet on the wall across the room. Soft whistles of laughter continued from her calm stature.

"Just how beautiful you look right now." It slipped out.

Lauren's maddeningly sweet giggles returned in full force. She was a picture of perfection as she slid her legs underneath her chest with a watered fluidity. She glanced up at him. "You're nothing like that wallaby I dated. You're cute."

Henry smiled. "Can I come down there with you?" It was a chance.

"I think it would be more comfortable up there." Lauren reached up. Henry gently helped her onto the bed. She softly caressed his cheek, feeling the stubble from two days of not having shaved, and stared meticulously at every wrinkle, every crevice, every imperfection. Without really understanding why, she pressed her nose to his, staring deeply into his mouth, half open, waiting.

"I haven't done this with anyone for years," she whispered. Henry could taste the bitter sting of alcohol on his tongue. It was nothing a kiss couldn't remedy.

"I've been waiting a long time," Henry whispered back. He sensed Lauren's lips birth a smile.

"Do you want to know a secret?" she said, her hand finding its way through Henry's hair.

"What's that?"

Lauren responded in the most secret of whispers. "So have I."

She pressed her lips to his. At the same time, Henry generously allowed Lauren to pin him down on his back. Rolling her tongue along the roof of his mouth, Lauren slid her thin frame up and down his stomach and then grabbed his penis. Henry jerked slightly, ending the kiss.

"Oh, I'm sorry," Lauren said, sliding off of him.

"No, no. It was just unexpected."

Lauren sat on the edge of the bed and placed her hand to her mouth, frightened she'd just made a monumental mistake.

"What's wrong?" Henry cautiously placed his hands on her shoulders. He thought about kissing her neck, but felt guilt tightened her shoulders.

"We shouldn't be doing this," she said, the alcohol giving her a slight headache.

"Don't say that." He started massaging her shoulders. Lauren felt her vagina heat up with pleasure. As she grew more relaxed, Henry took the chance to kiss her neck, which quickly led back to the sweet taste of her lips.

"Do you have a condom?" she asked, somewhat breaking the mood.

Henry's hands slid off Lauren in disappointment.

"You don't?" Lauren looked upset.

"I never thought —"

"Don't give me that," Lauren said. "No man I've ever known has ever been without a condom. Even if the piece of shit's sixty years old. They always have one just in case."

"I know," Henry said, believing he'd just lost his chance. "I wouldn't suppose you have one?"

"Why the hell would I have one?"

"Hey. Chicks buy 'em as a precaution, too, you know." Henry bent back on his elbows, forcing his pelvis to lift ever so slightly and rub the small of her back. A shimmer of excitement poured through her chest. She licked her lips and shifted her body against his, the itch between her legs becoming more unbearable as her breaths grew quicker. Henry slid back an inch to try and entice Lauren to follow. It worked, as Lauren's eyes squinted with the desire to devour him, her inhibitions ready to crack under his hunger for her body.

"Fuck it," she said and pulled off her shirt. She climbed back on top of Henry and shoved her tongue into his throat. She grew ever more eager as she pushed her ass hard against his crotch. Henry was quick to take advantage. He ripped her bra off as if it was latched with Velcro and took some time to examine her small, yet curved breasts with his tongue. Lauren held his head against them, closing her eyes and biting her lower lip. This was really happening and it felt as right as rain for them both.

*   *   *

Matthew wiped a bit of cold sweat from his forehead. Finding nothing of significance after digging down at least another five feet, he was beginning to fear this was about to turn out to be no better than his first solo expedition. He'd gone to Israel to find a piece of Noah's Ark, which he had traced there after having reviewed hundreds of journals, old parchments from the Socrates era and of course the Bible. The site was closed after two years of digging and sent Matthew's reputation into a tailspin. It took three years to find an investor for his next expedition, one that would hopefully lead him to Moses's staff. Though he didn't find anything that time either, his findings (which included several hundred pages of notes and resources) brought him an unexpected amount of gratitude from the archaeological community. For a few years after, Matthew became one of the most sought after archaeologists, but as financing dried up, he quickly found himself one mistake away from once again destroying his already tarnished reputation. He couldn't allow that to happen; he needed to dig. Even if it meant digging deep enough to discover a brand new volcano, Matthew would continue until his hands bled completely off.

Where is it? he thought. *Where is the secret?*

Ten minutes later, Matthew had dug two feet deeper (or a foot lower than the ladder, which rested on a carved out section of the hole) with still nothing to show for it. The stars twinkled bright above him and the music in the distance had gone the way of the wind. Matthew pounded the shovel into the ground and yelled in frustration. He sat against the stoop and rubbed his eyes generously as he slammed his head repeatedly against the dirt.

There was nothing more he could do.

He was done.

That is until he noticed a soft blue glow splinter his fingers. He lowered his hand and looked to the ground, which was flush in a bright blue hue.

What the hell?

The light, as far as Matthew could tell, originated from underneath the clay surrounding the edges of the shovel. He knelt down to examine the source of the light, which seemed to be some type of malleable liquid that smelled like blood with a hint of gasoline or oil. The surface was slimy and a little cold to the touch.

A smile sat on his lips. This was it.

He had found his secret.

Matthew grabbed hold of the shovel, but no matter how hard he pulled, it stayed wedged in the ground. It was only when he kicked it at the base nearest the ground did it finally pop loose, letting free a stream of bright blue light into the stratosphere. The force of the blast blew Matthew from the hole. The shovel flew even farther, some thirty feet in the opposite direction. Matthew tried to move, but his body ached beyond his own capacity of tolerance. His mind grew faint as his eyes turned upward into his head.

*   *   *

The covers had been shifted halfway off the mattress as the two passionate lovers lay squirreled together in the center of the bed. Henry was on top of Lauren, having taken control over the situation. He kissed every inch of her sweaty body, Lauren relegated to grabbing something — anything — that she could to stabilize herself as her body loosened into Jell-O, her legs tightly wound around Henry's backside.

Suddenly, a blue light washed through the room, accentuating every curve of their bodies. Lauren screamed loud enough to pierce bulletproof glass as Henry ejaculated a river. As her body dropped into numbness, a soft tingle running the course of her veins, Lauren's eyes filled with tears. She giggled uncontrollably. Henry pulled himself away and lied next to her. Lauren turned to him but said nothing. She simply closed her eyes and tried to hold onto that feeling as she fell into a deep slumber.

Connecticut – Friday, 7:23 pm

The party raged on around Kaleena as Dave continued to show tremendous interest in both her and her mind (or so her ego led her to believe). It didn't even register when they had sat down on the couch, or when Dave placed his arm around her. She was so involved in her own thoughts that everything else became irrelevant.

"And to understand physiology of the man's mind to that of the woman's, anyone can understand anything about any single person at any given moment."

Dave smiled as Kaleena finally ended her rant that started with Dave asking why men couldn't understand women. He stared at her with much more interest than he had given to the words streaming from her lips, finding himself more aroused with the way her mouth moved than with what was retreating from them.

"Totally awesome," he said, staring at her nose.

"Yeah," Kaleena said, finally realizing how close he was.

"You're so beautiful," he said, taking the moment to softly blow into her ear comb some stray hair behind it.

Kaleena slid away as far as she could. "What are you doing?"

Dave kept a grip around her shoulder and shifted back into her personal space. "Nothing," he said as he slipped his other hand coyly from his lap to her breast. Kaleena bent his fingers back as far as they would go before breaking and stood.

"Fucking asshole," she screamed. "Stay away from me."

Before Kaleena could move another inch, Kyla was standing next to her.

"What's going on?" she asked.

"You said she'd give it up if I listened to her damn nonsense," Dave said, adjusting his crotch.

"You what?" Kaleena was clearly outraged. She wasn't sure what else to say, so she simply walked back to the radio.

"Piece of shit," Kyla said to Dave. "You were supposed to keep her occupied, not try to fuck her." Kyla raced after Kaleena, grabbing her before she could turn off the music.

"Wait, Kaleena."

Kaleena tore her arm away. "Stay away from me," she roared. Aside from the drunks, who were too busy making fools of themselves, and the participants in the make-out sessions, which had become more intense and far less conservative, the majority of the partiers were staring at them, possibly waiting — and hoping — for a bitch fight to break out. "You're supposed to be my friend, Kyla. Instead you get some idiot you were about to have sex with babysit me so you could go fraternize your tits away to all of your other fuck-buddies."

"Kaleena…" Kyla was unsure of how to continue. She didn't want to hurt Kaleena; she *was* her friend. But it was time to tell the truth. "I don't know how to say this." Kyla had to reach deep down inside to find the courage. "Things change, Kaleena. You've been so distant these past few months."

Kaleena threw up her arms in bewilderment. "*I've* been distant?"

"Yeah, you have. I can't understand you anymore, Kal."

"Back at you, *Ky*. You've been such an outstanding role model."

"Don't put this shit back on me. I was trying to help you."

"Help me what? Become an alcoholic whore?"

Kyla looked ready to slap Kaleena, who stood her ground, almost stoically. "You know, this is just like you."

"Oh, yeah. Please. Enlighten me." Kaleena folded her arms, her foot tapping along with the beat of the music.

"Okay, miss high and mighty. Always going around thinking you're so much better than everyone else just because you're freakishly smart. I've got news for you. Smarter doesn't make you better. It just makes you more annoying and, quite frankly, controlling."

"I'm controlling?"

"Take a hint, Kal. Just because things don't go your way, doesn't mean they're wrong. You're different, I get that, but no one else does, so when you go around with your nose so fucking high up in the air, looking down on everyone else like they're immature little shits, you put a target on your back. I was simply trying to help you remove it."

"So you thought throwing a party in my apartment with a bunch of idiots I don't know, could care less to know, or despise with a passion, that all of a sudden, I would see things your way and understand why you, and all of your other slutty acquaintances, do what you do?"

Kyla wanted to scream, but somehow kept her anger in check. Maybe Kaleena was a better influence than she thought. "I was trying to help pull you from this goddamn manufactured womb you've crawled into."

Kaleena was stunned and a bit angry at the hidden truth within those words.

"I just wish you hadn't changed so much, Kaleena. I just wish you weren't such a…" Kyla turned away.

"Such a what?" Kaleena waited, but Kyla kept her back on her. "Such a what?" Kaleena repeated, forcing Kyla to face her. She averted her eyes a moment, then decided it better she tell her and get it over with.

"You're…" Kyla paused. Then, finally, "You're a virgin mother, okay."

"A what?"

"A virgin mother," Kyla repeated with more valor. "A teenage girl who goes around preaching abstinence without ever having tried to kiss anyone, let alone offer a blowjob or fuck anyone."

"That is the stupidest thing I've ever heard," Kaleena screamed.

"You may think it's stupid, Kal, but if I'm caught fraternizing with a virgin mother, I'll never get laid, no matter how many blowjobs I give away."

Kaleena stared into the frozen eyes of her old friend. "You're right," she finally said, calm and broken. "Things change. I've kept my pride, and it seems to me you lost yours when you couldn't come to terms with your own fucked up past." Kaleena shut the stereo off. "Party's over," she screamed.

All of the guests let out a sigh of frustration. Just then, Kaleena grabbed her head, feeling as if her brain had just grown two inches inside her skull. She let out a loud yelp and fell to her knees, vomiting uncontrollably.

The girls screamed with frightened disgust and bolted for the door; the guys whooped and hollered in a drunken frenzy. Kyla backed away, unsure. She wanted

to help Kaleena, but was angry with her for breaking their secret promise to never bring up the past. Everyone finally dispersed as the nauseous smell spread through the hot, murky atmosphere of the apartment. In less time it took for a politician to lie, the apartment was empty. The only person left was Kyla, who stood near the door, staring at her acquaintance.

When Kaleena stopped gagging, she rolled onto her back and cried heavily. Her chest was constricted and her legs were numb.

"Hey, Kyla," Dave called from outside. "The party's being moved to Gabe's house. You comin'?"

Kaleena looked to her friend and through spit-laced lips whispered, "Help," before closing her eyes. Though there was a soft haze of tears forming, Kyla decided it better for her reputation if she left to join her friends at the new party. Feeling slightly liberated, she closed the door quietly behind her and left Kaleena to lie in her own vomit under a soft blue haze.

Bermuda – Saturday, 6:35 am

It felt like a semi had parked on Matthew's head. He tried opening his eyes, but the rays from the blooming sun pierced into his retinas, forcing them closed. Fire-hot pokers to the groin couldn't have felt worse. He grunted as he tried to find movement in his legs.

What happened? Where am I?

The breezy, salted ocean air lifted his spirits as it tickled his lips, awakening his mind to the exotic sensation of the blue liquid he had found. How long ago that was, he wasn't sure; for all he knew, it could have been days. But if it had been, his team would have already discovered him. There was no way he'd still be lying out on the course patch of dirt that indented his skin. Shading his eyes, he looked at his watch. It was half past six. He'd only been out for six hours; it felt like six years.

He closed his eyes to mask the piercing pain in his head and pulled himself to his knees. Each breath, hollow and cold, overwhelmed the musicality of his

cracking bones. He coughed lightly to relieve some of the pressure, but all it did was send needles of tension to the rest of his body. He fell back to the ground, his cheek hitting the dirt near the hole. As he lay still, the ocean breeze steadily grew a slight oily stench. What was it? He lifted his head — his neck pushing to snap itself in half — and peered into the hole. The blue liquid had transformed into a dark turquoise pool.

"I found you," he squeezed out under his breath. He chuckled softly, ignoring the burn in his lungs. "I found you."

Though his body pleaded for more rest, he slid back to his knees and pulled his phone from the breast pocket of his vest. It was time he learned exactly what it was he had found. He quickly thumbed to his contacts, hit Lauren's name and coughed once more as he listened to the line begin to ring.

*　*　*

The theme song to *Indiana Jones* sang electronically through the silent room. The sound was muffled, but was still loud enough to arouse an incredibly light sleeper like Lauren. Peeling her tongue from the roof of her stale mouth, she couldn't quite grasp where exactly she was much less what the hell happened. She shifted her arm from off Henry's chest to clear the crust that had formed on the inner bridge of her eyes. After hazily sitting up, a wave of dizziness slammed her to the pillow, which felt like a bag of cement that had accidentally been doused with water. She untwisted her legs from Henry's and pushed the palm of her hand to the middle of her forehead, completely unaware of the music that continued to call out for her. Letting out a small tender grunt, something rustled up against her elbow. She opened her eyes wide to lock onto Henry's satisfied grin screaming at her with pleasurable force.

"Hey, sweetie," he said, still half asleep.

"Oh, god," Lauren said as the music ended. She sat up on her elbows and finally noticed Henry's naked body sprawled out next to her. "Oh, god," she said again,

this time more regretfully. Like the roadrunner escaping the coyote, Lauren slid off the bed and raced to the bathroom, almost missing the toilet as she vomited.

Henry wasn't sure how to take that reaction. After a moment, he chalked it up to the hangover and scratched his balls to make himself more comfortable on the comforter. He hugged the pillow and reminisced about the previous night, his dick hardening underneath him as he did. Music filled his mind — lovely and satisfying; the song of angels glorifying his sexual prowess. Then he realized it wasn't just in his head; it was coming from inside the room. Bending over the edge of the bed, Henry attempted to pinpoint where the sound was coming from. He concentrated his efforts on a pile of clothes near the nightstand and eventually found Lauren's cell phone in the back pocket of her delightfully scented jeans. The display read "Matt" in dark black letters and had a picture of Matthew and Lauren taking an awfully awkward selfie. (Was that her elbow or her knee?) Should he answer? He wasn't sure if he — if Lauren — wanted Matthew to know what happened, but it could be important. And with Lauren still singing to the toilet, he felt obligated to answer. So he thought up a quick lie and hit "Accept".

"Matt," he said, trying not to sound as if he'd just woken up. "What's up?"

"Henry? Where's Lauren?"

"Bathroom. It appears the night was not kind to our dear friend."

"Why? What's wrong?"

"Beats the hell out of me. She hasn't stopped throwing up since I came to invite her to breakfast."

"She was fine yesterday." Matthew's voice was shaky, but it didn't seem so because of concern for Lauren.

"It's probably just the hangover." Henry hoped he was buying all of this.

"Hm…" He wasn't. "Doesn't matter. I need you and the team to meet me at the dig site ten minutes ago." His voice was stronger and more excited now. It made Henry's voice that more energized.

"Why, what's up?"

"I found it."

Henry's eyes lit up. "We're on our way." He tossed the phone to the nightstand and jumped to the duffel bag on the chair near the door. He pulled out a fresh pair of shorts, a pair of boxers and a blue tinted Hawaiian shirt. "Lauren, get out of there," he called out. "We've got to get to the site."

When she didn't answer, Henry went to the bathroom, almost tripping over himself as he pulled on his boxers. Lauren sat with her head bent back against the sink, her bare buttocks warming the porcelain tiles. She hoped the nausea still swimming in her stomach would dissipate, but held her hand on the edge of the toilet near a few stray drops of vomit just in case.

"Lauren. Did you hear me?"

"I'll…" Lauren shut her mouth and forced another round of vomit back into her stomach, then let out a soothing breath. "I'll catch up."

"All right," Henry said pulling on his shirt. "I'll round up the rest of the team and meet you out back, okay?"

"Yeah," she said, masking the shameful quiver in her voice. "Fine."

Henry glanced into the mirror next to the door, quickly ran his hands through his hair to tidy it up a bit and winked at himself with a pleasurable grin. "See you soon," he said, slapping the door frame before leaving.

Lauren waited until she heard the door to the room close and banged her head against the sink. A stroke of fresh pain filled her already throbbing head, the nausea giving way to a slow churning of regret that culminated in her eyes. How could she have slept with Henry? After all she promised herself, how could she?

To bring her emotions and nausea under control, Lauren sat perfectly still with her eyes closed for several more minutes. When she felt ready, she flushed the toilet and used the sink to help pull her body into an erect position. She tried to find an ounce of respect within the shadowy, bloodshot eyes that stared at her in the mirror, but when that failed, she traced the contours of the flesh that had been consensually violated. How was she supposed to face her team knowing what she had done? Would they forgive her? Would they even care? She splashed some water onto her face and let it drip onto the sink as she waited for some recognition,

some idea of excitement. When nothing came, she pulled the towel from the rack next to the shower, wiped her face clean and then wrapped it around her body.

Stupid slut, she thought as she walked from the bathroom and collected her things off the floor. Her room was the one directly adjacent to Henry's, so hopefully she could sprint across without anyone seeing her. She opened the door just a crack and was relieved when she saw the empty hall. Peering out of the room, Lauren saw Kara float across the kitchen to the refrigerator, which was out of view of the hall. Lauren took that as her cue and in three steps was inside her own room. Within ten minutes, she had changed into a pair of washed-out jeans and a slightly baggy shirt, thinking it would keep from accentuating any of the features Henry might find enticing.

Would she ever be able to look at him again?

She sluggishly headed to the kitchen. Thomas, Kara and Henry were joking around at the table, patiently waiting for her.

"There she is," Henry blurted out happily. "Feeling better?"

Lauren nodded slightly, wondering if Kara and Thomas knew anything beyond the lie he told Matthew.

"Come on then." Henry stood up. "A discovery awaits."

Kara and Thomas left as Henry held back. He smiled slightly and shook his head, answering the question that had been haunting Lauren this whole time.

He hadn't said a thing to them.

Lauren forced a smile of serene gratitude and walked with him to the door.

Connecticut – Saturday, 3:56 am

Kaleena let loose a deep, hoarse cough that sounded isolated and tired, then sucked in a mouthful of the stench that enveloped the room. She gagged reflexively, the sandpaper in her throat forcing her to heave dryly several times after. When it finally stopped, she stared at the ceiling through heavily moistened eyes and waited for her stomach to settle. *What the hell happened?* The last thing she

remembered was getting called a holy matriarch; everything else was black. She thought maybe she'd experienced an extreme migraine, but her head didn't hurt. In fact, her mind was clearer than she could ever remember it being, as if it had been flushed of all negativity and weight.

Turning to sit up, Kaleena hissed. Her hair was stuck to the floor in the dry vomit that now acted like glue between her hair and the carpet. At the sight of this disgusting fusion, her first instinct was once again to throw up. She ate it back and grabbed a clump of hair inches off the floor, making sure to keep her head low so as not to feel any pain as she tugged. It took a few minutes, but her hair did eventually peel away, giving off an eerie Velcro sound while leaving several loose strands behind. Kaleena fell away from the spot and combed her hand through her hair, some vomit still keeping chunks of it fused together. As she wiped her eyes of sleep and uncertainty, the face from the woods reappeared, flashing before her in the sparks of the shadows — a watery form of a loving, nurturing elegance. Who was it? Why was her subconscious producing such a vision? Kaleena didn't want to think about it.

She got up and stumbled to the bathroom. Switching on the light, Kaleena caught sight of several beer bottles and a present someone had left her in the toilet, floating in the pool of yellow water. "Son of a bitch." She pushed the seat down to cover the repulsive sight and sat on the fluffy blue toilet cover, draping her arms over her lap and resting her head against the wall. The whole situation made her ill, especially whenever the thought of Kyla using her returned to the forefront of her thoughts. How long had it been going on? When did Kyla become a wolf in sheered sheepskin? Was she so desperately in need of friendship that she would sacrifice her own dignity to have friends that would leave her in an instant when they didn't need her anymore? It all seemed more like a dream — nothing seemed to make any sense.

Kaleena turned on the shower and let the water run over her, massaging what she thought was her skin eating her bone and muscles to hash. The shower ran for nearly a half hour as she cleansed the residual vomit from her hair, continually

reminding herself about the night Kyla was raped, and how her love for her went deeper than simple popularity or understanding. Or so she thought. She finally released herself from the water's magnetic touch when it had turned mildly warm and curled her skin onto itself. Without drying off or even attempting to get changed, Kaleena paced to her bedroom and dropped onto the bed as if it were her grave. It took nearly thirty minutes to fall asleep as she continued tossing and thinking about her friend's decline.

How could she have stopped it? How could she have helped her?

Kaleena had been tested as one of the smartest people to ever live, yet none of that intellect helped her find an answer. Was it simply because she didn't want to accept that her friend might have been scarred deeper than she could understand? Was it that Kyla was so jealous of Kaleena, she couldn't accept the support she offered without expecting something in return? Was it that the two girls, both young and fragile, both unaware of the dangers that possess the world around them, were too naïve to believe the experience could be hidden in the murkiness of the heart?

When her mind finally fell into slumber, her dreams were awash with water. She drank from the hose outside Kyla's house after running around the back yard in sweltering ninety-five-degree heat. Kaleena sprayed Kyla after she tried to pull the hose away from her. Kyla chirped a scream and let go, running a few feet away while using her hands to try and stop the water from hitting her. Kaleena laughed until Kyla fell to her knees and cried. *Had she gone too far?* Kaleena lowered the hose.

"The mind is the true spirit of life." The whisper was soft and cold in Kaleena's ear. She felt it in the air, echoing behind her. When she turned, she was looking out into the ocean. A majestic white gown draped her body, a loose strap sliding from her shoulder as the long skirt floated carelessly in the wind. Kaleena didn't feel her age; she was mature, much more so than fourteen. She watched the crashing waves and listened to the music they brought to the shores. The smell of the salt and the soft touch of the dirt through her toes made it feel as if she was flying.

As nature created, destroyed, and recycled itself, Kaleena thought she saw

movement within the deep blue rush of the waves, though it could have just been an illusion. The setting sun, lighting the sky in ripples of orange and red, hindered her view of the motion. That is until the water rose above the crashing mist and formed what resembled a human. As it shifted toward her, the figure's head wavering slightly, the shape changed, forming itself into a watery double of the object of its affection. It had no features, yet Kaleena felt she was staring into a mirrored waterfall that radiated her essence. Without even knowing it, her lips blossomed into a luminous smile.

She felt safe. When the replica held out its hand (unable to spread its digits, which appeared clasped together as if the figure was wearing mittens), Kaleena's own hand reached out for the figure. The tips of their fingers touched. Kaleena's heart stopped beating, and a rush of warmth flooded her body. She moved closer, allowing the shimmering replicas to wrap its hand smoothly around her own and lead her toward the horizon, where the sun had almost begun its slumber. Heaven awaited as the stars played peek-a-boo with the haze to watch the magic unfold. There was no doubt in her mind she would be born again, a spirit of light, a beacon for her heart to grow and nourish those that had no one else to turn to. She closed her eyes and allowed her mind to free itself of its boundaries and soar into flight.

Why was it, then, that Kaleena felt her movement stop? Her reflection had turned to face her. Its head was mere inches from her own, tracing its nose about her neck and cheeks. A soft, cold breeze tickled her skin and a liquid sensation itched beneath her toes. Darkening blue waves surrounded her as the ocean water lapped upon her feet, warm and soothing. When she reacted to a slight chill across her chest, the figure moved away slightly. Kaleena wanted to object, hoping to understand where, why and how. But upon opening her mouth, only puffs of air were released, snakelike streamers that wrapped themselves around the replica like a prey. A quick touch to Kaleena's lips forced them closed. The silky stream that ran down Kaleena's arm as the figure touched her shoulder killed any sensation to run or worry or hide or scream. There had never been — would never be — anything as comfortable; an illusion that lit up her senses and kept her from any

harm. When the liquid glass touched her hand, Kaleena closed her eyes again. Her replica traced itself around her body, the cold breeze once again caressing her neck. She raised her head to the sky, accepting her love, her body growing numb with anticipation.

Amen Dello Keli, a voice whispered in her ear.

And then her vivacity ended with a rush of pain in the palm of her hand.

Kaleena screamed.

She awoke on her bed, sweat dripping from every inch of her body. Her breaths were heavy and there was a soft ache in the middle of her hand. It hurt like an ice pick in the eye, but as she examined her palm in the hazy light of dawn, there was nothing there, not even the light remnants of a scar. She rubbed it slowly, hoping to coax the pain away. What had happened out there in the ocean — in her dream?

In her illusion?

Knowing she'd be unable to fall asleep again, Kaleena lowered her ice-cold feet to the floor, brought her breathing under control and played that vivid scene over and over again until it was just another memory.

Bermuda – Saturday, 7:45 am

"I'd say you struck oil, Matthew, but…" Henry knelt down at the edge of the hole and removed his tiger-striped, mirrored sunglasses to get a better look at the pool of liquid. "What the hell is it?" he finished under his breath. Thomas, glaring at the substance over Henry's broad shoulders, shot Kara a confused glance, which got a puzzled shrug in return. A few feet behind them all was Lauren, holding her arms tight around her stomach. She wanted to get up close and personal with the mysterious goo, but the slow tumbling of nausea kept her distant.

"It's not water, either," Matthew said, kneeling on the opposite side of the shimmering puddle. He glanced up at his team. Kara rubbed her mouth as she usually did when trying to contemplate the simplest of answers. The tip of her right index finger brushed the gap between her upper and lower lips with a gentle,

consistent stroke as her middle finger lay limp against her rounded chin. Thomas, on the other hand, rubbed his temples profusely as if trying to find the switch to turn on his brain. Matthew wished it were that simple.

"What do you think it is, then?" Henry said.

"That's what we need to find out." Matthew caught the uncontrolled glimmer of excitement in Henry's eyes. He quickly grabbed hold of Henry's wrist before the idiot had a chance to touch the unknown substance. Henry hissed his discomfort.

"What the hell are you doing?" Matthew scolded.

Henry lowered his eyes slightly in defeat. Matthew waited a few more seconds to guarantee Henry wouldn't try anything stupid and let go of his wrist. Henry pulled it in to his chest. It throbbed slightly, but he was far too proud to rub the pain away in front of Matthew, who wasn't really paying attention at the moment anyway. When his mentor turned to grab the shovel he had retrieved earlier that morning, Henry caressed his wrist, sliding his hand in circular motions to help the waning soreness fade completely. He stood with Matthew and turned to Lauren. She appeared to be freezing. A smile may have helped warm her, but then again, a smile may have appeared arrogant. Lauren wasn't ready to accept what had happened between them, Henry knew that. So he slipped his sunglasses back on without changing one wrinkle in his features and focused his attention on the liquid. As he did, Matthew tossed the shovel with a quick, "Catch."

Henry flinched, but found his grip near the center of the shovel's handle, which unexpectedly felt as if he was tossed a feather but caught the ostrich. Kara jumped a couple of feet back, afraid the shovel (or Henry) might hit her. Before the tip of the shovelhead hit the ground, Henry adjusted to the weight and turned the tool upside down, lowering the top of the handle into the ground for stability.

"What the hell...?" he said, "hell" coming out more of a whisper, leaving the sentence incomplete. He squinted behind his glasses, trying to avoid the bright reflection of the rising sun glowing off the metal. Kara got hit with a full blast of the light and had to retreat behind Thomas to wash the unexpected glare from her sight. Spots flashed above her vision as she fluttered her eyelids open and

closed. Thomas had turned in time to avoid catching the light by lowering himself below the head of the shovel. He noticed right away that it wasn't the shovel that brought on the blinding light, but the liquid, which had glued itself to the tip. It was somewhat transparent, revealing some of the dirt that had been pressed to the shovel, but appeared as smooth as glass without one visible flaw. Henry took notice of him and shifted the shovel away.

"Wait," Thomas said, pulling back. His nose nearly touched the liquid as he examined it.

"What is it?" Henry said.

"It's not moving. It looks to have solidified itself to the shovel's head."

"What?" Henry crouched down. From this angle, he could finally see the liquid. Thomas used the Harvard pen he always carried around with him (*for good luck*, Lauren always joked) to touch the substance. It generously allowed the pen to indent the clip into its surface. "It's not completely solid," Thomas reported. "It actually looks pretty flexible." After removing the pen, the substance returned to its previous shape.

"What is it?" Matthew asked.

"Satan suck my dick if I know," Thomas muttered. "It's soft to the touch but reforms when I let go."

"So, it's like a Twinkie," Henry blurted out. His small smile disappeared at the sight of Matthew's stern gaze. This wasn't a time for stupid jokes. He returned his sights to Lauren, hoping for some helpful recognition. But she was no help, completely unaware of what was going on as she stared into the sky.

"Get a sample from the hole," Matthew said to Thomas, who instantly went to his light tan duffel bag sitting near Lauren. "Kara," Matthew continued without hesitation.

Kara rubbed her eyes one last time, using Matthew's voice to locate him. "Yeah?"

"I collected some of the pieces of the artifact we found yesterday. There may be more. I need a carbon dating and a translation of whatever text we can salvage as

soon as possible." He then rattled off a bunch of jargon Thomas and Kara happily ignored in favor of their own thoughts.

"Right," Kara said, nonchalantly. The spots had almost faded and she could once again make out large shapes and defined colors. She took notice of the artifact pile and stumbled over to it.

"Did you see that container?" Thomas asked Lauren, who barely registered his appearance. He finally found what he was looking for without her. "You okay?" he asked.

"Huh?" Lauren mumbled, observing Thomas with lazy eyes.

"You okay?" he said again, with a bit more perplexity.

Lauren nodded as the words melted into her thoughts — thoughts that felt as if they had been coming from a hundred light years away. "Yeah," she finally acknowledged. "Yeah. I'm fine. Just a bit under the weather, I think." Her words were slow and precise. Thomas wanted to reply, but thought better of it. He had a job to do; he'd take care of personal matters later.

"Henry," Matthew said as Thomas returned to the hole. "Take the shovel back to the room with Thomas and get me answers on its molecular composition."

Now on his knees, vulnerable of being pushed into the liquid if Henry was feeling jovial, Thomas absorbed the soft odor of phosphorous and steam. He especially took notice of the steam, as there was no indication that the liquid was at all hot or capable of radiating heat. Not even when he placed his bare hand just centimeters above the liquid did he feel anything but the cool morning breeze. But the longer he held it there, the more the intricate scarring laced around every inch of his hand burned. He wanted to pull it away, but the more he tried, the more he was compelled to keep it there and let it burn. He screamed for help.

Henry pulled him away from the hole with ease. "What the hell are you doing?"

Thomas ignored him and tenderly massaged his palm, focusing on the wounds he acquired that night in the woods when he was forced to burn his hand. It was the only night he would spend in the woods and the only night Thomas would ever go anywhere without his mother until her quiet death when he was fourteen.

Her death hit him hard; not only did he have no one else to care for him, but he never got over his guilt, as her death, in a way, had set Thomas free — free from the protection that had kept him secluded from all outside activities. But no matter how hard he tried, he could never escape the words of his mother, words that kept Thomas from exploring, from expanding his mind, from going beyond the borders of his own insecurity —

"Better safe than dead."

Better, indeed, as the one time she allowed him the chance to explore the world around him and do something — anything — as a kid, he allowed himself to be severely scarred.

"You okay, Thomas?" Henry asked, tapping him on the shoulder.

Thomas took a minute to return to reality, but then nodded and eked out a quick, "Yeah."

"Well, hurry up and get the sample. I want to start testing."

Again, it took a moment to register, but Thomas shook it all off and nodded. "Yeah. Sorry." Taking his mother's words to heart —

Better safe than dead! —

Thomas pulled his excavation gloves from his back pocket and tossed it over his scarred hand before scooping up some of the substance. It was heavy, much like a thick pile of mud, and became solid the instant it hit the plastic. Careful not to touch any of it with his bare hand, he tried to shake the excess liquid off the container, but it had solidified itself to the side, unwilling to move.

"Henry. Grab me that knife out of my bag, will ya'," he said, staring at his reflection inside the hardened dark-turquoise plate. He looked young; his distin-guishable crow's feet and myriad of other wrinkles that had formed around his features over the last ten years had seemingly disappeared.

"Hey," Henry said, tapping Thomas's right shoulder with the butt of the small utility knife. "Earth to Tommy."

Thomas registered the knife quickly. "Thanks," he said, grabbing the red handle from Henry. Careful not to cut the container, Thomas slowly carved a line at the

top; a surgeon couldn't have been more precise. After reaching the outer edge, he lowered the blade of the knife underneath the top portion of the liquid and peeled downward. Surprisingly, the liquid seemed happy to be removed. The substance floated back to the hole like a feather and landed gently on top of the pool, where it once again became part of the liquid below it, as if it had never solidified.

"Magnificent," Thomas whispered. He slapped Henry on the back of the shoulder. "Let's get this party started," he said, doing his best to sound hip. Thomas tried to make eye contact with Lauren before picking up his bag, but she seemed to be avoiding both him and Henry without appearing to avoid them. Henry pushed Thomas forward before he was able to say anything, leaving nothing behind but a breath from his open lips.

"Come on," Henry said, pretending Lauren wasn't even there. It was the best he could do to keep her from completely breaking down. Thomas glanced back to Matthew, who was now helping Kara gather some pieces of the artifact by placing them each in small sandwich bags, no matter what the size. He wondered a moment if he should wait for her, if only to see if Lauren would show any recognition. But Matthew wanted the analysis ASAP, and it looked like Kara would still be several minutes. No point in getting chewed out for something so trivial.

"I'll see you guys back at the room," he called out, stalling just a bit longer. Kara waved a quick goodbye but kept her focus on the artifact. Matthew was far too focused on one of the pieces to even register his words. Thomas didn't much care that Matthew was off in his own world; he always was. But he had hoped Kara would have at least looked at him, maybe flash him one of her light smiles that showed her pasty white teeth. This wasn't the time to take anything to heart, however; things were starting to get interesting. That was when he realized if he didn't get the substance back to the room quickly, it would no doubt petrify. He flashed one last excited grin at Lauren and jogged off after Henry.

"That oughta do it," Kara said, placing the last piece in her duffel bag.

"Good luck putting it all back together," Matthew said, a slight wink in his voice.

"You're not coming?"

"I gotta get this hole covered up."

"Good idea." Kara fastened her bag and threw it over her shoulder. "Wouldn't want some frisky teenagers think it was some sort of natural hot tub."

Matthew chuckled.

"See you back at the room," Kara said, cocking her eyebrows in eager anticipation. She walked back toward the room at a steady pace that wasn't quite a walk, but wasn't quite a jog. Matthew kept his sights on her until Lauren took over his view. She stood statuesque without any sign of life. He knew he'd seen her like this before, but was having a hard time remembering when that was. She looked sickened by something, but at the same time, frightened. He tried to recall what happened last night, but his memory remained jumbled. From what he remembered, there was a bit of flirtation between her and Henry as they danced, but that seemed to be a very odd thing to be bothering her. Lauren had had some drinks, perhaps she was reacting to breaking her vow of sobriety. Then again, that still seemed a bit heavy of a reaction for just that. Had something happened between her and Henry after he left the bar? What he knew for certain was that she didn't want to talk about it and Matthew was far from one to push anyone into talking about anything he had no business knowing. If she *were* willing to open up to him, he would be there for her. Until then, he would keep his distance, emotionally.

"Lauren," he said, walking over to the hole. When she didn't respond, he called again. "Lauren."

Lauren broke from her trance and found Matthew's eye line. "Yeah," she choked out.

"Can you help me get this hole covered?" Matthew avoided anything having to do with her state of mind.

"Huh?" Lauren looked down at the liquid. "Oh, right," she said, a little less subdued. "Yeah, of course." She slowly worked her way to Matthew. Having not asked if she was all right must have helped. "We should get some sheets of plywood to cover the hole," she said, her eyes holding steady on the liquid.

"My thoughts exactly," Matthew said. "Let's go."

Lauren kept her eyes on her feet as she walked with Matthew to the jeep he'd rented after arriving on the island. Ever the gentleman, Matthew held the passenger door open for her. Her eyes remained opposite of his as he jumped in (appearing as cool as Bo and Luke Duke's cousins), instead keeping them plastered on the horizon.

The two of them spent the next two hours in near silence, Matthew speaking only when he had to. They covered the hole with a couple of eight-by-ten sheets of plywood and a couple of feet of dirt, making sure it was thoroughly covered. As Matthew finished packing the dirt down, Lauren dropped her shovel and sat on their man-made piece of earth. Resting her elbow on her knee, she raised her hand to her chin and stared out into the distant ocean. Matthew watched her, using his own shovel as a crutch to prop himself into a comfortable position. He could tell she seemed ready... for something, and felt it was time to find out how ready she was. He pushed the shovel deeper into the ground and joined her in her spiritual walk along the horizon. Unable to find anything to say to break the silence, he placed his hand in between her shoulder blades and gently rubbed her back. Small tears formed at the base of her eyes. Her lips quivered delicately as she lowered her head to Matthew's shoulder, wrapping her arm around his back and tightly grasping his other shoulder.

She cried. Matthew held her in silence as she finally let her heart pour out.

Connecticut – Saturday, 7:15 am

Kaleena woke up. Her eyelids were heavy weights and her back was sore in a dozen places. As her sight came into focus, she noticed she was lying on the couch in her living room and smelled the faint aroma of Pine Sol coming from the rubber dish gloves stuck to her hands. There was only one other time Kaleena could remember sleeping on this couch and that was the night her mother walked out on her. It had been a rough evening, watching her mother pack everything she

owned into two large suitcases. At first, Kaleena thought she was going on another cruise (which was what Kaleena called her mother's expeditions), but after a third suitcase was pulled from the closet and the last shirt was pulled off the rack, the hanger thrown to the chair across the room with all the others, Kaleena realized this was something much different.

An hour before, her mother had been fighting on the phone and neither noticed that Kaleena had picked up the receiver in her bedroom so she could listen to both sides of the conversation. Phrases such as, "I can't do this anymore," "Please just wait for me," and "It's just not working out," were bandied about over the course of the almost two-hour conversation, at the end of which, Kaleena's mother locked herself in her room. She couldn't be certain, but she could swear she heard her crying.

"Where are you going?" Kaleena asked, having taken a break from writing.

Kaleena heard the answer but never wanted to believe it. Her mother followed her words with a soft kiss on the cheek, the forehead and then on top of the head — all in between holding back tears with breaths of strength and defeat. Kaleena pressed her hand against the windowpane as she watched the cab disappear around the buildings ten minutes later. She was alone for the first time in her life and sleeping in her bed gave her nightmares. The only safe place she could find was the couch — the one the three of them sat on opening Christmas presents every year; the one Kaleena got sick on after eating her whole birthday cake in one sitting; the one her parents would hold each other on and kiss and hug as Kaleena watched *SpongeBob SquarePants*.

The couch where Kaleena heard those fateful words again.

"To find happiness, Kaleena. To find my life."

Kaleena's stomach turned a bit as the whisper faded from her thoughts. She hadn't spoken to her mother since that night, not even on holidays or her birthday, but deep down, she longed to see her again.

Stop it, Kaleena, she whispered to herself. *Forget it. It wasn't your fault.* Why she always had to remind herself that her mother's decision to leave was not her

fault was a question she may never know the answer to. No matter how much she felt it in her heart that her mother simply wasn't happy, her complicated mind constantly reminded her that she was part of the reason.

Hoping that moving around would help shift her thoughts to something else, she sauntered to the bathroom to take a look at herself in the mirror. Having spent the majority of the night cleaning up the remnants of the party — scrubbing the vomit from the carpet, throwing away all of the beer bottles and stray condoms, and vacuuming the entirety of the apartment — Kaleena looked dead. Her hair had been pulled up in a bun that had started to fall out, the rubber bands more than likely tangled within. Her eyes were slightly bloodshot and there was a slight hint of rolls forming underneath.

"Rough night," she said to herself before dropping her red and white checkered boxers and sitting on the toilet. She rubbed her eyes again, wiping a bit of sleep away, and peered up to the clock on the wall.

7:23

"Shit!" She rushed to finish her business and then dashed to her room, where she threw on a light blue tank top, a see-through shirt and a pair of washed-out jeans before grabbing her book bag and heading out the door. She didn't have time to fix her hair or put on any make-up; she was late — for the second day in a row.

Bermuda – Saturday, 10:26 am

Kara was at the kitchen table with pieces of the artifact spread out near a collection of sandwich bags piled off to the side. On her right sat a purple MacBook Air humming passionately to itself. Several books, from texts on ancient Babylonian to Aztec and Mayan histories, had been sprawled out on the counter behind her. She had spent the last few hours studying the inscriptions, trying to organize the symbols into any possible coherent thoughts and sifting through documents she'd pulled off the Internet. From what she could tell, most of the symbols looked very

similar to an early Aramaic dialect, but with slight nuances that led her to believe they may have roots in an old Yucatec Mayan language.

Kara had become fluent in Aramaic and Latin during graduate school, eventually teaching Sociolinguistics for a few years at Brown and earning a grant to spend a year uncovering a series of tablets in Babylon, which would take three additional years to fully translate. The texts were found to detail the history Kara didn't recognize, and given the nature and the scripture of the tablets, she believed she had just discovered a technologically advanced culture that existed long before the time of the first known humanoid. For years after, Kara searched for additional evidence, unwilling to seek advice from another historian. The find was too rich for her to part with. That decision led to writing an article for *Scientific American* called, "The Lives of Human Technology," which would be translated into a few dozen languages across the globe. She'd use the article's notoriety to finance a museum outside of Providence to showcase the growth, fall and rise of technology throughout history and return to teaching several anthropological linguistics classes at Brown. One day, while studying a new tablet found a few miles from Bethlehem, a knock on her office door caused her to lose her thought process.

"Office hours are two to three, Wednesdays and Fridays," she roared in frustration.

"I'm not a student," the voice chimed from behind the door. "My name is Matthew Stevens. I'd like to talk to you about your article in *Scientific American*."

It took her a minute to register the name, but when she did, the tablet was crumpling her notes within seconds.

"Matthew Stevens," Kara said as she opened the door. "It's an honor." She shook his hand, nearly pulling him into the room. "Please have a seat."

Matthew smiled and adjusted the sport coat that hid most of the wrinkles on his dusty-blue shirt. "Thank you," he mumbled as he sat. Not like Kara would have heard him anyway.

"To what do I owe the pleasure?" Kara said, slamming the door shut before taking her own seat.

"As I said, I came across the article you wrote about advanced technology in history and was genuinely intrigued."

"Thank you," she said. "Thank you. I've read some of your work as well. Very captivating."

"Then you know we have something in common."

Kara thought a moment, but couldn't come up with an answer. She shook her head, hinting for more information.

"Your paper goes into great detail about evidence you gathered to prove technology existed before technology existed."

"Correct," Kara said, unsure of where he was headed. "Not that I've earned much credence. Is that what you believe we have in common? People think we're insane?"

Matthew chuckled and leaned in closer, propping himself up on her desk. "I don't think you or your theories are insane."

"And why is that?" Kara said, slightly skeptical.

"You've read my work," he said. "You know my theories on the past."

"Yes, but what does technology have to do with 'magical powers'?" Air quotes and all.

"Humans, as you know, only use a small percentage of their brain's full capacity. I believe that the Pharaoh's 'magical powers'" (again with the air quotes) "was not magic at all, but a byproduct of accessing the percentage of the brain we refrain from using." Matthew leaned back in his chair, as did Kara, slightly more intrigued now.

"Okay… So, what you're saying is that the Pharaohs were the last of a line of humans capable of using a higher percentage of the brain's functional capacity."

"In short, yes. But I believe it goes beyond that. After reading your article, I started to look into the possibility that the Pharaohs were part of a culture that was also technologically advanced."

"Do you have any evidence to back that up?"

"Not yet. That's why I'm here."

Kara leaned back to the desk, folding her hands and resting them on top of the tablet. "So, you want my help to prove your new theory?"

"Not just that. I want us to help each other prove that there was advanced human life before the Genesis written of in the Bible."

"And how do you figure we do that?"

"By finding a lost city, one that was written about long ago by the great philosopher, Plato."

Kara leaned back, laughing. "You want me to help you find Atlantis?"

Matthew raised his eyebrows, his eyes registering an emphatic, "You bet!"

Kara toned her laughter down to a small chuckle. "And what do you plan on doing? Go down to the Bahamas and excavate the Bimini Road?"

"The Bimini Road is a hoax. Edgar Cayce wrongly interpreted natural occurrences of ocean floor seismology and lava flow as a road to the western ridge of Atlantis. Believe me, if Cayce had never made the prediction, it's unlikely anyone would have even made the connection. Plus, the stones were said to have been less than twelve thousand years old. I believe the civilization of Atlantis to be much older than that."

"And much more technologically advanced?"

"Reports say a giant wave buried Atlantis. Cayce believes a death ray killed the entire civilization. But whatever the reason, you know as well as I do that there have been shipwrecks with technology that we once believed were impossible for the time frame the ship was sunk. Not to mention the Library of Alexandria and its link to a technologically advanced society. Me, I believe some of the inhabitants must have survived in order to resurrect the human race and pass on their history."

Chuckles, and then, "It all sounds logical enough, but let me play devil's advocate for a minute. If what you say is true, how come we aren't as advanced as this unknown society?"

"De-evolution."

"De-evolution." She restated the word without an ounce of belief.

"The theory of evolution states that a species must adapt to their changing environments in order to survive. If it's true that technology destroyed Atlantis, then it's safe to say that the survivors would not want future generations to acquire the knowledge that would eventually destroy them. Each generation would know less and less about their past and how to tap into those regions of the brain, leading them to a point where only the essential areas could be accessed."

"Again, for the sake of argument, let's say that's true."

"Then we can say, in rare cases, people develop the ability to use the hidden areas of the brain, giving them what most would call supernatural powers."

"Okay. I'll buy that. So, assuming your theory is correct, and Atlantis existed only to destroy itself, what makes you think we'll be able to find even the smallest remnant when no one else has ever been able to do so?"

"That's where you come in."

Kara seemed mystified.

"I believe the answers to Atlantis's true location can be found right under your nose." Matthew tapped his finger on the tablet.

Again, a nice hearty laugh. "You think these tablets came from Atlantis?"

"And then kept in the Library of Alexandria until it was destroyed."

"And what, pray tell, makes you think that?"

"You mentioned the tablets appear to be a history... a type of journal that talks about a life of great technology, correct?"

"Yes, but there's no mention of anything referencing a lost city, a great destruction or even the name Atlantis."

"Well, there wouldn't be any reference to the name 'Atlantis.' As far as we know the term came from Plato, referring to where Atlantis resided."

"In the Atlantic Ocean."

"Right."

"But the explorers at Bimini have already gone through that song and dance."

"I'm not talking about Atlantis being near the Bahamas. I'm convinced it doesn't. But I do believe it exists *somewhere* in the Atlantic Ocean."

"So then answer me this. If the writers were descendants of Atlantis, why use sandstone tablets? Why not write on something more advanced? Paper or computers?"

"To disconnect themselves from technology for one. And, what better way to preserve your history over thousands, maybe hundreds of thousands of years?"

A glint of excitement finally sparkled the tips of Kara's lips.

"It also would have insured that when someone *did* find the tablets, we wouldn't freak out due to the unexplained nature of what we were looking at."

Kara tried hard to find a hole in Matthew's theory, but couldn't. It all made perfect sense to her. "You're good," she finally said. "Any ideas as to where we might find this technologically advanced lost city?"

"Not until we find out what's written on those tablets, word for word."

Kara nonchalantly laid her arms over the tablet. "What do I get out of this?"

"Recognition, some amount of fame and most likely several thousands of dollars in grants to continue your research and keep your dying museum afloat."

Kara couldn't argue. This was her chance to prove she was right. She handed Matthew the tablet.

"I've only been able to translate the first few sentences. It reads, 'So much to ignore, so much to fight, but for every last droplet, there was once a life. Rich in heritage, rich in humanity, rich in theory, rich in abomination, fear rises out of the water to blend with the myth of the land...'"

Matthew methodically scanned the tablet with awe. "Marvelous. Can I see the others?"

Kara and Matthew spent the next few months reviewing the tablets together, translating and re-translating every line, some changing due to discrepancies in text and symbols, others completely ignored due to lack of reference. One tablet talked about a white-haired woman dressed in white gowns ruling over a land of great power; another talked about the ability to control others and the ease of companionship among those that loved. The history was divided, though, and pieces were missing. Matthew figured there had to be more tablets, placed out of order so only the strongest mind would be able to decipher the documents and use them for unselfish purposes. "Only a true heart would find all the tablets," Matthew would say. However, he also knew he wouldn't need all of them to find what he was looking for. There were descriptions on one tablet, specifically, that described landmarks that led Matthew to Puerto Rico. Throughout all of it, Kara did her best to remain skeptical. But as she finished her translations on the broken pieces of Bermuda artifacts, her heart raced with exhilaration.

"We found it," she whispered as Lauren, less distant now and hanging onto a hint of a smile, walked into the kitchen with Matthew a step behind, his hand placed gently just above the edge of her spine.

"I think I found it," Kara said louder.

Matthew's eyes lit up. He swept past Lauren and looked over the scattered pieces. "Tell me," he said.

"It was difficult at first," Kara began. "It would have been a lot easier to translate if I had the whole thing, but I think we got most of what we needed. I started by translating some of the more recognizable symbols, which in itself was a pain. But once I figured them out, I used that as the base for everything else." She pointed to the computer.

Lauren was on the opposite side of the table now and leaned over to join Matthew in reading the text Kara had transcribed under scans of the broken pieces:

The tip of Trifecta... highest mountain will mark...
distance show light when in the center from home...
the map is read through...

"How do you know these combinations are correct?" Lauren said.

"Easy. The way the pieces fit together signifies which symbols go where."

"But there's no way to be sure," Lauren added.

Kara took a deep breath. "Not without the rest of the text, no," Kara said. "But changing some of the nouns and verbs still gives us the same overall message."

"What are you thinking?" Matthew asked no one in particular.

"The Bermuda Triangle," Kara said emphatically.

"Are you serious?" Lauren asked.

"Look. It talks about a trifecta and the center marking home," Kara explained. "It appears this may have been some sort of map, much like you'd see at a mall, except this one leads travelers to Atlantis."

Matthew carefully studied every word. He stopped on one symbol without any text. It appeared to be a pyramid wrapped in a faded star. "This last symbol. Is there any translation?"

"Not that I can figure. It seems like the symbol of home, two sides marking the three points of a triangle."

"San Juan, Puerto Rico; Miami, Florida; Bermuda," Lauren recited, recalling all the places they had been in the last few years. "They led us to each point of the triangle." She suddenly felt more confident in the find.

"And if we're right, Atlantis can be found in the direct center."

"Matthew." Thomas called out as he hustled into the kitchen. "Glad you're back. You have to see this. Come on."

Matthew, Kara and Lauren followed Thomas to Matthew's room, where several pieces of chemical analysis equipment, laptops and microscopes had been set up. Henry sat in front of an electron microscope, peering at what looked like a slide containing the blue substance. Next to him was a Petrie dish with a small flame dancing about in varying shades of blue and white.

"We ran several tests on the substance," Thomas started as he stepped up to one of the three computer screens, "and we found that it carried a high amount of hydrocarbon mixtures that sort of resembles light naphtha fractions."

"Gasoline?" Lauren asked curiously.

"That's what we thought at first, but there were also trace elements of petroleum and ammonia, plus some chemical that we have yet to identify."

"My god," Lauren whispered. "With that mix, that stuff could ignite with a slight breath."

"It's extremely flammable, that's for sure," Henry said, pointing to the flame.

"This was two milliliters of that stuff. We started burning it about an hour ago." It didn't look to anyone like it was ready to burn out.

"Which explains why it cools so quickly on the surface, as well," Thomas said. "If this stuff was underground, it was most likely being heated by the magma below the surface."

"If that's true, how on earth has it not exploded?" Lauren questioned.

"I think I know," Henry said. "Looking at this, that unidentified substance may be something similar to silica."

"So... a semi-distant cousin of magma?" Matthew asked.

"With a mid-range boiling temperature," Henry added.

"And," Thomas continued, grabbing a glass of water from the nightstand near the burning material, "an extreme resilience to water." He poured the water over the Petrie dish, but none of it made it to the base. It evaporated at the touch of the flame, which held steady and strong against the attack, breathing in any and all smoke generated by the evaporation.

"Any carbon dating info?" Matthew asked, seemingly unimpressed.

"Not yet," Kara said. "We don't have the right equipment here to get a precise reading. I'm going to need to get back to Brown to get a definitive answer."

"All right then. Let's pack it up. We're leaving."

"Where to?" Henry asked.

"Everyone take a few days for yourselves. We'll meet up in Miami in a week."

"Miami? What for?"

"To begin our trip to Atlantis." He said it as if everyone should have known the answer.

"You found it?" Thomas said, almost as excited as Kara.

"We hope."

"Where?" Henry asked, his interest piqued.

"Dead in the middle of the Bermuda Triangle."

"The Triangle..." Henry said, now a little nervous.

"I hate to bring this up," Thomas said, "but we have barely enough money

left to get back to the states. I don't think our friend's going to pick up the tab on this one."

"Let me worry about that," Matthew said calmly, grabbing his suitcase. "You guys just meet me in Miami-Dade next Saturday. Nine o'clock sharp."

Everyone watched Matthew throw stuff, unfolded, into his suitcase. Noticing their dead stares, he said, "What are you waiting for? Start packing."

Lauren and Kara shot from the room as Thomas and Henry tore down the equipment. "And someone bury that flame outside."

Henry did just that, passing Lauren as she closed her bedroom door.

Most of her stuff hadn't been unpacked, as she never felt it was worth the effort. The only items she had to pack were the clothes she wore the day before. Everything, piled in the center of the bed, reminded her of the previous night, from the shirt she had so quickly tossed away to the jeans that had been nearly chewed off by Henry. Her stomach once again tightened, leading her back to the bathroom floor, where she would stay until Matthew knocked on the door.

"Ready to go, Lauren?"

Lauren choked back her queasiness and coughed, "Yeah. Give me a minute. I'll be right out."

"I'll be in the jeep." Matthew's voice was calm and soothing.

Lauren flushed the toilet and balanced her slight dizziness by taking hold of the sink. Her head hurt, her stomach pinched and she felt hot. She wiped some sweat from her forehead and stepped out into the bedroom, where a small breeze of fresh air blew past her, calming her nerves slightly. It was going to be good to get back home. She grabbed her bag, refusing to pick up any of the clothes that reminded her of being knowingly sullied, and headed out. When she reached the jeep, her head still pounded but her stomach had settled. She figured it was because Henry had already gone.

"You gonna be okay?" Matthew asked.

"I think so," Lauren said. "I just need these few days."

Matthew didn't say another word.

Connecticut – Saturday, 9:53 am

Kaleena checked her watch. Her ninety-minute lab had started at nine. As she raced toward the computer lab on the south side of the campus, she hoped the professor didn't embarrass her the way he had the day before. Her fears gave way to frustration the moment she opened the door to find an empty room.

"Damn it," she hissed. After a foolish attempt to find someone, she kicked the nearest ergonomic chair and headed back out.

"Kaleena," the professor called, fast-walking toward her. He eyed her hair. "What happened to you?"

"I overslept," Kaleena sighed, avoiding any long explanations about her night.

"Well, I'm glad you made it," he said, standing a little closer than Kaleena felt comfortable with.

"Where is everyone?"

"It was a short lab today. Half hour."

"This may be a bit much —"

"Not at all," the professor cut in, placing his hand on Kaleena's right shoulder just above her tricep. "That's why I stuck around. I figured you'd show up at some point."

"Thank you," Kaleena said, not even realizing the professor was guiding her to her assigned station. As the computer hummed to life, the professor closed the door. Kaleena was too busy collecting her notebook to notice him sit down at the station next to her. He placed his hand on the back of her chair as she typed her username and password into the sign-in screen. The desktop took its sweet time to load, which gave her a moment to grab her pen and search through her notes. The professor watched every move like a vulture. What gave him away was the light grunt he let slip.

"What are you doing?" Kaleena asked.

The professor seemed lost in her eyes, when finally, he said, "Let's get started." He shifted his seat a little closer. Kaleena thought about sliding away, but she wasn't sure if her nervous paranoia was the result of bliss or anxiety, so she tried

to ignore her unease.

"We were working on relativity equations —"

"Kaleena, can I ask you a question?" The professor moved even closer, making sure to catch a glimpse of flesh peeking out from under her tank top. "Do you find me attractive?"

Kaleena was stunned. "Professor?" was all she could spit out. Confusion and panic laced her question Anxiety was definitely starting to take over. She tried shifting her chair backward, but he stopped it with his foot and set his hands on her knees. "Let go, Professor." Kaleena grabbed his hands, but he held strong. "Professor," she said again, growing ever more disturbed by what was transpiring.

"I've seen the way you look at me, Kaleena." The professor took a hold of Kaleena's hand and brought it close to his face, caressing it with his thumbs.

"Let go," Kaleena said more forceful. All of her strength meant nothing against the professor's.

"You're young, Kaleena," he whispered. "You're smart and extraordinarily beautiful." His eyes glazed over her body as he kissed her hand.

Aggressiveness filled her veins, which she hoped would fill her voice with enough strength to push him away. "What are you doing?"

"I'm teaching, Kaleena." He rested his hand under her chin. "Teaching you to be a woman." He leaned in to kiss her.

"No," she screamed, slamming her forehead into his nose. He let go, allowing her the split second she needed to flee. It wasn't enough.

"Damn it," he shouted just before bolting for the door and pushing her back to the computer. A slideshow of flowers, rainbows and other outdoor nature washed across the screen. The professor secreted sexual desire; Kaleena sweated the fear she saw in Kyla the night she lost her innocence. "Kaleena," he commanded, rubbing his cheek gently. "I'm not going to hurt you."

"You sick bastard," she whispered, witnessing Kyla pray through tears that the man approaching her would just go away. Her friend's heart raced as the man touched her breasts and pushed her to the bed. The betrayal was heavy; the complete lack of power, the pain and regret swarmed around her like a hive of hornets. Her body was numb, her legs stiff; she could do nothing but allow the man to use her — to deflower her. She smelled the stench of semen and alcohol as she lay curled on the bed, hurt, bruised. A shadow haunted the corner of her mind, a shadow that revealed a man Kaleena once held in high regard as someone she could trust; a man she thought was a caring, passionate friend and mentor.

"Please, Kaleena. Don't fight it," the monster said as he got within a few steps of her.

"Get the fuck away from me," Kaleena screamed.

He must have seen her next move coming, as when she threw her leg at his knee, he grabbed her ankle and pulled her away from the desk. Kaleena landed on the floor, but not before her head hit the side of the table at the base of her neck. Her head pulsated; she could hardly move, let alone feel the professor straddle her legs above the knee. She heard what sounded like a belt being undone, preparing himself to send her into a madness she wasn't ready to travel. He unbuttoned her jeans. The tips of his fingers brushed the top of her underwear as he pulled them down her chilled legs. Kaleena tried to scream, but only dry air escaped.

"Calm yourself," a soothing voice whispered in her ear, which was followed by a moist kiss on the corner of her mouth. Kaleena cried as she readied herself for what was to come. But as the professor's hands slid up her shirt, a fresh courage erupted in the back of her mind.

"Don't let it happen to you," Kyla said, her head resting on Kaleena's lap. "Don't be weak like me."

"You weren't weak, Kyla," Kaleena tried to comfort. "You were the victim. There was nothing you could have done."

"Sure there was." Kyla sat up. "I could have fought back."

"You could have been killed."

"You don't think I was?"

Kaleena screamed and flailed her legs as hard as she could. Her arms waved wildly about, striking anything she got close to, damn the pain. The professor

tried to avoid all of her kicks and hits to bring her back under his control. Within seconds, he had squeezed her legs in between his and slammed her wrists against the floor.

"Stay the fuck still, you bitch. I don't want to hurt you."

"Go fuck yourself, you piece of shit," she said with as much authority as she could muster. The spit in his face was a nice touch. The sick bastard just smiled and relished in the taste of the saliva that dripped down to his lips. "I can only hope everything else tastes just as good," he said, reaching into his pants.

"Fucking bastard!" she screamed. "Stop! Help!"

As the professor grabbed the elastic around her boxers, he was torn from Kaleena's body and thrown against the far wall near his desk. Kaleena immediately crawled on her elbows as far away as the room would allow. In between the two was a man (so she thought it was a man) wearing a long black coat with a hood covering his head.

The professor took his time to get back up, groggy as all hell. "Get the fuck out of here," he yelled to the stranger. "This doesn't concern you."

The stranger didn't say a word. He pounded his way to the professor and punched him in the jaw, sending the weasel back to the ground. Blood dripped from his mouth and nose as he attempted to stand again. But the stranger wouldn't let him. He kicked him in the balls and followed that up with a shot to the gut for good measure. When it looked as if the professor had caught his breath, the stranger sent another steel-toed boot to the professor's face, knocking a tooth from his mouth as he fell unconscious. Kaleena's tears held strong as the stranger knelt down to look the professor over. For a moment, she thought the man would break his neck, but all he did was turn to look at her. Bright yellow circles hid deep within the shadows of his hood. Kaleena cowered into the corner as the stranger knelt down next to her.

"Don't hurt me," she said in a small voice.

The stranger said nothing as he traced Kaleena's body with his eyes. As her breath grew heavy, sweat pouring from her brow, the stranger shifted her shirt down

her arm. She wanted to scream, knowing her rape had simply been transferred to this new attacker. But as he caressed his finger along a small scar just above her right breast, Kaleena felt his need to protect her.

"I have a message," the stranger finally said, sliding her shirt back up, hiding the scar beneath it. "Your father has found something very important."

Kaleena's terror filled with confusion. "My f-father," she stuttered.

"You must give him what he needs and do as he asks."

"What?"

"Do as he asks. But don't allow him to leave you behind."

With that, the stranger left.

Kaleena stayed huddled for a few more minutes, trying desperately to understand "the message." The need to be in the comfort of her father's arms was strong, but the urge to know more about her savior and those words raced through her mind. She stood, slowly — methodically — her eyes glued to the professor. Was he unconscious? Had the stranger killed her assailant? On the surface, she couldn't have cared less. She fastened her pants and ran to the door. But then an overwhelming need to check to see if he was alive washed over her.

The grunt was loud, but not as loud as her slow, steady steps that led her to the man she partially wished was dead and partially wished had somehow been possessed by some demon. It was the only explanation she could come up with for his odd, vile behavior. Then again, it's always the ones you don't expect, isn't it?

It took a moment for her to calm her nausea before she collected the strength to touch his wrist.

Boop-boop... boop-boop.

The pulse was slow, but steady. A bewildered relief swept over her. "Lucky son-of-a-bitch." She left him to bleed. Her first act once outside was to find the stranger, but obviously, he was nowhere to be found. "Dammit," she said under her breath. That was when her legs buckled with icy numbness. She sat down against the building and for the next hour, her body shook. Only then was she able to dial the police. She considered contacting campus security first, but after

the ineptness in dealing with her situation just twelve hours earlier, she thought better of it.

"911 emergency," the operator chimed. "Please hold."

"Goddammit," she yelled, lowering the phone to her side and taking one last look around for the stranger, whose message still rang loud and clear in the back of her mind.

Do as he says. Don't get left behind.

"Thank you for holding. What is your emergency?"

Kaleena raised the phone to her ear after a slight hesitation. "Yeah," she said, her voice a bit light. "I want to report an attempted rape."

Connecticut – Saturday, 5:25 pm

Minuscule steps were all Kaleena could muster as she walked along the sidewalk outside of her apartment. She had left the hospital four hours earlier but couldn't do anything but wander since then, blown away by how no one believed her. When the police arrived, Kaleena was waiting patiently in the computer lab, willing the professor to remain unconscious. She didn't know why she stayed, and was unsure of what she would have done if he had awakened to find her watching him. The thought of her mutilated body wrapped between the computers, blood dripping from her fingertips and toes forming small, drying puddles below her, made Kaleena ill. She spent twelve minutes on the cold, partially dirty bathroom tile, staring into the mucky toilet water. The urge to vomit was strong, but she was able to expel her sickness through her tears. Before leaving the stall, Kaleena stared at Kyla's picture on the screen of her phone, her thumb hovering nanometers above the call button. The slightest breath would have activated the call. She wanted to apologize for what happened the night before, to be the stronger friend, but the attack still controlled her emotions. It would be better if her mind was clear when she talked to Kyla, making sure she received her full attention.

Her nerves had calmed dramatically when she returned to the lab to find the professor lying on the floor, lifeless. Revenge fantasies spun through her mind in a wonderfully delicious web of reckoning. Part of her hoped he stayed unconscious, trapped in a dreamless coma for the rest of his life. Another part wanted him to be brain damaged, able to register nothing but light and dark, hardly able to chew his own food — a vegetable, awake but dead. But the more she contemplated her revenge, the less she wanted his life to be over. Being locked up for life in a cell with musclebound Bruce teaching him the real meaning of rape would have been the most deserving punishment. Witnessing his wife curse his name and his children finding out what a sick psycho their father truly was in hopes they would refrain from making the same mistakes in life would also be acceptable. Then again, with recent reports of rapists and child molesters getting off with hardly any jail time for their unthinkable crimes, Kaleena could only wish the professor received irrefutable justice, either by law or God himself.

The professor was still out for the count when the police arrived. Their first act of heroism was calling for medical assistance to aid the professor. *Let him lie there*, Kaleena thought. *Let him choke on his own blood.* It gave her a chill.

"What happened here?" asked a fully rounded officer, looking like Danny DeVito playing Chief Wiggum. A diet of doughnuts and Snickers would lead this cop to a really early grave. He scratched his balding hairline with the tip of his pen as he waited for an answer.

"The bastard tried to rape me," Kaleena said, suppressing her building rage.

"What were you doing here with him?"

"I was here for my lab."

"Lab?" the rotund officer repeated, looking Kaleena over. "How old are you?"

"Fourteen."

The cop seemed puzzled and entertained at the same time. "Is this a joke? Am I on some weird-ass reality program?" Was he looking for a hidden camera?

Profanities sat on the edge of her throat. Kaleena looked down, hoping that would be enough to calm the aggression. She caught sight of her bag and pulled

out her ID card. Even after handing it to the butterball, it was clear the cop still didn't believe her.

"I'm gonna have to check this out," the cop said. "Stay here." He labored his way out of the room, leaving Kaleena alone with her attacker. The paramedics arrived a short time later. They set the backboard next to the professor and placed a brace around his neck. Kaleena swore she saw the professor's arm move as the paramedics transferred him to the board. She had to close her eyes and turn away. A long, cool intake of air was enough to calm her stomach.

"How are you?" one of the medics asked. Her voice was delicate and soothed Kaleena's nerves even further. She checked Kaleena's pulse and then pulled her chin forward to examine her eyes.

"Fine, I guess," Kaleena lied. The paramedic smiled softly and looked at Kaleena's arms. The inside of her wrists and forearms were fresh with bruises.

"I'd like to transport you to the hospital for a check-up," the paramedic said, looking deep into her eyes with care and comfort. Kaleena couldn't refuse the offer.

"I'm not going with him," she answered.

"I wouldn't dream of it." The paramedic grabbed her radio. "Medic three-eight requesting secondary level four transport for a code fifty."

Kaleena had no idea what any of that meant. "Thank you."

"Lisa," the other paramedic called out. The professor had been securely strapped to the backboard and an oxygen mask covered his mouth. "Let's pack this guy in."

"I'll stay with you until the other bus arrives," she said, ignoring the confirmation report on the radio. The round officer came rolling back into the room as the paramedics lifted the professor off the ground.

"Don't leave without my go ahead," the cop said to the paramedics, who seemingly ignored him. "I apologize, miss Stevens," he continued, handing Kaleena her ID. She refused to say thank you. Not yet. "What type of altercation occurred between you and your assailant?"

"Do I have to spell it out for you?" Her frustration level was rising once again. "He. Tried. To. Rape. Me."

The cop wasn't amused. "What I meant was how did he end up like that?"

Kaleena felt foolish. "I don't know. Some guy came and stopped him."

"Some guy?"

"Yeah," she said calmly, avoiding the departure of the paramedics. "I was attempting to fight the professor off, calling out for help when suddenly some guy pulled him away and started beating him like a punching bag."

"May I ask why your footprints are in the accused's blood?"

Accused. As if he hadn't done anything. *Innocent until proven guilty my ass.* "After the guy left, I went to check to see if he was still breathing." Kaleena felt sheepish as she heard the stupidity of her own words.

"Why would you do that?"

"I don't know…" Kaleena no longer wanted to look at the cop, who made a quick noise with his throat as he wrote down a few notes on his pad.

"Can you describe this mystery man?"

Kaleena cleared her own throat. "Trench coat, hood… steel-toed boots. That's all I remember."

"Did he say anything to you? Maybe try and help you afterward?"

Those words came rushing back as if they were still being whispered to her. But this marshmallow didn't need to know about that. Not like he would understand any of it anyway. "No."

The officer scribbled out more notes. "Is there anyone we can call?" he asked, somewhat respectfully.

Kaleena shook her head. It wasn't time for her father to know about this.

"Thank you, miss Stevens," the cop muttered, closing his notepad. "If I have any more questions, I'll be in touch." The officer started to leave.

"Wait. Aren't you going to arrest him?"

"He's in custody. But we can't officially arrest him until the hospital releases him." The cop turned to her, as if this would help. "Sorry." He left the room.

Once the hospital releases him? Kaleena wanted the professor to go straight to prison, coma or not. But it was out of her hands; whatever happened to him now

was up for a panel of twelve bored individuals (most of whom just wanted to get away from work for a few days) to decide.

Kaleena only had to wait five minutes for the second ambulance to arrive. She got one last glimpse of the professor as Lisa escorted her from the room. It was the last time she wanted to lay eyes on the scumbag, but she knew better. If the man were ever going to be punished, she would have to confront him in court while explaining the details of what happened. Revealing her secrets to a room full of strangers as he undressed her on the witness stand gave her a cold chill. She felt like throwing up during the ride to the hospital, but Lisa's comforting touch gave her a sense of companionship that went deeper than mere sympathy. She gave Lisa a long, thankful hug when they arrived at their destination. Even though she didn't need it, Lisa helped Kaleena inside and stayed with her until the doctor came to check on her.

"You'll be okay," Lisa said with a reassuring smile.

"Thank you."

Lisa radioed someone as she disappeared down the hall of the emergency room. Kaleena didn't notice the doctor check her vitals. Only when he pressed his thumb to the bruise on her right thigh did she register his presence with a light yelp.

"Sorry," he said and continued his examination. He took an extraordinarily long time on her head. "Did you happen to hit your head?"

"Yeah," she said, her head throbbing slightly at the realization.

The doctor cleaned a bit of dry blood from the small wound. "You must have hit it pretty good," he said in a slightly playful mood, possibly thinking it would help cheer her up. "Good news is, it doesn't look like you're going to need stitches." He spent the next few minutes patching it up with a square bandage, humming a song Kaleena didn't recognize.

"It looks like you're going to be okay," he said, the mustache that crept just over his top lip bouncing with every word. "Would you like to take a rape test?" He asked the question as if it was a conversation piece you'd have over the dinner table with your family.

"No," Kaleena whispered. "He didn't get that far."

"That's good." The doctor did his best to lay her hair over the patch. "That's good." He grabbed the clipboard from the table next to Kaleena and wrote down some stuff. But Kaleena wasn't paying attention. Her focus was on the small woman, about five feet and rail thin, walking toward her. The woman's bloodshot eyes were tired, as if she'd been crying for hours.

"Excuse me," the woman said, her voice a low-pitched hum. "Are you the student that came in with my husband?"

Kaleena wasn't sure how to respond.

"Who's your husband?" the doctor asked for her.

"You accused him of rape," the woman said, her cold eyes piercing their way through Kaleena.

"I'm going to have to ask you to leave." The doctor stepped between Kaleena and her accuser. Before he could, the woman slapped Kaleena — once, twice — crying, "You bitch! Take it back!"

The doctor pushed the woman away. Kaleena held her reddening cheek. Security was quick to the scene. The doctor remained close to Kaleena as the hysterical woman was escorted from the hospital in front of a growing crowd of patients and staff. Kaleena was the only one who couldn't watch. She tried hard to coax the pain from her cheek as a cold brush of wind swept past her. She stepped up the stairs to her apartment and held the doorknob. It's cold, smooth texture felt satisfying against her palm. She thought about the dreadful display of human nature she had witnessed over the past twenty-four hours. What she wouldn't give to just lie in bed for a month, away from the world.

What would that accomplish?

No. If anything, she needed to abstain from giving in to the evil of the world. She had to stay strong; she could not let it beat her. She would not let it beat her. Ideas for a new book suddenly flooded her thoughts. All she could see were words and passages about the human condition. Getting to her laptop to write became her only focus.

She slammed the door shut as she dropped her bag in the corner. Her steps were swift and she didn't notice the rest of the apartment. Just before reaching her bedroom, a familiar voice called to her.

"Kaleena?" Matthew stepped out of the bathroom holding a small washcloth.

"Dad?"

"What the hell happened here?" he asked.

Kaleena fought hard to keep from rolling her eyes. *Typical.* "Yeah, it's good to see you, too, Dad," she said with slight disdain and walked to the living room.

Matthew slowly followed. "I'm waiting."

Kaleena gave in. "Kyla threw an unannounced party last night, okay? I was going to clean everything up." She paused, her mind spinning. "Wait. What are you doing home? I thought you wouldn't be back for another few weeks."

"We had a breakthrough, Kaleena." Matthew forgot all about the party.

"What kind of breakthrough?"

"Don't worry about that. You wouldn't believe me anyway." Matthew sat on the coffee table across from Kaleena and tossed the rag to the couch. "I do need to ask you a favor, though."

Kaleena was exasperated. "You need more money, don't you?"

"How much do you have?"

"I don't know... most of my royalties. How much do you need?"

Matthew sucked a whistle of air through his teeth before: "About fifty grand."

"Fifty grand?" The shock couldn't have been more pronounced. "What for?"

"The company financing this recent dig won't fund us any further without seeing some of our results."

"Then show them your results. What do you need me for?"

"Because I can't. Not yet."

"Why? 'Cause you don't have any?"

Matthew chuckled. "Oh, I have plenty of evidence. I just need to keep our most recent findings a secret until after this next expedition."

"Why?" Kaleena seemed somewhat curious.

"I told you. You wouldn't believe me."

"Try me."

Matthew was hesitant. Kaleena walked to the kitchen and filled a glass with pineapple juice she found in the refrigerator. "You want my money? I want to know what I'm financing. I'm not an idiot." She took a sip and waited for his answer.

When it came, it came as an almost undecipherable string of mumbles. "I may have found the location of Atlantis."

Kaleena was dumbfounded. "Atlantis? Are you serious?" Matthew's answer was layered heavily on his eyes. "Oh my god." She left her drink on the counter and walked back to the living room.

The whisper floated past her ears. *Give him what he needs.*

"You do know how I feel about this whole Atlantis thing, right?" Kaleena said.

"Of course. But you're the only one I can trust to keep this a secret."

"From who? Who are you afraid's going to find out?"

Give him what he needs. Still hushed, but more intense.

Matthew took his daughter's hand and guided her back to the couch. "I need proof before I can make this public. If word gets out and I don't find anything, my name — my career — will be irreparably tarnished."

Kaleena was listening. "And if you don't find anything, you'll end this ridiculous crusade for good?" Matthew couldn't answer her. Kaleena sighed. "I can't believe you," she said. "Atlantis is a myth, Dad. A story told to stir up controversy and create revenue flow." She paused, hoping Matthew would register a tiny hint of doubt. It didn't work. "I can't do it."

"Kaleena, please —"

Louder — *Give him what he needs.*

"I can't. Not this time." Kaleena started for her room. The whisper became crystal clear; so clear, she couldn't tell if it was a memory or a voice calling from somewhere in the room.

Give him what he needs. Give him what he needs and do as he asks.

Kaleena attempted to shake the voice away, but the more she resisted, the

more powerful it got.

Give him what he needs.

No, she thought. *I can't.*

Give him what he needs —

No!

Matthew paced the room, periodically running his hands through his hair when he wasn't squeezing his mouth tight. Kaleena could tell he wasn't going to push her if she didn't want to do it. She loved him for that and figured the least she could do was find out exactly what it was he was planning.

"Let me ask you something." — *Give him what he needs* — "Where do you expect to find it?"

Matthew perked up. No hesitation this time. "In the middle of the Bermuda Triangle."

Kaleena nodded — *Do as he asks* — and grabbed the sides of her head. There had to be a way to push the voice out of her mind. "What do you need the funds for?" she said, strained. "Exactly."

"I need to hire an oceanography team and rent a boat to take us out there."

"Us? Meaning" — *Give him what he needs* — "the oceanography team and" — *Give him what he needs* — "and your team?" Kaleena struggled to keep from yelling over her imaginary voice.

"That's right."

— *Give him what he needs and do as he asks —*

"Fine," Kaleena screamed.

The voice went quiet. Startled, Matthew waited for Kaleena to calm herself. It took a few seconds, but as she took her time to think, she felt this could be something she could use. "Fine," she repeated, softer. "I'll give you the money."

Matthew's smile was enormous.

But don't allow him to leave you behind, the voice whispered.

"On two conditions," she said quickly.

"Anything."

"You hire Mom and you take me with you."

"No," Matthew said without hesitation. "It's too dangerous."

"Then you don't get the money," Kaleena challenged. "I'm sorry, Dad. But this could be exactly what I need right now."

"What do you mean?" Matthew finally noticed a small scratch on Kaleena's upper cheekbone. "Kaleena, what happened?" He reached for her face, but she moved away. That was when he noticed the bruising on her arms. "My god..."

"It's too late for questions, Dad. Let's just say, I need a few days away."

"From what?"

"From everything. From school, from my friends... from life."

Matthew felt guilty for not being there for whatever happened to his daughter. But he couldn't dwell on it. She knew what she needed, and right now it seemed, in her posture and her voice, what she needed was him. Besides, without her, he had no other means of financing his expedition.

"Fine," he said. "You can come. But you have to listen to me and do as I say."

"And mom?" Kaleena asked, ignoring his command.

"You want her?" he said after quietly deliberating with himself. Even though she was exactly what he needed, he never once thought of his ex-wife as a possible candidate. Not that he would have considered it even if he had thought of her. She was a ghost to him — a memory. But Kaleena's steely gaze hammered him with pure authority, and Matthew knew it'd be unwise to resist. "You have to convince her to go." Matthew brushed past his daughter on his way to the bedroom and shut the door without another word.

Kaleena stared into the living room, dumbfounded. It was clear Matthew was convinced Atlantis truly existed, but she still had her doubts, having written two chapters debunking the existence of the lost city in the book that was about to pay for the expedition to find it. Kaleena cracked a smile at the irony, a smile that only got bigger as seeing her mother again overwhelmed her thoughts. She finally had a reason to call her, to get into contact with her.

Was she ready?

She grabbed her phone and found "Jamie S." in her address book faster than Speedy Gonzales on a date. She stared at the call button, deciding against pushing it —

Not yet.

She ran to her room and threw open her laptop. She settled in on her bed, tossing the phone to the side. Before she knew it, Word was open and her fingers were typing away non-stop. She needed to get the thoughts out of her head before she called, knowing full well, it was only her way of convincing herself to stall so she could figure out what she wanted — what she *needed* — to say.

* * *

Matthew sat on his bed. The room grew dark as he thought about Kaleena. What happened to her? Should he push for answers or give her space? He realized he hadn't been the father he always said he would be, but he couldn't help believe this expedition to Atlantis, whether he found anything or not, could be his chance to define a new relationship... as long as he didn't let his obsession with finding Atlantis interfere. That was his job.

Kaleena was his daughter.

He opened the bureau drawer and pulled out his wedding band. The gold shimmered lightly under the orange hue of the room. After some time of absent-minded reminiscing, he set the ring down next to his watch. He lied down and drifted off to sleep, the sun resting along with him.

* * *

9:36

Kaleena had been writing for four hours. Most of what she had written were notes on her attack, her mother's departure, Kyla's history and some general ideas on

the hypocrisies, conspiracies and selfishness that penetrated human nature. She rubbed her eyes and grabbed her phone. The screen popped to life, competing with the computer monitor to fill the room with light. At the command of the battery icon, Kaleena thought about charging it to make sure she'd be able to talk to her mom without worrying about her phone dying in the middle of their conversation, but once again, this was just an excuse, a way of avoiding the woman that hurt her three years ago.

If she was going to do this, she needed to do it now. No more vacillation.

She pressed the call button.

The phone rang. Sweat formed on Kaleena's forehead and her palms grew cold.

It rang again, then stopped.

Kaleena checked the phone. It was dead.

"Great," she whispered. She grabbed the house phone from off her nightstand and dialed the number that had been imprinted in her head over the last few hours. As it rang again, Kaleena tried to remember her mother. She saw her long, naturally curly brown hair hug her shoulders and her soft pink lips glitter with lip balm. But most importantly, she saw her eyes — bright blue that seemed to change color under different lighting. She would never forget those eyes, cold and hurt.

"I'm not around," her mother's voice said after the fifth ring. "Leave a message."

Kaleena's mind went into warp drive when that voice touched her ear. It was deeper than she remembered, but it was definitely her mother's. What would she say? Should she even leave a message? As the tone drifted off, Kaleena spoke in a quiet, dry tone.

"Hi, mom." She cleared her voice and continued. "Hi, mom. It's Kaleena. I have something very important to ask you. Please give me a call as soon as you get this. You can reach me on my cell." She paused after chirping off the number, wondering how to close. She couldn't say *I love you*; It just didn't feel right. On the other hand, she couldn't just say *Bye*; that sounded rude.

"Hope to hear back." Another quick pause and then, "Bye."

Kaleena hung up the phone and wiped the sweat off her brow. She had done it. She had called her. And now all she could do was wait.

BOOK TWO
THE EXPEDITION

Los Angeles – Saturday, 6:38 pm

Her cell phone hummed a familiar tune. Jaime caressed away the dry staleness that had set into her eyes from staring at the computer monitors for the last twelve hours. The room had grown darker than normal. A table lamp highlighted the keyboard and some sound mixing equipment hooked to a half-dozen hard drives working hard to render the data her associate, Gavin Kincaid, had been editing for her. The past thirty-six hours had been a bear as he tried to get the recent footage to work the way Jaime envisioned. It wasn't her fault; the production company producing the documentary was pushing to see a cut, and Jaime didn't want to give them something she herself disapproved of, or thought was going in the wrong direction. Having spent the last three months studying changing currents and their effect on ocean life off the coast of Baja, Jaime was not willing to have the plug pulled because she couldn't get a clear, structured piece of art while being fresh at the same time. The first cut had been questioned from beginning to end. Jaime gave him twenty-four hours to change the rough cut based on eight pages of hand-written notes. The second cut was better, but still dead somehow. She didn't know much about the software, but she stayed with Gavin to help get it to where she needed. It's a good thing Gavin didn't mind. He'd been working with Jaime for two years now and had grown accustomed to — even comfortable with — her perfectionism.

The phone stopped before Jaime even registered the noise.

"What if we bring the moray eel footage a few minutes up and switch it out with the finback whale?" Gavin asked, also unaware of the phone call. "It may give us a better progression into the larger species."

"No," Jaime huffed. "If we move the finback whale, we'll have to move the humpback whale, and there's no way we can transition from that into the warming of the convection currents."

"So why can't we talk about the convection currents earlier and lead everything into the loss of migratory mammals to the coast of Baja?"

Gavin felt the heat from the light bulb that just turned on inside Jaime's head. The idea seemed concise and might free up a few other possibilities. The more she thought about it, the more she saw a cohesive flow form. It wasn't exactly what she had originally conceived, but it could work in adding an original spin to the piece.

"You may have something," Jaime said, grabbing the pen that sat patiently above her ear. She scratched out a few notes on the legal pad as her phone started singing again. This time it was loud and clear. Jaime saw a crystal blue background with the word "Ex" printed in large letters under a prohibition sign. She tossed the phone to the side and continued writing.

"You gonna get that?" Gavin asked.

"It's just my ex-husband," she said thoughtlessly.

"What's he want?"

"I don't care." Jaime looked up to Gavin. "This may take a minute. Why don't you grab a quick power nap?"

Thank God. Gavin climbed to the couch that sat against the wall near the door. As soon as his head hit the armrest, he was dead to the world.

Meanwhile, Jaime wrote, occasionally scratching out words, sometimes complete sentences, whenever something started to feel more like word vomit than a viable idea. She had outlined a script when she was originally given the project, but after discovering the truth behind the life, migration habits, and current flow in the region, her initial ideas were all wrong. The footage and statistics she gathered were so extensive, it became a chore to find the right things for her narrator to say. With this new idea in place, now she might be able to create an enlightened, yet entertaining narrative. But the more she wrote, the more she felt she was forcing transitions, developing nonsensical attributes and creating false ideas without proof. After about thirty minutes, her hand started to cramp and all she had to show for it was a strong opening that would last about two minutes and a few key summery points. She needed a break.

After cracking her neck and rubbing the stress from her right shoulder, Jaime dropped the pad where she had been sitting, grabbed her phone and headed out into the hall of the facility she had rented from the studio. She pulled a box of Virginia Slims from her pocket and tapped out a stick. She usually smoked about three or four cigarettes a day — they helped her function better than coffee — but it had been eighteen hours since she last lit up. She felt it in every pore.

Her stomach turned as she set the tip of the cigarette between her lips. She tasted the nicotine on her tongue even before inhaling the first breath of smoke. Holding that first taste for as long as possible, Jaime set her head against the wall and relaxed her shoulders. She closed her weary eyes as she let the smoke slip high into the air. A few more inhales like that and Jaime would be ready to get back to it. She rested the cigarette on the corner of her mouth and checked her phone. A message was waiting. For a moment, she considered erasing it without even listening. She didn't care what he had to say. It had been over three years since she had last talked to her husband, and a few months since the last time she even thought of him. If anything, he was most likely asking her for

something she couldn't give him — or wasn't willing to give him. Then again, it very well may have been about their daughter, and if that was the case, she was obligated to listen.

After typing in her authorization code, she placed the phone to her ear and removed the cigarette from her mouth, crossing her arms in wait. The voice that crackled on the other end was like a jolt of adrenaline.

"Hi, mom," the soft voice said, a bit nervously. "Hi, mom. It's Kaleena. I have something very important to ask you."

As the name echoed in Jaime's mind, her stomach trembled with guilt. She couldn't recall the last time she had heard her daughter's voice, but as far as she knew, it was the day she had to say goodbye to that young, lonely face.

I love you.

"Just stop, Matthew," Jaime said into the receiver. It had to have been over an hour since Matthew had called. About what, she couldn't quite remember. All that mattered was the argument that erupted over her need for Matthew to come home. It was coming up on Thanksgiving, which Matthew had missed the previous couple of years. Jaime really wanted him there this year, if not for her, then for Kaleena. But it all seemed moot as the conversation spun into a web Jaime had been cocooned within.

"I think I may have stumbled onto something important," Matthew said. *May have stumbled onto something important...* words that played like a broken record.

"I'm tired of this, Matthew," Jaime cried. "How are we supposed to make this work if you're never here?"

"Jaime, I'm working."

Was he trying to avoid the question?

"I just don't think I can do this anymore." Jaime quietly held back her tears to keep from giving in to weakness.

"I just need a few more weeks —"

"And then what? You jump on another plane to search for something else that may or may not have a connection with whatever it is you find. It's never-ending,

Matthew. I don't know how much longer I can put my career on the backburner waiting for you to finally stop and give me a chance."

"Honey. This research is important."

"And mine isn't?"

"Look, I'd take you with me —"

"That's not what I want, Matthew," Jaime snapped.

"Then what is it?"

"I want my career back. I want the chance to explore *my* dreams for once."

"And I want that, too." Matthew's voice sounded sincere, but Jaime could swear she heard voices in the background, as if Matthew's attention was on his dig rather than on her needs.

"Bullshit. If that were true, you'd take a few years off and be a goddamned father."

"I would," Matthew said. "But I can't stop my research. We're too close." And then, distant, "No, cut it on the outside. We want the necklace intact."

Emotions closed Jaime's throat. She covered her eyes in hopes that it would keep her from fully erupting.

"Jaime, you still there?"

She took a moment to breathe before answering. "Not for much longer."

"I love you," Matthew said. "You know that."

"Do you? Because I'm finding it really hard to love you right now."

Matthew didn't have an answer. Drilling could be heard in the background. Jaime focused on her dreams, on Matthew's selfishness; but most of all, she focused on Kaleena.

"I can't do this anymore," she said after a few minutes of complete silence.

"Just give me two weeks, Jaime, and then we'll talk about this in person."

"It won't work, Matthew. It won't."

"Jay…"

"Goodbye." Jaime hung up the phone before Matthew could say anything else. She left it off the hook and let it sit, even after it started blaring at her with its

incessant beeping. She was glad now that her cell battery had been burned of its juice. It was an hour before she stopped crying and another thirty minutes or so before she moved from the comfort of her fetal position to sit up and stare at her reddened, puffy appearance in the mirrored closet door. She wiped some excess sweat and tears from her face with the sleeves of her blouse.

"It's time for you," she whispered.

She pulled a pair of large suitcases from the closet and slowly packed. There was a fervent desire to get out of the apartment as soon as she could, but Matthew was eight thousand miles away. She had time. And a small piece of her still felt the need to stay.

That piece spoke in a small, quiet, somewhat scared whistle. "Where are you going?"

Kaleena stood at the bedroom door looking like Mary-Lou Who, with her pink nightgown hitting the floor and her hair pulled back in a ponytail. Jaime's lips quivered as she squeezed out a smile. Could she tell her? How was she going to understand her decision to leave? She was only eleven; then again, not only would she begin college in the spring, she was already writing her first novel. There was nothing Kaleena couldn't understand. So Jaime let her heart speak for her.

"To find happiness, Kaleena. To find my life."

Tears rolled down her cheeks like molasses as Kaleena's disappointment hit. Jaime raised her arms ever-so-slightly, the need to hug her daughter overwhelming her better judgment. Packing had to be her priority. She didn't know when Kaleena left; all she knew was when she had finished filling the third suitcase, her daughter had returned to her room. It took her several minutes to carry her luggage to the front door, unable to keep from reminiscing about her life with Matthew. They had made a home together for thirteen years, but how much of that time was actually spent together? Before Kaleena, the two were inseparable, their lives flourishing in activity and work. However, Kaleena changed Jaime's life, essentially ending her career. She never despised her daughter for that; it wasn't her fault. Matthew grew more selfish after the birth, forcing her to become complacent to his whims

and wishes. The last eight years had been rough, but she fought through them for Kaleena's sake, setting her own dreams aside so that her daughter could achieve great things — including jumping multiple grades against Matthew's wishes. That didn't matter. Kaleena wanted it, and Jaime was never one to say no to her daughter, not when she knew how important something was to her — was to *her*. She loved Kaleena; she loved Matthew. But she no longer wanted to feel trapped.

When Jaime stepped out of her bedroom for the last time, Kaleena stood in the living room looking as if she had been waiting there for a lifetime. Jaime didn't say anything as she walked up to her, building a wall of false strength between them. She took hold of Kaleena's chin and kissed her on the cheek, her forehead, and the top of her head. It led to a long, soft hug, one she couldn't break for more than two minutes. When she finally let go, heavy amounts of love and pain, vitality and depression, innocence and shame danced across Kaleena's eyes. It hurt more than she could have imagined, but it also gave her hope that her young daughter would grow to be a much better person — a much better woman — than she ever could be.

Jaime kissed Kaleena once more before leaving the apartment without so much as a word or a second look back. As the latch clicked shut, she leaned against the door, dropped her suitcases, and broke down. She refused to allow her legs to give out; if she had, she may never have been able to leave. Instead, she shook away her tears and called for a taxi. Her legs felt as heavy as iron, making the trip down to the street a ten-minute slog. The moment she set her last bag on the sidewalk, the cab pulled up. The driver gave her a quick wink as he opened the trunk.

"Long trip?" he said, as he threw in the first bag.

"Something like that," Jaime said thoughtlessly. The driver continued cawing flirtatious niceties as he packed the rest of her bags. But her attention was on the apartment window, where Kaleena watched with her tiny hand pressed against the window. Jaime stretched her arm out, her palm out toward the window as if she were touching Kaleena's palm. And in a way, she had; she felt her daughter's touch. It would have to be enough. As the driver got back behind the wheel, Jaime

gave Kaleena one last smile and slid into the car, completely aware she was unlikely to ever see her again.

"Take care of her, Matthew," she whispered.

"Where to, gorgeous?" the driver said, ticking the meter on.

"Bradley International," Jaime answered without a hint of remorse. The last thing she needed was this chauvinist pig feeling sorry for her, or try to strike up some awkward conversation that would end up on HBO or some other stupid reality show. It would take her some time to figure out where to set down roots far enough away that she wouldn't feel obligated to return. Until then, there was one place she knew she could go to escape and fight the urge to turn around.

Three years later, one phone call brought all of the guilt, pain and doubt flooding back. Half of her second cigarette had been turned to ash as she rested her head between her knees, lifting it only to take another hit, each time sucking in the smoke as if it would be the last time. She stared at the black screen of her phone, which sat on the ground between her feet. Her daughter's words rattled about, her voice sounding uneasy but confident, residue from being on her own. It wouldn't surprise her in the least to find out Matthew had spent less than five minutes with Kaleena over the last three years. Even if that wasn't remotely true, it seemed her daughter had taken that time to become a mature young woman. She pictured her in her mind — tall and beautiful, fit with a bright smile that could outshine the sun; long, dark hair that flowed across her shoulders; eyes that read your soul with ease, but never in judgment.

"I am not a scholar; I am not a scientist," it read in chapter one of Kaleena's book, *Prove It: The Distinction Between Myth and Fact*. "I am a mere child that understands the difference between what is truth and what can only be defined as belief. I am seeking the honesty of nature and the reality of common sense."

Jaime smiled. Kaleena had spent months cycling through articles on the Internet (only one she could confirm through reliable sources, of course), books written by well-known philosophers, newspaper clippings and archival news footage. Thirty-eight chapters, six hundred and eighteen pages later, she had

pretty much disproved, through very intelligent, logical arguments, nearly every myth that had ever been devised. It was enough to make even Plato spin on his head in disbelief. Not once had Jaime even called her child to tell her how proud she was of her success.

It was time; there was no doubt she would return Kaleena's call. But it was past ten in Connecticut, and she didn't want to disturb her this late. She'd get to it in a couple of days, for sure. Whether it was an excuse to build up the courage to talk to her, or simply a need to finish her documentary, Jaime needed time. And that time was slowly slipping away.

She took one last puff on her cigarette and put it out on the concrete floor, leaving it to rest next to the pile of ash the cleaning crew would sweep up the next morning. She then grabbed her phone and tore back into the room.

"Get up," she said, slapping Gavin on the butt. "We've got a film to finish."

Gavin shot up and looked around, disoriented. After a moment he remembered where he was and slowly sat up.

"Yeah. I'm up…" he said. "I'm up."

Arizona – Sunday, 9:45 am

The smell of scented candles was quite soothing as Thomas stepped into the church. It was clear he had been absent for some time. The wall to the right of the foray had been torn down, expanding the entry to provide more room for the growing body of worshipers to mingle after the sermon. On the wall to the left, the small crucifix that was once displayed on the front of the preacher's podium now hung in the main hall for everyone to praise as they left. The cross was a humble wood, which looked old and worn, and the body that hung from it seemed to be at peace. A wreath of roses surrounded it while a group of candles sat on a small oak table, lighting the Lord's feet with a soft glow of warmth. Pictures of Mary, Jesus, Isaac and Moses, had been replaced for vases of lilacs and Orchids. Thomas assumed the pictures, much like the crucifix, had been moved to decorate another part of the church, possibly on the walls upstairs where the Sunday school classes were held (or at least had been, last he could remember). The wooden doors leading into the main hall had been replaced with glass partitions that allowed Thomas to watch everyone as they listened intently to their worship leader. He couldn't make out what was being said, but it was most likely something about the bake sale currently being set up outside. At least the pews had remained untouched.

Before Thomas could sit in the corner pew nearest the door, the congregation stood with light applause. The youth pastor shook the worship leader's hand and took his place at the podium. He began as any one leaving an old home for a new one would, with kind words for the people of the church, the ministers, the volunteers and everyone else who may have had some connection to the church or its parishioners. From what he could gather, the young man, nearing his late twenties if not early thirties, had just been hired as a minister in a small church in southern California. He finished with a few well-wishes, thanked those most important to him, pronounced both his sadness and good fortune, and then asked the congregation to bow their heads in prayer. Everyone except for the majority of the kids, most of whom were too distracted with their own feet or the hymnals to care much about what was going on, did so with great acceptance. Thomas took the moment to search the crowd for someone he hadn't talked to in over ten years. Caitlyn sat near the front next to an older gentleman, probably around fifty, who had his arm draped around her neck. He could only see the edge of her profile, but he knew it was her.

"Amen," the youth pastor said.

"Amen," the congregation responded, lifting their heads in unison. Caitlyn gave the man beside her an affectionate kiss as he moved his hand up and down her shoulder. A gold wedding band sparkled alongside Caitlyn's bliss. Thomas was happy for her. He held no animosity; he only wished her the best and would never interfere in her affairs. She was not who Thomas was looking for.

A soft hum brushed through the hall as the worship leader returned to the stage to announce the entrance of the youth choir. Several children, aged between about seven and fifteen, walked in wearing matching gold robes with purple trim. They formed two rows, one on the floor, the other on the first step of the stage. One of the younger kids accidentally stepped on the front of his robe before reaching his designated spot and landed nose first into the burnt sienna carpet. He cried as a middle-aged woman with graying hair ran to him. Thomas didn't see much of what happened, as his attention was on the oldest of the group, a heavyset girl with light brown hair and perfectly straight teeth. Her shock and surprise at the chaos below made Thomas chuckle. As the woman (who Thomas assumed was either his mother or the choir director) carried the boy past him, he thought that maybe if he made eye contact with the girl, things might all of a sudden become clear to her. That was impossible, of course. Chelsea, as she had been named on the day of her birth, didn't even know he was her father.

The commotion over the incident died quickly as the choir began to sing "Amazing Grace." Chelsea's voice was crystal clear over the others. Thomas wished he could run to her and give her a hug and kiss, but knew he'd lost that chance years ago. It was not a moment he had been proud of, but he was grateful for it anyway.

"Where have you been?" Caitlyn chided as Thomas walked through the front door of the apartment the two shared together after Chelsea's birth. It was small, with just one bedroom, and looked "lived-in" — paint was peeling off the walls and the windows had been sealed shut. Caitlyn had spent months trying to find something "affordable" (someplace that had working windows and a dishwasher). The only thing she could pay for on her salary alone was the cheap hell hole near the college. It would have been nice had Thomas actually contributed, but he hadn't worked in over six months, which forced Caitlyn to work two jobs, all the while taking twelve units of classes in order to keep her full-time status.

"Just out," Thomas slurred, a bit harshly.

"Out," Caitlyn said, tying her hair in a high ponytail. "With those fuck-off friends of yours?"

"Hey," Thomas said, angry. "Jason is not a fuck-off." He huffed a laugh. "You're probably right about the rest of them, though."

Caitlyn wasn't amused at his lame joke. She walked to the bedroom. "I need you to watch Chelsea this afternoon."

Thomas feigned excitement and walked to the small icebox they called their baby-fridge. He pulled out one of the last Miller's and chugged about half before Caitlyn returned wearing a yellow dress with "Famous Hamburgers" embroidered on the sleeve.

"Did you hear me?" she asked.

"Yeah, whatever." Thomas let rip a long, gurgled burp. "You look hot. Want to get in a quickie before you go?" He grabbed her waist and pulled her tight against his pelvis.

Caitlyn pushed him away. "Fuck off. I'm late."

Thomas chuckled and took another drink.

"Chelsea's asleep, but she'll need to eat when she wakes up." Caitlyn threw her coat on. "Don't you dare invite anyone over. And try not to get shit-faced again, okay?"

Thomas swilled the rest of the beer and sat down on the couch. He switched on the television, immediately flipping through channels.

"Thomas," Caitlyn said. He continued to ignore her. "I swear, you can be such a dick sometimes, you know. Call me if you need anything."

"Pick up a case on your way home, k?"

"We don't have enough money for that shit."

"Don't give me that."

"No, Thomas. I am not paying for any more of your goddamn alcohol. You want it, you get yourself a fucking job." Caitlyn slammed the door behind her.

"Damn it, Caitlyn," Thomas yelled. He waited two seconds for her to come back to finish the argument before shrugging it off in favor of the *Fresh Prince of Bel-Air*. Within an hour, he dozed off and almost didn't hear Chelsea. Registering her cries, Thomas groggily slid his way to the bedroom and picked his baby girl up. Her cries died down as he carried her to the kitchen and sat her down in her highchair. A jar of strained peas was all they seemed to have left for her, and the

only clean utensil he found was an old wooden spoon. "Splinters and vomit," he whispered as he sat down. "Best combo ever." After struggling a bit with the lid, Thomas was able to scoop up a mound of green slop and stuff the spoon into Chelsea's mouth. She immediately spit half of it up onto the pink dress Caitlyn's mother had gotten her granddaughter for Christmas.

"Damn it, Chelsea," Thomas sneered. He grabbed a towel from the bathroom and tried his best to clean the dress. Defeated, he attempted to give her more peas. She utterly refused him, continuing to push the spoon away whenever it got close to her mouth. "Would you eat, Chelsea. Jesus." He tried to force her, but that only led to massive wailing he believed could be heard in the next state.

"Fine," Thomas said, throwing the spoon to the sink and slamming the peas on the table. "Don't eat, then." He pulled her from the highchair and took her back to the bedroom. He checked her diaper, which, to his relief, didn't have to be changed, and then forced her to lie down in the crib. "Go to sleep."

Thomas left the room and spent the next couple of hours ignoring her cries. Every once in a while he would check her diaper, try to feed her a slice of pizza he ordered or get her to sleep with a cup of juice. Nothing helped, not even when he yelled at her to shut up. Thomas grew so flustered, he turned the sound on the television up to drown out her screams. But that didn't even work; Chelsea just raised the intensity of her voice with every push of the button. *Typical woman*, he mused. Finally, Thomas had had enough and stormed into the bedroom. He picked Chelsea up and screamed at her to be quiet, shaking her fiercely. It wasn't long before Chelsea's cries were softened by her inability to breathe.

"What the hell are you doing?" Caitlyn screamed, grabbing Chelsea from Thomas and pushing him onto the bed. She held her child close as her cries cleared. "It's okay," she whispered over and over, kissing her repeatedly on her head.

"I'm sorry," Thomas roared. "She wouldn't stop crying."

"And that was your solution?" Caitlyn cried.

"What else was I supposed to do? She won't eat. Her diaper's clean."

"Did you give her the teething ring?"

"Teething ring?" Thomas was completely unaware.

Caitlyn picked up a small plush blue ring and put it in Chelsea's mouth. The child's cries came to an end as she gnawed and sucked on the toy. Thomas was stunned.

"Yeah, you asshole. She's teething."

"I didn't know," Thomas said sheepishly.

"No fucking shit." Caitlyn left the room with Chelsea.

"Where are you going?" Thomas ran her down and stopped her from leaving the apartment.

"Get the fuck off me." Caitlyn tried to pull her arm away, but was unable to under Thomas's grip.

"Where are you taking my daughter?"

"As far away from you as I can get."

"You can't do that."

"The hell I can't." Caitlyn used every ounce of strength to rip her arm away from Thomas, getting a scratch in return. She wasted no time racing to her car.

Thomas chased after her. "Caitlyn, come back here."

Just as Caitlyn opened the door, Thomas shoved it closed and grabbed Caitlyn's jaw. "I won't let you take her from me."

"You need help, Thomas," she stuttered through gritted teeth. "Serious help."

Thomas hit Caitlyn, knocking her to the ground. The force of his slap caused her to lose her grip on Chelsea, who wailed as she struck the ground. Thomas leaned against the car in horror. Caitlyn, now also in tears, slowly crawled to her baby and tried to rock her pain away. Thomas offered to help them up. Caitlyn just swatted his hand away.

"Get away from us, you bastard," she screamed. "Just get away."

Thomas stepped back and then fell to his knees. Caitlyn strapped Chelsea into her car seat and drove away. Thomas was unable to move as the night grew thicker. It took him an hour to finally get to his feet and return to the apartment, where he became fully aware of his actions. He prayed that Chelsea would be okay; that nothing he did caused her any serious physical harm. The whole night was spent examining his life. He was failing most of his classes, he didn't have a dime to his name and he had just lost the one girl he thought he'd be with forever. He regretted not calling Caitlyn for help earlier and started to run through everything he could have done differently, from putting a limit on his alcohol consumption to actually listening to Caitlyn when she talked to him. It was clear a change was in order, or else he very well could wind up dead in the gutter with a bottle of Jack Daniels permanently glued to his hand. That next week, after several failed attempts to talk to Caitlyn, Thomas checked himself into a rehab clinic and stayed there for over three years. When he got out, sober and stable, Thomas asked Caitlyn to meet him.

"Can I get you anything?" Thomas said as Caitlyn stood staring at him at the Starbucks just down the block from the college.

"I don't intend to stay long," Caitlyn said. Her arms were crossed tightly just under her bosom. Thomas had to shake the sexual images that permeated his thoughts. "What do you want?"

Thomas folded his hands together and lowered his head. "How is she?"

"She's fine. Healthy." Caitlyn sounded compassionate.

Thomas smiled gently. "That's good… that's good. May I see her?"

"I don't think that's a good idea."

Thomas kept his eyes down as he folded his lips under his teeth. "I thought you would say that."

When he looked up, Caitlyn saw a glint of the man she fell in love with. They were soft and empathetic, far from the tired, glassy steel she had become accustomed to. "I'm sorry," she said.

"Don't be. It's my own fault. And I agree with you."

"You do?"

Thomas stood and pressed his hand gently to the middle of her arm. "You can't take the chance that I might fall back into the fuck I used to be. She doesn't deserve me. And I don't deserve her. Not yet, anyway."

Caitlyn held back a soft breath of tears. She felt his sincerity through his touch and for the slightest of moments, believed she would have taken him back if he had asked. Thomas gave Caitlyn a soft kiss on the cheek. "Take care of her," he said and left her standing at the table, stunned.

From that moment, he moved on gracefully, leaving Chelsea and Caitlyn to live their lives without intervention. It was all he could do to make up for what he had done and thank Caitlyn for not throwing him in prison for twenty years. He'd still make an effort to be a part of Chelsea's life, attending her school plays or graduation ceremonies, he'd do so in secret. He always believed she had a wonderful voice, and often went to see her sing, much like now.

As the group finished their somewhat off-key rendition of what Thomas considered to be the greatest song ever written, he quietly stood and left the room. He stopped outside to watch Chelsea exit the main hall. Seeing her smiling and laughing with her friends was all he needed to make the decision to break all ties with her for good. It was too hard for him. Besides, the man that stood next to Caitlyn was her one and only father now. He blew Caitlyn a kiss and walked away from the church, his daughter's voice singing forever in his head.

New York – Monday, 8:47 am

The sun broke through the thinning cloth of the curtains, silently shaking Lauren awake. She turned a few times, but after about ten minutes of trying to find renewed comfort, she gave up and stared at the digital clock on her nightstand for five minutes. Blinking, ticking, thinking; screaming. Her life was slowly ending with every new second, passing like a ship with a broken rudder on the open sea. Despite the dire ambiance, it was the most serene Lauren had been in over three days; her mind was finally focused on something other than Henry and her mistake.

Bermuda flashed through the darkness as she closed her eyes, pushing them back open into the present. *No*, she thought. *I will not let him get to me. It's over and done with. Move on, Lauren. Just… move on.*

It took a lot of will power to slide her legs from under the covers and force her body into a sitting position. The sun heated the nape of her neck and her bare shoulders. After a quick, phlegmy cough, Lauren picked up a generic bottle of Ibuprofen and chewed them delicately before swallowing. She held her forehead as a bit of nausea hit and then shuffled to the bathroom. The medicine cabinet was wide open, though Lauren was opposed to closing it. She grabbed the tube of Colgate Whitening (with Baking Soda, whatever that was for) and squeezed a bit of the green substance onto her white toothbrush that looked about twenty years old, the needles bent every which way, the blue center that marked the time to get a new toothbrush having become nonexistent. She leaned up against the wall with her eyes closed as she brushed her teeth.

Come back to me, a voice whispered as two bright yellow eyes flashed in front of her. Lauren shrieked and almost choked on the paste that had been filling her mouth. She coughed it out into the sink and looked around the room, finding nothing but towels, an overflowing hamper and various toiletries. Lauren quickly threw some water on her face and let it drip until it was dry.

What the hell was that? she kept asking herself. Various answers flowed through her mind, from a hallucination to a demented dream. When she felt ready, she slid out of the light red nightgown she received as a birthday gift from a boyfriend who left her stranded on Cape Cod to jet off to New Jersey or Florida, or some such place with a brunette with big tits, and stepped into the shower. Even though the nightgown reminded her of the asshole every time she put it on, she deserved to be pampered, even if it was out of spite. For several minutes, Lauren allowed the warm water to caress her neck and shoulders with every line of liquid that wrapped itself around her body before falling to its death at her feet. Whenever the heat dissipated, she'd turn the faucet deeper into the red, the renewed warmth sending goose bumps down her flesh.

After what could have been an hour, Lauren finally opened her eyes. She was just about to grab the shampoo when she noticed a small bump rounding her stomach. "What the hell?" She stood straight and stroked the odd bulge.

"It can't be," she whispered. "It's not possible."

Lauren turned off the shower and ran into her bedroom, her wet skin leaving light water marks along the white carpet. She threw on whatever clothes had been tossed on the floor (ignoring the sticky hugs they gave her), grabbed the keys off of the end table next to the door and left without even thinking of locking up. The gravel walkway crunched loudly under her heavy footsteps. She stayed calmed enough to unlock the car door without any problems, but it took a few tries to light up the ignition.

Every stoplight knew Lauren was in a hurry, playing games with her as she steamed down the suburban roadways. In the fifteen minutes it took her to go a few miles down the road to the local doctor's office, her thoughts screamed in a thousand different directions. She didn't notice — or much care — that she parked a bit crooked. When she reached the door with the name "Dr. Hunter Reed" plastered in block white letters, she ripped it open without even knowing if she was within the posted office hours. The waiting room was quiet; the only other patient surrounded by the pristine white walls, deplorable red shag carpet and fake plants that were meant to help add atmosphere, but just made the room look phony, was a lovely woman in her mid-thirties perusing a five-year-old issue of *People Magazine*. A young boy, probably around eight, played with some building blocks on the floor next to his mother's feet.

"May I help you?" a nurse asked from behind the plastic window in front of Lauren. She looked a bit worn, but her smile showed she was still very happy to help in any way she could.

"Yes," Lauren said, setting her keys down on the counter. She hadn't noticed they had made an indentation in her palm. "I need to see Dr. Reed."

The nurse slid a clipboard through the small rectangular hole in the window. "Please sign in with your name and symptoms," she said. Lauren was about to object to being treated like a child, but kept her mouth shut and wrote her name below *Cindy Sleight*, which was the fourth name written on the sheet. "Busy morning?" Lauren asked with a stupid grin. The nurse simply flashed a smile and went about

filing paperwork. Lauren turned her attention back to the clipboard and below *upset stomach* wrote *possible pregnancy.*

She was about to scratch it out to put something else but decided it would be pointless and slid the clipboard back to the nurse, who switched it out for a second clipboard. "Please fill this out, have your insurance information ready and we'll be with you as soon as possible."

Lauren took the clipboard with the best smile she could produce. "Thank you." She slid her keys into her pocket and sat in the maroon chair nearest the door. The woman eyed Lauren for a moment before turning back to her magazine. Her son, who appeared would throw-up at any minute, stared at Lauren as he took several minutes to place just two blocks together. There didn't seem to be any recognition in his features, but Lauren knew how he felt. She pictured him sitting on her lap, holding her neck as she sang him a soothing song to fall asleep, a bowl of uneaten chicken soup cooling on the table. Her son's heart beat as she kissed him on the forehead. Her stomach cramped and her eyes turned cold. It could have been a reality, one she gave up out of fear and insecurity.

"I can't be," Lauren said to the doctor in a hoarse, tearful choke. "I can't…" All she could think about was what her parents would do when they found out their sweet, seventeen-year-old daughter — who got good grades, stayed out of trouble and was secretary of the Junior class — had been knocked up by Wallace Langum, a dumbass senior charming his way through life in a hot-red mustang convertible with leather seats and a five o'clock shadow he sported to make him believe he looked cooler than he'd ever be. Her parents had always been wary of Wallace and warned her on several occasions to be careful. As any perfect teenager would, Lauren didn't care much what they said; she was in love with Wallace from the moment he slipped the silver promise ring with purple highlights onto her finger and gave her the most passionate, sincere kiss on that cold, crisp Christmas Eve. She had had a few boyfriends before Wallace, but none of them made Lauren's heart race whenever she heard his name. They became an official couple that night, but wouldn't consummate the relationship for another six months.

"I want it to happen naturally, Wally," she would say time and again. "I want it to be a special gift." Her love only grew stronger as he honored her wishes. The day he asked his beloved to the prom was the day Lauren knew in her heart she would give him her gift.

A deep nervous tension eclipsed her soul on that fateful morning. The urge to slow things down and choose a different fate was running hot, but her heart continued to palpitate with love. It comforted her to know that Wallace would support her, should she decide to go against the promise she made. She spent the entire day dolling herself up for the man she dreamed of every minute. Walking with him into the crowded ballroom, her arm draped around his, a pink corsage on her delicate hand, made her feel like a queen, her king escorting her through her subjects. The night went quickly; Cheryl Strutt won Prom Queen — no shock there; run-of-the-mill, head cheerleading slut — and Tony Parkinson won King, which was sort of a shock, given his inability to play sports. Nobody cared, as the crowning was just a cue for the kids to split. Some bolted for the elevators to head up to their hundred and fifty-dollar hotel rooms to do things that would make a porn star blush; others fled to the nearest party in hopes of getting smashed or high or utterly fucked up; and yet a handful stuck around, mostly lonely parties who came to the dance stag in a desperate attempt to appear social.

"So, what do you want to do?" Wallace asked as they slow-danced to some David Bowie ballad Lauren hadn't heard before.

Lauren's cheeks flushed. She touched her lips to his ear. "My parents are away this weekend," she whispered and then looked into his beautiful, loving brown eyes, flashing her own cute cherub grin. They were back at her small suburban home within the hour. As Wallace grabbed something to drink, Lauren lit a dozen candles she bought the day before to give her bedroom a soft, saccharine glow. Small talk was nonexistent as the two made out on top of the flowered bedspread. She lied back, his hand gently cradling her neck. Lauren felt Wallace harden as his pelvis pushed up against her thigh. Her doubts immediately washed back to the forefront. She was within a millisecond of pushing him away, but was able to

suppress her fears against her better judgment. From that point on, whenever a red flag was raised, she lowered it by talking her way through the experience step-by-step. At first, it was allowing him to rub her breasts and bite her neck, which led to giving him permission to remove her now uncomfortable dress and kiss her stomach, cleavage and the inside of her thigh. The more he touched her, the more he kissed her, the less strict she became and would eventually find out how much pain, excitement and love an act of mutual companionship inhabited.

"Stay with me," she said, lying next to him, a bit tired, breathless and numb. His answer was a kiss, short but in no way distant. Lauren used his lightly hairy chest as her pillow and slept until half past one the next day. She was disappointed to find Wallace had vanished, but quickly remembered he had to go to work that morning. A giant smile stayed plastered on her face as she lay in bed for the next two hours, eager for an encore of that magical unity.

Should she call him? Tell him she misses him?

It's too early for that.

Besides, her parents would most likely be home from Lake Tahoe around six and they would no doubt find having Wallace over a bit questionable. She would see him on Monday; that was going to have to be enough for her. It was around four when she finally got up, showered and changed. She ate a light snack of cheese and crackers with a bit of chocolate milk and then welcomed her parents home. The rest of the night was spent attempting to write a love letter to Wallace that she may or may not give him. It took her until two in the morning and when she finally fell asleep, she didn't dream.

Lauren carried the letter with her all day. She grew frightened when all of his normal haunts — his locker, the pool, behind the chemistry lab — were all void of his presence. Had something happened to him? Should she stop by his house after school to find out? Finding his car parked in his normal spot an hour after the last class had been dismissed gave her some relief. The top was up, which was a bit odd, but the weather did call for rain that afternoon, so Lauren didn't think much of it. There were only a handful of other cars left, including the abandoned

silver Honda down the hill a ways. If she were ever going to find him, there was no better spot to wait than there.

She was fifty yards away when she stopped, frozen in time. Her heart cracked and her throat closed as the car shimmied back and forth. *What's going on?* she thought, even though she knew the answer. She debated what to do — should she walk up to the car and confirm her fears or run the other way and deny everything until she died of depression and an overdose of sleeping pills? In the end she had to know for sure.

It took all of her strength to walk those last fifty yards. The windows were lightly fogged, but she could still see Wallace lying down in the backseat, his eyes glued to some brunette's chest. She couldn't turn away until Wallace caught sight of her. His words were vacant, but his lips didn't lie. *Shit,* they said, which ignited confusion in his brunette hussy. Lauren's eyes puffed up as large as a moist marshmallow. Wallace pulled his pants up and navigated his way out of the car. She wasn't going to wait; she dropped everything and ran. There was no way to know for sure what he had done. She imagined he tried to race after her in a need to expose his regret and claim he was truly sorry he had hurt her. It was believable to think he finished what he had started with that bitch in the car, the two of them laughing at her naïvety. Had Wallace gotten out of the car and found the crinkled letter, reading it to his new plaything with humor and insolence?

Lauren cried for two days. Her mother tried everything to calm her down, but it wasn't until the next week when Lauren went back to school and saw Wallace and Cheryl acting all lovey-dovey, holding one another, necking, whispering sweet nothings to each other, that she realized how stupid she was for believing Wallace would want anything to do with her but use her to score a bit of a reputation before going after his true goal of fucking the head cheerleader every night of the week until they separated after graduation. She didn't deserve the pain he had laid upon her. It was time to break free of the love she still harbored deep inside for the snake that had stolen her virginity.

"Wallace," she said as she stepped up behind him. The bell let out a horrifying ring that echoed through the halls. His loving features seemed to show a slight hint of regret.

No, Lauren said to herself. *Don't let him fool you.*

Before he got out anything but her name, Lauren sent a right hook to his left eye, knocking his head up against the locker. "Fucking dick," she said as the bell faded in the distance.

"What the hell?" Cheryl said, protecting Wallace like a mother. Surprisingly, Wallace showed her respect through his good eye.

"Enjoy him, Cheryl," Lauren said, pulling the promise ring from her finger. "Before he decides you're nothing more than a practice mitt for someone even more fetching and slutty." Lauren threw the ring at Wallace. It hit the ground in a metallic clunk as she walked away from him for the last time.

Two weeks later, Lauren felt sick to her stomach and realized she'd missed her period. Her thoughts roared with fear as she waited for the pregnancy test to reveal itself. That the test came up inconclusive didn't help. She didn't have enough money to keep buying tests, and there was no way she was about to tell her parents, especially if she was simply jumping to conclusions. So she made an appointment with a friend's mother at the local Planned Parenthood.

The doctor's eyes told her everything.

"I can't…" Lauren took in long, deep breaths to keep from crying.

"It seems the results of your blood test are positive, Lauren." The doctor pulled the chair sitting in the corner close to her and sat down. Lauren kept her eyes averted from hers, but she still sensed her looking for recognition. She refused her. "Would you like a minute?" she asked as Lauren wiped a tear away.

Why me? She kept asking herself, pleading for a reasonable answer. There were plenty of girls, including her best friend Janine (who first lost her virginity two years before at her sweet sixteen party), who constantly had sex, sometimes protected, sometimes not, without ever finding themselves in the situation she now found herself in.

"Lauren?" the doctor asked after a minute of silence. Lauren finally answered her with the shake of her head.

"I know this can't be easy for you."

Can't be easy? Lauren thought. *This is a fucking nightmare.*

"There are several options," she continued. "Adoption is very common among teenage parents."

"No," Lauren said. Having been thinking of nothing but what she would do with the baby if she had it, the one thing she couldn't fathom was giving her daughter to someone else; unable to ever see her child, talk to her, laugh with her. That would be more painful than finding Wallace cheating on her. Adoption was not the answer, nor was telling Wallace about the child. She wanted to leave him as cold as he had left her.

The doctor sighed. She read Lauren's confusion, fright and despondency on her brow. "Lauren, may I say that what you may be thinking is a viable solution, and I can help you through this if you don't have anyone else you can turn to."

"Yeah," Lauren said.

The doctor nodded, far from discouraged. She signed a paper on the clipboard and handed it to Lauren, which she accepted without ever looking at it. "I'm here if you need anything," the doctor said and left her alone. Leaving the office was difficult, and she did so without another word to anyone, not even the receptionist. She went directly to Janine's house, where she exposed her secret in a quick chatter that seemed to keep the tears at bay. It seemed if she talked fast enough, she wouldn't feel the pain.

"What are you going to do?" Janine asked when Lauren finally stopped.

"I don't know." Lauren paused. "I can't tell my parents. My father would throw me out of the house."

"Have you considered an abortion?" Somehow Janine knew. Lauren was unable to say the words out loud. "Well…" Janine prompted. "Tell me."

Lauren nodded with the slightest of movement and quietly answered, "Yes."

"Do you have the cash for one?"

Lauren shook her head, which led to uncontrollable shakes in every nerve.

"Come here." Janine hugged Lauren. "It's a crapshoot," she whispered. "You never know when it'll happen to you. It's not the end of the world."

"Even if I had the money, I'd still need my parents to sign off on it."

"That's not true. There are ways around that. Trust me, all you really need is someone to be there with you at the time of the procedure."

"Seriously?"

"Yeah. One of Tony's girls had an abortion a few months ago." Tony, as Lauren recalled, was one of Janine's friends with benefits who also had a working relationship with several other girls. Lauren didn't ask many questions; it was none of her business.

"How is she?"

"Fine, I guess. It's not really a topic of interest when we get together."

Lauren was curious, but her head was still spinning with anxiety. "I don't know."

"From what I've heard, it's completely safe," Janine comforted. "You have to go in and do some counseling and stuff, but the actual procedure takes about five minutes. You're lucky you're still in the first trimester. Hell, you could probably take the abortion pill if you wanted."

Lauren wasn't convinced of how lucky she was. She held her stomach tightly. "What if I don't want to go through with any of it?"

"I don't know. If it were me, I'd go and find out as much as I could and then figure out if it's worth it to tell my parents. But, it's up to you. It's your kid."

"Yeah."

Janine couldn't help giving Lauren another big hug. "Enough of this shit. Let's go pig out on some chocolate, chocolate chip."

"You're talking about ice-cream, right?"

Janine playfully punched Lauren in the arm. "Unless of course you know a deep double chocolate Chip."

The girls laughed delightfully. For the first time in weeks, Lauren felt good.

"Race you," she squealed as she bolted for the bedroom door, Janine right behind her. The two got sick on ice-cream while watching a couple of silly comedies before crashing. A few days later, Janine escorted Lauren to speak with an abortion counselor at Planned Parenthood. After two long hours, a million questions and digesting the pros and cons of having an abortion (both physically and mentally), Lauren's decision had been made — though she still had no clue where the money would come from.

"Give me a couple of days," Janine repeatedly said during the conversation with the counselor. "I'll get it for you." She said it one last time as they walked to Janine's car.

"Where?" Lauren finally asked.

"You let me worry about that. Just take it easy, make the necessary appointments and I'll take care of the rest. I promise." And when Janine promised, Lauren trusted her.

Over the next few weeks, Lauren took all the tests, filled out all the paperwork and sat through all the interviews required of her, but when the day came to have the procedure, Janine couldn't be found. Lauren stood outside the clinic an hour before the scheduled appointment, contemplating whether or not she should cancel the whole thing and tell her parents everything. To her relief, Janine arrived some ten minutes before the appointment. She had a scar on her upper lip and a fading black eye.

"What happened?" Lauren asked.

Janine pulled away from Lauren's attempt at touching her face. "Don't worry about it." She held out a rolled up ball of bills. "Here's the money."

"Where did you get this?"

Janine shoved the cash into Lauren's hand. "Take it," she said and headed into the clinic.

Lauren looked at the money. She could only assume Janine had performed a favor for whoever gave her the cash; a favor that at some point went wrong in more ways than one. She felt the need to give it back, tell her she would suck up her fear and tell her parents what happened. But she knew Janine wouldn't allow

that, not after what she no doubt had to go through to get it.

"Damn it," she whispered before trudging into the clinic. She didn't say a word to Janine during or immediately following the procedure. Janine left to run a few errands (or so she called them) during Lauren's recovery, giving Lauren time to reflect on her decision. The death that just occurred weighed heavy within her body, convincing her there was no possible way she would ever have a baby now that she helped kill her own flesh, no matter how small or undeveloped it had been. When Janine returned, she helped Lauren schedule her follow-up appointments and walked from the clinic a few yards in front of her friend. As they got in her car, Lauren bluntly asked, "What's wrong with you?"

Janine just started the car. The ride back to Lauren's was awkward and deathly silent. It was the last time Lauren would see Janine, who disappeared in her blue Jetta without so much as a wave goodbye.

For a while, it was difficult for Lauren to keep her abortion a secret, but over time, it got easier to wipe the incident from her mind. But waiting for the doctor once again to confirm her nightmare, she was no longer able to hide from the memory she had locked away so many years ago.

Lauren thought the doctor walking through the exam room door was the young woman who helped her in Planned Parenthood. But as she stepped closer, her features pruned and her hair silvered. It was the same doctor, having opened her own practice a few years after she originally spoke to Lauren that day, but it had been many years.

"I think we're having a bit of déjà vu, here, Lauren," the doctor said. "You're definitely pregnant and I'd say, by the look of things, you're approximately four months, give or take a week or so."

"Four months?" Lauren squealed.

"I can't be positive, not until we run an ultrasound, but yeah, it's a pretty accurate educated guess."

"That's not possible," Lauren said matter-of-fact. "My last period was just a few weeks ago."

"Spotting is quite normal, Lauren. Especially in the first trimester. Are you sure it wasn't just a little bleeding?"

"No. I wasn't fucking spotting. Up until a couple of days ago, the last time I had sex was… three years ago."

"There's no need to get angry," the doctor said in a soothing voice. "I'm going to give you the number to a very good pediatrician who can answer all of your questions. She's a friend of mine. She'll take care of you." The doctor wrote the number on the paperwork and gave it to Lauren. "I hope you'll go see her," she continued, softly hinting at the decision she knew she'd made before.

Lauren slid off the table, her eyes glued to the number. She felt a bit sick over losing her temper but let it pass. "I think I will," she said.

When she looked up, a strange man stood in front of her. A black shadow engulfed his body, filling the floor with a light smoke. Dark features hid most of his face, but Lauren recognized the bright yellow eyes that turned red as she bore into them.

"Come back to me," the darkness echoed.

Lauren screamed and dropped to the floor. She closed her eyes and covered her face. The doctor quickly tried to calm her seizure-like shaking. "Lauren. Lauren, calm down."

A repeated chorus of "Stay away" hummed under Lauren's heavy breaths. The doctor ran to the nearest cabinet and grabbed a small bottle of chlorpromazine. She sucked about 2 cubic centimeters into a needle and knelt back next to Lauren, waiting patiently for the right time to shove the syringe into her arm. It took a few seconds, but as the sedative worked its way through Lauren's body, she slowly stopped vibrating and passed out.

Providence – Monday, 3:25 pm

The sun broke through the cool afternoon breeze as Kara walked slowly through the cemetery. She placed a bouquet of daisies on top of a nearby headstone that read:

Diana Reisen
Loving daughter and sister
You will always be remembered

As she always did when she visited her sister, Kara kissed the tips of her fingers and pressed them to the name on the stone. It had been thirteen years since the crash that took Diana's life. She had begged her parents to allow her to go to France for her high school graduation, and though they continually said no (citing how young she was despite being eighteen), she went anyway. Her parents hardly ate or slept as they waited for their daughter to come home, which never happened. The return flight crashed somewhere over the Atlantic. Kara found out a few hours before leaving on a tomb raiding expedition in Babylon. It took her parents nearly twenty minutes to tell her what happened, as they couldn't stop crying; deep down she knew what they were going to tell her the moment she walked through the door. Kara postponed her trip to stay with her parents, waiting and praying Diana's body would be found, if nothing more than for closure. Six months passed and authorities found nothing relating to the crash. She bought a headstone and cemetery plot to try and help her parents — and in some ways, herself — a chance to heal and move forward, but she knew without a body, none of them would truly be able to do that. For all they knew, Diana was on some desert island, eating coconut all day and talking to the new best friend she found among the luggage. But Kara had to do something, just in case her body was decomposing on the bottom of the ocean. She invited all of their friends and relatives to the funeral. Some didn't come, but those who did confirmed what Kara had suspected — they needed to say goodbye in their own way and show how much Diana's life really meant to them all. Kara left the day after the funeral to join her team in Babylon. She would find the first tablet soon after her arrival, but all of her thoughts stayed with Diana and her parents. She needed to go back, but doing so would only bury her in depression. If she was truly going to get past this, she needed to immerse herself in her work. It was the only coping mechanism she knew.

"How you doing, kiddo?" Kara asked the headstone. "I just saw Mom and Dad. Looks like they're finally starting to get their lives back together. You'd be proud of them. Mom started a book club with some friends from church and Dad, well, he's been trying to fix stuff around the house. I think Mom lets him because it keeps him occupied." She paused and then asked, "Me? I'm doing okay. Remember the museum I told you about? It's holding steady, but an influx of business wouldn't hurt. I'm going on a trip in the next couple of days. You'd be amazed at this guy, Matthew Stevens. He's such a wide-eyed dreamer. He helped me decipher the text on those tablets I found. It led us to Bermuda, and guess what? We think we may have just found Atlantis. What's even more bizarre is we think it's in the dead center of the Bermuda Triangle." Kara chuckled. "I know, I know. Impossible, right? But you didn't see the evidence. We're heading out there on Saturday. I'll be sure to pray for you once we're on the water. You'll keep me safe, won't you?"

Kara wiped a small tear away and kissed the name once again. "I love you, kid. You're still my special nuisance." Kara pressed her hands together above her heart and then lowered them to the grave in one last loving gesture. She waved farewell and slowly walked away, turning back every few feet to take one last glimpse at the headstone.

Just before reaching her car, Kara's cell phone rang, scaring her to the marrow. After collecting her thoughts, she picked it from her pocket and checked to see who it was. She didn't have to think twice about answering.

"Hello, Paul. What's up?"

"We've got the results back from Purdue, Miss Reisen. You're not going to believe it."

"I'm about twenty minutes out." Kara didn't wait for a response. She jumped into her car and raced from the cemetery at about fifty miles per hour over the actual posted speed limit.

* * *

"Unbelievable," Kara said as she read over the results for a third time. Paul, one of Kara's thesis students who was now a graduate student helping as a teacher's aide, grinned knowingly behind her. "How accurate are these?"

"We ran it multiple times," Paul said, "and each time it came up the same way, with a three percent variance."

"This is unreal." Kara instantly dialed Matthew.

"Hello?" Matthew said after the second ring.

"Matthew, I have the results from the artifact."

"And?" Matthew's anticipation matched Kara's.

"And according to this, the artifact could be anywhere from two to three *million* years old."

Matthew was silent. Kara hoped he hadn't fainted. "You still with me, Matthew?"

"Yeah, I just… how accurate is that?"

"Within a three percent margin."

"Un-freakin'-believable. I never dreamt it would be that old."

"You're not the only one."

There was a long silence and then: "Are you ready for the trip?" Matthew sounded uneasy.

"As much as I can be," Kara said. "Aren't you?" It was the first time Kara felt Matthew had any doubts.

"Yeah… yeah."

Kara was quick to figure out what might have been bothering him. "How's Kaleena taking all of this?"

"Better than expected." The response was quick. "In fact, she's coming with us."

Kara smiled. She had never met Matthew's daughter — no one on the team had — so the idea stirred up a bit of excitement. "That's great."

"Yeah, I guess."

Kara now knew exactly where his anxiety stemmed from. "It'll be okay, Matthew. The stuff about the Bermuda Triangle is just rumor."

"I know that." Matthew sounded insulted. "I'm picking up some books about it tomorrow. Help prepare us a little."

"Prepare us for what?"

"For when the rumors turn out to be true."

Kara smiled. "Have you found an oceanographer yet?"

"Maybe. I'm still looking for a backup, though."

"Hey, you know who might want to do it? Remember David?"

"David? You think so?"

"I haven't talked to him for a few months, but you know how much of a triangle buff he is. Imagine how excited he'd be."

"What's his number? I'll give him a call."

Kara gave Matthew the number and hung up. Paul had been staring at her the whole time with a weird grin on his face. "You guys are headed out to the Bermuda Triangle?"

Kara winked and left.

Lucky bastards.

Connecticut – Tuesday, 11:43 am

Kaleena's feet hurt as she walked into the apartment. She had spent the better part of the morning running around campus gathering up all of the notes, topics and source materials she'd need for the next couple of weeks's worth of assignments and midterms. Kaleena wouldn't have even dared step foot on campus if it wasn't for that. She had much more engrossing things to do. She had written eight chapters over the weekend, some that she rewrote from scratch several times, some that poured out in near perfect condition, which is to say, she only had to edit once or twice to find the right way to phrase her thoughts. But she had obligations she wasn't willing to sacrifice.

When she first arrived on campus, her legs become concrete. It took a lot of time and concentrated effort to control the games her mind played with her and expunge the creature that was attempting to consume her. Fear continually tried to escape as she walked to each of her professor's rooms, prompting Kaleena to check behind her every few seconds, double check corners and hallways before passing, and jumping at the chirp of a cricket. It didn't matter where the noise originated, it felt as if they were right on top of her, whispering for the terror within to rise. She swore she saw *him* hiding in the shadow of the tall oak that stood outside one of the main libraries; sitting on the bench in the middle of the quad; pacing her up the stairs of the physics building. Each time, he stared at her, his face blackened with a fierce urge for revenge. Kaleena couldn't understand why she was acting so childish. His appearances had to be delusional; there was no way the Dean would have allowed a sex offender, even an *alleged* sex offender, back on campus.

She made it for the tail end of her geology class and when she picked up the last of the notes she would need, a slight relief warmed her; she could now disappear from the campus, collect her thoughts and find a way to overcome her trepidation. That comfort dripped away as she stepped from the building and saw the stranger leaning up against one of the trees lining the walkway. But he wasn't facing her this time; his focus was on the distant hillside — or so it seemed.

The thought of getting anywhere close to him chilled her blood, but it was the only way to get back to the main road. As she tiptoed past him, he stood motionless. Curiously anxious, Kaleena kept her eyes glued to his lean frame until she noticed him lift his open hand. Her first instinct was to run, get as far away from her adversary as possible. But something called to her, urging her to stop and find out what the man was holding. A gold chain dangled between his fingers. Kaleena couldn't see if the chain was attached to a pendant, and she wasn't about to step any closer to find out. Instead, she swiftly walked away, turning back just once. When she did, the man was gone. Undeterred, Kaleena went straight home, never losing a beat in the rhythm of her steps.

Though Kaleena's heart still chased her breaths, comfort took hold as she dropped her schoolwork on the table. She grabbed a glass from the cupboard and filled it to the edge with water from the Sparklets dispenser on the side of the counter. It was gone as soon as she started drinking, so she refilled the glass, this time taking a small sip and bringing the glass with her into the living room. She sat down on the couch, ready to focus on the work she had ahead of her. No matter how hard she tried, though, she remained distracted by the encounter with the stranger. Why was he there? What was on the gold chain? Why was he offering it to her? Was he trying to seduce her into something she would regret later? Was his rescue just a ruse for something greater? Or was he just some crackpot stalker who knew how to limit his interaction with his victims? Kaleena wiped all of those questions away as she tried to remember the instructions her professor's had given her in relation to the assignments. They all seemed muddled together, but if there was one thing Kaleena had learned, it was every professor had pretty much the same instructions for every paper that would ever be written. The research and arguments were what mattered, and based on the topics she had, everything seemed easy enough. Compare this idea with that idea, summarize this and explain the consequences of that, argue the case of something mundane with thorough support. There didn't seem to be any topics that screamed, "Write about me!" She'd choose soon enough. Right now, she just wanted to relax for once. It had been awhile.

"Heard from your mother yet?" Matthew asked as the front door closed. He carried some books Kaleena assumed were on Atlantis and the Bermuda Triangle.

"Studying up for the trip?" Kaleena asked.

"Just want to get all the info I can before heading out," he said, taking the books into his bedroom.

Kaleena shook her head in amusement. "You could have just asked me, you know. I am kind of an expert."

"That may be, but I'd rather get all sides of the story."

Kaleena let the jab at bias roll off her as she leaned back and closed her eyes.

"So," Matthew called as he bounced back into the living room. "Anything?"

"Not yet," she said wearily.

Matthew was about to say something but thought better of it. He rubbed his mouth and then said, "If you don't hear anything by tomorrow, I'm getting someone else."

"Right."

"I talked to an old colleague yesterday who's ready to go as soon as I say the word. In fact, he'd probably do it for free if it came down to it."

Kaleena knew what Matthew was doing. "She'll call," she said, a hint of doubt hiding beneath her voice.

"I'm sure she will," Matthew said. "I'm going to get some lunch. Want to come?"

Kaleena really needed to get to work on these papers, but it was the first time Matthew had offered to take her out to eat in some time. What would it hurt to get away for an hour and have lunch with her father? "Sure," she said. "Why not?" Kaleena tossed the papers back on the table. Matthew was a little shocked she agreed, but excited nonetheless. She still must love him, as a daughter would, or else she would have come up with some excuse to say no. As he escorted her out of the apartment, Matthew was delighted she could put all of his mistakes aside and give him yet another chance to be a father, even though she didn't have to. Or she just wanted a free meal. Either way, he now had the opportunity to talk to her. Whether she responded would be a miracle all its own.

*   *   *

It was a quiet lunch. Kaleena and Matthew sat at a table for two at Claim Jumper, one of Kaleena's favorite restaurants. She ordered her usual — chicken strips with a side of ranch for dipping and a bowl of French Onion soup. Her father ordered a turkey sandwich with all the trimmings — except lettuce, which Matthew couldn't stand; not on his sandwich anyway. Give it to him drowning in French dressing and he was in heaven. Give it to him dry with nothing but a bit of mayonnaise and tomato, forget it. Kaleena spent most of the meal staring at her food,

thinking about all the times her parents had taken her out to eat, most frequently to this particular restaurant. She remembered them smiling as they played their little games of observance, picking someone in the restaurant and coming up with a story for that person — what they were doing at the restaurant, why they wore what they wore and where their life was headed.

"Okay, hotshot..." Matthew would say through soft laughter after claiming a young girl with five piercings in her ear had escaped from the carnival and was hiding from an elephant that was being used to hunt her down — a claim that Jaime scoffed at with derision. Kaleena just laughed heartily. It was quite obvious Matthew didn't take the game too seriously, trying harder to get a laugh than to make a logical assessment. "You can do better?"

"You bet to shit I can," Jaime said.

"Well, all right." Matthew scanned the restaurant, spotting an old man sitting alone near the front door reading the latest John Grisham novel. He wore gray slacks with a blue and white sweater that looked to have been bought from a specialty store. "Tell me about the old man, there."

Jaime digested the man's features, his appearance and body language. She studied how he sipped his coffee immediately after the waitress came by to fill it up. His smile was bright, as she flirted with him before placing the check on the table.

"He's widowed," Jaime started. "Lost his wife maybe a year ago. He feels comfortable eating alone, probably comes here every day and orders the same thing: coffee, maybe a light sandwich, a hamburger on special occasions. Medium — not to cooked, but not rare enough to taste the blood. The waitresses know him, think he's cute, maybe a little funny when he's not remembering his wife. He doesn't worry about money; was probably a lawyer or a legal aid at some point. He misses his job, too, having been forced to retire 'cause he just can't seem to grasp the concept of defense or prosecution anymore due to his slowly decaying mind and body, for which he must take a dozen pills in the morning just to get out of bed. He probably wears nice clothes to present himself in the proper way, making sure everyone knows he's someone of high class and should not be looked down upon.

The slight comb-over and the trimmed mustache say he's still really enamored by his appearance and wants to put his best foot forward."

Matthew and Kaleena were silent, waiting for the punch line Matthew was so clever with. "What?" she asked.

"Why?" Matthew said.

"Why?"

"Yeah. Why is he so enamored by his appearance?"

"I don't know…" Jaime said, feeling a bit foolish.

"Come on. Is it because of the way he was brought up or is it just to impress the girls so he can get his groove on with a hot young thing?" Matthew made thrusting gestures with his pelvis as Kaleena laughed hysterically.

"That's it, I'm done," Jaime said, folding her hands to her face in awkward embarrassment. The couple sitting next to them shifted in their seats with disapproval on their brow. Matthew held his hand up in apology and calmed his laughter.

The memory put a smile on Kaleena's face as she took a sip from her Pepsi. That was a long time ago.

"What are you smiling at?" Matthew asked, wiping some mayo from his mouth.

"Nothing." After a brief moment: "Do you think she'll ever call?"

Matthew sat back in his chair. He didn't want to lie to her; she'd see right through him if he did. But he didn't want to say what he was really thinking, either. Jaime was never one to ever go back to the past, for any reason. Calling Kaleena now would only stir up feelings of regret — an emotion Jaime is not at all comfortable with.

"Have you tried calling her again?" he said.

"No."

"How come? Maybe she never got your message."

"Yeah, I thought of that," Kaleena said, shifting her body. "But I don't want to pressure her. What if she just doesn't want to talk to me?"

"You'll never know for sure if you don't try."

"I know." There was a short pause.

"Well? Go on."

"What, now?" Kaleena's stomach turned over. She wasn't ready to call her mother again and despised Matthew a little for putting her on the spot. What if she answered? Kaleena pictured her mother, overcome with guilt, hanging up as if it were an accident, just to avoid her. Then again, she didn't have to pick up. What if she sent the call directly to voicemail? Would she delete it without listening? Is that what she did originally? Until Kaleena came to grips with her own self-deprecation, she didn't want to dial her mother's number again. The memory of her mother was perfect and full of devotion to a beautiful child's smile and the sparkling eyes of youth and silliness.

"Why not?" Matthew said.

"I don't want to do it now." Kaleena forced a tone that would hopefully close the conversation. "I'll do it later tonight," she lied.

Matthew nodded and put his napkin on the table. "So what have you been writing recently?"

"Nothing," she said, scooping up the last of her ranch dressing with a luke-warm French fry. She was glad he had changed the subject, but not to her book. "Just some random thoughts about people and our society."

"Oh, yeah? What about society?"

Kaleena saw a hint of genuine interest. It made her blush slightly. "You know. Looking honestly at the human condition — who people really are, how no one seems to ever be truly sincere about anything. It's all just an act, every minute of every day."

Matthew listened to Kaleena for the next half hour. He would occasionally interrupt with an anecdote about Lauren or Henry or one of his other co-workers in regards to an idea she'd bring up. Some made her laugh, some she thought were a bit cruel, and others seemed entirely unrelated. But the more she learned about his adventures, his friends — his life — the closer she felt to him. For the

first time in three years, Kaleena was a kid again, not a fourteen-year-old going on forty. Her mind had been invigorated, cleared of all the events of the past week.

*   *   *

That night, after writing another chapter and making note of the relevant stories and tidbits Matthew had relayed, Kaleena went through with the promise of calling her mother. For some reason, she wasn't afraid of what might happen. So what if she answered and hung up? At least she would know she wasn't ready and could stop fighting herself about it. As she listened to the light ring of the phone, she ran over what she would say for both an answer and a message.

"I'm not around, leave a message." Kaleena's brow furrowed. She needed to say something that would give her mother reason to call her. But she didn't want to sound desperate or needy, or in any way hurting. She came to a conclusion.

It would be quick and short.

It would be a reminder.

Los Angeles – Tuesday, 6:26 pm

Jaime turned in her sleep, unaware of the setting sun. She still felt dead to the world as she sat up, tired of trying to get back to sleep. The sun had woken her up a couple of times throughout the day, flashing through the curtains like a peeping Tom with a flashlight. It couldn't have been more than a few hours, but it was the most sleep she had gotten in the last couple of days. She had spent all day Monday recording a mockup voice over for the completed rough cut of the film, knowing full well she didn't have enough time to hire the right narrator (which could take weeks if Morgan Freeman's agent never got back to her) and get the footage to the executives by eight the next morning. As Gavin laid the narration into the piece, Jaime rerecorded certain portions, rewrote and reedited small bits and pieces here and there and fine-tuned the entire project. By the time the sun

broke the horizon and the last bit of cheese from the solo slice of pizza was ice cold, Gavin had finally started transferring the footage to a DVD. It took a little over an hour, but Jaime was dead-set against getting any rest whatsoever, afraid that if she did, something would go wrong (God forbid) or she would sleep right through the meeting.

"Want some coffee?" Jaime had asked, shaking a Starbucks cup half full of cold black coffee.

"Nah," Gavin said, grabbing one of the last stale Dunkin' Donuts. "I want to sleep for a month. Coffee won't help." He took a bite and tossed the doughnut back into the ugly pink box, disgusted. The progress bar on the computer moved slower the more he watched it, so he let his head fell back on the couch and closed his eyes.

"I know what you mean." Jaime tossed her coffee in the small trashcan "We just need to get this to Jameson first."

"Yeah, I know." Gavin cracked his neck and gave it a squeeze. "Is it all right if I drop dead on his floor?"

Jaime choked out a chuckle and left the room to have a quick smoke, running through some things she was sure the studio would want to change. If nothing else, it kept her awake. At least she'd be able to sleep before they got back to her on it. She stepped out the cigarette and was about ready to convince herself to make one last change when Gavin came sleepwalking out of the office. He handed her the DVD.

"There you have it," he said, throwing on his coat.

An hour and a half later, they would finally get to see Kurt Jameson. After some quick pleasantries and a little bit about the film — making sure he knew it was just a rough cut and the voice actor had yet to be cast — Jaime handed over the product. She dropped Gavin off at his apartment and then headed back home, falling asleep a few times before she pulled into her driveway. She thought she'd be dead the minute her body hit the bed, but for some reason, either her body or her mind kept the sandman at bay. Something was bothering her; she just didn't know what it was. And now she was awake for good, and felt plastered.

She coughed a couple of times and grabbed a cigarette off the nightstand. The lighter didn't want to wake up either at first. When it finally did, Jaime inhaled a large mound of smoke only to cough it out. Regardless, she felt better. She rubbed her eyes deeply and ran her fingers through her gorgeously tattered hair before grabbing her phone. Three messages had been received while she was out. The first was from her technical wizard, Patricia Bannes, looking for an update on the project. The second was from her bank, trying to solicit some new theft protection thing on her credit card, which she deleted before it was even halfway finished.

The third brought life back to her eyes. The message was short, but it made her heart tense up. It was from Kaleena, whom Jaime realized she hadn't even thought about since she received that first surprising message.

"Hey, Mom. I may have found the life you were looking for. Call me. Miss you." —*click.*

"If you would like to replay this message…" the electronic woman chimed in.

Jaime wasn't paying attention. She pushed the one key and listened to the message… and again…. a different word emphasized with each pass; a different meaning within that sweet, kind voice. Jaime couldn't help but tear up. Not because Kaleena had mentioned the words Jaime had used to say goodbye. She cried for another reason; the real reason she kept listening to the message.

Miss you.

After another dozen rewinds, Jaime finally hung up without deleting the message and finished her cigarette. She thought long and hard about those two words — what they meant and the love they conveyed. Jaime went to her computer, but no matter how much information she looked up on fish that lived mostly near the Arctic, how much she studied weather patterns around the globe and what may happen in the future (most of which were conspiracy nuts trying to get a hard on by telling everyone the world would end), or how many times she bid on a really nice piece of equipment that could calculate the density of salt within a body of water compared with the amount of vegetation, she couldn't push those words out of her head. She kept peering over at the bookcase, which lying flat on its back in between all of her research papers, notebooks, charts and oceanography manuals, was Kaleena's book. How could she ignore her daughter like this? It was clear Kaleena wanted to talk to her, if not see her at least one time, maybe so she could tell her how she felt about her leaving, or maybe to try and beg her to come back, something Jaime wasn't willing to do. Whatever the reason, deep down, Jaime had the same level of desire to speak to Kaleena, if for nothing else than to attempt to begin a brand new relationship with her daughter.

It was time; Jaime had struggled long enough. She grabbed her cell and listened to the message again, jotting down Kaleena's number and dialing it up. It only took one ring for an answer, though no one spoke right away. Jaime took the initiative. "Kaleena?"

"Mom?" Kaleena's voice was young, chipper.

Jaime's cheeks brightened with the curvature of her lips. "Hey," she said with a nervous jilt in her throat.

"How are you?" Kaleena asked gently.

"I'm okay," Jaime said. "I read your book." Telling her this now was a bit foolish, but it was too late.

"Did you like it?"

"Yeah, I did. It had some fantastic arguments. A writer from my own heart."

Kaleena huffed a chuckle. "Thank you."

"So, what's up?" Jaime asked after listening to Kaleena's silence.

"I have something I need to ask you."

"Go on." Jamie braced herself for something horrible. Hopefully it was something about a boy, maybe how to prepare for her first date or what the right time was for a first kiss. It was something Jaime hadn't thought of until now, but Kaleena really didn't have anyone to talk to about these things. Then again, for all Jaime knew, Kaleena could be calling because she was pregnant or something even worse… if that were possible.

"I want to find out if you'd like to come on an expedition."

Jaime was relieved, then fell a bit confused. "An expedition?"

"Yeah. Dad wants me to fund a new expedition of his and he needs an ocean-ographer to go with him."

Jaime was flabbergasted. "You agreed to fund your father's work? Why would you do that?"

"Because he promised I could offer you the job," Kaleena bit back. "I thought you might like the opportunity."

"Why would you think that?" There was a slight tension in her voice.

"He's heading out to the middle of the Bermuda Triangle."

"The what?"

"Yeah," Kaleena said with excitement. "And I'm going with him."

"What? Is he insane?" Jaime's hands twitched nervously. She needed to get up and walk around. "What's out in the Bermuda Triangle that's so important he would risk your life?"

"Atlantis," Kaleena said, a bit apprehensive. Jaime figured it was because the thought of it sounded just as foolish and absurd to Kaleena as it did to her.

"Are you fucking kidding me?" Jaime clasped her mouth, realizing too late what she had said. "I'm sorry." Her voice was softer.

"It's fucking okay," Kaleena said with a light laugh, which brightened Jaime's spirit.

"Why would you agree to fund an expedition to find Atlantis? Didn't you argue of its nonexistence?"

"Yes." There was a slight pause, and then, "But it means a lot to Dad." Jaime took in a deep breath. She felt pride toward Kaleena for her seemingly unselfish behavior. "And I would really like for you to come with us and help, even if it is all a bunch of horse manure."

Jaime lit up a cigarette and gave the only answer she knew she could give. "I have to think about it."

"You have to hurry. If I don't have an answer by tomorrow night, Dad's going to hire some friend of his. Please. This would mean a lot to me."

"I'll think about it," Jaime said again. "I'll talk to you tomorrow, okay?"

"Yeah."

"Get some sleep."

Kaleena chuckled, "I will. You too."

Jaime hung up and paced the room. Her husband was out of his mind and now he was dragging her daughter into his fantastical whimsies. After lighting another cigarette, Jaime went to the window and watched the orange sky slowly burn to black.

New York – Tuesday, 9:45 pm

The first thing Lauren saw when she opened her eyes was the heart monitor. An IV had been jammed in her arm. The air was heavy, seemingly pressing her to the bed and keeping her lungs from gathering oxygen. She winced as she tried to move. The small curvature of her stomach had become the size of a grapefruit. A mixed bag of fright and confusion swarmed her features.

A nurse, about as tall as Lauren but with a bit more girth, strolled into the room. A bright, crooked smile appeared as she saw Lauren's eyes for the first time. "You're awake." She left without waiting for a response. A second later, an announcement rang over the intercom. "Doctor Keller, please report to room 109. Doctor Keller to room 109."

Lauren wondered if the announcement had been for her. According to the assignment chart on the wall next to her, it was. The nurse made her way back into the room a few minutes later with a tall, Irish-looking doctor whose stomach looked much like Lauren's. "How are we today?" he asked, pushing her eyelids open to check her pupils with a flashlight that seemed to be extremely brighter than usual.

"Fine," Lauren said with a scratchy, dry throat. Her eyes bit at her nerves as the doctor lowered the light and checked the monitors.

"Good," Doctor Keller said, paying more attention to the readings than to her.

"What time is it?"

"About ten. You gave us a bit of a scare." The doctor finally turned back to her.

"Scare? Why…? What happened?"

The doctor's lips curved into a boyish smile. "You've been out for nearly thirty-six hours."

Thirty-six hours? Lauren felt a cold rush of blood surface. "Am I going to be okay?" she asked.

"Everything looks good." Doctor Keller checked his notes. "I want to keep you overnight for observation, but I don't see why you couldn't check out of here tomorrow morning."

Lauren looked down at her stomach. "And the…" she couldn't find the word, or else she didn't want to hear the word out loud. She didn't have to.

"Your baby is strong and healthy. She's going to be perfectly fine."

A loving tenderness swept the chills away as she ran the words over in her mind. *She*, Lauren thought. *A girl. I'm going to have a daughter.*

Sleep never came for Lauren that night. Thinking about what life was going to be like now that she was finally going to have a child kept her mind moving. The next morning, after having her vitals checked one last time, she signed herself out of the hospital and thanked Doctor Keller. She wasn't sure why she should, but she had a slight inkling he had helped pull her out of wherever she had gone. Upon returning home, Lauren made herself a bowl of oatmeal and sat next to the pool. Her thoughts revolved around what might have caused her to lose a day and a half. It almost felt as if someone had wiped her memory so she wouldn't remember.

Lauren, get a grip, she thought as she finished her oatmeal. Sitting there didn't help as she hoped it would. She needed something else, something more soothing, so she removed her clothes and stepped slowly into the pool. The cool, fresh water felt majestic on her skin. As she immersed her entire body under the water, she felt the baby's heart beat calmly alongside her own. Lauren floated on her back, allowing her stomach to breathe with the heat of the sun. She digested the songs of the birds, the hum of the pool filter and the static of cars rushing along the streets downtown. Although they continued to move forward, living their lives

with harmony, time had stopped for Lauren. For the first time since losing her virginity, she was at peace with her body. There was nothing that could take this beauty away from her, not even the man that had created it.

A vision of Henry changed all of that. Her stomach tightened and she lost all sense of openness. She lowered her body into the water and looked frantically around her pool. As she expected, no one was there, but she couldn't help feel his presence. She pulled herself out of the pool and grabbed her clothes, covering her body as she ran into the house. For a second, she thought she caught sight of a body whisking through the wind. Though she knew it was her imagination run wild, she locked the sliding glass door just to be safe. It took some time, but Lauren eventually made it upstairs to the shower. As she washed the chlorine and shame from her body, she thought about Saturday, about Matthew and whether or not she could ever go back to him. There was no doubt she was excited about the expedition, about his dream of finding a place presumably lost for several hundreds of thousands of years, but with the speed the young child seemed to be growing, would it be a good idea to take a chance like that? If it kept up at this pace, she would undoubtedly give birth on board the ship. How would she be able to explain that to everyone? Just last week she wasn't pregnant at all. And now —

She rubbed her belly once more and smiled. Matthew could find Atlantis without her. He would understand; she was happy where she was.

"I love you," she whispered. The baby kicked back and Lauren took it as a sign that she, too, loved her mother.

Los Angeles – Wednesday, 1:14 pm

The city noises outside the restaurant were subdued. There didn't seem to be as many cars on the usually busy street and there wasn't any construction going on, which for a mid-week afternoon was astonishing. Jaime hardly noticed as she tried to hide from the sun under the washed-out purple umbrella that was barley being held up by the small hole in the metal table outside. Sitting alone, she watched

the pedestrians labor on, unaware of the decisions they would make in the near future or the mistakes that have led them to where they are. Tall, short, fat, thin, Asian, Hispanic, it didn't matter. In the end, each one had, at some point, done something they truly regretted. It made Jaime sad and remorseful. Smoking was her crutch; it's what allowed her to bury her own regret, and for the first time, it wasn't working. She couldn't stop thinking of Kaleena—

Miss you

— of Matthew and what he must have felt when Kaleena asked about her. She wondered if it had been the first time, or whether the two had ever discussed her absence before. Could she have been the only one that pushed to forget her past? Tears formed under her thin sunglasses as Gavin slid into the seat across from her.

"Hey," he said.

Jaime cocked her head in his direction with a sour grin. "Hey." She put out her cigarette.

"Get any sleep?"

"A little." Jaime waved for the waiter, who promptly hopped to their table.

"Yes, ma'am," said the young boy, most likely an actor waiting for his big break in a mega-budget film directed by Spielberg or Scorsese. He was fresh; must have stepped off the bus just weeks ago, leaving his quiet, small-town life behind. There was an abundance of anticipation in his eyes. He had yet to see the dangers and the failure and the sorrow that would haunt his eyes in years to come.

"I'd like a chicken salad with a side of ranch and a glass of Zinfandel." Jaime looked to Gavin, who became flustered.

"Oh, uh, yeah. Just a burger, extra cheese. And a beer. Thanks."

The waiter scratched the order on his pad. "Great. I'll get that started right away." He left, but Jaime kept her eyes on him for a little while longer as another patron asked for some more coffee, or some extra butter for his role.

"It's a shame," she said.

"What's that?"

The boy scurried off. *Stay true*, she thought. "Never mind."

"Oh, God." Gavin slumped back in his chair. "You've heard from Jameson. He hated it, didn't he?"

"No." Jaime said. She saw relief flush through him. "I'm just thinking out loud."

"So why'd you call?" Gavin asked.

"I needed to get your opinion about a new job."

"Already? Goddamn, Jaime. We just finished one."

"I know... believe me I know." Jaime lit up another cigarette.

"I thought we agreed to take a month off."

"This one can't wait. I need to have an answer tonight." The smoke Jaime exhaled brushed past the side of Gavin's face before floating off into the distance.

"What's the job?" he said, trying hard to keep from coughing.

"Routine observation," Jaime said.

"Where at?"

Jaime inhaled a deep breath of nicotine and let it out slowly. "The Bermuda Triangle."

Gavin's throat clammed up. "The Triangle? Are you fucking kidding me?"

"That's what I said," Jaime said, cold.

Pros and cons ran through Gavin's head as he contemplated the possibilities. A female waitress, also a bit young, but seemingly distraught, set down their drinks and flashed a tired smile before leaving. Gavin grabbed his beer and took a quick swig.

"So?" Jaime said. "What do you think?"

"It's dangerous."

"It has a lot of potential. If we made it out..."

Gavin nodded. "It definitely feels like it might be worth the risk."

"What do you think the others would say?"

Gavin couldn't hold in his amusement. "Tricia's gonna love it." As he took another sip of beer, Jaime let slip a smile, knowing full well Patricia's love for the Bermuda Triangle. "Who's financing the trip?"

Before she could answer, Jaime's phone lit up (*saving grace?*). She lifted her index finger to silence Gavin before taking the call. "This is Jaime."

Gavin waited intently, wishing he could hear the other side of the conversation. Based on Jaime's reactions, the brightening of her demeanor and the tone of her voice, Gavin felt really good about what was being talked about.

"Great. I'll come by tomorrow to pick it up. Thank you, sir." Jaime hung up the phone, took another hit of her cigarette and flicked the half-used stick into the street.

"Well?" Gavin said eagerly.

"Jameson loved it."

Gavin clapped his hands together. "I knew it."

"He said he's got some notes for us on a few things, but he's ready to show it to the higher-ups in the next couple of days."

"Music to my ears."

The young waiter brought the food and for the next twenty minutes, Jaime talked about how Jameson had mentioned Morgan Freeman or Sam Neill as possible narrators and what they might expect from the notes he had mentioned.

"When is it due?" Gavin asked, finishing up the last bite of his burger. Jaime had eaten all she could of her salad and started another cigarette as she slowly sipped the remnants of her wine.

"We have a week to get everything in shape."

Gavin nodded and then asked the inevitable. "So the Bermuda thing's off?"

Jaime fell into deep thought. The possibility of seeing Kaleena again had been diminished and it made Jaime sick. She hadn't realized how excited she was about the prospect before now. "How would you mind finishing it up on the trip?"

Gavin wasn't sure why, but even through her sunglasses he could tell she really needed this job. Somehow, going out to the Bermuda Triangle was going to change her life. "That'll work," he said. He swilled the last of his second beer.

"That's it then. Start packing your things and tell everyone to meet me at my house tonight."

"You got it." Gavin grabbed his wallet.

"I got this," Jaime said, placing her hand on Gavin's arm.

"You sure?"

Jaime bent her head so Gavin could see her eyes over the top of her sunglasses. "I'll see you tonight." She let go and a new life came to her as he left. This new endeavor was going to be one interesting gig. She just hoped being stuck out on a boat, lost in the middle of a mostly uncharted area with the husband she abandoned years ago wouldn't make her go insane. Then again, none of that really mattered. This was her chance to not only see Kaleena, but maybe, just maybe, help speed up her rise to fame.

She dialed the number she'd programmed in the night before. Once again, it only took one ring for an answer.

"Hey, Mom," Kaleena beamed.

"Hey, Kaleena."

"Have you made a decision?" Kaleena got straight to the point. Jaime liked that.

"I'm going to need twenty-five grand a week," Jaime said.

"That means yes?"

"Only if you agree."

"Oh, I agree. Twenty-five a week will not be a problem."

"Then you have yourself an oceanography team."

Jaime felt good. She put out her cigarette and leaned back, relaxed and vibrant.

Connecticut – Wednesday, 5:18 pm

"That's great," Kaleena held her pillow tightly in her lap. Her iMac hummed on the bed in blue brilliance. "We're going to meet at the harbor in Miami-Dade, Saturday at nine o'clock."

"Sounds like a plan," Jaime said.

Kaleena felt six-years-old, but held in her excitement. "Can't wait to see you. Bye."

"You take care, sweetie."

Kaleena stared at her computer screen for a moment until she knew for sure Jaime had hung up, then lied down and covered her head with the pillow to drown out the intense scream of joy she had to release. When she was through, she sprang off her bed and out the door. Matthew was going through one of the books — *The Triangle: Facts and Myths Revealed* — when Kaleena came pounding into the room.

"She's coming," Kaleena said. Her cheeks were bright red and her eyes beamed.

Matthew smiled, conflicted. "That's great," he said.

Kaleena bit her bottom lip and ran back to her bedroom.

Matthew waited until the door closed and then tossed the book to the table. He leaned back on the couch and stared out the window. He didn't know how he wanted to feel about the news. It was true Jaime was the only woman he had ever loved unconditionally, and in some ways, still did, but she left them for selfish purposes. And even though he wasn't innocent in the whole mess, he wasn't sure if he could respect her anymore. None of that could hold a candle to the anticipation running all over Kaleena, though, and knowing she was willing to forgive and reconcile with Jaime trumped his own ill feelings toward her. Though he was about ready to fix dinner (as much as he could claim he fixed dinner after picking up a phone and calling some pizza place or Chinese take-out), Matthew was no longer hungry and slid his way to his bedroom. If Kaleena came to him later, he'd order something for her, but until then, he just wanted to be alone. His wedding ring sparkled brightly under the glint of the sun coming through the window. He held it for near an hour, thinking about every loving moment, every fight, every experience he had had with Jaime and what lied ahead for them on the ocean in three short days. No emotion revealed itself as he thought about it; he was a stone of reminiscence. But as Jaime's voice once again poured her heart out for the last time, Matthew dropped a single tear that he wiped away before it ran the course of his cheek. He placed the ring back in the drawer where it had come and lied down on the bed.

Kaleena never came to him that night. She was either so deep into her writing

she had lost track of time or she just decided that making herself a sandwich was better than another night of take-out. Either way, he had gotten what he thought he wanted. But deep down, he wished she had come to him for something — just to know that he was still needed by someone in the world.

"Give me comfort," he said to the ceiling, "and protect her for me."

Unknown Location – Time Unknown

The path was a nearly endless slick of metal that poured with illumination from the round lights above. Cold, gray metal walls that felt watery to the touch lined each side. There was no wind to brush her hair, no sound to hurt her ears and no pregnancy to cause her discomfort. Staring into the deep, dark abyss in front of her, Lauren felt young, healthy and at peace.

Suddenly, the black hole was consumed by a dense, white light that filled the corridor with pure energy. The walls burst with every imaginable color, hidden behind what appeared to be a thin glass. The floor shimmered a royal blue and tickled Lauren's toes. A soft breeze blew past her, fluttering the light blue tank top and sweatpants she had worn to bed. She tried to say *Hello*, but no sound came out of her mouth. At least she didn't think it did; there was still no sound in the room. Had she gone deaf?

Before she could yell out again, a figure, shadowed by the light, appeared to be moving toward her. It got closer even as Lauren slipped backwards. Frightened and uneasy, Lauren turned to run, but she was stopped by a young woman, no more than twenty-five years old. She had a soft flow of blond hair, cheekbones that pronounced her femininity and eyes that glowed a bright shade of periwinkle. It didn't appear she was wearing any makeup, however her features were enhanced with a light shade of pink and purple. A white dress outlined her thin frame; the curvature of her small breasts and slightly rounded thighs were accentuated by the pattern of stars and snowflakes. Her ghostly stomach was exposed and the flesh of her shoulders smoldered under the lights. A ribbon that tied around the

back of the woman's neck held the dress in place. Should Lauren have seen it, the woman's back would have been completely bare, possibly exposing a small slice of the woman's shoulder blades and the very tiny indent from the small of her back.

As Lauren tried to find the words to scream for help, the woman smiled, the tips of her brilliant white teeth showing through the tiny crack of her wafer-thin red lips. "Hide your fear," she said. But she *didn't* say it; her mouth never moved.

A chill ran Lauren's spine. She opened her mouth but the woman raised her hand to stop her from speaking. Her nails showed just above the tips of her fingers and were painted a deep silver, which sparkled with some sort of glittery coating. *Please. Do not speak with your lips,* the woman said. *Speak with your mind.*

Lauren hesitated, unsure of how to do what the woman requested. But as she concentrated on her thoughts, she held them in the front of her mind and allowed them to vibrate through the particles in the air. *Who are you?*

The woman's smile grew deeper. Her eyes closed in a delicate gesture of kindness. *My name is Evestylyn.*

Where am I? Lauren quickly replied.

You are here to listen to my words, that is all you need to know.

Why should I listen to you? Lauren tried to move, but her feet were stuck to the floor as if they had become part of it.

Your life is connected to mine. If you do not listen, we may both die.

I don't understand.

Listen and you shall. Evestylyn offered Lauren her hand. She could see comfort and safety in the woman's eyes and felt a genuine urge to be closer. Lauren gently took Evestylyn's hand, the softness of her touch producing a sense of gentle warmth.

You have come a long way, Lauren, in a life filled with pain. But it's not over. You must continue on your journey to find your way to the home of your ancestors.

Lauren thought a moment before asking, *Where am I to go?*

You know where you need to be and how to get there. But you must not allow feelings of guilt or shame stop you from your travels. I'm waiting to be born to the light of the mother who will free the souls of those who were lost.

I need to go to Atlantis? Lauren thought, a bit foolish.

Your heart serves you truth, Evestylyn said.

How do I get there? Lauren asked.

Just follow the one that guides you.

Matthew, Lauren stated. *He will guide me to Atlantis?*

Quite so.

How will we know when we're there?

Don't worry yourself with trifles. When the time comes, you shall be free of any burden that has been thrust upon you.

What happens when we get there?

You will be provided nourishment, safety and love.

Why?

Evestylyn's lips brightened. *You were chosen.*

Why was I chosen?

You carry with you a token of guidance and strength that cannot be given life without the help of those you seek.

I don't understand, Lauren said, her stomach contracting slightly.

You are with child, Evestylyn sang. *If this child is born on the land of humanity, it will suffer, as you will suffer.*

I need to bring the child to you?

Evestylyn laughed a sweet comforting titter, one that didn't feel condescending at all. *No, no. But you will bring her to my family, for they will keep the child's heart pure and give you the love you deserve.* Evestylyn let go of Lauren's hand. A cold breeze washed through her, and with a small voice said, *I must go now.*

Will I see you again? Lauren asked as Evestylyn faded before her.

You shall, she said softly. *Just know in your heart what you must fight for.* And with that, she vanished with a flash of light smoke that smelled of cherries.

Lauren took up the smell with her eyes tightly locked. When she opened them, Henry was standing in front of her. A cold gaze wrapped through his dark, coal eyes.

"Come back to me," he said.

Lauren opened her eyes wide and sucked in a pound of air as if she hadn't taken a breath in an hour. She coughed deeply and sat up. A cold sweat had formed on her back. As she regained her composure, she realized she was in bed. The clock read 2:17. Her toes curled against the carpeted floor, a texture she couldn't remember ever feeling so welcoming. She then felt a small kick in her gut. Letting her lips curl upward, she rubbed the skin of her still growing belly, which had pushed her tank top to bunch up between her stomach and her slightly larger than normal chest. Lauren's internal fight about going on this trip seemed to have been resolved. But it was just a dream, wasn't it? How was she going to justify trusting a woman who haunted her fantasies? She didn't much care. There had been a deep connection with her, as if the woman was more than just a vision. Someone had spoken to her from within, and she couldn't fight it. She wouldn't fight it.

Trust your heart, Lauren heard Evestylyn whisper through the night. Lauren laid back down and let the soothing musical hum of a song Lauren didn't know the name of send her back into slumber.

Miami-Dade – Saturday, 6:02 am

The alarm clock crowed. Matthew hit the snooze button quickly and strained to open his eyes. Although he had gotten nearly two and a half hours of sleep, it barely felt like ten minutes. It wasn't by choice he stayed up so late; it wasn't even the anticipation of heading out to sea in the morning. What kept his thoughts moving was the prospect of seeing Jaime again. Every time sleep started to take him, her face would appear, snapping him back awake. Euphoria grew and faded as he tossed from one side to the other, trying hard to push her away. Kaleena didn't help, rapping away on her laptop like a possessed typewriter, the sound of which could still be heard as he sat up and attempted to rub the dryness from his eyes. A thin layer of sweat, which had caused the sheets to become damp, covered his

body. He couldn't remember having a dream, but he could swear he had. Trying to remember it would bug him all day.

"Hey," Matthew said with a heavy drawl. The room was dark, but Kaleena, her legs tucked under her on the soft, red sofa chair, was washed in the soft blue-gray glow of the computer humming gently on the table next to the window. She wore a white tank top and a pair of black sweatpants that covered most of her purple wool socks. She was wide-awake. *Oh, to be young again*, Matthew thought with an envious smile.

"Oh, hey," Kaleena said, halting her thoughts. She hadn't even seen him get up.

"You been up all night?" Matthew growled.

Kaleena checked her watch. "Yeah, I guess so. I didn't keep you awake, did I?"

"It wasn't you," Matthew said, hitting the light on. His cheeks were painted with a light stubble and his hair was plastered to his head. The bags under his eyes seemed darker as his eyelids fell halfway over his eyes.

"You look like crap," Kaleena said. "Rough night?" She remembered Matthew turning in bed a couple of times when she got up to go to the bathroom around one, but she had been oblivious toward him the rest of the time.

"I just need a shower," was all Matthew could say.

"No doubt." Kaleena looked back to the cursor on the screen. The anticipation to start writing was obvious, but she couldn't concentrate. It was hard for her to write with someone watching her, their eyes boring into her like a probe. Matthew knew how she felt.

"I'll be out in ten minutes."

"Enjoy," Kaleena said, taking that as her cue to jump back into the zone.

Matthew tried to sneak a peek at what she was writing, but his eyes were still blurred with sleep and the screen was just far enough away that the type became immersed in the light of the screen. "We leave at six-thirty," he said.

Kaleena waved her hand at him as the other continued to type. Matthew smirked and shuffled to the bathroom. The carpet felt soft and comfortable under his bare feet. He turned to Kaleena once more and caught sight of the sun rising

behind her, waking the ocean up along with it. Matthew's cell phone whistled for him just then, breaking the beauty from his mind. He sauntered back to his bed and pulled the phone from the charger. It was Kara.

"Morning," he said, trying to sound more chipper than he was.

"You're up." She sounded shocked.

"I have to get out to the docks and secure the yacht." Hearing the words out loud gave Matthew a resurgence of energy. "Did you just get in?"

"I'm at Miami International."

"Perfect. We're at the Intercontinental Miami. Come on by. We'll head out to the docks together."

"Sounds good," she said. "I'll be there shortly."

Matthew tossed the phone on the bed. "Kara's going to be here in a minute," he said to Kaleena. "Can you let her in if I'm not out of the shower?"

Kaleena nodded, obviously deep in thought. Matthew contemplated asking again to make sure she actually heard him, but he didn't want to get hit with teenage annoyance. So he went in to the bathroom without another word. The shower had only been on for a couple of minutes when knocking brought Kaleena back to the room.

"Who is it?" Kaleena asked, her eyes glued to the screen.

"It's Kara," was the shallow response.

Kara? Kaleena finished typing the paragraph, saved the document and closed the screen down on top of the keyboard. She stood up, feeling a quick twinge in the back of her right kneecap. The numbness in her legs nearly caused her to fall over. It took her a few steps to knock the sleep from them. She rubbed her calves gently as she opened the door. The first thing Kaleena noticed on the woman standing in front of her were the high cheekbones and crow's feet nested on her eyes, making her appear somewhere in her early fifties. The second thing she noticed was the light shade of yellow on her unusually small teeth. Even though Kara had spent the better half of her life digging up old artifacts and excavating ruins, Kaleena was still surprised to see her unmanicured nails and graying, mousy-brown hair.

It was quite a disappointment from the young (or younger) image she had originally envisioned.

"You must be Kaleena," Kara said, stepping into the hotel room without having been invited.

Kaleena smiled the apparent rudeness off and closed the door. "Yeah," she said.

"It's so great to finally meet you." Kara set her bags down and gave Kaleena an unwelcome hug. Kaleena wasn't much of a hugger to begin with, but she didn't even know Kara. It was more than awkward hugging someone she didn't trust.

"Yeah," she repeated as she waited for Kara to finish the embrace. "So, how long have you known my dad?"

Kara thankfully let go. "I think it's been about two and a half years now."

"That's all?" Kaleena had actually thought it was less than that.

"It feels longer," Kara agreed, taking a seat on the unmade bed. Kaleena sat down on her own queen-sized bed, creasing the bedspread for the first time since their arrival. Her laptop case still sat on the pillow where she had placed it the night before.

"So how do you feel about this trip?" Kaleena said, making conversation.

"Let me tell you. When your dad first came to me with the idea, I was skeptical. But the more we uncovered, the more I believed in what he was after."

Kaleena grinned. Her father had a way like that. "So you really think we'll find it?"

Kara laughed. "Honestly, I don't know what we'll find. But it's going to be a great trip whether we do or not."

"Aren't you worried about your reputation? I mean within the academic circles and all?"

"At first I was," Kara said after a brief moment of thought. "But it's not that important anymore. I'm just helping a colleague."

The entire answer felt calculated and rehearsed. Kaleena could tell Kara needed to be recognized for something, needed acceptance among her peers. Whether finding Atlantis was what she was hoping would give her that acceptance, or if she

was using Matthew for a larger goal, Kaleena still wasn't sure.

The shower turned off and the curtain was heard sliding across the metal bar. It would be another couple of minutes.

"What about you?" Kara asked. "You must think we'll find something."

"Me? Are you nuts?" Kaleena said quickly. "I think this is all a bunch of wild-eyed nonsense."

Kara looked confused. "But aren't you paying for this trip?"

"Yeah, but…" Kaleena paused. It was a bit odd explaining this to someone she knew only through the stories Matthew had recently told her. "That's not the reason I'm doing it."

Kaleena walked over to the window. The sun had finished rising above the water and was now casting its sparkling white shadow across the calm ocean. Kara sat quiet for a moment before softly muttering, "May I ask why you're doing it?"

Kaleena lowered her head. She felt her mother's soft kiss on her forehead and the touch of her hand on her cheek. The smell of Eternity perfume worn only when going out with Matthew hung heavy in her mind. She loved that smell. Would it be the same as she remembered it? *Not likely*, she thought. *Things change. Don't get your hopes up.*

"I'm sorry," Kara said, knowing full well Kaleena was not comfortable with the subject. "I didn't mean to pry."

Kaleena felt sorry for not answering, but happy she didn't have to. The awkwardness ended as the bathroom door opened. Kaleena immediately retreated inside with a pair of jeans, a small, red Roxy shirt and her toothbrush. She didn't once look at Matthew, who peered at Kara in bewilderment.

"I think I may have touched a nerve," she said.

"Why? What did you say?"

"I just asked why she was helping us out," Kara said innocently. Matthew lifted his head in acknowledgment and turned to the bathroom door. "Ten minutes, Kaleena."

"Okay," the bathroom door replied.

Matthew sat next to Kara. "You have to forgive her," he said. "It's a bit of a personal matter. I'll tell you about it later. How was your week?"

"Nothing to write home about."

"I talked to Thomas yesterday," he said, pulling the charger from the wall and shoving it in the small navy blue duffel bag at his feet. "He should be here around eight thirty with all of the equipment." He put on his worn, leather-strapped watch "Have you talked to Lauren or Henry at all this week?"

"No, why?"

"I don't know." He stood and went to Kaleena's computer. "I left Lauren a couple of messages but she never got back to me. Henry's phone was out of service."

"They're coming, aren't they?"

"I hope so. It would be a shame for them to miss this." Matthew flipped the laptop open. It had already been powered down.

Kaleena stepped out of the bathroom. "What are you doing?"

"Nothing," he said, closing the laptop; blushed.

Kaleena swiped her laptop away with a soft scowl. Kara hid a laugh as Kaleena looked at her the same way. She zipped her laptop securely in its case and shoved all of her stuff into her bag. As she threw on her tennis shoes, she had to pause a moment to calm the tightness in her head and the nausea in her gut.

"I'm sorry. I guess I should've gotten some sleep last night." She picked up her stuff and left the room before anyone could say another word. As she walked down the hall, a slight fatigue embraced her, giving her a small headache. Dizziness struck and she had to crouch down in front of the elevator to keep from toppling over. When the chime came, she slowly stood, hiding her spell from Matthew and Kara, who had finally made their way from the room. Kaleena held the door open as she waited for them to make sure the door was locked (not that they had to), and run to catch up to her. She remained wrapped in her own thoughts as Kara chatted away about the trip, Atlantis, some tablets that seemed rather important to them and some other stuff Kaleena was too preoccupied to register. It was only when she saw the sea of sailboats, fishing boats and yachts anchored at the marina

did she finally return to the world. Matthew escorted the girls to one of the larger yachts. Secured to the back was a dark maple nameplate with **ENDEAVOR** hand-carved in an elegant script.

"Hello?" Matthew called out. He walked a few feet down the dock, apparently looking for someone. "Benjamin?"

A few seconds later, a tall man, toned but showing signs of muscular decay, leapt up the stairwell at the far end of the large, fancy dining cockpit in the center of the boat. He was clean-shaven, but his hair was disheveled. It didn't seem he could make up his mind on whether to show a business-like appearance or go for an "I've been out to sea for a few days without any amenities" look. He wore what looked like a Rolex (which could have been a complete knock-off, had he not actually owned the *Endeavor*) but his clothes screamed, "ocean hobo." Kaleena wondered what else this guy was completely confused about. "Can I help you?" he said lazily.

"Benjamin," Matthew greeted as he saw him step onto the smooth white deck.

"Matthew," Benjamin said with a faint Australian accent that grew heavier the more he talked. "It's good to see you again, mate." The two men shook hands hard, Benjamin adding a quick hug and a slap to the back.

"Same to you."

"You look great," Benjamin said, looking for someone he evidently didn't find. "Where's Love?"

"She'll be here soon," Matthew said quietly. Kaleena quickly assumed 'Love' had to be Jaime. "Let me introduce you to my linguist, Kara Reisen."

"Good to meet ya', doll." Benjamin gave Kara's hand a tight squeeze.

"Same here," Kara said.

"And my daughter, Kaleena," Matthew finished.

"Of course. Love's young one. Precious." Benjamin took Kaleena's hand delicately and gave it a soft kiss. "You're the writer, aye?" Kaleena could only giggle softly at Benjamin's politeness. "Beautiful," he said. "Beautiful. I hear you're also the one paying for this mini-voyage, aye?"

"Aye," Kaleena acknowledged with a sense of fun.

"Well, let's not dilly." Benjamin hopped back on the yacht. "Let's get those papers signed, shall we? Then we can have a bite ta'eat." Benjamin left everyone bewildered as he headed below deck. He was back quickly with a black leather-bound book. That was Matthew's cue to help Kara and Kaleena onto the yacht. They met Benjamin in the cockpit, which was lined with six large glass tables on each side and a rather large bar near the galley toward the bow, above which were two rows of crystal champagne glasses. Kaleena wondered what was hidden in the cabinets behind it. The group sat down at the table near the bar as Benjamin unzipped his book. Inside were the usual business amenities, including a gold-plated ballpoint pen tucked into the side. Kaleena also saw a couple of credit cards peeking out from under the calendar pages and believed there to be a few more hidden underneath.

"These are the papers Love always signs when she hires the *Endeavor*," Benjamin said, flipping to the correct date in the calendar and grabbing a set of bound pages. "No surprises from me, mate." He went on to explain the short version of what the contract said, though Kaleena was more focused on the calendar as he did so. Saturday and Sunday had several lines of written text crossed out and replaced with

Matthew Stevens / Love / Triangle

Kaleena felt a little guilty knowing Benjamin had canceled other appointments for them. She never would have agreed to pay if she knew it was going to inconvenience other parties who no doubt had paid way in advance for a nice, relaxing vacation. Too late now. It would be insolent to call the whole thing off.

After explaining the basics of the insurance liability waiver, which said Matthew would have to pay up to a million dollars should any damage occur to the ship (*I don't have that much money*, Kaleena thought), Matthew signed the papers where necessary.

"How long have you known my dad?" Kaleena asked.

"Not as long as I've known your mum," Benjamin answered. "But quite a while now. I haven't seen this bloke in nearly, what's it been now, six, seven years?"

Matthew nodded. "About that." He signed the last page and handed the papers to Benjamin.

"Fantastic," Benjamin said, setting the contract in his book. "Now to the matter of mullah."

Kaleena grabbed her checkbook from her bag. "How much?"

"Because this is a favor for Love, you can write that check there for thirty. That's about two days's worth of rental for an undisclosed amount of days."

Kaleena filled out the check with a smile, noting "Atlantis" in the memo before scrawling out her signature. She handed the check to Benjamin. "Bonzer," he said enthusiastically. "Go ahead and have a gander around while I cook ya' up some grub. There's two berths down in the bow and two more aft, both of which have two pullout beds, case you need 'em."

The group grabbed their stuff and headed down the stairwell below deck. Kaleena seemed to be the only one fazed by the beauty of the interior, which shined of elegance and wealth. The walls were lined at the bottom half with maroon felt, dividing the white wood with a gold trim. There were several paintings hanging on the walls, which Kaleena guessed were originals, not reprints. A large, silver mirror with a rose pattern edge sat across from the stairwell so everyone who stepped down could see their lovely reflections. Kaleena knew then that despite his uneven appearance, Benjamin was vain in his subtle, metrosexual way.

"We'll take the rooms down this way," Matthew said, pointing to the rear end of the ship. "Jaime's team can have those."

Matthew and Kara headed into the rooms, which sat about fifteen feet from the stairwell. Kaleena took a few moments to admire the scattered plush, velvet chairs deliberately placed among the glass tables that held different colored vases filled with poppies and lilies. She wasn't sure if she should touch anything or go give Benjamin another check; she felt completely out of place and unworthy of this type of indulgence. She pushed her feelings aside as she entered the room on

the left side. Matthew was lowering a small, cushioned bed from inside the wall just above one of the twin beds that had been covered in maroon bedspreads to match the continued pattern of the wall. Hanging next to a small opening Kaleena assumed to be the bathroom was another mirror; not as fancy as the one hanging in the salon, but still plated in a slick silver.

"This is too much," Kaleena said, placing her bag on one of the two mahogany trunks that sat on the ends of each bed.

"Don't worry about it." Matthew wiped the creases out of the sheets of the hide-a-bed. "He's an old friend."

"I got that, but, Jesus." Kaleena sat and admired the room. She couldn't believe her parents had never told her about this before. It all made her question the validity of Benjamin's friendship, prompting her to pull out her laptop. As she waited for it to come to life, she found an electrical outlet just below the mirror, should she have to use it.

Kara came in a few seconds after Kaleena's desktop appeared. "You want to head up and see what Benjamin has cooking for us?"

"I could eat. Kaleena?"

"I'll be up in a minute. I have to get something down real quick." She opened up the Word file that held all of her notes.

"See you up there." Matthew led Kara from the room.

Kaleena spent the next forty-five minutes typing out her thoughts on the yacht, Benjamin and his friendship with her parents without once stopping to collect her thoughts or stretch. She still couldn't wrap her head around Benjamin canceling other appointments just because a friend asked. There had to be a larger motive. Had he and Jaime been in a relationship at some point in time? Was it before or after she met Matthew? Kaleena didn't want to believe her mother had had an affair, so she kept those thoughts at bay with the illusion that Jaime and Benjamin's relationship ended after she first met Matthew. When she finally stopped, Kaleena held the laptop for another few minutes before joining the team in the cockpit. Benjamin had just finished a story about something that happened on a tour of the Barrier Reef that

had everyone in stitches. Watching Matthew slapping Benjamin on the shoulder with some sort of macho congratulations, Kaleena wondered if he had ever speculated about Jaime and Benjamin's relationship, and whether he had been one of — or even possibly *the* — reason she left them in the first place. Thinking Benjamin could have had that much influence on her mother made Kaleena's stomach tighten.

"Hey, precious," Benjamin said. "I left some ham and eggs on the stove. Help yourself."

"I'm not hungry," Kaleena said, rubbing her temples. The headache throbbed lightly once again.

"You okay?" Matthew asked.

"I'm fine. Just a bit of a headache."

"It might help if you eat something," Kara chimed in.

Kaleena looked at her fiercely. Kara shied away, reading her loud and clear — she was not Kaleena's mother.

"Is this the right place?" Thomas called from the dock.

"It is," Matthew said, heading onto the deck. Thomas made his way to the side of the yacht and hopped on. He dropped his tan duffel bag and shook Matthew's hand. Kara quickly followed with a welcome hug. Kaleena stayed put at the table, watching through the windows that lined the cockpit.

"Where is everyone?" Thomas asked.

"I don't know." Matthew checked his watch. "They still have a little time. Let's get everything unloaded."

"You bet," Thomas said. Matthew and Kara followed him off the yacht.

"Are ya' sure ya' don't want anything, precious?" Benjamin asked as he collected the dirty dishes.

"I'm sure," Kaleena said. "And, please. Can you stop calling me precious?"

"Sure, love."

Kaleena clenched her jaw. "It's Kaleena."

"Yes, ma'am," Benjamin said with a slight chuckle. He walked to the galley, which was hidden behind the stairs that led up to the wheelhouse. Kaleena stood

and watched Thomas, Matthew and Kara unload the trunk of Thomas's car. She felt uneasy about what she was about to ask, but she needed to know, and there was no better time to find out. To ease herself into the heart of the conversation, she started with a compliment.

"I really like your yacht, Benjamin."

Benjamin returned to the dining cockpit with a wet rag and wiped down the table. "Thankee. I built it with my own two hands."

"Wow. How long did that take you?"

" 'Bout three years," he said. "But I needed somethin' that was mine. Somethin' that said I accomplished somethin' in this wayward piece of rock we call home."

Kaleena smiled and took that as her cue to change the subject. "How long has it been since you've seen my mom?"

"Oh, I don't know, mate. Two and a half years or so. Right around the time your mum —" He stopped. Kaleena didn't need him to finish; she knew exactly what he was about to say. "I'm sorry. I didn't mean…" Shame filled Benjamin's eyes.

"How did you know her?"

Benjamin was hesitant, but wasn't one to keep secrets. "Your mum and I met at a symphony in Australia when she was near seventeen. She was on a holiday with her parents."

Kaleena phrased her next question very carefully. "Did you have a relationship with her?"

"I shouldn't say," Benjamin answered. "You should really talk to your mum about that." Which to Kaleena meant a resounding, *Yes.*

"What ended it?"

Benjamin again hesitated. "We kept in contact for a bit after she left, but the longer we were apart, the more our conversations waned. I never forgot her, though. She was my Love. Things just didn't work out."

"What happened?"

"Well, by the time I built my yacht and traveled here, your lovely mum was engaged to a better man."

Kaleena absorbed those words — *better man*. They eased her headache and relaxed her body. Benjamin was turning out to be a better man than she first thought.

"I didn't want to interfere, though your mum and I stayed friends. Partners in some regards."

Kaleena sat down a few tables from Benjamin. "What happened the night my mom left us?"

Benjamin lowered his head, unsure whether he should say anything. When he looked back to Kaleena, her eyes were strong — she needed to know. He sat down and folded his hands together. It looked awkward, but the distance between them felt right.

"It was a couple of days after your mum left," he began in a soft tone. "She was still very upset over leaving and was unclear of what she wanted to do. It wasn't apparent at first, but it slowly started to hit her as we talked."

*　　*　　*

Jaime sat next to Benjamin in the *Endeavor*'s salon. Her hands were clasped between her legs. Benjamin was leaning forward, listening carefully to every syllable. "You have to understand," she said, her voice quivered by her tears. "I didn't want to leave her. I wish I could have taken her with me. But Matthew... he'll never understand."

"Have you called her?" Benjamin asked.

"How can I? What would I say?"

"Tell her you love her."

Jaime tried to force a smile. She chose instead to lean back and cover her entire face with her hands.

Benjamin rubbed her knee soothingly. Jaime didn't move away. "You can stay here as long as you'd like," he said.

"Two days," Jaime said quickly, lowering her hands. "I just need to figure out

my next move. I need to examine my options." Her tears had faded.

"I understand, Love." Benjamin took one of Jaime's hands, which she excepted with a light graciousness, and they embraced.

"Thank you," Jaime whispered. "This means a lot."

Benjamin looked into Jaime's eyes. The connection was simple, yet enticing. She remembered the time they had spent in Australia and the love they expressed over those twelve short days. It couldn't match anything Jaime had felt when she was with Matthew, but she knew nothing ever could. Benjamin's love was different; it always had been. It was soft and gentle, much more like a best friend than intense and passionate. His touch made her heart dance and his eyes were colored with a magnetic lull. She couldn't remember how, or even why, but she found her lips pressed against his. The sensation was obsessive and soft. She needed more of him to please the desire she had been missing over the last few years. By the time he lowered her naked body onto the bed and traced it with his supple fingertips, Jaime was no longer an adult having an affair. She was seventeen again and learning what it meant to be a woman.

*   *   *

"When I woke up the next mornin', she was gone. I haven't heard a word since." Benjamin sat silent as Kaleena wiped a sprinkle of tears from her cheek. It had been hard for her to hear, as the picture of perfection crumbled. How could she ever look at her mother the same way now? It seemed impossible, but no matter how much it hurt, she was glad Benjamin had told her. The truth was better than utter deception.

When Thomas, Matthew and Kara returned with several cases and bags, Benjamin handed Kaleena the rag. She used it to clean her face so Matthew didn't see she had been crying, even though she wasn't sure he would have noticed anyway.

"I'm heading down to the engine room for a bit, mate," Benjamin said to Matthew.

"All right," Matthew said as he led Thomas and Kara down into the belly of the ship.

Benjamin put his hand on Kaleena's shoulder. She wanted to push it away but it felt soothing to her somehow. "Your mum loves him, Kaleena. Trust that." He squeezed her shoulder, then rounded the cockpit toward the forward deck.

When Matthew returned, Kaleena held the rag firmly, as if it would answer her if she tortured it enough. He considered asking her if she was okay, but as he got closer to the table, all he could think of was how much she reminded him of Lauren. If they were in any way similar, Kaleena needed time to think about whatever it was that was bothering her, without Matthew butting in. So he walked out onto the deck without so much as a smile. Kaleena was glad he did.

Matthew took a moment to stretch and take in the beauty of the marina. He cracked a sly smirk as he pondered the story behind each of the boats — where they had come from; where they were heading. If only they could talk, the stories they'd be able to tell. No more so than the boat he stood on at that moment, for sure. But there were more than likely some wild stories coming off these boats that people would rather not have grace public knowledge. His thoughts broke when a taxi pulled up into the parking lot. Matthew hoped it was Lauren or Henry — or both, as he could see two people moving behind the driver. His hopes were dashed as a young man Matthew didn't recognize stepped out along with a representation of who Matthew believed to be Jaime. She was thinner than he remembered and her light brown hair, lying across the curvature of her shoulder blade, had been highlighted with auburn. The most disheartening thing about her transformation was the cigarette, which she promptly dropped to the ground and put out, blowing the remnants of her last puff into the cool sea air. She made no recognition of Matthew before reaching into the cab and pulling out a couple of small canvas cases. Her friend also pulled out a couple of cases, though his were a bit larger and appeared to be some sort of camera bags. The trunk held an endless stream of additional cases — some large, some small. After slamming the trunk down, they tapped it twice to tell the cabbie he could leave and collected their stuff.

Thomas and Kara's voices grew loud behind Matthew. "Can you give them a hand," he asked, pointing to Jaime.

"Sure," the two said in near unison. Jaime saw them depart the yacht and gave up trying to carry everything herself.

"Your mom's here," Matthew said to Kaleena, whose body tightened even more than it already had been. She stood and turned slowly, frightened of what she might see. Her vision of two people had been tarnished already this morning; she hoped it didn't continue. Matthew had moved to the opening of the rail, which gave Kaleena a clear view of her mother from the edge of the cockpit. For once, she didn't feel cheated. She couldn't tell if she was as vibrant or enthusiastic as her body made her appear because of the dark sunglasses balancing on her nose, but she saw a beautiful woman who, if she was anything like her, was carrying just as much trepidation as Kaleena. Though part of her wanted to run up to Jaime and give her a grand hug (as she pictured herself doing so many times over the last few days), she didn't move as the team made their way to the yacht.

"Jaime," Matthew said, his voice light but dead.

Jaime's tone was nearly identical. "Matthew."

Both gave trivial half smiles to each other as Matthew collected some of her things and placed them down on the deck. After helping her aboard, Jaime gave her daughter a brighter, more loving smile, which Kaleena could not return. "Hi, Kaleena," she said.

Kaleena lowered her head and focused on her shaking hands. The faint aroma of cigarette smoke hung heavy in the air, and though it was possible the man standing with her was responsible for it, in her heart, she knew that putrid perfume was coming from her mother. Unable to look back up, Kaleena retreated below deck. Jaime tried to call for her not to go, but found no words. It had been too long; she no longer knew what to say to her own daughter. It didn't matter that Kaleena had matured into such a lovely young woman, she still held out hope that she would get to see her favorite cherub smile in a welcome embrace. Instead, something had pushed her away. It was her own fault; Kaleena was reacting to an

absent mother's return. It seemed natural enough.

Maybe this wasn't such a good idea after all.

"I'm sorry," Matthew said. "She didn't get a lot of sleep last night…" He hoped the excuse was enough to explain Kaleena's inconsiderate disappearance.

"That's okay," Jaime said, waving the matter off.

"Was that your daughter?" the man next to Jaime inquired.

It took Jaime a second to realize he had spoken. "Yeah," she finally said. "Yeah, that was Kaleena. And this is Matthew. Matthew, this is Gavin."

Gavin shifted the camera bag and grasped Matthew's welcome hand. "Good to meet you," he said, mildly insincere.

"Gavin will be capturing all the footage for us."

"Great," Matthew said. "Welcome aboard. Thomas, help Gavin to his room."

"You got it, boss," Thomas said playfully. Gavin followed him and Kara through the dining cockpit as a second cab pulled up to the marina.

"There they are," Jaime said to herself. And then to Matthew: "I'm going to help them with their stuff."

Jaime walked back to the parking lot to meet two more women. One was African-American, slim and quiet. Her natural, curly black hair shone bright in the morning sun. The other was white, blond and heavier in both weight and personality. Her mouth was moving even before leaving the cab, chattering on about something Matthew couldn't quite make out through the soft noises of the marina. Both of them, as Jaime had done earlier, grabbed a couple of bags from inside the cab and then unloaded scuba equipment from the trunk.

Jaime took most of the smaller bags, allowing the black woman to grab the scuba equipment. She lifted them easily enough, making it clear she was a dive master. Her toned muscles came into shape as she walked toward the *Endeavor*.

"Would you look at this," the blond woman said with a giant smile. "Would you look at it? It's like a cruise ship tugboat." She put the bags on the deck and slapped Matthew on the shoulder. "Huh? A cruise ship tugboat, don't you think?"

Matthew brushed away the pain with courteous smile. "I guess," he said. The woman jabbed him again.

Thomas and Kara returned to grab some of the other bags.

"Hey there, kids," the blonde yelled out before saying, "How you doin'?" in her best impression of Matt Leblanc from *Friends*.

Thomas flashed Kara a light smile.

"Everyone, this is Patricia," Jaime chimed in quickly.

"Call me Pat or Patty," Patricia added, staring at Matthew carefully, "and you'll find out what it feels like to blow yourself."

Everyone looked at one another a bit awkwardly, unsure if it was a joke. Patricia eased the tension with a slap to Matthew's shoulder. "You'll be okay," she said.

"Patricia," Jaime cut in. "This is Thomas and..." She paused as she searched for a name. "...Kara?"

Kara nodded. "Reisen. Right."

"Are you a couple, Reeses?" Patricia asked.

"No," Thomas and Kara said repeatedly, each one growing a bit softer and more humorous. "My last name is Demeut," Thomas added.

"Demeut, ooh-la-la. It's a shame. You look cute together, you two."

Neither Thomas or Kara could think of anything to say to that, so instead they grabbed some more bags.

"And this is Matthew," Jaime continued.

"The ex!" Patricia squealed. "I've always pictured you a bit more..." Patricia looked Matthew over carefully as she grabbed his hand to shake it. "You know... manly."

"Patricia," Jaime said, embarrassed.

"I was just joking," Patricia smiled with a light wink. "He knew I was joking. Look at him."

Matthew had a smile that, for some reason, he couldn't shake.

"So where's the genius?" Patricia said.

"She's not feeling well," Jaime lied.

"Oh, that's too bad. I was looking forward to meeting the cutie."

"You will," Matthew said.

"All righty then. Where's my room on this little tugboat?" Patricia wrapped her arms around Thomas and Kara. "You my guides?"

"I guess," Thomas said quietly.

"Then lead the way." Patricia shoved Thomas, causing him to hit the edge of the door to the dining cockpit.

Kara chuckled and led them both below deck, listening to Patricia sing the first line to the chorus of "The Right Stuff" over and over, followed each time by the signature beat of "Ohs."

"Some character," Matthew whispered under his breath, though loud enough for Jaime to hear.

"She takes some getting used to," Jaime smiled. "This is Trishen," she continued, presenting the younger black woman.

"You can call me Trish," she said in a very light mutter.

"You're a diving expert," Matthew said, grasping Trishen's stone grip.

"That's right."

"Let me help you with those." Matthew pulled the large cases onto the deck as Benjamin came around the outside of the dining cockpit.

"There's my Love," he said immediately. For the first time, Jaime's features livened up.

"Benjamin." Jaime gave him a long, strong hug followed by a soft kiss on the cheek. "It's good to see you again."

"Good to see you, Love. How've you been?"

"Fine, fine," she said. They walked into the cockpit and took a seat, chatting about what Jaime had been doing over the past few years. Matthew tried to remember the last time he and Jaime had been that energetic with one another. It made him feel inadequate knowing he had lost the passion that was once so electric in their marriage. He lowered his head and glanced at his watch.

9:05

He instantly looked out into the parking area again. All he saw were a variety of cars that had been parked there for the last hour, with more unfamiliar cars coming in. A party of about thirty people had gathered near the far side. They were laughing together without a care in the world. "Where are you?" he whispered. Matthew shook his disappointment away and went to Benjamin. "Time to go."

Benjamin flashed a thumbs up, gave Jaime a soft kiss on the top of her right hand and climbed up to the wheelhouse. He ran a quick equipment check and flipped on the engine. It roared to life, kicking up a bit of water in the process. Benjamin leaned over the side. "Can you close that up, there, mate?"

Matthew grabbed the rail extension sitting against the side of the cockpit and locked it in place. Just then, another taxi pulled into the parking lot. The young woman inside emerged as quickly as she could with a small suitcase and a handbag. She ran — or rapidly hobbled — toward the *Endeavor*. Matthew almost tipped over the side of the yacht with elation at seeing Lauren; but on second glance, the woman he saw was pregnant, near eight or maybe even nine months. How could that possibly be Lauren?

"Matthew, wait," she called, waving her bag. The faster she tried to run, the more she seemed to slow down.

Matthew unlatched the rail and helped Lauren onto the deck. She dropped her suitcase. "Thank you," she huffed. "Sorry I'm late."

"You're right on time." Matthew latched the rail and looked up to the wheel-house. "Ready, Benjamin."

Benjamin gave another thumbs up and the yacht smoothly shifted away from the dock. As it coasted through the marina, Matthew stared at Lauren's unusually large stomach.

She smiled lightly. "Yes, I'm pregnant," she confirmed.

"How? You weren't pregnant last week. Not this pregnant anyway."

"No, you're right. I wasn't pregnant last week." Lauren rubbed her stomach with adoration. "Where's Henry?"

"I don't know. I couldn't get a hold of him."

Lauren felt both relief and a small ounce of regret. She was happy Henry wasn't there, as she wasn't sure what seeing him would do to her. Yet she was hoping he might see her, understand what happened and take Lauren as his, in love. She felt stupid for believing he would man up like that; any relationship with him was bound to be a failure. But the thought was there, nonetheless. He was her daughter's father and for a second, she thought she saw recognition of that fact in Matthew's eyes.

"Whoa. Who's the preggars?" Patricia came bouncing onto the deck and up to Lauren. "You are one kick away from popping, now aren't ya'?"

Lauren looked to Matthew for help. "This is Patricia," he said. "Patricia. No nicknames." Patricia winked at Matthew. "This is Lauren," he said.

"And the bundle?"

"I haven't decided yet," Lauren whispered, caressing her stomach. "I was thinking maybe Eve."

"Little Evey," Patricia squealed, placing her hand on Lauren's stomach. There was a soft double kick. "I think she likes it."

Lauren laughed as Jaime walked around the cockpit to the forward deck. She had been thinking about heading below to find Kaleena, but she didn't want to push her — or herself. Jaime needed a little time to relax and get things set up before she tried to create a new relationship with her estranged daughter. The yacht picked up steam as it entered the open ocean, and Jaime let the wind dance through her hair, washing all of her past away in a clear, hopeful view of what was to come.

Atlantic Ocean – Time Unknown

The darkness around her was deep. Her lungs contracted every few seconds, collecting the icy oxygen from the air around her and turning it to stone, choking it back out in a release of mist. With the moist texture of water moving between her frozen toes, she wrinkled them carefully so as not to snap one of them off. Faint voices drifted through the heavy air. As she tried to understand the words, she lost her balance. Her hands hit the watery pool. It didn't hurt; she caressed the ground, allowing the water to lick her fingertips. Suddenly, a second pair of hands wrapped themselves through hers. They tightened their grip as she pulled away. She screamed, but another hand covered her mouth, turning her skin to ice. She opened her eyes wide. The black became awash with color.

"Savior," one of the voices echoed through the red sky.

The hands disappeared; she was alone again. She swallowed a thick ounce of saliva that held the rich taste of blood and gagged up nothing but air. As she looked around, she coughed, spit falling from her mouth. She stood among the ocean, the horizon floating in the distance in all directions. Turning in a circle, her knees brittle and cold as glass, the only remnant of memory was found in the distance. The *Endeavor* sailed away from her. She ran to it, but with each step, the boat faded farther and farther away, as if she was actually running backwards. She soon gave up, realizing she could run as long and as fast as possible and never get any closer. Instead, she tried to yell for the boat to stop, to come back for her. But every time she opened her mouth, and no matter how hard she thought she was screaming, no audible sound crossed her lips.

Frustrated, she looked at her reflection, which stared back with a dark, pale expression. She moved her lips — *What do you want with me? What the hell do you want? Why do you keep doing this? Show yourself, goddamn it!*

"Show yourself," she screamed. It echoed through the burnt sky and, though she wasn't sure if it was because of her, caused the water to churn harder than it had been. She attempted to call out again, but her voice remained mute. When she stopped to think about what happened, her thoughts grew in amplitude. It was apparent now that she needed to control her thoughts in order to speak.

I said show yourself, she said, spinning around. Except for the few feet around the spot she stood, the water grew fiercer the more she screamed. *Why are you so afraid? Stop cowering beneath the water and talk to me!*

Suddenly, the water calmed; not a single ripple appeared in the blue sea. She waited, unable to see her reflection any longer. The sky grew steadily darker, almost

dripping blood from the heavens, when a familiar form — solid water, but human in stature — sprouted from the ocean. It rose, slowly and steadily, to meet her eye line and then paced around her. She was unable to take her eyes off of the mesmerizing creature as it stepped right next to her. A soft, cleansing breeze stroked her neck. Her blood became a warm flow of comfort. Her body opened up and she felt like falling into the creature's arms, allowing it to create a bond with her that could only be one of trust and love.

The creature pressed up against her back, caressing her navel and sliding its hand along the base of her neck. The sensation was numbing. When its hand reached the outside top of her ear, a moist ring spread across her head. Sharp needles, wrapping from the center of her forehead to the back of her head, pierced her flesh. Each one sat about a half inch apart, some above and below the main thread. Thin lines of blood flowed from each small pinprick. She tried to focus her thoughts and ask the creature what it was doing — what she had done wrong — but the more she tried, the deeper the pins went. She was afraid to do anything else in fear of them penetrating her skull, so she calmed the tension by erasing all of her fears and concerns. Within seconds, her body eased into a quiet slumber.

Who are you? The pins tightened as she asked the question, but not nearly as bad as before. *What do you want with me?*

The voice that returned echoed with high and low pitches, scarring her inner ear with pain.

You are my chalice.

The pins expanded, piercing the skull and attaching themselves to her brain. She couldn't scream; the pain was too much. She dropped to her knees. Blood poured more generously from the wounds and spilled onto her arms. But when she looked at them, all she saw were small hints of red in several tears of water.

Save us, the creature whispered. Kaleena was then shoved beneath the water and held there until she could no longer breathe.

The *Endeavor* – Saturday, 6:19 pm

Kaleena shot up in bed, inhaling a deep, hard breath. She coughed it back out from deep in her lungs and then sucked in another round of air, feeling it scratch at her throat. A lighter cough followed bringing with it a heavy throbbing in her head. She rubbed her temples, but it didn't help; it only made it tingle slightly with numbness only to return with greater force. For a minute, Kaleena couldn't move; not even to lie down. As she relaxed, she felt a cold dampness beneath her. She let out another phlegmy cough and shifted her legs. There, caking upon the sides of her thighs, was a pool of blood. Now she could move. Aside from her blood-stained jeans, there was an uncomfortable moist warmth trapped in her underwear.

"God," she whispered. The pounding in her head subsided as she pulled a tampon from the Playtex box she had accidentally packed along with her other toiletries. She never expected she was going to need them. Her last menstrual cycle had only been a week and a half before and she shouldn't have been due again while on the trip.

After latching the bathroom door locked, Kaleena lowered her pulsating head against it. Sweat bubbled on her forehead. She couldn't help but wonder if it *was* even her period. After all, she'd never had a period that flowed even half this much. But if it wasn't her period, what was it? Had she grown some type of cancer somewhere in her uterus or ovaries? Could it have something to do with a tear in her vaginal tissue, or worse?

Her head pounded harder just thinking about it. Not even the long drawn-out breaths could shake it. She ignored it the best she could as she threw her stuff on the small sink next to the toilet and removed her jeans. The blood had flowed down the inner part of her thighs on both legs, though her right seemed to have more than the left. Around the knee was a small circle of blood that seemed to have started a clot. Taking care to keep from getting any blood on the floor, Kaleena threw the jeans into the corner of the shower and removed her panties. A wave a nausea struck as blood spread across her calves and socks. Her once light pink panties were now a dark red and felt like a wool shirt that had been sitting in a sink of water.

The smell was a retched mix of fish and mucus that had been festering in a bed of pennies on hot asphalt. The squishy sound it made when hitting the shower made them seem like a sponge full of soda. Kaleena cupped her hand over her nose and mouth and turned on the shower. As she waited for the water to heat up, she looked into the mirror. Her eyes seemed dark, as if she were wearing a pound of mascara. Red strokes spun a simple web among the yellowing white canvas. She coughed to settle her stomach and opened the cabinet below the sink, hoping to find some aspirin. When she couldn't find any, she slammed the door shut and noticed the small hint of steam filling the room. She rubbed her temples one last time before disrobing and getting in the shower. It took several hard passes with the soapy rag to clean the blood from her thighs. She was glad it had stopped flowing (for now). Hopefully, if and when it started again (as it most likely would), it was nowhere near as strong as this. Once she finally felt cleansed, Kaleena ran a thimble full of shampoo through her otherwise clean hair and turned the water off. She rubbed down her legs once more with the rag to make sure all remnants of the blood were gone and then dried her body thoroughly, ignoring her hair, which crimped softly as it dried. As she inserted a tampon, the thought of her first period crossed her mind. She was almost twelve and was swimming at Kyla's house when she noticed a squishy sensation between her legs that resulted in small red drops floating and dissipating through the water. Kaleena gave a short shriek and pulled herself out of the pool, looking between her legs for the culprit.

Kyla smiled brightly. "What's wrong?" she asked, a bit sarcastic.

"I think I'm having my period."

"So," Kyla shrugged. "Get your tampons."

"I don't have any tampons," Kaleena cried.

"This is your first time?" Kyla seemed sincerely shocked. "Whoa. I wouldn't have guessed that." She pulled herself out of the pool and said, "Welcome to womanhood."

Kaleena allowed the fear to fade through her baby of a smile as Kyla wrapped her towel around her. "Come on. You can use one of mine."

It took three tries for Kaleena to finally position the tampon correctly so as not to cause discomfort. "I can't even feel it," she smiled.

"Then you're good." Kyla threw the used tampons into the trash and then told her all about what it would be like every month for the rest of her life (unaware they would eventually go through menopause), how and when to use a tampon and what her mother talked about when Kyla was going through "the change." Kaleena was grateful for her help. She would have been devastated — not to mention embarrassed — if she had to learn all of this from her father. Even though she knew it was simply a natural stage of growing up, her father was the last person she wanted talking to her about sex.

Kaleena wondered if her father even knew she had had her period as she stepped from the bathroom. She had to press her hand to her stomach to ease the discomfort of seeing the circle of blood that had formed on the comforter. It took a minute to relax her body enough to put on fresh clothes and remove the sheets from the bed. The mattress, it turns out, had also been spoiled. The stain was cold but nearly dry, so Kaleena carefully flipped the mattress over. It wasn't to hide the blood, necessarily; the sheets gave her away on that front. She remembered helping Jaime do the same thing one time with her mattress after Kaleena spilled grape juice on it. She was nine and had been distracted by something all afternoon. Her deadened eyes were locked on the television (not wanting to watch the History channel, or the Learning Channel, or whatever 'The' channel her mom was watching), when she accidentally lost her grip on the glass, layering the sheets with an inkblot psychiatrists use to discover more about how you think. Kaleena thought it looked a lot like the head of Falcor from *The Neverending Story*. She also believed she was in deep trouble, but instead of hiding her mistake like a normal nine-year-old might — and understanding that lying would just get her into even more trouble — she went straight to Jaime and confessed.

"What were you doing?" Jaime said, biting her lip to keep her anger subdued.

"I just wasn't paying attention," Kaleena said shyly. She sat on the edge of the

bed with her hands squeezed between her legs, holding her head so that her chin touched the bottom of her neck.

"I guess you weren't, were you?" Jaime was upset, but Kaleena felt unusually good inside. Her mother left the room without scolding her or giving her a quick pat on the rear that would sting for a few hours. Even then, she didn't move an inch as she waited for Jaime to return.

"Help me," she said as she set new sheets down on the small bureau beside the bed. Kaleena went to the opposite side of the bed without arguing and ripped the sheet off as far as she could. Jaime then did the same on her side, ripping the sheet off as fast as she could. It rested on the ground at the foot of the bed. Kaleena giggled and tried to do the same with the mattress cover, but the elastic on Jaime's end grabbed the corner of the bed, causing Kaleena to stumble to the floor.

Jaime laughed with her daughter as she pulled the rest of the sheets off to reveal the same dark purple stain. "What were you so distracted by?" Jaime asked, touching the spot. Kaleena didn't know why she did... of course it was still wet.

"I was just thinking about Kyla."

"Why? What happened?"

"She had her period this afternoon."

Jaime lowered her head in an attempt to hide a smile. It didn't work very well. "Come here. Help me."

Kaleena joined Jaime on the other side of the bed and the two of them (well, mostly Jaime, but Kaleena felt she did enough by helping to guide it) turned the mattress over. It landed with a soft bounce and teetered halfway off the box spring. Jaime and Kaleena grabbed the mattress before it could fall to the floor and pushed it into position. When it was done, Jaime put her hands to her waist in triumph.

"There," she said. "All clean. No more mess."

"What do we do if it happens again?" Kaleena asked.

"It's not going to happen again," Jaime stated with a stern face that Kaleena knew meant business. "Is it?"

Kaleena shook her head, her eyes a wee bit wider.

"Good." Jaime grabbed the clean sheets and unfolded the mattress cover with a flick of her wrist.

"Why do we have a period?" Kaleena asked thoughtfully. "I know it's baby eggs dying, but how come you bleed?"

Jaime set the cover on the bed and sat down. "Come here," she said, collecting her daughter onto her lap. Kaleena laid her head against Jaime's shoulder and listened carefully. "It's a punishment."

"Why are we being punished?"

"Because one day, a long time ago, a young women chose knowledge over blissful ignorance."

"Why was that bad?"

"I don't know, Kaleena. Why do you think it was bad?"

Kaleena looked her mother in the eye. "It wasn't. Knowledge isn't a bad thing. It's the people that use the knowledge for evil that are bad. If someone is capable of learning something new, they should be allowed to learn as much as they can and then apply that knowledge to enhance the quality of life."

"But what about the people that abuse knowledge?"

"They should be punished. Knowledge used to gain power for personal gain or exposure is the most dangerous creation. But those that have a pure heart shouldn't be punished for the acts of those who abuse it."

"I believe you're right. But how does anyone know if a person will use their knowledge to better the prospects of others until we learn the knowledge that's given to us?"

"It's impossible to know, I guess." Kaleena smiled. "Will I be punished like Kyla?"

"I'm afraid so, Kaleena. But as long as you don't abuse your knowledge, one day you may just find forgiveness and your punishment will disappear."

"I hope so."

"Come on, kiddo. Time for bed."

Kaleena hopped to her knees and kissed Jaime on the cheek. "Goodnight,"

she said before skipping out of the room, smiling internally. Kaleena loved her conversations with Jaime, especially the ones she knew were fables in their own right. She understood what the menstrual cycle was, having learned about it in health class way before Kyla had experienced it. But she also knew Jaime liked to believe, if only every once in a while, that her little girl was actually a normal, nine-year-old daughter, struggling through fourth grade, needing help on her assignments and crying when she fell off her bike after trying to ride without her training wheels. It was important to her, and Kaleena never wanted to take that away from her — at least not on purpose. But the older she got, the less Jaime felt she could relate to her daughter on an abstract, or childish level. Jaime grew more distant as Kaleena gained and applied deeper levels of knowledge. No more evident had this detachment been than this very morning after learning what her mother had done when she left and the absence of contact over the years that followed. She felt bad for the cold reception she gave Jaime earlier, but was it really time to make up for that? Could Jaime ever see Kaleena as a teenager and not as someone she had to fear? Kaleena wasn't sure. What she did know was they were going to have to talk at some point. How that conversation would go could only be left to the imagination.

*   *   *

Patricia reached through the slats of the rail on the port side of the *Endeavor* to collect some water into a small vile. She had spent the day setting up several buoys and small waterproof video cameras in the water to keep tabs on the flow, temperature, salinization and pressure of the ocean as the yacht made its journey into the middle of the Atlantic. All of the equipment were linked to four monitors humming away in the cockpit. The day had produced negligible fluctuating readings until about a half hour ago when the salt levels steadily dropped over the course of about ten miles. She triple-checked the readings with several oceanographic maps that outlined the currents and telemetry of the ocean floor. When nothing made sense, she cross-referenced the maps with the readings she had been gathering on the flow of currents. They matched, with only a slight discrepancy. At first, Patricia thought maybe the equipment was malfunctioning, so she decided to test the water by hand. Upon gathering her sample, Patricia placed a small stick into the vile for thirty seconds. The longer she held it there, the darker it got, indicating that the salinization levels the equipment was charting were accurate. She dumped the water back into the ocean, reminding herself to come back in an hour or so and retest to make sure it was correct. Until then, she needed a break, so she pulled out a package of cigarettes and lumbered to the forward deck. There, kneeling at the bow of the ship was Kara.

"Hey there, Reeses," Patricia called.

Kara didn't answer at first, then turned slightly. Patricia finally noticed her eyes were closed and her head was rested against her folded hands. "Oh, shitskin," she blurted out. "I'm sorry. Didn't mean to disturb your prayers. Hope I don't get a lightning bolt shoved up my ass."

"That would actually be Zeus," Kara said with a wink.

"I like you." Patricia lit her cigarette. "Go ahead. Pray your little heart out."

"I'm through," Kara said, standing.

"Afraid you might get kidnapped by aliens?"

Kara chuckled. "No." She took a moment to reflect on the prayer. She didn't feel ready to open up about her past to anyone but close friends and family, but saying it aloud might just very well help her grieve. "I lost my younger sister in a plane crash about thirteen years ago, right out here in these waters somewhere."

"Oh, God. I'm sorry." Patricia's vibrant smile faded for the first time since meeting her.

"It's okay. You couldn't have known."

"So you were saying hi?" Patricia asked.

"Something like that. Asking for her protection and, you know, opening up to her. She's really the only person I can truly talk to, even if she is no longer with us."

"That's beautiful," Patricia smiled. "Did I tell you I liked you, Reeses?"

Kara laughed. "Yes, you did."

"Well, get used to it, 'cause I like you." Patricia sucked on her cigarette. The smoke got caught in the wind. Kara coughed and tried to avoid it by sliding away from the source.

"I'm sorry," Patricia said, trying to find a way to hold the cigarette so the smoke didn't sail in Kara's direction. "These damn things. They're such a nuisance."

"Have you ever tried to quit?"

"Have I?" Patricia belted out. "Oh, you don't know the half of it! I've tried all the patches, tried weaning off 'em. I even tried to quit cold turkey once…" Patricia waved her arms up and down her body. "You can see how well that turned out."

Kara barely held back a smile.

"It's okay, Reeses. Laugh it up. I'm a fat bitch with a personality disorder. I'm not trying to hide anything." She then added with a wink, "Except maybe the thin bitch I used to be."

Kara wiped more smoke away.

"Ah, hell," Patricia said and pinched the cigarette out. "I have to go to the bathroom anyway." She looked out to the ocean. "I'll talk to you later, Reese's sister," she yelled, then turned back to Kara. "Might just keep me from getting a lightning bolt up my ass from *her*, eh?" Patricia slapped Kara on the shoulder, nearly knocking her over. Kara laughed softly and rubbed the pain from her shoulder.

It didn't take Patricia long to slide down to the salon. Sitting together were Thomas and Trishen. Two empty plates sat in front of them — one had been wiped almost cleaner than it had been before it was used, the other still had some parsley and remnants of sauce. There were also a couple of glasses of wine — one nearly half empty, the other almost gone — next to the plates.

"Hey there, peeps," Patricia said as she landed on the soft carpet. "You all fueled up?" Patricia had eaten dinner up in the dining cockpit as she watched the readings on her monitor, bugging the hell out of Gavin, who was trying to work on the changes to the documentary. She liked to bug Gavin; he was an easy target.

"Pretty much," Thomas said.

"That's good, that's good that's good. Now, I'm gonna go dump some toxic waste. You guys can just keep getting' your flirt on." Patricia shimmied her waist and shoulders in a little dance, at one point, pretending to slap someone's ass. Trishen's mouth opened wide, shocked. Thomas blushed, as if she knew exactly what he was doing. Patricia laughed to herself and was just about to leave when Kaleena stepped out of her room. Before she could retreat back in, Patricia caught sight of her.

"Well, would you look at this," Patricia boomed. "You must be the super computer." She walked heavily to Kaleena and grabbed her hand. "You're so damn young," she said. "I'm Patricia, the only other genius on this boat. Nowhere near as smart as you, but smart enough to know when I'm in good company."

"Thank you?" Kaleena said, sheepishly.

"You doin' okay? Still feeling a little floozy?"

Kaleena curled her brow, attempting to translate. "I'm fine," she finally said. "I just needed some sleep." She couldn't believe Patricia was still shaking her hand.

"Ooh. Wait. I almost forgot. Stay right here." Patricia made a couple of false attempts to leave (making sure Kaleena didn't move?) before going to her room. Kaleena raised her eyebrows, questioning for help from the other two, both of whom announced with their body language that they, too, had no idea what was going on.

Trishen, the young, very pretty black girl who could have been part African-American and part Caucasian, maybe a little Asian, added, "Don't mind her. She's harmless. I'm Trish by the way." She held out her hand, which Kaleena accepted kindly. It was a light grip, almost as if she were shaking a cloud.

"Kaleena."

"I don't think we've been properly introduced," Thomas, an older but semi-attractive man with graying hair, said. "I'm Thomas." His grip was a lot stronger and showed a lot of respect.

Patricia tumbled back into the salon holding a copy of Kaleena's book over her head. "Lookie-here," she said brightly. "Kaleena Stevens, teenage author — there

she stands. Take a bow for your damn self."

Kaleena's cheeks flushed slightly.

"All I need now is the marvelous author to sign this precious piece of brilliance." Patricia handed Kaleena the book and a pen. "This will make it worth more, no doubt. *And* give me bragging rights."

Kaleena chuckled, opened the book and quickly signed the front page. She would never get used to this — neither being asked for, or actually signing, her own books. It just felt so shameless. She blew lightly on the ink to make sure it was dry and handed it back to Patricia.

"Perfect," she boasted. "Now all I have to do is read it."

Kaleena stared at Patricia with mystified eyes.

"Come now, I'll read it. Just need to buy myself another copy first."

"Why do you need another copy?" Thomas asked.

"Are you shittin' me? I don't want to mess this copy up. This thing's going in the vault."

"May I read it?" No one had noticed Kara had come down the steps until just now. How long she had actually been standing there was anyone's guess.

Patricia was thinking of Kara's sister as she replied, "Sure," and handed Kara the book. "Just keep it in excellent condition. I don't want to see one mark on it, you got it?"

"You have my word," Kara said.

"Good. Now, if you don't mind, I need to go drop a few pounds." Patricia left as Kara thumbed through the pages.

Kaleena shook her head and then pressed her palm deep against her right temple. She could almost feel the physical maturation of pain.

"Headache?" Thomas said.

"A little one," Kaleena lied. "You guys wouldn't happen to have some aspirin, would you?"

"Sorry, no," Thomas said quickly. "Trish?"

Trishen shook her head apologetically.

"You should ask your dad."

"Okay, yeah. Where's he at?"

"Not sure. Last I saw him was in the mess."

"There's still some fish and steamed clams in the galley, too, if you're hungry," Trishen added. "Maybe that will help."

"Maybe." Kaleena labored up the stairs. Kara watched her a moment before turning to Thomas and Trishen. "I'm heading to bed," she said.

"Okay," Thomas replied.

"Have a good night," Trishen said.

"You too," Kara said and headed into her room. She looked at the back cover of the book as she sat down on her bed. Kaleena stared back at her with a light smile. Matthew talked about this book all the time and Kara had always wanted to buy a copy, but she never seemed to get around to doing it. Now that she had it in her hands, she was excited to finally get the chance to burrow into the young girl's mind, something she couldn't seem to do in person.

She ran her finger down the table of contents, and she almost flipped to the chapter titled, "The Fountain of Youth: A drink of immortality or a placebo of insanity?" but there was a more relevant chapter she was eager to get to. She immediately went to the chapter titled, "The Lost City of Atlantis" and started reading. The first thing that caught her attention was the fluidity of the writing, which only helped strengthen the already persuasive arguments Kaleena used to explain how Atlantis could never have existed. Kara couldn't help but smile knowing the child had just placed a check for thirty thousand dollars into the hands of a man who was taking them out into the middle of the ocean in order to track down a city, Kara was now convinced, never existed. The question that lingered — *Why would she do that?* — haunted Kara as she continued reading, though she knew full well the answer didn't lie within the pages of the book. But as the argument deepened, the less Kara really cared. She was entranced; there was no other place she wanted to be right now.

*   *   *

The aroma of cooked fish rumbled Kaleena's stomach even before she reached the top step of the cockpit. She hadn't eaten since the night before, and even that was only a piece of rough chicken and stale mashed potatoes that came with the flight. Grabbing a bite before tracking down Matthew was a brilliant idea. But before she could grab a plate and dig in, she saw Jaime on the deck, leaning up against the railing with her left arm tucked under her stomach. Her right elbow rested on the rail as she soaked in the glowing sunset. As she took a steady round of hits from the cigarette tucked between her fingers, Kaleena's thoughts bounced between what she had learned, what she had remembered and everything she had hoped would occur upon seeing her mother again. It all made her wonder is she might have taken things too personally. *She's your mother*, she kept telling herself.

Kaleena hadn't noticed she had paced down the cockpit a ways until she saw all the equipment Jaime's team had set up while she was asleep. Several expensive looking monitors sat on a couple of the tables near the aft side of the cockpit. Streams of wires flowed all about, some sprawled out through the back of the cockpit, some connected to other pieces of equipment Kaleena didn't recognize — though they looked like computers or monitoring consoles of some kind. Across the aisle were some photocopies of text written in a language Kaleena had never seen before. Next to them was a pad of paper with her father's handwriting scrawled all over it, probably a translation of the text he was looking at. The man that had arrived with Jaime was sitting nearest the bar. He looked worn out and tired as he rubbed his hand through his hair in what appeared to be frustration. The laptop glowed in front of him looked to have some sort of editing program, and two external hard drives — one plugged into the computer, the other linked to the first — sat tucked behind the laptop. By the sound of their static vibrations, both were working extraordinarily hard to render the images streaming on one of the small windows in the corner of the screen. There was a second display window that sat frozen on a massive whale leaping out of the water — an image that looked award-worthy from where she was standing. Kaleena flashed a smile as the man caught her watching and stopped the playback with the click of the spacebar. "Sorry," she whispered, taking his return gaze as her cue to have a closer look at her father's notebook. She didn't get a chance to read any of it as Matthew distracted her, sauntering up to Jaime. She couldn't quite hear what they were saying, so she tiptoed to the table nearest the outside deck and took a seat, resting her head against the side of the cockpit to listen.

"She's doing well," Matthew said, answering a question Kaleena assumed was about her. "Her grades are the same as always and she seems to like it there." He refrained from telling her about the incident. Why scare her when *he* didn't even know what really happened.

"That's good," Jaime said. It seemed she wanted to say more, ask more detailed questions, but for some reason she bit her tongue, unwilling to talk to Matthew about it.

"How have you been?" Matthew asked cautiously.

Jaime shrugged. "Fine." She didn't ask how he was in return. She just placed the cigarette in her mouth.

"What have you been up to?" At least he was trying.

"Not much." Jaime's voice was low and monotonous. "Just my work."

"Anything interesting?"

"Not anything I'd care to talk about right now."

Matthew folded his hands together, separated them and then folded them back together, resting his body against the rail. Jaime took another deep hit of nicotine. "When did you start smoking?"

Jaime blew the smoke out and finally looked at her husband. "What do you care?"

"I don't," Matthew said defensively. "I just thought you hated the sight of 'em."

"Yeah. People change."

"I wish you wouldn't. It doesn't flatter you."

"Well, then. I better stop, huh?" Jaime straightened up and shook the small glass of scotch she held in her left hand. "Maybe I should stop drinking too? Maybe stop swearing. Would that make me more *fucking* attractive?" She took a hit from her cigarette and blew the smoke into Matthew's face. She followed that up with a sip from her glass and then turned back to the ocean. "Can't let that happen."

Matthew looked uncomfortable and didn't seem to know what to do. Jaime lowered her head and calmed her voice. "What do you want, Matthew?"

He searched long and hard for an answer that never came.

"I'm not looking to get back with you, Matthew, if that's what you're hoping for. I'm not here to reconcile and become a family again. I'm here because my daughter asked me to come and I didn't want to disappoint her. So I would appreciate it," she continued, turning to face him, "if you would just let me do my job and leave the past in the past." Jaime took a drink and looked back to the horizon. The sun had almost set.

It took Matthew a while to move again. Kaleena could only imagine what he was thinking, though it was more than likely on par with her own thoughts. The woman they thought they knew had vanished with the smoke Jaime huffed into the sea air. Kaleena straightened as Matthew walked into the cockpit. He didn't say a word as he grabbed his papers, but his piercing eyes were full of regret. Feeling a light sprinkle of water round the corners of her eyes, Kaleena turned back to Jaime as he left for the salon. The idea her parents would use this trip to rekindle their love was a child's wild-eyed hope that had now been extinguished. It may have just been to drive Matthew away, but the conversation made it clear that Jaime was there for no other reason than to do a job. As time continued to slowly drift into night, Kaleena wondered if there was anyone left in the world that truly cared for her, who was honest with her about who they were and their reasoning behind their actions.

Her chest constricted when the memories she was trying to escape came rushing back to her, knocking her nerves into near shock. For a second, Kaleena wasn't sure she would escape them this time. But with a deep, stuttered breath, she

released it all through one last relaxing exhale. That's when she heard the familiar rattle of aspirin inside their little plastic home. She turned to see a beautiful young woman. Her large round belly was exposed underneath the small tank top the woman wore underneath a long-sleeve button-down shirt that draped over her shoulders.

"I heard you were looking for aspirin." The woman sat down across the table.

"Thank you," Kaleena said, popping the top of the bottle open. She spilled two aspirin into the palm of her hand and tossed them in her mouth, swallowing them quickly.

"I'm Lauren," the woman said politely.

"Kaleena. But I'm sure you already know that."

Lauren's cheeks puffed gently up. "Yes. I've heard all about you."

Kaleena could only remember a little about Lauren, and a lot of that was vague or had faded from memory. She couldn't recall ever being told she was with child. "How long have you been pregnant?"

"You wouldn't believe me if I told you," Lauren said.

"It has to be at least eight months. Right?"

Lauren's smile brightened. "You'd think."

Kaleena was outright confused, but didn't press the matter. It wasn't her place to pry anyway. Her thoughts were already swarming with too many questions and she didn't need any added confusion.

"I hear you're writing a new book."

Kaleena leaned back and sighed, clearly not wanting to go through this song and dance again.

"Something about the human condition and the problems in society."

"Not the problems in society," Kaleena interjected. "It's more about the dangers of society and how hypocrisy and selfishness are destroying the world around us."

Lauren nodded. "What prompted such a cynical view of society?"

Kaleena wondered why Lauren was trying so hard to be Kaleena's friend. But the more she looked her over, the more she felt a connection with her, as if they

were somehow sisters or had been a family in some other existence. She felt comfortable; trusting. Kaleena turned to watch Jaime put out her cigarette on the soul of her shoe and place the butt into the ashtray on the bench next to her. "Can I ask you a question?" Kaleena said, her eyes fixated on following her mother to the forward deck, passing her without even acknowledging her presence.

"Sure." The soft smile remained spread across Lauren's face.

Kaleena made eye contact with Lauren as Jaime disappeared around the cockpit. "Do you think there's any humanity left in the world?"

Lauren looked perplexed and delighted at the same time. "That's a heavy question." She shifted in her seat to find a more comfortable position. "Do you mean love and support, that kind of thing?"

"Yeah, I guess…" Kaleena paused to find the heart of what she truly meant. "More along the lines of humanity in terms of unselfishness, honesty and self-sacrifice."

Lauren nodded, looking like a bobble head on the dashboard of some hippie's car. Kaleena waited patiently as Lauren took her time to build a response. "Honestly, Kaleena, I really believe there is," she finally said, peering down to her stomach. "I think everyone sacrifices something of themselves for someone else at some point in their life."

Kaleena was quick to respond. "But are they really doing it without any predilection toward gaining something for themselves?"

It was Lauren's turn to look out to the darkening horizon. Kaleena knew right away she didn't know or didn't understand what she was asking.

"Let me ask you another question," she said. "Be as honest as you can. Let's say, for whatever reason, someone on this boat was about to get shot. Would you step in front of the bullet to save their life?"

Lauren rubbed her stomach, thinking.

"Pretend you weren't pregnant and have never had a child. Would you do it?"

It was hard for Lauren to come up with an answer. Would she give up her life, one that was still young and just now growing into a fruitful existence, for someone

she either didn't know or was minutely friends with? There was a lot Lauren still needed to do to spiritually and physically make up for the mistakes she had made. Giving up her life would prove she was someone you could admire, but was that enough for personal redemption?

"I don't know," she answered. "I guess it would really come down to the circumstances of the situation."

"By which you mean, if you had no regrets, or had already lived a long fruitful life, you probably would?" Kaleena eyed Lauren thoughtfully.

"I… I suppose, a little."

"Which demonstrates my point. You would only sacrifice yourself if you felt you had done everything *you*" — Kaleena strongly emphasized the word — "needed to accomplish for *yourself.*"

Lauren was shocked into submission. Kaleena felt she wasn't being fair. "Okay, let's change the situation a little. Say you did have a child and someone you cared deeply for is about to get shot. Would you give up your life, knowing your daughter would grow up without a mother? Or would it take the threat of your daughter's death to sacrifice yourself?"

"If someone told me that my daughter would be killed if I didn't take a bullet for someone else," Lauren summarized quickly, "then yes, I would do it, no question. But if it simply meant my daughter would grow up without me, probably not."

"Because your daughter's life is more important than your own. A mother's instinct. But if it meant being able to watch your daughter grow up, regardless if a friend or loved one died, you'd choose your daughter, even if it made you look like a coward. Why?"

"Probably because I'd rather look like a coward for her than look like a hero to everyone else."

"And I bet you one hundred percent of the population would say the exact same thing. It's in everyone's nature, as human beings, to think of themselves first, no matter what, regardless of whether they have to lie or cheat to get what they want, or act like hypocrites to make themselves feel better. Answer me this. What would

you do if you were handed a million dollars that you could do anything you wanted with? If you decide to spend it on yourself, nothing bad will ever happen to you. However, down the street, there's an orphanage where ten kids will die in a week unless they had a million dollars. But if you spend it on the orphanage, you lose everything you've ever owned. Would you save those children? In a hypothetical situation, a lot of people would say yes, who in turn, getting the actual opportunity, would do the exact opposite. Most people, if not everyone in the world, would spend that million dollars on a new sports car or mansion somewhere in Beverly Hills, pay off debts, or buy a million lottery tickets before they spend a dime on people they don't know and risk becoming destitute in the process. Why? Because people look out for themselves, no matter what their decisions are or where their lives are headed. The cripple on the street corner? Ignored. The child that gets abused? Forgotten. People turn a blind eye to everything around them because they don't want to lose the safety they've built for themselves. If it doesn't help the self, the self will never help."

Lauren took a breath and then said, "But what about the woman that puts up her own money to build that orphanage, without any help or reason? Just simply to help those that don't have anything. Doesn't that make her self-sacrificing?"

"It depends. Is she truly doing it for no other reason but to help, or is she doing it because she needs the acceptance to get through the day? Or maybe she's doing it so she can slide on her taxes? Maybe it's because she needs to prove she can change the world, become a famous "savior" and make all the headlines. A desire to be needed is still selfish."

"I don't believe that. A desire to be needed is nothing more than an emotion that helps drive people in a certain direction. It's human to want to be needed."

"That's true. But it's not sacrifice to be human. To sacrifice, you need to give up everything, for no other reason than because it's the right thing to do."

"Wait," Lauren said softly. "If you give up everything for no reason but to do the right thing, isn't that in and of itself, selfish?"

Kaleena's teeth glowed bright. "Exactly."

Lauren's lips curled as she finally understood.

"I've seen the face of our future," Kaleena finished, "and within it, humanity has become extinct."

Lauren felt like crying. It was hard to watch such a young girl think the way Kaleena did. What had to have occurred for a fourteen-year-old girl, flourishing in life in more ways than any one person could ever dream of, to believe the human race could be such a dark and dwindling species? She didn't want to give up on her.

She wouldn't.

"Can I ask *you* a question?" Lauren said, softer than before.

Kaleena nodded.

"What about hope?"

"Hope?" Kaleena urged Lauren to expand on her question.

"Yeah. Do you believe in hope, no matter how small it may be? Don't you think that people can learn from their mistakes, simply by having hope in the future? Isn't that worth more than sacrifice?"

Kaleena smiled. She knew there was a reason she felt connected to Lauren. "There's the rub. Hope doesn't exist without sacrifice."

"Why not?"

"Because unless there's someone out there willing to display pure sacrifice, what's there to hope for?"

"That one day, someone will."

"That's a dream."

"And a dream, Kaleena, is hope."

Kaleena clicked her teeth together, excited. The stars shone bright across the sky. She had plenty to think about now that she had spoken to Lauren. "Thank you," she said. "This was nice."

"Thank you," Lauren said politely. "I'm always here if you need an ear." She smiled as the baby kicked. "Or if you just need to argue." She used the table as leverage to stand and waddled to the stairs, flashing one last sweet smile at Kaleena before heading down.

Mixed feelings continued to torment Kaleena. Facing her mother now that she knew who she was, who she had become, and what she was doing here was going to be incredibly awkward, but how could she remain so upset with her mother when Kaleena herself was guilty of her own selfishness? She may have convinced herself she needed to get away from her life (which was selfish in its own right), but in reality, the only reason she came on this trip was to convince her mother to come back home. Jaime was looking toward the future — always has been — and Kaleena finally understood that's why she herself was never going to be able to grow as a daughter, or as a woman. It terrified her.

Jaime walked back along the outside of the cockpit (probably heading for the stairs), striking Kaleena with a slice of pain that tightened every muscle in her body. Even if it was only to say hi before going their separate ways, Jaime was the last person she wanted to see right now. So she sprinted for the stairs.

"Yeah, that was refreshing," Patricia said before nearly taking a tumble back down the stairs with Kaleena. "Whoa, what's the hurry speed racer?"

"Please excuse me." Kaleena pushed past Patricia (which wasn't easy), indifferent to whether she appeared rude.

"You gonna be sick?" Patricia said as Kaleena disappeared below deck. She shrugged as one of the doors to the rooms closed. "I'm lightning in a bottle, baby. I'm rubbing the right way," she sang as she entered the cockpit. She sang the same line over (but louder) to Jaime. "Sing with me," she said before repeating it again.

"Did Kaleena just run downstairs?" Jaime said, ignoring the song.

"I think so. Didn't get a good look. She bolted out of here like a firecracker on steroids."

Jaime sighed as Patricia took a seat in front of the monitors, picking up her repetitive song where she left off. What had she done to scare Kaleena so bad? What happened to that buoyant excitement she heard through their electronic communications? Matthew developing into a headache she wished she could shake was expected, but the way her young daughter was avoiding her — almost as if she were afraid of her — sickened Jaime deeply. That wasn't what she wanted.

Not at all.

Instead of heading down and knocking on Kaleena's door to try and reconcile, Jaime stayed with Patricia to discuss what may begin to happen as their journey headed deeper into the Bermuda Triangle over the next couple of days. It was just enough to push Kaleena to the back of her mind. She couldn't forget about her, but at least she could ignore her. That would have to do for now.

The *Endeavor* – Sunday, Early Morning

Thomas woke abruptly. His body shook as a tinge of cold air washed over him. The scars on his right hand began to burn. He closed his eyes and rubbed them. Flashes from his dream rolled back through the spray of sparks and changing pattern of lights in the darkness of his eyelids. He stood above a fading fire, looking over a younger version of himself — a child of about ten — sitting on a rock in a small clearing of the woods, counting the stars above him. No one was around as he drifted into the sky without even realizing it. The air around the little boy grew warmer, but his concentration remained fixed on the small dots in the sky.

"I'm coming," he whispered before a hint of tightness in his palm knocked him from his focus on the stars. Ignoring the heat surrounding him, he examined the indentations of his knuckles and each small wrinkle that formed the spirit of his palm. The most prominent one was a small line on his pinkie, signifying the time he cut himself when helping his mom slice tomatoes for the chicken salad they were preparing for dinner. There was nothing to signify pain, though, which seemed to be coming from an invisible source outlining a weird pattern along his hand. He eventually gave up and looked back to the stars.

And caught fire.

Thomas tried to scream for him, but his own body tightened as flames licked the souls of his feet. He couldn't do anything as they swarmed his younger self and shot straight into the sky. But the boy experienced no pain as the fire painted the night with morning and engulfed him in the explosive blaze.

Realizing he'd forgotten to breathe, Thomas opened his eyes and sucked in air tainted with a hint of perfume. Trishen's head lay against his shoulder, her hand resting gently on his chest. Her hair fell across her face, highlighting the tip of her petite nose and cheek, where Thomas noticed a small hint of a smile on the corner of her lips. He curled his hand into a fist to ease the pain that tickled his palm as he tried to move the arm wedged between her neck and the couch the pair had moved to later in the evening to get more comfortable as they talked. To keep from waking her, he decided to let his arm stay where it was and unfurled his hand to rest it on her warm shoulder.

It had been a while since he held a woman like this. The difference was, Caitlyn would only lie with him like this after a passionate night of sex, her small breasts, visible against his side, warm and soft among the aroma of sweat, alcohol and occasionally cigarette smoke. With Trishen, Thomas felt a kinship he never felt with Caitlyn. It was nice to have a relationship — or friendship as it were — with a woman that didn't involve sex. That's not to say he wasn't sexually attracted to Trishen, he just didn't feel the need to act on that attraction, giving into his ability to show respect rather than diving into her with animalistic desire. He slid a few strands of Trishen's hair behind her ear and saw an angel he could never ask anything from but love and honor —someone he could see living a full, healthy life with, regardless of sex or beauty. Trishen shifted as he pushed a little more hair behind her ear, but she quickly settled and remained asleep. He smiled as an affectionate burn muddled through his chest, followed by the echo of her voice in the back of his mind.

"My parents were never really around," she had said around one in the morning. Everyone else had retired for the night and the *Endeavor* had been anchored, softly tumbling against the buoyancy of the ocean. "I mean, they were around, but they would often eat out or go on vacation, and when they weren't doing that, they were either working or sleeping. I rarely ever saw them for more than ten minutes, usually for breakfast or maybe before I went to bed."

"Did they at least support you?" Thomas asked.

"How do you mean?"

"I mean, like in school plays, or your choice of college. That kind of thing."

"Oh, they took an interest in what I did. It wasn't like those primetime CW soap operas that show these supposed teenagers running around without parents."

"But with them out of town all the time, it must have been easy to throw parties or have boyfriends over, right?"

"Probably, I guess. I wasn't much of the social butterfly, if you know what I mean. I stayed pretty much to myself, really." Trishen turned away. Thomas wasn't sure if it was shame or embarrassment. Either way, she didn't look at all comfortable.

"What did they do?" Thomas said, shifting the subject back to her parents.

"My dad's a broker and my mom's a DA."

"Really? Wow, okay. Now I know why you were always alone." Thomas winked, trying to urge a smile out of her. But she wasn't having it. Time to change the subject again. "So what got you into diving?"

It took a second, but the subject changed Trishen's demeanor and her voice became more engaged than before. "When I was younger, my parents would take me on some of their trips… places like Cabo, Hawaii, the Virgin Islands…. My dad loved snorkeling and deep-sea fishing and always took me with him. I guess you could say I became addicted to it — it was just so beautiful and amazing."

"Sounds awesome." Thomas moved in a little closer, wrapping his arm around her shoulders. She shied away at first, but quickly became comfortable, moving in to rest her shoulder against his side, giving him a look of a childlike wonderment.

"What about your parents?" she said, her voice softer and less defensive.

The brightness in Thomas's features, though, faded with the question. He turned his eyes downward. Trishen realized she may have just made a mistake. She was about ready to move away, give him some space, when he answered in a soft, low whisper.

"My dad died when I was about two." He caught the sadness in Trishen's eyes.

"I'm sorry," she said, placing the tips of her fingers to her bottom lip. "I didn't mean to…"

Thomas forced his smile to return, but with a reconciliatory charm. "No, it's okay," he said. "I just don't talk about it much."

"Do you even remember him?"

"Not really. My mom told me stories from time to time and I had a picture of him above my bed. It made me feel safe believing he was always watching over me."

"I'm sure he was." Trishen shifted to put weight on her legs, which had up to this point been sitting beneath her. At first, Thomas tried to coax her back, but he let her go, choosing to wait for the right time to ask her back in. "I'm afraid to ask about your mother," she said.

Thomas couldn't help break out a laugh, quick and louder than he wanted. He closed his mouth and waited to see if he had woken anyone up. Trishen covered her mouth to keep from letting out her own burst of laughter and lowered her head to his chest. After a minute, she giggled the last remaining bits of hysteria from her body and allowed Thomas to once again hold her close.

"So, what about your mom?" she said cautiously. "What was she like?"

"She was pretty protective… didn't let me do a whole lot without her."

"That sucks." Trishen felt her laughter start to return.

"Yeah, it did. Didn't help me after she passed on, either."

"Oh, my god," Trishen said, sitting back up.

Thomas chortled softly at her reaction. "Don't worry. It was a long time ago."

"That's not the point. Here I am, boasting about my parents and you…" Trishen was unable to find an end to that sentence that didn't make her seem cold or heartless.

Thomas finished it for her. "I got screwed."

This time it was Trishen that let slip an explosive laugh. She clasped both hands over her mouth and held them there for what seemed like an hour as tears poured from her eyes. Her chest punched her heart as she buried her head into Thomas's stomach, her face flushed. Whenever she relaxed enough to remove her hands, her laughter would start right back up again. It was hard for Thomas to keep from joining in. When she finally brought it under control, she shifted her

body upward, stretched her legs out along the couch and rested her head against Thomas's shoulder.

They would talk for the next three hours about their political beliefs (Thomas claimed to be an independent, but Trishen, through dissecting some of his thoughts, believed him to be a Democrat, like her), some of their unusual habits, what they thought about the difference between white meat and the other white meat, and just who was that kid in the window in *Three Men and a Baby*? Trishen fell asleep first, but it didn't take Thomas long to do the same. As he faded into slumber, his thoughts were on her beautiful laugh, which sang through his mind once again now as he stared at her gorgeous eyelids shaking slightly in REM.

"Would you look at the two little love birds?" Patricia howled as she walked into the salon.

Trishen immediately woke, bouncing up into a sitting position.

"You guys look so cute together," Patricia said. "My husband wouldn't ever cuddle with me. It was more of a 'Wham-bam, thank you, ma'am, hit the snooze' with him. It's a wonder we lasted as long as we did, huh?"

"Oh, my god," Trishen said, her cheeks heating to a bright red.

Thomas rubbed her shoulder softly. "What's wrong?"

"I'm sorry," she said and shot across the salon into her room.

Thomas sat still, frozen in confusion.

"Whoops," Patricia said. "My bad. I can squeeze in a chat with her if you'd like. It's damn hard to ignore me, don't you know."

Thomas took some time to answer. "No... no. Don't worry about it. Let her be."

"You sure, lover?"

Thomas squeaked out a grin. "Yeah."

"Okay. But if you change your mind, you know where I'll be."

Thomas pointed a finger at her in sly recognition, which Patricia returned graciously before heading upstairs. He rubbed his eyes as sleep fell back on him. He lay back, confounded by Trishen's reaction. Had he done something to upset her? She must have been feeling the same thing he was, but for whatever reason,

didn't want anyone to know. He couldn't understand why… maybe it was just too soon, a thought that had crossed his mind as well. He hadn't waited with Caitlyn, sleeping with her mere hours after they first met, knocking her up on their fourth date and losing her to a drunken stooper two years later. Had he waited, things may have been different. Maybe, just maybe, he might actually know his daughter; may actually have been a respected husband and father. He didn't want to rush into anything this time, afraid he'd lose once again. It was more than possible that no matter what her past relationships may have held, Trishen felt the exact same thing.

Slow and steady wins the race. Always.

*   *   *

"Hey there up there," Patricia called out. She had put her sunglasses on to avoid the glaring rays of the sun beaming down on her as she stared up at the wheelhouse.

Benjamin looked down from his perch. "Ahoy, mate."

"How long have we been on the move?"

" 'Bout an hour and a half now," Benjamin guessed after checking his watch, which seemed to have slowed down.

"How are your instruments running?"

"I'd say 'bout expected. Y'know, a little off center but manageable if y'know what you're doin'."

"You're sure we're headed in the right direction, then?"

Benjamin was growing somewhat irritated by the inquisition. "I know how to read these waters, doll. I've sailed them plenty a time before."

Patricia's lips curled into a petite smile. "Don't get me wrong, Ben. I'd trust your skills to the edge of the world if I had to. Just humor me."

Benjamin couldn't read Patricia very well, so he decided to oblige. "Aye. East, southeast. Straight into the fires of hell." Benjamin laughed. "Not gettin' scared, there, are ya'?"

"I'm not afraid of hell," Patricia replied. "You weren't married to my husband. I'm just getting anxious, is all. How long 'til we get there?"

"I'd say we're about a hundred miles out, yet. Maybe 'nother half a day or so."

"All right, then. You keep up that top-notch captaining… or whatever… Captaining," she repeated to herself softly. "Is that a word?" she asked Benjamin.

"It is now, doll." Benjamin flashed a sly grin and raised his thumb in acknowledgment before double-checking the idiosyncrasies of the instruments.

Patricia squeezed herself back toward the cockpit, sipping the apple cider she poured herself minutes ago and looking out over the calm ocean. It was eerie yet pleasing; it made Patricia calmer than normal without having smoked a pack of cigarettes or chewing someone out for their stupidity over cutting her off on the highway or eating the last block of cookie dough in the freezer. If she didn't know any better, it felt as if it was coaxing her to enjoy the cool texture and fragrance of an unknown world. *Maybe another time*, she thought as if she were speaking to the sea. *There's much too much to think about right now.* She smiled and hummed a tune, the words volleying through her head — *My body lies over the ocean, so bring back my puppy to me.*

She sat down at the monitors and shoved a piece of toast with butter and strawberry jam into her mouth. It wasn't her ideal breakfast, but as she saw it, making a full on feast would have taken way too long. *Toast and a sweet cig's enough for me,* she thought. *I have to lose weight anyway, right, funny girl? Someone else will whip something up and I can just mooch off of them.* After licking the jam from her fingers, she noticed a few of her readings were rapidly fluctuating. She had expected something like this to start happening as they entered this part of the Atlantic, but still wanted to make sure her equipment wasn't malfunctioning. Now that she knew Benjamin's equipment was also acting funny, her inconsistent readings made more sense. That was until she saw something she couldn't explain away by magnetic anomalies. She leaned in closer to the monitor to get a better look. The salinization readings had dropped below ten percent and continued to drop a tenth of a percent every minute. Patricia went back through the previous night's

numbers and about around the time Benjamin said he got the *Endeavor* moving, the percentages had been increasingly dropping. Perplexed, Patricia checked some of the other readings: the hydrostatic pressure claimed the density of the water was slowly decreasing, which Patricia found odd until she realized the sonar pointed to land approximately 325 feet below them.

That couldn't be. Patricia flipped one of the monitors to the camera readings and took a look-see at the crystal clear vision of the ocean floor — through slight flips of static and magnetic interference. She didn't notice it at first, but there wasn't one living creature swimming about. In fact, there wasn't any plant life either, just miles of sand forming some type of underwater oasis. As she panned the camera to get a better look, something else caught her eye, stopping her heart in amazement.

A structure, a wall…

A throne.

Patricia raced onto the deck.

"Benjamin. Stop the boat. Quick."

Benjamin looked down, a bit frantic. "What is it? What for?"

"Just stop," she yelled, adding "goddamn it," under her breath. She bolted downstairs before Benjamin could even get a squeak of an interjection past his lips. Apparently she was in too much of a hurry to enjoy a quick argument. His first instinct was to ignore her. Under normal circumstances, unless the person whose name is on the agreement said to stop, he would finish the job as per the contract. But Matthew was nothing if not part of a team, and this little tour was an expedition — a trip intended to wield fancy treasures of some kind. If he didn't stop, he might just flitter over something extremely important, and there was no guarantee they would be able to find it again. Matthew, and for the better part, Jaime, trusted their teams. More importantly, they trusted him; it was better to waste ten minutes at a standstill than hours trying to retrace their steps — especially in these waters. It was enough to convince him to go ahead and shut his baby down. She could use the rest anyway.

No harm, no foul.

*   *   *

"Jaime, I've got something." Patricia pounded through the door to Jaime's cabin before noticing it was Gavin grumbling and shifting around under the covers. The other bed was empty, but had clearly been slept in. "Jaime?"

"Yeah?" Jaime said from the bathroom. She stepped into the doorway, brushing her hair. She wore a pair of gray sweats and a tank top that showed maybe a little too much cleavage. "What is it?"

"Hell just froze over and puked up a snowstorm."

Gavin looked at Patricia through his uncontrollable hair. "What?"

"Just get your asses upstairs," Patricia said and left.

"What the hell is she talking about?"

"I don't know," Jaime said, looking at the door as if Patricia was still there. "But we better do as she says before she has a conniption."

Gavin slammed his face into the pillow, grumbling under his breath. After having spent the last twelve hours working on the documentary, all he wanted to do was sleep for the next twelve hours. He knew it had only been about four hours since he crashed, but based on the way he felt, it seemed as if he had just gotten to sleep. "Do I have to? Can't I just stay here and sleep?" he said into the pillow as if Jaime was trying to wake him for school. He slipped back into unconsciousness as he waited for an answer he never heard — if she had said anything at all.

Jaime, in fact, didn't even hear his request, having turned back into the bathroom before he made it. As she changed, she wondered why Patricia was acting so hyper and insane. The two of them had worked together for the last two and a half years and in that time seemed to have seen everything. Fissures in the ocean bed near the arctic that spewed heated magma; a chasm that registered near eight thousand feet deep (or so they claimed), in the northern Pacific. They once even saw live fish nearly glow fluorescent in the deep hollows of the ocean caverns. Each time, Patricia had some wise comment, funny thought, or song tucked in

her back pocket that summed everything up. She had always been that way; it was her nature.

When Jaime first got to Los Angeles, it didn't take her long to find her first job — tracking the migration patterns of the Pacific bluefin tuna and their relationship to other migratory and stable sea creatures over a three-month period — with a sea life conservation company in Newport Beach. The founder of the company, a ratty little toad named Mrs. Pesterfield, was writing a novel (so she thought; as long as she got paid, she didn't care much about the end result) and knew she had only gotten the job because she was cheap. But it was an opportunity she couldn't pass up. Mrs. Pesterfield needed someone that could handle the technical side of the job as well — that is, tagging the fish and acquiring accurate readings — while Jaime focused on the community side, watching their behavior with all other life around them. Patricia was one of the first to respond to an ad Jaime posted on Craig's List for "an oceanographer with expert skills in the technological side of the ocean." Jaime thought her response was wordy and not nearly professional enough. But under the abrasive, sarcastic, rambling text full of groan-inducing jokes and puns, were some very intelligent information and a tight resume. She called her the next day for a pre-interview and found her to be very quick on her feet, answering every question with precise detail and overwhelming zeal; so much so that it was easy to overlook the constant chatter in between all the wise comments. Of the other eight responses that came in, Jaime only found one other person that didn't seem to answer the ad as an overall binge to see what sticks. She was a sweet student at UCLA and her response and cover letter were very professionally written. The pre-interview only lasted ten minutes. Though the girl was sweet and gave succinct answers — short, to the point and robotic — she seemed to be distracted by homework, or a boyfriend, or just her own fear of having to actually apply her skills and knowledge to the real world. Jaime pictured being out in the middle of the ocean, the girl's nose stuck in a copy of *Twenty-Thousand Leagues Under the Sea* or *Moby Dick* to avoid eye contact unless absolutely necessary. Jaime needed something more than that.

Suffice it to say, Patricia was hired and the two spent the next three months collecting necessary data and writing journal entries in several spiral-bound notebooks. Though she occasionally got on Jaime's nerves, with her nonsensical banter and constant tone-deaf singing, she hardly noticed it after a few weeks. It became like the sound of the ocean waves — background noise in an otherwise stressful environment. With her high intelligence and keen sense of logic, Patricia was an asset. After delivering the findings and getting her first paycheck, Jaime would be near dead-broke by the time she acquired her next job, which Patricia was the first contact. Once again, annoyance laid way to a dear friendship, one that helped in the development of several new ways of tracking the habits of the sea while working with old, malfunctioning computers and cameras. For two and a half years, Patricia would chatter on about the Bermuda Triangle, the current theories and published papers about the area and how excited she was about acquiring a new book, fiction or non-fiction, that dealt with a place that wasn't even acknowledged as a real entity in many intellectual circles. Even the dimensions and the locations of the invisible triangle itself were often under contention. But Jaime was enamored by her eagerness to get out there some day to find the truth behind the mystery. It was no shock, then, what Patricia's response would be when that opportunity finally arrived.

"Hot damn," Patricia said, slapping the leather couch and almost dropping the plate of cheese and crackers she was holding. Trishen sat on the far side of the room, her legs crossed together with her hands folded delicately above her knees. Gavin stood next to Jaime by the full glass door leading out to the porch. "This calls for a drink." Patricia set the plate on the oak coffee table and tramped into the kitchen.

"I told you," Gavin whispered. Jaime cracked a smile.

"Told her what?" Patricia hummed as she opened the refrigerator door. She didn't seem to care for a response as she found a bottle of Dom Pérignon. "Here we go," she said, ripping the cover from the neck of the bottle with her medium-sized fake nail attachments.

"What do you think, Trish?" Jaime said, ignoring Patricia for the moment. Trishen sat still a second and then shrugged lightly.

"Come on, Trish," Patricia said. A slight pop occurred as she pulled the cork from the bottle, allowing for a small amount of foam to leak from the top. She immediately shoved the bottle into her mouth before letting the champagne pour all over the countertops. "Anyone else want some?" she asked, holding the bottle up for everyone. Trishen lifted her hand modestly with a slight shake of her head. Jaime gave her a polite, "No, thank you."

Gavin drank the rest of the water he had in his glass, held it up and said, "Sure."

"You can't have champagne in a cheap three-dollar hooker," Patricia groaned. "I'll get some wine glasses."

As she walked to the china cabinet near the back wall of the dining area, Trishen, slowly shifted in her seat, re-crossing her legs in the opposite direction and placing her hand to her chin.

"You don't think it's a good idea," Jaime said as a statement.

"You have got to be shittin' me," Patricia belted from the dining room. She pulled two tulip-shaped glasses from the hutch and poured the champagne, filling one a little too full. The froth spilled over the edge and down the long stem, settling on the linen tablecloth on the dining room table. "The Triangle is the greatest piece of ocean in the world," she continued, setting the bottle down. She picked up the wine glasses and took a quick swig from the overflowing glass. "Mm," she groaned. "This is some sweet stuff. Kinda like me, but bubbly." Patricia handed Gavin the half-empty glass, staring at Trishen the whole time. "I mean, just exploring the lore alone should excite your nethers." She sat down and took another drink.

"I just think it might be too dangerous," Trishen said, taking offense at the remark.

"God, that's the whole point," Patricia said.

Trishen took a deep breath, her eyebrows bent together. Jaime and Gavin were both waiting for an answer she didn't want to give. "Whatever you guys want," she finally replied, trusting her friends — her companions.

"We're not going unless everyone's on board. No second thoughts," Jaime said.

"Shit," Patricia whispered, setting her champagne down and grabbing the pack of cigarettes off the table. She lit one up with the silver lighter that Jaime kept out for guests. After taking a few puffs, she shook some of the ashes into the wooden ashtray and scooped the champagne glass back into her hand.

"It's just… you haven't given us any details about this trip except where it is," Trishen said, feeling she had to explain herself.

"Who cares," Patricia countered.

"No, seriously. What's the trip about? Who's paying? Why is this so important?"

Jaime chose her response carefully. "My ex-husband has an expedition set up to try and locate a lost artifact."

"Your ex?" Gavin said before Patricia could. "You didn't tell me that."

"I didn't think it was important," Jaime said, a little defensive.

"To hell it wasn't. Why the shit are you agreeing to go on an expedition with your ex-husband?"

"What's it matter?"

Gavin held his tongue. From his own experiences dealing with an ex-wife (two, in fact, the second of which lasted just a month), he knew nothing good could come of this. Plus, Gavin hadn't realized it until now, but he didn't want Jaime to put herself in the position of a possible reconciliation. It wasn't in his best interest for that to happen. For him, the best thing she could do would be to stay as far away from Matthew as possible.

"What's the artifact?" Trishen asked, barely audible.

Jaime lowered her head and shifted her feet. If she told them what Matthew was searching for, she might lose her only reason to see Kaleena. But she counted on this group of people — of friends to whom she had grown a strong, treasured bond — and didn't want to lie to them; they would find out eventually anyway. Better to take her chances than to have them find out on the boat and lose all of their respect.

"Don't you know?" Trishen said.

"What's the big secret?" Patricia said before Jaime could respond. "Is he trying to find Atlantis or something?"

Jaime made eye contact with a look no one could deny.

"No shit?" Patricia said, stunned.

"Atlantis?" Trishen added. She uncrossed her legs and sat forward. "Are you serious?"

Jaime nodded. "Yes. My lunatic ex-husband is trying to find the claimed 'Lost City.'"

Trishen sat back. "I can't believe this. You want to except a job from your ex-husband to find Atlantis?" The word *Atlantis* melted from her mouth with each syllable accentuated.

Jaime walked to the coffee table and lit herself a cigarette, hoping the soothing taste would help her relax.

"My god," Trishen hissed out.

"Look, I didn't expect any of you to want to do this," Jaime said. She looked to Gavin for help.

"Don't look at me. I was on board this afternoon."

"Do you expect to find anything out there?" Patricia asked, blowing out a stream of smoke. "I mean, do you think there's a chance we might actually find Atlantis?"

"About as much chance as Hell becoming Santa's winter wonderland."

"Then why even consider it?" Trishen said.

Jaime had never seen her so tense before. She shoved the cigarette into the ashtray. It wasn't helping. "Because it wasn't my ex that asked," Jaime finally revealed. She turned her back to the group and crossed her arms, which amazingly helped ease that stress a little. "It was my daughter."

"The genius?" Patricia's usual smile popped to her face.

Jaime chuckled. "Yeah."

"Hot damn," Patricia said. "You got my vote," she said.

"I'm still in," Gavin said wryly.

Jaime smiled. She didn't think anyone would understand, but they must have. They all had heard tales about Kaleena, tales that stopped about a year ago. Knowing she seemed to have forgotten about her daughter for that much time certainly hit her hard, killing her slowly as she fought with the decision of having to face the young girl she abandoned. She knew what the stakes were, what she had riding on this now, and it felt good to have all of their support. At least, *almost* all of their support.

She turned to Trishen, who was still clearly undecided.

"Come on, kid," Patricia taunted. "How many people can say they've snorkeled in the middle of the Bermuda Triangle?"

"I'm sure not many. They're probably all dead." She didn't seem to be joking.

"So you can be the first to tell 'em all what's out there. Who knows? You just may find a new species of shark or finally get laid."

"Patricia," Jaime scolded, trying to keep a laugh from breaking free.

"Much good it would do me if I'm dead."

"Trish. The triangle is not a killer. Most of the shit people talk about is just myth. Do you know how much cargo goes through that part of the Atlantic every year?"

Trishen shook her head.

"A boat load," Patricia said, finally getting a smile out of her, if only one that barely curled the corners of her mouth. "Trust me. You'll be perfectly safe out there."

When Trishen didn't answer, Patricia finished her champagne and then said, "Besides. It's not the ocean or the methane gas or even the wormholes you need to be afraid of. It's those damn aliens you gotta watch out for."

She finally got to her. Trishen broke her stern façade with a bright smile, which was followed by steady laughter from Jaime and Gavin.

"All right," Trishen said. "All right. You've convinced me." She looked to Jaime and with honest eyes said, "I'm in."

Patricia set her cigarette in the ashtray and gave Trishen a rough noogie. "That a girl," she said as Trishen screamed for her to stop. "Who knows? Hell may just freeze over and give us all a fucking kick in the ass."

The rest of the night was filled with a light aura of fun and excitement as they discussed the specifics of the trip.

Three days later, Jaime still didn't know what would have happened had Trishen said no, but she couldn't think about that now. She finally understood what Patricia had meant. Had she really found something relating to Atlantis? Jaime was professional enough to refrain from ignoring her colleagues and trusted Patricia enough to know that she knew what she was talking about.

After sliding into her sandals, Jaime pulled her hair back and clipped it in a ponytail at the base of her neck. "Get up, Gavin," she said as she walked by.

"All right," he said, muffled by the soft, unrelenting comfort of the pillow. "All right." Gavin pushed himself up and dangled his legs over the side. He shivered as the air hit his bare skin, covered only by his smiley-face boxer shorts. "I'll be up —"

Jaime was gone. Gavin thought about lying back down — *Just one more minute, mommy* — but decided against it. He stood and shuffled to the bathroom.

*　　*　　*

"Get up, big guy," Patricia said, peaking her head into Matthew's room. Lauren was lying in the bed opposite Matthew and Kaleena, who slept above him in the wall bed. Lauren arched herself up onto her elbows as Matthew slowly lifted his head to focus on Patricia through blurred eyes.

"What's up?" Lauren asked.

"You're going to love this," Patricia said.

"You find something?" Matthew asked, perking up a bit.

"I can't be positive, but it sure as hell seems to have something to do with your little lost city." The words sounded odd to Patricia, but she knew it was what Matthew wanted to hear. "Now stop charging the crank and get your ass up." Patricia closed the door before anyone could say anything else.

Matthew threw the covers off and sat up, rubbing his face with the palms of his hands. He had spent most of the night trying to decipher some of the translations he and Kara had pulled from the tablets. Almost everything they'd found had some kind of double meaning, either within the words, the structure of the sentences or the phrasing of the words in context to other sentences. The two of them had only understood maybe three percent of all that was written, but Matthew wouldn't give up on deciphering as much as he could. Of course, as he noticed from time to time, deciphering one passage relied on passages from other tablets, so without all of them (of which Kara figured were up to two dozen; they only had eight) it was going to take forever to figure out even ten percent. If nothing else, Matthew was at least going to memorize them all.

"Is it possible?" Lauren asked with an excited smirk.

"Why not? We've been right so far. This could be what we've been waiting for."

Matthew had fallen asleep in the clothes he was wearing the day before, so he pulled a fresh pair of shorts and a button down shirt from the trunk at the edge of his bed and swapped them out as Lauren pushed herself out of bed. Her large, round stomach gleaned in the morning sun peeking through the window. She rubbed it softly, feeling a hint of tightness.

"Hang in there, kid," she whispered. And then: "Do you really think we're on the right track?" Her voice was soft, most likely to keep from waking Kaleena.

"There's only one to find out," Matthew said, grabbing a pair of light blue flip-flops from the side of the bed and jumping to the door with a large step. "Hurry and get changed."

Lauren felt a couple of kicks as Matthew left. She giggled lightly, then kissed the tips of her fingers and rested them on top of her stomach. "Love you too, Evey. Love you too."

She watched Kaleena for a minute, trying to picture her young infant slumbering across from her, sleeping sound and still, a perfect picture of innocence; the child's chest rising and falling without thought, without fear. She stood on Matthew's bed to meet Kaleena's eye line and combed the child's hair from her face to better take in the beauty of a young woman, unafraid, unaware and far from the knowledge that would haunt her waking life. For a minute, she peered

at Kaleena's thin lips, curled downward in a faint frown, open just a centimeter to allow only the slightest bit of air in. She wanted to give her a kiss, wake her quietly to the hum of a lullaby and find the love expressed within her delicate eyes. It was overwhelming; Lauren fell in love with the child that would one day sleep as silently as Kaleena slept now.

It took another few minutes and a few more kicks to the gut (each a little stronger than the last) to knock Lauren from her enchanted condition. She let a breath of air wash over Kaleena's thinly brushed eyelashes and then gave her a gentle kiss on the cheek — a kiss that would not affect Kaleena's deep slumber.

"Sleep well, Kaleena." She stepped down from the bed, grabbed a few things from her bag and went to the bathroom. Excited to know what it was that had Patricia so energized, but needing to clean up (even though it had only been twelve hours since her last shower), Lauren switched on the water and stripped. For a brief moment, she saw the woman from her dreams staring at her. Lauren blew her a kiss, which the woman graciously excepted by curling her lips around the air in front of her and pressing her newly formed fist to the top of her bare left breast, just above her heart. The woman bowed and then vanished. A tear fell from Lauren's eye as she stepped into the shower.

*   *   *

Before Matthew closed the door to his cabin, Jaime caught a glimpse of Lauren in nothing but lacey, somewhat sexy-looking lingerie. Not sexy enough for Victoria's Secret, but a lot sexier than Wal-Mart. Jaime suddenly had a picture in her head of her husband lying in bed with the little vixen, a thought that chilled her a bit — especially because of how young Lauren appeared to be. Could she be carrying Matthew's baby?

"Hey," Matthew said sweetly, seemingly ignoring the small fight they had had. It may have just been he was too excited to care about their petty differences at the moment.

"Does Kaleena know?" Jaime said.

"Does Kaleena know what?" Matthew had an inkling she wasn't talking about Patricia's news. He followed Jaime's eye line as she looked past Matthew to his door, then turned back with a huge grin plastered to his face.

"Lauren?" he chuckled. "We're just friends. Besides, what does it matter if we were more than that?"

"It doesn't," she said, more defensively than she would have liked. "Fuck every eighteen-year-old in the world for all I care."

"She's not eighteen," Matthew fought back.

"Whatever," Jaime said, heading up to the stairs. "I don't want to know. Just make sure it's not in the same room as our daughter."

Matthew stood dumbfounded as Jaime walked up the stairs. She was wearing a pair of jeans that lifted her backside into a small supple roundness that made Matthew feel like grabbing her and once again becoming her husband. He shook the thought away and kept his eyes on his feet as he followed Jaime to the cockpit, staying as close to her as he could without making it awkward. Patricia and Benjamin eagerly awaited them at the monitors.

Benjamin gave Jaime a quick peck on the cheek. "Mornin', Love."

"Morning Benjamin," Jaime said through a flirty smile.

"All right," Matthew said, walking around them to get a look at what Patricia had been talking about. "What's up?"

"Check this out." Patricia stood and nearly pushed Jaime and Benjamin into the opposite table. Matthew slid down to the seat as Jaime blushed the event away and stood behind him. Neither of them saw anything.

"What am I looking at?" Jaime asked.

"Looks like a giant, underwater wasteland to me," Matthew added. He looked to Benjamin. "You stopped the boat for this?"

"You can't see it?" Patricia said. "I'm half blind and I can see it." She pushed Matthew against the window so she could sit directly in front of the monitors. "Whoops," she said. "Camera must have shifted. Hold on." She fudged with the

joystick on the compact console sitting next to one of the monitors and stopped when she reached the image of a stone surrounded by what looked like a man-made structure.

Matthew leaned in close as he saw it. From what he could tell, the four-foot wide stone sat flat, about three feet high off the ocean floor. It didn't look like any type of stone he'd ever seen before, but the camera had been fogged and was a bit fuzzy, breaking in and out every few seconds. Attached to the rock was a carved outline of what looked to Matthew to be a giant set of wings, arched at a near twenty-five-degree angle. The tips of the wings were connected to the stone at the top two corners and fell down, seemingly submerged into the ground below it. Lying across the edge of one of the wings was a sword or a staff of some sort. The head or handle sat above the stone, the blade hanging just above the ground.

"What is that?" Jaime said, mesmerized.

"Pretty cool, huh?" Benjamin grinned.

"It looks…" Matthew paused. He couldn't tell through the soft snow of the monitors, but he thought he saw several more stones forming a circle, each fixture spaced about six feet apart and angled at about a ten-degree difference than the fixture next to it. "Could it be?"

"Looks like what?" Patricia asked eagerly. "What? What is it?"

"What's up guys?" Kara said as she made her way out of the stairwell. "Any breakfast?"

"Kara, come here," Matthew said. "You need to see this."

"What?" Her demeanor became instantly more vibrant as she traced her way to Matthew. She pressed her cheek against his as she leaned in to view the monitors more carefully. "What the…?"

"Tell me you're seeing what I'm seeing," Matthew said.

"We lie our peace in the center of the crown to allow our brethren the ability of flight?" Kara turned to Matthew. Their lips almost touched.

"What?" Patricia said. "Now I'm more confused than a teenage boy with his first erection."

"This is it," Kara said, standing upright. "This *is it*."

"Someone better start explaining things around here," Patricia said, "or I'm gonna go bitchtastic on everyone."

"It's a cemetery," Matthew said, the words leaving his lips in an unnerving glow.

"A cemetery?" Patricia and Jaime both bellowed.

Matthew nodded. "The translation from one of the tablets Kara uncovered talks about a crown that gives the ability of flight. We assumed they were talking about an actual, physical crown, but this has to be it."

"What makes you think it's a cemetery?" Jaime asked, hiding her enthusiasm.

"'We lay our brethren in the center of the crown'."

"And look at the wings, symbolizing angels or flight," Kara added.

"Damn," Patricia said under her breath.

Matthew stared at the stones. He wanted to touch them, caress the texture and just be one with their prominence. "I need to get down there." Matthew leapt over the back of the seat (believing it would take too long to get past Patricia) and headed to the stairwell.

"Matthew, wait," Jaime said, nearly knocking Kara over to follow.

"You can't stop me," Matthew said.

Jaime wanted to go down there as much as Matthew, but she knew better than to jump into something like this without more evidence and exploration. "We don't even know how deep that is."

"It's only about two hundred and fifty feet," Patricia said.

Jaime turned to Patricia. Her trepidation was quite noticeable. Patricia couldn't understand why, but she figured it must have something to do with Kaleena.

"There you go," Matthew said. "Safe enough."

"Wait," Jaime said before he could get to the stairwell. "My team and I are coming with you."

"Fine. You've got a half hour."

Matthew flew downstairs as Benjamin grasped Jaime's arms in his secure hands. "You sure you want to do that, Love?"

"Yeah," Jaime said, bringing whatever fear she had under control. What did she have to be worried about? She'd done this a hundred times. "Yeah," she said again with more confidence. "I have to see this up close." She gave Benjamin a light kiss on the cheek and headed down the stairwell.

"Damn," Patricia said with a sigh. "I was hoping someone would make breakfast."

Benjamin laughed heartily. "No problem. I'm on it." He snapped his fingers and headed for the galley.

"Make me something, too," Kara called out. Benjamin gave a thumbs up and disappeared around the corner. Kara smiled and looked to Patricia. "I thought you'd be headed down with your team."

"He-ll, no," Patricia squealed. "You ain't about to squeeze my wide ass into one of those cat suits. Not a chance in hell," she added under her breath.

Kara smiled brightly and focused her attention back on her graveyard.

* * *

Trishen lay on her bed with her forearm covering her eyes. Her thoughts ran rapid as she tried to convince herself she didn't have feelings for Thomas and how she would tell him that the next time she saw him. It wasn't in her nature to fall for someone so quickly and she wasn't ready to be that close to anyone. She liked Thomas, could probably grow to love him given time and nurture, but for now, she only wanted to consider him a friend, one she could open up to — which was strange unto itself. When she was sad, she wouldn't shed a tear unless she was alone; excitement was consistently muted; and love was hidden under a mask of shyness. But somehow, Thomas had already broken some of those walls, and she was afraid he would tear down the rest. How could she have opened up to Thomas so freely? It very well could have been his friendly nature, his smile garnering a respect of admiration; it may have been the gentleness of his touch and the kindness in his laugh. Of course, none of that compared to the glow in those dark brown

eyes, which hinted at sincerity, honesty, deep regret and sympathy that continued to burn through her heart. Those eyes that never turned away except when haunted by a question Trishen never should have asked, questions that he eventually always answered without objection. But why? Could it have been her own freedom of answers that prompted his openness? Maybe the ghost of a lost love Trishen had unlocked within him? Whatever it may have been, Trishen couldn't stop thinking about their late-night conversation, the way she succumbed to his graciousness and the comforting aura that surrounded their bodies as she lay upon his chest. It was enough to make her want to hold him, kiss him, love him. But she couldn't. It went against everything she believed. Her longest relationship only lasted a few months, and she always waited at least a month for a first kiss — with one exception. She didn't love that boy (which is what he was — a child compared to her own sense of maturity at sixteen); she only kissed him because she felt obligated during a session of Seven Minutes in Heaven at a sweet sixteen party she didn't even want to go to. Her best friend received an invitation and didn't want to go alone, so Trishen agreed to accompany her, only to lose her among a gaggle of her sex-crazed peers.

Locked in the closet with the boy she knew from her American history class, Trishen fought with herself over what to do. If she did nothing but stand two inches away from him for seven minutes, she might get the reputation of being a spinster, which was fine with her; at least no one would think she was a slut. Then again, there was that small chance that if she didn't do anything, he might just spread the rumor she sucked him dry for seven minutes.

(*Yeah, like it would've taken him that long to shoot off*, she had thought.)

She decided to kiss him, lightly at first and then harder as he came forward for another. She liked it enough to allow him to slide his tongue in — for a few seconds anyway. Up until now, the only other person she had ever kissed was her mother, quick and loving. Now she experienced the kiss of a jackal, passionate and moist. His saliva ran into her throat as his hands crawled around her back, lowering every few seconds, until they neared the small of her back. Trishen pushed him away before he could get any lower.

"That's enough," she said. She licked her lips, keeping her eyes fixed on the boy of whose name had completely escaped her. It wasn't his name that mattered; it was his eyes, which lusted over her in the dim light leaking through the slits in the door that opened a minute later to the caws of flirtatious teenagers. Trishen bolted for the kitchen as a couple of white kids that looked about ready to attack each other even before getting into the closet fell in and shut the door. She grabbed the first drink she could find (a warming beer that may have been spiked with something more powerful) and guzzled it down, trying to figure out what she would do next. Should she leave the party? Should she make her closet mate understand her trepidation? He made the decision for her as he sauntered up to her with those same lustful eyes that only wanted one thing — a gift she would never be able to give him. It was this that was missing from Thomas. No lust; no deep-rooted sexual desire; just an admiration for a young woman who showed an interest in his thoughts.

Trishen's muscles tightened and her heart raced when someone knocked at the door. Should she answer? She didn't want to ignore Jaime or Patricia, but if it was Thomas, what would she do? Tell him to go away?

Fortunately, Jaime's voice rang on the other side of the door. "Trishen?"

Trishen calmed and sat up. "Yeah?" She said dryly.

Jaime opened the door and got straight to the point. "Get the gear ready. We're heading down in a half hour."

"Okay," Trishen nodded without asking any questions. It didn't really matter why; she loved diving, and any chance to do it was one she was prepared for. Her anticipation grew heightened as she pulled two large cases from under the beds. Inside were two oxygen tanks a piece, placed side-by-side, bottom to top. Each one had a regulator and hose attached to them. A mask sat at the foot of each one. Thomas fell to the back of her mind as her focus was placed directly on the safety of those she would be taking down with her. She pulled one of the tanks from the case and checked the pressure levels and connections to the hoses. Trishen prided herself on being overly cautious. After all, every time she took someone diving, their life was in her hands. To this day she has never lost anyone, though she came close once. Taking some bored housewife on her first dive, the connection to the pour soul's oxygen mask loosened and started spitting out into the water. They had only dived some fifty feet, though, and the woman had enough air to be escorted back to the surface without any harm. She was frightened (who wouldn't be) and refused to try again with a different tank. Trishen would never force the matter; she had built her career around "safety first, fun second." Today would be no exception.

*   *   *

Gavin was dozing above the covers when Jaime entered the room. He had put a pair of shorts and a t-shirt on and by the looks of it, had sat down to put on his shoes when he decided to rest his eyes. Jaime slapped him on the top of the head.

"Get up, Gavin."

He shot up. "What the hell?" Jaime stood over him like a British sentry. "Oh," he said solemnly as he rubbed his eyes. "What's up?"

"Get your wetsuit on." Jaime turned to her bag and pulled out a black wet suit with yellow stripes down the sides.

"I just got dressed," Gavin moaned.

"Too bad. Matthew thinks we may have found something and I want to get footage of it."

"What did you find?" Gavin asked as Jaime headed for the bathroom. When she didn't answer, he repeated, "Jaime? What did you find?"

Jaime flashed him a smile, raised her eyebrows and winked before closing the door.

"Great," he whispered to himself. "What's that supposed to mean?" He pulled his bag from under the bed and yanked out his matching wetsuit. He set it to the side and pulled out a black canvas camera bag that held the waterproof gear he used every time he needed to film underwater by hand. The cameras set up on the

sides of the boat were good for scanning — much like a security camera installed in any low-rent liquor store — but occasionally he needed to get up close and personal. Gavin didn't mind; he loved getting the chance to film underwater. He just wished he'd gotten more sleep. What would happen if he nodded off down there? Then again, if this supposed find was as exciting as Jaime made it out to be (she only acted this way when she was super excited), then Gavin was sure sleep would be the furthest thing from his mind.

*   *   *

There wasn't anyone in the room when Kaleena woke up. She was happy about that, especially her dad, who had seemingly given her the silent treatment after running from Jaime. He sat on the bed in some type of deep trance, most likely going over his conversation with Jaime, wondering if he'd made a mistake in allowing Kaleena to ask her to come on this trip. Her muscles tightened as he turned to her. It took all her strength to make eye contact, her arms crossed tightly against her chest as if she had just walked into a freezer. Though for a moment it looked like he might say something, he never did. Kaleena strode into the bathroom. It wasn't as if she was in the mood to talk, but she had thought he might at least try and explain what her mother meant. She sat against the door and wrapped her arms around her legs. She didn't cry; she didn't have an urge to cry. She just needed time to figure out what she wanted to do — what she needed to do — to talk to her mother; to return to a time when they had a special bond full of playful love. Where had it gone? Would she ever be able to get it back? When she couldn't take the conflict of her thoughts any longer, she brushed her teeth and freed her tampon. It was dripping with blood and fluid. Kaleena coughed her nausea away and tossed the tampon in the toilet. The water quickly became a soft pink, growing to a dark red before she flushed it all down the drain. Blood continued to drip down the inside of her leg, so she inserted another tampon, wondering if it would ever stop. After pulling on her boxer

shorts, she stepped back out into the cabin. Lauren sat on the bed across from Matthew. They both looked at her like she was a disease.

"I was telling your dad about our little talk," Lauren said.

Kaleena shot her a near sickening look, which to Lauren felt angry, as if Kaleena was disappointed in her.

"I'm sorry… was that supposed to be between us?"

Another look, this one screaming, "No shit, Sherlock." Her eyebrows were raised and the corners of her mouth curled with a sneer.

"I'm sorry, Kaleena."

Kaleena hoisted herself up to her bed and turned her back on Lauren, holding the covers tight against her shoulders. "Damn it," she heard Lauren whisper. "I'm so sorry, I didn't know."

"Don't worry," Matthew whispered back. "Let's just get some sleep."

Lauren got up and went to the bathroom as Matthew laid down on the bed. Kaleena didn't hear Lauren come back into the room, but saw her sleeping silently in her bed when she got up three hours later to go to the bathroom. There was something about Lauren, her stomach in particular, that looked different in the soft glow of the moonlight. It looked as if it was shining, much like a glow-in-the-dark toy. After landing softly on the floor (and checking to make sure she didn't wake Matthew), Kaleena knelt down next to Lauren to get a better look. She held her hand just above Lauren's navel. It emanated a warmth that tickled her palm. The longer she held it there, the more the sensation consumed her body, causing her to feel like a child stealing her first kiss from the boy next door under the kitchen table, or a teenager holding hands with the boy of her dreams for the first time on the walk home from school. As it made her legs and toes nearly fall asleep, she gazed at the same soft glow highlighting Lauren's lips and eyelids. There was a calm about her that soothed Kaleena's mind and gave her something she had never expected — hope.

Kaleena used that feeling to draw circles on Lauren's stomach with the tip of her forefinger, a painting of what she imagined this child becoming: the world's

foremost thinker of science and technology; the first astronaut to colonize Mars and start a brand new civilization of peace and harmony; the president of the United States, ushering in a change that would lead to the growth of the spirit and the end of civil and global strife. The love Kaleena sensed through Lauren's skin was just the beginning. When the baby kicked, Lauren shifted a little in her sleep but didn't wake up. Kaleena absorbed the bright smile on Lauren's lips as if she could feel her connection in her dreams, and then went to the bathroom. She replaced her tampon, mixed the red toilet water with bloody urine and went back to bed. The process was repeated four hours later, and Kaleena had a feeling this wouldn't be the last time. Fear that she may die if it never ended crept into her mind as she sat alone in her room, the intense sunlight crushing her eyes. She tried to coax the pain away to no avail. It just felt like her brain was about ready to pop her skull at any minute. Sliding off the bed, she had to lower her body when one of her legs nearly gave out. They both felt extremely brittle as she walked to the bathroom. Her skin had become pale, accenting her darkening pink lips.

God damn, I'm dying.

What could she do, though? Going to the hospital was the most logical course of action, but would Matthew turn this boat around for her? Not likely, not without absolute proof she wasn't just faking the whole thing in order to end the trip before it had a chance to start. Her responses to Jaime would no doubt convince him it was all psychological, fear of facing her mother after the perfect image she had built up had been tarnished. But after pulling another blood-red tampon from her body, she knew she wasn't going to be able to piss much more blood before her heart decided to stop trying to replace it and cease functioning altogether. The Bermuda Triangle wasn't going anywhere; Matthew had to believe her life was more important than a flight of fancy. And even if he didn't, it seemed to her, in a logical and maternal sense, that the way to convince her father to abort the mission would be through her mother. Jaime would see the truth and force Matthew to do the right thing. Kaleena still wasn't sure she was ready to talk to her, but it might just be her only option if things didn't turn around.

After finishing up in the bathroom, Kaleena felt fatigued as she got dressed. She hardly exerted herself, but she still felt winded and had to sit to catch her breath. Then she shivered, her veins filling with ice. She wrapped a blanket around her shoulders and left the cabin. Walking to the opposite side of the salon was draining. She took a moment to relax before knocking on one of the doors. "Mom?" When no answer came back, she turned to the other and did the same. Again, no response. Kaleena quickly assumed everyone had adjourned on deck, possibly for breakfast, which she wasn't hungry for at all. Her stomach felt like a twisted mash of rubber bands. Each step she took up the stairs was cautious, hoping the ascent wouldn't cause her to pass out. She smelled a hint of eggs and bacon, which tightened her stomach to the point she had to stop or else vomit all over the stairwell. When the tightness subsided, she finished climbing the stairs. No one was in the galley or the cockpit. *What the hell? What did they do? Abandon ship?*

That's when she saw them all gathered on the port side of the *Endeavor*. The young black woman (*Trish*, she thought, but couldn't be sure) stood by the rail, going over the details of how to use and manage the weight belts and air tanks each diver wore. The muscular tone of her body showed through her wetsuit, as did the weight gain on Matthew, who stood to the right of whom she assumed to be Jaime's editor friend. He was toying around with a video camera, seemingly ignoring everything Trishen was saying, though Kaleena assumed the speech was more for Matthew than anyone else. All of the divers wore vented hoods, so she couldn't tell who the fourth person in the group was, but after further deduction of who wasn't wearing a suit, it had to be Jaime. Kaleena trudged her way to the edge of the cockpit as fast as she could, Trishen's voice growing louder with each step.

"If your tank should accidentally run out of air, do *not* panic," Trishen was saying. "Signal your partner by tapping your mouthpiece. Your partner will then share their mouthpiece with you. Take two breaths and then allow your partner to do the same. Continue this until you are both able to reach the surface."

"We all know this," Matthew said eagerly.

"Matthew," Jaime said harshly.

"I do not allow anyone to dive without first going through safety procedures," Trishen said. "Not even professionals."

"Can we just hurry up?"

"Those stones aren't going anywhere," Thomas chimed in. "Let her do her thing." Matthew glared at him with what could have been contempt, but possibly just anxious anger.

Trishen blushed. "Thank you." She sheepishly let slip a smile and then got back to business. "Now, I don't normally do this, but we'll be diving deeper than a hundred and thirty feet, which could cause nitrogen narcosis to set in. If you see anyone begin to act irrationally or start doing anything foolish, tell me immediately and start heading back for the surface. I will not have anyone killing themselves down there."

"Killing themselves?" Kaleena asked through a slight cough. Everyone finally acknowledged her presence.

"You okay?" Patricia was the first to ask. Kaleena nodded, though her eyes were heavy and worn.

"Don't worry," Trishen said. "The condition is rare, but it does happen."

Kaleena coughed again.

"Are you sure you're okay?" Jaime asked. It was the first time she felt like a mother in a long time. Kaleena felt her insincerity.

"I'll be fine," Kaleena said. "Just go do whatever it is you need to do."

Jaime was tempted to tell her she wouldn't go, but didn't want to push her too fast. There were a lot of people here that could keep an eye on her while she was down there. Kaleena would be okay.

Matthew saw real concern in Jaime's eyes, but she didn't allow him in for long, opting to throw her mask on and step up to the rail rather than deal with him. Trishen grabbed her arm before she could jump into the water.

"Remember," she said. "Stay with your partner at all times and do not stray from the group. I will be monitoring our decompression rates and n-two levels the entire time. Everyone will also be able to hear Patricia through their earpieces, so if either of us see anything out of the ordinary, I am ending the dive. If I tell you to rise, you will listen."

Jaime nodded, placed the regulator in her mouth and jumped in. Gavin followed suit, tucking the camera into his stomach before diving in after her to avoid stray impact with the water. Matthew hesitated. The last time Kaleena was in a state like this, he made the mistake of believing she would be okay, be strong enough to fight her own fall. But she hadn't, and that regret still lingered to this day. She now seemed to need him more than she had in a long time. His priorities were torn between her and the artifacts below him. She was older than before, though — stronger, more independent. And he wouldn't be long; several minutes, tops. He would be there for her when he got back. He nodded to try and comfort her, then got his gear ready and fell in, hitting the water with a thud rather than a natural splash.

"Is my camera on," Trishen asked Patricia, who skirted around the corner to look at the monitors. Kaleena noticed a small pocket on the right side of Trishen's mask that held a small micro-camera. Patricia gave a thumbs up when she saw Thomas, Lauren and Kara looking odd on the monitor farthest to the left. Trishen flashed her thumb back and prepped her gear, which included flashing the light she held in her hand on and off to make sure it was functioning properly.

"Good luck," Thomas said with a wink. Trishen simply jumped overboard. Thomas wasn't sure how to take that. It was likely she hadn't even heard him, so he didn't strain over it. If she had heard him, she apparently still needed some space to sort through whatever she needed to sort through.

Kaleena sat down across the aisle from the monitors and lowered her head to the table. She pulled the blanket tight around her, shaking off a slice of chills that breezed through her chest and head.

Benjamin and Thomas placed the rail back into position as Kara and Lauren joined Patricia to watch the divers. Lauren glanced over at Kaleena and could tell she was upset. About what, she wasn't sure. She didn't want to try and act like her mother (even though from what she's seen, Jaime wasn't doing a very good job in the position), but maybe Kaleena would accept a friend. So she sat down across

the aisle and placed her head on the child's knee.

"Can I help?" she asked.

Though she liked Lauren, and wished she could tell her everything, what Kaleena needed to say was something she could only say to her parents. "Not this time," she moaned. "But thank you."

Lauren removed her hand but kept her eyes on the pale face of a once vibrant young woman. She hoped one day her own child wouldn't feel the same way toward her. The thought of a child keeping secrets from their parents nearly pushed her to tears. "All right," she finally said. "But I'm here for you, Kaleena."

"I know. And I would tell you if it wasn't so personal."

"I understand."

"You want to watch your parents?" Patricia said from out of nowhere.

Kaleena pushed her lips into a quiet smile. She took one last glance at Lauren, then stepped across the aisle to sit down next to Patricia. Thomas and Benjamin had joined Kara to stand behind Patricia. They all saw Jaime and Gavin swimming alongside each other toward a circle of stones. Kaleena leaned in closer to get a better look.

"What is that?" she asked.

"We think it might be some sort of cemetery," Kara answered.

Kaleena turned to her. "A cemetery?"

Kara nodded with a bright spirit in her eyes.

"Why would a cemetery be built in the middle of the ocean?"

No one answered. Kaleena felt the heavy apprehensiveness and knew what they were all thinking. "You think this is a cemetery from Atlantis?" The silence was again overwhelming. Kaleena looked directly at Kara, who nodded softly. "You have got to be kidding me," she mumbled under her breath, turning back to the monitors.

"I know what you must think, Kaleena," Kara said. "But open your mind. You wrote in your book that there was no way an entire city, or country, could have been buried by the sea."

"Right," Kaleena said. "Because a civilization as advanced as Plato and Cayce pictured wouldn't have been able to grow between when the ice age ended and the current topography of the land."

"I agreed with that at first. But what I found to be missing was the idea, or possibility, that Atlantis and all of its people, lived *during* the last ice age."

"During?" Kaleena repeated.

"I have evidence of an artifact from our last dig in Bermuda that has a carbon-dating of over two and a half million years. And as you probably already know, an ice age only covers the northern and southern poles with ice. This region of the planet would not have been affected."

"Except with lower sea levels." Kaleena was beginning to understand.

"If the stories are correct," Kara continued, "and the people of Atlantis did destroy themselves, then when the ice age ended twenty-two thousand years ago, there's a possibility it would have covered the city without anyone ever knowing it existed."

"Okay, let's say you're right and Atlanteans lived during the ice age. How do you explain the supposed vast mountains Plato claimed surrounded the city? There's no evidence that any mountains ever existed in these waters, and even if it were true, that would mean the tallest peak was less than three hundred feet. Not a very massive mountain range if you ask me."

"Actually," Patricia interjected, "that might explain the massive difference in topography."

"How so?" Kaleena and Kara asked simultaneously.

"The floor of the Atlantic is very chaotic, with both low level land masses like the one we're looking at, and extremely deep trenches. If there was a mountain range out here, that might explain why those trenches even exist."

"But it doesn't explain the low-level height of the mountains," Kaleena countered.

"Sure it does. It just means Atlantis sat on a plateau at a higher elevation than the base of the mountains."

Kaleena fell silent. Everything she had written was being unraveled. But it felt good to debate. She never got this type of cerebral back and forth in school. "But what about the remnants? If Atlantis did destroy itself, there would be clear evidence of that destruction. Some sort of radiation or chemical debris. From my knowledge, nothing like that exists."

"Well, some scientists have claimed there's evidence of wormholes or time displacement riffs within certain parts of the ocean," Patricia said.

"Really?" Kaleena said, skeptical.

"Yup. That's why no one ever finds shipwrecks or pieces of planes that crash in these parts of the Atlantic. I don't really believe it myself, but the theory is out there. And it's pretty popular."

"I did not know that." Kaleena felt rather stupid. She apparently hadn't done enough research on the Atlantic Ocean before analyzing why Atlantis was a myth. Could she have been wrong on other things as well? For the first time, doubts against her research were heightened. The lack of knowledge could be attributed to her rather young age and inexperience, but she needed to trust what she had written. It was all she had. "Your arguments are sound," she said. "But I still have my doubts."

"Doubts?" Patricia said. "You don't believe Atlantis exists?"

"You didn't know that?"

"Well, what the hell's high heaven are you doing out here, then?"

Kaleena looked at the monitors without a word and watched Gavin swim over the top of Jaime, giving her stomach a playful squeeze before sliding to the opposite side. Jaime then turned to the camera as if she had sensed Kaleena watching. "Are they safe down there?" she mumbled as the divers arrived at the stone structure Kaleena refused to call a cemetery.

Patricia saw the sadness radiating within Kaleena's features. "They'll be fine," she said. "Trish knows what she's doing. And as far as I can tell, there aren't any fissures that could spit out any methane gas."

"Methane gas?"

"Yeah, you know… small bursts of methane gas that some scientists have attributed to missing ships."

Kaleena didn't ask anything more. She was a little angry Matthew hadn't gone over any of this before leaving the dock, but she knew him well enough to know he wouldn't put himself in a dangerous position; at least she hoped. The team circled the structure as Gavin filmed from a bit of a distance. At one point, Jaime posed with one of the stones. In some ways, Kaleena felt she should be down there with them. It looked like a lot of fun. Suddenly, a flash of light flickered on the screen and disappeared.

"What was that?" Kaleena said with more life than she had been able to exhibit all morning.

"What?" Patricia's eyes jostled around the monitors trying to locate something. "What did you see?"

"I don't know. I thought I saw some kind of light move through the water. Must have been the sun or something playing tricks. I don't see it anymore."

Patricia nodded, her eyes glued to the monitors. If Kaleena did see something, she was going to make sure she didn't miss it if it happened again.

*   *   *

Side-by-side Trishen, Matthew watched Jaime and Gavin swim together to the ocean floor. Jaime had accused him of sleeping with Lauren and he now saw a faint connection between these two *friends* as Gavin gave her a loving squeeze when he passed over the top of her to swim to the other side of the stone cemetery. Jaime was a very personable woman, caring and open — someone for whom anyone would feel comfortable around. She made friends with anyone as long as they didn't betray her or make her feel trapped. Gavin, as far as Matthew could tell, allowed Jaime to control him, but if that was how he wanted it, who was Matthew to say anything. It was quite hypocritical of Jaime, though, to be jealous of Lauren if she were in fact more than just friends with Gavin.

As Gavin paddled off to the side, Jaime waved her hand, signaling for Trishen and Matthew to head around to the opposite side. Trishen waved back and then urged Matthew to join her. He did as she requested, happy to swim alongside these man-made tombstones — which were absolutely beautiful up close. The center stone had to be at least six feet high, looming over the rest of the fixtures that sat about half its size. The delicate features of the woman's face at the head of the statue held his gaze. Her eyes felt alive, as if she were watching him swim up to it. She was lovely and something to be admired; and dreaded. He removed one of his gloves so he could feel the texture of her cheek. Based on the amount of time these statues had to have been buried under the water, Matthew had expected to find signs of decay or erosion. But the stone was completely smooth, free of any nicks or bruises.

Matthew's observation ended when Trishen ran her hand across his back. She pointed at the statue. He nodded and pulled a pick from the pack he wore around his waist. Not wanting to do any harm to the perfection in front of him, Matthew curled around to the wings on the statue's back. He hammered one of the edges of the feathers, but nothing broke as he chipped away at it. The more he tried, the more dented the pick became until the edge was nothing more than a small stub. Astounded, he replaced the pick in his pack and carefully studied the flow of each curve, as well as the quality and precision of what had been done as he glided down the side of wings. He believed the statue couldn't have taken more than a year to construct — that is if the builders worked sixteen-hour days, ate one meal and slept less than five hours. Of course, that was based on how something similar would have been built with modern tools, not necessarily with tools that a technologically advanced race might have used. Matthew imagined hand held or computerized lasers (much like ones used in eye surgery) cutting the stone with pinpoint accuracy. As he reached the angel's feet, he looked up at his team. Though Trishen was curiously examining one of the fixtures, Jaime was posing for Gavin next to one of the stones. He shook his head in disbelief. They no doubt didn't understand the importance of this cemetery, not like he did. As

Gavin inched in for a closer shot, Matthew swam to the closest tombstone and saw what might be text inscribed upon it, much like a regular tombstone would. He waved Trishen over. She complied quickly, possibly thinking something was wrong with his oxygen tank or regulator. When she arrived, slightly wide-eyed, Matthew stole the flashlight and pointed it at the stone. He could now clearly see several lines of symbols that matched those written on the tablets he and Kara had translated. He swam to the next statue and found the same, though some of the symbols at the end of the inscription had changed. He turned to Trishen and pointed to Gavin. As she went to retrieve him, Matthew studied the text, trying hard to translate it without any success. He didn't like it, but without Kara, he wouldn't be able to understand any of it. When Gavin reached Matthew (with Jaime in tow behind him), he saw the symbols sparkling under the light and knew exactly what Matthew was after. He focused the camera on the stone and let it film for several seconds before moving to the next. Upon reaching the fifth stone in the circle, Trishen and Jaime decided to have a look at the center of the ring. Trishen picked up some soil samples from what looked like a darker patch of sand and Jaime simply took in the magnitude of all the stones. When she caught sight of the center statue, she suddenly felt she was being judged.

*　　*　　*

"There," Kaleena chirped, pointing at the monitor. "Did you see it?"

"I think it might have just been the flashlight reflecting off the camera lens," Kara said.

"No, it wasn't. Trishen had the flashlight the first time. This is something else."

"What do you think it was?" Lauren asked. She had joined Kara and Thomas behind Patricia.

Kara was adamant. "I'm telling you, it looks like a lens flare."

"And I'm telling you," Kaleena said forcefully, "it looked like it was swimming."

"I agree with the kid," Patricia said. "It didn't look like a normal lens flare."

They all kept their eyes on the monitor as Trishen moved to the center of the stones and collected some sand into a small vile.

"Oh my god," Kara said under her breath.

"What?"

"I think I saw it. Tell Trish to look straight at the stones ahead of her and slowly turn her head."

Patricia switched on a small microphone attached to one of the computers.

"Trishen? Can you hear me?"

The camera moved up and down. Jaime came into view.

"Jaime, swim behind Trish. I need you out of view of the camera so Trish can scan the stones."

Jaime obeyed. Once out of view, Trishen scanned the stones quicker than Patricia wanted.

"Slow down, Trish. Scan them as slowly as you can." Trishen did as she was asked. Everyone watched stone-faced.

"What's the hullabaloo?" Benjamin said, returning from a much needed bathroom break. No one paid him any attention.

The connection to the camera cut off.

"Wait," Kaleena said, frantic. "What happened?"

"Trishen," Patricia yelled into the microphone. "Emergency. I lost video. Repeat — I have lost visual. Get your bony ass back up here ASAP."

"What's going on?" Kaleena yelled.

"How the hell should I know?"

"Well can they hear you?"

Patricia didn't know how to answer her.

*   *   *

Matthew barely made out Patricia's voice through all of the static and interference blistering his earpiece. Gavin must have been having trouble too, as he tapped his ear and shrugged. He turned off the camera when Trishen gestured for everyone to rise. Before he could start swimming, Matthew tugged at his arm and pointed at the remaining stones. Gavin shook his head and motioned to Trishen, who had already started up with Jaime. He kicked his feet, but Matthew wasn't about to let go of this. Jaime, clearly angry with Matthew's stubbornness, swam to them and pushed him aside. She grabbed Gavin's hand and swam with him for a few yards before he was yanked away with tremendous energy. He landed with impressive force in the center of the stone ring, spitting out a cloud of sand around him. Jaime's anger fumed until she saw Matthew swimming upward about ten feet away. It wasn't him. Relief didn't last long when the sand cloud dissipated enough to notice Gavin wasn't moving. She swam back toward him, but didn't get very far. A tight compression against her chest kept her from moving forward. It was only when she moved away from Gavin that she could breathe again. As she pressed her hand against her chest to figure out what had happened, a light flashed through the water toward Gavin. It reached him at lightning speed. As it frantically circled him, Jaime thought she saw the shape of a human living inside of it.

Matthew had made his way back to Gavin and was only a few meters away when the light shot past him. Matthew was stunned breathless. It wasn't until he saw his oxygen tank surrounding him with a flurry of bubbles that he understood why. The cold ocean chilled his lips as he pulled the regulator from his mouth and waved for Jaime to help. She didn't have to, as Trishen appeared almost out of nowhere to supply Matthew with her regulator. He sucked in a refreshing gulp of oxygen and then took a few more breaths before Trishen pulled the mouthpiece away. She tucked her hand under his armpit and kicked away from the ground. Matthew stripped his arm away and gestured for her to wait and swam to Gavin. The closer he got, the more his lungs contracted. When he reached him, he grabbed the camera. That was Jaime's cue to start back down. Her lungs tightened again, but nowhere near as bad as before. Matthew met her a few feet from the ground and rested his hand on the side of her face. The moment was kind and compassionate.

Jaime covered his hand with hers and then let him flutter his way alongside Trishen to share her air as they rose for the surface.

Jaime watched them a moment before turning back to Gavin, only to watch him rise off the ground. For a moment, she thought he may be convulsing. There was no more time to waste. She tried to pull him away, but he was glued to the ocean. She curled underneath him to see if he was being held by something.

Nothing.

Rising to his side, Jaime nearly lost her regulator as she let rip a muffled scream. Glaring at her from the other side were two bright white circles in the shape of eyes floating in the middle of the water. Jaime saw the faintest outline of what she could only assume was a head as they shifted up and down. Something tightened around her neck and she was pulled forward within inches of the circles. Staring into them turned her body to ice. Something was searching her mind and body. Jaime wanted to push away from it — anything to just be somewhere else — but the more she moved, the deader she felt. Soon, the pressure around her neck shifted to her head, forcing her to look at Gavin. His eyes were open wide with unmitigated fear. A reflected shape of a hand removed his regulator and then caressed his cheek, soothing his anxiety. Tears fogged Jaime's mask as the hand slid down into Gavin's throat, flooding his body with what Jaime could only imagine were gallons of water. His eyes slowly lost the vibrancy of life. By now, all Jaime could see was a fuzzy gray nothing, but she sensed Gavin's dead stare. When she went to place her hand on his cheek in a concerted effort to revive him, she was thrust upwards as if she had been shot from a cannon. The pressure stung her back with pin needles. She hardly felt it though, as the thought of Gavin lying dead among the silent sea below overwhelmed her senses.

Matthew and Trishen stopped to watch Jaime fly past them. Trishen had never seen someone move that fast through the water. She prayed Jaime's body could handle the force. Once she disappeared into the dark abyss, Trishen saw two small circles turn and flash toward her. She couldn't be sure what they were, but once they reached her, Matthew was pulled away. She caught his arm, and though the

power of this invisible creature was more than Trishen thought she could handle, she wasn't about to let him go.

Not without dying with him.

*   *   *

Jaime's body landed with a hard crack on the deck of the *Endeavor*. It smashed into the cockpit wall, just behind Thomas, Kara and Benjamin, who was ripping off her gear before he even got to her. Kaleena moved a few feet away to see who it was. Lauren stood behind her, lightly grasping her arms.

"What happened down there?" Benjamin roared as he pulled off Jaime's hood. Her wet hair fell around her shoulders.

Jaime was unflinching, staring out to sea with haunted eyes.

"Jaime?" he said sterner than before. He lightly tapped her cheek to get her attention. It didn't work; there simply wasn't any recognition.

"What the hell?" Patricia said as the monitor flashed on again. Thomas and Kara turned to see Matthew fighting to get something off his leg. Trishen held his arm, but was struggling to sustain her grip.

"Fuck this," Thomas said, pulling off his shirt. He ran to the back of the *Endeavor* while pulling off his shoes.

"No, Thomas," Kara screamed. "What are you doing?"

"They need help," Thomas climbed onto the rail.

"Wait." Kara ran to him and gave him a swift kiss on the cheek. "Good Luck."

Thomas dove into the water without much of any acknowledgment. He kicked as hard as he could until he saw Trishen, then kicked even harder. When he reached her, he wrapped his arms around her waist. Attempting to swim upward was futile. Whatever was pulling at them was unyielding. He swam around to face Trishen and tapped on her regulator before removing it and sucking in a few breaths. After replacing it in her mouth, Thomas grabbed a hold of Matthew's waist. The circles lit up brightly, reducing his muscle mass to liquid mush. His body felt as if

— 240 —

it was about to be ripped apart when a screaming roar blasted through the water.

The eyes disappeared.

Matthew's body was light as ever. Trishen quickly pulled him upward and supplied him the regulator. Thomas let go and looked down into the depths of the ocean. Mesmerized was too weak a word to describe what he felt. Trishen snapped him from his trance as she gave him the regulator. Both men then followed her back to the surface. The fresh air couldn't have been more invigorating.

Benjamin threw out a lifesaver as everyone except Kaleena gathered around the side of the *Endeavor* to help the three of them up onto the boat. Matthew ripped his mask off and coughed up some water the instant his knees hit the deck.

"You okay, mate?"

Matthew caught his breath and leaned against the rail. Thomas helped Patricia pull Trishen onto the deck. He then climbed himself up, receiving a great big hug from Kara as he did.

"Are you okay?" Thomas asked Trishen, who leaned up against the cockpit window. She nodded but couldn't seem to catch her breath enough to speak. "What was that?" All Trishen could do was shake her head in confused anguish.

"Get us out of here, Benjamin," Matthew finally spit out.

"Wait," Patricia said. "Where's Gavin?"

"He's dead," Matthew said, staring at Benjamin with purpose. "Get us out of here."

"You got it, mate." Benjamin ran through the cockpit.

"No," Jaime mumbled softly as Benjamin climbed the stairs to the wheelhouse. He was prepping the engines when Jaime yelled, "No!"

He peered down to watch her pick up her mask and stumble for the back of the yacht.

"What are you doing, Love?" Benjamin called down.

Jaime turned to him. "Don't you dare move this fucking boat," she screamed. She threw her mask on as Matthew found strength in his legs.

"Jaime, where are you going?" he said.

"We can't leave him."

"It's too dangerous."

"The shit it's dangerous. I need to save him." Jaime bit her regulator and climbed onto the rail. Matthew didn't hesitate to pull her down.

"Get the fuck off me, asshole!"

Matthew fought to hold onto her as she screamed and violently thrust her body. "I can't let you go back. If he's still down there, Jaime, he's gone."

"No. He's not dead. I can save him."

"Listen to yourself," Matthew said, letting go of her. "What do you expect to find?"

"We do not leave our people behind, Matthew. Ever."

"You want to get yourself killed?" Matthew looked up to Benjamin. "Go."

"Don't you touch a fucking thing." Jaime grabbed the rail, but Matthew kept her from climbing up. "I said get the fuck out of my way, you inconsiderate prick. You left him down there — *you* did this." Jaime belted Matthew in the jaw with a right hook, sending him to the deck. "You fucking killed him," she screamed.

"What the hell?" Thomas yelled.

"Don't," Jaime said with a crazed glow in her eyes. "Just… don't."

Matthew sat up, caressing his jaw. He opened his mouth to say something, but wasn't sure if he should. But it was time. "You know what, Jaime. I've tried. I've tried to put our past where it belongs. For Kaleena. But apparently you just haven't been able to get over your own self-centered immaturity. So go ahead. Go back down there to your boyfriend and get yourself killed. We don't need you anymore anyway."

Jaime was stunned. The only thing she could think to say was, "He's not my boyfriend," in a very loud voice.

"Could have fooled me, you chain-smoking drunk."

"Fuck you."

"Shut up," Kaleena finally screamed. "Just shut up. Both of you." Her eyes burned with a fire neither Matthew or Jaime had ever seen before.

"You two are acting like a couple of jackasses. I mean, seriously. What happened to you two? You both used to love each other more than anything. Where did that go? You know, mom, I asked you to come on this trip because I thought I would be able to forgive you. But you fucked that up the second you slept with your old boyfriend. Honestly, I was scared you had changed from the mother I remembered. And now I know you have. You've forgotten everything we went through, everything we were as a family, and I can't bear to be around you knowing who you really are. I wanted to believe in you; believe you had changed, but it's clear to me now that it's impossible for you to stop acting like a fucking teenager with a tree up your ass."

"Kaleena," Jaime said, trying to calm her daughter down.

"No, mom." Tears streamed down her eyes, her words slowing. "It's too late. Dad's right. You just aren't the person I remember and you probably never will be again. I'm sorry, but I can't..." Kaleena held her head. She stumbled and grabbed a hold of the table. "I can't keep..." Her breaths became erratic and her eyes rolled to the back of her head. She fell to the ground like a marionette being clipped from its strings and hit her head on the deck with a hard *thud*.

"Kaleena!" Matthew yelled. He clambered to his feet, collecting her in his arms as he slid in next to her. "Kaleena."

Jaime took a step forward but froze, unable to get close while Matthew held onto her. Guilt ran cold through her veins as Matthew pushed Kaleena's moistening hair from her face to check her forehead for a rising temperature.

"Is she okay?" Kara asked.

"She's burning up," Matthew said, checking the back of her head for any signs of blood. Thank god there wasn't any. "Kaleena," he said again, praying she'd respond.

Suddenly, a low grunt came from the edge of the deck. "Oh, shit."

Lauren clutched her stomach and nearly fell over as her legs became like Jell-O. The veins in her right hand glowed a rich purple as she grasped the rail of the *Endeavor*. She tried to suck in a breath through clenched teeth, ("Shit, shit") but the pain was too much to do anything but slide her butt to the deck.

Kara ran to her. "Lauren, what's wrong?"

Another grunt. "Oh, I think I'm in labor." She moaned and took in several quick breaths, wishing the pain would go away.

"What can I do?" Kara asked frantically. "Do you have any breathing techniques or Lamaze or something?"

"I've only been pregnant a week, damn it." Another slice of pain tightened her body.

A deep sorrow filled Matthew's eyes as he kissed Kaleena softly on the forehead. Jaime watched him for a moment longer before another hollow scream from Lauren forced her to head to the forward deck. She slipped the tank off her back, grabbed a hold of the rail and opened her mouth wide in a desperate need to let everything go — to find relief that would end the madness. Saliva dripped from her teeth as she waited for air to fill her lungs. When it finally came, she fell to her knees and laid her chest onto them. She wanted to cry, but her eyes were as dry as stone and unwilling to blink. All she could do was lay her head against the rail.

"Benjamin," Matthew yelled. "We need to get to a hospital. NOW!"

"I'm on it, mate." Benjamin grabbed his radio and spun through stations to find one that wasn't complete static. With every turn of the knob, he pressed the communication button and called out, "Mayday, mayday. This is the *Endeavor*. We have a medical emergency. Please respond." Static would resume and he'd try the next channel, all the while attempting to get the *Endeavor*'s engine to turn over.

Nothing but silence and a few — *click click*'s.

"Damn it all," Benjamin yelled after the eighth attempt at both the radio and the engine. He threw the receiver against the console and stormed back down to the cockpit.

"What's going on?" Matthew screamed as Benjamin raced toward him.

"Something's wrong with the engines and I can't get anyone on the radio." He stopped next to Patricia. "I need you to continue to try for medical help while I scurry down to the engine room. Can you do that?"

"Of course," Patricia said, her eyes wide. "Yeah, I've got your back."

Benjamin turned to Lauren, who was taking slow, deep breaths. Depending on how long it took for the next contraction would give him an estimate on how much time he'd have to get this bucket moving or get help. A seething breath and a slow squeal told him he'd better hurry.

He brushed past Patricia and stopped at the back of the forward deck. Jaime looked awash with a haunted nothingness. He wanted to comfort her, but Lauren's screams reminded him he had a more pressing urgency. His sweet Love was going to have to figure things out on her own. Without wasting another second, Benjamin headed down into his cabin to gain access to the engine room.

On the stern, Kara lifted Lauren to her feet as the latest contraction dissipated. She walked her to the cockpit, where Matthew was carefully scooping Kaleena into his arms. He walked as fast as he could to the stairwell, Kara and Lauren following behind. It wasn't long before they all swiftly disappeared into the belly of the *Endeavor*.

Trishen remained stunned. The world seemed to have come to a complete stop, a sickness spinning her vision into a whirlwind. Her heart pumped with the speed of a racecar as Thomas lay his hand on her shoulder. He removed it quickly in reaction to the hysterical jump of fright that followed.

"I'm sorry," he said. "Are you okay?"

It seemed at first she didn't know who he was; then she cried, shoving her face into his chest. Thomas was hesitant, but slowly massaged her back and combed his fingers through her wet hair. He didn't say a word. Not that he didn't want to; he just felt the moment called for silence. For the first time in the last ten minutes, Thomas felt at peace and just wanted the hum of the ocean to calm Trishen's vibrating nerves. He was completely unaware that Patricia was watching them.

"This calls for a drink," she said and rushed to the bar to help herself to a gin and tonic before heading upstairs in the hopes of hailing someone —

I'd settle for a damn pirate —

on the radio. *Not fucking likely*, she thought as she sat down in the captain's chair. *Not fucking likely*.

The *Endeavor* – Sunday, Late Evening

"Don't do this to me again."

Matthew sat in his cabin, his elbows relaxed on the tips of his knees. His eyes were puffy and streaked with dark red highlights as he stared at his daughter lying deathly still on the bed across from him. The smallest of breaths pushed Kaleena's chest up and down every few seconds, letting Matthew know that she was, in fact, still alive.

"Not now, Kaleena. Not now." Matthew's whisper was so low, it almost seemed more like a prayer. "I don't know where you are right now, sweetheart. Some far-away place you can't understand, I'm sure. But I'm here for you, Kaleena. Hear my voice."

Looking away to peer out at the darkening sky, Matthew saw a swarm of threatening clouds invade his view. It almost felt as if he were looking at a representation of his mind.

He turned back to Kaleena, afraid that if he kept his eyes off of her for too long, those clouds would devour her without remorse. As he washed his face with his hand, he saw her eyes shift in a heightened state of excitement. It didn't last long. Almost as soon as he saw them twitch, they fell dead again. Was it all in his head? Did she know he was watching? If so, was there a possibility she could hear him? Matthew never believed anyone in a coma could actually hear them, just as he never believed plants lived longer if you talked to them, told them stories, acted as if they were your best friend or pretended they were your little babies. But Kaleena was a prime example of how much more mysterious and complex an organism the human brain was. But when it came down to it, isn't that all the brain really was? An organ. Blood and oxygen was all it needed to survive, just as all a plant needed was light and water. Matthew couldn't help feeling, however

(as most parents, relatives or loved ones would attest), that talking to her would help. It may have been a cry of desperation, or possibly a security blanket to help his own mind cope with his daughter's current state, but whatever the reason, he was helpless. Talking was all he could do to keep his sanity in check.

"I think Lauren may have had her baby," he said, choosing a topic that had no relation to Kaleena's "sickness", as he termed it in his own mind. He picked up Kaleena's hand and held it gently between his, warming the icy, stiff texture. "She went into labor just after you… well, after. I haven't heard a baby yet, but Kara took her into the other cabin, so I don't know. I suspect we'd still be able to hear Lauren, though. If she had had it, Kara would have boasted the delivery by now, so, maybe it turned out to be false labor. Did you know it took thirty-six hours to finally push your way out? That was a day and a half of pure torture, and I'm not talking about your mother." He had to let out a soft chuckle. No reaction from Kaleena. *What am I doing?* he asked himself, letting her hand slip from his.

He paced the room, keeping his attention on Kaleena's chest (making sure it continued to rise and fall), yet avoiding her at the same time. It hurt too much to keep watching her. He hated seeing her like this, but unlike other parents, he had seen it before, though on a much more heightened level. He tried hard to keep those three very long, very strenuous days from his mind; a reality he'd been able to successfully evade, allowing him to pretend it had all been a very bad dream. But with Kaleena lying nearly still like this, he could no longer hide from those torturous memories. All he could see was Kaleena on the couch, her arm draped over the side, holding onto the phone as if it were part of her. Whether it had been like that in anticipation to hear from Jaime, or if she had been like that when he talked to her that night, he didn't know. But her voice and her speech had warned him of the impending scene.

"How are you doing, sweetheart?" Matthew's voice was low, yet nurturing. After a long breath, he said, "Kaleena?"

"Not good," she said softly. Matthew couldn't tell if she was scared, sad, in shock, or all of the above as her whisper was only slightly coherent. What he noticed

most about it, though, was how long it seemed to take her to say it.

"Have you talked to anyone? Kyla, maybe?"

A small noise, possibly a sniffle, preceded her short long drawl of a, "No…"

Matthew's thoughts moved a mile a minute, none of which left his shaky, nervous lips.

"Are you coming home?" Kaleena asked. Her voice seemed more alert, yet it still held a lower than normal drawl.

"I'm going to be home soon, okay?" Matthew said, trying hard to comfort her.

"Why aren't you home?" she said, this time with much more sadness. He could hear her tears spill out. She wasn't alone.

"Kaleena, I'm getting there as fast as I can. I promise."

"She promised…"

Matthew's legs fell weak. He had to lean against one of the seats overlooking the runways. "I know," he choked out.

"She promised…" Kaleena repeated, but followed it up with, "You did too."

The promise to always love her and be there for her. Now neither of them was. It killed Matthew to know that.

"Kaleena. I promised. I'm promising again. I will be there soon. Call Kyla. Ask her to come over and before you know it, I'll be there." He paused and then added one more time with clarity, "I. Promise."

Matthew only heard her soft breath over the receiver. He imagined her sitting in their apartment, staring at Jamie's picture (or a picture of all three of them) happy, carefree — an image of joy Kaleena didn't want to (or was unable to) let go of.

"Now boarding B-class for Southwest flight three-sixteen," the flight attendant announced over the intercom.

"Kaleena?" he asked, knowing he would have to hang up. He didn't want to, but missing his flight would be an even greater mistake. "Can you hear me? I'm coming home right now. Can you do as I ask?" After another pause: "Kaleena?"

"Okay," she said, and this time Matthew could tell, through a layer of tears, that Kaleena had given up on him.

"I love you, sweetheart," he said, hoping to relax her. He wasn't sure why he thought it would work, but a fool's hope was better than nothing.

"Yeah," Kaleena said, followed quickly by silence. Matthew tightened his grip on his cell phone, the pressure of which was enough to break it. The flight attendant's next announcement, allowing the rest of the passenger's access to the plane, eased his stress. He placed the phone in his pocket and handed the flight attendant his boarding pass. Her smile irritated him; she was far too happy. After handing it back with a perky thank you, Matthew stepped into the terminal without a word. Another far too energetic flight attendant greeted him at the door. There didn't seem to be many people on this flight and he was glad. He didn't need all the distractions. He tried to get some sleep, something he hadn't done for nearly forty-eight hours, but Kaleena kept him wide-awake. He couldn't get her *Yeah* out of his head. She was too smart to do anything to herself —

I hope —

however, he wasn't sure if the emotional impact he noticed in her voice would push her to act irrationally or to simply stop doing anything at all. He wouldn't feel right until he got back home and was able to look into those beautiful brown eyes that were probably filled with a depressive quiet instead of the roaming excitement they usually held.

About six hours into the fourteen-hour flight, Matthew decided it best to call her again. After the initial first two rings, the voicemail picked up. He listened to the familiar message, which included Kaleena's sprightly ten-year-old voice in full bloom. Just comparing that to the sadness and emptiness of the conversation he'd just had with her sent a fierce wave of fright and nausea throughout his body. An overwhelming urge to take over the cockpit and show these pilots how to fly a damn plane was silenced as he left a quick message he was afraid Kaleena would never hear —

"I love you, Kaleena. I'm almost home."

He settled back into his seat (if that's what you could call it — his nerves were as tight as a nun's nether region) after hitting the *end*. Time slowed down; in some

instances to a complete stop. Would there be no end to this flight? Was it possible he would be stuck in the air for the rest of his life?

Matthew was dead on his feet, his eyes saucers of exhaustion and sorrow, by the time the plane landed. He grabbed the first cab he could get (he didn't care he had to steal it from a woman with a heavy southern drawl and a pantsuit that screamed, "I'm a lawyer, and I'll sue you, you bastard"), foregoing the even longer wait he would have had to endure at baggage claim (*It'll still be there tomorrow,* he thought). He arrived back at the apartment at 7:28 on Friday evening, a time he would never forget for the rest of his life. Five minutes earlier, Kaleena would have been fine; five minutes later... Matthew would always wonder.

"Kaleena," he called even before the door was open. There was no time to close it behind him. He ran for her room, but stopped cold when he caught sight of her lying on the couch, looking like a porcelain doll that had been absent-mindedly abandoned there. The phone was nearly welded to her right hand, which rested softly on the carpet below her. Her left arm was stuffed under her body and her legs were sprawled across the back of the couch, one foot dangling over the arm rest, the other waiting for gravity to break it off and drop it to the floor. In what seemed to be a soft slumber, her mouth sat slightly open, allowing saliva to begin pooling under her nose on the throw pillow. It was obvious she hadn't washed her hair in a few days as it sprawled clumped and greasy along the curvature of the sofa. Even the pink nightgown she wore looked worn. By the looks of it, Kaleena had most likely spent the last two days on this couch waiting for the phone to ring.

Matthew knelt down and shook her shoulders. "Kaleena, wake up. I'm home." He shook harder the more Kaleena refused to do as he asked. Eventually, the phone fell from her hand, landing on the rug Jaime had picked up on the side of the road from an immigrant hoping to feed her family for a week.

It was no use. Kaleena would not wake up.

Her head fell against the couch without the slightest of movement as Matthew sat her up. He pulled the end of her nightgown to her feet and shifted her body,

causing her head to roll only because it was attached. That's when he noticed it. His daughter — a child with his bloodline flowing through her — wasn't breathing.

"Kaleena!"

Without thinking, Matthew lowered Kaleena to the floor and started CPR, breathing hard, warm air into her lungs as he was taught at the YMCA he used to go to in high school to gain extra credit and pass his health class. Not a moment did he think he would ever need to use it. After a few seconds of trying to find the right placement for his hands on Kaleena's chest, Matthew pushed down, at first lightly (in fear of doing more harm) and then harder when he realized it wasn't working. He tried again — a breath and then a constant barrage of chest pumps — before making the hardest decision of his life —

He would need to stop and call the ambulance. He pulled his cell phone from his pocket and dialed 911, all the while watching Kaleena drop even deeper into death.

Thankfully, it didn't take long for the operator to answer. "Nine-One-One emergency. Please hold," the static voice said.

"Damn you, I can't hold," Matthew screamed, throwing the phone across the room. He didn't see it smash a small hole in the window; he was too busy lifting Kaleena into his arms to care. He hustled her out to the street as if it were right outside his door, but his first instinct wasn't to hail a ride. He simply walked as fast as he could, desperately needing to keep moving. Stopping would have just killed her.

About a mile up the road, as Matthew's legs started to burn, a car slowed to match his speed. The driver, an older gentleman with just a wisp of white hair on his freckled head and a small pot belly that pushed up slightly against the steering wheel, leaned over across the passenger seat. "Do you need a lift?" he said in a scruffed voice that revealed the man to be a long-time smoker.

Matthew turned to him but didn't want to stop moving. How fast could this old man go, anyway? Twenty, thirty miles an hour? *A speed demon for sure.* Then again, how long could Matthew go without his legs buckling underneath him?

What good would that do?

"Sir?" the old man asked again. This time Matthew stopped. For a moment, he just stood, seemingly unable to move. "Are you okay?" the man said. "What happened?"

Matthew finally turned to the man and said under heavy breaths, "I need... hospital..."

The old man's small eyes grew into giant saucers as he noticed Kaleena draped across Matthew's arms like a blanket. "Yeah, yeah... get in." He struggled to open the passenger door for Matthew, who slowly forced it all the way open and slid into the car. "Hurry," Matthew said in between breaths. The old man, after resettling in his seat, stepped on the gas, helping the passenger door to close without much strength from Matthew, who continued to cradle Kaleena tight. For the entire trip to the hospital (which seemed to take hours even though the old man was driving about sixty in what was most likely a thirty- or forty-five-mile zone), one arm remained propped under her head, the other combed through her tattered hair. He continually urged her awake with repetitive soft whispers, willing to give up everything to get her to open her eyes and smile brightly in seeing he'd kept his promise. But nothing happened — just a dead bounce with every bump in the road. The old man remained silent, occasionally peering over to look at the small child, afraid to ask what happened.

Upon arrival at the hospital, Matthew kicked the door open before the car had come to a complete stop and flew from it without even as much as a glance at the old man, who stepped out to get a good view of Matthew running into the hospital, Kaleena's limbs flailing about.

"I need help," Matthew screamed as he dropped to his knees in the center of the emergency room, unable to take the weight of his daughter or the weight of the stress any longer. "I need help," he said again, quieter in fear that he may never see Kaleena again.

It didn't take long for a doctor and a couple of nurses to take Kaleena from him, a task much easier said than done. Matthew, knowing he needed to let go,

couldn't get up the courage to do so. Finally, after several long seconds of urging from the doctor, Matthew succumbed and allowed the nurses to carry her into one of the beds nearby. The second nurse stayed with Matthew, repeatedly asking if he could stand.

"No," he croaked, watching the doctors cut Kaleena's nightgown of, spouting some things Matthew couldn't register — stuff about IV's and cc's and whatever other doctor babble he'd heard all the time on those repetitive doctor shows like *ER* and *Grey's Anatomy*.

"Come on," the nurse repeated, tucking her hand under his arm and coaxing Matthew to his feet. He towered over the nurse by at least a foot and a half. "I need to ask you some questions and get some history."

Matthew barely heard the nurse's request, but when it did finally register, he peered to her as if she were mad. *Leave my daughter*, he screamed in his mind. *Are you shittin' me?* He kept his composure, though, as he realized all she wanted to do was help. He finally felt her hand grasping his upper arm with a tender grip and decided it best if he did as she asked.

"Is your daughter allergic to any medications?" She saw the distraction in his eyes as she waited for his answer, which came slow and silent in the form of a simple headshake. "No?"

She sounded distant to Matthew as his concern remained with the small hum coming from Kaleena's bed. He turned in time to watch the doctor place the defibrillator paddles on Kaleena's chest and send somewhere around three or four hundred volts of electricity through her heart. It didn't help, as he heard the doctor call out a new number and repeat the action. The nurse once again asked, in a confirming tone, if his daughter was allergic to anything. He didn't look at her as he shook his head more prominently, eking out a slow, "No…" At least he couldn't remember her being allergic to anything. How could he not know if she was allergic to anything? Had Jaime actually been right about him? A sharp pain pinched his chest as he realized his idea of being a good father was being challenged at the darkest moment in his life.

"Can you please come with me?" The nurse's hand was still cupped under his arm. Matthew finally looked to her. He could tell right away, through her somewhat tired but understanding eyes, that she was a mother. One more shot of voltage to Kaleena's chest urged him to do as he was asked instead of forcing himself to watch his daughter's inevitable death. The nurse guided Matthew into the safe, yet utterly isolated waiting room. She handed him a clipboard with paperwork Matthew wasn't even in the mood to look at, much less fill out. He set it down on the chair next to him (knowing he may never be in the mood, not even if Kaleena somehow pulled through) and sat in silence, keeping his eyes averted from the three other people who were also, no doubt, waiting for answers about loved ones.

It was about a half hour later when Kaleena's doctor finally came into the waiting room. His face answered every question Matthew had running through his head. "No, no, no... don't you dare," Matthew stuttered, his eyes heating as his skin chilled.

"I'm sorry..." the doctor said in a thick whisper. "We did everything we could."

"It's not possible," Matthew roared, wanting desperately to send a fist to the young kid's jaw and turn him into his own patient. He fought the temptation and sat down. His body shook uncontrollably as he pet his mouth. A cloud full of questions and thoughts haunted his mind until one rose to the surface, clear as day — one that would leak from his lips without much knowledge.

"How did she...?" He couldn't finish it; he still didn't want to believe it.

"We won't know until we perform an autopsy," the doctor answered.

All Matthew could do was cover his bright red, puffy eyes and shake his head. The others in the room sat still and quiet, most likely dreading the possibility of receiving the same news.

"I'm very sorry for your loss," the doctor said after a few stagnant moments. "Is there anyone else we can call for you?" When Matthew didn't respond, the doctor lowered his head and left.

It took Matthew four hours to compose himself enough to stand. He walked to the nearest phone and dialed a number he wouldn't ever dial again.

"What is it," Jaime said, scratchy and tired.

"Where are you?" His mouth was dry.

"None of your business," she whispered. Matthew wasn't sure why she was whispering, but he didn't really care.

"We can't do this now, Jaime," he said as his voice cracked.

"What's wrong?"

It took a minute, but was finally able to say it aloud for the first time. "She's dead…"

There was a long silence, and then, "Who? Who's dead?"

"You left her and now she's…" Once was enough; he didn't need to hear it again. He hung up the phone and rested his head against it, trying to keep from crying. It was impossible as he sat with her, once again urging his teenage daughter to return from her comatose state and give him a big hug. He remained convinced that Jaime had sent her here for a second time. What angered him, though, was the fact Jaime hadn't once come down to see if she was okay. Not like he would allow her to, but knowing she had the forethought to make the attempt was expected — at the very least to make up for never saying a word after Kaleena made her full recovery the first time. Why should he care? Maybe he still held out hope that she had changed. But with everything that had gone on over the last twenty-four hours, the only thing that had changed was her weight and habits. Jaime was the exact same selfish person he remembered.

"You can't quit on me," Matthew said. "The past three years have been a miracle. For both of us. You can't waste them, you hear me? I won't let you."

He stopped, seemingly waiting for an answer he knew would never come.

"Your mother… she…" He needed to recite his next words carefully. "She doesn't know what she wants. She's lost, Kaleena. She doesn't understand how much you really mean to her. I know that probably sounds crazy, but I don't see any other explanation. You may be the only one that can make her understand. But you can't do that like this. You can't leave us a second time. Not when we're so close to…"

What was he doing? Not that he thought she was listening, but if by some miracle she could hear him, he was leading her down a line of thinking that ended where he wanted. As he watched Kaleena's chest rise and collapse… rise and collapse… Matthew realized that maybe Jaime was right. Maybe he had been the selfish one in all of this. What Jaime did was wrong and he would never forgive her for that, but for the first time, the thought that it was all his fault corrupted his thoughts.

"My god, Kaleena. I'm sorry," he continued through a light puddle of watery eyes. "I'm so sorry." He picked up her hand. For a second, he thought he felt her fingers wrap around his, but quickly wrote it off as his own optimistic imagination. "Don't leave us, please."

It all started to become too much for him. Simply waiting and wishing for her to wake up made him feel unproductive. He didn't want to leave, but fresh air was probably the only thing that would calm his nerves. If he had a choice, he'd be in three places at once: holding onto Kaleena until she opened her eyes; tearing the *Endeavor* apart until he found Jaime; and doing everything he could to find Atlantis and make this whole mess of a trip worth something. He gave Kaleena a light kiss on the forehead, took one last glance at her beautiful, yet deathly ill face and left the cabin.

He went up to the cockpit. Thomas had his arms wrapped around Trishen's stomach as they cuddled at the table closest to the galley. She had changed into a pair of jeans, a white tank-top and a pink button-down shirt that wasn't buttoned at all, but tied in a knot at the ends. Thomas hadn't changed; it seemed he opted to drip-dry instead.

"Hey, Matthew," Thomas said with a forced smile, hoping to get one back. He did.

"Hey," he said solemnly, trying his best to hide his anguish.

"How is she?" Trishen asked before Thomas could.

"She's still alive." Always the one to stay positive.

"That's good." Trishen laid her hand over the top of Thomas's and gently

played with his fingers. Matthew could tell she was grieving over her loss as well.

"I'm sorry. I didn't mean —"

"It's all right," Trishen whispered. "I'm glad your daughter's okay."

Matthew felt stupid and didn't know what to say to make up for it. Thomas curled her delicate fingers around his, showing a warm compassion Matthew hadn't really ever noticed in Thomas before. He felt better knowing Trishen had someone to comfort her, even if it was someone she'd just met. Choosing to leave them be, Matthew stepped into the galley and poured himself a cup of cold coffee. It would have to suffice.

*　*　*

The reddening rays of the sun were barely visible through the single porthole in the sparsely decorated room. Compared to the rest of the ship, Benjamin's sleeping quarters could be considered a shack. However, as the events of the last few years spun in constant circles through Jaime's head, the room remained exotic in its simplicity. The walls were lined in a wood, finished with a dark redwood glaze that accented the smooth wooden floors that felt like ice against Jaime's bare feet. Aside from the bed, a small bureau, and a shelf that hung just above the headboard, nothing else cluttered up the condensed quarters, making it a place Jaime could find the solace she needed.

It had taken her nearly an hour to find strength enough in her legs to lift herself up off the deck. The cool breeze pricked at her skin. She didn't know where to go now that she was standing. Gavin's death kept her from retreating back to her room. His eyes had been so cold with fear; whenever Jaime even thought his name, they would pierce her mind. It wasn't enough she was unable to help him, now he haunted her with questions over his final thoughts. Had he spent his last breath disappointed in the one person he trusted the most? Was he angry with her for doing nothing to help him? Was it arrogance to believe he was even thinking about her? He could have simply been fighting to find a single breath, praying for

a reprieve, for a second chance, for some hope...

For a savior?

There was no way to know for sure; his death was far too quick and far too sudden to have become so detailed. And everything Jaime imagined felt so empty, just as his mind may have been as his lungs filled with seawater, leaving only darkness and a stab of pain in his chest before... what?

Her inability to answer that question kept Jaime from facing anyone who would remind her of Gavin. It didn't occur to her that she hadn't thought of Kaleena at all. Not once over the entire time she sat huddled on the deck in her disassociated state. Even now, as clouds started to roll in, she wasn't her number one priority, though she did wonder how she had known about Benjamin. Was Kaleena really trying to hurt her or was it simply a frustrated outburst? As she played the verbal attack over and over again, Kaleena's words passing through with a ghosted resonance

(*I thought I would be able to forgive you; you fucked that up the second you slept with your old boyfriend; I can't bear to be around you knowing who you really are*)

Jaime felt a light pinch in her gut. She hissed through her teeth, willing the pain to go away. But it persisted. Jaime leaned over the rail of the *Endeavor* and regurgitated air. Then it was just a matter of waiting. That's all she could do.

Wait.

The pain subsided, but Jaime knew it would come back if she didn't have a cigarette — and soon. A dry, nicotine aftertaste painted the inner walls of her mouth. The problem was, her cigarettes were in her bag... in her cabin. She couldn't go back there. She would just have to go hide somewhere and deal with the withdrawals; somewhere no one would look for her. But every place she thought of on the tiny piss-ant boat would remind her of Gavin or lead to someone she didn't want to see. Then it hit her — there *was* one place that could offer her sanctuary, and it was sitting right underneath her.

Light leaked from the open floorboard leading to Benjamin's cabin. He was definitely down there, though Jaime figured he'd be in the engine room. If he

was, perfect. She could be alone. If he was in the room, waiting patiently for her to come to him, so be it. Benjamin was really the only person she would be able to tolerate right now, and his comfort may prove to be just what she needed.

She slid quietly into the hatch, each step a cautious search. Once she could peer into the room, she was slightly disappointed, yet overall relieved, to find Benjamin nowhere to be found. Jaime lowered the floorboard above her and stepped down into the room. Her wetsuit was beginning to irritate her still moistened skin, so she opened the top drawer of the bureau. A pack of Marlboro Lights sat off to the corner on top of a cluttered pile of boxer shorts, white T's and socks. Jaime felt a weight lift off her shoulders. They weren't her regular brand, but right now, a smoke was a smoke. She swiped them up and frantically looked for a lighter or a pack of matches — something she could light up with. Nothing. Her hands shook with desperation when the sun glinted off a lighter on the shelf. She climbed onto the bed, pulled a stick from the red and white pack and lit it up, inhaling the nicotine with sweet satisfaction. Though she still felt a heavy fatigue weighing her down, her mind was clearer.

It didn't take long for her to finish the cigarette and light up a second. By that time, a light haze of smoke was filling the room. Jaime ignored it, more interested in the picture she picked off the shelf of her and Benjamin standing in front of the Sydney Opera House the night before she first made love to him.

The night before she would have to leave him behind.

The girl looked so happy holding onto her lover — her love — with a whimsical adoration of fantasy and spirit.

Jaime didn't recognize that girl.

As she finished the second cigarette, Jaime felt an awkward humiliation as she finally noticed the heavy smoke floating around the unventilated space. She set the picture down and went back up the stairs to prop the floorboard open, hoping the smoke would find its way up and out before Benjamin returned. It didn't help much.

Fuck it, she thought and walked the butt of the cigarette back to the dusty, glass ashtray on the bureau where she let it burn to ash. The cigarettes had helped her clear her head, but they weren't helping the burning irritation under her breasts and between her legs. Only one thing could cure that. She opened the bottom drawer of the bureau to find an array of cotton, wool, and silk button-down shirts. The blue-striped Hawaiian shirt would do wonders, along with the one pair of jean shorts she found among the pile of board shorts and Khakis. She tossed them on the bed and pulled the top half of her wetsuit off. The air was cold as it hit her skin, but she remained nearly motionless as the smoky air help fry the remaining moisture from her upper body. When the icy exhilaration wore off, Jaime checked under her breasts to see how bad a rash had formed. After concluding the redness was insignificant, she threw on the shirt and buttoned it to the second topmost button, allowing the collar to weigh the top down a bit to reveal a slight hint of cleavage Jaime was unaware of having exposed.

Oddly, the smell of the shirt brought memories of Gavin back to the surface. She climbed onto the bed and lit herself another Marlboro Light. But this time, she settled in and savored the fresh taste. She watched the sunset through the porthole until the stick expired. The heat nipped the numbness of her fingers as she pinched the butt out, unwilling to move to reach the ashtray. The next half hour was spent figuring out how she was going to convince herself to go see Kaleena (and Matthew, for that matter), and how she would find the energy to rise above her sadness and show strength among the rest of her team. Without her leadership, how could they possibly move forward? On the other hand, had their reliance on her strength caused her to become something she never thought she'd be — cold and heartless?

"Love?"

Jaime didn't move as Benjamin stepped closer, his flip-flops making small sticky patters along the floor. "Are you okay?"

"Do you know I haven't cried once since that night?" Jaime said quietly. Benjamin stopped, but Jaime heard him breathing. He was right next to the bed. "Not once. What does that mean?"

"I don't think it means anythin'," Benjamin said after a short pause.

Jaime's eyes darted about, unable to focus on anything as she contemplated the answer.

Benjamin continued. "People deal with grief in their own way, Love. Some cry 'til their eyes are sore, some eat, some smoke." He wiped his nose, apparently affected by the smoke in the room. "I think you're just —"

"A bitch?" Jaime looked up at Benjamin. Grease striped his arms and covered his hands. He was perspiring heavily, even though the soft breeze whistling through the floorboard had cooled the room enough to make Jaime feel she needed a sweater.

"Now, Love —"

"That's what I am, isn't it?" Jaime said forcefully. "A heartless bitch with a tree trunk shoved up her ass?" Kaleena's words echoed across the walls of the room.

"I don't think you're a bitch." He looked at her, for some reason needing to expand on what he had said. "*No one* thinks you're a bitch."

"Sure they do. I can see it in the way they look at me."

"Who, exactly?"

She knew Benjamin was trying to get her to say Matthew, to hear it out loud and get it out in the open. But she couldn't. She pondered naming someone else, but doing that would be an outright lie and he'd know it. There was no reason to think her team didn't completely respect her and her decisions, and she hadn't even barely said three words to Thomas and his friend (or as far as she knew, his girlfriend) to know, or even care, what they thought about her. But as she opened her mouth to get it over with, she realized it wasn't even Matthew. Yes, it was true he had scorned her, but the feelings for him that would have caused her pain were long dead — or dormant — and she was no longer affected by anything he said. As far as she was concerned, anything he did say to or about her was out of spite and anger. No, it was Kaleena's sharp-tongued attack that stung the most. It was believing Kaleena thought she was a bitch that broke her heart. That, she was not willing to say.

She turned away, unable to look at Benjamin any longer.

"It's all in your head, Love."

Jaime shook her head. "I'm still not sure about that, Ben. With everything that's happened…"

"With everything that's happened, you're feeling lost."

Jaime turned back to Benjamin at hearing this. Her chest and throat tightened as if she were about to cry, but her eyes remained dry as a desert. "You might be right," she choked. "This whole trip has just been so…"

" 'Orrible?"

"I was going to say fucked up, but I guess that'll do," she said to force a smile out of him. Apparently, he didn't find it funny. She lowered her head and picked at the bedspread. "I'm sorry. It's just… ever since I agreed to do this thing I've had this anxiety about it, like it was a bad idea." She looked back to Benjamin. "So far, I haven't found any reason to think otherwise."

Jaime paused and eyed Benjamin's body. "I feel like it's been such a long time since I've had a real, fulfilling relationship. Gavin…" it hurt her to say his name, but she had to say it again. "Gavin was the closest thing I had to that and now… because of me… he's gone."

"You can't blame yourself for his death, Love." Benjamin rested his hand on her shoulder.

"I know," she returned softly, caressing his hand. "But I can't help but feel I should have done more to help him." She tightened her grip just enough to show loving affection. "I haven't told anyone this before, but I think I was falling in love with him."

Benjamin sat down and pulled her head into his chest, knowing full well how hard it must have been to admit that Matthew was almost right in claiming Gavin had been Jaime's boyfriend. The grease on his hands that hadn't dried colored her hair slightly. It didn't matter that they were rough and scratchy; for the first time in two years, she felt comfortable in her own skin.

"I love you," Jaime whispered. Benjamin returned the salutation with a kiss to the top of her head.

"Me too, Love."

Jaime lifted her head and placed her palm against his cheek.

"I always have. It's hard to admit, but there was a time, early on in my marriage, that I regretted leaving you."

"Don't say things like that, Love," Benjamin said.

"But it's true. You should have been the one I married, Benjamin." She followed this with a kiss. Benjamin attempted to pull away, but Jaime grabbed the back of his head and held him close. After a moment, he succumbed to the nurture and honesty in the kiss, enjoying the sweet taste once again. Jaime felt him return her affection and allowed him to take control. She slipped her hands around his shoulders before lowering them to her chest and unbuttoning her shirt. She picked up one of his hands and guided it to her breast. His warm touch sent a hot rush of goose pimples across her flesh. It was enough to push her back into being the aggressor, coercing Benjamin to lie down on the bed. She moved her pelvis up and down his before reaching for his shorts.

Benjamin pushed Jaime away, holding her shoulders tightly. "No, Love. We can't do this."

"Shut up and fuck me," she scolded, going back in for another kiss.

"No," he said, turning his head.

"Why not?" she asked, rejected.

"Love, your daughter is sick. Your best friend, near lover, just died. You're in mourning."

"So what? I need you right now." Jaime leaned in again. This time, Benjamin pushed Jaime off his lap and slid away from her.

"Please. You don't know what you're doin'."

"I know full well what I'm doing," Jaime said, her voice a bit heightened with rage.

Benjamin stood up. "I'm sorry. I can't do this."

"That's odd. When I left my husband you couldn't wait to fuck me."

"That's why," he said sternly. "This isn't the Jaime I love. I can't, and won't,

simply *fuck* you to make you feel better."

"You bastard."

"Stop, please."

"You told her, didn't you?" Jaime said out of nowhere.

"What?"

"You told Kaleena about us? What we did that night."

Benjamin's eyes fell guilty as he stared at his old lover, wishing now that he could have taken that whole night back.

"How could you?" Jaime pulled her shirt back around her chest and buttoned it back up.

"You don't understand," Benjamin tried to say.

"That was a private moment, Benjamin. You had no right to tell my daughter. No right." Jaime slid off the opposite side of the bed and ran for the staircase

"Jaime, come back. Please."

Only silence was returned.

*   *   *

It was cold, dark…

And wet.

Kaleena's body danced in the midst of nothing she could feel. She tried to open her eyes, but they seemed to have been forced closed by the thin fingertips of some type of spirit. There were no sounds that she could discern. The inside of her mouth tasted salty and pasty with a bit of iron, and it felt as if they had been sewn together. However, even with all of this, Kaleena felt comfortable; so comfortable in fact, she didn't realize her mind was quiet. Not one question about where she was or how she had gotten there; not one memory of where she had come from or what she even was. It was as if she had no need for them; as being here, she was free. And she felt a strong need to do just that:

Free herself.

Allowing her body to fall limp, her limbs extended into the wind (or water) around her. The more she let go, the more she experienced — the dust whisping through the air of a desert; a flower, blossoming under the heat of the warm sun; a butterfly breaking from its small cocoon and flapping its brand new wings for the first time; a baby, cold and wet, crying in a state of shock and wonder as she's wrapped in a warm blanket... the blanket with each of its soft threads... threads that intertwined with companionship and strength. Kaleena felt it all. And she was in glorious content.

Suddenly, her chest tightened (she hadn't even realized she still had a chest) and her heart contracted — squashed, really — under the vice grip of what felt like a large hand. Everything she had been touching (as she would later claim) disappeared, leading her back into a conscious state where she could only feel her own restricted lungs, her fingers (which felt painfully arthritic), her stomach (which turned over on itself in a heap of nausea) and her thoughts, which now flooded her mind as if she were seeing her entire life for the first time.

Then the pain in her chest disappeared and her lungs grew heavy.

She was drowning.

Finally, realizing she was deep within a body of water, she pumped her arms in the only direction that felt right. The more she rose, the more she longed for air. And though she was still couldn't open her eyes, she knew she was getting close to a surface as the darkness under her eyelids steadily grew a bright orange-red. Her mind told her she was almost there and urged her lungs to continue to hold on until finally, after a minute of slowly ticking seconds, Kaleena opened her mouth wide and sucked in the oxygen from the air above the water. Taking in each new breath with a sense of relief and power, the thoughts jamming her mind faded into the deep recesses of her subconscious. She was finally able to open her eyes. It took a moment for her pupils to adjust to the piercing light that flooded the horizon, but as she focused, she realized that what she was looking at was not the sun. It was a small light — much like a firefly — floating approximately four feet from her eyes, seemingly investigating her features. A burst of sleepiness then fell

upon her even though she was not at all tired. She grew determined to keep her body from pushing her into sleep so she could find out where she was. The firefly was as good a place as any to start.

"Where am I?" she whispered.

The light instantly went out, leaving Kaleena in the darkened pale light of the setting sun. *What the hell?* she thought, spinning her body in the calm water to locate — *what?* What was she looking for exactly? She wasn't quite sure. All she knew was she needed to find someone (or something, for that matter) that would give her answers.

"Hello?" she called out. "Can anyone hear me? Please? Is anyone out there?"

We can, a soft, musical voice echoed around her. It vibrated through her ears like chimes hanging from the porch of a suburban home in a town that no one's ever heard of since the invention of the extreme time saver known as a freeway.

"Who are you?" Kaleena called back. Her voice didn't echo — it just fell flat among the heavy air.

Soft giggles floated by her, followed by a soft hum, a tune Kaleena had never heard but which made her feel warm and at home. A smile fell upon her lips and, for a short instance, Kaleena forgot she wanted answers. But the burning in her legs from treading water woke her senses. "May I see you?"

A short pause with a little more music and then, *Yes, you may.*

A bright light rose from the water behind Kaleena. She turned to face it, having to hide her eyes until the bright glow faded. After refocusing her pupils, Kaleena saw the form of a beautiful woman, shaped in every man's fantasy with just the right proportions and just the right features — eyes that sparkled in purple mascara and lips that glistened with the radiant sun. Her white (*blond?*) hair fell gently against the long white gown flowing gently in the soft breeze. She held Kaleena mesmerized as she floated toward her, each step delicate and soft against the water. Her brilliant white teeth peeked out from under her thin lips like a curtain waiting to be raised to reveal the feature presentation. When she was within inches of Kaleena, the woman held out her hand. It didn't take long

for Kaleena to accept it. Her thin palm was smooth as glass, with no markings whatsoever, and the vibrant silver nail polish had a soft glazed coating. Kaleena's body rose until she was completely out of the water, her bare feet taking in the gleeful tickle of the ocean. It was then that Kaleena noticed that she, too, was wearing a similar white gown that wasn't wet at all. In fact, it was quite warm. She curled her lips with graciousness.

"Who are you?" This time she knew she'd get an answer.

"I am your destiny, Kaleena," the woman said.

"How?"

The woman's cheekbones lit up. "You have finally arrived to save us."

"How am I supposed to save you? I don't even know who you are."

"But you do."

Kaleena's brow furrowed and the woman giggled, sending what sounded like a hidden crystal-like chorus to chime all around her.

"Open your mind, Kaleena. I have been with you since you set sail upon the ocean."

Kaleena pondered the woman's words. What was she trying to tell her? She was usually good at figuring out the hidden messages and meanings within cryptic or vague statements, but she was having a difficult time with her new acquaintance — until the woman stared deeply into her eyes.

"Oh my god," Kaleena whispered. "That can't be."

"Trust your heart, Kaleena. It will never fail you."

"But that's impossible. How can that be?"

"Nothing's impossible, Kaleena, when you set your mind free. I know you felt me that night. I felt you, too. And I knew you were the one we were looking for."

"But —"

The woman placed her fingertip to Kaleena's lips to hush her words. Kaleena smelled a small hint of cherries.

"Your mind will always hide that which it cannot understand, Kaleena. You must find your way through the fog and accept that truth is a powerful and sometimes unexplainable thing." The woman lowered her finger.

"Okay," Kaleena murmured. "I will give you the benefit of the doubt. If you are who you say you are, then why do you keep saying that I'm here to rescue you?"

"A very good question," the woman said. "The answer lies in the existence of that for which you do not believe."

"Atlantis?" Kaleena stated. "You have a connection to Atlantis?"

The woman simply closed her eyes and lowered her head.

"How?"

"When the triangle of fire is set, you will bring freedom and truth to the darkness of the past."

"What are you talking about? How am I supposed to do that?"

"Listen to the words of your father."

"My dad?"

"No," the woman interjected, placing her hand just above Kaleena's temples. "Your *father*."

"How…" Kaleena closed her eyes as pain bit her head.

"You will know him when you meet him. Listen to him, know that what he tells you is truth and help him bring peace to his people."

Kaleena didn't know how to respond. The pain subsided and she opened her eyes.

"Please. You're my last hope, Kaleena. Save us." The words rang through the air, filtered by the soft hum of music. The woman then burst into nothing more than sparkles, a firework of bright silver lights that floated around Kaleena before dissolving into the water.

Kaleena had no time to breathe before being pulled back into the water with a powerful suction. Her lungs tightened before she was even a foot below the surface. She struggled to climb back up as all light faded from view and all sounds disappeared into a gentle haze of silence. And then —

Gasping for air, Kaleena sat up. She tumbled out of her bed as she coughed and vomited in a fit of disbelief and subjection. An aroma emanated off the pile

of liquid on the floor, activating her gag reflex, but nothing else came up. She sat back against the bed, needing to get away from it (and fast). As she did, an itchy discomfort burned between her legs.

Water outlined her eyes as she crawled her way to the bathroom. It took her nearly five minutes. When she finally settled between the shower door and the toilet, she pulled off her pants and underwear and grabbed hold of the tampon strings. She softly pulled them away from her body but stopped when the tampon wouldn't slide out as easily as it should have. She moved her body to find a better position and tried again. This time, the tampon moved but burned as if it had taken some of her skin with it. She screamed in short bursts as she continued to pull the tampon from her body. It felt like brushing her gums with sandpaper, but she didn't stop. She couldn't stop.

When the tampon had been completely removed, Kaleena relaxed her muscles and fell to the floor, resting her head against the shower. The burn in her vaginal cavity faded quickly, almost as if it was healing itself. A minute or two later, Kaleena slid to her knees and tossed the dark red tampon into the toilet. She stared at it, wondering if that was finally it; if whatever was happening with her body had finally been expunged. Other than the small amount of dry blood stuck to her legs (some from earlier, some chunks from the tampon she just removed), there was no evidence that she was bleeding.

Relief washed over her as she flushed the toilet. She didn't know if it was temporary, but for now, at least, it was over. Yet her body was still in a state of fatigue: her muscles sore and weak, her eyes heavy and, even though still coated in salted moisture, uncharacteristically dry. If she could pass out and not dream, she would sleep for a year. But it was her dreams — dreams that felt as real as this very moment — that kept her from doing so. Had they even been dreams? The water, the forms of angelic perfection, the spoken words of thoughts, the pain, the torture — maybe they were premonitions of some sort; the world's way of telling her she was about to be tested. Tested for what, exactly, escaped her. The more she tried to understand them, the more disbelief filtered into her theories... into herself. Her dreams could very well have been her mind's way of dealing with whatever it was her body was rejecting. The thought of not being able to bear children because of what was happening crossed her mind more than once, which may have been why she dreamt of Lauren's baby in that way. But her words... the idea that Kaleena would save her — save them, actually...

For only the second time Kaleena could remember, she didn't have a logical, reasonable explanation for what was happening. It frightened her. The last time she felt this way, it almost killed her. Was she about to let that happen again?

Listen to your father.

She wouldn't let it happen again. She couldn't leave Matthew like that; not this way. Knowing Jaime was nowhere near ready to be a family again, Kaleena — and Atlantis — was all Matthew had. She wouldn't give up on him a second time. She was stronger now. Her mind was stronger and she would use that strength to prove she could survive; that she could save herself. The child — her old lost soul — would be reborn and grow to become the woman she knew she could be; the woman that Jaime was not, and was far from ever being.

Kaleena used the toilet to prop herself up on her knees and reach the sink, which she used to lift herself to her feet. She once again saw the pale, white skin of a ghost in the mirror, accentuating the heavy, dark red rings circling the war between fear and bravery. Her hair hung in thick patches of wet, sweaty strings. This was not the vision she was hoping to see, but she had time to change it. It was all starting to make sense.

Without warning, the *Endeavor* shook dramatically to the right, knocking Kaleena to the floor. She rose to her feet as the yacht shifted back to the left to stabilize itself. When she looked back to the mirror, though, there was no image of a teenage girl; there was no image of life. There was simply a blue triangle of fire — flames burning and crackling above the rough sea.

When the triangle of fire is set, she heard the crystal voice say again, as if it were speaking through the shimmer of light in the mirror. A bright flash of light lit up the center of the triangle — all but a small dot in the center, where Kaleena now,

once again, saw her reflection.

"Oh, God," she whispered as the low rumble in her gut told her something terrible was about to happen.

*   *   *

The cup of coffee swirled like a pile of mud as Matthew absorbed the sway of the boat from left to right, forward and back. The horizon looked beautiful, flashing with a moonlit shimmer. He couldn't help feel conflicted about his purpose. The oceans seemed to be calling him, asking him to find Atlantis. It would help his career, help his reputation and possibly help him fill the loneliness he's felt for the last two years. Yet none of that was as important (*or was it?*) as his little girl — white as a sheet and growing visibly weaker by the second — lying in an eerie coma below him. After six months of watching over her, caring for her and making sure she was okay, this very project fell into his lap. The hardest part was telling Kaleena he was going back to work.

"Okay..." she said, a little unsure.

"I'm not leaving right away. I've got to collect some information and translate some tablets with a colleague, so I'll still be here for you if you need me."

"That's okay." Kaleena got up from the couch and walked to the kitchen. She pulled a cookie from the jar shaped like an Oreo. "I've been busy here, anyway," she said. Matthew heard a little resentment, maybe some disappointment, but, oddly, acceptance. Had she been waiting for this to happen? "I'm going to start promoting my book next month and classes start soon." She took a bite of her cookie.

"Look," Matthew said. "I know the last few months have been rough..."

"I'm okay, Dad." After a short pause, "I'll be okay. You've done enough. It's time for you to get back to work."

Kaleena flashed a warm smile and Matthew couldn't help himself. He pulled her to him and gave her a huge hug. "We're going to make it, aren't we?"

"Of course," Kaleena said.

"I'll always be here. Remember that."

"Always."

It wasn't until just before agreeing to let her call Jaime that Matthew realized he'd let his job consume him to the point of completely ignoring his daughter. Looking out at the ocean, he tried to understand how much that emotional abandonment must have felt. She would never show or tell him, but he knew it was there. When he saw those bruises on her arm, he knew — he wasn't protecting her the way he should have been. But it was never too late to start acting like the father he promised he'd be. Atlantis was a dream he would continue to have. But the myth wasn't worth killing his daughter over. He decided —

He was not going to be like Jaime.

Setting the cup of mud down on the counter, Matthew felt Atlantis calling for him to reconsider. He fought the temptation as he stepped from the galley. Unfortunately, Atlantis found him again in the next room.

"Matthew, check this out," Kara said.

His response was almost automatic. It was a reflex he didn't realize he had, but once he acknowledged her, he was stuck. Or was he? "I need to get back to Kaleena."

"Just a sec. I think I got those stones translated."

Matthew finally noticed Gavin's video camera sitting on the table next to Kara. It looked to be plugged into the computer's hard drive. A fresh exhilaration flushed through his veins. He went to his colleague with a pace of masked excitement. Trishen moved up and away from Thomas just enough for him to sit up. He wanted to hear what she had to say as much as Matthew.

"Is it okay for you to be using those?" Matthew asked out of courtesy. He didn't care about the answer. The video display of the stones was all that mattered.

"Patricia said it would be fine," Kara said. "And Trishen agreed."

"Gavin never would have put personal matters before his work," Trishen said in a voice that made her sound like some kind of oracle. "Who am I to go against that?"

Matthew nodded with a real, heartfelt smirk. It felt good. "Speaking of which,"

he said. "Where is the eighth wonder?"

Trishen let slip a nip of laughter before covering her mouth to hide her amusement. Tried to, anyway. Thomas pressed his nose gently to her cheek and gave it a little rub.

"She's down in the cabin with Lauren," Kara finally answered with her own hint of amusement.

"Lauren?" he said, his mind reconnecting to present events. How had he forgotten about her? "How's she doing? Any news?"

"I haven't heard a butchered rendition of *She's Having a Baby* yet," Trishen quipped, then buried her head in Thomas's chest. He gave her a hint of a kiss on her cheek, a gesture she accepted by cuddling even closer. It reminded Matthew of when he and Jaime first fell in love, holding each other under the stars on the beach in Kauai with nothing on their minds but the love they had for each other. He wanted to believe the two of them could be as happy as they were on that day for the rest of their lives. But Matthew's father told him from an early age: "The world can be a fun place, son. But watch out, 'cause it can, and will, always kick you in the ass. Sometimes just to get your attention."

Matthew never believed it, until it did just that.

Good luck, he thought to himself.

"Her contractions seemed to be getting less frequent when I left her," Kara said. "So I assume the whole thing was a false alarm."

Matthew returned his attention to the her. "A reaction to the stress?"

"I guess."

"So, what do they say?" He pointed to the screen. Smooth subject change.

"We're havin' a baby," bellowed from below. "My baby and me." It repeated over and over, louder and louder. The four laughed as Patricia reached the top of the stairs and sang the lines one last time in a deep, diaphragm-induced baritone. Everyone felt at ease. It was nice.

"Damn it, I missed a joke, didn't I?" Patricia said. "I hate it when that happens. Tell it again."

"Don't worry," Trishen said with a wide smile. "It just wouldn't be as funny."

Suddenly, Matthew realized what the inside joke actually meant. "Wait a minute. Does that mean Lauren —"

"Save your hyperventilating for another time, ex. The kid hasn't had her kid yet."

"Well, how is she?"

"She's a trooper, let me tell ya'. But the contractions have stopped completely. Leave it to gas to make your unborn baby go shit-nuts." No one had a response for that. Patricia felt a little awkward. "What?"

Matthew chuckled the whole thing off. "Anyway," he said, turning back to Kara. "You were saying?"

"How's that stuff workin' out for you?" Patricia cut in as she went to her own set-up at the other end of the cockpit.

"Fine," Kara answered.

"Figure everything out okay?"

"Yeah." There was annoyance in Kara's voice now.

"Excellent." Patricia sat down and looked over her own readings. "Let me know if you need anything else."

"Okay." Kara glanced up to Matthew with a gentle eye-roll. "So…" She paused to see if anyone else wanted to interrupt. When they didn't, she pointed to the middle section of the text. "It took me a while to crack this portion here, but once I figured out that the words in this order caused a couple of the other meanings to change, it all started to make sense."

She grabbed the yellow legal pad sitting next to the camera. "The stones, as you may have already guessed, all say exactly the same thing except for the last few words, which change on each stone." She looked at Matthew. "I don't think it was a cemetery."

"*Not* a cemetery?"

Kara shook her head.

"Well, spit it out already," Patricia said, loud enough that it sounded like a yell.

"I think," Kara started, staring down Patricia before turning back to Matthew, "it was a place of worship. Or, someplace they used as a gateway for the dying."

"Like a prayer circle," Matthew affirmed.

"Yeah, in a way. One that may have given them hope that their faith would help lead their souls to heaven, or a higher existence, or whatever it was that they believed in."

"What was that, Reeses?" Patricia interjected. "I didn't quite translate."

"It was like a wake, of sorts. A place to free those who were dying from their earth-bound existence."

"What did they do? Kill 'em?"

"It wasn't about death," Kara said, trying hard to hold back her heightened annoyance. "It was about renewed life."

"They prayed for them to become angels," Matthew clarified.

"Yeah, something like that. Listen to this." Kara wrapped her legs over the edge of the seat, leaned in close to Matthew and read from her pad. "'For those that have lived and those that have believed now find truth in the face of their existence. One becomes all and all becomes one in the heart of destiny with the spirit of…'"

"The spirit of what?" Patricia blurted out, ignoring the readings that indicated a change in water pressure.

"That's what changes on each stone."

"Sounds romantic," Trishen said, raising her hand to Thomas's cheek.

"You think that's romantic. Just listen to the list of words that complete the saying."

"Jaime, come back. Please," Benjamin called out.

Everyone watched as Jaime stormed past the cockpit toward the back of the yacht. Benjamin was quick to catch up to her and grab her arm. She pulled away, whipping around to face him.

"Don't you dare touch me, you bastard," Jaime screamed.

"Jaime, listen to me," Benjamin fought back.

"Listen to what? You betrayed me. You betrayed me and turned my daughter against me."

"I told her because she needed to know," Benjamin said.

"Oh? And how is that?"

Benjamin took a moment to find the right words to clarify. Meanwhile, Patricia noticed the sudden change in water temperature and expanded the range of her readings to fifty miles. The farther out she got, the more the water's temperature and pressure rose. "What the shit?" she whispered. She looked through the cockpit window to the south, then made her way to the yacht's stern.

"If I had lied to her, she would have known," Benjamin finally spit out. "She needed the truth. I could see it in her eyes."

"You told her because you felt guilty." She could see the truth in his eyes. "Thought so." Jaime turned into the cockpit, where she finally noticed everyone looking at her. More importantly, Matthew. Her cheeks instantly flooded dark red and her stomach swam. "Oh, God," she whispered, digesting Matthew's saddened, disappointed gaze.

Benjamin came up behind her and looked directly at Matthew. A slow burn rose to Matthew's eyes that extended to his mind like a wildfire. Before he knew what was happening, he was moving rapidly toward the two.

"Shit," Thomas said, nudging for Trishen to move so he could get up. Though she obliged quick enough, he wouldn't get to Matthew in time.

"Don't do this," Jaime said, her eyes glued to Matthew's.

"Now, mate —" Benjamin said before finding a right hook to the side of his face.

"You bastard," Matthew yelled as Benjamin staggered across the deck. He collected himself against the rail and wiped away some blood coming from the cuts inside his gums.

Matthew stormed toward Benjamin with purpose but Thomas was able to curl his arms around Matthew's and grip them behind his back. "Matthew, stop this."

"Let go of me," Matthew screamed. Jamie had made her way to Benjamin. He

winced as she placed her hand to his cheek, but was soon in a position to hug her. Matthew didn't like it, but he could see now that Jaime truly cared for Benjamin in a deeper, more meaningful way than she would ever admit.

"You don't want to do this," Thomas said in Matthew's ear. "You're better than the both of them." He could already feel Matthew's muscles relaxing. "Just go back to Kaleena. She needs you." He waited a moment longer (just to make sure) and then let go of Matthew's arms.

"Did you sleep with her?" Matthew asked Benjamin in a calm, deadened voice.

It took a while, but Benjamin answered honestly. "Yes. But only once when she was with you. After she left you, actually."

Matthew thought of Kaleena as he processed his old friend's answer. It was clear now that Jaime might have left him, not because she wanted more freedom, not because Matthew was never there for her, but because she wanted to be with Benjamin. He couldn't say it out loud, though. By how she held her arms across her chest, her hands resting softly on her shoulder blades, she already knew what he was thinking. He simply shook his head and walked to the stairwell.

Jaime wondered if she could say anything to him that would matter. Should she even try? "Matthew, wait."

Matthew froze at the edge of the stairs. "I'm going to take care of my daughter," he said in a low growl.

Suddenly, the yacht nearly tipped on its side. Matthew caught himself from tumbling down the stairwell as Trishen jammed her stomach into the side of the table, forcing her to lose her breath. The equipment crashed against the wall, some collecting on the seat and cracking Kara's back as she was pushed against it. Out on the deck, Patricia held tight to the rail, trying hard to keep from falling into the ocean, which at the height of the tip, nearly touched her nose. Next to her, Jaime rolled to the corner of the starboard side. Benjamin, trying to keep her from sliding away, struck the corner of the railing with his forehead, knocking him out as he joined Jaime in the corner. Thomas stumbled, but held tight to the side of the cockpit, allowing him a chance to watch as metal and

sparks flew from Patricia's equipment. It smoldered as the yacht settled back in its original position.

"You guys okay?" Thomas asked. Kara grunted as she pushed away from Gavin's equipment. "I'll take that as a yes. Trishen?"

Trishen waved and nodded as she caught her breath.

"What the hell was that?" he asked no one in particular.

"Damn it," Patricia screamed as she saw the destruction of her equipment. "Goddamn shit." She picked up one of the keyboards. It had snapped in half. "Do you know how much this shit costs?" she uttered as she threw it back to the pile.

"Benjamin!"

Thomas and Patricia turned to see a pool of blood forming under Benjamin's head. Jaime put her hand on the wound to try and stop it, but the blood simply leaked through her fingers. "Somebody help," she screamed. Thomas tore off his shirt and pushed it hard against the wound, checking Benjamin's neck for a pulse. He didn't want to tell Jaime the truth, but she was going to find out eventually. Jaime cupped her mouth and slid backwards as Thomas shook his head and dropped his shirt to the deck. He fell against the rail and set his head between his legs.

At this point, Matthew had found his footing and was assessing the scene. Kara, Trishen and Patricia looked a bit banged up but relatively fine, so his focus remained heavily on Jaime, who now stared at the blood covering her vibrating hands. Matthew's instincts told him to help her, comfort her, but he wasn't even sure she needed comforting. Jaime was completely devoid of tears; not a single glimmer of anything resembling sadness.

"What was that?" Kara asked, picking up the unanswered question Thomas left dangling.

"I don't know," Matthew said, unsure if she had asked him directly. He cautiously stepped forward, expecting something else to strike the boat. "A rogue wave maybe?"

"A rogue wave would have toppled this dingy," Patricia said, giving up on salvaging anything from the pile of rubble.

"What do you think it was?" he said, seeking a way through the mess. "Jaws, perhaps?"

"We're gonna need one helleva bigger boat."

A sting of irritation curdled Matthew's blood. It looked as if Thomas and Jaime felt the same way.

"What?" Patricia shrugged. "I'm just tryin' to lighten the fuckin' mood here."

"We don't need the mood lightened, *Pat*," Jaime said, sneering. She held her hands out away from her as if she were deathly afraid of them. "We need to get the fuck out of this goddamned wasteland."

Matthew couldn't see her, but by her sudden silence, he knew Patricia was fuming. He shifted his legs forward in an unconscious attempt to hide his family jewels from Patricia's wrath.

"Look. We all just need to calm down," Thomas said. "We need to take a breath and figure out how to get help —"

"What in the devil's fucking dick is that?" Patricia, along with Kara and Trishen, peered through the window at something in the distance. Curious, Matthew turned his attention to the horizon. Through the clouded darkness he saw it.

Blue flames had risen from the ocean and touched the sky above. They formed a giant wall across the Atlantic, stretching from the northeast (or so he thought, believing the yacht was still on course) to the southwest, slowly — no quickly, upon second glance — sprinting toward what appeared now to be the edge of the world.

"What the hell?" Matthew whispered. He stepped from the cockpit and realized the flames weren't so much moving as they were growing from beneath the water. If he had to guess, they appeared to have been triggered by something… but what?

Thomas tried to see what they were all looking at, but could barely make anything out as Patricia and Kara joined Matthew against the rail.

"Is that fire?" Patricia asked.

"It looks like it's traveling on a guide," Matthew said, using his finger to follow the path it made. Jaime got to her knees to get a better look at this supposedly

remarkable flame.

"As if it had been built," Kara said.

"What in the world could produce that large a fire?" Patricia asked.

Matthew looked to Thomas with large eyes, igniting a smirk — a revelation that made both of them want to jump with excitement.

"The substance..." Thomas whispered, mimicking Matthew's wordless lips.

"The substance?" Kara said. "You mean that blue stuff we found in Bermuda."

Thomas looked like a kid who just had his cherry popped.

"Whoa there, boys," Patricia said, taking a step back. "You want to catch me up? What the hell are we talking about here?"

Jaime slid back down; the strain on her neck was too much for her. The flames had moved what she considered to have been a hundred or so miles since she first saw it, and it didn't look as if it was about to slow down any time soon.

"A week ago," Thomas started before Matthew had a chance, "we were on a dig in Bermuda. Hidden about... what would you say?"

"It was about fifteen feet," Matthew answered.

"Fifteen feet deep into a dig, we —" Glancing up at Matthew, Thomas quickly corrected himself. "Well, Matthew found this weird blue substance... actually, come to think of it, I think I still have some." Thomas clambered up and headed below deck. Matthew picked up the story.

"We weren't sure what it was. All we knew was it attached itself to any surface it made contact with. But when inserted back into the main pool, or body, or whatever you want to call it, it became liquid again."

"The shit was alive?" Patricia said.

"I wouldn't go that far. But it did have an extreme sense of itself."

"And don't forget about the Twinkie," Kara chimed in.

"You hungry, Reeses?"

Kara shot Patricia a contemptible look. "No. Some of the stuff attached itself to my shovel, and when Thomas pressed his pen into it, it formed back into its original shape."

"Like a Twinkie," Patricia smiled. "Ha. I get it." She slapped Kara with a snap on the shoulder. "Good one."

The sting burned Kara's clavicle. She rubbed it deeply, but it seemed to just make it worse.

"Check it out," Thomas said, pacing his way back to the deck. Trishen followed him to join in on the discovery. As he removed the cap of the vile that stored the blue substance, a beam of bright blue light lit the sky to the south. Matthew was the first to notice the flame wall was now heading northwest.

"It changed direction." He traced the wall back to its origin point with his finger. "It's heading for Florida…" he said silently, though loud enough for everyone to hear.

"How do you know that?" Kara said.

"Look at its trajectory. Assuming we're still on course, the flames start in the east, which, if I'm not mistaken, puts it directly in Bermuda. It then travels south-west to San Juan, and Northwest to Florida."

"Oh, my god," Kara hissed. "Oh, my god…"

"Do we really have to get God involved?" Patricia said.

"It can't be," Kara said, ignoring Patricia's inane comment.

"If I'm right," Matthew continued, "we'll see another one of those bright beams of light in a minute, changing the direction of this thing east, back to Bermuda."

"God damn it," Patricia said. "Would you two spit it out already."

"It's forming the triangle," Kara said, annoyed.

"And it's picking up speed."

Everyone fell silent. The flame did appear to be moving faster along the horizon, but was that just an illusion?

"Wait, what?" Patricia said loudly after the stunned shock wore off (which for her wasn't very long). "How can that be? The Bermuda Triangle is just an imaginary line that some scientist came up with to get rich."

"There's always a hint of truth behind any rumor or myth," Kara said, watching the line of fire with amazement. "Stories all need to come from something."

"What are you guys saying?" Jaime said. Her voice was deathly dry. "That the Bermuda Triangle is a giant blue wall of flame that we're about to get caught in the middle of?"

Out loud, it sounded ridiculous and Matthew wasn't sure if he wanted to answer. Then he figured, *what the hell?* "Yeah."

Jaime laid her head against the yacht and slapped her hand over her eyes. "I can't believe I thought you might actually know what you were doing."

"Jaime —" Matthew said, but stopped as the yacht rocked to its side once again, this time on the starboard side. Jaime slid across the deck with Benjamin's lifeless corpse right along with her and slammed her head into the rail wall. Thomas and Kara grabbed hold of the rail just in time to keep from flying backward along the deck. Before she fell, Trishen wrapped her arms around Thomas's leg, both of which left the safety of the deck as the yacht reached the height of its climb. Kara also dangled from the rail, her grip loosening before the boat splashed back down quicker than before, causing a large splash of water to wash the deck. Thomas, Kara and Trishen grunted with pain as they slammed hard against the deck. Thomas wasn't so much concerned for his own injuries as he was for Trishen's, who moved as if every bone in her body was broken.

"You okay?" Thomas asked, helping Trishen sit up.

"Yeah… yeah," she said, stretching every muscle she could think of to try and help relax them.

"Is everyone all right?" Matthew said, examining the deck. He'd been able to hang onto the cockpit wall with no ill effects.

"I think so," Kara said from his left. She was rolling her ankle. "I may have sprained my ankle."

Thomas was already attending to Trishen, so Matthew turned to Jaime. She inched away from Benjamin's body and lowered her head into her hands. "You all right, Jaime?" Matthew asked more out of courtesy than concern.

She looked to him but didn't answer. She simply rubbed the pain away from the bump forming on the side of her head.

It appeared everyone had survived. Everyone except… "Where's Patricia?"

Jaime and Trishen both looked around. Patricia was nowhere to be found. Trishen slowly stood. She didn't want help from Thomas, but accepted what she could nonetheless.

"Patricia?" Jaime called out. She stood to peer over the edge of the yacht. "Patricia!"

"Where is she?" Trishen said, joining Jaime at the rail. "Patricia!"

"What the hell hit us?" Kara said to Matthew.

"I'd only be guessing, but it might have been a shockwave from the ignition of the blue beam."

"You think?"

"I don't know. We've been hit twice now, and two corners of the triangle have been lit up.

"But we only heard one explosion," Kara said.

"Patricia!"

"And we only saw one beam of light," Thomas added. "We didn't even notice the fire until it was nearly half way to San Juan."

"But I did see the beam of light," Matthew interjected. "In Bermuda."

"The night before we found the blue stuff," Kara said.

"Patricia!"

"I may have caused the explosion after digging it up," Matthew said a little sheepishly. "It may be what knocked me unconscious."

"But what was the trigger?" Kara asked. She wasn't the only one wondering. Matthew shook his head, bewildered.

"You people are insane," Jaime yelled. "My friends — my crew — are getting killed one by one and all you idiots can talk about is science fiction bullshit."

"Well, hold on," Matthew said, "because if it's not bullshit, another beam is about to light up Florida with the final explosion."

Jaime shook her head in disbelief as Matthew's team watched the flame so intently, they all looked like statues.

"I'm going in after her," Jaime said to Trishen. She climbed up and slid her legs over the rail.

Trishen grabbed her arm. "You can't." The fire in Jaime's eyes told her she was in no position to talk her out of it.

Just then, another beam of light shot into the air, followed closely behind by the low rumble of an explosion, sending the wall of flame soaring off, even faster this time, back to Bermuda to complete the triangle.

Jaime couldn't believe it. "You have got to be kidding me."

"Everyone brace yourselves," Matthew yelled.

Thomas and Kara hurried to the stern and wrapped their arms around the rail. Matthew stood against the back of the cockpit wall, gripping the corner as best he could.

"Come on," Trishen said before joining Thomas and Kara. "Jaime, hurry."

Jaime saw a love in her eyes, a need for her to think about what she was doing. She looked into the dark, almost black depths of the water below her. Even if Patricia were near the surface, how on earth would she ever find her in this? Jaime finally came to her senses just before the next shockwave blast tipped the back of the yacht upward. She slipped from the rail and landed with a crack on the deck.

"Jaime!" Trishen lost her grip on the rail as she reached out for her friend. As Thomas and Kara lifted off the deck, Trishen slipped to the cockpit wall and forced a web of cracks to open up in the glass with the smash of her head. Jaime, meanwhile, followed Benjamin's body down the side of the yacht to the forward deck, the tip of which had been completely submerged under water. She grabbed hold of a buoy affixed to the cockpit wall as Benjamin's body hit the ocean. For a moment, she thought about joining him, letting the water take her as it had done with the rest of her crew. But she couldn't let the tragedies of everyone else kill her as well. If the ocean wanted her, it would have to come and take her. Benjamin's body disappeared as the *Endeavor* came crashing down once again. Jaime kept her grip on the buoy for a moment longer, frozen. When she finally got control of her nerves, she made her way to the back of the yacht to check on Trishen.

Apparently, she didn't have to; Thomas was already with her, holding tightly to the back of her head.

"You okay?" Jaime asked.

"Yeah," Trishen said. "Just a bit of a bump."

Jaime knelt down next to her. Thomas could see the need for affirmation that Trishen was telling the truth. He nodded with a quiet smile. Jaime grabbed his shoulder in recognition of her thankfulness.

"Look," Matthew said. "It's almost complete."

"What happens then?" Kara asked.

"We'll just have to wait and see."

The wind blew harder and a light drizzle began to fall. Matthew and Kara remained focused on the flame wall. His heart pounded with anticipation for what might happen — if anything would happen — when the triangle was complete.

"Come on," Thomas said as the rain got harder. "Let's get you back down below."

Matthew watched Thomas help Trishen to her feet and then noticed Jaime settle against the wall, exhausted — more mentally than physically. And it hit him.

"Kaleena," he heard himself say under his breath. His eyes grew three sizes and everything disappeared as if the world had been extinguished. All he saw was Kaleena, sprawled across the floor like a small misfit toy, unaware that anything had happened, unaware that she could be hurt — bleeding for all he knew. And all the while he had been more interested in a dream.

"What is it?" Kara asked. He didn't answer; he didn't even turn to her. He simply ran for the cockpit, shoving Thomas and Trishen out of his way as he passed them.

"Matthew, what's wrong?" Thomas called out, a yell that dissipated so quickly, Matthew didn't even register it.

"Oh, God," Kara said. But her mind wasn't on Kaleena. She yelled to Thomas but no sound seemed to come out. It was as if she, and possibly everyone on the boat, had gone deaf.

The rain came harder. Lightning flashed around them. Kara limped toward the cockpit, a twinge of pain biting at her heel. She was knocked back when one of the bolts struck her feet from the *Endeavor*, giving the yacht a little shake and triggering a burst of gale force winds to hit the yacht in all directions in unison.

All of the glass exploded. Jaime curled into a ball and rolled to her side. Thomas covered Trishen to protect her. The cockpit crushed inward a few meters, causing Matthew to duck down and tumble to the ground just before reaching the stairwell. He was lucky — Kara felt the tremendous force of the wind first hand as it crushed her body inward as if she were Popeye's spinach can, about to be opened to help rescue Olive Oyl from whatever scheme Bluto had gotten her into this week. Small cuts traced along the veins of her exposed skin. Blood formed around her eyes and ears.

The wind nipped at Jaime's back, causing the rain to prick her body like a storm of needles. Each drop sliced her skin and tore holes in her shirt and pants. As she lifted her head to see what was happening, her hair was nearly ripped from her head. With what she could see through the slits of her eyes, the larger rain drops appeared to have been frozen in time and were keeping her locked in place. She lowered her head back to the deck and remained still. Any sudden movements and the rain or the wind would rip her skin right off.

But the yacht could only withstand the pressure for so long. The rail soon started to bend in on itself to become a thin string of metal; the cockpit walls had nearly collapsed; the wheelhouse had been obliterated; and the deck was about to be completely uprooted. In one fell swoop, all of it — the cockpit, the rail and the deck — all compressed together. Everyone remained floating above the bottom half of the yacht, which held strong among the harsh winds.

Inside, Kaleena lied unconscious and half naked in the bathroom of her cabin. A small cut, bloodless, yet scarred, appeared on the top of her head. Lauren was washed up against the wall of her own cabin, desperately trying to stay afloat among the water that had found its way inside the yacht. She only just felt the piercing rain strike her body when the massive line of wood and glass crashed

down into the center of the yacht, splicing a hole into the middle of the *Endeavor* and splitting the once exquisite double-family cruise ship into two dozen pieces to be buried in the middle of the Atlantic.

*   *   *

Kaleena couldn't tell if she was conscious or dreaming. It was as if she were flying, wishing she could see the clouds below her. But a cold sweat poured around her, washing her body clean. She couldn't move any of her limbs, not even her head. In fact, her neck felt broken. The odd thing was, she didn't feel dead. Her body was numb but her thoughts were clear, concise and fluid. Maybe she *had* broken her neck, paralyzing her body. But how could she know for sure? She wondered where Matthew might be, whether she was in her bed, with her father watching carefully over her, or if something bad *had* happened, as she felt in her gut before the boat started twitching.

The boat started twitching…

That's what it was. She'd woken up, had seen a strange triangle of fire in the mirror. But Matthew was nowhere near her at the time. Had he forgotten her? Had he decided Atlantis was too important to stay with her? Was he simply getting a breath of fresh air (which she wished she could do right now) when all of the havoc started? What about Jaime? Where was she?

(*Fucking her boyfriend, maybe?*)

Stop that, she thought. Jaime was of no concern to her. She had to find a way out of wherever she was at the moment. But how?

It was then her lungs grew cold and her chest constricted. She realized she was under water and about to drown. Had she done this to herself? The more she thought, it seemed, the more her body ached, though she still couldn't move anything. It became her goal to find strength in her arms and legs again, to swim. It was impossible; there was no escape for her this time. Her mother and father were on the yacht, either completely unaware of her disappearance or too caught up in

the destruction to care about where she was or if she was okay.

Then it happened — a tiny movement across her arm. It wrapped around her, sliding along her bare stomach (under what she believed to be her shirt), her spine and then back to her arms. It felt like a set of smooth fingers, but could have been anything. Would it save her? Protect her?

Kill her?

Is this it? she thought for the briefest of moments. *Have my visions finally led me to my own vibrant death?*

As the touch spread to both arms, a warm softness caressed her neck and cheek. Was it breath? Was it warm pockets of air within the ocean water? She couldn't tell, but didn't necessarily care either. The warmth helped heat her freezing body and send a stillness to her brain, calming her fears. She didn't know if it was her imagination or not, but she thought she heard a soft hum of music surround her, much like what her mother used to sing when putting her to sleep as a baby. It made her feel safe, regardless. She felt needed; she felt loved. It was exactly where she wanted to be. She no longer felt her chest tightening, even though she knew it still was.

After a few long seconds (*minutes?*), a pair of lips came together with her own. She wasn't quite sure what to do — allow it to happen or pull away. But the longer she allowed it, the more right it seemed, and the more willing she was to just let it happen. Her lungs were soon alive with oxygen. They still hurt, they still throbbed, but she no longer felt she was going to die. Whatever was helping her — whoever was there with her — was trying to rescue her.

She didn't fight it; she couldn't, as the more she received oxygen, the more tired and dizzy she became. Eventually, she passed out and let the ocean sweep her away.

BOOK THREE

KNOWLEDGE IS POWER

France – Friday, 9:35 pm
(*Thirteen Years Ago*)

The plane was nearly empty. Only about a dozen or so passengers mulled about, some who were already seated, some still trying to situate their bags in the cramped overhead compartments. A young woman who appeared to have stepped right out of an eighties Madonna video walked to the far aisle. She wore a black skirt that fell just shy of her knees, a couple of tank tops (one black and shorter than the red one underneath), a couple of necklaces that fell past what she considered her twelve-year-old chest, and several rings that covered nearly every finger on her hand, some of which she had before she left the states, a few she picked up from vendors around France. It was her first solo trip and her first jaunt outside of the U.S. She had been talking about traveling abroad for about four years, and even though her parents had probably disowned her by now, she was proud of the steps she took on her transition from dependency to pure escape. She had no regrets over anything she'd seen or done. In fact, she did exactly what she needed to become a strong, independent woman in a world she still knew almost nothing about. Whether it be taking tours of landmarks, hiking through country sides, eating everywhere from high-caliber restaurants to hole-in-the-wall eateries, or expressing her inner desires and discovering what it meant to be uninhibited, everything she did was her choice, and each of those choices pleased her beyond empowerment — especially on her final night when she made what she believed was pure love to a man she'd been flirting with over the last three weeks. It wasn't the first night she spent with him, or even the first night they'd been together sexually, but her last night with him felt more powerful than anything she'd experienced before. From losing her virginity to Ryan Grace the night before she left for France, to the three or four other men she slept with in the first six weeks of her trip, this was the first time she ever had a real orgasm. It was exactly what she was hoping it would be, and just the right gift to say goodbye. And through it all — or because of it all — she was happy to be heading back to familiar ground after ten incredible weeks of ravishing freedom and embracing desire.

If now she could only find love.

She reached one of the seats near the center of the right side of the plane. Even though there were still plenty of seats up front, she always liked to sit near the middle. It gave her a better view of those around her, but didn't make her seem as if she were trying to avoid something. She grabbed the top of her tan canvas messenger bag that brushed across her hip as she walked and pulled the strap over her head. The bag was nearly empty except for her necessary essentials (laptop, magazines and Kleenex), her diary, for which she wrote almost every detail of every day, and a couple of first printings of French books she found to be very overwhelming in theme and structure. Even though her French was still mostly basic, what she understood of the beautiful words that made up the poetic, romantic prose inspired her to continue her education in French literature.

After placing the bag in the overhead compartment, the woman noticed the plane filling up quickly with passengers. She took a seat next to the window and gazed around at the others, getting a better sense of what the eight-hour trip would be like. In the back near the galleys and bathrooms was a woman who looked like she hadn't had any sleep in the last three days, cuddling an infant (possibly breast feeding him) and trying to keep another child (about six from what she could tell) quiet and in his seat, a feat that would turn out to be futile, as he never shut his mouth during the flight. To her right, a couple of rows behind her and in the center aisle were a couple of teens, possibly French, maybe British, around seventeen, maybe eighteen. The boy was tall with a fair complexion and business-like wardrobe; the girl was sweet, blond, and a bit more liberal with her tight fitting clothes and nose ring. They were nearly sitting on top of each another, their eyes never leaving the other. The fingers of one hand were intertwined tightly together, while their other hands moved around each other's face, shoulder, leg — usually finding their way to the erotic zones as they whispered nonsense into one another's ears, savoring each kiss by lying her head on his shoulder or placing her forehead to his chin and giggling. It was only a matter of time before the mile-high club inducted them as members. Up front, just getting onto the plane was a large, husky gentleman, British, judging by his accent, and near drunk, if not completely smashed. His eyes were swelling, sweat seeping from every pore of his body. His speech was slurred and about five decibels louder than it should have been. To the woman's relief, the man took a seat near the front of the plane and not next to her. She just hoped that when the man's liquor got the best of him and the dinner he ate a few hours ago decided to come back up for another round, she was either asleep or was quietly listening to the headphones she'd make sure she got from the stewardess after lift-off.

"Is this seat taken?"

The woman turned away from the fat drunk to eye a young man standing above her, smiling graciously, his brow curled into a questionable puppy curvature. Her smile melted into her throat. Breathing a sheepish sigh, she suddenly felt quite

shy. Could it have been his gleaming brown eyes, his soft professor-type haircut or the pure white teeth that made her feel ten years old? Or was it the way he looked at her, as if she were the most beautiful creature on the face of the planet?

"I don't know," she said coyly. "Is it?"

He now seemed to be the one turning red as a lobster. "You sure?"

"Hey, better than having that guy sitting here," she said, nodding over to the fat drunk, who reached for the flight attendants blue skirt, coming within millimeters of touching her rear end, making it appear as if that was what he was reaching for to begin with. "I said I need a drink, doll," the fat drunk said.

The flight attendant slipped away from him and said, with a bright, cheery smile (and disgrace in her eyes), "And I said you have to wait until after lift-off."

"I've already lifted off, cheeks," the fat drunk said, trying to wink, but unable to figure out how. The flight attendant just walked away, but not before the man got a quick pat of her backside, to which the flight attendant replied, "Horse-fuck."

The young man turned back to the woman, his smile rich with enthusiasm. "I could go get him if you'd like."

She let out a quiet huff of laughter. "You do and I make sure you don't leave this flight with all of your extremities."

"Is that a threat?"

"Only if you want it to be."

The young man pushed what appeared to be a camera bag into the overhead compartment. "The seat's officially taken," he said. "I just need to use the facilities real quick. Don't let anyone, especially your boyfriend over there, take my seat."

"I won't. As long as you wash your hands." She winked and the young man walked away, continually looking back, at times attempting to hide the fact that he was ever looking back. She knew he was because she was doing the same thing. He took one last glance at her before entering the bathroom, prompting the woman to face forward, giddily unable to stop blushing. It felt wonderful and serene, something she'd never felt and hoped would never end. Waiting for him to return, the woman slipped off her strapless shoes and rubbed the balls of her

feet. It was going to be nice to spend a day relaxing in her favorite spa, treating herself to a foot massage, manicure, pedicure and mud bath. After a few minutes, she leaned back, thinking about what she might say when her new neighbor came back from doing whatever he may be doing in the bathroom. She closed her eyes and couldn't help but breathe a soft chuckle of seventh-grade immaturity she'd no doubt try and hide when he returned.

When she opened her eyes, the boy from the back of the plane looked at her with curiosity from the seat next to her. "Hi. I'm Kevin."

The woman sat up a little. "Hi, Kevin."

"Are you from America?" he asked, his legs freely moving back and forth. "I am. We're in France right now, but not for long. The plane's taking us back home. Do you know how big the ocean is? My dad says it's ninety percent of the earth. I don't believe him. He's a priest. We're visiting the Cardinal. Do you know that's a bird? I had a bird once, a parakeet, but it died when I was five. My mom won't give me another pet. She says I'm not responsible enough. I think I am." Kevin lifted his foot up to the seat and tied his shoes. "I asked for a dog last Christmas, but I didn't get one. I got a skateboard instead. I use it all the time. I like it. But it hurts when I fall off. It gave me a scar on my knee. My mommy used bacteria to get the blood off, now it's scabbed. I pick at it. Want to see?"

Kevin lifted his pant leg before she could respond and started picking at the small scab on his knee. "Why aren't you wearing shoes? Mine are old, but my mom says I can't get new ones. I want some with wheels, but my mommy says they're too expensive."

"I knew it. You dropped me for a younger man."

The woman looked to the young man, disappointed, but playfully so. "Well, you know," she said, "I do like 'em young."

"Kevin," a voice called from behind them. "Kevin, get over her. Stop bothering those people."

"I have to go. Bye." Kevin hopped off the seat and ran back to his mother.

"All yours," the woman said.

"I don't know. How do I know you won't cheat on me again?"

"You don't. But that's what makes it exciting."

The young man nodded. "I guess it is," he said and took a seat next to her, barely able to keep his eyes off her.

"So, you don't have an accent," the woman said.

"Damn, you noticed."

"I mean to say, you're heading back home."

"Yeah. Boston. And judging by your lack of accent, would I be correct in assuming the same of you?"

"You would. Except I'm homeward bound to Rhode Island."

"Were you on vacation?"

"Sure was. First time overseas. You?"

"I wish." He rolled his eyes and looked away for the first time since he sat down. Their eyes reconnected immediately.

"Business?"

"Research, actually. For school."

"In the summer? That kinda sucks, doesn't it?"

"Not really. I'm only taking eight units. I'm hoping to get into a master's program early, so by taking a couple of classes each summer, I should have enough to graduate in the fall and move into a program next spring."

"Sounds like you've got things figured out."

"You don't?"

"I don't even know what college I want to go to, much less what I want to do with the rest of my life."

"You're not in college, then?"

The woman wasn't sure if the question was accompanied by nervousness or simply a question to get to know her better. She decided to answer honestly. "I just graduated high school."

"Wow. I wouldn't have thought. You look much more mature than that."

"Older, you mean."

The young man chuckled. "No, not at all. But your eyes... they just feel more experienced."

"Well, thank you, I guess." She knew he didn't mean anything by it except as a compliment. "I was hoping time away would clear my head a bit."

"It didn't help, I take it?"

"Only in making me more mature." She was being cryptic, but she could tell he understood exactly what she meant. And she didn't seem to mind one bit. "Maybe that's what you're seeing."

"Could be."

They sat together in silence for a moment before the woman broke the awkwardness. "So what do you study?"

"Archaeology."

The corner of her lip rose ever so slightly. "So, you're, like, an Indiana Jones?"

He chuckled, matching her joy. "Huh. More like a low-rent Alan Grant." He waited for recognition that never came. "Have you never seen *Jurassic Park*?"

"I don't watch many movies. They're a waste of time, if you ask me."

"Books, too?"

"Literature," she said, pronouncing each syllable carefully, "is what I care about."

"And judging by the glow in those beautiful eyes of yours, you know exactly what you want to pursue in life, even if you don't realize it yet."

The woman turned away sheepishly and looked out the window. She needed to hide the dark rush of blood to her face. The flutter in her chest that had been present since first laying her eyes on the young man grew faster and harder.

"You okay?" For a second he thought he might have gone too far too soon.

"Yeah," she said, turning back to him. "Sorry."

"You have nothing to be sorry about," the young man said before being interrupted by the flight attendant, who began her speech about oxygen masks and floating devices.

"Looks like we're about to take off," she said.

"Yup. And it looks like it'll be a pretty good flight."

Her eyes glowed. "I'm Diana. Reisen," she added as if as an afterthought.

"Henry Green." They shook hands and didn't turn away from one another throughout the entirety of the flight attendant's very exuberant speech.

Connecticut – Thursday, 11:36 pm
(3 years ago)

Case number M2-816-L2420. Here to assist with cleaning the body and collecting all evidence is pathology assistant Dr. David Fallon. We've taken initial pictures of the deceased and will now begin our initial review.

Appearance upon arrival shows no immediate signs of cause. A pink nightgown, cut down the center by ER doctors, has been folded flat across her body with the right side having been placed over the left and kept in sleeping position. There is no apparent forensic evidence on the nightgown.

Removing the gown, subject is wearing pink and white underwear. Crash cart paddle marks appear on subject's chest and side, as does bruising in the center of the chest between the subject's nipples to signify performance of cardiopulmonary resuscitation.

(Click-click)

No other marks appear on subject's chest or stomach.

David will now remove subject's clothing to begin external examination.

(click-Click)

No additional bruising appears on any part of subject's body, arms, legs or neck. Nails are dirty and bitten. Subject's hair is heavily greasy, but otherwise clean. No visible wounds or fresh bumps on the skull. Eyes are clean without reddening or trauma. Lips and mouth are also clear. Pubic region does not show signs of aggression or forced physical contact and there are no signs of external liquid, including blood or semen.

Help me turn her over.

(unghh... thwump)

Back and buttocks are also clean of external fluid, cuts or bruising.

Turn her back over, please, then take your samples and move her to the wash table.

*   *   *

Case number M2-816-L2420 has been cleaned, weighed and measured. Subject is eleven-year-old Caucasian female, brown hair, brown eyes, four foot eleven, ninety-six pounds. There is a small birthmark shaped like a cross on the subject's thigh just below her left buttock, and there's old scar tissue on her left knee. We have taken samples of subject's nails and gums, hair and skin. We have also taken a small sample of skin from the pubic region to test for trace of sexual activity. Based on my completed external review, I have found no evidence for cause of death. I have scheduled an internal examination for Saturday evening, to be performed with the assistance of Dr. David Fallon and witnessed by forensic examiner Mark Kinkaid.

Connecticut – Saturday, 11:59 pm
(3 years ago)

Kaleena's body lay still on the examiner's table, covered by a thin baby blue sheet. A light hanging above her stomach made her already pasty skin glow an unnatural white. Dr. Jon Warner stood over her, examining her features. He had been a pathologist and coroner for nearly fifteen years and whether it be murder victims, car accident fatalities, or shocking twists of fate — not much bothered him. Except when he had a child on his table. The youngest he'd ever worked on was an infant who died after his mother shook him so dramatically, his brain was knocked loose. "Children should never end up on an autopsy table," he always said. But life is never what you hope it will be. Sometimes, it was just cruel.

"Are you ready, doctor?" Mark Kinkaid stood on the opposite side of the body. Jon averted his moist eyes and nodded.

"Yes, David. Go ahead and remove the sheet so we can begin our internal review."

David Fallon, standing at the foot of the table, nodded, "Yes, doctor," and removed the sheet from Kaleena's body. Jon looked her over to make sure he hadn't missed anything in his external review, which was his way of stalling the inevitable. *Get it over with*, he thought. *It'll be much harder if you continue this sulking.* He picked up the rubber body brick from the table next to him. As he did, David slipped his arms underneath Kaleena's body — one arm under her shoulder blades, the other near the small of her back — and lifted her off the table about six inches. Jon set the body brick just under the curvature of her shoulder blades. After lowering the body back to the table, David adjusted the light to point directly at the center of Kaleena's chest. Jon checked his gloves (another stalling tactic) then picked up his scalpel.

"I will now begin my T-incision," he said, placing his hand just above the right breast bone. He set the scalpel about two inches in from the edge of her shoulder.

Need to go back… It was a soft whisper.

Jon looked up. "Did you say something?"

"No," David said.

Mark shook his head quizzically. Unsure of what he had heard, Jon wrote it off as another way to keep himself from cutting this young girl open. He readjusted his shoulders and dragged the scalpel slowly across the top of Kaleena's chest.

Blood bubbled and then poured from the cut, dripping down Kaleena's collarbone and into her hair. Jon stopped his incision immediately, having cut less than an inch of her body.

"Is there supposed to be that much blood?" Mark asked curiously, snapping a few pictures off before Jon could grab a towel and wipe the blood away.

"I've never seen that much," David said.

Jon pressed the towel to the wound when it wouldn't stop bleeding. "David, hold this, will you."

David did as instructed. "Why is it still bleeding?" he asked as the towel slowly grew red under his hand.

"I don't…" Jon looked Kaleena over carefully. There was only one reason that would warrant that much blood. He knelt down to give himself an eye line level with Kaleena's body and carefully watched her chest without blinking.

"Shit," he whispered after a moment. "Would you look at that?"

It took a few seconds for David to see what Jon saw, but when he did, his face flushed white. "Is she breathing?"

"Fuck me," Mark whispered. "She's alive?"

Jon bolted to his office. "Keep pressure on that wound. Mark, grab a med kit from under the shelving there to your right. We need to sew up that wound ASAP."

"Where are you going?" David said.

"To call Dr. Klein." Jon slammed the door behind him and had the phone receiver in his hand within seconds.

David reiterated Jon's demands, then turned to Kaleena. "My god," he whispered, mesmerized by the slow, rhythmic rise and fall of her chest.

"I need…" Kaleena whispered, her lips barely moving. "I need… honor… I need… trust… I need…"

Unknown Location – Time Unknown

… love.

The word echoed softly throughout the darkness.

Kaleena smelled a light mold in the otherwise freshness of the air. To her left, she heard a small trickle of water. The moisture in the air nipped at her cold skin as she moved her arms into a more comfortable position closer to her body. Her knees rose inward to her chest. After closing her arms around them, the chill quickly gave way to a serene warmth. As she allowed her exhausted body to regain its energy, she realized she was wearing some sort of dress or nightgown, which aided in helping warm her legs. She couldn't remember putting on any clothes, especially a dress, which she hadn't worn in nearly five years. Not since her mother stopped taking her to church.

"You don't need a church to praise God, Kaleena," Jaime told her when asked why they weren't going. "All you need is your heart."

"Then why did we go before?"

Jaime took her time to answer. "Because, sweetie. You can't praise God if you don't know how. You now know everything you need to know."

Kaleena was upset; she wanted to see her friends — the only friends she had that were her own age. In Sunday school, she was equal to everyone else. Solving math problems, examining history lessons, creating science projects, and reading the most comprehensive literary texts came easily and naturally to her. Bible studies were a different beast altogether, and she was always excited to learn something new from her Sunday school teacher. Her classmates never sneered at her for being "better." They simply saw another kid they could play with, do arts and crafts with and have fun with. But she didn't want to argue with her mother on the day of our Lord, so she whispered, "Okay," and skulked back into her room. She spent the rest of the day flipping through her mother's Bible, writing out little stories on characters she read about and prayed whenever she thought about her friends, her mom, or her dad. She prayed for their health, for His comfort and His love; she prayed to give her mom space until she remembered what church was really about; and she prayed for strength, asking Him to help her remember that when she was old enough to go on her own, that she would; that she would never forget Him.

At dinnertime, she finally took off her black dress highlighted with sprinkled daisies and put on a pair of shorts and a pink shirt with the phrase, "I believe... in nothing that isn't there." The dress would sit untouched until Jaime gave it to the Salvation Army two years later. Kaleena had outgrown the dress by then and had found meaning in science. She hadn't completely forsaken the Lord, but she didn't take His word the same way anymore either.

It only took a moment for the memory to fade into the pitch black of her current surroundings. A shallow tear streamed down Kaleena's nose. Before it hit the tip, she wiped it away and then dried what little moisture was left in her eye. Her heart skipped as thoughts of blindness struck her.

How? Why? What happened to her?

A flash of the blue-flamed triangle eclipsed her mind and pushed her to remember the *Endeavor* being hit by —

What? What hit the Endeavor?

—something. That's when she first saw the triangle, her visage huddled in the center as if she were being caged within. But it wasn't her; not really. It was more her spirit, her mind removed from her body and taken captive by whatever it was that controlled the flame. The sight held her, unflinching, unmoving, until the yacht was hit once again, this time smashing her head against the wall. She fell to the ground, groggy but still conscious. Her head pounded red-hot with fury. A scream in the distance urged her to crawl toward the door and try to pull herself to her feet. The higher she rose, the dizzier and more nauseated she became. The only thing she could do was allow her mind to shut down. That's all she could remember...

Except it wasn't.

She saw the flame, smelled the salty, methane-tainted air and tasted the ashy-texture of water on her tongue. And there was someone there with her, a hidden force of resurrection who touched her, felt her, supported her... tasted her.

Loved her.

Kaleena touched the tips of her fingers to her soft, moist lips, feeling the pressure of the other's lips on hers; the cold rush of life enters her lungs; a euphoria striking her body as she fell back into a deep sleep. Did it save her, or...

Was she dead?

Her fingers traced the contours of her lips as her palm covered her mouth. Her eyes grew wide. She couldn't be dead. Death was supposed to be gentler — freer. This felt too real; too heavy. She still felt confined to her own mind, trapped by her own insecurities and fears. But how could she know for sure? She was once considered dead for three days, but she couldn't recall anything from that time. She'd tried to convince herself she'd only gone into a coma that slowed her heart rate down to immeasurable levels. She couldn't comprehend how death could

be simply nothing at all, having fallen asleep one night on her couch to wake up on a coroner's table wearing nothing but a blanket, four men standing over her, awestruck. One she knew right away was a doctor; another she assumed was the pathologist. The other two she assumed may be a reporter and his photographer or forensic assistant. She couldn't tell through her blurred vision; all she knew for sure was that none of them were her father.

"Where am I?" she asked, her throat hard.

"Miss Stevens. I'm Doctor Klein."

Kaleena tried steadily to focus on the two men near the lockers, but her normal eyesight wouldn't return. It frightened her a little.

"Can you look at me?" Doctor Klein asked, placing his fingertips lightly on her chin to turn her head.

"Where?" she repeated, finding it easier to focus on the doctor.

"You're in the medical examiner's office of St. Mary's Hospital."

"A hospital?" Kaleena sat up and was immediately knocked queasy. She lied back down and readjusted the sheet that nearly slipped off her body.

"Why am I here? Where's my dad?" Her voice was growing stronger.

"He's on his way."

"What happened?"

"There's no way to really sugar coat this, Miss Stevens, so I'll just say it."

Kaleena focused on the doctor's dour, somewhat frightened appearance. "What?"

"You've been dead for the past three days."

Kaleena sat up this time. A cold chill bit her back as she held the sheet tightly to her chest. Even though she really hadn't blossomed yet, she was still aware that there were four strange men in the room. "What do you mean I've been dead for three days? Where's my dad?" The fear overwhelmed her to tears.

"I'm here," Matthew said loudly as he rushed into the room. "My god. It can't be."

Kaleena wanted to run to him, but he beat her to it, wrapping her in his arms

with a loving, welcome hug. "I can't believe this," Matthew said through a river of tears. "I can't believe it. It's a miracle."

When he pulled away, he held Kaleena's cold, bare shoulders in his hands as he looked her over (afraid, maybe, that if he let go, she'd slip away again). Her skin was still a pasty white, but she was staring right at him as if nothing had happened.

"Dad, what happened?"

"I don't know, Kaleena," he said, embracing her again. "I don't know, but that doesn't matter anymore."

"It does, actually," Doctor Klein said, disturbing their reunion.

They both turned to him. "What?"

"Mr. Stevens, your daughter was declared dead."

"I know that. In fact, I should sue the hell out of this hospital for it."

"Mr. Stevens, please. You know as well as I do that she was DOA when she got to the hospital."

Matthew couldn't argue the point. He just rubbed his hands down Kaleena's arms, hoping to warm her up. "It still doesn't matter."

"It does matter, Mr. Stevens. No one has ever returned from the dead like this. We need to keep her here for observation and tests."

"No," Matthew said immediately. "No."

"Mr. Stevens. We need to make sure all of her organs, muscles, nerves and especially her brain are functioning properly before we're able to release her. After what she's been through, it's a miracle she's even sitting up, much less talking right now."

"You're right," Matthew whispered. "It is a miracle." He carefully wiped the remaining tears from her cheeks. "I'll give you two days. Do what you have to, but I'm taking my daughter home tomorrow night."

"If we find everything is normal and stable," Doctor Klein said.

Matthew heard him but didn't want to acknowledge him. "You're going to be okay?" A question? A statement? It was unclear.

Kaleena nodded. "Yeah," she said. "I'll be okay. You'll stay with me, though, right?"

"Yeah, of course. Where else would I go?"

"Did you call mom?"

Matthew let go of Kaleena for the first time since arriving.

Kaleena knew right away. "She's not coming."

Matthew's head dropped. Was it out of shame, or could he just not look his daughter in the eye any longer?

"It's okay."

Matthew looked up, his eyes bright red.

"I'll be okay." Her lips curled and she looked to the doctor. "If I can get another sheet, and maybe my clothes. It's damn cold in here."

A slight shiver crawled up Kaleena's spine. She told Matthew she'd be okay, but those missing days changed her. Everything about the experience led her to believe that it was all for some larger purpose, which she spent a few endless nights attempting to understand. She never could, not until she stared at the darkness that now enveloped her. It occurred to her that since her death, she's relied heavily, and almost solely, on sight, able to see things in nature, society and cultures that wouldn't have been there had she been ignorant of her surroundings. Whatever rescued her from the ocean must have needed to strip her away from her weakness in order to give her a second chance to find out what really happened, and for what reason. Her darkness had become a symbol. She realized now that nothing would change if she simply gave in and allowed her fear to guide her. She needed to keep moving forward to find her way home.

Kaleena stood with caution so as not to hit her head on a low ceiling or platform that might be settled above her. The dress slipped from her knees and fell softly against her body, as if it didn't want to hurt her. Arms outstretched, she took a step forward. The floor was glassy, but despite the smooth moistness that left her feet warm, the balls of her feet gripped the ground as if she were on asphalt. After a few yards, Kaleena was ready to try a new direction, but then her hand hit some

type of surface. Much like the ground, the it smooth, wet and glassy. She quickly assumed this was the source of the dripping water, however, she couldn't feel any nicks or cracks. There wasn't even an edge to connect the wall to the floor, just a smooth curvature, melding the two into one. Confused, Kaleena stood on her toes (which still gripped the ground with ease) and reached as high as she could. If there was a ceiling, it was too high for her. Based on this, Kaleena had only one choice left — she'd have to walk the room in hopes of finding a door, a seam or a trigger of some sort… anything to illuminate her situation and guide her to the answers she needed to escape her glassy confines.

Time seemed to stop as she made her way around the wall that never ended. At first she wondered if the room was endless, but the more plausible answer was that it was circular, and she had simply gone around and around. If that was the case, there was no way out, not by normal everyday means, at least. The only way out of this situation was to use the one tool she knew she'd always have.

Based on the construction of the wall, she knew she had to be in some sort of domed room that did not include any corners whatsoever. Water painted the surfaces, which also could be glass. However, if it was glass, why was there no light? Was it a dome inside of a cave or underground? Was it covered by a large black cloth? Maybe it had to do with what she was doing there, rather than where she actually was. She was sure no one on the *Endeavor*, including her father, had brought her here. The only other person she thought of was the woman — that beautiful woman who spoke to her just before the yacht was attacked. It couldn't have been a mere coincidence, though according to Patricia, the shaking could have come from methane gases that apparently roamed the Atlantic. But it didn't feel right; it couldn't be that simple. Then again, this all could very well be a dream that didn't make any sense to her.

Find your way through the fog…

Her voice was clear. Kaleena needed to interpret the words. The woman had said she was connected to Atlantis and that she would save them. But how? Was she, right now, somewhere in Atlantis, if it did in fact exist? Could there still be

survivors living in a city under water? That was impossible. Wasn't it?

Don't think of impossibility, Kaleena thought. *Think with an open mind. Everything is true; everything is real.*

It would be hard, but Kaleena needed to believe in the impossible, the improbable, the unscientific. If Atlantis existed, it would be much more advanced than she could possibly know. And if that were true, she'd have to think far beyond the confines of what she knew. If Atlanteans had to test someone to find out if they were strong enough to believe, then placing them in a pitch black dome and waiting for them to figure out how to once again see would prove that they were ready to understand the complexity of Atlantis and its demise. If her dreams had been real, Kaleena was meant to save Lauren's baby and bring peace to all of Atlantis. But until she understood how to leave the darkness behind, she wouldn't be able to understand what awaited her.

How, then, could she understand? Maybe the answer wasn't in the unknown, but in the simplicity. Perhaps, all she needed to do was ask.

"Lights on," she said, softly, disbelief filling her voice.

Yeah, like that was going to work, she thought.

After a few seconds of contemplation something occurred to her. She pressed her palms firmly against the wall. The water spread across the back of her hands, warm... alive. A light smile crossed her lips as she lowered her forehead to the wall in between her hands.

Illuminate, she thought forcefully.

The entire room lit up as if the sun had reached its zenith in the middle of the night. Kaleena spun around. Dozens, possibly hundreds of reflections of varying sizes and weights mimicked her every move. Above her, below her, she was everywhere — a maddening dizziness of a carnival hall of mirrors that produced a radical uncertainty of which one was really her. The size of the room was indistinguishable. Her other selves all wore the same form fitting white dress with thin shoulders and even thinner laced sleeves covering her arms. The gown was decorated in what looked to be butterflies or dragonflies, though it could have been

something different, something more meaningful. The top covered her back, but dropped down in the front just enough to show the tiniest bit of cleavage. Around her waist was a white lace belt, tied in the back, the tails dropping to her feet. Her hair was layered, the underbelly, clean and smooth, draped down and across her shoulders. On top of that, another portion of hair was tied in the middle of her head with a small white ribbon, allowing the ponytail to lay flat against the back of her head. As she admired her doppelgängers, she noticed her makeup, which included a light silver eye shadow that made her heavy black eyelashes stand out among the white of the room. Soft pink blush highlighted her cheekbones, and dark, maroon lipstick lit up her mouth.

Kaleena reached out for her doppelgängers, all of whom extended their arms to her, each one needing to touch her but unable to. The young girls staring back at her weren't her, and yet they were. She moved closer, but the room faded away from her with every step. It was no longer confined to a solid space. Instead, it changed in order to keep Kaleena at its center, if that was where she truly was. Her head spun; she felt like throwing up. As she lowered her head to her knees in hopes of calming her stomach, her sister stared up at her with bewilderment. Which side was she really on? Or was that the trick? Was she literally on every side simultaneously, pieces of the same person that must be put back together to become whole?

Very good, a voice reverberated off the glass.

Kaleena followed the voice around the room, all of her other selves helping to try and find the source. "Who is that?" she called out. "Where are you?"

Please refrain from speaking.

Kaleena was puzzled, then realized the voice wasn't in the room. It was in her head.

Where are you? she asked in her mind, searching every eye for her captor. *What do you want?*

That's better.

The dome suddenly shimmered. Her reflections, though, remained solid, each

one curious as to what was happening to the room itself. A man stepped through the shimmer, appearing out of thin air. He wore a black cloak with dark red lining that fell all the way to the floor. His manicured hands were folded together and rested gently just below his stomach. She couldn't make out his features under the thick hood but his presence was far from menacing. Rather, it felt kind and, in a way, needed. As the tail of his cloak entered existence, the shimmer quieted until the room was again a solid window of on-lookers.

"Where did you —"

The man put his finger to his lips (or what Kaleena believed to be his lips). *Speak softly.*

Kaleena complied without question. *Where did you come from?*

In time.

Whether the man meant that he came from some other time or if her answer would be given to her later, Kaleena was unsure.

Your question will be answered in time, the man said, answering her confusion.

You can read my mind.

Of course.

How else would we be able to speak like this? Kaleena's cheeks flushed red, embarrassed for asking the question.

Precisely.

Who are you? Kaleena asked.

The man lowered his hood carefully to his shoulders. *You may call me Adamus.*

Adamus, Kaleena said, repeating the name as if it were the first time she spoke a syllable. His features were healthy, but fading. Lines of age formed around his eyes and mouth, and his light brown hair was beginning to gray. Kaleena figured him to be in his late thirties, possibly early forties. Regardless, she found him to be quite handsome, drawn into eyes that glowed a light yellow. Within the blackening pupils she saw a hint of deception, though oddly enough, one that produced a sense of comfort and truth. Somehow, she knew this man, Adamus, but he was a stranger to her; a figment of her imagination.

"I know you," she said out loud. She needed to hear her voice say it.

Adamus lowered his head in a shallow bow of acknowledgment.

You helped me, she said. *The day I got raped.*

Adamus didn't say a word. He didn't even blink, causing his eyes to gloss over with what appeared to be the same mirrored glass that filled the room. She saw herself in those eyes; her soul inside of him. It felt cold and unnerving.

How did you know it was happening?

I know everything about you, Love, he said.

The name chilled Kaleena. *Don't call me that*, she said fiercely, repetitively, as if every one of her reflections were yelling it in succession.

But it is who you are, Adamus said. *I cannot call you different.*

You may call me Kaleena.

Kaleena is not the true nature of your soul, Adamus continued. *Humans have turned names into labels to identify a living body. But a true name belongs to a person's soul. It is who they are, and you, my dear… are Love.*

No. "No," she said again in a whisper.

Adamus held up his hand to stop her from saying anything more. *I will succumb to your wish, young child, and give you the pleasure of using your label.* Adamus's eyes were dark and rich with anger. *For now.* The voice filtered throughout the dome with a tone so deep, it outmatched even Darth Vader's menacing rumble.

How do you know so much about me? Kaleena asked after pausing to allow the circulation to return to her body.

I have been following you for some time, he said.

Why have you been following me?

I cannot answer that question now.

Why not?

Because you are not ready.

Why am I not ready? Ready for what? Where am I?

You are where you need to be.

Kaleena rolled her eyes, making sure her mind was empty of thought. *How did I get here?* she asked shortly after.

You were brought here after your boat was destroyed, Adamus answered, quick and without pause.

Destroyed? Kaleena said, though it wasn't a surprise.

Yes.

How?

A hurricane came upon your boat without warning. It tore a hole in the hull and sank it instantly.

Kaleena hesitated to ask the next question, the one she dreaded the most. *Am I alive?*

Adamus's eyes lit up with humor. *Yes, of course,* he answered softly.

Relief quieted Kaleena's mind, that is until she thought of everyone else that had been on the boat. *What about my dad?* she asked quickly. *Is he still alive? Can I see him? What happened to everyone else? Kara, Lauren...*

Adamus raised his hand. *Please, calm yourself. You will know their fates in time.*

Why in time? What am I doing here? What do you need from me?

You have communicated with the child.

Kaleena thought a moment, then: *Lauren's child?*

Adamus again gave an approving nod and continued without a word from Kaleena. He already knew what she was going to say.

Dreams are a window, Kaleena. You must be willing to go through that window to see its completeness. The child has given you everything you need to become your destiny.

I'm supposed to help her, Kaleena said, somewhat timid. *How do I do that when I'm stuck in a room with no way out?*

That is a question I cannot help you with.

Why not? If my destiny is to help Lauren's baby, then why have you trapped me here like this?

Look around you, Kaleena. Take a deep, long, look. Because until you understand, you will be unable to comprehend anything more.

Understand what? They're a bunch of mirrors! Kaleena raised her arms as she said this, looking around with her eyes. *What am I supposed to do?*

Understand.

God damn it. She lowered her arms and slapped her thighs, giving her wrists a biting sting. Adamus was deathly quiet. A fiery anger flared up underneath his darkening eyes. Kaleena cowered as she shrank in his presence.

Do not ever use that phrase in my presence, he groaned, each word hitting her slowly and succinctly.

Kaleena didn't say anything, though she sensed he was waiting for an apology before returning to his normal, serene state of being. She gave a small flinch of a nod, pushing acknowledgment to the forefront of her eyes. Soon after, Adamus's appearance became far less forceful.

Your mind is capable of tremendous knowledge, Kaleena. But it has been weakened by the perception of law and society. Until you can reach your true potential, your mind will not be able to comprehend any of what I must tell you.

And this will bring me that potential? Kaleena asked softly, still slightly afraid of saying the wrong thing.

Adamus nodded.

And when I am able to understand, you will answer my questions?

Another nod.

And let me see my parents.

This time, Adamus didn't nod. *Open yourself, solve the puzzle, and truth will be revealed.* He turned around. The shimmer across the mirrors once again appeared.

Wait. Where are you going? You need to help me understand.

Only you can help yourself.

What if I can't?

Adamus glanced at her over his shoulder. *Then you are not the one we thought you to be.*

Adamus raised his hood before stepping through nothing to disappear as he had once appeared. As the end of his cloak slipped through the shimmer, Kaleena

attempted to follow him, running toward the shimmer that would be forever out of her reach.

"Shit!" her reflections screamed as the dome trapped them all once again.

She spun around, anger clouding her mind. But was it anger over Adamus not helping her or fear that she would never find the answer she was looking for? Fear that this room — this mirrored casket — would soon become her deathbed? How would she keep herself from going mad?

Kaleena had to sit down and calm her mind. She closed her eyes and took in a few, long deep breaths, contemplating whether or not she could trust Adamus. She had to, though, didn't she? He must see the potential for her to find her way out of this. Why else would he have kept her alive? Why else would he have protected her at her weakest moment? To prove that he could be trusted. That was the only reason. That would have to be enough to convince Kaleena that what he said was true. There was a door to this room, somewhere, she just had to find it; she just needed to discover what the meaning of the dome truly was.

After she cleared her mind of anger, Kaleena scanned the room, each doppelgänger staring at her with cold, hazy eyes. But they weren't all the same. Each pair reflected something new; each displayed a different side to every event in her life: the death of her father and the possibility that he had survived; her mother's decision not to leave and the choice to stay with Benjamin; Kyla's life without having being raped and her suicide. Seeing all of this at once sent a pounding throb through Kaleena's head. She couldn't keep looking. She had to close her eyes. But if she couldn't see, how could she pass Adamus's test?

She forced her eyes open and kept them locked on the fourteen-year-old girl that sat directly below her, looking into eyes that felt empty and without hope.

"Help me," she said, the girl on the other side whispering the same request. A tear dropped to the floor as she again closed her eyes. Kaleena was lost, unprepared and vulnerable. She lied down, needing rest, needing strength; needing someone to hold her, to calm her and protect her. For the first time in three years, she simply did not want to be alone with herself.

Unknown Location – Time Unknown

It took Lauren a minute to fully realize she was awake. The last several minutes had been spent lying on a smooth porcelain floor, staring at the reflection of her naked body in the shallow pool, which was actually more like an underground fountain she believed to be no more than a couple of feet deep, maybe reaching just below her kneecaps if she were standing. She ran her fingers through the warm water, brushing ripples across her stomach, smiling at the strong brightness in her eyes. She was overwhelmed with the urge to slide into the pool and let the water lap over her body until she could no longer breathe, though she didn't know why. Her child was about ready to be born. Why would she even contemplate giving that up? However, there was a hole in her mind, a memory she could sense was there but couldn't find. Whenever she scanned for the missing time between the shockwave that rocked the yacht and her waking up here, in a room full of elegant statues, calming waterfalls, and hand carved marble fixtures, her thoughts would be diverted to memories of swimming in her pool at home, spending time with Matthew, and guilt over losing Janice… it was enough to believe that something (*someone?*) was keeping her from knowing the truth.

"Give me strength," she whispered, scooping up a handful of water and dropping it on her stomach. It ran down her skin in all directions, heating as it traveled. Lauren didn't feel cold as she rolled onto her back and stared at the ceiling. There were several paintings depicting young nude women of all ages — all of whom were giving birth, or had given birth — among the thick wooden beams that encased the windowless room.

The pool was also very prominent among them. Lauren had heard of underwater births, but had never contemplated actually ever having one. It frightened her to think the child's first encounter with the world would be as a near drowning victim. But, as she always liked to joke, it was a good way to get them into swimming. She remembered hearing about one of her friends from high school (the term friend was used loosely; she was more of an acquaintance actually, talking in class from time to time and signing each other's yearbooks) that had this type

of birth. As far as she knew, it was a success in reducing the pain of childbirth without having to resort to drugs. Thinking about it, the idea that underwater births were first established hundreds of thousands of years ago in the age of Atlantis would make for one terrific story. A Pulitzer for sure, if she could ever prove it. And find a way out.

The baby kicked; *playfully*, Lauren thought — knew, in a way. "It's okay, Evey. I'm not going anywhere." She couldn't if she wanted. Standing from her current position was hard enough at nine months pregnant without having to deal with the slippery floor that would no doubt lead to cracking her head open if she tried. There was nothing she could do right now but wait. For what? To give birth? For someone to come? A midwife perhaps or the person who was responsible for bringing her here? Or maybe to waste away, eventually finding an end to her life? Another kick from the child warned her off of any negative thoughts. "Sorry," Lauren calmed, lifting her head to gaze at what appeared to be a giant mountain of a stomach, knowing she'd offended her little girl. "You told me if I came, I would get help. I trust you." She lowered her head. "I trust you," she whispered, unsure this time.

You can trust her.

Lauren sat up as far as she could, quickly covering her exposed breasts with her arm, but still couldn't see much. Slowly (and in a little bit of pain), she slid onto her side and stretched her neck as far as she could to get an obscured view of what was behind her. When she didn't see anyone, she carefully rolled onto her back, able to see nothing but the tips of her toes playing hide and seek behind her stomach.

"Who's there?" Lauren called out, keeping her voice deep and firm.

As she waited for a reply, she heard soft footsteps behind her. She propped her head back to see what, or who, was moving toward her. Eventually, as if becoming an extension of the shadows, the form of a human stepped into the soft illumination of the room. Lauren slid away from the figure, her bare backside making it easy to do so on the wet porcelain.

"Who are you?" she said, her voice shaky.

Calm yourself, the shadow said. She wasn't sure if it was coming from the

figure or from outside the room. Was she being watched by hidden cameras in some sick voyeuristic fantasy?

Lauren wrapped her right arm over her breasts and slid her legs up, folding one over the other. "Who the fuck are you?" she screamed, assertive and fierce.

The man removed the hood that covered the black hollow of his face. As the soft light streamed across his features, Lauren's breath grew rapid with surprise and confusion.

"Henry?"

"Hello, Lauren." Henry stepped fully into the light (a source from which Lauren was still unsure of where it came), his eyes glazed in a yellow hue, his smile large and comforting.

"How — what — what the hell?"

Henry placed his finger to his lips. "Shh."

"My god, fuck," she whispered, averting her eyes from those familiar features. She slid away from him as he stepped closer. She couldn't look at him but only for a split second at a time. "What the fuck?" she said under her breath before stopping. She didn't know why she stopped, but she no longer felt compelled to move. Or was it more she was being kept from moving?

"It's okay, Lauren," Henry said. "I know how this might look."

"Shit you do," Lauren said, finally able to keep her eyes locked on him. "How the hell did you get here? Did you know where this place was from the start? What the fuck is that thing you're wearing? And where are my clothes, you perverted fuck?"

"Lauren."

"Fuck."

"Shut up, Lauren." The yellow of Henry's eyes darkened as a hint of red grew around the outer rim of his pupil. Lauren's mouth was agape as she tried to keep from igniting a total panic attack. A slight chill ran through her body, which she knew automatically had come from him. "Just shut up, okay. You're acting like a fucking child. If you'd shut your fucking mouth for just one minute, I might be able to explain what the fuck is going on."

Lauren's eyes were sharp with anger, not only for speaking to her that way, but also for being here in the first place. She didn't want to see him. Not after he didn't show up on the yacht.

As seconds ticked away, Henry's eyes faded back to their normal state (if you could call yellow eyes normal) and his demeanor, which had become a dark, haunting image of a demon, once again eased into comfort and warmth. Lauren's body also became very warm, though with it came with a sharp pain to her stomach. She winced, trying not to show she was in pain in front of her baby's father.

"How can you explain this, Henry?" She sucked a small breath through her teeth and the pain faded.

"First of all, I have always known about the existence of Atlantis. You may not believe this, Lauren, and I don't expect you to, but I was born here."

"What...?" Lauren wanted to say more but another sharp pain, this one longer than the first, kept her mouth shut. Either Henry was making sure Lauren didn't say another word or her daughter wanted to hear Henry out. Either way, she would have to oblige.

"I can't go into the details just yet, but my home is, has been, and will always be this glorious city."

Lauren shook her head. Had Henry gone completely insane? The truth in his eyes said otherwise, so she decided to go along with it to see what other nonsense he might come up with. "How could you survive here?" Lauren spit out as the pain faded. "Under three hundred feet of water?"

"We're an intelligent people, Lauren. We surpassed the technological advances of human kind long before they ever existed among the land. One of those advances was the capability of sustaining one's consciousness over many millennia. That's all this is."

"So, what you're telling me is you're over thousands of years old?"

"In a manner of speaking, yes."

Lauren let out a squeak of a scream, unable to hide the pain inside. She now knew for sure her contractions had returned. Hiding her naked body was the least of her worries.

"You're going into labor, Lauren," Henry said, kneeling down and placing his hand gently on her knee.

"No shit," she hissed back, slicing her leg away from his hand.

"Let me help you." Henry found Lauren's knee and held it. This time, she let it stay, concentrating more on wishing the pain away than fighting him away. "Our child wants my help."

Henry spread her legs apart and examined her cervix. "You're almost ready."

When the pain from the contraction had passed, Lauren slammed her knees together, nearly smashing Henry's knuckles.

"What the hell Lauren?"

"Get away from me," she growled. "I don't want your help."

Let him help.

Lauren shook her head as the whisper of a young girl's voice floated through her mind. "Who...?"

Let him help. He will be good to you. Set your mind free.

"Who are you?" she screamed. Henry waited patiently at her feet as if he knew what was happening; as if it were him giving her this advice.

"Tell me who you are!"

A scream tightened her stomach. Lauren couldn't help but stop breathing altogether. The pain was gone a second later, and Lauren's breath returned. "Shit," she choked. "Shit." This one longer, stretched out over several seconds. She didn't want to obey, didn't want to give him the satisfaction, but realized she would have to. She had to obey her daughter.

Lauren, tears and sweat mixing together upon her moistened face, relaxed and opened her legs for Henry,

"Good," he said, pulling her to him until her knees were touching his shoulders. He cupped his hands under her back and carefully lifted her. Another

contraction. Not having had the time to take Lamaze or learn any other medical techniques to handling the pain, Lauren relied on how movies and television shows depicted labor for support. However, as she started to breathe ("Hee-Hee-Hooo... Hee-Hee-Hoooo....") she realized those shows were full of shit.

"God, this hurts," she moaned, her eyes pinched shut.

"Ease your mind, Lauren. It only hurts because you let yourself believe it does."

"What?" Sweat poured from Lauren's skin, dripping into her mouth and eyes. She let out a long hiss through her teeth and rotated her body to find a more comfortable position.

"Labor only hurts because you let it. The pain is just your body trying to rid itself of something it can no longer nurture. Your mind doesn't want to let it go. That conflict is what's producing your pain. Allow yourself to let it go."

As the contraction subsided, Lauren realized she was squeezing Henry between her legs. She loosened her grip. "You're full of shit, you know that."

"Take deep breaths, Lauren. Calm your muscles," Henry said, ignoring her comment without even a flinch. He slid himself toward the pool, pulling Lauren's legs with him.

Lauren attempted to pull away. "What are you doing?"

"I need to get you into the water before your next contraction."

Henry waited for Lauren's approval, which eventually came as another contraction pinched her lower abdomen. He stepped into the pool and took a hold of her lower waist, just below the cusp of her stomach. Surprisingly, his hands were the gentlest she'd ever felt. Lauren clenched her teeth as he helped guide her into the pool. The water was warm and soothing, and helped to calm the contraction before it took full swing and bite her hard. She screamed and slipped, but Henry caught her head before it hit the edge of the porcelain floor.

"Deep breaths, Lauren. Use the air to soothe the blood." Henry set Lauren on the floor of the pool. The water came up to just above her chest, blanketing her in a sparkling clear sheet. She rested the back of her head on the edge of the

pool and attempted to take a deep breath. But it was impossible. The pain was too much. She let it out and had trouble taking in another.

"I can't," she said, her voice squeaky and rough. "I can't..."

"You can." Henry placed his right hand behind Lauren's neck, caressing it with just his fingertips. The massage distracted Lauren from the pain, but only a little. He placed his other hand on the top of her stomach; that eased the pain more than the neck massage.

"God, it still hurts like a bad fuck —" Lauren grunted. She then hummed softly, lifting herself up off of the bottom of the pool as if she were about to take flight. Henry pushed her back to the floor.

"Lauren, you're not listening to me."

"You're not making any sense," Lauren hissed.

"You're not relaxing," Henry bit back. "Stop resisting it. Let it become you."

Lauren's eyes were wide and hot as her eyebrows arched inward, connecting above the tip of her petite nose. It was all she could do to get Henry's attention.

"Sit, rest," Henry said, succumbing to her inability to understand. He slid to her side, and with one hand still resting gently on the tip of her stomach, he combed his hand through her silky wet hair, then cupped his hand firmly under the base of her skull, his fingers tickling the middle of her neck.

"Relax, now, Lauren. It will be over soon." Henry set his lips upon hers. Lauren's first reaction was to pull away, but she quickly surrendered to his sweet, sugary taste. The pain subsided as she became enamored with the kiss, which was much more than just a kiss — it was the trepidation of her first kiss; the true kiss of a fiancé upon the altar; the numbness of the gentle touch after the first time she made love as a married woman. It was gentle, salty. It was hot and moist. But she stole as many as she could as her body collapsed from the high.

"Justin," she huffed, pecking the corner of her husband's mouth. "God damn."

Justin's jet-black hair was strewn all over in wet clumps. His stubble was much more prominent covered in sweat. But Lauren liked it that way; she loved it that way.

She rubbed the bristles with her palm and cuddled up to him with another kiss. She wore nothing but her wedding veil, which by now was more than likely tangled up in her matted hair that took her nearly eight hours to get right… and even then she wasn't completely happy with it.

"I love you," she whispered.

"Me, too," he said, as almost a cough. Lauren didn't notice.

The two lay together in deep silence. Lauren listened to Justin's heartbeat, enjoying the quickened, race of a pulse. As it steadily slowed to a calm rhythm, Lauren thought about her first experience with a man — how much love she felt, how much ecstasy was involved, how much pain it had caused her. This was different; this was a true love, one that may go through some rough bumps along the way for sure, but which would survive the heartache and tears. She'd never had that before. Justin would support her, she knew that, whatever the problem. No matter what disasters came their way.

Right?

"Justin?" Lauren bit her lower lip.

"Huh…" Justin groaned, popping back from the light sleep he was entering.

"Will you always support me?" She mumbled as if she didn't want to ask the question.

"What?"

Lauren sat up. "Will you always support me?"

Having to fully wake himself, Justin sat up slightly on his elbows. "What kind of question is that?"

"Just answer."

"Of course I will. I took the vows, didn't I?"

Lauren hesitated. "I haven't told you everything about my past."

"Lauren, whatever it is, I don't care. You're my wife now. None of that matters."

"I know," Lauren confirmed, playing with the sweaty hair on Justin's chest. "It's just…" She paused, searching for the right thing to say without sending Justin into a complete frenzy.

"What is it?" Henry was now awake and very interested.

"We've never talked about having kids," Lauren said sheepishly.

"Kids? Wha —" Justin stared into Lauren's simple brown eyes. "We just got married. It's a bit early to be talking about kids, don't you think?"

"I know. That's not what I'm talking about." Lauren held her legs to her chest. She always knew it would be a touchy subject, not for his sake, but for hers. Whenever they got close to talking about it, she changed the subject to keep from having to get into this very argument, fearing deep down that if he knew what had happened, he would have run, never to be seen from again. She loved him too much for that. But now that it had become official, it was only right to tell him. Even if it did make her look like a complete whore for not revealing the truth until after he proclaimed to honor her under God. This was her first night as a married woman, and the possibility of it being her last was evident.

Justin wrapped his arm around her shoulders. "What is it? You don't have any do you?" He laughed until he saw the lack of humor on Lauren's face. "You don't, do you?"

"No. Just forget it."

"Lauren, what is it, then?"

"I said forget it. Let's just get some sleep. It's been a long day."

"No. No, you started this."

Lauren felt like crying but remained strong. "I almost did," she finally spit out. "She would have been about six now."

The shock made it appear as if Justin had just found out she wasn't a virgin. He stuttered a few nonsensical syllables and then: "What happened? Did you miscarry?"

Lauren took in a deep breath. "I had an abortion."

"It was probably for the best," Justin said without sympathy.

"Really? And what if I had chosen to keep it? What if it was your child, and I decided to keep it? Would you have supported me?"

"Oh, God. You're not pregnant, are you?"

"Justin, God. This is serious." Lauren shoved his arm off her shoulders and started pacing the room.

"Lauren, I don't understand what you're asking me."

"Fu… I just want to know if you would support me in whatever decisions I choose to make."

"About kids?"

"About everything!"

"Lauren, of course I'll support you."

"So, if I were pregnant right now and I wanted to keep it, you'd be okay with that?"

Justin took a long, silent moment to himself before finding the answer he hoped she wanted. "I couldn't make you go through another abortion, Lauren. Even if I do prefer kids I can ship back home when I get fed up with them."

Lauren held back a smile, which told Justin he could now move closer. He walked over to her and wrapped his arms around her, holding her tight as she closed her arms around his back. "I love you," he said, following it with a kiss on the cheek. "I will support any decision you felt was right. And I hope you would do the same for me."

Lauren felt sympathy this time, mixed with a fervent amount of love. She kissed him. "Thank you," she said and lied Justin back down on the bed. She climbed on top of him and made love to him one more time. As Lauren fell deep into the black abyss of sleep, she thought of nothing that could make her happier than being where she was at that moment. One day she would have a child. Deep down she just felt it. When that would be she didn't know, but her spirit was bright in knowing that when she did, Justin would be the father. Love for this led her into her dreams.

Mirrored Room – Time Unknown

Half melted into the slick abyss of the glass, Kaleena wondered if there was anything

left for her. She'd spent what felt like a few hours attempting to come to terms with her self-described "assignment." But in this room, time was lost to the shimmer of her existence. She had peered into her own eyes a hundred times over, watched every variable unfold in her mind, each one successively richer with pain, frustration, urgency and depression. Every time she turned to a new identity, the glassed-mirror stole a small piece of her, whether it be her heart, her mind or her soul. As she pursued a reason, sought out a definition, looked for a meaning, the light became hazy, darkening but not completely burning out, leaving her the slightest amount of hope and resurgence… if she was willing to take it. But it was hard to hold onto hope as the girls around her taunted her with their sharp words, each one whispering (screaming, it seemed to become after a while) over the top of one another, caught in a dizzy song of truths and haunted dreams. One of the girls on her left, a little older than Kaleena, slowly chanted away Kaleena's willingness to stand.

"You've spent the last three years running," she had said, the whisper an echo behind her thoughts. "You run and hide, like a rabbit from a predator. Run and hide with fear. Run and hide, run and hide. When you're found (you're always found), you run some more, and run and run and run some more until the bite takes hold and you fall to your knees. Even then, you're almost caught and you stand and run. But it's all you know, it's all you can believe, and it's all you can do, so you run."

"I can't," Kaleena told the girl in front of her, who mimicked Kaleena, moving her mouth to a hollow sound that never reached her ear. "I can't… not anymore." Her breaths were light, her knees weakened. "I can't run… I'm too tired, I need rest…" Kaleena dropped to one knee. Her leg shook and her calves cramped up.

"Run… run until your breath is heavy; run until your legs are on fire; run until your heart can take no more and then run, run, run… it's all you know."

"No." Kaleena slid her other leg to the floor and sat on her feet. "No more running," she said and looked to the girl to her left, who had dark, wet hair and sweat dripping from her forehead. "Where can I go? Who would I find?"

"Run to nowhere... it's all you know. Run run run... run run run... runrunrun..."

Kaleena shifted her head to evade the exhaustion. The girl to her right beamed with power, one of three as one, a dragon that could suck the hunger from her stomach.

"You've tasted the past," the middle girl said, followed in quick succession by the second

("You've tasted the present")

and the third

("*You've tasted the future*"),

each one quieter and more distant. Kaleena's tongue began to dry and her throat grew cold and clammy.

"Bitter

(sour)

(*pungent*)

you've become accustomed to the distaste of it all. Nothing comes sweet

(nothing comes loving)

(*nothing comes pure*)

but still you eat from the fruit that has been given to you, without thought

(without objection)

(*without understanding*).

But it's all you know, and it's all you can taste. So you eat

(you eat)

(*eat*)."

Kaleena gagged dryly. Again. She held her stomach and looked away from the monster, drawing her legs out from underneath her. The moistness of the floor leaked through the gown and touched her skin. It felt familiar — the tub in her home as she played with her Malibu Barbie, her mother carefully making sure the shampoo didn't run into her eyes; the edge of the pool at her best friend's house (*what was her name?*), learning for the first time what a kiss really looked

like after (*what the* hell *was her name?*) dared some faceless boy to stick his tongue into her mouth, at which point, the boy went deep red, laughter erupting over the boy's unexpected erection. Kaleena laughed because (*will I ever remember her name? Will I ever remember her face?*) laughed. Was it funny? She didn't know, but it didn't matter.

And it was the coroner's exam table. Where everything became…

"Dark."

Kaleena turned to the girl behind her, glimpsing the silhouette of a ghost. She shook her head, afraid of what else might be taken from her as the taunting continued from all directions, slowly becoming a monotonous tonal hum, with just one voice overpowering them all — Kaleena's shadow.

"You've been part of the dark, you've sought it out… you've hunted it. You crave it; you're addicted to it. You cling to it like a parent, like a friend, like a lover. You dream of it, you desire it, you relish it. You cannot live without it. It's your soul and it's all you know, and it's all you see."

Kaleena closed her eyes and allowed her body to fall completely to the floor, unable to keep herself up, unable to look at her attackers any longer.

"So you die…" the voice whispered.

She wanted to vomit; she wanted to fade away into a nothing, allow the room to swallow her and take whatever it was they wanted. They could have everything, except…

Except for one small piece that had left without force, disappeared into the deepest well to remain as quiet as it could so as not to be found. They wouldn't be able to take it from her. Not unless she knew where it had gone.

Tap-Tap-Tap…

Kaleena opened her eyes. Below her, pressing her cheek to Kaleena's, was an eleven-year-old girl, curious yet knowing, strong yet docile, close yet still very far away. The girl tapped the glass, playing a game with her sister in the musical notes of their fingernails. A soft smile kissed the corner of Kaleena's morose lips. It was warm and comforting — a kiss of hope drowned by the bittersweet taste of the

fluid that disconnected the two girls from one another. Opening her mouth made her want to gag; keeping her eyes open hurt more than a knife through the heart. But she had to know the reason; she had to find out where the girl had gone and why she had left Kaleena to run her fate through the sickening darkness.

"Where did you go?" Kaleena asked the little girl, barely able to open her mouth.

"I died," the girl said, continuing to enjoy the tapping. Her eyes were fixed on the two sets of fingers, one hand smaller than the other, yet the same exact size.

"How did you die?" Kaleena asked, closing her eyes. They were heavy; they were stone.

"I don't know. I didn't want to live anymore."

"But why?"

"I don't know." A child's answer.

"You have to know." Kaleena felt water around her eyes, but wasn't sure if they were tears or the water flowing across the floor.

"I asked God to save me," the little girl said, happy.

"And he did."

The little girl continued the *tap-tap-tap* on the mirror.

"Are you happy for what God gave you?" Kaleena opened her eyes when the little girl didn't answer. She was gone, replaced by a dark pit that burned of smoke and hate.

"Kaleena," she said, pulling her head from the floor just enough to remove it from the rising heat. Her stomach turned and her head spun, but she fought the dizziness. "Kaleena, come back." She looked everywhere in the pit for the little girl. "You can't leave me like this again."

Then an image appeared. It was a fluid appearance, a movie pulled from Kaleena's mind and projected upon the dark mist. She saw the little girl sitting on the couch of her apartment wearing a pink nightgown, her hair dead against her face. She grasped a cordless phone in her hands. It seemed as if she was ready to crush it into a mass heap of diodes and resistors. The little girl's eyes were hot

with red electric streaks compressing her pupils inward. She was a statue. Would she ever move?

The phone lit up. The little girl jumped in fright by the loud ring that echoed through the eerily quiet apartment. As if a machine, the little girl hit a key on the phone and brought it to her ear, a surge of energy racing through her features.

"Mom?"

"Kaleena? It's Dad. How are you doing, sweetheart?"

Kaleena's excitement drained from her body when she heard her father's low, nurturing voice. She didn't feel like being nurtured right now. She needed so much more than that.

"Kaleena?"

A second later, after trying to pull her voice from deep down inside, she answered in a deathly grave, scratchy voice, "Not good."

"Have you talked to anyone? Kyla, maybe?"

Who's Kyla, she thought, trying to imagine a friend from another life. She vaguely remembered a girl, a few years older than she was, laughing and smiling her way through the mall, chatting away as if she had anything real to say.

But it had all faded, an old black and white photo that was beginning to lose its original zeal. She sniffed and spit out, "No…" She was unable to let go of the word, just as she was not ready to let go of…

"Are you coming home?"

"I'm going to be home soon, okay?"

"Why aren't you home?" The question was meant more for her mother than her father.

"Kaleena, I'm getting there as fast as I can, I promise."

"She promised…"

Kaleena was unable to hold the phone to her ear as another round of sadness struck. Everything around her blurred as it became harder to breath. She tried lifting the phone to say something more, but every time she did, her arm grew heavy. Finally, she mustered the strength to set the phone on her face and quietly

hummed, "She promised…" and then, after a second of hesitation, added, "… You did too."

"Kaleena. I promised. I'm promising again. I will be there soon. Call Kyla. Ask her to come over and before you know it, I'll be there. I. Promise."

It took Kaleena time to come to terms with what he was saying. She wondered if she could trust him, if she wanted to trust him. She had trusted her mother for the last eleven years. How could she trust anyone now? He *was* her father. But… she *was* her mother.

"Kaleena? Can you hear me? I'm coming home right now. Can you do as I ask?"

Can I trust him?

"Kaleena?"

"Okay," Kaleena said, unsure if she really meant it (or believed it).

"I love you, sweetheart," Matthew said.

Kaleena was quick to answer. "Yeah." She pressed the button to hang up the phone. She didn't want to hear him anymore; she didn't want to think about him or listen to promises that would eventually, she knew, be broken. She didn't need it. And she didn't want it.

Sleep, a soft voice said from somewhere in the room. At first, Kaleena thought it was her mother, hope hitting her like a lead brick. "Mom?"

You must sleep, now, sweetheart.

"But, mom," Kaleena said, unable to find anyone in the apartment.

Just listen, Love. You must sleep now.

"I want to see you."

You will. Once you rest. Now sleep.

"Okay," Kaleena said, a heavy drowsiness hitting her. She still grasped the phone tightly. It had become a lifeline, her last visage of hope in what had become a black hole of despair. "When will I get to see you?"

Patience, the voice said. Before Kaleena's eyes closed, she saw her — a vision of her mother, smiling, gently caressing her cheek. *That's it. Sleep.*

Sleep, she said again as the images within the deep, glass pit faded. Kaleena

rested her head between her legs, lightheadedness overwhelming her. "Why did you leave?" she called out. "Why…?"

She looked at the ceiling and reached for the lives that seemed free, wishing she could be with them floating in the nothing. "You have to come back," she said. "I need you."

A woman appeared among the reflections, weaving through them and meeting Kaleena nearly within inches of where she sat. She wasn't sure who it was at first, but then realized it was her mother. Not the woman she saw on the yacht — her mother, the bright, healthy vibrant woman who helped her with her homework even if she didn't know the answers to anything; who would talk to her when a bully wouldn't stop picking on her; who would make her favorite chocolate strawberry cake on her birthday and write little sayings each year to celebrate.

"Why?" she asked the woman, who asked the question right back to her in return.

Kaleena saw a new reflection within her mother's eyes — the reflection of Kaleena, every piece connected with maturity, with knowledge, with…

"You," she said, reaching for the girl within her mother's eyes. "Where have you been?"

Her mother replied. "Where have you been?"

Kaleena looked around at friends who had been pulling her down.

Running… I've been running…

Eating… I've tasted the sickness…

Dying… I've been deep in the dark of…

Her mother was gone, but her reflection remained; the only reflection left above her. She nodded acceptance. "…my mind."

The tips of Kaleena's lips curled up. Those who remained hidden in the glass seemed hollow, forgotten. Their flesh was real, they looked like normal girls, but their eyes were glazed over. Kaleena was stronger, unafraid. Her mind was clear; the ambient fog that had filled her head grew thinner. She stared at one of the ghosts

in the walls, knowing something was missing. Something that had happened, or had been said, was just out of reach of her understanding. But what was it?

Look around you, Kaleena. Take a deep, long, look.

The little girl below her had returned from her black hole. "Take a look around, Kaleena," she said. "What's missing?"

"What's missing?" Kaleena whispered back. The confusion didn't appear on the child. "What's...?"

Kaleena looked up, eyes wide open. *What* was *missing*?

"His reflection."

Reflections... all the hollow bodies around her whispered back, one after the other like a wave flowing around the room.

The little girl had her hands clasped together. Her shoulders were scrunched up, hiding her neck. A giant, bright smile laced what appeared to be her whole head, except for the joy in her bright brown eyes.

"Adamus didn't have a reflection," Kaleena explained to her young doppelgänger.

"And you know what that means." The little girl nearly jumped into the air (or down into the air, perhaps).

"Well, either he's a damned vampire..." Kaleena looked around, her reflections having begun to fade. "Or, none of this real."

Kaleena stepped forward and reached for her near-invisible self, pushing to touch the wall, which at first, slid away from her. But as she focused on her goal and the reality of where she was, she was able to rub her hand against the slick boundary, whisking the watery texture around in a wavy pattern that washed the rest of the reflections completely away. When she turned around, all she saw was a dead white wall. She was no longer in a room, but floating on air. It felt good. But it wasn't real; she knew that now. It was time to erase the wall and find her answers.

She closed her eyes, held her breath for thirty seconds, and then let it out, opening her eyes to the mesmerizing beauty surrounding her. Elegant, almost God-like in their quality, nude women in several different phases of birth covered the

ceiling thirty feet above her in the massive, windowless room that was at least three times the size of her apartment. Pillars, about two and a half feet in diameter, rose in successions of three along the walls. Each pillar was made of a majestic purple and rose marble with a ring of silver and gold about every three feet. Purple silk curtains draped between the pillars, pleated across and reaching the floor with a curl that brought the curtain to a point at the center of each pair of pillars and up to the first gold ring from the floor. The wooden walls were painted with a dark finish, highlighting each line of age in the wood. The floors were white marble that felt cold yet soothing against Kaleena's feet as she walked. In the center of the room was a small hole filled with water that looked a lot like a wading pool of some sort. Four marble statues guarded the four corners of the room in their own graceful nude poses. The first was a thin, shapely woman holding her arm across her chest, touching her shoulder, the other arm, held outward, as if inviting someone in. The second was a pregnant woman cupping her round, supple stomach. The third was sitting, her legs arched and open. The expression on her face was modest, quiet. The fourth held a young baby to her breast, a look of hope and what seemed to be smugness on her lips.

What Kaleena couldn't see was a way out.

You can't let your eyes tell you what's real, she thought. *There's a way out. You just have to concentrate. Think. Where would the door be hidden?*

It was then that a large piece of the wall opened behind her. Adamus gracefully slid in to greet her.

Well done, Kaleena, he said, issuing a gentle bow.

Next time challenge me a little, Kaleena replied quickly with no trace of even a smirk.

Adamus let out a deep, hearty chuckle. *Quite good,* he mused.

You promised me answers. Kaleena moved to the edge of the wading pool.

Yes of course, Adamus said, walking to the other side. *And you will get them —*

You know, I'm getting really sick of these childish games. Just tell me what the hell is going on.

Of course, Adamus said, more out of honor than intimidation. *What would you like to know?*

Where am I? It seemed like an easy question to begin with.

You are in the labor room in the bottommost quarter of Life's Blood.

What's Life's Blood?

It's one of three central towers that make up the city of Atlantis.

How did you do that dog and pony show with the mirrors? Again, a question Kaleena didn't really need an answer to, but had to ask.

That was none of my doing.

Really? So, what? It was just a figment of my imagination? Her contempt was searing.

A mind, Kaleena (the name came out as if Adamus was afraid of it) *is more powerful than you can fully understand.*

Enlighten me.

Adamus paused, hesitant of whether he should give her an explanation. Based on Kaleena's posture (arms crossed, shoulders back, head forward), not giving an answer might keep her from doing what he needed of her.

When faced with great stress and circumstances out of one's control, a mind can manipulate the truth. Before you can understand what needs to be seen, your mind must first come to terms with what it cannot understand.

So... a figment of my imagination, Kaleena summed up.

No. It is much more than that.

Yeah, I get it. I needed to come to terms with my own sordid past in order to fully accept where I was. A way to fight off what I didn't want to believe.

More a way of concealing the truth until you were ready to confront whatever conflict your mind and spirit were fighting.

Whatever, Kaleena chided. *Point is, I'm ready for real answers now, so you better not fuck around with me.*

I would never do such a thing.

Good to know. Kaleena waited for a flinch, some movement that would tell

her he was lying or was about to lie. But he was motionless, his features calm and honest.

Where is my father? she asked, scared of the inevitable answer that came quickly and without remorse.

It will take time for you to come to terms with this, Kaleena, but your father perished among the sea, along with all of the other passengers on your boat.

Kaleena fought back her tears. She didn't know why she had to remain strong, but if she broke down in front of Adamus, she would be of no use to him; no use to the people that she was supposedly going to protect; and absolutely no use to herself. If she collapsed now, she would never find her way back. She didn't want to believe it, though. Not yet. Not until she got more answers. If Adamus was lying (as her gut was telling her) and her parents were alive, she would've allowed her selfishness to turn her into nothing but a doll to sit on the bed and stare at the wall of space until they decided she was nothing more than a living corpse and end her miserable existence. Her strength was in making sure she showed no weakness and the willingness to fight off the demons in the possibility of the lies.

Adamus felt Kaleena fighting her disbelief in his words. *All but one,* he finally said, attempting to ease her stress.

Who? Kaleena said after a short pause, hoping to hear… she wasn't sure. But the answer she got was one that helped calm her mind and allow the stress in her shoulders to fade.

The label she was given was —

"Lauren," she said aloud.

Adamus nodded. Kaleena tried to contain her joy. If Lauren was alive, the chances that her parents were also alive grew exponentially.

Is the baby okay? Kaleena said.

The child is fine. She is healthy.

I want to see her.

And you will. First, I must explain to you that which has been plaguing you since you woke.

What I'm doing here, Kaleena said.

You are here to save our civilization.

I got that part. But how? What makes me so special?

Your mind.

Kaleena's silence prompted him to expand on his explanation.

You are a very special woman, Kaleena. You've been given a gift that far exceeds the parameters of what the human mind wants to comprehend. Because of this, you've hidden your potential for fear of what might happen if you allowed it to become whole.

How do you know that?

We have been following you for some time.

Yeah, no shit.

We've watched you struggle to fit in and be normal, yet needing to be above those that live life with anger, contempt, jealousy and fear. You've taken your first step to solving that conflict. At the same time, your mind and spirit have grown strong enough to create new life.

But how? How am I supposed to create life? Hell, how am I supposed to save your so-called civilization?

Ask the city.

The city?

Adamus nodded, his eyes closed in pleasure.

Kaleena grew more agitated. *What does that even mean?*

Your inquiry is unclear.

Well, if you're saying the city's alive, then why haven't you already asked it to do whatever it is it needs to do? You're the damn Atlantean, or whatever you want to call yourself. Your minds must be much stronger than mine will ever be. Why do you need me?

You speak the truth. However, never allow your eyes to fool you. The vessels you see are not the vessels we held long ago.

After a moment, Kaleena asked: *Your bodies are hosts?*

In a manner of speaking.

Kaleena needed a moment to absorb the absurdity of it all before she continued. Could she believe anything else Adamus would tell her? She had to find out. *Where did you get the hosts?* Kaleena already believed she knew the answer, but Adamus's silence wiped away whatever doubt she held.

How many others are there? In the city?

There are many, Adamus said. *But only a few that live and breathe as we are now. In order to revive the rest of those whose lives were stripped from them so long ago, we must give life to a dead city. And only you are capable of providing us that life.*

And what makes you think I'm going to help you bring life back to the city? The last part of the question held a strong weight of sarcasm.

Because Atlantis has been greatly wounded and you're the only one who can ease its pain.

Kaleena shuffled her feet across the floor as she tried to figure out Adamus's angle. He was holding something back, but if she was, for whatever reason, the only one powerful enough to bring the city back to its former glory, she needed to dig deeper before she let herself fall victim to her own compassion.

What happened? she asked. *To your city? How did Atlantis fall?* She doubted she would believe a word of it, but she wanted to hear it.

A tragic story, I must admit. And a long one.

I have time. Kaleena sat down on the edge of the pool and allowed her feet to sit in the water. She set her folded hands in her lap and looked up to Adamus with a child's curiosity. *I'm listening. Convince me.*

Adamus remained standing, his eyes fixed on Kaleena, unblinking, emotionless. *Atlantis once thrived as a city of the mind,* he began, *one that grew and nurtured the people among it, just as the people grew and nurtured one another.*

The city was their mother, Kaleena stated, matter-of-fact as she peered at the statues.

Not as you would understand it, not yet. But you will, in time.

Perhaps, Kaleena said, drawing an interested smirk to Adamus's lips.

Perhaps, indeed. Nevertheless, Atlantis was healthy and thriving, a life in harmony.

Or so we all thought.

* * *

Atlantis, long ago, sat in the center of a plateau overlooking the Sena and Gydra mountains, which surrounded the city in a beautiful spectacle some hundred miles off in each direction. The city itself stretched twenty miles from tip to tip, the land surrounding them a lush, glorious green of plants, flowers and crops. Wild animals grazed for miles in the freedom of their own spaces to do as they pleased. We were not a farming people; the men of the city were hunters, only eating what they killed, providing food for the women and children, and providing the seed to which life would be given; the women were caretakers, nurturing the children they bore until they were grown enough to bear, or provide life to, their own child. Marriage, as it has developed into today, did not exist; all citizens of Atlantis lived as one community, one family. And it was a woman's right to choose to give birth and to whom would provide her with that life. It was an honor, as a man, to be chosen. Jealousy, betrayal, anger and rage did not exist among the people because there was one thing no one ever conveyed to just one person.

Love.

It was a communal love for life, for nature, for the world we lived in. To love just one person and none other was against our beliefs and our laws. We were taught at a young age to respect everyone else, to honor the decisions made and care for everyone equally. We saw each person as the same; no one was ever more beautiful or handsome, better or worse than another. There were occasions when one man and one woman became enamored with one another, but it was very rare, and when it happened, the couple would have a choice — they could leave the city and live with one another with nature, or live as all others in the city apart from one another, rejecting the love they possessed. Most often they would choose to live outside of the city, but at a cost. Those that chose that life did not live long, unable to bear the extreme conditions of the mountains. Those that chose to stay

could barely function when faced with being apart. To fall in love, though accepted, was not something you wanted to have happen to you. But more often than not, it was unavoidable; and one day, it happened to me.

I had just reached the point in my life when I was able to produce the seed to provide a child, and as I waited to be chosen, I spent my days learning to hunt and my nights cooking and providing nutrients to the city. One morning, as I was heading out to try my hand at hunting alone for the first time, Tylyn, child of Joana, child of Mary, was playing a game with some other females. She didn't see me come around the corner and knocked us both over. I offered to assist her back to her feet. She placed her soft hand into mine with a touch as light as the air. The electricity between us was magnetic. Her silver eyes sparkled; her smile was full and bright. We didn't have to say a word to convey what we felt; we read it in our eternal touch and knew what it was as soon as it happened. But it didn't matter. When her friends came to find her, Tylyn said thank you and kissed my cheek before running off with them. She turned back once before disappearing around the corner to finish the game. My heart sank. Going out to hunt, I was unable to kill anything and was almost caught in the jaws of a boar. I simply could not stop thinking about her — her smell, her touch, her smile. When I returned that night, I retreated directly to my room (hiding my inadequate first hunt) and lied in bed and dreamed of once again seeing the girl who would pleasure me in my dreams. It turned out to be some time before we ever saw one another again, but when we did, everything changed.

It was the night of the crystal moon, when the women who were ready to bear a child would select the giver of the seed. All of the men gathered in the center of the city surrounding the women who stood on top of Foxlight Fountain, seductively enticing the men with their silky smooth bodies. This was my first crystal moon ceremony and I was running late, having been caught up in thoughts of my love. About a half a mile from the center of the city, I saw Tylyn standing in the shadows, waiting for me, dressed in a sparkling purple gown that accentuated her feminine stature. She pulled me close and kissed me without saying a word. We

held that kiss during the ceremony. As the horn sounded the end of the selections, she told me she loved me.

"I too, feel love for you that haunts my dreams," I confessed, kissing her once again.

"We must find a place to be together," she said, our bodies growing warm against the other.

"We can't," I said, unable to stop kissing her.

"We have to," she said. "We are destined to bear a child together."

I agreed with her, in my heart, for a child born in love is a child destined for the greatest achievements known to man. But my mind fought the idea because it was against the law to do so. By law, only women that were given permission to bear a child and participate in the crystal moon ceremony were allowed to have a child.

(*What kind of stupid law is that? Kaleena asked, interrupting the story for the first time.*

It was the law of the magistrate, *Adamus explained.*

Magistrate?

My apologies. Allow me to explain.)

Much like your modern cities and empires, Atlantis relied on rules to survive. In order to create a life free of chaos and fear, laws were created by the magistrate — our leader, our queen, our maker. She sustained our serenity by making sure all who went against her laws would be reprimanded. The most common punishment was abandonment into the mountains, leaving behind the sanctity and the protection of the city to live the rest of your days alone. In order to allow for new life and death of elders to equal one another so as to refrain from overpopulating the great, miraculous city, our magistrate created the Law of Children, which stated that only those women chosen by her hand were allowed to bear a child.

In the event a child was created without the magistrate's explicit authorization, the man would be exiled into the mountains while the woman and fetus were burned as a spiritual sadist. To avoid such punishment, the couple would usually pronounce their love and, at that time, be given the choice mentioned earlier.

(My god, *Kaleena exclaimed.* I totally understand why Tylyn wanted to keep your love a secret.)

To love one another would mean banishment. To live in the city would mean staying apart. But we needed one another as a plant needs light, and as she touched me, kissed me, loved me, she convinced me the only way we would be able to live as one and remain in the city was to keep our love a secret.

"Okay," I whispered. "We will love in quiet."

"Meet me along the terrace of the upper greens in the northern city," she whispered. "Tomorrow night."

She kissed me and slipped into the shadows. Just then, the men of the city passed by to prepare themselves for the next crystal moon. I joined them, love allowing me to float among them.

Sleep alluded me and the next night I met my love in the upper greens where she awaited me, her body exposed, ready to become one with me. We made love twice that night, and every night for the next complete moon cycle. One night, as we lay together under the near circle of the blood moon, Tylyn, my love, my only, revealed to me that we had been blessed with a new life, after which, she cried. For the next few days, she remained hidden and in tears. I spent those days considering our next actions. I didn't want to leave the city but I didn't want to live without my love, in life or death. It became clear that if we were going to be happy, we had to tell the magistrate everything and choose life in solitude. When I went to her, though, she presented a different idea.

"I will not live in the mountains, my love," she said, her tears soft and delicate. "I will not. It is not fair to us, or our blessed young."

"I know, but what other choice do we have? If we stay, I will lose you and the child."

"That would be better than a slow death of nature." Her voice was soft, quiet.

"To suffer life without you in my arms would be too much pain to bear."

"I know, my love. Which is why I ask this of you. The next crystal moon will rise soon. I plan to approach the magistrate and request my participation in the ceremony." Her tears were still vibrant but restrained. "At the ceremony, I will choose you to give me life. We will not have to suffer the death of our child or the exile into the mountains. We can live here, in love as we are now, with a child that will rise to be the greatest mind of our time."

At first I objected, unable to allow my truest heart to lie and deceive the magistrate. But as I held her in my arms and kissed her, I realized she was right. It was the only way to continue our lives as we felt best for our child. So I agreed and we made love.

The next day she went to see the magistrate. Living in the highest tower in the center of the city, the magistrate was the most beloved, most admired among any in the city below her. She lived in elegance and beauty. Everything she wore, everything she ate, everything she touched could only be the best in quality, stature and perfection. All wished to be like her, all wished to be with her. But never in the history of the city had the magistrate ever chosen to lie with a man. Some thought it because she never found a man to match the perfection she most admired. Some say she was barren, unable to produce life. Whatever it may have been, the magistrate was still the wisest, most respected and most cherished being the city had ever known. Her word was obeyed without question. Bowing before the throne, carved in gold and silver stone decorated in silk and fur, my love awaited the presence of the magistrate. Wearing layers of smooth cotton striped with lace, her hair done up with pearls and jewels of every nature, the magistrate was guided to her throne by the hands of two other women who were made to appear humble in her presence. My love didn't look at her, out of respect and fear that she would somehow read the truth that laced her eyes.

"My child," the magistrate sang, her voice light and rich. "You come to me today as an innocent young girl seeking the gift, do you not?"

"You know truth," my love replied.

"You wish to participate under the crystal moon, to create a life, to nurture a young child under the law of my own."

"I do. Bless you, say I."

"Unfortunately, my child, I cannot grant you this wish."

My love looked to the magistrate with wide eyes. "No, please. Why can you not grant me my wish for life, magistrate?"

"Because you have lied, and proven deception in my presence."

"No, you are wrong," Tylyn claimed. "I have not deceived you."

"Stop your begging," the magistrate said, walking down the marble stairwell that separated the magistrate from her disciple. She took my love's chin, placed her other hand to my love's stomach and peered deep into her soul. "You have fallen in love, my child, and have gone against my will to produce a child outside of my law. And then you come to me, as if you were not already with child, claiming yourself innocent and pure."

My love felt the embryo grow cold as the magistrate pressed harder against her stomach. "Because of your deception and your lack of respect for me and my name, you and your child will face extinction from this city, from this world — from this life."

"No, please. I am sorry for my indiscretion. I have made a mistake. Please, spare my child. You may take me, but spare my child."

"I cannot. Your child is a remnant of that which I have tried hard to keep from tainting my beloved city. It cannot live because it was conceived through the existence of dishonesty and fraudulence. That is all it knows now. It will know nothing more."

"You are wrong," my love proclaimed, tears pouring. "You are wrong. My child will do great things. It was conceived in the presence of love."

"And that is what I cannot have," the magistrate said, removing her hands. "We cannot love and live in harmony as a people." She turned her back to my love. "Take her to the cell and await my orders."

The magistrate's subordinates dragged my love to the cells below the city and then came to arrest me. When I learned about what happened, I hid. I could not be sentenced to watch my love tortured and killed. I needed silence to plan how I would rescue my love from inevitable death. Then I heard through whispers and

gossip that the magistrate had ordered the death of one child with the rise of every moon until I was found. I didn't believe the word until that first night when a young male was taken to the Foxlight Fountain and slain in front of the entire city. As I watched the blood wash through the water, the soul of the child lost forever into the darkness of death, I couldn't allow it to continue.

"I am here," I called out, removing the cloak that kept me hidden among the group. I stood in front of the magistrate, a stone of peace. "Do not harm another child. I give myself up."

"You are wise to do so, dear Adamus," she said with a scolding smile. "You have defied my law and you must accept the consequences of that indiscretion."

"I will accept my consequences with a steady mind," I said, lowering myself to my knees. "My wise and gracious magistrate, I will respect and honor your final verdict. However, I wish to request that you spare my young love and my child and take my life instead of hers. She is innocent of all deceptions."

"I will determine who is innocent, young Adamus," she said, taking soft, gentle steps to me until she was looking over me like a god. I could not look up to her; I was shamed in front of all my peers.

"Bring up the prisoner," she commanded. I was unable to move, unable to think of anything but my love as they brought her up to me. When she arrived, I finally lifted my head. I wanted to steal her away into the horizon, kiss her, even make love to her, but I stayed still and unmoving.

"Adamus, I am sorry," Tylyn said as she was brought to the magistrate's side.

"Do not be sorry," I told her. "You are innocent. I have hurt you and the people of this city, and I must be punished. It's not your fault."

"But it is, Adamus. You are as innocent as I am."

"Take a look, my people," the magistrate spoke. "Standing before you are a man and a woman who have defied my law and produced a fetus outside of the crystal moon. They are cowards and are both guilty of deception and sadism. They must, and will, be punished for their crime."

"I love you," I said aloud, hoping the chattering crowd would hear.

"I love you," she returned to a quieter crowd. "I always will, with all of my heart."

"Your love cannot save you," the magistrate proclaimed to a deadened crowd. "Love is an illusion, a sickness brought on by the demons of the world around us. We have lived in harmony within the circle of mountains all our lives, able to keep the powers of darkness out. But occasionally, a spirit breaks through our barrier to infect one of us, and we must eradicate that spirit quickly before it takes control and spreads. By destroying the womb and the mother, we rid ourselves of this infection."

"No, you are wrong," I said, in a desperate act to save her spirit. "Love is holy, bestowed upon us by the god's grace to give us hope."

"Quiet, you heathenous demon," the magistrate bit back. "Can you not see," she advised the crowd. "Can you not see what they are?"

The crowd said nothing. It was the first time in nearly eighty centuries that a love so strong had occurred among the city. It was the first time any of the people had ever seen it. I took the opportunity to continue.

"Can you not see," I shouted, completely defying the magistrate and what she stood for. "Can you not see what this is? The magistrate, our leader, our life, is nothing more than a witch, her heart and mind filled with jealousy and rage over not having the ability of falling in love herself."

"Quiet," the magistrate said. She grabbed my neck and sent a surge of electricity into my body. I dropped to my knees, screaming in pain. "You will not listen to this demon soul," she said.

"But you must," my love yelled out. "You must believe we are truth. Do none of you ever feel something more in the eyes of another, a connection that hinders you both weak and brings you complete joy and happiness all at the same time. Do you not ever wish to be with someone forever, to take care of them, and only them, and feel only their touch so long as you should live?"

The magistrate knocked Tylyn to the ground. But she rose, confident and strong. She was going to die one way or another. She might as well fight to her end.

"I beg you to believe," she said. "Trust yourselves to know and understand

what I say. It is wrong to force us from loving and it is wrong to be forced into barrenness should the magistrate deem it ill. She cannot love, she cannot produce life, and that is why she does not allow others to have it. Believe me when I say, I have loved and I am happy to die for that."

"Very well." The magistrate grabbed Tylyn by the neck. My love screamed and cried as the magistrate boiled her body into flames. When the fire burned out, and all that was left was an ashen corpse, the magistrate was about to take me up as well when someone from the crowd yelled out, "I too have loved, but have hid it in fear. I no longer fear the law."

"I too have loved," another said.

"I, too."

This was followed by an eruption of agreement from the crowd. The magistrate's eyes turned blood red.

"You have all been infected," she screamed.

"I agree," a voice from the crowd followed.

"I, too. Kill them all," a voice said. I'm not sure when it started or how long it lasted, but soon, the entire city had been enveloped in a chaotic confrontation amongst themselves. Men, women, even children fought, some on the side of love, some on the side of law. The fight eventually progressed into war. The magistrate led the warriors of law, I led those on the side of love. It raged for many cycles. Hundreds of our people perished. The city burned. The land was ravaged and everything we once knew as a people died.

Over two of what you consider years in your time, my side had almost defeated the other. We had an attack strategy to take the magistrate's tower and in that victory, we would end the war and bring peace. The magistrate knew her reign was over and before we could strike, she released a bomb high above the city, discharging toxic radiation among everything over a hundred-mile radius. The magistrate had won, destroyed all of the demons, the infection that plagued her people. She would take her victory to her grave with the knowledge that Atlantis would die along with her.

* * *

Or so she thought. A few of us had fled the city before the radiation hit. We lived in the deepest caverns of the mountains and learned how to keep our spirits alive among the land until we were able to find the one that would help us bring Atlantis back to its full glory.

Kaleena sat captivated. Even though Adamus had concluded his story, she was unable to move, trying to come to terms with what she believed to be true. As far as she could tell, Adamus was being completely honest. She would remain cautious nonetheless.

So, what say you, Kaleena? Will you help us?

There was only one answer she knew to be right. *I want to see Lauren.*

Of course. Immediate and without question. Kaleena wasn't sure what to make of it. *But first, I must give you something.*

Adamus pulled a necklace from around his neck. The chain was long enough that it slid over his head quite easily without having to unfasten the latch. Kaleena wasn't sure if it even had one. He cupped the necklace in his hand and motioned for her to stand, which she did without really thinking about it.

This necklace is one of which was once worn by my love, Adamus said as he walked around the pool. *And now I wish for you to have it.* He took Kaleena's hand and dropped the necklace into it.

The chain was laced magically in a sparkling gold made of hundreds of little hearts. The pendant that hung from the chain was of a beautiful woman, her features nearly perfect, if not completely so, her body the vision of an angel. She was standing in front of a heart pierced by what Kaleena considered to be a sword.

Beautiful, she said. *A little obsessed with naked women, maybe,* Kaleena added sarcastically. *But beautiful. Thank you.*

You are welcome, Adamus said before bowing and waving his arm toward the door. Kaleena flashed a sweet smile as she placed the necklace around her neck. Adamus then escorted her from the room. The door shut behind them without

making a sound. The hallway was narrow, but still large enough for four or five people to walk side-by-side. The walls were giant windows that looked out into the depths of the ocean. Kaleena imagined sitting on one of the marble benches that lined each window, writing as she looked out onto glorious vegetation, mountains, sunsets and wondrous beauty of the city around her, dreaming of life, death and the future of what all of it held for her and her friends, her family and her spirit.

As they reached a second causeway that paralleled the one they were in, Adamus ushered her to the right. The two walked for the rest of what could have been near a mile without speaking one word in their minds.

The *Endeavor* – Time Unknown

Matthew groaned after spitting out a few splintered coughs that cut his throat. Shards of glass dropped from his body, leaving behind a simple rhythmic tune as he rubbed his neck to sooth the burn. After one last garish cough that nearly tore his lungs, Matthew pressed his palms to the glass surrounding him. He hissed and swept the pieces away. More glass took rest on the ground as he rose to his knees, which felt more brittle than a thin sheet of ice. He looked around the cockpit, rubbing even smaller pieces of glass from his hair. One cut his forefinger from the tip to the knuckle. His finger turned red before he wrapped a rag around the cut, stopping the leak for now. What he could see through the light glow of the moon sitting just above the horizon was nearly unrecognizable. The tables and seats had been obliterated, as had the walls, leaving behind bent studs and metal rods that once held the tables in place to shape the room. Patricia's equipment was mostly intact, minus what had been broken prior to the explosion.

It was an explosion, wasn't it?

What he didn't see were any other signs of life.

A sting punctuated his legs and groin as he stood. He ignored it as he traipsed his way through the sea of glass to the deck. It was difficult to see anything without the glow of the cabin lights. He called out several names, hoping for a response. The only sound that came back was the calm lapping of the ocean against the yacht's hull. He traced his way around the cockpit to the forward deck and turned his ankle on the corner of a large hole. As he bent to catch himself, he caught sight of the hatch to Benjamin's cabin. It was pitch black inside with absolutely no noise. The quiet calm was eerie.

"Hello?" he called into the hatch. His own voice came back. Matthew could swear he saw the opening get wider, tempting him to go down. He almost accepted, but one last look around gave him reason to stay put. As he suspected, the top of the cockpit had been crushed, the sides having been pressed inward as if being crunched like a tin can.

"God," he said, his thoughts hovering around Jaime. Although he couldn't stop picturing her lying down in that hole with Benjamin — touching him as she never touched Matthew, kissing him with a sense of relief instead of obligation — in a bizarre way, the fresh night air actually relaxed him. The ocean took all of his concerns, jealousy and anger and washed them away. He didn't understand, and didn't want to. It was enough to believe he was finally able to move on, let her go. Perhaps with a little more serenity, he would finally find room in his heart to bring others back to him that had somehow been locked out. But who? Who could possibly fill the empty space in his life? He couldn't think of anyone who needed, much less deserved, his affection. It might be time to stop trying. He could be free from it all, accept his place among the world without a care or a duty to anyone... anyone except...

The one person who had been lost to the bowels of the yacht —

Who? —

the child who fell ill and was near death for the second time in her life —

I can't remember her face —

the young woman who was always lost when she was in need the most —

I can't remember her name —

the daughter who has had to endure the hell of adulthood in the presence of youth and has fought the world for acceptance in her adolescent maturity.

"Kaleena," he shouted.

In less than a second, Matthew had leapt through one of the shattered windows of the cockpit. He landed at the top of the stairs, unable to stop punishing himself for having forgotten about her until just now. But what good was it doing? What mattered was getting to her — if she was even still there.

The carpeted floor on the lower deck sloshed under his feet. Matthew couldn't see anything but the thin line of moonlight that sprayed through the portholes, which wasn't near enough to see where he was going. It took him several minutes to navigate the salon and reach his cabin door, which almost came off its hinges as he ripped it open. "Kaleena."

Once again, Matthew was faced with nothing — pitch darkness that somehow breathed and pulsed in front of him. Stunned by the ripe hollowness, Matthew stumbled backward. The door swung back and forth, repelled by the black hole, yet drawn to it at the same time. He felt the same way, needing desperately to get as close as he could but compelled to avoid the darkness at all costs. Whether that was for Kaleena's sake or not, he wasn't sure. Regardless, he forced himself to step toward it. As he did, he thought he heard a low growl behind him. Turning revealed nothing but the same, usual darkness. Another step toward the room activated another growl. This time, Matthew ignored it, but with his next step, his foot became glued to the floor. Pulling didn't help it budge, neither did stepping back for leverage. It was only when he brought both feet together was he able to move it. So he took another step, this time his back foot attaching itself to the floor.

"Damn it," he said under his breath. He placed both feet together again. They were both free. It was evident now. Jumping was all the darkness would allow him to do.

Jumping… was all he could do.

Matthew rubbed his hands together and stretched his shoulders, concentrating deep into the heart of the black hole. It was the only way. He had to do it. After bending his crackling knees to help give more force to his decision, he jumped forward.

The door flung from its hinges as a wind hit his chest with the force of a wrecking ball. Matthew flew across the salon, smashing his head into the cabins on the opposite end. He attempted to stand, but was unable to lift his body. Before blacking out, Matthew saw the outline of a woman, old, dead almost, peering at him from within the darkness. He tried to speak, but his mind wouldn't allow him to, opting to fade into unconsciousness to avoid an answer he wasn't ready for.

Woods – Time Unknown

The wind whistled through the trees. Thomas had been conscious for some time, but had been unable to open his eyes in fear of being crushed, or worse, dead and somewhere he didn't want to be. But if he was alive (and if the pain in his legs was any indication, he was), how long could he lie here before hunger sent him into death? If he *was* already dead, he'd much rather lie here for the rest of eternity, damned in having only his thoughts and memories of his god-awful existence for company. It wasn't so much the regret in what happened in the past, or how much he missed in his daughter's young life, it was having finally fell in love and having to give the reality of his dreams up for… what? What had he given his life up for? A dream of something that couldn't ever be proved or ever have existed? Then again, it was that dream that led him to the love he so cherished.

A dream he ultimately was not ready to give up on.

Thomas opened his eyes, cautiously waiting for a sharp pain or bright light to hinder his sight. His fears were laid to rest as the stars literally twinkled through the thick brush of leaves. Last he knew, he was in the middle of the ocean. How long had he been unconscious? Where was he, exactly? How did he get here? Why was he brought here? Valid questions that would never get answered.

It took a minute to stand, his withered body still feeling the effects of what he endured on the yacht. Small amounts of dry blood stuck to his face and arms. Trying to wipe it off yielded nothing but fierce stings. So he looked around the dense woods, a sense of dreadful familiarity washing through his mind. Being here

made his heart flutter… something bothered him about it. He thought back as far as he could — past the yacht, past his rehabilitation, past his life with Caitlyn — but his mind grew darker the farther he went, clouded by a haunting mysterious black hole that seemed to have sucked his memories into oblivion. Seeking help from the stars didn't help either. The only way he was going to remember was if he sought it out, in the here and now. So he started moving.

An hour later, Thomas had traveled just over a mile. Everything felt familiar, but it was all new to him. He sat, distraught, tired and ready to give up. His body screamed for him to lie down and let out the stream of tears that had been building up in his sore body. But his heart told him to keep going, that he was almost where he needed to be to find his answers. Just before falling victim to his festering depression, Thomas saw, through glistening eyes, a shape in the distance. It appeared to be a woman dressed in a wispy white gown. By the time he cleared his eyes to get a better look at the feminine creature, she had run away from him.

"Hey, wait," Thomas cried out, running after her with everything his legs would allow, and maybe a little more. His knees felt as if they would break from his legs at any moment, but he continued on, chasing after what could have simply been a trick of his mind. The more he ran, the more he believed he was running after nothing. The woman had disappeared. Where had she gone?

She was the wind — there, but nonexistent.

He tried to recall what she looked like, but her face was a shadow. The more he tried to remember just one small feature, the more he saw Caitlyn, her bright smile producing a tingle in his chest and a soft erection. The same happened the first time he met her.

His roommate had spread the word around campus about a wild keggar, which it seemed every student had made their way to their apartment to fit as much alcohol into their bodies before it poisoned them to the brink of vomit. Eighteen-year-old freshmen, away from home for the first time, scoured the party like small insects, their eyes wide and uncontrolled as if they were trespassing. Twenty-two-year-old seniors made sure the freshmen (and any other lower primate) received the correct

initiation into the world of hangovers and reckless abandonment. Thomas was not one of those freshmen. His high school career was all about getting wasted, getting high, and nearly failing every subject. How he even secured a spot in college was beyond him, but it probably had a lot to do with the ability to pay for the whole thing with the money he received from his mother's death.

Thomas had spent most of the afternoon swilling Heineken's and channel surfing a dozen or so channels of nothing, wishing they had paid their Internet bill so he could find some porn to jack off to before his roommate returned with the kegs. By the time the party was in full bloom, he was chatting up all the hot girls (and even some of the ugly ones he convinced himself were hot because they would be more willing to put out). But nothing popped him more than when Caitlyn, her soft brown hair laying gently across her shoulders and her eyes dark with mascara and purple eye shadow, walked through the door. Her friend was a little shorter than she was, which gave the impression that beneath Caitlyn's tight fitting jeans, were some tall, splendid legs that led to a completely waxed center. Thomas couldn't keep his eyes off her small, pixie smile as she followed her friend around the room searching for no one in particular. He had to move quickly before some other schmuck looking for some ass could claim her.

"Need a drink, beautiful?" Thomas said, coming up behind the two of them with a fresh red Solo cup of beer. Caitlyn looked Thomas up and down as if an angel had just arrived.

"Thank you." Her voice was soft but energetic.

"You new here?" Thomas said as she took a sip, barely pressing the cup to her lips. She was gentle; her kiss would no doubt be the same.

"Yeah." Her eyes darted around the room. "I'm afraid I don't know anyone. Except my roommate." She gestured to her friend, but Thomas didn't acknowledge her.

"You do now," Thomas said, his voice a bit louder than it should have been as he tried to sound cool over the music, conversation and drunken lightheadedness. "I'm Thomas."

"Caitlyn." She took another drink, this one a bit more forceful.

"Caitlyn." Thomas stole a peek at her breasts through the slightly open cut in her blouse.

"How long have you been coming here?" Caitlyn's friend (or roommate, as she had so precisely pointed out) was slowly becoming a third wheel.

"Not long. This is my first year too."

"How'd you hear about the party?" Caitlyn seemed interested, especially after having peaked at Thomas's crotch a little while earlier.

"It's mine," Thomas said, pushing her roommate away. He wasn't sure when she might have left, but it didn't bother him one bit. Caitlyn was the prize. "Well, not mine, but it's my place."

"Awesome," Caitlyn said, taking another look around the room with another sip of beer.

"You want to dance?"

"It's about time you asked," she said and pulled him close, shaking her hips across his waist. He hoped she didn't feel his penis grow with every swipe, though if she liked what she felt, it could very well lead to the end game. It would stay that way for the entire three hours they were together — dancing, hanging out, drinking, laughing, telling stories and eventually making out. By the time the party wore down, Caitlyn and Thomas had stripped down in Thomas's bedroom. Starting with some light, playful oral pleasure, the two quickly worked their way into a full out attack of sexual aggression. Though it was only the first night of many, it was probably the best night they would ever have together. When she woke up the next day, and walked to the door with nothing on but her socks, Thomas saw a girl he might be able to fall in love with, one whose aura shone bright and untainted. It was that same unadulterated aura (which he somehow managed to destroy over the course of two years of doling out nothing but shit to a woman that deserved better) that he saw in the woods. Or at least he thought he saw. It could very well be his mind playing tricks on him.

He was about to collapse when he heard screams in the distance. They weren't

frightened screams; they were excited and playful. Thomas found new energy as he followed the rising yells. He slowed to a walk when the amplitude of the voices had hit their peak. As a small, open encampment came into view, he slouched down and used the thick brush to keep himself hidden. Off in the trees was a group of boys playing some game of tag or football or something. A couple of adults stood off to the side, chatting about news that seemed to be nearly thirty years old. And sitting all alone, roasting a marshmallow in the dying fire, a sad, lonely, disconnected look on his face, was Thomas.

Atlantis – 4 hours 32 minutes after arrival

Silence followed Kaleena and Adamus through hallways and stairwells that all looked basically the same. Dark stone pillars decorated with tiers of gold and silver were covered in several different species of plant life, vines and ivy that woke up the moment they stepped into a new room or hall. Several bore buds that bloomed into fresh fruit or flowers as Kaleena brushed past them and shriveled in her wake. Kaleena recognized some of them, but the majority were unidentifiable, possibly having gone extinct along with Atlantis. The vision of a young woman with long flowing hair, built from thick, heavy wood and coated with a hand-brushed lacquer that helped the beauty grow more elegant with each step among the light, also remained a prominent fixture throughout. She had sad, but soothing eyes that never once looked straight out. They were always pointed toward the floor, always hidden by the woman's hair or her ever-heavy eyelids, as if she were humbled by their presence. Each representation was displayed near a doorway, melting away in a corner, or occasionally floating above, singing among the ceilings. Kaleena first believed the woman to be the magistrate, reminding (or scaring) her people of who was in control and reinforcing her ever powerful hold over the city. But why would such a powerful force — such a powerful woman — be so self-effacing before her subjects? For the magistrate to have the effect Adamus had explained over her people, she would no doubt relentlessly express her supremacy, keeping her eyes directly on the city at all times. If that was the case, who was the woman being portrayed? Based on her stature and her meekness, there was a chance she might just be the first woman — an Eve of Atlantis so to speak; the woman of earth and love before the magistrate's reign of power. What was even more curious was the absence of male-centric portraits, statues or carvings, which indicated that men were quite inferior to the women in this society, a pre-kingdom monarchy that honored and revered a woman and her ability to give birth rather than the reverence of a man for his strength.

Knowing Adamus was listening to every one of her maddening thoughts, Kaleena watched for any sign of recognition for any of her theories. But he never responded or changed his stature in any way, not until he escorted her up a spiral staircase leading to the center of a grand ballroom made of glass and smelling of ginger and roses. Kaleena was awed as she looked out upon the entire city. Giant steel and concrete buildings spread out for what seemed like miles in all directions, representing several different structural styles, from Japanese or Asian to French and modern American. Some were tall, some were warped, some had round, mirrored towers on their ceilings, some came to a sharp edge as if the city were pointing to the heavens above. One building looked a lot like the Sydney Opera House except for the long staff that connected the tiers to the ground; some others reminded her of the Las Vegas skyline, yet more mesmerizing in their shapes and textures. The most impressive buildings, though, were oddly-shaped orbs with an organic asymmetry, shaped in the form of living creatures and plants, like a leaf or a blade of grass. Below all of this, there were a few under-developed structures made of mud, rock and wood that seemed out of place yet in perfect harmony. It was the two giant towers that Kaleena couldn't ignore. Along with the building she was currently standing in, the towers created a triangle around a large courtyard, each connected by several glass walkways and smaller buildings she had just spent the last half hour walking through. In the center of it all stood a massive eight-foot statue. The core was cut glass shaped to look like the flow of water. Porcelain decorated the round base along with what appeared to be dead ivy, which ran up

the core, almost hidden inside the glass water and connecting several tiers leveled about a foot apart, each one smaller than the next. At the top was a small hole, where, once functioning correctly, real water would spray, allowing it to run down from tier to tier, covering the glass and making the entire statue come alive. Sitting on the base, surrounding the central core, were a half a dozen wolves — or which Kaleena guessed more likely foxes — guarding it from intrusion.

Foxlight Fountain, Adamus said.

It's beautiful. Which was true. Despite the statue having been covered in seawater for all of these long years, it looked as if it had just been constructed. No marks of corrosion or war were apparent. Not from where she stood, at least.

We must keep moving, Adamus informed. *We have almost arrived.*

Yeah, okay. Kaleena took one last look around the underwater city before following Adamus into another dark corridor.

Watch your step, he said.

Wouldn't want me to trip and bust this special brain of mine, huh?

As always, Adamus didn't respond.

Kaleena carefully stepped forward, feeling another step. With her weight, several small lights lit up around it, displaying the height and size of the steps. It reminded her of going to the movies. *And yet people still trip over themselves,* she mused.

Pardon?

Never mind. With every new step, lights illuminated. It was the first time the city lights had reacted to her… unless, like the plant life, the city had been reacting to her the whole time as opposed to Adamus, which she had originally thought. *This is cool.* As expected, when she pulled her foot up off the step, the lights turned off, replaced with the lights on the next step. This continued for nearly twelve flights of stairs. "Where's an elevator when you need one?" she quipped under her breath halfway up.

Why let someone else do the work when you're quite capable of doing it yourself? Adamus said in his usual monotonous tone. Nothing fazed this guy.

Because it's quicker, Kaleena shot back. Her expression revealed sarcasm, if it was even visible.

Time is an illusion. His voice sounded as if it was coming from a flight above her, but she couldn't be sure. *When you're patient, the entire world will bow at your feet.*

Really? The whole world? The playfulness of doubt was evident, however, she didn't think Adamus would care that she was only kidding with him.

When you go too fast, you ignore importance, and that's when you become nothing but a wind to be forgotten.

Good advice, Kaleena said after a moment of running the statement over again in her head. *I think.* But as she climbed the stairs, the meaning of those words became more clear. She eventually came to the conclusion that it was, in fact, the best advice she had ever been given.

Upon reaching the top of the thirteenth stairwell (to her count, at least, it may have been more), Kaleena felt pressure on her chest, just between her breasts. She let out a high-chirped scream and grabbed Adamus's hand, digging her nails into it as hard as she could.

No, she exclaimed.

A pair of chilling, yellow eyes appeared out of the black and glared down at her. She shied away and knelt to the floor, a bit shaky. She held her hand to her eyes, covering potential tears she was able to fight off. As she wiped the rising sweat on her forehead through her hair, she looked back up to those eyes — eyes she remembered now as protective. It took a moment to calm her nerves enough to stand.

Sorry, she said, unsure of why she was apologizing. The eyes turned away and she enjoyed a refreshing new bite of air. *Why haven't the lights come on?* Her voice still held a little quiver.

I don't know, Adamus said softly, his eyes disappearing for a split second. *This is the first time I've experienced it.*

Really? Had she really been lighting up the city as they walked? *How is that*

possible? Kaleena cautiously slid closer to the floating eyes, wondering what might be in front of her.

I've said you're very special to us, Kaleena. This has just been a taste of what you can do and what you're capable of achieving, should you decide to help us.

What are you saying? I can light this whole place up if I wanted?

Once you are willing, the eyes said before disappearing once again. Shortly after, a green light was ignited, outlining Adamus's hand. It vanished within seconds and gave way to a crack of soft blue light extending from the floor to about two feet above Kaleena. Adamus stood in the shadows to the side, which allowed Kaleena to step past him into the crevice. Before she could open the door any wider, Adamus grabbed her shoulder, startling her.

"Hey." Her tone was heightened with anger.

This is very important, he said without looking at her. It seemed he was trying hard to avoid eye contact. *Do not discuss what you have learned or reveal to her who I am.*

Why?

Promise me.

Kaleena didn't want to make that promise. It wasn't out of the ordinary for him to keep secrets from her; ever since she first spoke to him, he was vague and allusive. But with the unbound openness he's displayed since then, she trusted him enough to believe he meant well, that he wanted to help his people. Which meant just one thing: Lauren wasn't ready to know.

Okay, she said, wondering if she could help Lauren in any way.

Adamus bowed his head in recognition and let go. He let his arm fall across his body and slid his hands together in front of him. With his head back and still, he resembled a haunted statue.

Kaleena's eyes remained fixed on Adamus until she was through the opening in the wall. Once through, the soft bluish-green light turned to the bright reddish-gold of the walls covering a smaller room than she was used to. It looked like a studio apartment with a few miniature fixtures and decorative carvings. Large, arched windows that were covered with colored mosaics of animals, woman and children sat in-between a bevy of shelves, routed and carved in a variety of gorgeous floral patterns. Each one was full of leather-bound books, porcelain and stone statues, and nick-knacks Kaleena wasn't quite sure what to make of. Once again, several plants covered in buds that had yet to bloom — some potted, some allowed to grow free along the walls —filled the room. Kaleena's steps were silent as she walked across the smooth red rug covering the floor. It wasn't normal carpet; in a way, it seemed as if it might have been made of some type of animal fur or skin, much like a bearskin rug. When she reached one of the potted plants, she finally figured out where the strong aroma of oranges and mangos was coming from. It reminded her of the picnics she and her mom took after church on the first Sunday of every month. They would always pack the same lunch: a couple of turkey sandwiches and a variety of fruits and vegetables, including apples, oranges, broccoli and mangos. Sometimes they brought a piece of watermelon or strawberries as well. It was their communion, of sorts, but the picnics were never about the food. Down the hill from where they sat, under the same oak tree where a robin built its nest and always sang, was a lake that shimmered in the noon sun. It was surrounded by lush hillsides of vibrant green grass and trees that once fall broke became a beautiful array of colors. In the winter, the lake froze, accentuating the winter wonderland — a sight that, despite the cold, always brought them out for the purity of its pleasures. Matthew went with them whenever he wasn't on a dig or expedition, but for Kaleena, it was always meant to be a mother-daughter bonding time, where she was free to open up about her fears, anxieties and desires. She could tell her mother anything, and in return, her mother would never make her feel bad or uncomfortable about what she revealed. The last time they went (two weeks before Jaime left), they talked about the nature of love, marriage and what it took to be unselfish enough to always support the person you vowed to love beyond death.

"It takes a lot of patience," Jaime said. "Sometimes, it can be deeply daunting. But you have to be able to rise above it."

"But how do you rise above it?" Kaleena asked innocently. "It seems so unnatural."

After a long silence: "It is. But if you really love someone, any selfishness you may have had simply disappears."

"But what if it doesn't work? What if jealousy and the strain of selflessness just makes you weak and tired?"

"Why are you asking?" Jaime said.

"No reason." Kaleena turned away, a shy redness hitting her cheeks. She didn't notice her mother glow.

"Is there someone in your life I should know about?" Jaime's lips curled into a mischievous grin and her eyes tickled with amusement. She loved the thought of her daughter having a crush on someone, even if that someone was twice her age, which it could most possibly have been.

"No." The blush filling Kaleena's cheeks turned as red as a tomato.

Jaime chuckled and winked. "Come here." She lifted her arms and Kaleena laid her head in Jaime's lap. "I guess when things get a little tough, you just have to talk about it, tell the person you love what bothers you the most. If you don't talk, you can't fix what's wrong." Jaime sifted her fingers through Kaleena's soft, full hair.

"And what if talking doesn't work?"

Jaime scanned the distance for a long time before answering. "Then you probably never loved them."

"What do you mean?"

"I don't know. Love is way too chaotic to define. I mean, you can love someone and not be *in* love with them. You can say you love someone but deep down know you're lying to yourself because you don't have the confidence to know what you truly want. It's really all just an insane game." Jaime looked at Kaleena, a soft hint of tears running through her eyes. "Unless you're willing to play honestly, you're always going to lose."

"How do you know when you've lost?" The question was nearly hidden under Kaleena's breath. She wanted to know what her mother felt, but was afraid Jaime

would finally figure out why she started asking the questions. In the end, she had to know if there was anything to the distance she had seen grow between Jaime and Matthew over the last few years. She just couldn't come straight out and ask.

Jaime forced strength in the face of a complete breakdown. "Some never do."

The two of them didn't say another word for the rest of the day. It was then that Kaleena knew her feelings about them were right and couldn't face the fact that simply inquiring about the whole thing may have been what finally tore them apart. She never went back to that tree and isn't even sure if it's still there. But much like her inability to go to church or wear dresses after waking up in the morgue, Kaleena felt heading back there would conjure memories of her mother she didn't want to remember.

Kaleena absorbed the memory like she absorbed the smell of the plant: cautious but willing. She cupped her hand around one of the buds. It bloomed into an orange rose-type flower. As she stepped away from it, all of the vines bloomed, spanning out from that single bud until the entire room had been transformed into a giant Zen-like garden. Lauren was in the center of the room on a stone structure that was shaped like a bowl but looked more like a large, uncomfortable beanbag chair. She lay in a slouched, sitting position, her legs dripped over the edge of the stone and her arm draped over her stomach, which no longer seemed to hold a baby. She wore the same style gown Kaleena had on and her hair was tied in the same fashion. The only difference was the lack of makeup. On the headboard were a couple of carved swords, crossed to create an 'X' that burst out of a flash of streaks surrounding the rest of odd beanbag bed. As Kaleena got closer, it was no wonder Lauren looked so peaceful. Underneath her, a cotton or plush material filled a hollowed out center to create a soft, relaxing surface to sleep on. She stood over her for a long while, wanting only to take in her sweet slumber. But no matter how long it may have been since she had rested this well, Kaleena needed a familiar face to talk to until she was allowed to search for her parents. She sat on the side of the bed and looked to the door. When she didn't see Adamus, she shook Lauren's shoulder lightly and lowered her lips to her ear.

"Lauren," she whispered.

Lauren groaned and shifted her body with an unconscious hope of finding a more relaxed position and falling back asleep. When it was apparent Lauren wasn't really awake, only stuck in a mid-dream reactive daze, Kaleena shook her again and repeated her name until she finally opened her eyes. "Lauren?"

It took a moment of dazed mindlessness before Lauren placed her hand gently to her daughter's cheek. "Evey," Lauren whispered. "Evey, you look so beautiful."

Confused and a touch frightened, Kaleena took Lauren's hand and shook her head. "No, Lauren. It's Kaleena. Do you remember?" She waited patiently for Lauren to come out of the dream.

"Ka... lee... na..." Each syllable was stretched over several seconds. Suddenly, Lauren woke from her sleepless daydream. Her eyes were awash with acknowledgment. "Kaleena." She sat up, quicker than she may have thought. Pain pierced her abdomen. She hissed and gripped the bed as best she could.

"What's wrong?" Kaleena asked.

"Nothing," Lauren said, relaxing. "You're looking better, though."

"I'm feeling better." It wasn't a lie, though she still felt a hunger that made her more tired than she would have liked. Lauren didn't need to know that. "Did you have the baby?"

Lauren was somewhat surprised. "I did..." she whispered, caressing the loose skin underneath the gown. Another quick pain bit her, making it feel as if her appendix was about to burst. Either that or she had eaten something bad and was on the verge of food poisoning. A glow of a new mother filled her face as the pain subsided. "I did. But..."

"But what?"

"I... I haven't seen her." Lauren looked around, an act Kaleena followed, assuming they were looking for the baby girl. "Where is she?"

"I don't —"

"Henry." Lauren said gravely. "It was Henry."

"Who's Henry?" Kaleena supposed it was another Atlantean who had taken over a host body, but she had promised not to say that type of thing out loud.

"Henry... Henry's the..." Lauren was unable to finish her thought. Deep down, she still didn't want Henry to be a part of her child's life. Even more, she didn't think Kaleena would believe her if she told her the truth. But what did she have to lose? "He's the father of my baby."

"The what?" Kaleena paused a few seconds and then, "How can the father of your baby be here?"

"I know it sounds crazy, but you need to believe me."

Kaleena chuckled, producing a puzzled look on Lauren's face. She was quick to calm her. "You don't have to worry about that. After what's happened to me, if you say Henry was here, I have to believe it. It was more a question for myself."

"Why? What happened to you?"

A glance at the door kept her from saying more than, "I can't tell you that right now. But, yeah."

"Okay," Lauren said, looking at the blue sliver against the wall. She then leaned in and whispered, "Is there someone out there?"

Kaleena pressed her finger to her lips and cleared her mind. "I can't talk about that right now."

Lauren nodded, but didn't want to leave the subject. "I need to find out what happened to Evey."

Kaleena turned to the door and then back to Lauren, who took her cue by asking, "I wish I could see her. Why won't they let me see my own child?" She may have come off as over-doing the desperate mother act.

"If they wanted you to see your child, they wouldn't have taken her away," Kaleena said, hoping to sense something — anything — from Adamus. Everything remained silent, so she produced some fake tears and asked, *Where's Lauren's daughter?*

She is safe, came the response.

"It's so cruel," Kaleena responded in kind to Lauren's blubbering. *Can we see her? We want to see her.*

As you wish.

Kaleena wasn't sure if he had left to go get the baby, but she no longer sensed his presence. She held her hand up, stopping Lauren's charade, and jogged to the crevice. She didn't see Adamus's outline. He must be gone.

"What is it?" Lauren asked, sliding forward to sit on the lip of the bed.

"I think he's gone, but he may still be able to hear us," Kaleena answered in a loud whisper. "So forgive me if I can't say exactly, but the person that led me here... saved my life, really... is going to get Evey."

"He fell for it? How do you know?"

Kaleena's face brightened. "He fell for it," she said, simply.

"What?"

"Never mind." Kaleena walked back to Lauren. "I'll explain later."

Lauren was utterly confused, but she knew Kaleena well enough — through her father's stories and their pleasant talk — that if she had something to say, she'd say it. She may not have as high an IQ as Kaleena, but she was just as intuitive. "All right," she said and slid off the bed to take in the smell of the freshly opened flowers.

"Beautiful, huh?"

"Very," Lauren said. Then: "How did he save your life?"

Kaleena was silent. The light that had made her face sparkle just a second ago had disappeared.

"I'm sorry."

"No, it's okay," Kaleena said, lowering her head. Lauren rubbed her shoulders, helping to release the ever-growing tightness.

"What happened?"

Kaleena looked directly into Lauren's eyes. Standing in front of her, the two looked like twins, sisters that held an unspeakable connection with one another; even stronger than what she felt on the yacht. She could tell her anything. "I was nearly raped by one of my professors about a week ago."

"Oh my god," Lauren exclaimed. "Oh my god."

"It's okay."

"No it's not. Shit."

"No, really. Someone came and stopped it before it went too far."

"So what. Kaleena..."

"Please. Don't make a bigger deal out of this than it is, okay. My point is, the person that stopped my professor was the same person that rescued me from the ocean."

Lauren was stunned, unable to find any words to console Kaleena. So she scooped her into her arms, kissed her head and held her. "I'm sorry."

"Thank you." Kaleena wrapped her own arms around Lauren. It felt good to hold someone like this again. It felt safe, comfortable, and oddly familiar.

"Just don't tell anyone."

Lauren let go. "No one else knows? Not even Matthew?"

Kaleena shook her head. "And I'd like to keep it that way."

"Kaleena, your father should know."

She didn't think it was possible, but Lauren saw her mood drop deeper into depression.

"Shit," Lauren whispered. "Don't tell me... Matthew..."

Kaleena lowered her head, hiding.

"How do you know?"

"I don't," Kaleena whispered. "But that's what he alluded to. No one else made it."

Lauren covered her mouth. "No..."

Kaleena wanted to cry, but somehow couldn't bring herself to release her tears.

"But if you aren't certain..."

Kaleena's eyes said enough. She fought to keep them alive in her mind, even though she held a constant doubt that her savior — *captor?* — was telling the truth.

"Kaleena," Lauren whispered. "My god..."

What's wrong?

Kaleena looked to the door, prompting Lauren to do the same. Adamus stood just in front of the crevice holding a young infant that looked much older than a few hours.

"Evey?" Lauren said. The stranger held the infant out to Lauren and lowered his head with honor. Lauren looked to Kaleena for an answer, or reassurance, or permission to go over and take her daughter from him. Kaleena nodded, a hint of joy swimming in her eyes. Lauren nodded in return and then swept the young child into her arms.

"She's so beautiful," she said, though it didn't feel as true as she wanted it to be. The baby seemed deathly white, almost albino. Her thin, silver hair looked as if it had just been transplanted from a hundred-year-old corpse. The baby hardly moved, hardly breathed as she slept. Lauren was glad the silk blanket covered the rest of her body; she wasn't sure she wanted to see the whole of her daughter this way.

"What's wrong with her?"

Adamus stood motionless.

Answer her, Kaleena said.

The child is sick, Adamus replied. Kaleena knew Lauren had heard his cold, shallow voice when she looked at him with confused fear.

"What do you mean, sick?" she said, rocking the child gently.

She's dying, Adamus proclaimed.

"No, she can't be…" Lauren's eyes welled up. "She was healthy. I know she was."

What can we do to help? Kaleena said. Lauren was unaware she hadn't moved her lips.

There is only one way to save the child.

Lauren's eyes were desperate with fear. Kaleena knew right away what had to be done and she wasn't going to let her lose her child.

Okay, she said. *I'll do it.*

She felt Adamus's dark smile underneath the hood of his cloak. *I must return the child to her room.*

No, Lauren thought. *I won't let you take her away from me again.*

I must. She will not live unless she is returned.

Lauren's eyes were wide as she realized Adamus had heard her.

You can trust him, Kaleena said, smiling to try and keep Lauren calm.

Lauren wasn't sure she was ready for this, but calmed her mind as she looked at her daughter. *I want to come with you.*

I'm sorry, but that's not possible.

Don't give me that shit. I want to come.

Adamus didn't answer.

"Damn it!" Lauren's eyes were on fire.

Lauren. Kaleena rested her hand on Lauren's arm. She knew exactly how she felt but had to convince her to allow Adamus to take her baby. *Just let him do what he needs to do.*

Why should I? This is my baby. Lauren spoke with her mind as if she had been doing it her whole life.

I know. But we all want the same thing. To protect her. And we will. If you don't trust Adamus, trust me. I won't let anything happen to her. I promise.

Lauren didn't want to let go of her baby, not when she had just gotten her in her arms. But she knew if it meant saving her, then that's what she was going to have to do. And it was better if she didn't fight with them about it.

I'm sure it'll only be for a few hours, Kaleena said.

Lauren handed the baby to Adamus, who accepted the child graciously. *Come,* he said and left the room.

"I'll be back," Kaleena said after giving Lauren a tight hug. "Everything will be fine. I was chosen to protect your baby, and that's what I'm going to do."

Lauren accepted her honesty with a kiss to Kaleena's cheek. "Go. Save my child."

As Kaleena left, the room was draped in a hazy darkness and the flowers sank back into their buds. Lauren sat down on the bed, helpless and worthless, and watched as the crevice joined the growing darkness.

Woods – Saturday, 9:35 pm

The kids were now off in the distance playing a new game (after they got bored with the first one). The leaders of the group, Jacob and Phillip — best friends for over six years; next door neighbors their entire lives — had split everyone into two groups, slapping the hands of their new recruits with zeal each time they chose someone new. When they conceived of this little trip, their parents (friends in their own right) invited all the boys from their class for the sake of "fairness". They would have invited the girls as well, but according to Jacob, they were immature and gay and wouldn't fit in. Each team had five players when the school-yard pick was done, leaving one odd-boy-out: Thomas.

But that was the plan.

When the trip was announced, Thomas was the only other boy in the class that wasn't already one of Jacob's good friends to take them up on the offer. Thomas didn't have any real friends, except for Rebecca, who everyone teased was in love with him and wanted to hump him (he didn't know what "humping" was, but he knew it was bad, or in the very least, something the rest of the kids could make fun of). This was his mother's attempt to help him get past his debilitating shyness and prove he was one of them. So after being teased on the car-ride up to the campgrounds, forgotten about on the hike, scolded for wandering off on his own, unable to catch any fish when the rest of the boys had caught nearly a dozen and forced to nearly starve when it came time to eat those fish ("You eat only what you catch," Jacob conceitedly proclaimed, his father allowing the rule to stand instead of forcing Jacob to share), he got super excited when they asked him to participate in a game.

"Hey Thom-bag," Jacob said with a devilish smile as he and his crew walked up to Thomas, who accidentally dropped his blackening marshmallow into the fire to burn completely away.

Thomas stood nervously. "Hey." He tried to keep from slouching, but he was three inches shorter than Jacob (he swore he saw a whisker on his chin at one point) and the rest of the boys held him hostage with the intensity of their stares.

"You up for a game of 'Soldier'?"

"What's that?"

"It's a game," Phillip said sarcastically.

"What kind of game?" Thomas shot back, innocently enough. He wanted to say, "No shit, Sherlock. You just get out of crime school or are you just a fucking genius?" but even though he didn't have a clue what the phrase meant, he knew it was an insult and didn't want to get beat up. It came from a movie Rebecca stole from her sister's room and watched him when his mom was out shopping. The film was disgusting in its frankness and made them both wonder if they were supposed to do the things the people did in the movie. Rebecca was more open to it and asked to see his penis, prompting Thomas to lock himself in the bathroom. She apologized and swore never to tell anyone about the movie, and he agreed. So no matter how much he wanted to tell these guys he'd seen a dozen girls naked, or repeat some of the funny lines he remembered from the film, to do so would be to break his promise. And these fools weren't going to keep their mouths shut; they'd probably spread rumors that Rebecca did kiss his penis, and then where would he be? No, keeping his mouth shut and succumbing to Jacob's tyranny was his best defense.

"It's like tag," said Greg, a shorter kid with a mullet.

"Yeah, except there are ten taggers and one baby possum," Jacob explained.

"You're the possum," Phillip clarified for his own amusement.

"Exactly."

"What do I do?" Thomas was slow with his words. His excitement was waning.

"Don't get caught," Jacob said slyly.

"What happens if I do?"

"You get integrated, like, for real, when a bad-guy is caught."

"Does someone else become the new possum?"

"No. that wouldn't make sense. We're just going to integrate you until we get all of the information we want."

"What kind of information?"

"I don't know. We'll figure that out after we strap you to the integration chair."

All of the boys smiled like little lunatics preparing to shave the next-door neighbor's kitten. All except Jacob, that is. He looked irritated and pissed.

"Well, are you in or what?"

"I…" Thomas lowered his eyes. He wanted to, so bad, but knew it was a trick — a game designed to end badly for him. Either he'd be captured and forced to tell them stuff he didn't want to tell them or he'd be left out in the woods to fend for himself for who knows how long as the rest of them packed up and moved the campsite. Jacob and Phillip's fathers weren't any help; they just guzzled their beers, waiting for him to answer.

"I told you he'd be a chicken-shit," Phillip said.

"A big baby," Greg added.

"A little wimp," another boy said.

"My baby sister," from another.

"A terrified thumb sucker."

"Shut up," Thomas finally said, nearing tears.

"Look, Thom-bag," Jacob said. "Play the game or get called names for the rest of the trip. It's up to you."

"He won't do it," Phillip said. "He can't do anything like a real boy. He might as well give up his dick. If he even has one." Phillip's father laughed.

"Shut up," Thomas said again. "I'm not a girl."

"Prove it," Jacob said. "Let's play the game."

"Okay," Thomas said without thinking it through. "I'll play your stupid game." The boys perked up and slapped and punched each other like a pack of wild monkeys. "What do I have to do?" he asked, his nerves rattling his body.

"Just start running." Jacob opened up the circle.

"And. Don't. Get. Caught," everyone said together.

Thomas took one last look to the adults, who simply urged Thomas to get going, and then took off into the woods.

"Okay," Jacob said to his friends. "You know the rules. The first team to capture the enemy wins. Anything goes. Our dads can help find him, but not capture him."

The kids agreed and then split into their groups to secretly discuss strategies before heading into the woods — Jacob's group with his dad, Phillip's with his.

The entire scene brought tears to the now thirty-eight-year-old man sitting with his back turned to the encampment. He was unable to come to terms with the odd out-of-body-type experience or endure the debacle a second time. It wasn't over, either. His younger self would eventually be back, a thought that brought with it a painful itch to his scarred hand. For a moment, he considered putting out the campfire, hoping that would somehow change everything. But unless he had mysteriously traveled back in time, trying to do anything to stop the inevitable was pointless.

He lowered his head to his knees, awash with a strong sense of regret, abandonment and stupidity. Should he wait for his memory to play out, or should he push the whole thing to the back of his mind and look for the woman that brought him here in the first place?

You don't have to, the wind answered.

Thomas's head shot up. "Who's there?" he spit out of his hardened throat.

Footsteps crushed the leaves to his right. Thomas saw a shadow form in front of him. He eased up a little, ready to rabbit if it came to it. But as the shadow stepped into the soft glow of the fire peeking through the brush, he saw the soothing face of a lost love before him.

"Caitlyn?" he trembled.

Caitlyn closed her eyes, a gesture that turned Thomas's fears into a radiant glow. When she reopened them, her elegance was unmistakable. She was not frightened; she was not angry; she was kind, forgiving. Based on the beam of her intense eyes, she was there to protect him; save him from his nightmare.

"Caitlyn, what are you doing here?" The question was warm, but held a hint of frightened confusion and disbelief.

"No, Thomas. The question is, 'What are *you* doing here?'"

Thomas shook his head, unable to take his eyes away from hers. He couldn't; they held his sight in the magnetic grasp of love and serenity. It took him a moment before he realized he hadn't answered her question.

"I don't know…"

"You know," Caitlyn said, her voice soothing. "You know why you've returned."

Deep down, he knew she was right. But he wasn't ready to admit it. "I don't…"

"You do, Thomas. You just have to accept it."

"Accept what?" Thomas knew the answer before she said it.

"Your past."

Thomas looked up to the stars. He heard Jacob yell. The younger Thomas had just evaded Jacob's capture by an eyelash, after which Jacob tripped on a tree root, giving Thomas more space between them. Thomas used the time to duck into a thick brush of trees. It was only a few more minutes before the return to the campsite.

"I can't…" Thomas pressed the butt of his palm to his forehead, trying to push the ever-growing pain away. "I can't…"

"You have to." Caitlyn touched his chin. Thomas lowered his hand and re-connected their eyes. He didn't know why he was allowing what could only be a figment of his imagination to coax him into reliving the worst day of his life. But there she was, a star in a black hole, whose mere presence was enough to make him do whatever she asked of him.

"Why?" he asked, fighting her as long as he could.

"That's not for me to answer." Caitlyn picked up his scarred hand. She caressed it and kissed it gently. "You are the only one who can answer that question. But only after you do what you came here to do."

"But you brought me here."

Her soft smile covered a hint of laughter. "No, Thomas. I didn't bring you here. I just guided you to the answer."

"The answer to what?" Thomas grew more frustrated. He could tell Caitlyn knew that.

"You can't move forward until you've made peace with a past mistake. Everything you see is only here because you need it."

"But how can I make peace with it? It's not even real."

"That's up to you to figure out."

"God," Thomas exclaimed, turning from Caitlyn to hide his fear.

"Listen to me, Thomas. Your mind is trying to tell you something. Unless you listen to it, you'll never be free."

Through red, watery eyes, Thomas turned back to Caitlyn. "What am I supposed to be listening to?"

"Let's find out."

Caitlyn urged Thomas to his feet and walked him to a space where they could get a clear view of Thomas's younger self, who was darting toward them through the thin layer of trees. The younger Thomas sprinted to one of the tents and sat down, taking a cautious look around it, back the way he came.

"I can't watch this." Thomas tried to pull away from Caitlyn.

"You have to," Caitlyn said, tightening her grip on his arm. "Trust me."

Unable (or unwilling) to argue, Thomas succumbed to Caitlyn's wish and watched his memory unfold.

The younger Thomas, thinking he was safe, closed his eyes and wiped sweat from his forehead. Coming up with a plan was pointless. There really wasn't a way out of this mess. Unless he wanted to spend the rest of the night in the woods with the snakes and bears and God knows what other slimy, creepy little insects and spiders lived out there, he was going to have to be caught. On the other hand, if he gave up, he would be considered weak. What was he going to do?

A cracking twig brought Thomas back to the game. But it was too late. Jacob, Greg and one of the other kids Thomas thought would grow up to become addicted to drugs and eventually homeless (or so he hoped) formed a triangle around him. Although there was nowhere to run without getting tackled, he had to try.

He ran away from Jacob. As he swerved around the outside of the fire, Greg leapt to him and grabbed him around his ankles, bringing Thomas crashing to the ground. He tried to kick him loose, but the stubborn brat only grabbed harder, even though his chest and arms must have been killing him. By the time Thomas got one foot loose, Jacob and the other boy had reached them. Jacob rolled on top of him, pinning his head to the soft dirt.

"You're mine, Thom-bag!" Jacob yelled. He then lowered his face so that their cheeks were nearly touching. "Time for the integration."

Jacob grabbed a chunk of Thomas's hair and pulled his chin off the ground.

"Tell me, slime. Have you ever wet your bed?"

The boys laughed as they waited for the answer.

"No," Thomas said.

Jacob pulled his hair even harder. "Don't lie. Have you ever wet the bed?"

Thomas figured Jacob wouldn't stop until he said what Jacob wanted to hear, so he gave in and answered, "Yes," which incited a more boisterous round of laughter.

"Thought so. You probably still drink from your mommy's boobs, too, huh?"

"Yes," Thomas admitted, even though it wasn't true. He had been bottle fed his entire life. But Jacob didn't care. Thomas hoped Jacob's dad would put an end to this whole charade, but knowing the boys had ditched their fathers some time ago, he knew he was on his own.

"What about your girlfriend," Jacob said, which turned Thomas's stomach. *Please don't do this*, he thought, clenching his teeth. "Has she ever seen your teeter?"

Thomas took forever to answer. Jacob tightened his grip with every second that passed. "No," he said, unwilling to answer yes to that question.

"Oh, come on. You're best friends. You've seen each other naked."

"No," Thomas said. "No, we haven't."

Jacob leaned closer to Thomas's face again. "You want to kiss her, don't you?"

"No," Thomas said, lying for the first time.

"Sure you do. You wouldn't be friends with her if you didn't want to kiss a baby out of her."

"Shut up," Thomas said, finally fighting back.

"I knew it. You love her. Admit it. Rebecca and Thomas sittin' in a tree.

K-I-S-S-I-N-G." Everyone sang together. Thomas grew redder with both fury and embarrassment.

"Just shut up." He struggled to push Jacob off of him.

"Admit you love her and want to kiss her and see her naked."

"No," Thomas groaned.

"Fine." Jacob stood up, still pulling Thomas's hair tight. "Hold him down."

The nameless boy sat down on Thomas's legs and Greg grabbed his left arm. Jacob took his right and pulled it over to the fire so that his hand rested just over the top of the flame, slowly scorching his skin. All three of them laughed with psychotic glee.

"How long do you think it'll take to burn your hand off, Thom-bag?" He slowly lowered Thomas's hand to the flame. "Admit it!"

Thomas tried to get the feeling back to his fingers by curling them into a fist. He wished he could just deck Jacob. He recalled reading a comic one time about some guy that was part flame and wished to God he could become that guy. It didn't work.

"Admit you're a little cry-baby girl who loves his sissy girlfriend."

"No," Thomas said.

Jacob lowered Thomas's hand a little more. The only heat he felt licked his cheek because his palm was near numb. The other two boys anticipated his hand combusting.

"You're hurting yourself. Just tell the truth."

"Okay, okay," Thomas finally said. He wanted to throw up. "I love her. I want to kiss her and I want to see her naked." Thomas's words were collected by a round of laughter, but Jacob didn't pull his hand away from the fire.

"I thought so, pervert," Jacob said.

Suddenly, someone (to Thomas's recollection, it was Jacob's dad, but he couldn't be certain) yelled for Jacob to stop. In shocked reaction, Jacob let go of Thomas's hand. But because Thomas could barely feel his arm, which had nearly been bent the wrong way for several minutes, his hand dropped into the flame.

And he once again felt everything.

He rolled from the fire, screaming. His arm burned numb as he held his hand tight against his chest. None of the boys said a word, standing as still as emotionless robots in need of a charge. Jacob's dad was the first adult to arrive. He picked the young, sobbing boy into his arms and walked briskly into the woods. Phillip's dad rounded up all the boys and followed shortly after, everyone appearing to have been victims of the body snatchers.

The fire eventually burned out, leaving Thomas and Caitlyn alone in the glow of the large full moon. Caitlyn rubbed Thomas's shoulders to help ease his nausea. Her touch was like a dream, relaxing him enough to wrap his arms around her and cry for several minutes. Caitlyn didn't say a word. Not until he was ready.

"I never forgave them," Thomas said. His forehead sat inches from hers. "When they got back to school, they told everyone what I said. I didn't know Rebecca heard until my mom tried to set up a play-date and her mom refused, saying I saw her naked. I had to explain to my mom about the video and I never left her side after that. The next four years, I was home-schooled and it wasn't until after my mom died that I saw any of them again. Rebecca was so beautiful. I tried to apologize, but she claimed she didn't remember who I was. Her friendship meant a lot to me, so to hear that, whether it was true or not, was devastating. I lost her that night. I learned later that she had become Jacob's on-again off-again girlfriend — a fuck-buddy, really. Over the next few years, I thought I had to prove something to them, that I had become a man, that the incident had hardened me in some way. I don't know why. But it led to a lot of shit I'm not proud of."

Thomas looked into Caitlyn's eyes. "It led to a lot of shit, period. You just happened to be there when it was at its most fucked up."

"I know," Caitlyn said.

"I'm sorry, Caitlyn." Thomas cried again and Caitlyn took him in her arms. "I'm so sorry. Everything I did to you, to Chelsea… neither of you deserved the shit I put you through."

"It's okay," Caitlyn soothed.

"No, it's not. I fucked up. I didn't know what I was doing, running around, seeking answers in booze, pot and any pussy I could get my dick into… I thought they all made me stronger, but they just made me a weak little toad. You loved me for all those years, or at least tried to. I blamed you for taking my daughter away from me but it was me. I fucked up and I'm willing to accept the consequences. Promise me you'll never let Chelsea know who I am. Oh god… God… forgive me, Caitlyn. You deserved so much better… please, just…"

Thomas lowered his head to Caitlyn's shoulder. She brushed her fingers through his hair and lowered her lips to his ear.

"You're forgiven," she whispered, softly and kindly. She then lifted his head up, combed some of the wet hair from his eyes, looked lovingly into his soul and kissed him. With it, Thomas was hit with a sense of renewal he had been trying to find ever since Caitlyn left him. Suddenly, Thomas was kissing nothing but air.

He opened his eyes. The silent woods were his only companion. The clearing where he remembered the fire pit being held nothing but a few branches and a sea of leaves. He walked to the center, slowly reminiscing about where he had been when his hand was burned. Some of the rocks they used to build the pit were covered in dirt, leaves and ash, which he sifted through with his fingers.

"I loved you, Rebecca," he screamed into the night sky. "And I forgive you. I forgive everyone. I am free of my loneliness. You hear me, Jacob? You can no longer hurt me."

Thomas let out a long, loud yell he couldn't let go of. He just kept screaming until he was faint and had to lie down.

Sleep was nearly instant.

The *Endeavor* – Time Unknown

A jolt cramped Matthew's calf stiff and woke him up. He instantly bent his leg in various new directions, quietly repeating, "No, no, no," hoping it would ease the tension. Most of the pain faded after a few seconds, though he remained cautious,

fearing any movement might cause the charlie horse to return. He rubbed his calf lightly as he looked around groggily, unsure of where he was. His head hurt the more he thought about it, but as sleep became a memory, it occurred to him.

Kaleena...

He was still on the *Endeavor*... or at least what appeared to be the *Endeavor*, and Kaleena could be lying dead just a few feet away. However, there was also the possibility she might not even be here, having vanished like everyone else. The funny thing was, the room kept him from finding out. How in the world was a room keeping him from saving his daughter? The whole thing sounded insane, but if Kaleena was here, he had to find out if she was hurt. Then...

...what? Let death take you? You can't allow that.

No. He couldn't. He needed to stay strong. For Kaleena; for Lauren and the rest of his crew; for himself. Kaleena *was* here, waiting, possibly dying. He needed to get to her. If it took the rest of his life, he wouldn't ever give up.

Holding his leg, he shifted into a sitting position and stared at the darkness blanketing the cabin door across the salon. He suddenly smelled something that had been in the air the whole time, but hadn't noticed until just now. On the ground next to him was a plate of food. It looked like mashed potatoes, white and fluffy, but smelled a little like salmon. He took in a deep breath and his stomach tightened; he was starving. Although he couldn't find any reason to trust the food, he couldn't deny his hunger. He scooped a little into his mouth. It was smooth and silky and tasted much like it smelled with a hint of relish. The mash wasn't the best thing he'd ever tasted, but it went down easy enough. By the time he had finished half of it, the taste was no longer a concern. When nearly three quarters of it was gone, he let out a soft, bitter burp. He felt stronger, both mentally and physically. His head no longer hurt and he was wide awake with a resurgence of energy. There was nothing left to do now except get into that room, no matter what it took. A sharp twinge bit at his calf as he stood, but only caused a slight limp as he walked to the door. He stood still, contemplating how to go about his task. Defying the nonsense and ripping the door from its hinges was all he wanted to do, but would determination be enough to keep from being attacked? Any slight hesitation or fear of what *might* happen could cause him to be knocked out again, and the more he fell unconscious, the less time Kaleena had of making it out alive. He had to be strong, be brave, but how could he do that when all he could think about was losing his daughter for a second time? The trepidation turned his stomach.

Do it, you coward.

His hand was on the knob when a shadow in the stairwell caught his eye. It moved, allowing fresh moonlight to sweep into the salon and light Matthew up in a soft blue hue.

"Hello?" Matthew said, attempting to see if the shadow maker would return or if it had just been a hallucination. Forgetting what it was he was about to do, Matthew cautiously made his way up to the dining cockpit, where the moonlight seemed to light the boat and the sea around it in an eerie spotlight. The rest of the ocean was like tar, hidden in the depths of nothing.

"Hello? Is anyone there?" Matthew checked the boat without moving his feet. No one was there, so he slowly moved to the rear of the yacht and then slid along the side to the forward deck, calling out every few seconds. He stopped when the forward deck was in full view. A young women stood at the tip. In the current light, Matthew couldn't be sure if it was Kaleena or a simple trick of the shadows. He stepped closer and said, "Hello?" in a quiet, calm voice.

The girl turned her head and gave him a soft, glowing smile.

"Kaleena?" Even though she didn't turn around fully, there was no doubt.

"It's beautiful, isn't it?" Kaleena said after turning back to the ocean.

Matthew's instinct was to run to her, hug her, kiss her and keep her safe. But he refrained from doing so in the slight chance it was all a trick. Instead, he took another few steps toward her and said, "What are you doing out here?"

"You know," she said, and then: "It's beautiful, isn't it?"

"What? What's beautiful?"

"Everything." She turned around. "Take a look around you. What you see, what you don't see, who you are, who you aren't. It's all just so beautiful."

"Kaleena…"

"Just look around you," Kaleena said, her smile never once fading.

Matthew was confused. All he could see was the darkness surrounding the torn, broken *Endeavor* and his daughter, standing in what could have been a black dress, but looked more like a shadow hiding her naked body. "What am I looking for?" he finally asked.

"If you can't figure that out, you'll never find me." Kaleena's smile was gone.

"What do you mean? You're right here."

"Look deeper. Am I *truly* here?"

For a second it seemed as if Kaleena's body had been swallowed by the night, leaving her head to float above the yacht. He closed his eyes and shook his head. When he opened them again, her body had returned. "What was that?"

"What?" Kaleena seemed authentically dumbfounded.

"Nothing." Matthew leaned against the rail.

"Don't," Kaleena said, shifting slightly away from him. "Don't ignore it."

"Ignore what? Kaleena, you're not making any sense."

"I'm making perfect sense." Kaleena looked out at the water. "You just don't want to understand."

"Then help me understand."

"I can't do that." Kaleena's features turned dark as her demeanor became tense.

"Why not?"

"Because if you can't help yourself, you'll always be too weak to ever help anyone else."

"So, what? Am I just supposed to stand here, look around at 'everything' and hope the answer just hits me."

"Do you want to help me?"

Matthew took the question seriously. He thought about it deeply before attempting a response. "Yes. Whatever it is, whatever's happened to you, I want to help you."

"No you don't," Kaleena said, her eyes locked on the darkness in front of her.

"How can you say that?"

Her silence spoke volumes. She had already answered that question.

"I'm afraid," Matthew finally admitted. Kaleena turned to him, her eyes bright.

"I'm afraid that…"

"What? Tell me."

"That you've died," he said. "I remember the first time it happened. You looked so peaceful, yet I didn't want to let you go. I let you down; it was as if I had killed you by not being around for you, by not telling you that I loved you every day. When your mom left and I wasn't there to protect you, that was my way of letting you slip away."

Kaleena stared at Matthew as if everything he was saying was true. She listened with an open mind and an open heart. And a loving curl on her lips.

"I knew it was beginning to happen again. When you came home that day and your arms were bruised. I was more concerned with this damn trip than I was with what happened to you. I put this expedition ahead of your safety and didn't care what you may have been feeling. My god, I was totally sending you back into that state of mind, wasn't I? I let you down again and now there's a chance you've paid for that mistake again. Kaleena, I'm sorry. I can't believe I put you aside like you never existed… How could I have been so selfish? Had I just given you the attention you deserved and not acted like such an inconsiderate prick, we wouldn't be here, would we?" After a short pause of recollection, Matthew added, "I'm sorry, Kaleena."

Matthew had succumbed to tears as he finished his speech.

"Thank you." Kaleena touched Matthew's cheek, setting a gentle kiss on the other.

Matthew wiped a bit of water from his eyes.

"Now look around you."

Matthew gazed into the darkness, and though he still couldn't see anything, he understood what he was looking at. The darkness was what he was truly afraid of.

"That's right," Kaleena said. "And if you can't fight that fear…" Her eyes had

turned bright silver. Before Matthew knew what was happening, Kaleena sprinted down the side of the boat.

"Wait, Kaleena."

Matthew followed her around the cockpit and down the steps. The salon had been lit up except for the gaping hole behind the now wide open door of his cabin. An intense wind blew from inside the room. Matthew's heart beat fast, but his fear over what had to be done was gone. Whether or not Kaleena was dead was something he needed to confront, like it or not. If she was alive, he would rescue her from whatever fear she held toward him and her mother. If she was dead, he would accept her anointment into heaven. She wasn't afraid to die; never was. Why should he be afraid to follow her if there was even a remote possibility he could save her before that happened? In his heart and in her kiss, she wasn't dead. All of this was trying to keep him from knowing the truth — that she was alive and waiting for him. He knew now, deep down, the only way to protect his daughter was to accept his fate and allow the darkness to swallow him whole.

"I love you, Kaleena," he yelled, followed by a long scream as he ran to the door at top speed. When he reached the threshold, he covered his eyes with his arm and leapt. For a second, he thought he might fly forever. Then, without warning, he landed hard on the ground. He curled onto his back and rolled a few feet before coming to a stop. The pain in his calf spliced through his leg and made its way up to his spine.

The strong force of wind had stopped and the ground had a rough, rocky texture. He took a look around as he attempted to sit. Moss and dripping water filled the surrounding red rock that was lit by several small torches hanging from the walls. For a moment, Matthew thought he'd see Brendan Fraser come running around the corner chasing a milky, degenerative corpse (or more likely, running away from one). But he laughed the thought away as he played his confessional fantasy over again in his head and tried to understand what it all meant. In the end, it didn't matter. Unless he had literally landed in Hell, he was alive. The only thing that mattered now was finding his daughter, a task that seemed easy and impossible at the same time.

He slowly stood, hardly able to put any weight on his leg and feeling as if he had just gone twenty rounds with Ivan Drago. As he stretched his arms and back the best he could, Matthew saw a body lying on the ground about a hundred yards away, hidden around the corner through another tunnel. He hoped to God it was Kaleena and that she was alive. Disappointment hit when he found out it wasn't her, but a resurgence of energy followed when he realized who it was.

"Thomas."

Matthew ran to him and cupped him in his arms. "Thomas, are you okay?"

Thomas didn't respond; he just lay limp against Matthew's chest. At least he was still alive.

Atlantis – 5 hours 47 minutes after arrival

Other than a little bit of faded light swimming through the windows of the tower, the maze of rooms and stairwells were awash in darkness. Kaleena thought maybe she was right — that Adamus had been the one turning on the lights, only making it feel she was the culprit in order to give her a deeper sense of purpose. Then again, with the silent state he'd placed himself into, it was just as likely the lights had been trying to illuminate, but Adamus was forcing them to remain off. Why he would feel the need to do that was unclear. She couldn't help but think it was his way of hiding something. But what?

Mom and Dad, she thought.

I assure you, Kaleena, that is not the case. Adamus said. *Your parents have perished. The sooner you accept that, the sooner you'll embrace your destiny.*

That's starting to get real old, you know.

Your thoughts are shared, Kaleena.

Which is kind of an invasion of my privacy, don't you think?

That is of no concern to me. Your mind speaks more than you would like. If you don't wish me to listen, you must learn to control it.

Yeah, okay, Kaleena said sarcastically. *So I can be like you and hide all my secrets?*

I am not hiding anything from you, Kaleena.

The hell you aren't.

Adamus stopped cold as her words left her mind. *Do not accuse me of deception when it's your own fear that has hid you from the truth.*

Kaleena felt his breath on her cheek as his skin brushed hers. She sucked up air as if she were drowning and then the sun poured into the room. They were in the middle of what seemed like an enormous indoor jungle.

You see, Kaleena, Adamus said, *the fear your mind holds will hinder you until you learn to let go. When you do, you will see that the world is much more beautiful than you can imagine.*

Though her lungs were tight, Kaleena felt safe. Adamus nodded and looked to the baby in his arms. *Come. We are nearly at our destination.* He walked the dirt path that traced its way through the flurry of trees and brush.

Kaleena took one last moment to absorb the beauty around her and then caught up to Adamus, needing to stay as close to him as possible, if nothing more than to make sure Evey remained safe. It didn't take long to reach a stone archway, which was wrapped on each side by what looked like giant Bonsai trees. The room on the other side couldn't have contrasted more with the room they left. There wasn't one plant to be found in the gray, steel room that seemed to go on forever in all directions. It was so clean, Kaleena felt if she coughed, the whole room would need to be sterilized. As she paced her way to a dark opening on the opposite side of the room, she wondered if she had inadvertently entered an alien spaceship and was being led to a chamber to have needles shoved into her eyes and be experimented on until she went insane. A slight disappointment set in when Adamus led her down into the hole and descended yet another flight of stairs. The room below lit up, revealing a medieval dungeon. A light trickle of water streamed down one of the thick, muddy rock walls. Again, it was such a contrast to what she believed the rest of the city represented.

Where are we? Kaleena asked.

We are underneath Foxlight Courtyard. In a few hundred yards, we will be directly underneath the fountain at the center of the city.

What are we doing down here?

Foxlight Fountain is the source of life. The key to resurrection is directly beneath her.

Then let's not waste any more time, Kaleena said. She glanced at Evey, who looked more like a corpse than she remembered.

As you wish. Adamus guided Kaleena through the dank, moist caverns that looked as if they had been dug by some kind of a rodent, left to its own natural devices of decay.

After about a half mile down a small hill that led them even deeper into the earth, Kaleena deliberately asked, *Is there a reason these tunnels aren't like the rest of the city?*

I'm not sure I understand your meaning.

If this area is so important, it seems to me it would have been obnoxiously plastered with protection and security. I don't see any of that down here.

Appearances can be deceiving, Kaleena.

Apparently.

You'll learn.

Right. Kaleena accepted his answer without argument. Looking ahead, she saw a wall in front of them. *What's that?*

The gateway.

Kaleena picked up speed as massive wooden door that not only filled the entire tunnel, but actually matched the age of the city, drew her closer. It was warped in various places, splintering portions of the faded colors and leaving it black and moldy in others. The center, though, was in near perfect condition. There was a carving (or better yet, what the door itself had been carved around) of the humble woman seen all over the city. Unlike all of the other carvings, this time the woman was looking up, making it seem as this was the source for which all of the others were looking, seeking guidance. Kaleena ran her fingers over the smooth curvature of every inch of the woman, who floated in the air, a thin gown dressed casually around her, flowing in the wind, her arms held out, ready to accept the heavens. Her legs were slightly spread apart, one a bit higher than the other, both knees bent, making it appear as if she were running or was being picked up by an invisible hand. Looking up at the matriarch's face, Kaleena tried to understand where the woman's mind was. The eyes were closed but she was smiling, her mouth slightly agape as if she were about ready to accept the first kiss of true love.

Welcome to Spirited Wind, Adamus said and gently placed his hand to the woman's stomach. The wall shook, stunning Kaleena when it split the woman in half to open into another room. She hadn't even noticed a crease that would indicate a double door. Yet she didn't hesitate to cross the threshold when the doors were wide enough to enter. She immediately felt she was back in the city above, though the room appeared to be much silkier. Directly in front of her was another door (or so she assumed) made of glass or ice, which gleamed in the light of the room. She hoped she might discover where it might lead, but all she could see was a fuzzy reflection of her and Adamus staring back at her in the shimmer of the colorful tunnel behind it.

It is not of concern, Adamus said, attempting to focus her attention away from the door.

What is it?

A prison, if you must know.

A prison? Kaleena looked deeper. *Is that where Tylyn was held? I mean...* She turned to Adamus to convey sadness and regret for his loss. *Before...*

Adamus lowered his head. Kaleena felt bad for even bringing it up. She was about to apologize but thought better of it. *Better just move on.* She shied away from Adamus's cold stare and tried to picture what could be hidden beyond the tunnel. She now understood what kept most people away from here — the security, so-to-speak, which made sure the citizens of Atlantis stayed on the surface.

She rested her hand on the glass. It was cold and dry, yet she didn't feel death or solitude within its confines. What she felt, or at least thought she felt, was sanctity, spirituality —

Love?

Kaleena dropped her hand from the door when a powerful sense of anger exploded from Adamus. She attempted to block the numerous situations that ran through her mind before Adamus could pick up on them. She wasn't sure if it worked; all she knew was that her best bet of calming Adamus was to forget about the doorway and its prison. She stepped away from the door. A light glistened off of a carving hidden under the rock dust that had settled on the walls over the years. Wiping her hand across the wall and blowing away the dust revealed several symbols. It soon became clear that the symbols had been carved into the entire wall, possibly the entire room. She turned to Adamus, more excited than she thought she should have been.

What is it? she asked. *Some sort of history?*

The text chronicles the genesis of Atlantis. The birth of man and the gift of life.

Kaleena let out a soft chuckle of exhilaration. *What does it say?*

I'm sorry, but the discussion of the texts will have to wait. The child will not live much longer if we do not proceed quickly.

Kaleena scanned the history she had uncovered and then moved backward toward Adamus. "Right," she whispered. When she was within a foot of her guide, she turned to him with a resurgence of energy.

Okay, so, what do I do?

Adamus handed Evey to Kaleena, who gently rocked the dying child in her arms. What she got in return was an eerie warmth wrapping itself around her, cupping them both in a bright aura of relaxation. She felt incredibly healthy and protected. *Adamus,* she said happily, but Evey wouldn't let her continue. It wasn't just her thoughts, either. When she opened her mouth to speak, her voice was stripped away. She was left to watch Adamus uncover a massive amount of text across from her. He blew dust away from the entirety of the wall except near the center, where a smooth, unabated gap had been created. Adamus caressed the text, apparently reading it to find out what needed to be done, and then returned to collect the child. The moment Evey was removed from her arms, the aura of

protection faded. Kaleena felt fatigued.

Ah… what was that? she said as she fell to one knee, pushing the butt of her hand to her forehead to urge the throbbing away.

Fight it off, Adamus said. *It is time to do what you came here to do.*

Kaleena stood cautiously, wishing the pain away. It didn't help.

Step up to the wall and place your forehead into the center.

Kaleena peered at Adamus as if he were nuts, but complied when all she saw in his eyes was complete honesty. She placed her hands to either side of the gap in the text and gently placed her forehead to the empty space.

Now what? she asked, unconvinced anything would happen.

First you must believe in your ability, Adamus said.

What ability?

The power of your mind.

Oh, of course. How stupid of me.

Your sarcasm will not help, Love.

Kaleena pulled her head from the wall. *Hey. What did I say about calling me that?*

Adamus grew dark with anger. Kaleena held her ground. *Do not defy me,* he scolded.

Don't fuck with me, she shot back. Suddenly, Evey cried; more of a sickly whimper, but a cry nonetheless.

Adamus's anger softened as Kaleena sank into a shallow sadness, matching what Evey must have been exuding. She sank back to the wall and softly whispered, "I'm sorry," more to Evey than Adamus. He took it as an apology anyway.

Now, will you help us? he asked solemnly.

Yeah, yeah. Believe… Kaleena pressed her head to the open space. She had no idea what she needed to do, or what power she was supposed to have, but she figured she'd know it when she felt it. Unfortunately, the longer and harder she tried to find it, the more it seemed to distance itself from her

I can't, she finally said. *I don't know what I'm supposed to do.*

Free your mind.

I can't do that. Damn it. Kaleena pounded the wall. Any harder and she would have broken her knuckles. As she pushed away, she sensed a bit of disappointment coming from Evey. *I don't know how.* She wasn't sure whom she was speaking to anymore.

Let go of what you know and focus on the city, Adamus said. *On the fountain… on its people.*

How?

By opening yourself up to them.

How do I know when I'm doing that?

You'll know.

Kaleena curled her hands into fists and roared frustration. She was ready to break her hand if it meant making everything make sense.

You're still fighting it, Kaleena.

Okay, she said, clenching her teeth. *I'll try again. Relax, focus…* Kaleena set herself in position in front of the wall. She thought about what she'd seen roaming the city, about her father, about Evey and Lauren. When her mind gravitated to the fountain, a light jolt of electricity tickled her fingertips. And just as fast as it had come, it faded away, leaving her holding a wall in a cave under a dead city.

It's not working.

Silence filled the room. All she heard were light footsteps walk toward her. Adamus placed his hand on the back of her head. *You can do this, Kaleena. You just need to believe you can.*

Focusing on the fountain, sensing it flourish with bristling, clear water, the plants alive and healthy, blooming in every home and along every walkway, tasting the sweet aroma of fruits and berries, Kaleena felt her hands sink into the wall and her feet melt into the floor. A human presence filled the room. It doubled and then tripled until hundreds of lives were on top of her, each one becoming part of her, downloading their consciousness into her mind. Men, women and children all took turns showing Kaleena their lives before dissolving into the wall to travel the

earth into the city. After the last child made his way through the portal, Kaleena examined the wall with nothing but her spirit. She allowed the city to consume her, eventually absorbing the energy that had been gathered within. Her thoughts of flowing water lit up the fountain with fresh water that poured through the center of the statue to mix with the sea. The ivy wrapped around the base became a lush green as if it were summertime at Wrigley Field. The riveting burn in Kaleena's soul urged her to continue. She used the fountain as her source of energy to travel through the rest of the city, lighting each building up with ease. When the last of the structures had come to life, she brought her consciousness back to her body. That's when the sickness set in. She followed the sensation across the courtyard to a room underneath the building, which Adamus passed through to travel to the historical archive. It was full of large, bright cryogenic tubes, spread out away from the courtyard for what seemed like miles. Steam surrounded bodies hidden behind invisible glass barriers. They were cold, lifeless — but they weren't. Kaleena saw memories of planes crashing and boats sinking. She saw a sailor, caught in a storm, thrown overboard and strangled to death by the water; a child on a cruise with his parents, crying for his mother as he waited to be eaten by the sea; a young woman, fearing for her life, praying for redemption as she headed for her tomb alongside a dozen or so strangers. The woman held someone's hand for protection, a face Kaleena couldn't quite make out. As she probed deeper into the woman's mind, a force blocked her. It was similar to a lot of others, but the woman seemed special somehow; more important.

After being pushed out a third time, Kaleena scanned the rest of the room. Adamus stood in front of a console connected to all of the tubes. One such wire broke away from the bundled packs and wound its way to a chair where Evey sat, stiff and proper. A small strap was laced around her forehead. Kaleena felt new life spreading through her and into each of the bodies, none of whom seemed good or loving at all. In fact, all of the worlds she sensed were filled with jealousy, fear, aggression and desire. Their memories soon evaporated in favor of one specific consciousness — a soul of someone important; someone who had once lived in Atlantis.

Adamus, what are you doing? Kaleena screamed, letting her voice reverberate around the room.

You've done your job, Love. Leave me to mine.

Kaleena's consciousness was then slammed back into her body, knocking her across the enclosed room. She landed a few feet from the glass door, unconscious, her forehead smoldering with a reddening scar.

Caverns – Time Unknown

Hidden in the shadows of a small tunnel, she watched the man crouched next to the other, sweep him into his arms, clearly having found his way into the reality of the world he was once too afraid to know. The second, having taken time to expel the anger, anguish and despair from his mind, had been slumped in a small, fetal ball to lie in unadulterated quiet. He had yet to wake, though she didn't know whether it was because he was still trapped within himself, or because he was unwilling to return, content to remain in the place he'd found himself — a lonely dungeon deep within the hollowed mind where he could punish himself for whatever he was fighting. His friend, breathing in dangerous levels of rapidity, looked frantically around the caverns, searching for something — or possibly someone. It was an oddity to see this act, as she wasn't unaccustomed to it. She had seen it before, but mostly within those that had lost their hope, and for some, their sanity. Humans had always seemed odd in that way. In her lifetime, before that which destroyed the world she tried so hard to keep from crumbling, fear was held only by animals, which instinctively craved to survive. Man, as she knew, never feared death, not until false hope, aggression and hatred had been introduced and blossomed into the dominant trait in the weak mind of the young. Her hope for a blissful future was torn apart and her decision to test that hope had failed, as evident by this man's tortured heart.

It wasn't long before the first man yelled unclear rubbish. Although she should have understood the words that leapt from the man's tongue, her age and failing

health limited her ability to comprehend. Keeping both men alive had expended so much energy, she was now all but dead. She could have let them pass on — become what she knew they would eventually become — if she didn't need their help so desperately. How she might convey this to them was unclear, and she wasn't willing to spend another ounce of her strength to speak.

The man stopped calling out and sat comfortably against the wall, lying his ill friend in his lap. Watching the man protect this person like his own kin, his own blood, was deeply moving. Had she the ability, she may have shed a tear. She had no possible way of knowing what the man (and to a greater degree, his friend — his brother, as it seemed) had gone through in his mind, who he had encountered and what fear he had to overcome to break free of his deception, but her instincts told her it had to do with his young daughter, of which the man, through his lonely eyes, felt deep regret toward. She had yet to understand the full extent to which the father had lost his way, but she was determined to find out, hoping whatever he'd lost would help her in her inevitable quest.

Above her, events were taking place that would turn the tide of a long dead war from which she had lost her most precious gift. She had to stop the madness from rising again, as it once had so long ago upon the devil's return from isolation, a test that ultimately failed a man for whom she was very close. He was her first, her last and her only, though it was always clear that, with a piece of her own, he would become her exact opposite. All she desired was peace, to be held in the interim of a continued life, the bridge to a better tomorrow; her other half wanted a life in the here and now, to dominate and domineer, to rule over those that were weak and guide those who were willing to be taught a path the intricacies of the mind were not ready to understand. It was of his own volition that he left that day to travel the earth and find what it was he was missing. He took all of his emotion with him and a piece of her always hoped his return would never come to pass. She was content; but she was also naïve. She would not allow it to happen again. It was his mind she used to lead the world into what it was now accustomed to; however, she let it be. The world would not be ready should he be given a new life.

Just then, pain sliced through her heart. With a little focus, she sensed the daughter (Kaleena, as she was labeled by the man resting his fractured body) become one with the city. She felt the beat of her soft heart, the warmth of her giving mind, and the rising heat of a necklace, one that had once been a sign of hope and vivacity. Her thin lips etched a joyous smile, one that was premature. The death of the young girl would not be in the woman's best interest. She needed her alive to give her the chance to be whole again.

As she listened to her soul, her own energy grew. Her heart beat faster and her body began to flesh. Eventually, upon searching the city, the girl came to a room where a younger, healthy man toiled with a device she didn't recognize. The words from the young girl —

What are you doing? —

were clear, confused and angry.

You've done your job. Leave me to mine, came the response from the young man, seething with a voice that chilled her mind. Her connection to the girl was severed by a piercing sting to her mind. The presence of the necklace also vanished. But the energy she'd collected from the child was enough to gain access to the quiet mind of the unconscious, without losing the body she now inhabited. It was time to reveal herself to the men before her and convince them to help her in her quest. She crawled from the hole she had buried herself in and walked feebly up to them, knowing it would take one last act of strength and will to prove herself their friend. She just hoped it wouldn't be her final act.

*   *   *

Matthew lay against the damp wall when he first caught a glimpse of her.

After first attempting to shake Thomas awake, wishing he had a large bucket of ice water he could throw on his colleague, Matthew called out for help. It was a futile act, as he never expected anyone to come help in the blazing red darkness of the caverns. He was about ready to explore the caverns, learn a thing or two about

them and possibly find a way out or track down any sort of help, but he couldn't leave Thomas alone. Who knows what was down there with them, capable of dragging either one of them off into a smaller, more secluded hole somewhere, leaving no trace of its prey's whereabouts. And even if there weren't any other creatures roaming the caves, Thomas could wake up at any time. After having gone through it himself, he knew it would be best to wake up alongside someone familiar than to be alone in an unfamiliar environment. He moved to the wall to rest. His legs and back hurt and a running tightness pinched his nerves as if it was toying with him. His breathing was labored — forced at times — and his stomach decided to play along with the rest of his body, producing small, abrupt burps that left behind an aftertaste of relish and vomit. Thomas lay at his feet like a large dog after having run for miles, seemingly content. Matthew wanted to believe he was comfortable, but couldn't fight the feeling that Thomas was in the same state of mind he'd been in and had yet to find his way back from it. He wished he could see inside his friend's mind and help show him the way back, the same way Kaleena helped Matthew understand his own personal struggle. But it wasn't her. At the time, she felt as real as the walls around him now, her eyes familiar, genuine and kind. But the more he thought about his experience, Kaleena's eyes had been much too cold. They looked at him like a child meeting a stranger, more in love with the blindness of her surroundings than she was with the safety of having him close. His mind had been unable to produce those sweet, nurturing eyes without revealing them to be false, making her body nothing but a shell. He didn't know where she was, but his gut told him she was alive but distant. Had she been forced to examine her own mind? Could she find her way back before she grew defeated, dropping into a similar state as Thomas? She was strong, there was no doubt; but was she brave enough to accept the truth of who she really was? Nothing was certain. He just hoped he would be able to wrap his arms around her at least once more, to look into those pearly eyes and say, "I love you."

Matthew was fatigued and lightheaded. He forced himself to stay alert, but his eyes continued to grow weary, and eventually, he had to close them. He didn't

know how long sleep held him before snapping awake, believing he heard something. Had it been a dream? Had it been a muscle spasm, or a slight crack of a bone as his body twitched among his drowsiness? Then he heard it.

It was soft and subtle, but no doubt a footstep. And another. Someone (or something) was coming closer. The light from a torch three feet above and a few feet to the left of Matthew highlighted what at first looked to be an undead corpse, walking its way into the moonlight after having been cursed. Its features became more acute as it drew closer. It wasn't a corpse, but a very frail, old woman. She wore nothing but a thin, nearly see-through cloak draped over her shoulders and tied loosely around her waist, where the end of the looping gap (which ran from the top of her shoulders, past her flat breasts, to the knot of the cloak's ribbon) exposed more than Matthew really cared to see. The gap returned underneath the ribbon, allowing an ease to the flow in the woman's short, cautious steps. Her back arched forward, allowing the thin veil of white hair that seemed to float on its own against her skull to fall past her shoulders and dangle just inches from the ground. Matthew didn't say a word. He backed away a few inches at first, then remembered Thomas and wrapped his arms around him to pull him away from the woman. As he struggled to slide the body away, the weight of which pulled on every strained muscle (and possibly creating even more along his arms and thighs), the woman raised her hand, all five bony fingers revealing long fingernails that curled into themselves. The woman's chest rose and fell against her skeletal form and her dark eyes, hidden within the large round holes of her skull, looked afraid. Matthew stopped pulling Thomas, hoping his decision to do as he was prompted wouldn't backfire. She lowered her hand, and though he couldn't see a hint of any lips, Matthew thought he saw a faint smile.

"Who are you?" Matthew asked, though he wasn't sure if he had or not. The woman didn't answer with her voice. She raised her hand once again, this time her fingers pointed at him, her palm face-up, as if she was asking to take Matthew's hand. She then turned it graciously toward Thomas and then back on herself, pointing at her delicate chest. Matthew wasn't sure what she was doing until she did it again, pointing at Thomas and then herself. She wanted to help. His head unconsciously fell forward. The woman slid to them, but this time Matthew didn't try to pull away. He shifted a few inches to Thomas's side, giving the woman plenty of room to do as she needed, but remaining close enough to make sure if anything went wrong, he could intervene, possibly break one of her bony arms in half.

It took several minutes for the woman, appearing as if she were moving in super slow motion, to kneel down. She dropped her chin in Matthew's direction, apparently nodding a gracious thank you before resting her fingers to Thomas's temples. For a few minutes, nothing happened. Then, the woman bent her head back and let loose a piercing scream, shallow and callous. Thomas jerked in hysterics, appearing to have a seizure. But Matthew couldn't do anything to stop the old woman out of fear of going deaf should he let go of his ears. He ducked away as dirt and rock fell from the ceiling and kept his ears covered even after the screaming had stopped. It was only a matter of chance that he opened his eyes to see the woman slumped next to Thomas, who coughed as he tried to sit up.

"Thomas," Matthew screamed, though he could barely hear himself over the pulsing ring vibrating in his ears. Thomas looked to him, disoriented.

"Matthew?" Thomas let out a deep sigh as Matthew lowered his hands and got to his knees. They embraced with a warm, welcome hug. "God, am I glad to see you," he said, though all Matthew heard was, "God — see —".

"Good to see you," Matthew roared back. Thomas shifted away slightly and Matthew realized he was talking too loud. He'd have to trust the vibration of his vocal chords and rely on his ability to read lips until his hearing decided to return to full strength.

"Are you real?" Thomas asked. "Not another hallucination?"

"I'm real," Matthew whispered (or so he thought).

"Thank God." Thomas sat back, making sure to face Matthew at all times. "Where are we?"

"I don't know," Matthew responded.

"Ediinis." The low, cracked voice came from behind Thomas. He turned and saw a corpse struggling to rise up. Thomas slid away with a squeak.

"Don't," Matthew ordered, holding out his hand. "She's only here to help."

"Help... She?"

"Yes," the corpse said. "Help." Her features had waned considerably. She now looked like the skeleton that hung from the wall in a biology class, her thin skin having become nearly transparent.

"Who are you?" Matthew asked again.

"My name..." It looked as if she was searching for the answer. But then she cleared her throat, spit out a large mound of what looked like mucus mixed with blood, and then continued, her voice a bit less scratchy, though still deep and hard. "My name, in your tongue, is pronounced Gydressina."

"In my tongue?" Matthew asked, peaking over at Thomas.

Gydressina nodded.

"Do you mean our language?" The tone in his ears was still present, but had died down to a low hum.

"Yes, of course. Your language." The last word was pronounced delicately.

"How do you know our language?"

"That is of no concern. We have much more urgent importance to discuss."

"Where are we?" Thomas asked.

A smile rose to Gydressina's non-existent mouth. "As I have said. You are underneath Ediinis."

Thomas looked to Matthew, who knew that confused expression well.

"Where is Ediinis," Matthew said as if asking a child.

"Ediinis is where it has always been," Gydressina said, answering nothing. She noticed Thomas roll his eyes. "Were you not seeking the city?" she said.

"We were seeking a city, yes," Matthew said calmly. "But we were looking for Atlantis." He felt a surge of energy in Gydressina's mind. If she weren't so old, he knew she'd be laughing, possibly hysterically. "Do you know of it?" he asked.

"Of course," she said, her voice suddenly bright and cheerful.

"Do you know where it is?"

Gydressina seemed to avoid the question. Matthew waited patiently as she rose to her feet, though the same could not be said for Thomas. He rolled his eyes several times and shifted every few seconds, tapping his leg with a constant beat. When she finally stood tall amongst them, she raised her arms and said, "You are sitting right below it. The city you seek is the great, majestic city of Ediinis."

Thomas still looked confused. "Ediinis is Atlantis?" Matthew asked to confirm what Thomas didn't understand.

"You speak truth."

Matthew stood. "You have to show us. We have to see the city."

"Patience, my friend. I must ask something of you first."

"What's that?" Matthew's impatience to see Atlantis with his own eyes was clearly evident in his voice and lightly shaky hands.

"Wait a minute," Thomas said, standing. "How do we know she's not lying to us."

"Thomas —" Matthew scolded.

"God, Matthew, look at her." Thomas ran his hands up and down, grasping the reality of how unattractive the 'woman' was. "She's barely alive… if she's even alive."

"I assure you, my life is whole."

"What is she doing here? Who is she? Where did she come from? Wouldn't these be good things to know before we trust everything she says?"

"Your hesitation is understood, Thomas."

"Don't use my name." Thomas turned his back to Gydressina and stepped away.

"I will tell you all everything in time," she assured. "But I must ask for your trust now, even though you are blind to my knowledge."

"What?" Thomas whipped around, his arms crossed tight against his chest.

"I have something I must do and I need your help to do it."

"What do you need to do?" Matthew asked, filling the silence that had fallen among them.

"I need to save my city."

"*Your* city?" Thomas scowled.

"Ediinis was built with my life. I cannot have it fall to those that seek its destruction."

"Destruction?" Thomas looked back and forth from Matthew to Gydressina. "Matthew, are you honestly going to believe this shit?"

Lauren and Kara raced through Matthew's mind. What happened to them? Were they okay? Had they somehow made it off the *Endeavor* as he and Thomas had? If so, where were they now? Had they been taken captive by, as Gydressina put it, those who seek destruction? For a split second, he also thought of Jaime and wondered, with a small ounce of love, if she, too, was all right. But there was only one he really cared about, and it was she he spoke to Gydressina about now.

"Answer me one question," he whispered, before looking Gydressina in the eyes. "What happened to my daughter?"

"Kaleena is alive," Gydressina happily pronounced, to Matthew's devastating relief. "And she is fine. For now."

"What do you mean 'for now'?" He hadn't realized he'd never said Kaleena's name out loud.

"She is an intelligent, caring person, Matthew. However, I fear for her safety. Which is why I need your help."

"You need us to help rescue her?" Matthew wanted to make this clear — if only to himself. Gydressina nodded courteously.

"Hold on," Thomas interjected. "Matthew, no disrespect, but why is she so concerned about *your* daughter? What does she have to gain from rescuing her?"

Gydressina showed what seemed to be frustration. Her voice remained calm nonetheless. "She is important to me, I admit. Without her, I cannot complete my objective."

Thomas gestured to Gydressina while looking at Matthew with an "I told you so" expression.

"Why?" Matthew coughed. "Why do you need her?"

"Because she is the only one that can resurrect my youth."

A piercing shot of fear hit Matthew's heart. "How?"

"I wish to explain everything, but not here. We must move quickly."

"Wait. Why?"

"I am dying," Gydressina said coldly. "Kaleena is my last hope. I need her help. I promise I will not take her life."

Matthew sought solace from Thomas, who shrugged, unsure of what to say. Matthew finally nodded. Kaleena was far more important to him than his own selfish pride. If the only way to see her again, to hold her tight and keep her safe, was to help this old woman, then he was going to have to do it. Even if it meant betraying Gydressina once they found her. Getting his daughter back was all he cared about.

"Okay," he said. The ring in his ears had all but dissipated, but his answer felt a mile away. "We'll help you."

Gydressina took in a relaxing breath. "Thank you, Matthew." She turned to Thomas. "Thank you."

Thomas threw up his hands. What else was he supposed to do?

"What do you need us to do?" Matthew asked.

"Follow me, do as I ask, and all will fall into place. Grab those torches. We will need them."

Matthew slipped one of the torches closest to him from its frame. Thomas, after a slight hesitation, knew it was best to stay with Matthew and grabbed the torch on the opposite wall, hoping they weren't being taken into a trap.

"This way," Gydressina groaned and the two men fell in behind her.

"I'm happy she's safe," Thomas said after a few feet, which, following Gydressina, took several minutes to walk.

"Thank you," Matthew replied.

"I just wish we knew about the others. I can't stand knowing Trishen might be —" He couldn't finish; he didn't want to finish. Not after what he'd been through.

"She is alive." The voice before him was sweet, almost intoxicating.

"What?"

Gydressina turned to face Thomas. "Your friends. They are still alive." Her black eyes shifted to Matthew. "As is your wife."

Unknown Location – Time Unknown

Jamie woke with a sharp cough. She couldn't feel her right arm, which she'd been lying on for who knows how long. As she lifted her arm to regain blood flow, a light, cool breeze brushed past her face and neck. She was unable to see anything, but the smell of Benjamin emanated from the cotton shirt she wore, causing a brief moment of grief to strike before she came to her senses. There was no time to feel sorry or mourn; she had to find out where she was. Ignoring the burning itch from the still wet plastic of the diving suit she had yet to remove, Jaime followed the hard dirt floor with her hands until she reached a dry, rocky surface in front of her. There wasn't any type of opening or doorway. Only a corner that led across another small wall to another corner, until finally, she had traveled the entirety of the wall and returned to where she had started.

She was boxed in with no clear exit.

Jaime pounded the rock with an exasperated yelp and fell back against the wall behind her, which couldn't have been more than a couple of feet away. Stretching her legs out straight would be impossible. The top of her cell was a little less than arm's length away, again with no possibility of escape. Tears warmed her cheeks as claustrophobia settled in. She curled her knees up tight to her chest. Where was she? And if there's no way out, how could she possibly have gotten in? Every conclusion she came up with, no matter how mundane, insane or otherwise, was absurd and always led back to Benjamin. It was only when she gave up trying to decipher her whereabouts and thought exclusively of him that a slit of light broke through one of the corners of the room. Her eyes weakened, but Jaime now knew exactly where she was — the cave where she made love to Benjamin for the first

time. It wasn't a night Jaime was very proud of, and it sent a chill up her spine whenever she brought herself to remember it.

Her parents had been packing their bags for their seven o'clock flight when she told them she didn't want to go with them. Their reaction was expected.

"Out of the question," her mother said. Jaime sat on the queen-sized bed in the motel room.

"Mom, why?"

"You're only seventeen."

"I don't care?" Jaime screamed with a hint of water forming in her eyes. "I love him."

"You've only known him for a week."

"Twelve days."

Her mother gave her that look. Jaime shied away.

"How old is this boy?"

"Why do you care?"

"How old?" her mother demanded.

"Twenty-one," Jaime whispered, hoping her mother heard something different. She wanted to lie, but her mother would see right through it if she had.

"Twenty —" Jaime's mother's face turned red as she paced the room.

"Mom, please," Jaime pleaded. "You have to understand. I'm in love with him. I don't want to leave him."

"You're not in love," her mother yelled. "You're too young to understand what love means."

Jaime's mouth was agape.

"Tell her," her mother screamed to her father. He sat at the desk in the corner, writing some notes on a legal pad he brought with him in case some inspiration hit. She didn't know what he was writing about, but it must have been something incredible. He could barely take his eyes off the page as he spoke.

"You're too young," he muttered, hardly audible above the scratch of his pencil.

"You guys are total hypocrites, you know that." Jaime stood to match her mother's gaze, hoping it would help her show strength.

"Don't you dare talk to us like that, young lady." Her mother's finger nearly poked Jaime's eye out.

"You are. Shit —"

"Watch your mouth."

"No. Fuck." Jaime saw flames rise in her mother's eyes. Jaime turned and walked across the room. When she was ready, she turned back, confident. "You guys were married when you were twenty, right?"

"And we had been dating for six years before that."

"*And?*"

"We took our time, Jaime. We made damn sure what we felt for each other was real. That we could trust each other for life."

"I trust him," Jaime said, her tears overwhelming her.

"You can't know that after just a few days."

Jaime didn't have a response. All she knew is she wanted to be with him now, tomorrow, the next day and the next. She wanted nothing else but to hold him, kiss him, be with him. Life felt empty without him by her side. Her parents wouldn't understand, no matter how hard she tried to explain. That killed her.

"This isn't some wild fling, Caroline," Jaime finally spit out. Calling her 'mom' made her feel childish and referring to her as 'mother' would keep her in a state of dependency, something she didn't want her mother to take advantage of. She needed to prove she was old enough to make her own decisions. "We are going to be together."

"You both agree?" her father asked, pausing his writing. He looked at her with intensity.

"What?" Both Jaime and her mother couldn't believe what he had said.

"Do you both agree? Or is it just you who feels this way?"

Jaime held her mouth steady, slightly open. She couldn't understand what her father meant.

"Answer your father," her mother said.

It was another few seconds before she said, "If you're asking if I'm forcing him into a relationship, you're wrong." She looked back and forth from mother to father, eagerly waiting for one of them to flinch. Neither did.

"He asked me to stay."

Both her parents were stunned. "Wh-when," her mother asked, breaking the eerie quiet filling the room.

"Two nights ago."

"Before or after you told him you were leaving."

Jaime wasn't sure why her mother was asking, so she answered honestly. "After."

Her mother shook her head. She couldn't look at her daughter any longer.

Jaime suddenly realized the mistake she made. Flustered, she softly said, "We love each other."

"And how many others has he 'loved'?"

"I don't —"

"How many other girls, how many other vacationers, has he courted like this?"

"I —"

"Has he ever had a girlfriend? Has he ever been married? Does he have a child?"

Jaime tried hard to answer her mother, but was consistently cut off before she could. The sound of her mother's voice became quicker and quicker. Questions began to run into one another, overlap each other. "What about his parents? Are they alive? Dead? Are they divorced? Separated? Does he have a pet? A dog? A cat?"

"Shut up, just shut up," Jaime screamed, halting her mother's attack of questions. She stood silent, furious over her mother's lack of respect for her and her wishes.

"How can you say you're in love with someone you don't even know?" Her eyes seemed sad and weary.

"I just know," Jaime responded with a crack in her voice.

"Well, if it's real, then he'll still be here, waiting for you when you've completed college and you're ready to make that decision."

Jaime could only muster a head shake.

"Until then," her mother continued when Jaime didn't fight back, "you're coming home. End of story."

"You just don't want to see me happy," Jaime screamed, hitting her parents with her own barrage of questions that would go unanswered. "You don't want to see me become independent, do you? You're too scared to let go of me, aren't you? Too scared that something's going to happen to me like what happened to him. I've got news for you, Caroline. I'm not Steven, and he's not coming back. So give it up, move on and let me live my fucking life the way I want to live it."

Caroline's eyes were wet with sorrow. "Don't you dare talk about him like that, Jaime. Don't you dare."

"Fuck you," Jaime sneered.

"Don't you dare —"

"Fuck, fuck, fuck," Jaime yelled, charging for the door.

"Where do you think you're going?"

"You can't stop me from staying."

"Jaime! Come back here."

Jaime opened the door and turned to her parents. "Just leave me the hell alone."

"Jaime, please, wait," her mother pleaded.

Jaime stopped halfway through the door, hanging tight to the handle. When her mother didn't say anything else, she said, "I love him, and I'll always love him. I won't leave him."

"Just tell me where you're going."

"To give my future husband the fuck he deserves." She paused and then finished with, "Which won't be the first time." The door slammed shut behind her.

She didn't leave right away. She stood in front of the door, waiting for (deep down, possibly hoping for) her mother to chase after her. When the door didn't budge after a few minutes, Jaime let out a stream of tears she'd been hiding from her parents. She covered her mouth to control the level of her voice so her parents wouldn't hear and held her forehead against the door until the emotion passed. Walking away from them was one of the hardest things she'd ever done,

but she needed time to think, to be alone. As she ambled through the streets, huddling her bare arms close to her body in a futile attempt at keeping them warm, she thought about her parents, about Benjamin and her love for them all. She couldn't figure out why she told them she had slept with Benjamin when he hadn't even attempted to feel her up. All the two of them ever did together were take walks on the beach, go to ice-cream shops, have picnics, and check out a few movies. But she wanted to severely hurt them for forcing her to leave. Making them believe their only child, their baby girl, was a woman was the only way to sever the umbilical cord for good. It was all she could think to do to weaken them. Then again, leaving them as she did might have been enough of a punishment. Why did she have to go that far?

It was an hour before Jaime figured out where she wanted to be. She remembered the first time Benjamin kissed her. He'd taken her deep within a system of caves not a lot of people knew about. Her heart pounded briskly, wandering around in the dark without a clue as to where they were or if they'd ever find their way out. His hand was sweaty against hers as he stopped and grabbed her shoulder. He whispered a sweet poem into her ear, his breaths heavy. Wondering if he had written the poem (as it sounded like something she felt toward him), his lips pressed to hers, a little dry, but warm. She didn't resist, opening her lips a little to allow her saliva to moisten the kiss. It was then that his tongue pressed lightly against hers, almost as if it was afraid of entering without permission, something which was quickly granted as Jaime pushed her tongue hard against his. Other than a quick kiss from her mother before school, or a gentle goodnight kiss from her father after having been tucked into bed, Jaime had never been kissed until this very moment. She didn't want it to end. The next ten minutes flew by, and when Benjamin finally did pull away, and she sucked the fresh air through her still open mouth, the electricity and passion held strong between them. Though she couldn't see him with her eyes, his touch told her everything she needed to know. She lay against his chest for another hour, neither saying a word. This was where Jaime needed to be right now.

When she arrived at the mouth of the cavern Benjamin had brought her to that night, it was nearly midnight, two hours after storming out of the motel. Her nose was frozen and her body shook. After feeling her way through the thick darkness, Jaime found a nice, small space to sit and possibly sleep the night into day. She thought of a great many things, mostly of living a full life with Benjamin and what she might miss out on if she stayed with him. On one hand, Benjamin was sweet, tender and in love with her. He was a gentleman and would care for her, teach her, and give her a life full of joy and happiness. At the same time, she might not be able to hammer down a serious career, possibly living on dimes, barely able to make ends meet. She was young, and that meant she would miss a lot of exploration, of both her mind and her body. Going to college, living the gamut of frat parties, college exams and hanging out in the dorms with friends would give her the opportunities to learn how to better herself, to grab hold of the world and contribute to it in ways she wouldn't be able to if she stayed with Benjamin. Had her mother been right? If Benjamin really did love her, and she him, then they could wait for one another. But if she was wrong, she might lose him. She couldn't allow that to happen.

No clear solution was evident as she grew drowsy. Jaime didn't know what time it was when she saw the flash of light and heard Benjamin's clear voice ("Jaime") echo through the caves, but it woke her up.

Tears raced to Jaime's eyes as she tucked herself as far as she could into her hiding place. It wasn't enough. The flashlight shifted in her direction and she saw the smooth outline of Benjamin through the backwash of light. His silhouette was calming, yet made her feel sick to her stomach.

"Jaime," he said, relieved. "Jaime, love, are you okay?"

Jaime kept her head low, her eyes away from Benjamin, whose aura was too much for her right now. There was nowhere she could go as he slid in next to her and wrapped his arm around her shoulder. Setting the flashlight on the ground, leaving just a fog of light around the cave, Benjamin took hold of her chin. "Look at me, Jaime," he whispered.

He waited to say anything more until she did. "Your parents are worried." He cupped her head into his chest. "I was worried."

"They were right," she muttered, her tears moistening Benjamin's shirt.

"Right about what?"

It took Jaime some time to actually say the words, but as she did, she felt incredibly free. "I have to leave."

Benjamin's chest rose and fell deeply. He then lifted her head. "I know," he said and kissed her. It was salty and a bit cold, but deep and alive.

When he removed his lips, Jaime whispered, "I love you."

"I love you," Benjamin whispered back. "I will never forget you."

Jaime answered with another kiss. "I want to stay."

"I want you to stay. But it's not meant to be. Not yet." They kissed again, this time for several minutes.

"You won't forget me, will you?" Jaime's moist hand was placed firmly against Benjamin's cheek.

"I could never forget you. You're my love. You are Love."

The obsession in the kiss that followed convinced Jaime this was the moment she had been waiting for since the first kiss. Benjamin became extremely hard as he lied her on the rocky floor, inadvertently sliding his pelvis against her leg. It wasn't enough. She needed him inside of her, to feel his desire between her legs and become the woman that would be brave enough to leave her family behind. She grabbed his ass and pulled him hard against her waist. After a moment of confused hesitation, Benjamin saw Jaime biting her lower lip. She didn't need help getting her shirt off. Her breasts looked supple within her black bra. He kissed them, sending a heated chill across Jaime's skin. Before she knew it, her pants were unfastened and he was rubbing her on top of her black underwear. She didn't want him to stop, but felt a bit selfish. Her hands grabbed his belt buckle as she leaned up to kiss him. Together, they enjoyed the fruit of their lust, a whirlwind that led them to lie together, nothing between them but icy sweat. Jaime had felt nothing like it, and was euphoric as they held each other's frozen, nude bodies. They fell asleep together for the first time. She wasn't afraid any longer.

The next morning, he kissed her awake, respecting her body lit only by the dying hum of the flashlight. They collected their clothes and got dressed, slowly, neither wanting to take their eyes off the other. When they reached the light of the cracking sunrise at the mouth of the cave, she hugged him tight and whispered in his ear, "I'll write to you every day."

"I will anticipate every word." They kissed and walked back to the motel, hand-in-hand. She hugged him, wanting everything to take him with her. His smile held true as she slipped from his grasp and waved goodbye, her hand hovering above the door handle. She would see him again, possibly love him once more. At that moment, she could never have fathomed witnessing his death, a vision that brought with it a renewed rush of tears as she sat, alone once again in those caves, wondering if there was any possibility of Benjamin coming to rescue her as he did that night. She knew in her heart he wasn't coming for her. He was gone, as was the other man she cared deeply about, lost together in a matter of a few hours. But whose fault was that? The walls closed in on her as she learned the awful truth: she had killed them all, including her daughter. Maybe not by her own hand, but leaving Kaleena the way she did, unable to come to terms with her own selfishness, she had led everyone to this moment. And she was helpless to save them. She couldn't even save herself. She was trapped in a hell she created and was ready to succumb to her fate.

"Jaime?"

Jaime opened her eyes as the soft voice trailed off. It sounded familiar but very far away. For a moment, she thought she might have imagined it. Then,

"Jaime? Can you hear me?"

Louder this time, closer. She knew the voice well.

"Patricia?"

"Hot damn."

Jaime's smile couldn't have grown any larger. She stood, having to lean forward

slightly, and searched the walls around her for any sign of Patricia's whereabouts.

"Patricia. Where are you?"

"I'm right here."

"Where? I can't see you."

"Pay attention, kid. I'm standing right in front of you."

Jaime hissed exasperation. "Where?"

"Right here. Look harder." Her voice was stern — like a mother to a child who just wouldn't listen.

"I can't —" Jaime stopped moving and felt the air around her. "I can't see you. It's too dark."

There was a short pause.

"Where are you right now?" Patricia asked.

Jaime was confused, but decided to answer the question. "I'm in a cave."

"Think again."

"What?"

"Trust me. You are *not* in a cave right now."

"The hell I'm not," Jaime argued.

"The shit you are," Patricia returned. "Have I ever lied to you before?"

"Yeah, I believe you have."

"Well, forget all that. You're just gonna have to trust me. It's all in your head, boss. You're not really there."

"What are you talking about?"

"We're in a room, not a cave. I'm looking right at you. I can see you twiddling around like a drunken, blind rat. If you can't see me, it means you're blind or you don't want to know where you really are."

"Damn it, Patricia. Stop fucking around and find a way to get me the fuck out of here."

Suddenly, a scorching sting ripped across her cheek. Jaime grabbed the side of her face. "What the hell?"

"You like that?" Patricia asked. "I can give you another one if it'll help."

Jaime ducked away from yet another sting she sensed coming and held out her hand. "No, wait. Stop." Jaime rattled her brain for an answer and then, "How did you do that?"

"Easy sneezy," Patricia said. "Did it wake you up?"

Jaime rubbed away the residual irritation from her cheek and focused on the wall. *She's gotta be here. How else would she have been able to do that?* But no matter how hard she concentrated, Patricia never appeared. "Goddamn it," she whispered and then fell over as another hard slap spread across her face. When she looked up, pain welling her eyes, she saw a soft, ghost-like fog of Patricia's face. She fixated on those dark blue eyes. The fog cleared, forming around the curves of Patricia's body until, like a complete apparition, she was standing in front of her, full and real. "Patricia?"

Patricia let out a hearty laugh, turned to someone behind her and said, "I told you I could slap some sense into her." She turned back to Jaime. "I told 'em."

Jaime flexed her jaw. The last slap felt as if it had been from a fist rather than an open palm. "You okay?" Patricia held out her hand. Jaime accepted it, a little angry with her for hitting her so hard, but happy she had. She stood cautiously, avoiding hitting her head, but quickly learned the ceiling that felt so low before had vanished. She didn't question it as she stood fully erect.

"God, Patricia. It's good to see your ugly mug."

"Your mug ain't bad either."

Jaime grabbed Patricia into her arms. When she let go, she said, "Who were you talking to?" The sting in her jaw still made her teeth ache a little.

"Trish and Reeses."

"Trish? Where?" Jaime could only see a resonating black behind Patricia.

"Right there," Patricia pointed. "You can't see them?"

"I can't see anything but you."

"Damn, girl. You're still in the freakin' cave?"

Jaime gave Patricia a look that yelled, "DUH!" Patricia just rolled her eyes. "Don't make me have to hit you again," she said.

"Don't you dare," Jaime shot back, stepping back as far as she could.

"Well, maybe they have to do it," Patricia contemplated.

"No."

Patricia chuckled. "I got something. Watch closely, hon. If this works the way I hope, you're about to see some fascinating shit." Patricia took a step back, her eyes fixed on Jaime's. "First you see me." She took another step back and disappeared.

"Now I don't." It was becoming clear. Jaime was trapped all right. But was it really as easy as simply releasing herself?

Patricia appeared again — half of her body anyway. "That's right, now get your tiny ass in gear and follow me out." Patricia grabbed Jaime's arm and pulled her forward. Jaime closed her eyes, afraid she'd smash her face into the wall. Which she did, with full force, crushing her nose against the rock. She would've fallen backward if Patricia's severed arm wasn't holding on so tight.

"Damn, these hallucinations are real as steel, you know?" Patricia said.

Jaime felt a trickle of blood run from one of her nostrils. "You're telling me."

Patricia's head reappeared. "Come on, boss. You've gotta believe there isn't really anything in front of you for this to work."

"Okay," Jaime said, still a bit cautious.

"Not good enough," Patricia said disapprovingly, before her head disappeared "Maybe if you guys said something."

"Come on Jaime, you can do it." It was Trishen, her sweet delicate voice was music to Jaime's ears.

"I don't know you very well," said a voice that must have been Kara, "but I believe you're smart enough to figure it out."

Patricia's head appeared again and for a second, Jaime swore she saw a glimpse of a dark room lit with a bluish-green hue and two shadows standing on either side of Patricia, maybe a couple of steps behind her.

"You heard 'em. They're here. All you have to do is come with us."

Jaime rubbed her eyes and wiped some blood from her nose. She could taste it now on her lips. "I —"

"Don't do it. Don't sell yourself short. You're the smartest, toughest bitch I know, besides me. Prove me wrong." Patricia disappeared from the cavern. "I can't help you anymore. You have to free your own ass."

Jaime waited, hoping the wall would somehow disappear. Part of her kept screaming she was making her rescue up as a coping mechanism, but deep down, she knew it had to be real. Patricia, Trishen and Kara were all waiting for her to figure this little mind game out and break from its torture. She closed her eyes and brushed the final bit of pain away from her nose. *I'm walking out of this shit,* she thought before taking a step forward. And then another. As she took her third step, she knew she was no longer barred by her own depression and opened her eyes. Standing there was Patricia. Trishen and Kara stood just behind her, waiting impatiently for a response.

"It worked," Jaime said.

"Hot damn!" Patricia wrapped her thick arms around Jaime. "I knew you weren't mental enough to stay put."

Jaime laughed. "I'm surprised you aren't still in one of those mind fucks."

"Hell," Patricia said, taking a step back. "So am I. But it wasn't hard to figure out mine wasn't real."

"How's that?"

"My husband was way too nice. And my baby girl, damn if she wasn't the perfect little princess."

"Sounds like something you would've wanted to keep," Kara said.

"Shit, yeah. But the whole thing creeped me out. I couldn't handle it."

Jaime and Trishen laughed. Kara remained unsure of why it was funny. Finally, she let out a bit of a chuckle, catching the infectious noise. As the laughter died away, Jaime took Trishen in her arms. "It's good to see you," she said. "Thank God you're alive."

"Same here."

Jaime then gave Kara a warm greeting as well. "You, too."

"Right now, I'm just happy to see anyone from the yacht."

"Ain't that the truth," Patricia said.

"Have you had a chance to figure out where the hell we are?" Jaime finally asked. She walked to a large window the size of the entire wall. Everyone else watched with glee as Jaime gazed at the massive cityscape sprawled out below her, covered in seaweed, masked only by the slight haze of the sea.

"Holy shit."

Patricia scooted up behind her and slapped her on the back of the shoulder. "Ain't it just the shittiest shit you've ever seen? The ex may be a pathetic bastard, but he was right on the money with this one."

"Actually," Kara interjected before she could stop herself, "that credit would technically go to me." The last few words rolled out under her breath, unsure if she was coming off too conceited. Her own team would have bounced the statement off of her with a fun barrage of sarcastic barbs. But this group — she just hoped they didn't think she was honestly taking credit for what Matthew had done. She suddenly felt extremely uncomfortable as the women glared at her like contemptible stone. Then Patricia exposed her teeth and widened her eyes. "That a baby!" Kara relaxed as everyone smiled their acceptance.

Jaime turned back to the city. "Can it really be Atlantis?"

"It better as hell be Atlantis," Patricia said. "Or else we have some serious explaining to do."

Jaime cracked a bigger smile. "How high do you think we are?"

"I'd guess about twelve stories up," Kara deduced. "And by what I could assess, we're most likely in one of the three tallest buildings in the city. Where that is, I'm not sure, but take a look here." Kara stepped next to Jaime "Do you see that large open space there, below us?"

Patricia spoke first. "You mean the quad with the fountain?"

"Yeah."

"What about it?" Jaime asked.

"I think it might be the direct center of the city."

"How do you figure?"

"By the way the buildings are structured around it. I mean, from here, the city looks like it spreads out about the same distance in all directions. Add to that those two identical buildings that form what I'm assuming are two additional corners of an isosceles triangle, with this building as the third point. Perfect geometric construction." Kara's mouth slid open in near awe.

"Does it hurt to think so much?" Patricia asked.

"You'd be surprised how much," Kara quipped.

Patricia wasted no time slapping Kara's shoulder blade. "Have I ever said how much I like you?"

"On occasion," Kara said, smiling despite the light pain Patricia massaged into her shoulder.

"What's that there?" Trishen said. It was the first time anyone really remembered her speaking.

"Where?" Kara asked.

"There, between the towers. It looks like it could have been a lake." A large hole, which appeared to be about a hundred feet deep in the direct center with an edge that dropped like a wall closest to them and slowly ascended until it became the top of the ground a few hundred yards in the distance, seemingly connected the two distant towers. By how the smaller buildings surrounded the lake, it appeared as if it could have been somewhat of a miniature Venice.

Jaime ignored the chatter that continued as she thought about Benjamin and Gavin and the sacrifice each made to help them find the whereabouts of the lost city. She also wondered where Matthew and Kaleena's fates had sent them. The exhilaration drained from her as the need to get answers to questions she wasn't even sure anyone could answer overwhelmed her.

"Where is everyone else?"

The silence was deafening until Patricia, in an unconventionally soft voice, said, "We don't know."

"We're not even sure they're alive," Kara added.

Jaime nodded, a great pressure forming in her chest. She had a feeling the

other members of Kara's crew were alive, but wasn't quite sure she believed it.

"How do we get out of here?"

"We haven't figured that part out yet, either," Patricia said, more spirited.

That was when Jaime saw something in the ocean. "What is… that?"

"What," Kara said, a bit frantic.

"Look."

Just above the statue, a small brush of bubbles sprouted from the top and mixed with the sea.

"What the hell?"

A moment later, lights turned on all around the city, spreading out systematically from the center outward in a giant circle. The group watched the magic intently until their room came to life, delivering a soft pain to each of the women's eyes. They all had to close and slowly reopen them. Patricia looked immediately to the large doors on the opposite side of the window; Trishen was taken by the plant life that blossomed along the walls; and Kara's attention went to the extremely high ceiling.

"Where is it coming from?" Kara asked, unable to find any source for the light.

"I think we might have found our way out." Patricia headed for the door as Trishen and Kara studied the room. Every pillar, every decorative wall, every piece of art was meticulously thought out in carved, intricate detail, creating a bevy of authentic purity. Trishen picked up one of the insanely soft, felt pillows lining the three windowless walls as Kara examined one of the dozen wooden fixtures spaced in front of the pillows every two to three feet. They stood about two feet high and resembled what most people perceived to be the cup Jesus used at the last supper. The center of the room was empty except for a large, hand-woven rug. There seemed to be a design sewn into the center with red and gold, but no one could make it out as they stood on its edge.

"My word," Trishen whispered. "Would you look at this place?"

Jaime never turned from the window. She felt Kaleena running through the glass in front of her, felt her tickle her feet from the floor beneath her. She was

certain her daughter had found a way to generate the light. Everything throughout the city was alive and Kaleena was right in the middle of it.

"We need to find a way out of here," she said, turning to the rest of the group. "Kaleena's alive."

Atlantis – Lauren's Quarters – 6 hours 32 minutes after arrival

The lights had been on for several minutes before Lauren slid out of bed. She hadn't been sleeping; she couldn't. Her mind was flooded with thoughts of her daughter, of Kaleena and the possibility she had walked into a trap by agreeing to help these people. Every time she tried to convince herself Adamus and Henry were good people — that all they wanted to do was help — questions with no viable answers would arise: How was Henry connected to all of this? Was she his pawn? Did he create this giant puzzle to deliver his baby? Why was Kaleena supposedly so special? What was her purpose? If they wanted to harm them, why rescue them? Or was Evey always the end game? The second-guessing, the triple-guessing — it made her all but insane. Changing the subject never helped, as every thought would connect back to Kaleena, leaving her to wonder how she could have been so selfish. After all she had discussed with her —

Your daughter's life is more important than your own. A mother's instinct —

Don't you think that having hope in the future, that it, or the people that live in the world, can learn from their mistakes? Isn't that worth more than sacrifice? —

Unless there's someone out there willing to display pure self-sacrifice, what's there to hope for?

— how could she possibly have let her do what she did? Even if she didn't believe any of it, Kaleena was the real deal — a true selfless person. Lauren thought she understood, thought their conversation had been a moment of clarity, one that had been accepted by the child waiting to be born. Evey had kicked her after Kaleena so quickly departed. She didn't care to listen to Jaime and Patricia discuss water pressures and landmasses any longer, so she walked to the stern. Once

against the rail, Lauren watched the wake from the yacht form a soft white froth in the moonlight. Her daughter took the opportunity to speak to her. Not with actual words, but with an intense telepathic connection, as if Evey was telling her to believe every word Kaleena had to say, to really think about it and absorb the meaning beneath the surface. She urged her to remember not only the way the words were said, but how Kaleena's eyes spoke with them. Sad and serene, layered with deep conviction. She had never seen that much intensity in anyone before, not even Matthew. But had she really seen it, or was Evey playing games with her, making her see what she wanted her to see? When her stomach cramped up at the thought of it, she knew her child was not to be ignored.

The cool breeze soothed her as she stood on the stern for nearly three hours before heading down to the room, where she would tell Matthew everything. It wasn't to hurt Kaleena; it was her way of protecting her, to make sure Matthew knew his daughter was watching him, watching Jaime and in desperate need of someone to show her they cared about her. Matthew didn't have anything to say in return, but Lauren knew he felt horrible about the whole thing. Quite like what she felt right now. If Kaleena really did sacrifice herself, how was she going to tell Matthew about what she'd done (or to what Lauren herself hadn't done)? It was a bit foolish, really, to think Matthew was even still alive. But holding onto that hope kept her sane and was enough to keep her believing Kaleena would also be okay.

Then the room lit up and the plants bloomed with life, much how they did when Kaleena was in the room. As she pressed her hands to the wall to lift herself into a sitting position, it was as if Kaleena was somehow there with her. It was as if she was producing life across the room from inside the walls. But how was that possible? She thought about leaving to seek out the answers and make sure she was okay, but doing so might sever the link (whatever that meant) with Kaleena. She had to believe that as long as she felt her presence, Kaleena would be safe. Lauren pressed her cheek to the wall. Her ear burned against the side of her head. She heard a soft hum, but more importantly, felt the kiss of Kaleena's life.

It warmed her heart as if she was becoming one with the wall — until her spirit was wrenched away. Lauren pulled her head back, a slight heated pain pinching her cheek. She no longer sensed that mysterious bond. Kaleena was gone. But the room still flourished with life.

Lauren touched her reddened cheek and was happy to realize there was no blood. It had just been a sting, like a slap to the face. When Kaleena didn't return to her after a few minutes, Lauren went to the door. There were no handles or keypads of any sort; just the wall and no idea of how to open it. Lauren was stuck for the time being. But it was probably for the best. If Kaleena was still alive, as she so strongly felt, then someone would most likely bring her body back to her. It was all she had to keep her calm.

In the meantime, Lauren kept herself busy by searching the room. Along the walls were several shelves of books. The spines were written in the same language she remembered seeing on the artifact. At that moment, there was no one else Lauren wanted to see more than Kara. She pulled one of the books from the shelf. The fabric looked like washed-out suede, but felt more like hard cotton. It was worn, not because of its age, but because it appeared to have been handled quite often. She ran her fingers over the fine paper and then flipped the book open, which automatically fell to the page marked by the silk ribbon kept inside. The symbols — or writing — on the page were in ink, faded slightly, but nonetheless readable and no doubt written by hand. There was something scratched at the top, which, after flipping a few pages backward through the book, seemed to be a date, or a number of some kind, leading Lauren to the conclusion that the book was actually someone's diary. She looked back at the rest of the books, of which there had to be at least three dozen more of the same. Did every room in the city have a collection of diaries like this? What had they said? Why were they displayed so prominently where any one could just pick them up and read them? Had they personal secrets hidden within? Or were they all the same — a chronicle, so to speak, written by all who had lived? Different perspectives of the same events, told by different voices that would all, one day, be collected and read as one long, ripe history.

Lauren flipped through the pages, gently and delicately. Even though she couldn't read any of it, she felt connected to it, like she knew exactly what was being said. She dropped the book when she heard the large doors of the room crack open. The cloaked figure walked in, Kaleena draped lifeless across his arms.

"What the hell?" Lauren exclaimed. She ran to Kaleena and attempted to take her from Adamus, but he pulled her away. "What did you do to her?"

She's fine, Adamus said as he walked past her. He lied Kaleena in the bed and brushed some of the hair from her face. He looked at her delicate features in the dead silence of the room and then turned to Lauren, his head whipping around with fierce motive.

I am not what you claim I am, Tylyn.

Lauren was stricken with a cold chill. *What did you call me?* she thought.

Your true name, as it's written in the scrolls of ancestry.

"What?" Lauren whispered.

I knew you wouldn't believe. Love is the only one that can understand the true nature of her mind.

"Love?" Lauren immediately thought of Jaime. She'd heard Benjamin call her 'Love' on several occasions. Could she still be alive?

The one you think of as Love is wrong, Adamus corrected. *She is right here, among us.*

Kaleena?

Adamus nodded. It seemed odd that Kaleena would now be referred to as 'Love.' It gave Lauren the impression that, much like Henry, Benjamin was Atlantean. If that was the case, then he may not have died on that boat and could possibly be standing right in front of her.

Your thoughts are incorrect, Adamus said. *I am not who you believe I am. The man you speak of has perished, just as the rest of your friends.*

"Yeah. Kaleena told me all that," Lauren said. *But I don't believe it.*

Believe it or not, it is the truth. Adamus seized one last look at Kaleena as she took in soft, slow breaths. *Give her time. She will wake.*

What about Evey?

She's fine as well. Love did as she promised.

Lauren was relieved, if not a bit guilty for feeling that way with Kaleena half-dead across the room. None of it mattered. Lauren still felt as if she were being kept in the dark. It was time to be read in on everything that was going on.

I want to see her, she spit out with a sharp tongue. *I want to see Evey.*

You will see her in time. Adamus walked to Lauren. He placed his hand on her cheek, gently and with a kindness she was used to only from Matthew. For a moment, she felt safe again, willing to do whatever it was she was told. But she fought the urge to back down and swatted Adamus's hand away, a cold glean washing across her eyes.

"No. I want to see her. Right now."

Adamus lowered his arm and stared at her. She could make out a little of her captor's chiseled features within the darkness of his hood, but he lowered his head and stepped back before she could really see anything recognizable. Quickly, he stepped past her toward the door.

"Where are you going?" Lauren's stern voice echoed along the walls. The flowers pulled back slightly in their heightened bloom. "I want to see her, goddamn it."

Adamus didn't say another word. The doors closed slowly behind him. Lauren's gut said to rush him and beat the living shit out of him until he agreed to let her see Evey, but she instantly thought better of it. Not only would he know what she was going to do before she did it, but he may have hurt her beyond what her own mind and body were capable of enduring. Which would leave Kaleena where?

Alone, without anyone.

If everyone else really had perished in the attack on the yacht, Lauren was essentially all Kaleena had left. She couldn't risk leaving her alone, so she sucked in her pride, watched the doors fuse shut, and then hurried to Kaleena. Brushing her hair gently, she finally saw a large cut that spanned Kaleena's forehead from temple to temple. It had been scarred over and there were no traces of blood

coming from the wound, but Lauren couldn't help wanting to heal it somehow. There was nothing she could do for her right now except stay with her — become her mother in a way. It was at that moment Lauren glanced over at the book she had dropped. She went over and picked it up, then slid her lap under Kaleena's head, resting the young girl's weakened body against her own. After opening the book to the marked page, Lauren started talking as if she were reading Kaleena a bedtime story.

Some time later, when her throat became dry, Lauren closed the book, lied it next to Kaleena's arm and started humming the song her mother used to sing to her when she was a child — the one she hoped would pull Kaleena back to full health.

Give it time, she thought. *My love is with you.*

Caverns – Time Unknown

Gydressina slowly shifted her feet across the thick rock, barely able to bend her knees enough to raise them up. Matthew and Thomas kept to themselves several feet in front of her, turning to their new guide only when she spoke to direct them through the darkening caverns. At least the torches they carried gave them plenty of light to examine the relatively smooth walls that showed no signs of erosion and hardly any crevices.

"It's true, isn't it?" Thomas had muttered to Matthew a half hour earlier. "It's as if the entire cave's been embalmed."

"Not embalmed," Gydressina said. "The earth has simply chosen to live."

Thomas didn't think much of it. In fact, Thomas hadn't given much credence to anything Gydressina said, passing it off as some old woman's psychosis. He knew Matthew only defended her because of the possibility Kaleena was still alive; that alone was worth more to him than his own life. But with Thomas's constant fear of Gydressina leading them into some sort of trap, was it enough to risk Thomas's life as well?

"This is such bullshit," Thomas finally said, expunging his growing madness.

He turned to Gydressina. "Are we even close to getting out of this hell hole?" His voice echoed endlessly through the caverns.

Gydressina didn't stop moving. She slipped past Thomas as if he hadn't even spoken. His rage rose to his cheeks as he grabbed the old woman's arm, ending her ghostly stride. He kept his grip light, believing if he squeezed too hard, her whole arm would become nothing more than a handful of dust. "I asked you a question," he said. "And don't you dare fuck around the bush with some spiritual bullshit."

"Thomas," Matthew said, finally realizing what was happening. "Let her go."

"Listen to your friend," Gydressina choked out, her eyes fixed on the ground. Thomas couldn't tell if she was frightened of him or if she was hiding her own bubbling anger.

"I don't have to listen to him." Thomas tried to conceal his heightened anger with a calm, forced monotone.

"True. But to ignore his warnings will be your eventual downfall."

"Are you threatening me?"

Gydressina finally turned her eyes up to Thomas. Underneath the dying skin and hollow skull, her eyes seemed warm, friendly even. It was enough to make Thomas feel sorry for the way he was acting. "I do not threaten anyone," she said softly. "I am only trying to warn you so that your death will not be in vain."

For the first time, Thomas took in her words carefully. Was she threatening him or prophesizing his death? His grip on her arm loosened even more, leaving only his fingertips on the woman's dry skin. "I —"

Gydressina raised her long bony finger to Thomas's lips. He tasted dirt and smelled a hint of decomposing flesh as the cold bone touched the tip of his tongue. It didn't turn his stomach but it did make him feel a bit weak in the knees, as if he were about to faint. "Quiet," she said. "You believe I'm leading you into a fate that will end in your death. I know this because of your voice and the manner of language not spoken through words. But you must know that is not my wish. I am trying to protect you both, to help you all find your way back home. If you do not listen to me, heed my words, trust each other and listen to one another, then

none of us will survive what awaits us." Gydressina held her finger to Thomas's lips for a while longer, pushing her words into his mind and holding them there until they were understood — and hopefully adhered to. After a minute of silence, Gydressina's eyes glistened. She moved closer to Thomas, raised her skeletal structure up, kissed the corner of his mouth and then began walking once again, leaving Thomas standing firm as a statue. Matthew couldn't even tell if he was breathing.

"What do you mean?" Matthew said for Thomas. Gydressina's questioning gaze (at least that's what it appeared to be, hidden under the whisper of her thin white eyebrows) prompted Matthew to rephrase his inquiry. "You said to continue to make sure we survive."

Gydressina nodded. Her gentleness was evident. "I have been protecting you for some time now, Matthew."

"How have you been protecting us?"

A moment passed. "If it were not for my help, you both would have perished among the sea."

"You pulled us from the ocean?" Matthew somehow knew this was true, but still felt stunned by the revelation.

"I had to. The others would not have been as kind."

"The others?" Thomas said. "What others?"

"It's too much to convey in my current state. What I can say is it's not in their interest to protect any man from harm, or else put themselves into possible eradication. The only breed of human life they cherish is that of the female, as they are the vessels of new life. To them, you were expendable."

"But not to you?"

Gydressina shook her head ever so slightly, her eyes strong.

"Why?"

"Because life isn't just a matter of reproduction and power. Life is opportunity, a chance to learn, grow and develop into much more than what can be imagined within the confines of the blood that courses a man's veins. They don't trust that, and thus must hide in the fear of their own inadequacy."

Matthew stood silent. He thought Benjamin's death had simply been an accident, but now wasn't so sure. The attack on the *Endeavor* now seemed less of an accident and more of a controlled attempt to exterminate the male presence. That idea made even more sense as he recalled the events at the stones when the sea itself seemingly attacked him and Gavin, going to great lengths to keep Jaime and Trishen from rescuing them.

"Why did it run?"

Gydressina and Matthew turned to Thomas, whose stature was surprisingly relaxed. Matthew could tell he was thinking the same thing, though maybe still unable to truly accept that Gydressina had been watching over them the whole time.

Thomas turned his gaze up and looked deeply into Gydressina. "When I went to rescue Trishen. It fled."

"Yes."

The connection between Thomas and Gydressina grew stronger as the kiss on his lips burned. Not in a painful way, but in a loving touch. It was simple, caring and tingled with a bright sensation of warmth and harmony. "I didn't do anything."

"You did more than you realize," Gydressina said. "There was nothing you could have done physically. What you did came from the heart." Gydressina rested her cold palm on Thomas's chest. His heart began to beat faster and harder and his penis hardened. "In that moment, you reacted unselfishly. That is much more powerful than any weapon you could have wielded."

"But what was it?" Matthew asked.

"I suspect, but cannot be certain. Not until we reach the surface and track down your daughter will I know for sure."

"Well then, let's go," Thomas said brightly, his breath heavy.

"We do not have much farther," Gydressina said, lowering her hand. Thomas's heart instantly slowed back to its normal rhythm and the blood began to leave his penis.

Gydressina pushed forward once again, moving past Matthew and disappearing into the darkness before them, faster than either of them remembered her

going since they met. Matthew stepped to Thomas, his gaze glued to the black in front of them.

"Can we trust her?" Matthew wanted to confirm.

Thomas adjusted his softening crotch. "I don't know." He brushed the corner of his mouth, licked the dryness from his lips and bit them before striding forward to catch up to the woman he now knew had saved his life. Matthew followed and quickly took the lead. Thomas stayed by Gydressina's side, as if she was now his partner — his girlfriend in some twisted way.

After another couple hundred yards, everything around Matthew became blindingly dark, even though, as far as he knew, the flame from the torch remained as crisp as it had been when he first picked it up several hours ago. He whipped around to his fellow exhausted travelers, but they too were gone in a void of darkness. Not even Thomas's flame showed any signs of life. But they hadn't been more than a few feet behind him. Had they?

"Thomas? Gydressina?" Matthew spun around. The heat from his torch flashed across his face.

"Where the hell are you?" Thomas responded.

Matthew started to spit out a response when Gydressina choked out, "We have arrived."

"Arrived where? Where the hell are you?"

"Take a few steps toward my voice," she said delicately and with intense calm.

Matthew did as he was told without arguing. Within seconds, Thomas and Gydressina appeared like apparitions. Gydressina's arm was raised like a roadblock, keeping Thomas from walking into the void that sat like a giant wall in front of them. Matthew held the torch up to the wall and pushed it forward. The closer he got to the darkness, the more the flame disappeared. If he kept at it, he suspected the flame would eventually die out — without really dying out.

"What the hell is this?" he said. To Thomas, Matthew looked a couple of years older, sporting a few additional wrinkles and a slight dust of gray hair behind his ears. But he refrained from saying anything; it was probably his imagination.

"It's known as a black hole," Gydressina quietly advised.

Thomas stepped past her to join Matthew at the wall. "I can see that," he retorted. "But what is it?" Though he knew he wouldn't feel anything, he lifted his hand to touch it. As expected, his fingers faded away, leaving behind nothing but an arm. He could still feel his fingers, though, wiggling them for a few seconds before pulling them back into the light, his hand reappearing as if nothing had happened.

"It's a barrier used to keep out the unwanted. Not only does it filter out all light so you cannot see, but the longer you stay within its confines, the faster your body deteriorates."

Thomas's eyes grew wide as he examined his hand a bit closer. Matthew's aging wasn't his imagination. "You're kidding."

"I have seen young boys return wilted and prepared to die after mere hours within."

"No shit?" Thomas kept moving his fingers and rubbing his palm, hoping it would help it from growing old.

"I do not lie. I myself have tried to escape it, but to no avail."

"What is it doing down here?"

"It's a story too long for our purposes," Gydressina said calmly. "What matters most is finding a way through it."

"How are we supposed to do that?"

"You're both fairly young."

"Hold up one second," Thomas roared, backing away a few steps behind Gydressina. "You expect me to go into that thing without knowing why it's here, or if we'll even make it out alive?"

Gydressina slowly twisted her body to face Thomas. He could've sworn her eyes glowed a slight red. "You do not have to do as I ask. But if you do not do this, I'm afraid there's nothing I'll be able to do for Kaleena." And with a dark determinate stare: "Or any of the others."

Thomas's throat dried as he thought of Trishen. Her smile, her touch, her body,

her mind all evaporated slowly from his mind as time continued to drift forward. It was enough to silence him from any more disputes.

"How did we get here?" Matthew interjected.

Gydressina whipped back around to Matthew so fast, it was if she had stopped time. "Pardon?"

"If the barrier has kept you trapped here, how were you able to bring us here?"

There was a long pause, and for a minute, both Thomas and Matthew weren't sure if she would ever answer them. But just before Matthew gave up to join Thomas in his reluctance:

"I spirited you here."

"You what?"

Gydressina stepped to the wall and laid her back against its cool texture. She knew she owed these very patient and loving men an explanation, or else lose their help completely — even after using Kaleena's life as leverage. She lowered her head and started her story. It took nearly ten minutes to explain.

"Though you may not understand some of what I'm about to say, I pray you keep your minds open, as all I am about to reveal to you is true." She took a breath, which Thomas felt was like a dramatic pause you'd only find in a tearful, pompous film seeking to score Oscar gold, and then:

"From the moment your vessel first crossed into the barrier of the Ediinis Triad, I've been keeping track of you and your friends. As have others, including one whose true name has always been that of Cephis. I will not talk about him in detail. Just know that Cephis is, was and in this life, will always be my exact opposite. In the same way that I helped you from the water, Cephis attacked your vessel and took your female companions through the art of spiriting, a metaphysical transformation that allows a person's soul to disconnect with their corporeal self. This state of being requires great knowledge and complete control. Other than myself, there is only one other who has ever mastered it. To live in such a way also requires a lot of energy from the body of whom has disconnected. Because of this, and because of the destruction my current body had already been subjected to,

— 429 —

I could not be there to protect you from him at all times, as I should have been. One of those absent periods yielded the attack you speak of; the other occurred during the rise of the Kliestian Flame. I was in a deep trance when I felt the connection occur and knew I had to get to you quickly. By the time I was able to once again spirit myself to your position, the vessel had been destroyed, Cephis had taken what he believed to be his and left all unnecessary pieces to perish. Your minds were crumbling and your spirits were dying. Knowing my body was deteriorating rapidly, I spirited you here, where I could monitor the progress of your bodily transfers, which can be a maddening, if not a deathly, process for even the strongest of minds."

"Whoa, okay, one second," Thomas finally said. "Our bodily transfers? What the hell is that?"

"To do as I did, I needed to pull your spirits from your bodies."

"Okay," Thomas said, slow and concise. "And how do you go about doing such a thing?"

"With a kiss."

"A kiss?"

"Yes. It's the only way for the body to follow the spirit wherever it must go."

"This is insane."

"I asked you to believe."

"Yes, we believe," Matthew interjected, throwing Thomas a glowering stare. "Go on."

"Once your spirits are rested, your shells are able to reform around them. To reconnect the body to the spirit, though, takes time and occasionally, it refuses to reconnect. When this happens, the spirit must go through a trial of sorts, one that I know you both experienced."

Thomas knelt down, hard of breathing, looking as if he may throw-up at any moment. Matthew could tell he was finally starting to believe her.

"Only when the spirit reconnects the heart to the mind does it become whole with the body once again. It was at that time, when I knew you had both passed

your trials, that I appeared to you."

Matthew wasn't sure how to respond. "And the same thing happened to Kaleena?"

"Most likely. And to all the others as well."

"And instead of taking us to the city, you brought us here," Thomas choked out. He was obviously holding back tears. His experience must have been aggressively affecting.

"You would be dead if I hadn't. And there was no way I could enter the black hole again without help."

Thomas refrained from saying what was on his mind, knowing full well that if she hadn't have been there, Thomas and Matthew would be lost in the city somewhere. At least here, they were protected somewhat.

"I'm still a little confused," Matthew said, changing the subject.

"Yes?"

"If you could physically touch us in order to bring our souls — our spirits — here, then why can't you do that spirited thing to unlock the barrier?"

"It doesn't work like that. When a spirit leaves its body, it can only touch that which has life. The black hole is essentially nothing, and thus has no life within it. The only way to break the barrier is to physically deactivate with flesh."

"I still say this whole thing is completely insane." Thomas stood, his knees slightly weak. "But…"

"But we will help you," Matthew finished, aware that it would be hard for Thomas to admit he was wrong. Thomas nodded recognition.

"I thank you, with all of my heart."

"So how do we 'deactivate' this shithole?"

"It's not simple, and you may lose many years while doing so."

"Right, I figured that," Matthew said softly. "You gotta do what you gotta do."

"Then give me your hands." Gydressina reached out for both Thomas and Matthew. After a slight hesitation, they took her hands gently.

"Now take one another's hands," she said. The two set their torches on the ground and took each other's hands. They both felt dry and scratched.

"I will guide you through each phase of what needs to be done. But first, you must clear your mind and let me in. No matter what happens, do not resist me and always believe I am with you."

Matthew closed his eyes and wiped every thought from his mind. Suddenly, a flash of bright white light blinded him, even though his eyes were still closed. When he was ready to open them, Gydressina had vanished, leaving him and Thomas alone.

"Where'd the hell she go?" Thomas questioned. "God —"

"I am with you," Gydressina said. At least they thought it was Gydressina. Her voice was now light and young.

"What do we do?" Matthew asked to the cavern.

"Go forward."

"Into the black hole?"

Matthew felt a slight giggle, though he couldn't hear anything. It made him want to laugh as well, his gut tickling a bit, but he didn't. He just turned to where the black hole should have been. In its place was the cavern, fully lit without torches.

"How —"

"Do not ask questions. Just do as I say."

Matthew nodded and looked to Thomas, who was still holding Matthew's hand. The two men released a little nervous chuckle before heading forward, silent and unafraid.

Atlantis – Women's Quarters – 8 hours 10 minutes after arrival

"Goddamn it!"

Jaime had been fussing with the door for the last half hour, about an hour longer than Patricia, who had given up pretty much after they found out there were no door handles. She stuck to it for a while because Jaime had all but ordered

her to help. They tried everything from kicking to pushing with everything they had. At one point, Jaime thought she saw the doors budge, but Patricia figured it was all in her head. It wasn't until Kara, after devouring every inch of the room, came across a strange pattern in the wall next to the door, which she determined to be some sort of keypad or lock, that Patricia officially gave up. Trying to decipher and understand the unusual mold was far too intricate for Patricia's taste and she was soon splayed across a couple of the pillows near the window. Jaime stuck to it, doing her best to help Kara figure out the pattern. Through the course of her experiments, she learned that as she passed her fingers across each line in the symbol, a stream of light would follow it along its chosen path. She figured (and Kara excitedly agreed) that they would need to figure out the correct sequence or pattern of light to open the door. But with approximately twelve separate lines, each stretching nearly three inches in length, all intertwined with one another, and not knowing how far she needed to go on any which one, or how many lines needed to be connected, Jaime grew easily frustrated and had reached her breaking point.

"Just give it a rest," Patricia sang from the opposite side of the room. She flipped her lighter open and closed every few seconds, her hand faintly shaking.

Jaime pounded her fist against the wall and then turned to Patricia. "At least I'm trying to get us the fuck out of here."

Patricia waved her hand and tilted her head back. Jaime scowled.

"We all want to get out of here," Kara said calmly.

"Who asked you?" Jaime hissed, and then turned back to the wall.

"I'm just saying that someone had to have brought us here, right?"

Jaime peered over her shoulder to catch a slight glimpse of Kara, who stood near Patricia. "So what?"

"Think about it." Kara walked toward Jaime, who folded her arms together, not much caring for what she had to say. "If someone brought us here, then that someone will most likely come back."

Jaime eyed Kara. She was probably right, but Jaime didn't want to admit it.

"So. What then?" Trishen asked. She had slid into one of the pillows across

the room from Patricia and huddled herself together in a failed attempt at rest. She looked at Jaime with tired, reddening eyes. Had she been crying as well?

"What do you mean?" Kara asked.

"When whoever brought us here comes back? Do we ask him to let us go? Do we tie him up and escape? What?"

Kara didn't really know what they should do if someone ever did come back. She still wasn't even sure if anyone would. All Kara was trying to do was calm the tension in the room. Apparently, that plan had backfired.

"Thought so," Trishen whispered before lowering her head to her knees.

Jaime rolled her eyes and for the first time in an hour and a half, stepped away from the door. "I need a fuckin' smoke," she said.

"Oh, God. You and me both," Patricia said delighted. "That would be heaven right now." Patricia sat up, snapping the lighter closed. "Can I bum one?"

"You don't have any?"

"My smokes were washed away when I went overboard."

"Shit." Jaime grabbed her forehead, which had been pounding since she woke up.

"It would have been pointless anyway. Even if we did have a stick…" Patricia opened the lighter and flicked the igniter. Each time, not even a spark was produced. "We'd have no way to light up."

Jaime lowered her head to the window with a large sigh and closed her eyes. She hadn't felt Kaleena for some time now and was beginning to believe that it really hadn't happened; that it was just her way of convincing herself Kaleena was still alive. The idea her daughter never even made it off the *Endeavor* was flourishing, and yet, the possibility she had been brought to the city and was recently killed was very real. Whatever the case, her hope was diminishing. If she ever did find a way out of this room, her fear was that it would only be her first step to finding Kaleena's dead body.

How would she even handle that?

Jaime felt someone's soft touch settle on her shoulders.

"I know how you must feel." Kara rested her head against Jaime's. "When I found out my sister had died in a plane crash, I could barely eat or sleep for weeks. I spent most of my nights swearing to God and blaming Him for taking her from me. She was only eighteen, you know. Just out of high school, traveling Europe and looking forward to a bright future. She called me the night before her flight back home to tell me she wanted to apply to my alma mater and study French and literature. It was the first thing she said when I answered the phone, even though we hadn't talked since the night she left. I asked her why and she talked all about her trip in precise detail — what all had happened, her numerous sexual experiences she had had. I was upset, granted, but it was her life. I had to respect it. She was exploring, and that was where her adventures took her. God's will."

*   *   *

"I'm thinking about staying a few more days," Diana said near the end of the conversation.

"Why?"

"The man I was talking to you about, the French guy." There was a pause. It felt extremely light and airy. "I think I'm in love."

Kara was happy for her, yet part of her wanted to reach through the phone and pull her back home to knock some sense into her. "What makes you think you're in love?"

"I don't know. I mean, he's great. Honest, caring and sensitive. Not to mention he can do some incredible things with his mouth —"

"I don't need to hear that." After another short pause (as Kara attempted to push the thought from her mind): "Diana, I don't want to be mean, but I think you might be letting what can only be a very good sexual experience influence you."

"That's not it, Kar. When he's around me, I feel like I'm floating. And when he's not... I'm only thinking about the next time I'll get to see him. How can that not be love?"

"I'm not saying it isn't love. All I'm asking is how can you be so certain? You're eighteen. You're away from home for the first time. Your independence may be overwhelming you."

"You think I should take a few weeks and think about it?" Diana wasn't scolding Kara for suggesting it. It's as if she knew it was what she needed to do.

"Yeah, I do."

"Okay. If that's what you think I should do, I'll do it."

Kara's smile was light. The trip seemed to have done exactly what it was supposed to.

"Will you be there to pick me up at the airport? I have so much more to talk to you about, and there's no way I can tell Mom and Dad about any of it. Not yet anyway. Maybe when they're already on their death beds."

"I don't know. That might make them live even longer."

Diana giggled. Kara loved it. "Thanks sis. My flight leaves in a few hours, so I better get ready to go."

"Whatever you do, don't get inducted into the mile-high club."

"I'll see you tomorrow."

Kara chuckled softly, unsure if Diana even knew what she was talking about. "See you tomorrow."

*　　*　　*

"That was the last conversation I had with my little sister," Kara concluded. "I couldn't accept that I had a hand in her death. I was convinced that had I just trusted her when she said she was in love, had I not convinced her to come home that day, she might still be alive. A few years later, I read an article in my college newspaper about a young girl. She was a smart, well-adjusted student who lost her life after letting one her friends drive drunk. There were three other people in the car when it wrapped around a telephone pole. Everyone except that girl walked away with nothing but a few minor scratches and bruises. She had just turned

twenty-one and with one bad decision, her life came to an end. 'Why her?' the article asked. It went on to talk about fate, God's overall plan, the reasons for why things happen and why we shouldn't question them. It sent me to tears. I couldn't stop reading it. Over and over, I replaced that girl with my sister and questioned how it all pertained to her. I tried like hell, but could never answer the why. But as the days passed, I began to understand the true meaning of the article. Sometimes, the reason why something happens will never be clear because it's so much bigger than you or I. That idea helped me lay my sister to rest and end my self-afflicted turmoil. A few months later I learned the parents of that girl started a memorial center for families of teens who have tragically died, a center that has not only helped hundreds of families deal with their unexpected losses, but has donated money to several charities, including cancer research centers, in an effort to save as many lives as they can. None of that would have happened had this family not gone through that very personal loss. I know now that there was a specific reason my sister had to die that day. I don't know what it is, but I have no doubt I'll find out why before I die."

Jamie had been in tears for some time, some soaking her cotton shirt, some having fallen to the floor or gotten stuck to the window.

"What I'm trying to say is that you don't ever know what the future holds, or how decisions you make will affect other's lives. But nothing you do will ever change the past. I believe as much as you that Kaleena's alive. And we'll find her, I'm sure of that. But we all have to stay patient and let God take care of the situation. When it's time for us to act, the situation will present itself."

Kara let her hands slide from Jaime's shoulder. She waited as Jaime collected her thoughts and without another word, Jaime took her into her arms and simply held her. Behind them, Patricia sat still and quiet, the lighter now on the floor. There would have been tears if Patricia ever cried.

Trishen, on the other hand, hadn't heard anything, her thoughts bouncing between her need to know if Thomas was alive and the mistakes she'd made in Gavin's death. Her head rose quickly when she (along with everyone else) heard a deep rumble and saw the doors begin to open. Everyone stood in awe as they spied someone that looked to be lined by flowered vines standing in the center of the hallway outside. He (or she, though the figure's height and weight definitely exuded a male vibe) wore a long black cloak with a dark red trim, tied together just below the stomach region with a long, silk belt. A hood rested over the figure's head, hiding any features within its shadow. Jaime's first instinct was to run like hell, bolt past the eerie figure and go find Kaleena. But like everyone else, she was held frozen by its mere presence. She would heed Kara's advice and remain patient, hoping that she would get some answers before attempting to trek through the unknown world outside.

Once the doors finally came to a stop, the figure walked into the room. The doors slowly started to close as he stepped past the threshold. By the time they had fully sealed, the figure stood statuesque in the center of the room. Jaime let go of Kara (she hadn't even realized she was still holding her) and wiped her eyes clean, blinking several times to try and dry them quicker. Unsure of what might happen, Kara stepped back, seemingly hiding behind Jaime. Trishen held steady where she was, waiting for someone to say something. The atmosphere had become incredibly tense when Patricia decided to break the ice.

"Darth Atlantis, I presume?"

Jaime turned to Patricia so fast it was amazing her neck didn't break. "Patricia," she said through her teeth.

"What?" Patricia stared directly into the center of the hood. She smiled and said, "No, huh? Well, I'm out of guesses. Anyone else want a shot?"

Before anyone even thought about answering her, the figure walked to Patricia and knelt next to her. She quickly gave him a "Hi, how you doin'" gesture that he ignored in favor of lowering his hand to her stomach. The man's other heavy, rock-like hand was pressed firmly against her back, keeping her from slipping away from him. "Hey watch it now," she said as a soft swirl in her stomach that she wasn't sure she should like made her sweat with pleasure. Before the growing tickle reached a climax, the figure retracted his hand and stood. "Whoa..."

Without a word (or a breath for that matter), the figure walked to Jaime. The shifting of his hood from side to side made it clear he was looking her over. "Please, be not afraid," the man said, his voice a gruff rumble. Jaime allowed the man to place his hand on her stomach, unwilling to let him get the better of her. He left behind a whirlwind sensation of laughter and an odd sense of sexual pleasure as he moved on to Kara, who did back away, only to be stopped by the cool glass.

"Let him," Jaime said, unsure of why she would. Kara, though, saw the reason in her eyes and gave in. The man did what he had done to the other two, then flowed over to Trishen, who was no longer pouring out tears of loss, but tears of fear. He carefully nodded and presented Trishen his hand. She looked at Jaime, who nodded, and then graciously accepted it. He helped her to her feet and then applied his hand to her stomach to provide her with the same pleasurable ride the others had experienced. For some reason, the sensation had cleared her mind of everything she'd been conflicted over. Her tears had disappeared. It seemed to take a bit longer than all of the others, but when he was through, he slid back to the center of the room.

"Who are you?" Jaime asked, allowing her leadership to overwhelm her.

It took a few seconds but the low growl rose again. "You may call me Cephis."

Cephis? Kara thought. Where had she heard that name before? Was it something that had been written on one of the tablets? The stones in the ocean? What did it mean? She didn't hear much of the rest of the conversation as it became background noise to her own reflective deliberation.

"Where are we?" Jaime said.

"I believe you already know the answer," Cephis responded.

"Atlantis," Jaime said aloud, receiving an expected nod. Confirming it gave her a warm sensation that could have been the joy of actually knowing she was part of the team that finally found the city of legend… but it could also have been happiness for her husband and daughter and what they must be feeling. Matthew believed in the city when Jaime and Kaleena both blew it off as just another dream.

Thinking about it now, it was his emotion that was overwhelming her, not her own. "How did we get here?"

"I brought you here," Cephis said. His authority and directness gave Jaime the clear impression he was telling her the truth.

"How? Why?"

"There have been many who have come and many who have died within our borders. None of those I have rescued have been as important as you."

"Important? Why are we important?"

"You are all young, fertile females. For us, that is our heaven."

Jaime fell silent. Patricia took the opportunity to jump in with her own comment. "I hate to break it to you, Cephilicious, but I am nowhere near as young as you think."

"But you are. Fertility is what determines how young a soul is, not their outer shell. All of you are still very young."

"That doesn't explain why we're important," Jamie said. "What about the others you claim to have rescued. I'm sure some of them had to be young, fertile females."

"Quite so. But they, my dear, were destined for other purposes. You... you are the bearer of our queen. Our souls."

"Your queen?" Jaime thought she knew who Cephis was talking about, but for the life of her, she couldn't place her face or her name. "Who else lives here?" she said, inadvertently changing the subject.

"My brothers," the man said quickly and seemingly without thought, as if he knew the question was coming.

"Brothers?"

"Ooh, brothers," Patricia said with a slight grin that vibrated her eyebrows. "Do any of them look like you, by chance?"

A slow chuckle that sounded much like an oncoming earthquake vibrated out of the man's throat. "When I speak of brothers, I speak of those souls that I deem my friends. My family in spirit."

Patricia's shoulders slumped forward. "Damn. That's too bad."

"How many of your *brothers* are there?"

"Do not worry about that. You will meet them all in time."

Jaime's determination overtook the puppetry of the conversation. She no longer wanted to hear any vague or inconsistent answers. "That doesn't answer my question," she said sharply. "How many of them are there?"

The silence that filled the room turned Jaime's skin to ice.

"When can we leave?" Jaime finally asked. It was the question she'd been waiting to ask, but was afraid of encountering this very reaction. Nonetheless, she figured she might as well throw it out there; if she was as important as he said, she felt secure in pushing the limits of the man's tolerance.

Instead of finding an even stronger rage, though, Jaime saw a soothing calm blanket Cephis's demeanor. Patricia and Kara held their breaths as they waited for him to say or do anything in response to the question. Trishen sat cold as stone just to the right of him. If Jaime didn't know any better, she would have sworn she was an exhibit in a wax museum.

"I cannot allow any of you to leave," Cephis finally growled.

"What?" Jaime's voice was high. "Why the hell not?"

"I have said enough." Cephis turned from Jaime.

"Bullshit. You can't keep us here like this."

"I can do as I please."

"The hell you can." Jaime sprinted toward Cephis. She wasn't quite sure what she'd do when she got to him; he outweighed her by at least a hundred pounds. But she hoped the others — especially Patricia — would back her, an assumption she found would turn out to be false. Just before she reached Cephis, her hands curled into fists, he turned and swiped Jaime's neck into his large steel grip. Her feet dangled three feet above the ground as she choked for air, kicking at nothing.

I am Lord Cephis. You cannot defeat me. If you try, you will find death, but not before you watch as I send the rest of your friends into a living hell with the simple touch of my finger. I am here to give you the fruits of life, unexplained pleasure and knowledge beyond your comprehension. You are their leader, young Jaime. Choose

wisely. When I return, either you bow at my feet and agree to be the vessel for my children, or you will live in hell.

Cephis released his fingers. Jaime dropped like a stone, landing in the puddle of piss that had poured from her as that loud, gruff voice numbed her mind, making her feel less than human — ghost-like in a way. She couldn't open her eyes or breathe after hitting the floor, but she knew she was still conscious, wishing she wasn't. Her entire body trembled. She was limp, tired and hungry; sick, violated and cold. If she were about to die, she would do so without hesitation.

But *he* wouldn't let that happen.

His footsteps pounded the floor, echoing against her eardrums as if they were enhanced a hundred times over. As the doors closed tight, her friends rushed to her aid. But their touch was missing; the only sensation she had left was that voice trembling every inch of her nerves.

Unknown Location – Time Unknown

The darkness surrounding Lauren felt eerily familiar. Not because she had been there before, but because of the way it made her feel as if it was everything she had ever seen, had ever touched, had ever loved. At the same time, it was cold and empty in a way that felt lifeless and disconnected. From her mind? From her body? She wasn't quite sure, though she thought she felt the touch of her fingers on the surrounding darkness, the rich iciness of her toes and a tingling itch between her legs. She tried at times to speak, but nothing could be heard. She tried at times to move, but went seemingly nowhere. It was maddening — it was dangerous — it was...

...Kaleena — above her.

Or was it? She couldn't tell much beyond the shadowy shape of a young body highlighted by the hum of a soft glow caressing the child in a silhouette of still-ness. Lauren didn't notice that she could now see a light outline of her own, aged body because all of her attention was on the one hanging above her, tilted about

thirty degrees forward, held in position by nothing. Her arms were spread out to either side and her legs were firm and straight, held together by an unseen rope of some kind. The young child's clothes had been shredded, clinging to her as if they were afraid to fall.

Kaleena, Lauren thought, and although she didn't see the body move, it seemed to come alive. It was enough for her to keep talking. *Kaleena, it's Lauren. Can you hear me? Are you all right?*

A quiet hum followed Lauren's inquiries, one that grew louder with every passing second. But no vocalization was heard among it. Or was she simply not listening?

Kaleena? Can you hear me?

Another hum, this one louder than before and for the first time, Lauren was able to filter a word from it. She didn't understand what it meant, but as she prompted Kaleena to talk even further, the word became attached to a short phrase Lauren heard with crisp clarity, the hum having disappeared completely.

My destiny come forth.

Lauren remained silent, able to sense a slow heartbeat from within the shadow. She tried to deconstruct the message, if that's what it truly was. What did it mean? What was Kaleena trying to tell her? The more she thought about the statement, the deeper the pain in her head grew. Lauren eventually fell to her knees directly under Kaleena. In an attempt to stop the increasing pressure, she lied down on her back. She felt the child's pain and anguish as she stared at Kaleena's flat black face. Where was she? How had she gotten here? Would she find her way back home?

My destiny...

The whisper floated past Lauren's ears before a large drop of something

(*Saliva? Mucus? Blood?*)

fell from Kaleena's body. The liquid dropped directly into Lauren's slightly open mouth, leaving a trace of moist tenderness on the edge of her lips. Before she could do anything — taste the sweet mix of salt and iron, wipe the gooey texture from her mouth, spit the foreign entity away — she was caught in a whirlwind of Kaleena's worst nightmares. She was frozen stiff as she watched Jaime step into a cab, her hand placed firmly on the living room window, creating a cold, foggy handprint around her little, chubby fingers; she witnessed the dread of a girl Kaleena's age petrified with blood red, tearless eyes, afraid to even come close to her outstretched arms; she saw a man attack her, trying to put his hand down her pants, the emptiness of a dark, quiet apartment, the tightening pressure of a dozen eyes squeezing her body with nowhere to run and nowhere to hide. All were chilling, real and chaotic, leaving behind a swirl in Lauren's stomach that wasn't really there; a deep sinking feeling, much like heading downhill after the apex of a roller coaster's highest point and then never reaching the bottom of that hill to relax before the next thrilling and sickening moment. From what she could tell, she wasn't actually seeing those events as much as she was feeling them, the emotional impact of each forming the pictures in her mind and driving the maddening state of awareness. Then, after the dizzying pressure reached a height of unbearable proportions, it all stopped. A light breeze whipped through her hair, calming her urgency to break free from her lack of control.

She found herself standing on a hill, lush with grass that covered the plains for miles, lined with blossoming flowers delicately shaded by a bevy of trees, which were no doubt homes to an array of small animals. It took a moment to realize she could move. When she finally took that first step, all of her fears fell away. She no longer felt any pain. A smile rose innocently to her lips, lighting her features as she walked to one of the nearby trees that seemed to be calling to her. Lying her hand on the soft bark of its trunk, Lauren sensed several heartbeats working together to heal the wounds left by storms, age and human contact. She pushed her entire body upon it. In almost an instant, it was as if she had become the tree. No longer a human with a single mind, a single conscious or a single soul, Lauren was one with the millions of whispers that echoed from every leaf upon the branches. She was at peace — she was at home.

But she wasn't.

That one thought of once being a single entity eventually knocked her from her peace. Lauren stepped away from the tree. The soft smile never left her lips and the warmth of her conception lingered upon every organ of her body, but she was not a tree. She was not a leaf. She was not just a body of cells and organisms. There was so much more to her than conformity. She was an independent woman who didn't take any shit from anyone else, who was comfortable with her body, her mind and her life. But was that the only reason she remained this way? She felt something — a voice, a touch, a mind — that asked her to stay, that scared her. Or was it a hallucination? Lauren couldn't remember and like déjà vu, wasn't sure if she could trust her own instincts. If there had been, Lauren was sure she would face those fears again when it was time. But until then, she was going to avoid it at all costs.

The trees around her whistled as a hard gust whisked past the hilltop. Lauren had to grab hold of the tree to keep herself from falling down the hill. As she brushed her hair from her eyes, she saw something cut into the lower part of the tree, about three or four feet above the ground. She wondered if a couple of teenage lovers had cut into the tree as they lay under the shade, holding one another after losing their virginity. Or maybe it had been a child, pronouncing their love for whatever Cory was stealing the young girl's hearts at the time (which wasn't unfamiliar to Lauren, who did just that when she carved a heart around the words "Johnny Depp and Lauren Depp 4ever" into the fence with a steak knife she found on the kitchen counter, a dream Lauren still secretly wished would come true, despite his wife and kids). But this carving was different. It wasn't a heart holding two names together, or an 'I heart whoever.' This marking told a different story altogether.

The JK tree stands with God's love

The mark held Lauren still for quite a long while with one question: Who was JK? At first Lauren thought of Jesus, even though the initials were wrong. Perhaps the carving was made in a time or language when people spelled Christ with a K, just as Jehovah was spelled with an 'I' because the Latin alphabet never included a 'J'. Lauren didn't recall any historical evidence for why that might be true, but she wasn't about to expel the possibility, not after what she'd been through over the last week. Hell, for all she knew, the Man Himself carved the message into the tree with a bolt of perfectly shaped lightning just for her to see at this very moment. Lauren laughed at the preposterousness of the idea and left the symbol to linger in the back of her mind as she gazed down upon the glistening lake at the bottom of the hill. She closed her eyes and imagined herself floating lightly within it, the water licking her bare skin, caressing her to sleep. The refreshing touch of the water was suddenly all around her. She opened her eyes. The blue sky shone bright, faded only by the intense sunlight. A rush of ice ran the course of her veins as her body collapsed into the water. Her toes then went numb and her nipples hardened like rocks. Lauren chirped a squeal of shock and wrapped her arms around her bare breasts. She was somewhere near the center of the lake, hundreds of yards from any shoreline, but she couldn't worry about how she had gotten there. A light trickle of liquid traced her upper thigh like a snake and the clear blue water slowly turned red. Her stomach tightened as she finally felt the small discharge spitting from between her legs. Even though she knew it was only her period, she was eerily frightened, as if it were the first time she was experiencing it. But it wasn't... or was it? Lauren couldn't remember. The pinch in her stomach got stronger as she realized she couldn't really remember much past her own name. Memories were distant or just weren't there. Her body shook as the fear of having everything erased caught up to her and she began to cry uncontrollably.

Quiet. You are in no danger.

Lauren's tears forced her to cough before she was able to control her nerves long enough to call out, "Who's there?"

Please. Hush my child.

"Who is that?"

Hush. You are safe. You are protected. Relax.

"Who are you?" Lauren roared out under her gushing tears. After a bout of

calm silence, she noticed a soft shadow circle her under the water before coming to a stop in front of her. "Please don't hurt me."

I don't want to hurt you, the shadow whispered.

"Who are you?"

The water rose up, a shell of which flowed constantly like a fountain. It grew high — ten feet, maybe twelve — and stared down on her with hidden eyes. Urine filled the bloodied water as Lauren's lungs tightened, preventing any breath from reaching them. The water continued to flow as the shell split in half, revealing the form of a young woman, maybe twenty or twenty-one. Her long, glistening silver hair covered her breasts like a coat and she was devoid of any trace of genitalia. She kept her eyes lowered and her arms crossed delicately across her body, curled around one another. She appeared shy and humble, a presence of radiant beauty and elegance.

Do not fear the mother. Lauren sensed the song come from the woman but couldn't tell if her lips had moved. *Do not fear the sacrifice. Fear only the mind of man.*

That was when the woman raised her head to reveal a pair of glowing silver eyes that radiated the truth behind the shell of Lauren's reflection. In those eyes, Lauren saw Kaleena. The flood or fear that poured through Lauren's body at that moment pushed her into a silent room surrounded by vines of ivy, flowers and plants; into all of her memories, from the day of her birth when the cold whisk of air made her miss the warmth of her mother's safety to the moment she had fallen asleep with Kaleena on her lap and a diary in her hand; into a place where she knew someone was about to lose a life, while others would escape with a new outlook on all that is life.

There was nothing more for Lauren to do but expunge the remnants of her fear through a sickening attack of vomit.

"Are you okay?"

Coughing, Lauren looked up to see Henry standing near the door. He was holding the hand of a six-year-old girl with dimples that shined even without a smile and flowing blonde hair tipped with silver.

"Mommy!" the little girl screamed, joy overwhelming her face. She ran to Lauren, who pulled her legs out from under Kaleena and rolled them over the side of the bed just in time to catch the child's small, thin arms around her neck. Lauren felt incredibly happy but confused. The little girl had called her mother, and her hug... she just didn't know.

She wanted to reciprocate the child's warm and passionate feelings, but it was impossible to connect with a child she had nothing to do with.

Though for some odd reason, she felt her daughter.

The little girl stepped away just enough for Lauren's fingertips to hover on her arms. As Lauren looked her over, the child crossed her arms and playfully folded her fingers together. Her smile was bright with extraordinarily white teeth and her eyes were a light periwinkle that glowed so bright, the color was nearly missing from them. After a moment of staring at one other, each one waiting for the other to say something — a simple hello, perhaps — Lauren looked at Henry. He seemed pleased.

"Who..." Lauren served up a forced smile for the child's sake and then stood. "Who is this?"

Henry chuffed a light chuckle, but then answered the question without judgment. "It's Evey, honey." When Lauren didn't respond, Henry continued, "Our daughter."

Lauren peered back to Evey. "Daughter..." she whispered as she placed her hand to the little girl's neck, feeling her warm skin through the silky smoothness of her hair. "How can that be?"

Henry finally walked to the girls. "What does that matter?" He stroked his fingertips along Lauren's cheek and then looked at Evey. "She's your daughter. Isn't that enough?"

Lauren started to say something then stopped. It was hard for her to believe that the little girl standing in front of her, who should be getting picked on by the cooler girls in her first grade class, crying over not being able to figure out her math homework and worrying about which one of the hottest new toys she was going

to ask Santa for, was her newborn baby. "But…" Lauren took her time, wanting to get what she had to say off her chest, but unwilling to say it with the little girl standing right in front of her. If this was her daughter, did she really want her to hear her objection? Lauren leaned in close to Henry and lowered her voice to where even Henry could barely hear what she had to say. "This isn't Evey."

Henry pressed his lips to Lauren's ear. "But it is. The sooner you accept that, the easier it will be for you." He nodded, his eyes strong with a forceful urgency. Lauren wanted so bad to object again, but how could she? A small part of her knew it was true: Evey had grown six years in just over eight hours. But another part of her couldn't comprehend how or why, and wanted desperately to object to the insanity of it all. Then she remembered that she'd just gone through an entire pregnancy in just a week. Everything she ever knew to be real had been flipped on its head. What makes this situation any different?

"Mommy?" Evey tugged on Lauren's dress. When Lauren looked at her, her eyes were laced with worry. "Mommy, are you okay?"

"Yeah," Lauren said under her breath, her doubt hidden behind a loving smile. "Yeah, sweetie." Lauren knelt down to meet Evey's gaze. A sense of motherly love washed over her. Even if this was somehow a hoax, the child needed Lauren to be her mother right now, and she was willing to accept that — for now. She swept Evey into her arms and hugged her tightly. "I'm perfect."

Evey giggled and kissed Lauren on the cheek. "I love you, mommy," she whispered and squeezed Lauren a little harder.

"Does this suffice?" Henry asked.

Lauren was a bit confused at the formation of the remark, unsure of what it meant. "I'm sorry?"

"You requested to see your daughter to make sure she was okay. Now that you've seen her, are you happy with her condition?"

Lauren's confusion remained steady. The tone of Henry's voice seemed condescending at best. It felt as if he were treating her as his child as well. But she kept any abrupt outburst from breaking free (for the sake of Evey?) and nodded,

a simple gesture that felt extremely forced, as if someone else was guiding her reaction.

"Good," Henry stated and then held out his hand. "Come, Evey. We must go."

"What?" Lauren said. Evey tightened her grip on her arm. It felt good to feel her daughter's love for her soaking through her fingertips.

"We have a lot to do."

Before Lauren could object, Evey said, "I want to stay."

"I said come."

Evey grasped Lauren even tighter and rested her head on her mother's shoulder. "I'm staying." The command was abrupt and forceful. Henry's eyes glazed over with a minute anger, which then transformed into a deathly calm as he stared into Evey's eyes. Jaime couldn't see what was happening, but the power the child held over Henry was strong, as if she would kill him if he didn't oblige.

Henry lowered his arm. "Very well. I'll return shortly with a visitor. You have until then, Evey." He left, but before closing the doors, he turned to Evey with red eyes. "And then you will come."

When the doors locked shut, Lauren sat stunned, unsure of what to do next. Evey's grip on Lauren loosened as she stared at the door as if she were waiting for Henry to return. Lauren suddenly felt the need to pull her daughter into her bosom — *protect her?* — and connect in a meaningful way. She had been pushing the child away, grappling with the reality of her sudden growth spurt, but as a small bead of sweat moistened her grip, Lauren finally felt Evey's heart — her soul in a way — and knew they were part of one another.

"Mommy." The sweet angelic voice chimed in Lauren's ear. Her heart jumped, not in fright, but anticipation. All of her uncertainty seemed to wash away as she peered into those tiny, gentle eyes.

"Yes, Evey?"

"Do you love me?" The question was so innocent and kind.

Lauren took hold of Evey's upper arms. She didn't want her answer to be false, or contrived. She wanted her daughter to know that it was honest, from deep within her heart. "Yes, of course. You're my daughter. There's nothing that could keep me from loving you."

Evey's cheeks lit up as her mouth gently opened, showcasing two delicate rows of small, pure white teeth. She wrapped her arms around Lauren and squeezed. Lauren was hesitant to reciprocate, but soon closed her arms around the child. They held each other for quite a while, unable to let the other go, feeling that if they did, they'd lose each other forever.

Lauren only loosened her grip when something important popped to the forefront of her thoughts. "Can I ask you something?"

"Yeah."

"How old are you?"

Evey looked around the room, scanning everything from the decorative fixtures to the diaries and then caught sight of Kaleena. For a moment, her skin chilled. But it didn't last long. Evey turned back to Lauren, this time, distracted.

"I don't know. Not years. Maybe hours."

"Hours?"

"Yeah. I was only born a few hours ago, wasn't I?"

"What do you remember?"

Evey took a second, shocked by the question. Finally: "Everything."

"Everything?"

"Yeah." Evey couldn't stop fixating on Kaleena. Her body remained stiff as she methodically walked over to her.

"What's wrong?"

"She's hurt." The response wasn't quite what Lauren had expected. It was colder, more concise and a bit menacing. For a moment, Lauren thought Evey was happy Kaleena was hurt, but that was just ludicrous.

Wasn't it?

"She's a remarkable young woman," Evey continued.

"Yes, she is." A shallow chill haunted Lauren, though she didn't understand why.

"Her mind is strong…" Evey placed her hand on Kaleena's chest just below her collarbone and began to take short breaths that matched the slow beats of Kaleena's heart. "But her heart is even stronger." She paused, her eyes seemingly attached to the necklace that lay humbly against Kaleena's neck.

"She's very special, and very beautiful, though she bears a lot of sadness. Her mind may have been developed well beyond her years, but her soul has yet to catch up. She's become more than a child because of the turmoil, the grief of the recent past that's changed her view of those around her. A woman has yet to emerge, but in time, she will be released and give the child the love she deserves."

Lauren finally figured it out — Evey spoke with a sophistication that didn't match the outer shell of her body.

Evey removed her hand and used her tiny fingers to trace Kaleena's facial features, delicately touching her soft lips, the round tip of her nose and the sturdy gel of her eyelashes. She eventually rested her hand on Kaleena's forehead. Taking a deep breath, Evey looked up to the ceiling and released all of the air from her lungs. Lauren was nearly hysterical as she watched, but her outward appearance remained as hard as stone. She was frozen, as was Evey — until the pint-sized adult took in another deep breath and lowered her head. A flash of round light shot from between Evey's hand and Kaleena's forehead. It passed through Lauren with the warmth of lava, but didn't linger. A sense of health and joy echoed through her body as Evey lowered her mouth to Kaleena's forehead and expelled the air she had just gathered. After a moment, Evey removed her hand. The scar was gone, as if nothing had ever happened to her. She still didn't wake, but her breaths became steadier.

"What was that?" Lauren said, nearly out of breath herself.

"I helped her."

"Will she wake up?"

"In a little bit." Evey lowered her lips to Kaleena's and gave her a gentle, but seemingly passionate kiss. "Time will heal her," she said as she stepped away. "And time will defeat her." She turned to Lauren. "That was fun." The maturity Evey

had displayed just seconds earlier had vanished.

Lauren was mesmerized — and frightened. It did seem as if Kaleena was healing, as life was returning to her cheeks. She had to trust that Evey meant them no harm.

"Let's play a game."

Uncertainty painted Lauren's features. To play a game with the child after just having gone macabre was unsettling to say the least, but she still felt a powerful connection between them that couldn't be ignored. And the more Evey joyously waited for an answer, rolling back and forth on the balls of her feet, her hands clasped behind her back, the more the fire of admiration welled up within Lauren.

"Okay," she finally answered, glowing with childish glee.

Black Hole – Time Unknown

He couldn't tell it physically, but Matthew felt older — much older — than he did twenty minutes ago. Gydressina seemed to have been right about the black hole sending its effects through him and Thomas, who never left Matthew's side as they inched their way through the caverns looking for —

What?

— anything that appeared to be a door or a pathway to anywhere but here. The farther they walked, the longer they took to traverse the black hole, the more it ate at them, squeezing them in a tight grasp of dread. But as Gydressina continued to explain as she helped guide them through — keep their spirits up, as it were — the more constricted and tired they felt, the closer they were to reaching their ultimate goal.

So intent on finding a way out, Matthew hadn't noticed he'd fallen back a ways from Thomas, though part of him told him it was Thomas who had fallen back. "Thomas," he choked out.

Thomas turned to Matthew

(or did Matthew turn to Thomas?)

and quickly took a hold of him. Matthew felt quite weak as Thomas held him in his arms. "Hang in there, Matthew.

"Hang in there…

"We're almost out of this shithole.

"Almost out of shit."

He strained to pull Matthew to his feet. "I know it." *I know it.*

"Truth is an illusion, Thomas" The crystal song of Gydressina breezed past like a wind.

"We have to be close," Thomas hollered out.

Matthew reacted to Thomas's strength. "We've got to be.

"Got to be…

"I'm okay," he finished, pushing Thomas away slightly. "I'll be okay." *Okay!*

"You sure?" *Sure?*

"Yeah.

Yeah.

"Let's just keep moving.

"Keep. Moving."

Matthew started forward again, Thomas in lock step behind him (or maybe in front of him). After another few minutes of hopeless wandering, Matthew caught sight of something up ahead. His body filled with a light resurgence of energy.

"What's up?" Thomas asked quickly, noticing the change in attitude.

"Do you see it?

"See it?" Matthew pointed at the wall in front of him.

"See what?

"What?

"Matthew, it's a wall.

"A WALL!"

"No, it can't be.

"Can't… be…

"It's the way out.

— 454 —

"Way out."

"Matthew, you're looking at a wall.

"You're a wall."

"No, no.

"No. No.

"It's a door.

"A door.

"It has to be the way out.

"Be our way out."

"Trust not your eyes, Matthew," Gydressina quickly interjected. "They can deceive you quicker than your mind. Trust your friend. And trust your heart."

"No, I'm trusting.

"Not trusting.

"It's the way out.

"Out!

"I'm sure of it.

"Sure of shit."

Matthew ran toward the wall. But instead of smashing his face into the rock, he went straight through the apparition. Thomas's eyes were saucers. He immediately jogged up to it. He was apprehensive about doing anything at first, then placed his hand on it. It was smooth like the rest of the caverns, and as expected, completely solid.

"What the hell?"

"You are close, Thomas. The black hole is attempting to control your minds; cause you pain. Be wary, but find Matthew. He isn't strong enough to continue alone. Find him and convince him of his own reality. Only then will the door reveal itself."

"Where do I find him?"

"Trust your heart to guide you, but don't allow the hole to swallow you with temptation."

"Right." Thomas's chest hurt as he sprinted through the cavern in search of his lost friend.

*   *   *

Matthew had run so fast and was so determined to reach the door that he didn't realize Thomas had disappeared. He also hadn't paid much attention to the fact that the farther he ran, the farther the door moved away from him. His destination continued to allude him, but it wasn't really the destination he was attempting to reach. His goal was in his desire to escape all that he found himself in, and if that made him have to run until his heart exploded, then so be it.

His legs started to give out before that could happen. With each step, his knees tightened and his calves burned to numbness. Occasionally, Matthew would slip to the ground, but his need to reach the door kept him from staying put for long. After about five minutes of running, Matthew was out of breath and ready to vomit for hours. He was bruised and cut, blood unable to dry because of the heavy perspiration that covered his body and weighed down his clothes. Matthew fell to the ground and this time, he couldn't get up. His legs wouldn't allow it, buckling underneath him every time he tried. To give up would be to admit defeat, but what could he do? As he rolled onto his back, his entire body beating with heat, the tears that had been building started to pour out. It wasn't out of fear of being unable to find his way out; it was knowing that if Gydressina was right and Kaleena was alive, she would have to fight her way through the madness alone. His desire to reach the door spun a web of longing for his daughter mixed with the fear that she would not forgive him for what he put her through over the last few years, for not being there when she needed him and for his lack of effort and inability to continue on. How would she react if she knew he'd given up when he was so close?

He couldn't allow her to believe he'd given up on her, that he had given up on himself. He didn't want that to be her last memory. He would fight his way through this. He had to.

He had to for Kaleena's sake. For Kaleena's love.

For Kaleena's life.

A resurgence of strength soon returned to his legs and his chest no longer burned with fatigue. He slowly stood and finally realized that Thomas was no longer with him. But he'd be okay. If either one of them got out, it would allow the other to find their way out — or at least that's what Matthew repeated to himself to keep from laboring on the idea that he wasn't willing to track down Thomas over Kaleena. Gydressina would protect his friend and guide him out. And if she didn't... Matthew didn't want to even think about the consequences of that decision. He pushed the nubs of his fingers into his eyes and rubbed them intensely. As he reopened them, he saw something near the door. It looked like a body, but he couldn't tell from where he was standing. For all he knew it was a giant bag of rocks. The door continued to stay at an equal distance from Matthew as he stepped forward. Lucky for him, the object remained in place, growing larger as he got closer. The black hole was going to allow him to reach it. For a second, the idea that all of this was just an illusion, that he was lying dead or unconscious somewhere, his mind walking up to his own body as some sick, twisted test that he'd have to pass before he was allowed access to the city, chilled his whole body. But that notion faded as the body he saw lying there wasn't near large enough to be his, much less any man's. It was far too petite. Then his organs shut down. What was left of the female's clothes had been ripped in several places and her undergarments appeared to be soiled. The body was dirty with blood caked throughout her hair. Matthew couldn't see the girl's face, which was hidden under her arm, but he could see a small, familiar bruise. Part of him didn't want to know who it was; the other part knew exactly who it was. The need to know for sure grew heavy; the sooner he confirmed it, the sooner he could free himself from everything. He got down on his knees, a small pop exploding from both of them, and reached for the girl's arm. Fear of what Matthew was about to see flushed his spirit in a rush of guilt, sadness, anger and regret. Her face matched her body — bruised and cut. Her mouth was split open in several places and her nose was broken. This young, delicate flower had been beaten, abused, and by all signs, possibly raped and left here to waste away into a corpse.

This young spirit — with no hope of finding someone to love her and take care of her when she was ill.

This young girl — who would force Matthew into a fitful rage of tears and screams.

This girl...

Kaleena.

Atlantis – Lauren's Quarters – 8 hours 52 minutes after arrival

Lauren's eyes were wide as she tried desperately to come up with the answer to the question Evey had proposed. Both sat cross-legged on the floor about two feet from the other. Lauren knew that in just a few seconds, if she didn't answer, she'd once again lose, as she had at least a dozen times already. She really thought she had control over the game now, but the last question rattled her. Evey had all but given her a pass on the first few rounds, which Lauren understood to be somewhat like a reverse twenty questions, wherein one player would state an object and the other would then describe that object, at which point the first player would ask follow-up questions about the object. When either player ran out of questions or couldn't possibly answer one, the game was over.

"What is a flower?" Evey had asked after guiding Lauren to sit on the floor.

"A flower?"

"Yes. What is a flower?"

Lauren looked down at her knees, but Evey leaned in and pulled Lauren's face forward to meet hers. "Never look away from your inquisitor. It makes you seem dishonest and is an automatic disqualification."

With a short breath of laughter, Lauren situated herself a bit more comfortably. Evey did the same, backing up into a very statuesque, proper position. "Okay," Lauren smiled. Evey nodding her appreciation. "Okay, a flower." Lauren made sure her eyes remained on her daughter and then said, "A flower is a plant that includes a bud, pollen and sometimes thorns."

Evey didn't hesitate: "What is pollen?"

"Pollen are the seeds that flowers use to reproduce. I think."

"How do they reproduce?"

"Usually with bees. As they travel from flower to flower, they carry pollen with them. Wind can also carry pollen to a new destination."

"Why do the bees like flowers?"

"Because they're attracted to them."

"Why?"

"Because of their color and their scent."

"What if a flower doesn't have a scent? Or doesn't bloom a color?"

"I've never seen a flower without color."

"That doesn't answer my question."

Lauren paused a moment. "I guess then the bees wouldn't find the flower attractive, unless the scent was really strong."

"Why not?"

"Because it wouldn't be appealing anymore."

"Why not?"

"Because…" Lauren couldn't answer the question, and she knew Evey could sense it, just by looking into her eyes, which glowed with a gleam of satisfaction. "All right. You win."

"Fun, huh?" Evey said, breaking the solid concentration she'd been locked into during the game. "Let's go again. Your turn to ask the questions."

Lauren proceeded to ask Evey what a rock was, and with every question Lauren threw at her, Evey was right on top of it with a logical, coherent answer that made all the sense in the world. Eventually, Lauren couldn't come up with a new question. They continued on, Evey winning every time without even seeming to try, though Lauren started to answer quicker and with more detail, doing her best to match Evey's confidence. Finally, it was Evey's turn again to ask the question and

Lauren felt absolutely ready to win — until the question was asked.

"What is love?"

It took her nearly two minutes to formulate an answer, one which was so simple, she hoped Evey wouldn't understand how to question it. "Love is an emotion that connects your heart, your mind and your spirit with another in a way that if you were to lose that other, it would be like losing a piece of yourself."

Evey's eyes beamed. She really liked that answer. "Is that all it is?"

Lauren was flabbergasted. Here she thought she was being clever, but Evey somehow responded with a much cleverer question. How was she supposed to answer that? Before she could, an answer came from behind Evey.

"No, that's not all it is."

Evey turned around. Kaleena was still lying in the bed, her eyes closed and motionless.

"What else is it?"

Kaleena answered sweetly and direct. "Attraction, desire and lust."

Evey looked Kaleena over carefully, and then: "What do those attributes have to do with love?"

"They make up the first stages of love, and evolve into traps that blind the mind when dealing with the profound impact of the emotion."

"What do you mean by traps?"

"Humans are set apart from other animals by their ability to control their needs and inhibitions. They've learned to fight the desire to lay with anyone at any time because of emotions that have developed, such as guilt and remorse. This filter, this ability to control those desires, is called love. Attraction to another is the first stage, at which point, if we didn't have the filters, we'd simply have sex with them whenever we pleased without ever batting an eye. But our minds tell us that doing so would be wrong, that there are other feelings to take into account. We can't just go up to anyone we feel attracted to and get what we want. This filter is broken on some people, which is why we have nymphomaniacs, pedophiles, and rapists — people who believe they can have anyone they so

choose at any time. That is desire. They don't feel guilt or remorse after they've done what they believe is their animalistic right. Which, without the filter of law, it truly is. Animals don't obey man-made law; they simply obey nature. But humans have grown accustomed to obey law, thus the filter keeps the majority of people in check. When someone is able to control their filters and pass the tests of attraction and desire, then all they're left with is lust, a base emotion that makes you feel needed, wanted, excepted and happy when you're around someone that attracts your desire. In order to control the lust, the need to have someone even if the law says you can't, whether it be because of marriage or age, the mind builds a new filter that stops that person from following through on lust. That is when you, as they say, 'Fall in love.'"

"So are you saying love doesn't truly exist?"

"I'm saying love is a false hope we wield so we can feel good about ourselves. As a society, we've been bred to believe that there's simply one other out there — our soul mate — who will somehow make us whole, who has been chosen for us by a higher power, and if we're lucky, one day we might actually find this someone. Most, if anyone, never finds this true soul mate, but because of our attraction to someone, our desire to be with them is enough to make us happy and satisfies our animalistic needs, we choose to manufacture it through the filters of lust, law, guilt and remorse. We make believe that we've found our one true love because deep down, our minds know there's no such thing."

Lauren held her knees against her chest in an odd attempt to hide herself from the speech Kaleena just gave. She couldn't believe what she had just heard, but couldn't help but believe every word of it. Evey, on the other hand, sat stunned, but with a hint of a smile on her face. "But why do we fight our natural animal urges?"

"Jealousy."

"What is jealousy?"

Kaleena slowly opened her eyes and sat up, still a bit weak and groggy. "In a word," she said after a light cough. "Selfishness. The need to keep others from having what you have, or having what you can never get."

Now it made much more sense. The root of Kaleena's cynical view was based in selfishness. Lauren's heart roared back to life, bringing with it a jolt of energy that urged her to join Evey as her teammate against Kaleena. "What about other types of love? Like motherly love, or love of a fine wine?" Evey's face lit up as she accepted her new partnership with grand appreciation.

Kaleena hinted at hiding a satisfying grin of her own. She liked this game. "Love of a fine wine, or any other object, like a toy or a movie, is simply an objectification of something you enjoy. But because law doesn't prohibit taking and acquiring that of an object, we can enjoy it more, without the filters of guilt or remorse. But because we still want to be the only ones to have a certain something, when we aren't, our selfishness kicks in, expressed in the form of jealousy. In that way, love for an object is exactly like love for another life, as most men only see a woman as an object, a goal, or a treasure they and no other can have."

"But what about women?"

"Women see men as a toy of their own, able to mold and shape them into what they believe is the ideal. This, too can be traced back to jealousy and selfishness."

"And motherly love?" Lauren said softly.

For a second, as Kaleena contemplated her answer, Lauren actually thought she might have stumped her. But then: "A motherly love, or a fatherly love at that, is, I believe, what real love actually is. It doesn't root itself in jealousy, or selfishness. A child is a part of you, and thus, you have a desire to protect that child at any cost, even if it means killing the child to save others. *That* is the only way love can truly exist."

"Wait. So you're saying that killing your child to protect others is a form of protecting the child?" Lauren seemed a tad disturbed.

"No. I'm saying that when you kill your child to *save* others, it's in this unselfish act that you save yourself."

"So how is that protecting the child?" Evey said.

"Because the child is you."

"And if killing the child doesn't save anyone else?"

"Then you will never be saved from your own selfishness."

Lauren felt fatigued. All she could think about was her lost child, the one she never gave a chance to breathe, the one she felt every day, even though, in her mind at the time, it was still only a viable embryo when it was destroyed. It was her selfishness that killed that child, and all of the guilt and remorse surrounding her death finally caught up to her in one simple sentence. Kaleena was spot on in her assessment, and it sickened her. It made her want to trade places with her unborn child and give her the life she was meant to have, replacing the one Lauren didn't feel she deserved. Then she saw Evey and it all became clear. If she had not had an abortion, where would she be right now? Would Evey have even been conceived? In a very unorthodox way, killing one child may just have saved another. But was that reasoning enough to believe that what she did was right?

"Does that mean I win?" Kaleena said, breaking the eerily dark silence.

Evey's eyes became saucers. "Yes it does." She stood and ran to Kaleena, wrapping her arms around her with a big squeeze. As Kaleena reciprocated the hug, Lauren felt serene, especially knowing Kaleena had no idea who the child was. Or at least she thought.

"Good to see you awake," Lauren said after a light chuff. She gave Kaleena a welcome hug of her own.

"Thank you," Kaleena said, her eyes fixed on Evey's dimpled brightness. "Glad to be awake and not dead." Kaleena laughed lightly, though Lauren had no idea why. "And who might this little darling be?"

"Kaleena…" Lauren took in a deep breath. "This is my daughter, Evey."

Kaleena's eyes darted to Lauren as her happiness faded faster than a light in a black hole. "What?"

Lauren raised her eyebrows and shrugged in recognition of the truth.

Kaleena shook her head, looking over Evey as if she were some alien cyborg hybrid form the planet Nonsense. "That's impossible. I just saw her. She couldn't have been more than a few days old." She looked back to Lauren. "How long was I out?"

"I'd like to say six years, Rip Van Winkle, but it hasn't been more than a few hours."

"That doesn't help."

Lauren shrugged again. She didn't know what else to do.

"I'm special," Evey said, and waited for Kaleena to turn back to her to continue. "I'm not a child in the way your minds perceive a child."

"Well, yeah. That's obvious."

"I've grown at an extraordinary rate, and I will continue to do so over the next few hours. The next time you see me, I'll be as old as you, and by tomorrow, I'll appear as old as Lauren. But don't let that fool you. My physical appearance is one thing. My mind is quite another. On some level, it's already more mature than yours."

Lauren couldn't deny her statement. It was unbelievable how much Evey sounded like Kaleena.

"But how is that possible?"

"You shouldn't dwell on such trivial things. It's unimportant. There are much more imperative events we must discuss before my father returns."

"Your father?"

"Henry," Lauren cut in, reiterating what they had discussed earlier. The expression on Kaleena's face told Lauren everything — she had no memory of anything they'd discussed before she left to 'save' Evey.

Kaleena racked her brain for a moment longer, and then remembered a couple of her father's stories. "You mean one of my dad's students, Henry?"

Lauren nodded.

"Ah, this just keeps getting weirder and weirder."

"Again, don't fret. It's all irrelevant."

"How is all of this irrelevant?"

"Because it's not necessary to our ultimate goal."

"And what's that?"

"You and I, Kaleena, are the same. As I, you were chosen to help us fight the

evil that plagues the remnants of Atlantis. You were all chosen, my father included."

"And my parents?"

Evey responded coldly and methodically: "A means to an end."

"What?" Kaleena's grip tightened around Evey's arm, though the child didn't even seem to notice — or care.

"Your mother and father's only purpose was to lead you and Lauren to Atlantis. You wouldn't be here without them."

"But once they led us here, they were expendable? Is that what you're saying?"

"Yes. But it's for your own good."

"Are you kidding me?" Kaleena refrained from using the expletive she so badly wanted to use.

"Your continued attachment to your parents would have kept you from doing what you're destined to do for us."

"And what *exactly* have I been *destined* to do for you?"

"There's a woman. She was once ruler of this city until her selfishness destroyed us all."

Kaleena's anger began to ease. "The magistrate."

Evey tilted her head down in acknowledgment.

"She's still alive?"

"Very much so, though she is very old, very haggard. But she's been taking steps to build her power once again. If she's able to find her way out of her prison and walk the city, she will destroy all that's left of it. And the life, the history as we know it will die."

"You want me to stop her?"

"You need to help me kill her."

Kaleena finally let go of Evey and sat down, her back uncomfortably set against the bed. She wasn't sure what to make of all of this, but knew something wasn't right.

"How am I supposed to do that?"

"By sacrificing yourself to Atlantis."

"Evey, no," Lauren said. She'd been listening to the whole conversation, but stayed silent, fearing her daughter might do something terrible if she spoke her concerns. But telling Kaleena she needed to die was unacceptable.

"Mother, please. Don't attempt to keep her from her destiny."

"I'm sorry, but I'm not about to let her kill herself."

"You must. If she doesn't do as I ask, the magistrate will destroy the city, killing me, you and all the others who wish to roam these halls in peace."

Lauren couldn't fight Evey on this point; she didn't want to die as much as she didn't want to see Kaleena die.

"Why do I have to die to stop the magistrate?"

"Because I can't stop her without your soul."

"My soul? Is that all?"

Evey was confused, then registered the sarcasm. "You become much more powerful to me in death. I need your strength to tear down the old woman's defenses. Without your death, she will continue to flourish."

"What are you saying?" Kaleena said quickly. "The magistrate is using me to build her strength?"

Evey's lips curled, raising her cheeks. Kaleena couldn't tell if the smile was joy toward her recognition or something more. "Yes," Evey finally whispered.

Kaleena's mind swirled in a fireball of questions, doubt, eagerness and respect. She wanted to believe her, to protect her, but she had to remain cautious, to protect herself. When the time came, she didn't know if she'd be able to do what Evey needed. Would that decision put all of their lives in danger? She didn't know what to do, and looking to Lauren, who stood cold and stiff, didn't help. Before she could register her lips moving, a soft, "Okay," escaped under her breath. Evey's smile grew twice as large and twice as delicate.

"I knew you would," she said in a very childlike manner, then fell on top of Kaleena to apply another big hug. Her lips eventually rose to rest on the bottom of Kaleena's ear. "But you need to do something else first," she whispered.

"What's that?" Kaleena whispered back.

"You need to give me a sister."

Kaleena's mind grew curious as a new, unfamiliar voice rose through the room, sending goosebumps marching across her skin. *What a lovely moment.*

Evey turned to the door as two cloaked figures entered the room. Kaleena quickly stood in an attempt to show strength where there was still a cloud of weakness and fear. Lauren remained frozen; everything about this had gone beyond her comprehension. But Evey skipped happily to the figure standing a few steps behind the other, utterly subservient in demeanor. He scooped the child up and gave her a ravishing hug, then lowered her back to the ground and took her hand. Evey looked in love.

Adamus? Kaleena asked without moving her lips.

He gave a slight nod as his 'master' walked to Kaleena. He flowed smoothly from side-to-side, as if he had no spine — or any bones at all.

Adamus, who is this? Kaleena's trepidation grew more intense as the ghost drew closer.

You may call me Cephis, child, the booming growl seethed. The monster towered over Kaleena, turning her skin a pale white.

What do you want from me? she asked.

I believe you already know. Cephis caressed her cheek, then slid his fingers past her lips and down her neck toward her chest. *My love,* he whispered. *My heart. My chalice. So beautiful you are. So young.*

Kaleena tried to look away from the cold, dark cloud of nothing filling the hood, but her head had been frozen in place. There was nothing she could do to stop this monster from what he was about to do. But before his hand reached her breasts, Cephis removed his hand and grabbed Kaleena's stomach, just above her hip line. He started tapping a tune above her naval with his thick fingers. Kaleena felt her gut warm slightly as Cephis raised his head to the ceiling, appearing to have an orgasm. Even though Lauren was unable to move, she swore if this freak lowered his hand just one inch, she would find the strength to rip the asshole's arm off.

She didn't have to. As the seconds ticked away, Lauren sensed a growing dissatisfaction. Cephis's intensified breathing became a low murmur, which quickly turned to a low growl. Kaleena's body fell cold and a slight needle sharp pain bit her stomach. All of the plant life across the room withered and the lights dimmed.

A loud scream erupted from behind the hood and for the first time, Evey looked frightened. She clasped Adamus tightly, her lightness gone. Cephis removed his hand from Kaleena's stomach and whipped around to Adamus, whose stature remained strong. Kaleena grabbed her side and fell to her knees, prompting Lauren to follow her to the ground to break her fall. The instant her head hit Lauren's chest, she passed out and lay motionless in her arms.

What is this? Cephis rumbled.

My Lord? Adamus's voice was a bit shaky.

She's been cleansed. Evey let go of Adamus's hand as Cephis grabbed his neck. *How is that possible?*

I don't know. I swear.

Gydressina is more powerful than we thought, Evey chimed in. Her voice sounded older, more mature.

Cephis looked to Evey. *This is not acceptable.*

It's a setback. But inconsequential. Love will still guide us through.

Can you trust her?

Evey turned to Lauren and flashed a gentle, loving smile. "I know I can."

Then we move forward without her.

Evey nodded and Cephis turned back to Adamus. He stared deep into the man's hood for a long time without thought, then lowered him to the ground. Lauren heard the creature pull in a hungry gasp of air.

The others are ready for implantation. Take her back to Spirit and then join me in Firelight.

Cephis took one last look over the girls before leaving the room. Adamus held his ground until Cephis had completely vanished from their sight, then reached out for Evey. She took his hand and they walked to the door.

"Who was that?" Lauren asked, a bit of a jitter caught in her throat.

Adamus and Evey both turned to Lauren without a word.

"What did he do to Kaleena?"

"She's not hurt," Evey said. "She'll wake up shortly. Just be patient."

The two started out the door and Lauren couldn't help herself. "Where are you going?" she screamed. "Tell me what's going on here!"

Evey waived a loving goodbye as the door closed behind her.

Black Hole – Time Unknown

It seemed to take Thomas a lifetime to wrap himself through the suddenly maze-like formation of the caves. Dead-end after dead-end led Thomas to come to the conclusion that he needed to calm down and think before he reacted to a new twist or turn. The black hole had been sucking him into a twisted version of his own mind so that he wouldn't be able to locate Matthew, who could be sitting right next to him, for all he knew. Was any of this real? Or was he still only a spirit trying to acclimate to his dying corpse?

With Gydressina ignoring his cries for help, Thomas was on his own in finding his way out. At first, he thought it would be as easy as believing none of it was actually real; that he could walk through any wall at any time. But after continually walking into every single wall he encountered, he figured the only way to accomplish his goal would be to focus on something much deeper. Thinking about what Caitlyn had said to him in the forest, it became clear that he needed to let go, not only of his regret over pushing her and his daughter away, but what that meant to everyone else around him. To find his way back to consciousness, he had to find it in his heart to forgive the boys who had burned his hand, an incident he now realized had led him to where he is today. Every step, every drink, every hit he took or gave was manufactured from that one moment, defining who he was, and in the process, hurting many more people than he probably ever knew. How many lives had been hurt or changed because of that one simple act of cruelty?

How many lives changed for the better? For the worse? His reprehensible actions may have hurt Caitlyn, but he also gave her Chelsea, and essentially led her to the man she now loves, the man that loves his daughter as his own. Where would the family be if he hadn't been the way he was? And in turn, where would he be if he hadn't tried to make himself better after realizing what he'd lost? With or without Thomas, Matthew would have been able to find Atlantis. Then again, without Thomas, Matthew may have died while investigating the underground cemetery. It was all becoming clear. Everything in his past, everything that caused him so much pain and sickness, greed and depression, had led him to this point for one reason — to protect Matthew.

That rationalization was all he had left.

"No, it's not."

Thomas turned around. Standing about six feet from him was a thin redhead with long legs and freckles tattooed all over her exquisitely naked body. She seemed older, but nevertheless, just as exotic as he remembered.

"Rebecca?"

She smiled and snaked up to him, wrapping her arms around his head and moving her body against his like a wave lapping the ocean. Thomas felt her breasts against his bare chest and a new vibrant sensation poured through his body, turning him nearly numb.

"Rebecca..." He tried to choke out more, but couldn't as Rebecca moved from sucking his neck to eating his lips. Thomas couldn't move as his mind dissolved into a smoke of nothing.

When she had finished tasting his saliva, she stared into his eyes. "You've always had me, Thomas. Even when you didn't believe it, you always had me. You never fought for me, but I was waiting. And now, you can have me. Do you want me, Thomas? Can I taste your penis?"

Rebecca grabbed Thomas's ass and pressed his pelvis to hers, shoving her tongue into his mouth. Thomas wrapped his arms around her and took control of the kiss. It felt right, it felt natural, it felt... unreal.

Thomas pulled away. "No. You're not real."

"I am, Thomas. Feel me. You know it's true."

"No. I can't." Thomas stepped away from his dream, who stood stunned and angry.

"What are doing? Don't you want me? Don't you want my friendship back?"

"This isn't real."

"I love you, Thomas. I only fucked Jacob because I was mad at you for leaving me. I didn't want to fuck him, believe me, he wasn't that good. All I wanted was you. You were the only person I ever wanted to hump."

Thomas held his tongue. Whatever he had to say wouldn't be kind.

"I know you feel the same about me. You've wanted nothing more than to see me like you saw all those girls in that movie." Suddenly, Thomas saw a half a dozen other naked women in the distance behind Rebecca, caressing one another, kissing one another, touching one another. Thomas grew extremely hard and felt like he needed to run into the bathroom and do what he used to do every time he thought of Rebecca. "That's right," she continued, her tongue sliding gently across his face, neck and chest. "Just like you dreamed of every day. You can have me now, for real. All you need to do is take me, love me. I'm your fantasy, Thomas, and I am much more real than your hand." Rebecca took in a few sensual breaths as she ran her fingers around her smooth breast. The girls behind her became as aroused as Thomas.

"And I can give you the family you always desired."

The word *family* echoed across his mind as Thomas returned to his own reality. The girls in the distance faded into a light haze of smoke.

"No, Rebecca," he finally uttered under his breath. "You don't understand. Matthew is my family. Kara, Lauren. *They* are my family. Trishen..." the name rolled from Thomas's tongue with a fluid calm. His heart pounded quicker than normal as he thought of her smile and, more so, her soul.

"Trishen is my love, now, Rebecca. I once thought my life revolved around you, but I know better now. You betrayed me when you slept with Jacob, and

I forgive you for that. But it doesn't change the fact that when that happened, the girl I lusted over had died. I don't need you anymore. I don't want you anymore. You are no longer a part of my life and I have to get back to those that are. I've moved on, and so have you. It's time to put you back where you belong. In memory."

Rebecca's eyes turned ice cold. "You will not leave me again, Thomas. The child you knew did die when you left, and it was because you didn't fight for me. Fight for me now, goddammit. Bring back the friend you so dearly remember and fuck me already."

"No. I won't do it."

"Fuck me, you bastard."

"Fuck yourself, you bitch," Thomas quickly shot back. "FUCK YOURSELF, YOU FUCKING BLACK HOLE!" The echo of his words blew Rebecca into millions of bright lights, like a swarm of lightning bugs scattering after a large object invaded their hive. Thomas closed his eyes and dropped to his knees as a sharp pain crushed his head. As the pain weakened and his nausea waned, Thomas slowly opened his eyes, hoping that Rebecca had truly disappeared. To his relief, she had, and in the distance, Thomas saw someone else sitting on the ground, rocking back and forth. As he cleared the blurriness from his eyes, he could make out the saddened features and knew right away who it was.

"Matthew!" Thomas ran to his friend, who held his arms out in the air as if he were holding something and crying over it. Thomas knelt down next to him and grabbed his shoulders.

"Matthew, what's wrong? What happened?"

"She's dead, Thomas... she's dead," Matthew choked out under his tears.

"Who's dead, Matthew? Who?"

It took a long time for Matthew to reach deep into his throat and say the words. When they came out, it felt as if Matthew was vomiting up his soul. "Kaleena."

Thomas lowered his head in a knowing sigh and then moved to the front of Matthew to try and look into his eyes.

"Matthew. Kaleena's not dead. Do you hear me?"

"No," Matthew whined. "No. She's gone. She's gone and I wasn't there to help her. I wasn't there to stop them."

"Matthew. It's not real. Nothing happened to Kaleena."

"I wasn't there to stop the monsters from attacking her."

"Matthew."

"I wasn't there to keep her safe."

"Matthew!"

"I wasn't ever there when I should have been."

"Matthew look at me." Thomas grabbed Matthew's head. The man put up a fight at first, unwilling to take his eyes off of his dead daughter, but quickly gave up, finding weakness much easier to handle than strength.

Thomas looked into those reddened, puffy eyes and made sure he was acknowledging him before: "Matthew, you have to listen to me. Kaleena is not dead. The black hole wants to keep you from opening that door. It's trying to kill you and has chosen your daughter as the means to do so. She is not in your arms right now, Matthew. It's an illusion to keep you from finding your true goal. We're close. We're almost free. But you have to fight it. You have to believe that what I'm saying is true. Matthew. Do you believe me?"

"She's dead, Thomas…" Matthew squeaked out.

"Take another look, Matthew. She's alive. And she needs you now."

Matthew closed his eyes, allowing more tears to roll down his cheeks. When he opened his eyes, he saw Kaleena, eleven years old and smiling brightly up at him.

"Can you protect me?" she said.

Matthew's troubled tears turned to joy and he kissed his daughter's forehead. She giggled ecstatically. "You're not dead," he said. "Thank God. You're not dead."

Thomas remained silent as Matthew continued to kiss the air between his arms. All he could do was wait for him to release his guilt for good.

"Daddy, I never blamed you for what happened. It was never your fault. You were the one that came back for me when it mattered."

Matthew curled his lips into a regretful, yet loving smile as Kaleena reached up to touch his cheek. "Close your eyes now, Daddy. Close your eyes."

"I don't want to lose you again."

"Just close your eyes," Kaleena whispered. Matthew couldn't fight it anymore. He did as his daughter asked. As he did, her touch faded from his cheek. He heard a light whisper in the air around him.

Now help me, before I am lost forever.

Matthew opened his eyes. His daughter was gone. "Kaleena?" he asked cautiously, lowering his arms. He looked up and saw Thomas kneeling in front of him.

"Thomas?"

Thomas sighed relief, letting out a breath he hadn't even realized he was holding. "Thank God, Matthew."

"Where's Kaleena?"

"I don't know. But we're going to find her."

"How?"

I need you both to listen to me now. Gydressina's light, beautiful voice rose among the walls. *The door we are all seeking is right behind you.*

All Thomas could see was a wall. "There's nothing there."

There is. But you have to believe there is.

Matthew wiped his eyes clear before standing with Thomas and walking to the wall.

Believe in it.

"What do we do?" Thomas asked, knowing Matthew was still too distraught to do so.

Place your hands onto the wall and look deep within to find your reflections. When both of you have found them, call out for the door to open in your minds and feel the glass shatter among your hands.

"Thank you." Matthew pulled Thomas into his arms and hugged him.

"No problem."

Matthew composed himself quickly, and then: "Let's do this."

Thomas cracked a real smile for the first time since arriving in the catacombs and gave Matthew a slap on the back of the shoulder that turned into a tight squeeze. Both men placed their hands to the wall and stared into it as deeply as they could.

"Anything?" Matthew asked seconds after placing his hands on the wall.

"Give it time," Thomas said quietly. "Concentrate."

"How will we know when we've found our reflections?"

"I don't know. Just do it."

Matthew nodded, knowing Thomas couldn't see him, then looked intensely at the wall, trying desperately not to blink. Before long, the rock started swimming around him. His eyes became foggy and dry. But no matter how hard he concentrated (or thought he was concentrating), the pulsating rocks wouldn't allow him a reflection.

Until he blinked.

For a split second, a ghost of a shadow popped across his line of sight. So he blinked again. This time, the shadow was much larger, and with each consecutive blink, the ghost grew. He started blinking faster, and soon, Matthew could make out his own reflection blinking back at him.

"Blink, Thomas."

"What?"

"Blink. Quickly. And don't stop."

Thomas did as he was told and he too saw the growing shadow become his reflection. Suddenly, Matthew and Thomas were both staring at themselves inside the rock. The only word either thought of at that moment was:

Open!

The rocks suddenly became slick and smooth. Thomas wanted to pull away, but he heard Matthew say, "Steady," so he held strong and waited. The more the two men concentrated, the smoother the rock became until they felt small cracks begin to form underneath their warming fingers.

"Hold on," Matthew said as a small wind that seemed to be coming from between the gaps in their fingers blew around them. The men held their ground as the wall continued to crack until it shattered like a sheet of glass. They fell forward and hit the floor without noticing that no glass surrounded them. As the wind settled and the loud high-pitched echoes faded from their ears, pain sank into their bodies. They looked at each other and saw an old man staring back at them.

"Matthew?"

"Thomas?"

Both men looked over their frail skin in the soft green light coming from the center of the room. Layers of wrinkled skin drooped from Thomas's arms. Matthew's neck and chin waggled loosely. Thomas found a party of liver spots covering his arms, while what was left of Matthew's hair was wisped in white.

"What happened?" Matthew croaked, his voice dry and scratched.

"We must have been in there too long," Thomas said.

"You got out just in time." Gydressina added. She was standing next to a door, her own withered body looking more decrepit than ever.

"Where'd you come from," Matthew choked out.

"I was with you the whole time," Gydressina explained, her voice slow and withered. She slowly slid her way past the men. "I was simply within a separate plain of life."

"A separate plain...?"

"Yes. More to the truth, it was you who were in an alternate existence."

"How?" was all Thomas could utter in his own softened voice.

"It's not something of which you would understand, Thomas. The point is, you were both integral in helping us all make it through."

"But look at us," Matthew said as he stood, his bones cracking with every slight movement.

"Your bodies have deteriorated, yes," Gydressina said. "But your minds are as young as they've ever been."

"What does that matter if our bodies are dead?" Thomas asked, he himself feeling as if he needed a cane to even move his legs.

"Do not allow your mind to believe that your bodies control them. If you believe that you're young, your bodies will react as such." Gydressina continued to move forward, sliding ever so slowly toward the opposite wall. "To an extent," she added before chortling a coughed laugh.

Matthew and Thomas couldn't help but laugh a bit themselves. *Mind over matter*, Matthew thought as he looked around the room for the first time.

He noticed a small patch of the wall behind him that seemed to have been cleared of all dirt. As he sauntered up to it, he also noticed something had been etched within it. He rubbed his bony hand along the wall, wiping more dirt and dust away. And though his vision had become incredibly impaired, he could tell that the etchings were the same symbols that had carved onto Kara's tablets, as well as the stones in the ocean and the artifact from Bermuda.

"Would you look at this?" Matthew whispered. Thomas turned to him. Apparently, his hearing hadn't gone the way of the old man. He saw Matthew staring at the wall and then noticed the symbols. He turned to the wall behind him and rubbed some of the dirt away to reveal even more.

"My god," Thomas muttered.

Matthew and Thomas wiped all the dirt from the wall as far as they could reach, uncovering text across every inch of the room. They were so enthralled by their discovery, they hadn't noticed Gydressina step up to the spot that had already been cleared before their arrival and place her forehead against it with her hands on either side. She stood perfectly still.

"I've found them," she said after Matthew and Thomas had stopped cleaning to admire what they had uncovered. They no longer registered the aches and pains in their bodies, the text having driven their minds away from their age.

Gydressina pulled her head away from the wall and turned to Matthew. "Come."

"We can't leave," Matthew said quickly. "Look at all of this."

"It is the origins and history of Ediinis," Gydressina said softly, unfazed.

"Its origins," Thomas chimed in. "You mean a genesis?"

"Yes."

"What a find," Matthew said.

"We cannot stay, Matthew."

"Why not."

"Because I've found your daughter. And we must get to her before it's too late."

It was the words "too late" that woke Matthew from his trance.

"What?"

"We must get to Kaleena and seek her help. If we do not, then Ediinis will fall."

Matthew finally remembered what his true goal had been. Kaleena was alive and she needed him — as much as he needed her.

"Well let's go, then," Thomas said. "We can come back for this after we find her."

"And save the city," Gydressina added.

Matthew nodded. "Lead the way."

Atlantis – Women's Quarters – 8 hours 52 minutes after arrival

Trishen sat in the corner by the window, half of her focus on the cityscape, the other half on Jaime being comforted by Patricia and Kara. She thought about going over and calming her as well, but she somehow couldn't get up the strength to do it, believing she was just as in need of comforting as Jaime. She felt violated by whatever Cephis had done; it was almost as if he'd raped her — which didn't seem to be the case for the others, who appeared to be no more affected than if their boyfriends had felt them up in the basement while their parents were out on a date. But if that were the case, why had he chosen her over everyone else? Perhaps it was because she'd never been pregnant before, but as far as she knew, neither had Kara. In fact, Trishen seemed to have more in common with her than she did anyone else. So why wasn't Kara as affected as she was?

Unable to watch the shower of condolences being lavished upon Jaime any longer, Trishen turned her entire focus to the city, toying with the possibility that

she was only feeling this way because, unlike the others (probably even Kara, though she couldn't be completely sure), she had never been with a man. It didn't mean she'd never loved before, far from it. Trishen chose to keep herself chased throughout life, even with the advent of love in her life. And even if it was never reciprocated, her love for others always remained strong. None more so than with Gavin. A richer friend than she could ever have imagined, Gavin was one step away from Trishen's first sexual experience. From the first moment she glimpsed that ghosted visage of him through the water glistening in the warm sun, she felt a connection to him that would never be fully realized. In fact, when she first saw his scuffed features looking down on her as she climbed the depths of the sea, it was the first time she actually couldn't wait to get to the surface, if only to quell her curiosity.

Coming out of the water, she couldn't see much through her fogging goggles, blurred also by the tears of water stuck to them, but she could tell that the stranger was watching her closely. Her muscles contracted as she pulled the mask off and locked eyes with the man that somehow appeared on the boat like some kind of angel. *How long have I been down there?* was her first thought.

"Trishen, yeah?" the man said holding out his hand. Trishen flashed a smile and took his gracious help out of the water and onto the boat.

"And you are?" she said nonchalantly, hiding her soft blush of embarrassment.

"Did you find it?" Jaime called out before the man could answer. She came around the side of the fishing boat they'd rented from the docks to find a rare species of crab that got caught up in a fisherman's net. Jaime had been excited about the find because that specific type of crab should not have been where it was found and she needed to find out if it was a stray — a fluke really — or if it was a change in migratory habits. The find could have led her to a much more substantial payday.

"Sorry, Jaime," Trishen said, removing the rest of her headgear and releasing a clump of wet, tattered hair down her back. "I couldn't find anything. If there were more, they're long gone. My guess is it was a stray, pulled here by another fishing boat, or even a shark."

"Damn," Jaime said under her breath, a cigarette dangling softly from her lips. "I had a good feeling about this one." And then again, "Damn."

Trishen turned back to the man still standing next to her. Jaime took a hit from the cigarette and, noticing Trishen's steely gaze, pulled it from her mouth. "Oh, sorry," she said, blowing the smoke out before finishing. "Trishen, this is Gavin. Gavin, Trishen."

Gavin gave Trishen a quick wink to go along with his gorgeous smirk and adorable salute.

"And what net trapped him aboard?" Trishen said, trying to mask her attraction.

"Gavin's that new videographer I told you about," Jaime said without really thinking. Her focus remained on other possibilities she may have missed or what else she might be able to find to keep the trip from being a total bust.

"Ah," Trishen said. A new flare of excitement rose to her eyes. This boy was in it for the long haul. "Well, I do hope you're better with a camera than the last guy."

"Yeah?" Gavin said, flashing that carefree smile again as Trishen stripped herself of her oxygen tank and weight belt. "What happened to the last guy?"

"I can't confirm, but I think a shark may have been involved after he lost about three days's worth of footage."

Jaime watched curiously. She'd never really seen Trishen this witty; at least not with someone she'd never met before.

Gavin chuckled. "Look, if I lose three days's worth of footage, you have my permission to turn me into chum."

Trishen blushed as Gavin never looked away. It was almost as if they were trading secret thoughts behind Jaime's back. "Don't worry," she said. "You'll find out soon enough that we'll keep that promise, and maybe more." Trishen winked, feeling a bit foolish afterward, suddenly wanting nothing more than to hide in a hole for the next few days. She chose the next best thing. "I've gotta go take myself a quick shower. I'll see you back out here for a bite."

"As long as it's not me you're biting," Gavin said quickly without a hint of shyness.

Trishen shook her head sheepishly and walked past Jaime, tapping her hand on her shoulder as she did. "I think he's a keeper," Trishen whispered, taking one last glance at Gavin before heading down below deck. Jaime chuckled lightly.

Over the next few months, as Trishen tried to find even the slightest amount of courage to stop flirting and just tell Gavin how she felt, she took a back seat to Jaime and Gavin's blossoming relationship. The more time they spent with each other, the more they flirted, and the more Trishen separated herself from the possibility of ever having that kind of relationship with him. She liked him, more than she'd ever liked anyone before (she wasn't ready to call it love, though deep down she knew it had to be), but she didn't want to cause trouble, or turn this into some soap opera love triangle that wouldn't end well for her. Gavin was a great friend and a great videographer (in her humble opinion; the footage he shot was masterful and brilliant). She didn't want to lose him as either. She'd always hold a small spot for him in her heart, one which now seemed more like a hole that could never be filled. Thomas, with his kindness and compassion, had started to find his way into filling it once again, but he, too, was lost to her now. But the more she thought about it, hoping to catch a glimpse of Thomas running through the causeways across the city, or coming to her rescue like Superman for Lois, the more it became clear that Thomas wasn't just filling the hole vacated by Gavin's death. It was much more than that — a new type of love Trishen had never encountered. As she compared Thomas to Gavin, the attraction she held for the latter wasn't love at all; it was a simple infatuated adoration. Both men were kind and gentle, funny and understanding, but what set Thomas apart was his clear affection for more than just her body or her mind or her friendship. It frightened her. Within what could only have been a twenty-four-hour period, Trishen had lost not one, but two great friends and possible loves. And so, it seemed, had Jaime. It made her feel a bit sick to her stomach, really. Not because of the nausea swimming through her body; not because Jaime had garnered all of the attention; but because, turning back to Jaime, it looked as if she had just taken a ride through hell, and Trishen could do nothing more but sulk in her own jealousy. If it hadn't been for the graciousness of that woman, she'd probably be living on the street with a boat full of debt. Jaime had given her her first real job, and she never truly thanked her for that. It was time she set her grade school pettiness aside and do what she could for who she considered her best friend.

Trishen climbed to her feet and inched over to Jaime. She held her arms across her stomach, hoping she wouldn't suddenly vomit all over the place. *Deep breaths*, she thought. *Deep breaths.* As she got closer, she couldn't hear anyone talking aside from a few murmurs of, "Are you sure you're okay?", "How can I help," and other such chattering. Jaime looked as if she were ready to throw up herself, out of sickness of having to continually repeat the same things over and over. To break the monotony of the comfort hounds, Trishen stepped around Patricia, took a deep breath to make sure regurgitation wouldn't be attached to her question and asked, "What did he say?"

When Jaime looked up, everyone saw the ghostly pale color of her pupils, hidden behind the red stroked eyelids that looked as if someone had sliced a razor around them. She didn't blink (possibly couldn't blink) and her voice was pitched as if she had something clogging her throat. It could have been a small lump of fear, but most likely it was a remnant of her being strangled.

"It's so clear," Jaime began, seemingly unable to talk about what happened, but completely aware she needed to let it out. "When he had me up, I could hear him in my head, and at the same time, I could see... see... images." Jaime's breaths became labored and her mouth hissed a subtle amount of air between her slightly agape lips.

"What were they?" Kara asked, intrigued.

Jaime shook her head. "I... I... don't know, really..." Suddenly her body convulsed in a quick bite of freezing pain that left a river of goose bumps in its wake.

"Are you okay," Patricia asked again for the hundred-and-umpteenth time.

"Yeah, yeah," Jaime stuttered. "It's just the images... thinking about them... they... they..."

"Okay, that's enough," Trishen said. "You don't have to say anything. We get it."

"No... no you don't," Jaime said, more forceful now. "Those images, they were like a mind-fuck so rich, so dark, so fucking roasted... I couldn't believe I even still existed. It was as if a flood of memories I never experienced poured into my head and tried to eat my flesh." Jaime started laughing hysterically, unable to control it. "Actually..." more whimpers of laughter before: "Actually, they weren't really memories at all. It was more like a ghost raping my body to the point of excruciating blindness." Her eyes glistened with incoherence. "Does any of that make any sense to anyone?"

Kara didn't want to press the matter, feeling as if it would drive Jaime even deeper into hysteria. Trishen felt her stomach grow more nauseous even thinking about it. Patricia, on the other hand —

"You just described a life with my husband."

Kara reacted the strongest, calling Patricia an inconsiderate bitch under her breath (and possibly a few more swears no one could make out). Trishen felt a bit awkward about it, as it did seem somewhat inconsiderate, but knowing Patricia for as long as she had, she wanted to laugh. Luckily, she wouldn't have to hold it in for long. It took a few seconds for what Patricia said to register, but once it had, Jaime fell into another fit of uncontrollable laughter. Trishen and Patricia were unable to contain themselves and joined her.

"What the hell?" Kara asked as Jaime fell to her knees, coughing through the pain in her chest that had been inflicted by the laughter.

"Hell doesn't describe my husband, Reeses," Patricia said, doubling down on the laughter. Kara wasn't sure if it was a release of the pent-up tension that had been hovering over the group for so long, or simply one of those fits someone gets when they're stressed... or drunk. Kara watched a moment longer as the three women wiped tears from their eyes. Eventually, she joined in, though her laughter seemed more out of courteousness than actual humor.

After a while, Jaime felt her lungs burning. She tried to contain the laughter and regulate her breaths, but both seemed to be unstoppable as thoughts of Patricia's comment continued to fuel the fire... or was it simply thinking of Patricia that kept it going? She had to think about something else quick before her lungs burst apart. Then again, dying of laughter wouldn't be the worst way to go.

"Oh, yeah, and which way would that be?" Matthew asked. Jaime had been seeing Matthew for about three months and they had reached that point in their relationship where they seemed to hold hands everywhere they went, didn't care about where or when they conducted an extreme make out session, and talked for hours on end while cuddling on the couch watching some old movie on AMC with the sound off or canoodling in bed with the light sounds of Kenny G sending them into blissful dreams.

Though she was ready to go the distance with him, they hadn't slept together yet. Jaime admired Matthew for that. She respected his tenacity to keep things slow. But it never stopped her from testing the waters with an accidental touch of his groin or dressing in front of him, lingering in her lingerie a bit longer than she normally would have otherwise. Every so often, he allowed her to go a little farther, reaching the point to where she could gently pet his penis over his pants, which she found herself doing without really thinking when they broke into the discussion about the worst ways to die.

"I don't know," she answered, shifting her head to rest it against his neck. "Probably after being tortured for answers to something, which you finally give up after hours, only to find out they always intended to kill you."

"Okay," Matthew said. "Way to spoil the mood."

Jaime laughed. "I'm sorry." She kissed his neck, setting the table for a long-standing hickey. It seemed to help, as Matthew grew more aroused. As Jaime sucked on his neck for the next several minutes, Jaime felt his hands begin to explore her breasts. She wanted to take off her top and allow Matthew the freedom to roam her chest without obstruction, but she restrained herself, instead asking a simple question. "Do you think I'm sexy?"

"Yeah, of course," he said through a jitter of arousal. Her hand had sped up along his crotch. It seemed as if he wanted her to stop, but couldn't ask her to.

"Then why don't you want to have sex?"

"I do," he said. "God, I do. But I don't want to be foolish. I want to wait until we both know for sure."

"Know what for sure?" Jaime said.

"You know." Matthew shifted slightly. Jaime lowered her head to watch as she finished the job.

"Aren't we?"

"I-I… just need to know for sure."

For some reason Matthew held back the word Jaime clearly knew he was inferring. But she wasn't about to let him off the hook so quickly.

"Know what for sure?" she giggled.

Matthew reached his climax, and as he was about to release, the words came out in a high-pitch squeal. "That we're in love."

A wetness formed around Jaime's fingertips and she started to laugh, both because of the ejaculation and for the girlie outburst. "Oh, right, perfect," Matthew said, tearing off for the bathroom.

"No wait," Jaime tittered as she tried to stop laughing. "Come back, please."

Matthew walked back into the bedroom, his cheeks fire red. Jaime couldn't control another sudden outburst of joy and Matthew had to mask a hint of anger. He was about to leave when Jaime got up on her knees and wiped some tears away. "Wait. Come back here." She slid across to the edge of the bed and grabbed the top of his jeans. "Come here," she giggled softly, pulling him toward her. "I wasn't laughing *at* you." She wrapped her arms around his neck. "I am so grateful for your sincerity and your kindness, Matthew, and I am so in love with your integrity." Holding his gaze for a long while in silence, Jaime cracked a smile every so often as her heart fluttered, feeling his doing cartwheels much the same. Finally:

"I do love you, Matthew. I love you so deeply." She kissed him with a passion she hadn't ever felt with Benjamin. Somehow this love was different, deeper, more alive, yet much subtler at the same time. "I love you," she said again.

"I love you," Matthew returned and laid her back on the bed. One hand filtered

through her hair as his other caressed the form fitting curvature of her butt. "I love you," he whispered.

"I love you," she whispered back. "I truly do…" Jaime paused a second, wondering if she should even say the other thing she was thinking, but it escaped nonetheless. "Even if you are a premature ejaculating little prissy."

Matthew let go as Jaime erupted in laughter. She rolled around on the bed, her lungs and stomach growing tense with joyful pain. "Laugh it up," Matthew said, real anger tickling his eyes and voice. He returned to the bathroom and leaned against the sink, unable to acknowledge the cold reflection in the mirror as his girlfriend laughed hysterically in the background. Jaime felt extremely guilty, but knew he'd get over it. It wasn't as if he'd never teased her plenty of times before. But unlike being ragged on for her cooking skills, she had attacked his manhood, and that helped her laughter wane quickly. She had to make up for it.

As quietly and as lightly as she could, Jaime slid off the bed and walked to the bathroom. Matthew must not have heard her because his muscles snapped a bit when she wrapped her arms around his cold waist. "I'm sorry, sweetie." Her own breath ricocheted off his neck as she unbuckled his pants. Matthew turned around. Jaime could tell whatever resentment he may have had toward her jocularity had been washed away. She slipped her hands between his thighs and his pants, helping them crumple to the floor. In recognition of his acceptance, Matthew picked her cheeks into his hands and kissed her. They were soon out of their clothes and in the shower, making love for the first time that night. It was the night Jaime truly fell in love with Matthew and it was the first memory she could recall that hadn't been bent in despair by Cephis. It led to several other memories she'd forgotten that brought her joy and contentment, and she began to cherish each and every moment that helped banish the sinister, deathly thoughts from her mind. Kaleena once again rose to the forefront, and she knew her daughter would be the strength to help her lead her team out of this damned captivity.

"He wants to impregnate us," Jaime finally whispered, her throat clear and soft. Her eyes were no longer glazed over and she appeared more vibrant.

"What?" Kara asked quickly. She wasn't sure she heard her correctly, but it was confirmed when Jaime grabbed Patricia's hand to help her to her feet.

"He's going to impregnate us." Jaime looked around at the other girls. They all looked stunned and confused.

"I don't think so," Patricia said with a deep chortle. "If you think this bitch is going through another three-day pregnancy, you're shittin' yourself."

"How?" Kara said, ignoring Patricia completely. She could tell Trishen had the same question on her mind.

"When he had me up there," Jaime said, walking to the door, "I felt everything." She looked like a new woman, determined and fresh, as if nothing had ever happened. She started playing around with the keypad again as she rambled on at a lightning pace. "Cephis spoke to me about why we're here and why we're so special. He mentioned I was the leader and that I'd either talk you into what they wanted or lead you to your deaths. During it all, I could sense something fiercer and deceptive. He wasn't trying to hide it from me, but he was, you know? It was like he knew I was listening, and in a way, he didn't. I could feel his desire, but it wasn't for me. It was for my womb. In fact, I felt a growth swelling inside me as he held me up, like there was a child growing inside. I knew it wasn't true, because all I could feel was Kaleena. It was her old presence; I know it was. You know, like how I felt when I was originally pregnant with her. But he tried to make me believe it was something different. That was when I heard his plan. He's going to impregnate all of us and the children that are born will be sent around the world, to grow and live as normal children until the day of…"

Jaime's fingers ran the course of the keypad, quickly and methodically. Her brow furrowed every so often, but her determination grew with every new combination.

"The day of what?" Trishen said for the rest of the group.

"The day…" Jaime started, but couldn't finish.

Kara could tell there was something stopping her from saying what she so desperately wanted to say, but instead of prying further, she had a different question,

one Patricia seemed to have as well, since it was her that spoke up first. "And what if we don't want to have a kid? What are they going to do? Rape us?"

"No, no. No, of course not. The Atlanteans don't need to have sex."

"What?" Kara asked, curious. Her thoughts began to float through the tablets. In an odd way the entire idea made complete sense. Trishen felt the same and tried to hide her unease by tightening her arms across her stomach. She started to believe Cephis had already begun the process on her and that something was growing inside of her.

"Hell... what's the fun in that?" Patricia asked softly.

"Do you know how they do it?" Kara said.

"When Cephis was here, he touched us. Do you remember?"

"How could I forget," Patricia said with a small shiver of excitement.

"He was checking us."

"He needed to find out if we were fertile enough to have children," Kara finished. She could hear Matthew reading one of the translations from the tablets — *"And with the touch of my hand to her soft, smooth stomach, I lay to rest the absence of life within the womb of the lady gentle."* She hadn't quite understood what it meant, as the other pieces of the text seemed to be out of sequence, but now that she understood how Cephis planned on reproducing, it was all becoming clear.

"Yes."

"Whoa, whoa, whoa. Wait just one fucking minute," Patricia interjected. "Are you trying to tell me that this fucker wants to implant me with a child, force me to give birth, and then send it away like a piece of meat?"

"That about sums it up," Jaime said.

"My god," Kara whispered, turning and looking around the room.

"Hell no. If I'm forced to go through that pain again, I'm damn well gonna raise that damn thing myself. You think I'm gonna have a kid against my will and then let some other bastard family take care of it?"

"What are you doing?" Trishen asked as if Patricia hadn't been rambling on and on.

"I don't believe he's going to kill us, at least not before he gets the children he wants. But whether I can convince you or not, there's no way I'm about to allow us all to be incubators for our own destruction."

"But the code's impossible to break," Kara said.

"Not impossible," Jaime said under a thin smile. "Not if you saw the way to reconfigure the formula."

"Formula?" Kara walked to Jaime to get a closer look at the pad. Jaime's fingers seemed to move faster through each line. "Is it alive?"

"Not as much as it is artificial. The entire city is connected. Through what, I'm not sure, but you only need to know what connects it all to understand how to use it. Kaleena knows. She doesn't realize it, but Kaleena's the key to running the city. She's the one that lit this place up. In a way, it's her blood that runs through the walls of this entire thing. So…"

"It's just a matter of knowing her genetic code and transferring it in."

Jaime lit up, her eyes still locked on the keypad.

"It's so simple."

"Not that simple. It's getting harder and harder to see the code. It's like the longer I'm not around Cephis, the more the memory fades. But I'm trying my damnedest to hold onto it. Because once I get it…"

Jaime's attention fell attune to the keyboard. Everything and everyone around her disappeared. It was just her and the door, and she was going to get it open. She had to, for the sake of her friends, but more importantly, for the sake of Kaleena. Before she could get the words out of her mouth, the keypad flashed a bright green and a soft musical note shocked her fingers and rang through her ear.

"…we can get the hell out of this shithole." Jaime stepped back. A light burn rested in her fingertips, which had been deeply reddened. After a few seconds, the doors cracked open. Jaime couldn't have been more excited.

"Fuck me," Patricia blurted out, enthusiasm and intrigue floating though the sentiment.

"You can say that again," Kara said, watching the door open.

"Fuck me," Patricia said again.

Everyone stood motionless as the doors came to a stop. None of them were sure if it was because they were afraid of what would be waiting on the other side of the door, which for now simply looked like an empty hallway and stairwell, or if they were simply stuck in this room, unable to move by some weird mind control force field.

Patricia was the first to brave the possibility of what may or may not happen to them if they took a step out the door. Her breaths were heavier than normal as she passed the threshold of the room, but she didn't seem to notice. When she was a few feet into the hall, she looked around, believing she would be shot dead on the spot. But nothing happened. All was quiet and serene. She turned back to the others. "Well, what the hell are we waiting for?"

Kara and Jaime turned to one another with a great appreciation for the other. In a way, it had been Kara's speech that helped Jaime believe in the possibility of Kaleena still being alive, and what it meant if she wasn't. If she was still alive, she was going to find her; if she wasn't, there was a purpose for her death and she wasn't going to wait around to keep that purpose from fruition. Kara saw an extremely vibrant, intelligent woman. She was genuine, special, and Matthew was right to regret losing her — letting her go the way he did. Kara was now determined to follow her wherever she needed to go.

"Let's go find your daughter," she said.

Jaime nodded and the two of them joined Patricia just outside the door.

"So, which way do we go?" Patricia asked.

"I have no idea," Jaime said, taking in the majesty of it all.

"Down." Trishen still stood like a rock in the center of the room.

"What are you doing, Trish? Come on."

"No, I can't."

"What are you talking about?" Jaime's desire to track Kaleena faded slightly.

"I can't do this," Trishen said. "I need to stay here."

"Don't make me have to knock you upside the head," Patricia said, storming

toward Trishen. She reached out to grab her arm, but Trishen was quick to step away from her before she could.

"I'm not going."

"Trishen." There was a sweetness in Jaime's voice that Kara had never heard before. There was a love there that she once felt, and in a weird way, still felt for Diana. Even in death, Kara had a deep connection to her sister, one that would never be broken. This unexplainable bond between Jaime and Trishen was powerful. Even though Kara still didn't know any of these women very well, she knew they thought of themselves as a family. Diana felt closer to her than she had in a long time.

"You can't stay," Kara said softly.

"I have to."

"What are you talking about?" Seeing Patricia angry was really odd. "You're coming with us."

This time Patricia was able to grab Trishen's arm, but she yanked it away so fiercely, she lost her footing and fell to the ground. A sharp pain stung her stomach as she landed. She rolled over onto her back to try and ease the pain.

"What the hell?" Patricia yelled.

"Patricia," Jaime called out. She started to head back into the room, but Kara placed her hand on her arm. Jaime looked back with a bit of a sadness hovering above her features. Kara simply shook her head. She saw what was happening here; it was the same type of situation she was in when Diana packed her bags.

"They're not going to let me go, Kar," Diana said, slamming a handful of jeans into her suitcase. "They're dead set against it. I mean, I thought I could count on you to be more supportive about all this."

"Can you blame me. You're barely eighteen."

"What does that matter?" Diana scoured her drawers for other parcels of clothes she might want to take with her on the trip. "I'm suffocating, here. I need to just be by myself and explore."

"Look, I'm not saying you shouldn't go. I'm just saying we should talk more about it. Get more of a plan squared away before you flitter off into the unexpected."

"Kara, believe me, I wish I could." Diana finally acknowledged her presence. "But if I don't do it now, I'm never going to be able to." She grabbed a few more garments of underwear, some of which looked like strings of dental floss, others that laced around her fingers with a silky fluidity. Where had she gotten those anyway? And what was she planning to do with them? Kara wanted to support her sister so badly and hated her parents for asking her to talk her out of it. She knew her sister better than anyone, and knew once she had an idea stuck in her head, it wasn't going anywhere. Besides, she needed this time to herself, to see the world before she was tied down to a job, a husband, a few kids that would throw up all over her and tear up everything she'd worked for just to swear at you because they won't allow them to go off to Europe for a summer. But she was also her little sister. She had a duty to protect her. Not from life, which always seemed to come up and bite you in the ass when you least expect it (whether it be with the venom of pain or the elixir of love), but from herself.

"Just tell me you have some sort of plan," Kara finally said as Diana zipped up her bag.

"Not really. I just want to let the world carry me where it pleases. I want to let go and see different cultures and lands that are out there waiting to be explored." Diana sat down on her bed and cupped her hands together in her lap. "I'd expect you to know better than anyone what that feels like."

"What do you mean?"

"You're traveling the world all the time. You get to see new places, you get to meet new people, understand new cultures."

"Diana, that's my job. I have to do all of that."

"But it wouldn't be your job if deep down you didn't want to do it." Diana walked over to Kara and took her hands. "Admit it. You love being able to swarm the world with nothing more than your suitcase in tow and just open your eyes and discover."

Kara wasn't sure how to answer. By agreeing with her, Kara would be condoning

Diana's insubordination. If she disagreed, she probably wouldn't speak to her ever again, and that was far more important to her than any level of recognition from her parents.

"Look me in the eye and tell me you don't love traveling," Diana said.

Kara squeezed her sister's hands as she explored those beautiful, young, hazel eyes, full of loss with a hint of wonderment and joy just ready to escape. How could she possibly talk her into staying when it was clear she needed to spread her wings and become a woman on her own terms? Kara never once thought of ever going against her parent's wishes for anything; she trusted them to know better. But a small part of her always believed that she missed out on something because of it. Kara had gone off to college right out of high school, got an internship while studying for her Master's degree and dated three guys in the process, each one a little bit worse and less compassionate than the next.

Her high school sweetheart went to school on the opposite coast and when the phone calls got fewer and fewer, and Kara began to spend more time studying, the relationship faded away like a cloud on the wind until she had completely forgotten about him. She tried calling him once after breaking up with a boy she met in a French class who was more interested in kissing than in an actual relationship, but the phone had been disconnected. She figured that either he no longer wanted her in her life or he had just forgotten about her too. The third was a date her room-mate set her up on, a childish dog of a man who was so disgusting and rude and perverse that Kara wished that it had all been a dream. She never had the chance to date anyone else since then, as her love and passion was stolen by her job. She knew she'd never been in love and was hoping her sister wouldn't be offered up to gorge on the same fate. She prayed her sister would find love someday, and to get that chance, Diana had to discover herself first.

"I love it, I'll admit," Kara finally let slip.

"Then you know why I can't stay here. I need this."

Again, Kara saw the truth in Diana's eyes. She may not physically look like it, but she was more than ready for this.

"Talk to them," Kara said, hoping to convince her one last time to at least reconcile with her parents before leaving. "Let them know all of this."

"I've already tried. It won't work."

After a short pause: "Will you at least call them? After you've landed?" Kara felt shame race through her body, but it was all she could ask. She knew her parents wouldn't understand any of this. They got married out of high school and have never left the small burg they were both born into. They were traditional; they were routine. Anything that broke that routine scared them, and in a way, Kara grew to enjoy that idea as well. Diana wouldn't be able to handle it.

Diana let out a hiss of a scream and gave Kara a huge hug. "Thank you, thank you."

"Promise me," Kara said again, waiting for her sister to let go. When she did, she looked at her with a parental gaze. "Promise me."

"I promise. I'll call them the minute I land."

"And when is that?" Kara asked slyly.

"I don't know exactly. Why?"

"Because I want to be as far away from the wrath as possible when you do." Kara finally broke her own smile as Diana's grew even larger (if that was even possible). She scooped Diana into her arms and held her, a feeling that this might be the last time she saw her as a young sister. Something in her gut told her that when she saw Diana again, she would no longer be a child, so she wanted to hold onto this moment for as long as possible, knowing she'd eventually have to let go and let life do as it pleased.

"When's your flight?"

"In a couple of hours. I've told Mom I'm going to hang out at Jessica's and probably sleep there."

"And if she calls?"

"Jessica knows the plan. Don't worry. I've got it all covered."

"I can't believe I'm doing this," Kara whispered as Diana grabbed her suitcase off the bed. "I come over here to talk you out of this and here I am helping you.

I'm going to Hell, I just know it."

"Not if I have anything to say about it," Diana said. She gave Kara a wink and a kiss on the cheek before jumping out the front door, unable to get to the car fast enough. Kara lingered by the door as Diana put her suitcase in the trunk of Kara's beat-up Mazda Hatchback and wondered what amazing, eye-opening experiences the young girl was going to have and how much she would take away from it.

"Protect her, Lord," Kara whispered, grabbing hold of the cross that dangled from her necklace. "Protect her. For me."

Just as Kara had to let her sister go, even if it meant her death, Jaime would have to do the same for Trishen. And Jaime read it all in Kara's eyes.

"Let her go," Jaime said, more to herself than anyone else. She needed to hear the words before she acknowledged her decision. It wasn't long ago that she was on the opposite side of this dilemma when she tried to force everyone to let her go back into the ocean to rescue Gavin. She now understood what they all felt, and knew it had been the right thing for them to do.

"Trishen, come on," Patricia yelled, grabbing her arms and pulling her to her feet. "You never leave a man behind, isn't that your whole shtick?"

"Let her go," Jaime said louder. Patricia looked angry and confused.

"What?"

Jaime turned to Patricia with stern, motherly eyes. "We need to let her go."

"No, no way. I'm not leaving her here to die."

"I'll be okay," Trishen said, trying hard to catch her breath against the sharp pains flashing across her gut. "Trust me."

"But… we can't." Patricia now appeared soft, vulnerable. Any remnants of laughter and sarcasm were completely gone.

"I don't want to leave her, either," Kara chimed in, hoping she could use her own experience to help persuade Patricia. "But we have to trust her. She needs to do what she believes. If we don't let her, we're just going to suffocate her."

Tears filled Jaime's eyes as a flood of old memories came roaring back. She kept them under control, unwilling to let the others catch a glimpse of her own personal vulnerability. "She'll be okay," she said. "We may not like it, but she'll be okay. We have to listen to her."

Trishen had moved away from Patricia and was looking at Jaime with a great degree of appreciation. They knew what each was speaking of; their friendship — their love — grew in that moment.

"You better go before they realize what's happening," Trishen finally said, stronger and more assertive.

"She's right. Come on, Patricia."

Patricia was torn. She didn't want to leave Trishen behind, but knew her boss was right. She hadn't really seen it until now, but Trishen needed time to sort through her recent losses, to find whatever it was she was looking for. There was something she wasn't telling them and Patricia figured that whatever it was, it would most likely end up saving them all. In a way, the group wasn't leaving her behind; they were saving her from some unseen madness. And to understand where it stemmed from, she needed time, something that wouldn't be given to her if she came with them. Patricia was sure, when she was ready, she would find them again.

"You better come back to us," Patricia said sternly. "You got that."

Trishen cracked the slightest hint of a smile and nodded. "Get out of here. Go find Kaleena. She needs you more than I do."

Patricia waited a second longer and then left Trishen alone in the room. As the team disappeared down the stairwell, Trishen walked to the door, fighting back another round of nausea. The door was extremely heavy, but she somehow found a small extra bit of strength she didn't think she had to close them tight. Laying her head against the door to catch her breath, she fought with herself over whether she was actually doing the right thing. In the end, she knew Kaleena's life was more important than her own and she'd only slow the rest of the group down in searching for her. At least this way, she'd be able to face her inevitable death with dignity and the slightest bit of heroism.

Let it come; she was more than ready.

Atlantis – Lauren's Quarters – 9 hours 37 minutes after arrival

After Evey left with her companions, Lauren spent some time brushing her fingers through Kaleena's hair, thinking about her child and wishing it was her in her arms right now. She couldn't shake the feeling that Evey was making sure the two of them stayed linked. In an odd way, Lauren felt she was still feeding her daughter, connected to her by some energy-emitting umbilical cord. Whether it was a psychic energy that Evey needed in order to grow as fast as she was, or something much more than that, much deeper, Lauren sensed Evey's need for her strength, even when they were apart from one another. In turn, Evey gave Lauren a heartbeat that kept her quiet, calm. Stuck in between them like a symbolic womb, was Kaleena.

It wasn't long before Lauren's thoughts grew darker, spreading themselves across her mind in twisted revelations. It wasn't clear why they had become so dark, but they were instantly too much for her to handle. She lifted Kaleena up to the bed and grabbed the diary, opening it up to about the middle. She sat down on the floor beside Kaleena's head and started talking, flipping the pages every so often. Like before, Lauren didn't care that she wasn't reading anything; she just needed a reason to pour her thoughts out into the air around her. What she didn't expect was for the writings in front of her to change such that her thoughts were suddenly on the pages. She knew it couldn't have been possible, but she wanted to believe she was once again seven, sitting on her bed, her feet dangling in the air, rocking back and forth to the tune singing in her head as she wrote down her thoughts about school, her teacher, why she thought Bobby liked Sarah, and how they teased her about it all day. She could remember writing everything about her parents and her dreams of one day becoming a cooking girl who would work at the best, most fantastical restaurant that served only hamburgers and chicken fingers, and fries and milk. Ice cream, too, for that special occasion. Oh, and cake. She couldn't forget about the cake.

Lauren's cheeks sparkled as she saw Evey's smile laced upon her own childhood memory, relishing in the idea that she was doing the same exact thing right now. The problem was, she knew that wasn't the case. Whenever she thought of Evey, she couldn't help but feel a danger. Not for Evey, but for those she cared about. It was that thought — that Evey could possibly have some sort of evil agenda — that frightened Lauren enough to continue reading, hoping to subdue those feelings in favor of warmer ones. It didn't seem to help in the way she first hoped, though, as she rattled on about her relationship with Wallace and her devastating, inevitable trip to the abortion clinic. She spoke about her marriage, the calm before the storm and the hurricane that ripped her to shreds emotionally and damaged her physically. But then she started talking about her metaphysical resurrection when she met Matthew and started to believe there were actually nice men out in the world she could trust and respond to, that she could have a relationship with that had nothing to do with sexual attraction or lust. He'd taught her that the only relationship that can make a person happy is the one that person had with themselves. If that relationship were ever broken, no other relationship would be able to fix it. That was when her mind started to clear.

Even after the water forming around the rims of her eyes fogged her vision, she continued speaking, knowing that the simple act of letting it all out was, in a weird way, cleansing her. She had realized she'd never spoken to anyone about any of this before and it felt good to finally get it off her chest. No one was there to hear it (unless Kaleena was picking it all up in her sleep, which, for Lauren, didn't matter much if she was; she trusted Kaleena enough to keep all of her secrets, just as Kaleena trusted Lauren with hers), but she was the only one that needed to hear it. Her comfort was what she desired, and she was finally able to come to terms with the fact that she hadn't really grown at all as a person in the last few years. She'd simply chosen to hide her past and pretend it hadn't existed. And as she reached the last page of the diary and spoke her final words to the slumbering Kaleena, Lauren couldn't help but wonder if Evey had anything to do with washing all of her grief and regret away.

"I love you," Kaleena said. Her voice was lower than normal — almost a mix of Kaleena's natural voice and that of Henry's, as if he was using her as some kind of human bug to listen in on her conversation.

"What?" Lauren looked up to Kaleena. Although she was still asleep, the answer that came back was soft and sweet.

"Your life is a love you have hidden. Can you accept your future now that you have come to terms with your past?"

Lauren wiped away what moisture was left in her eyes and stood up. "I don't think I understand," she said, hoping for more that wouldn't come.

Kaleena instead opened her eyes. Upon seeing — and recognizing — Lauren: "What happened?"

Lauren quickly reached down and wrapped her arms around Kaleena. It was a hug, not just in the acknowledgment of Kaleena's awakening, but of her own as well. That and a warm hug for Evey, hoping that somehow Kaleena would act as a bridge in providing Evey the affection she most deserved.

As she let go, Kaleena couldn't help but chuckle.

"I'm sorry," Lauren said, laughing a few rogue tears away. "It's been a long time coming."

"What has?"

Lauren waved her hand nervously. "Nothing."

"Are you okay?" Kaleena giggled with confusion.

"I'm fine. The better question is, are *you* okay?"

Kaleena took a good long look at Lauren. She could tell she was telling her the truth and, in fact, Lauren looked a little more beautiful than before, freer in a metaphysical way. Her eyes were calm and there was a soft glow about her, which radiated a joy that felt almost addictive. She nodded and looked curiously around the room. "Where's the kid?" she asked, the infectious joy beginning to well up inside of her.

"She left with Adamus and his escort," Lauren said, her smile fading.

"And you just let her go?"

"I had to." After a contemplative pause: "She seemed happy, like she wanted to go with them. In fact, this may sound a bit stupid, but it almost felt like she was in control of them."

Kaleena remained confused, but saw that Lauren was even more so. Instead of pushing the matter any further, she said, "Do you know where they went?"

"I don't know, but before they left, I think I overheard them talking about you."

"What about me?"

Lauren paced away from Kaleena. When she wouldn't answer (say anything, for that matter), Kaleena feared the worst. She hadn't really believed Matthew or Jaime had died, but with Lauren's reaction, she felt maybe she'd just confirmed it. She had to be certain. "Lauren, don't do this. What is it?"

Lauren turned to her, realizing what Kaleena must be thinking. "Oh, God, Kaleena, no. It's not that, I promise."

Kaleena sighed in relief. "Then what is it?"

"I was a little distracted with you and Evey and everything, so I'm not sure I remember the exact words they used, but I think they said you were... cleansed."

"Cleansed? What does that mean?"

Lauren chuffed. "Your guess is as good as mine."

Cleansed, Kaleena thought, trying hard to think of what they may have been talking about.

"What do you remember when they were here?" Lauren said, thinking it might help her understand it better.

"Not much. I remember the smell of his breath and his hand on my cheek, thinking the whole time that he was about to rape me. Then I was ice cold and..." Kaleena raised her arms in a quiet shrug. "Nothing."

Lauren rubbed the corners of her mouth. "That's it?"

"Yeah. I mean, I can't even remember dreaming. Why?"

Lauren was silent a moment and then: "They mentioned something else... something that seemed to piss off the dominant one. I think it was a name..."

Kaleena waited patiently for Lauren to remember. When she did, she spit the name out as if she'd gotten shot with it. "Gydressina."

"Gydressina? Are you sure?"

"Yeah. Positive. Does it mean anything to you?"

Kaleena couldn't wrap her head around the name, but the more she thought about it, the more it made sense to her, as if she'd heard it before, had felt the name on her lips and was meant to help. "No," she said, knowing it wasn't the answer Lauren was hoping for.

"Are you sure?"

"Unless it's the name of the magistrate," Kaleena said without thinking.

"The magistrate?"

"The one that destroyed Atlantis and all of its people."

"Well, whoever she is, they all seemed rather scared of her." Lauren played with the wording in her head for a moment and then, "No, not scared. More annoyed, really."

"Annoyed? Like how?"

"Like they were mad at her for the whole cleansing thing. They said she was more powerful than they originally thought." Lauren's words came out a bit robotic now, as she hoped Kaleena wouldn't realize it was Evey that said those words. She still didn't want to believe it herself.

Kaleena nodded, unable to respond. She tried to understand it all, but couldn't seem to grasp the reality of any of it. Just a few days ago, she never would have thought she'd be standing in Atlantis. None of this made sense; then again, it all seemed to. "That must be why I'm here. To help Evey and her friends stop Gydressina once and for all."

"Why would you think that?"

"Simple deduction. Based on what you overheard and what Adamus has told me, Gydressina has been trying to destroy Atlantis for centuries."

"Yeah, okay. But how do you know we can trust them?"

"You trust Evey, don't you?"

Lauren hesitated. The circumstances wouldn't allow her to fully accept the premise, but deep down, she had to believe Evey wasn't out to hurt them, that she was fighting for the betterment of Atlantis and its people. "Yeah, yeah. I do," she finally said.

"Then trust me. If Gydressina is alive, I may be the only one that can stop her. Besides, if you're right and she did do something to me, well, then, she sure as hell is going to pay for it."

Don't be so quick to accept the truth.

The voice rang clear and vibrant. Though it sounded like it was only in her head, Kaleena could tell Lauren had heard it too.

"What was that?" Lauren asked.

Kaleena raised her finger to her lips and wiped her thoughts away. She then focused all of her energy on Lauren. *Quiet. Clear your mind.*

Lauren was aghast and couldn't help but stumble back. She'd spoken to Henry like this a little bit, but she had no idea Kaleena could do it too. What exactly had they done to her? It frightened her because it made it seem as if the Atlanteans were somehow transforming her into one of them.

She couldn't worry about that now; she had to do as Kaleena asked. So she nodded and tried hard to keep from thinking about anything. But the harder she tried, the more she thought. To fight the urge to drum up any memories, she selected a single word and repeated it over and over.

Evey. Evey. Evey. Evey.

Do not be frightened, the voice said. Kaleena couldn't help but feel whoever was communicating with them could read her thoughts no matter how much she suppressed them. She was a powerful being, that's for sure.

Gydressina? Kaleena asked.

Yes, child. I am she. Kaleena wanted to convey anger, but the crystalline voice wouldn't allow her to feel anything but warmth and compassion.

Where are you?

I am near.

What do you want with me?

I only wish to bring to you what you desire most.

Kaleena's heart stopped. She had to consciously force herself to take a breath before her lungs stopped as well. *Could it be possible?*

The answer came as the door of the room opened. The skeletal figure of a decaying old woman stood in the center of the hall, staring at Kaleena with hallowed eyes. This was the great beauty of the magistrate that lined the walls like a goddess?

Kaleena's attention was quickly drawn to the older looking gentlemen who stood next to the magistrate. They had to be nearing their nineties, but their steps seemed light and quick. As she took a harder look at the one on the left, she swore she saw a resemblance to someone in her past. Her breaths quickened and her body stiffened as the whisper of the man she most wanted to see stepped into the room.

"Dad?"

"Kaleena." His voice was rough and slow, but Kaleena instantly knew it was real.

"Dad," Kaleena said again, unable to produce any other words. Before she knew it, her feet were moving, ever so slightly at first, and then faster the closer she got to her father. Lauren stood firm as Kaleena embraced Matthew without the slightest of hesitation. It was clear the love they had for one another went beyond physical appearance. Everything that had happened to them in the past week — past years — evaporated as they held each other. Just being able to see the other, touch them, even for a second, was enough to overpower their indifferences.

"You're alive," Matthew whispered. Kaleena finally recognized Matthew's true voice hidden under the gruff tone. As she let go, hoping in some way that he wouldn't let her, the anticipation that Matthew had magically reverted back to his regular self was quashed. But it wasn't enough to quell her excitement.

"I was told you were dead," she said.

"They lied," Gydressina said slower than a tape player with a dying battery. Kaleena's enthusiasm dissipated with the speed of Secretariat as she looked at the old woman. Though she was always one to keep from rushing to judgment, with all that she had been told, and all that she had been through recently…

"Don't you speak to me," she said.

"What's wrong." Matthew tried to keep Kaleena close to him but her hand slipped from his as she backed her way to Lauren and took her hand instead. For the first time, Lauren felt like a true mother.

"She murdered them all." Kaleena kept her gaze tight on those dark cylinders that never changed expression, no matter how much she hoped they would.

"I know how much anguish you feel, Kaleena," Gydressina said. "But you cannot trust those who have helped you."

"But I can trust you, is that it?"

"No, and I would expect nothing less. You must not trust in my words, or those of any other except for that of those you love and trust. Use that bridge to find the truth behind the facade."

"You want me to trust my father."

Gydressina slowly lowered her head and then raised it again. For a moment, Kaleena wasn't sure if Gydressina was nodding acknowledgment or simply dozing off.

"I wish I could," she said coldly, a statement that nearly crushed Matthew.

"Kaleena, please." Matthew felt like falling to his knees and begging her to trust him, but he wasn't ready to go that far. It wouldn't work anyway. If anything, it would have made him appear even more suspicious.

"Dad, you can't possibly expect me to trust this woman just because she brought you here. How do I know it's not part of some grand scheme to kill us all?"

Because I am not the destruction of life, Gydressina sang in her angelic voice. Kaleena felt a wave of acceptance wash over her, but she was able to fend it off and keep control of her mind. She quickly focused her energy at Gydressina, hoping that no one else would be able to hear her.

So burying this city under water was not *your doing?*

There is a much richer meaning behind it than you realize, Kaleena. The facts you've been given have been distorted in order to convey to you what you needed to hear.

And I'm supposed to believe what you're telling me hasn't been distorted?

I would never lie.

That's what all liars say.

I'm not hiding anything from you, Kaleena. Search my mind if you must.

Kaleena moved her shoulders against Lauren, who could sense her discomfort. Matthew, who had been focused on Kaleena the whole time, looked to Lauren and shrugged. Lauren lifted her hand slightly, making sure Kaleena didn't notice. Matthew nodded slightly, knowing full well he had to remain patient.

I can't, Kaleena said. *I don't know how.*

Then I must show you the answers you so richly deserve.

Of course, Kaleena said, her shoulders loosening. *How convenient for you.*

I do not expect you to believe me, or even trust me. But I must ask that you trust your father and come with us so that I may give you what you need.

Kaleena looked to Matthew. His eyes were sad and…was it lonely?

"What did you do to him?" Kaleena said out loud, asking the question that had been weighing on her mind since she first saw Matthew step into the room.

"She didn't do this to us," the other old man said before Matthew could. For Lauren, the voice was more familiar than Matthew's. How had she not figured it out already?

"Thomas?" Lauren let go of Kaleena, who at first didn't want to let go, but eventually let her slide away. She had her moment with her father; she wasn't about to keep Lauren from hers.

"Yeah, it's me," he said, shying away a bit as Lauren touched his near bony figure and wrinkled features. Her touch was cold against his bare chest.

"How?"

"It's complicated."

"We've got time."

"That's not true," Gydressina said. "Our time is very short. Cephis will return and we cannot be here when he does."

"Cephis?" Kaleena said for both her and Lauren. They didn't need Gydressina to answer them, as they already knew who she spoke of. Believing she'd said enough to convince Kaleena to follow her, Gydressina turned to go.

"No."

Gydressina stopped and lowered her head. Matthew let out a "Kaleena" with clear disappointment.

"I'm sorry. I can't."

"And what of Cephis. You're no longer useful to him. He will kill you."

"I don't believe that."

"What do you believe?" Gydressina turned her head. It looked as if her neck would snap if she tried turning it any farther.

"Honestly, I have no fucking idea what to believe right now."

"Then believe me," Matthew interjected. "I trust Gydressina. She saved our lives."

"And Adamus saved mine," Kaleena said, fully aware Matthew had no idea who Adamus was. But he had to understand her argument, regardless.

Matthew took a moment, unsure of how to phrase his next words. They needed to be strong and forceful, but loving and convincing. "Do you remember what your mother always taught you about strangers?"

Kaleena looked confused, but decided to play along. "'Don't trust the words of anyone you don't know.'"

"And do you remember what I always told you?"

"'Don't trust anyone willing to give you something for nothing'." Kaleena's stature changed. She seemed annoyed at the query, as if she knew exactly where it was headed. "'But keep your mind open to those that want something more in return'. Yeah, okay Dad, I get it. So what does this woman want from you?"

"My help, my trust and my loyalty."

"Bullshit."

"Maybe. But what does your friend want from you?"

Kaleena hesitated. She didn't want to answer that question, not with Gydressina standing right there.

"Must not be very acceptable if you can't even say it," Matthew chided. "Have they given you anything besides a flurry of words or promises?"

"And what has Gydressina given you but a bunch of words and promises?"

"You."

Kaleena squeezed her lips tight under her teeth. Matthew was right; she had been lied to about her parents. She thought at first it had simply been a mistake, that Adamus and Evey simply didn't know. But now, thinking over what Lauren had told her, the lie may have been much bigger than that. She wouldn't be absolutely sure without speaking to them first.

"Answer me honestly," she said to Gydressina. "Were you the magistrate of this city before it was buried?"

"I was."

"Did you choose the women who were allowed to give birth?"

"Yes."

"And you destroyed this city."

"I did."

"Why did you rescue my father?"

"To convince you to help me."

"Why do you need my help?"

"To bring life back to my body."

Kaleena dropped her eyes to her feet, needing to keep from making eye contact with Gydressina, and to some extent, her father. It didn't seem Gydressina was trying to hide anything. Either that or she was letting Kaleena hear what she wanted to hear so she'd trust her. She could only think of one other question and asked it in the silence of her mind.

Are you trying to manipulate me?

I am not. Your choice is yours. But if you do not help me, all of our lives will perish. Including your mother's.

"My mom's alive?" Kaleena's eyes were suddenly alive with an awkward excitement. She was happy, but still felt betrayed.

"Very much so," Gydressina said. "And I will take you to her if you help me. You will get no such offer from Cephis. Or Adamus, both of whom will continue to claim that she's dead."

"Wait," Lauren interrupted, her own excitement level hitting eleven. "Does that mean —"

"Your other friends are very much alive."

Lauren looked at Thomas. "Kara."

"Trishen." Thomas felt a new birth within him. Just knowing Trishen was alive gave him energy enough to counter the age of his current body. He hoped the news would be the final factor.

"We have to find them," Lauren said.

"And we will. But I cannot help them in this state. We must first heal my body. Only then can we help your friends."

"Okay," Kaleena said, looking to Lauren, who had been holding Thomas's hand this whole time for affirmation. She wasn't about to let Lauren down, not when the possibility of everyone being alive was almost certain. That, and she knew Matthew would never allow Kaleena to be harmed. Not intentionally. If Gydressina was deceiving them, the time would come for vengeance. But if she was telling the truth, it meant Adamus had a nefarious purpose, one Kaleena couldn't allow to be executed. Kaleena ran her hand through her hair accompanied by a frustrated grunt. The decision was on her shoulders. If it was the wrong one, she would never be able to live it down. "Okay, I'll trust you. But if I even sense at any time that you're lying to us or manipulating us for some sadistic purpose, I will not hesitate to do as Evey requested."

"And you have that right. But I assure you it is not *I* who is manipulating you."

Kaleena shook her head before cautiously walking to Matthew. He took her in his arms again and gave her a kiss on the cheek that felt more like some giant lizard than her father.

Gydressina lowered her head slightly (was that an attempt at a wink?) and then turned from the room and headed down the corridor. Kaleena gave Matthew a look of distrust. He acknowledged it with another kiss on the forehead. "We have no reason not to," he said quietly. Though no one wanted to admit it, Matthew,

Lauren and Thomas didn't want to spend hours, perhaps days, following someone they just met into a possible trap. The question of who was telling the truth and who was lying was gray at best, but Gydressina seemed to know exactly what she was doing. If they didn't continue to help her, their efforts may all be for naught. If the others were in any danger, Matthew was sure she would have told them. "Come on." Matthew escorted Kaleena after Gydressina.

Lauren followed, but was pulled back by Thomas's steadfastness. "What's wrong?"

Thomas ignored Lauren as he looked around the room. For some reason, he thought he could hear Trishen, and felt a bit of her pain. But how was that possible?

"Thomas?"

Lauren's eyes looked sad and confused. Thomas shook the feeling off. "What? Oh, nothing. Let's go."

The group walked together in silence, finally able to enjoy the city and the lush wildlife that grew across the walls in the company of those they originally thought were dead.

Atlantis – Incubation Room – 9 hours 44 minutes after arrival

Adamus stood at the console in front of the sea of cryogenic tubes. He kept his fingers moving along the plasma screen, lines forming along the path he traced with his fingers and then disappearing with every touch and move. Steam billowed from the base of each of the tubes, filling the floor with a soft fog about a foot and a half thick. At the top of each tube was a small round pipe that stretched to the ceiling and then turned back to connect with the hundreds of other pipes. Small puffs of a red liquid systematically dropped into each of the tubes at a steady rate, joining the swirl of blue liquid swimming around the stiff, naked bodies within, creating small, subtle patterns that looked like artwork created by a Renaissance master. As Adamus worked to regulate each of those red deposits, a hidden, muffled scream could be heard. A hint of pain nipped at him with every one and all he wanted was to make it stop. But he had a job to do, and bearing the screams was part of that job. He needed to make sure each body received the right amount of the liquid and couldn't stop the process until it was finished. What hurt even more, though, was knowing this was only the second round. The first, which was slightly less traumatic, lasted only a few minutes, producing and distributing only a slight amount of nutrients. The third round, he knew all too well, would last even longer. The only thing that eased his mind was knowing the current round was about to end. It couldn't happen soon enough.

After a few more minutes, Adamus moved his fingers across the screen in a star-like pattern with a line down the center, ceasing the muffled screams as expected. A calm alleviation washed through his chest and he lowered his head. The puffs of red substance had also stopped dropping into the tubes, though the swirling of the liquids didn't, slowly shifting into a darkened purple. Taking a refreshing breath, Adamus once again tapped along the screens, bringing forth a slew of statistical information. One piece in particular caught his eye. He left the console and slipped through the field of tubes to locate one with a young male child around the age of eight or ten. Adamus knelt down and after studying the contents carefully, saw what his readings had told him. There was a very faint movement in the boy's chest — the boy's heartbeat. Adamus smiled lightly and bolted back to the console. As he slid into position behind it, a piece of the cavern in front of him broke away from the rock wall like a door and Evey stepped through. She had grown about two feet and her hair had grown about just as much, the silver tips now reaching just above her knees. Her lips had become beautiful thin lines and her eyes were lined with a glittery silver, her lush, black eyelashes flowing out from them, curled and soft. She had blossomed as well, her white gown now forming around a pair of small, rounded breasts and the slight curvature of her thighs. She slid across the cool floor and took a place next to Adamus, lightly touching his back with her smooth, thin fingers. She leaned in close to him, hoping to smell a hint of his breath and feel the beat of his heart as he worked. It had been a long while.

Where are we? Evey asked, her cheek swiping against his just enough to feel it — a gentle, momentary touch.

We're on track. The hearts of the children are beginning to react.

Brilliant, she said, soft and with a hint of perfection. Adamus began to feel her presence for the first time. Her smell was of sweet cherries and he could taste her skin, her hair — her entire body. The longer she stood next to him, the more he wanted to act on his now uncontrollable lust for her. But he had to resist. If he were to take her now, her body would become impure and their work would become worthless.

One more round of creation and we'll be ready, Adamus said, his voice wavering. He tried all he could to keep his thoughts on anything but her.

Good, she said, pushing in closer, the corner of her lips slowly moving across his cheek until the corners of their mouths were touching with the slightest of contact. *I will stay here and monitor the progress.* A spark jumped from her eye that made Adamus's heart nearly explode with hunger. Her smile grew as her eyes became more aggressive. *Go to the conception room. Cephis is waiting.*

Adamus fought the magnetic pull Evey's lips created and the urge to lean in and take what was his. *Yes, of course,* he finally said, finding enough strength to step away from her. Evey watched him intently with that luscious come hither stare.

He walked to a ladder near the end of the first row of tubes and turned to her. *I will be back.*

My love waits. Evey gave him a quick wink with the soft touch of her tongue to her lips. Adamus couldn't help but follow suit before breaking the grip she had on him and climbing the ladder. Evey stared at it for a long while, enjoying the playful sexuality of her maturing body.

Atlantis – Women's Quarters – 10 hours 18 minutes after arrival

Trishen held herself in the corner of the room, as far away from the door as physically possible. She kept playing over and over in her mind what would happen when Cephis returned and no one but her was there to greet him. She figured he would torture her for answers as to the others whereabouts, but thoughts of him killing her were also robust, though not as likely, especially if she was right in believing he had already placed a child within her. Whatever her fate, she'd take it with the greatest of strength. She knew she may never see her friends again, but her desire to know the truth was much greater than dying in a selfish attempt to save herself. Besides, the world had given her pretty much all it could... or all she could handle. In her mind, she had nothing left to gain and nothing left to give, so why not allow it to end in honor? The only fear that held her trapped in the corner was the thought that it all would be in vain.

A possibility that sickened her greatly as the doors opened.

Standing dead center was the form she recognized as Cephis, his body larger than she remembered, possibly because he knew the others had escaped before he even got there. His pace as he entered seemed calm, though, and in a way, pleased. Could it be possible that he was *hoping* the rest of them would leave so he could have her all to himself? The thought sent a chill up her spine, even more so than the shadow of the man standing above her, looking down on her like a father ready to scold his child for stealing the keys to his Mercedes and getting arrested for a DUI.

Where are they? His voice boomed through the room like thunder.

Trishen's body shut down, stunned. She wasn't quite sure why he was even asking her that question. In turn, she wanted to get answers from him, but his mere presence turned her to stone. The lack of a response impelled him to wrap his large muscled hand around her throat.

I asked you a question.

Trishen felt the force Jaime must have endured as he pulled her up off the floor. She smelled ash swarming around her and felt the pain, anguish, fear and heat of everything that seemed to make up the man that called himself Cephis. The longer she stayed trapped in his grip, the more she saw his memories. Not as pictures, but through the intense struggle of her own mind. Within a short time, Trishen was able to pull the answers she was looking for from these feelings and found them all to be a bit warm, a bit unexpected. She was comfortable, relaxed, ready to fall asleep as if she were in her bed, her head resting among the soft pillows, the sheets keeping her warm from the nip of the breeze coming through the window, her dreams about to be filled by the chiseled fisherman she'd been trying to flirt with over the last few months, hoping one day he'd finally ask her out, or in the very least, ask her to head out on a fishing trip with him. Just the two of them, out on a boat, wrangling some fish with the possibility of falling in love painted on the horizon. Trishen would never admit her virginity to anyone, and her dreams were filled with finding the perfect man she could hook into a sexual experience of love and harmony in the sanctity of marriage. As she fell deeper into her dreams, the fear of what might happen if she exposed herself to the possibility that someone would take advantage of her — like that boy in the closet — washed her ability to act on her attraction into her subconscious. She was hindered by the memory of the boyfriend she had in college who wouldn't stop trying to get her into bed. Every time they'd make-out or get anywhere near intimate, he'd attempt to take it to the next level. She allowed him to rub her breasts, and even reach down between her legs; it was exciting, stimulating. But the moment he tried to remove her pants, or reach under her bra to grab the rare skin upon skin, she'd stop him, leading to massive arguments and eventually a disastrous break-up. It was then that she reserved herself from even talking to anyone of the opposite sex unless it was as part of her church group. Joining Jaime's crew kept her from needing that type of romantic companionship, even though she wished, for a long time, to have it with Gavin. She knew, though, because of her insecurities, she may not ever know what it would feel like to lie with someone in such a passionate, animalistic ritual. But she didn't care. She was happy. She was happy, as she was now, without even realizing she was about to lose her life.

Her comfort grew more devastating when she heard a series of whispers. At first it was just a few, which quickly became thousands, and then hundreds of thousands, all overlapping, all screaming at her in a language she didn't understand. She couldn't tell if it was a language she should know, or if it was one that no one had ever heard before. It was probably the latter, as she no longer felt her heart beat. Had she died? Was she going to her final resting place and, in the process, becoming one with the rest of the voices? She was about to resign herself to death when she heard a clear voice ring in her ear. It was familiar and loving, one that Trishen had thought she'd never hear again.

Trishen. Stay strong. Fight your fear.

She tried to speak, but couldn't move her mouth. Her vocal chords had closed and clipped. No voice was ever going to leave her lips again. But could she still talk? Could she control her thoughts enough to find the voice within to speak for her?

Gavin... the whisper was hardly audible, but it worked. Gavin responded quickly.

Don't let him take your spirit. Fight it.

I'm trying.

You are not trying. You're giving yourself up to him. Don't allow him to take you.

But I'm scared.

Don't be scared, Trishen. I know you can fight this.

Trishen tried. She tried to find her way back to her mind, to her body, to do something with the legs she no longer felt, to do something with the arms that were dangling at her sides. To do something to stop her death because —

He is coming for you. Your love is coming.

He was coming? Who was coming? What was his name? How did he love her? Did she love him back?

He's coming, and he'll help you. But you must fight. Find your voice and stop him from this torture.

He is coming?

And you need him.

And I need him. Confirmation. A light of energy pushed Trishen back to the pain of Cephis's grip upon her bleeding neck. She felt her toes again, and her feet beginning to fling back and forth. Through the haze of her slightly open eyes, she

saw the ceiling and smelled the horrid funk of dead fish plastering her nostrils. She took hold of Cephis's growing, thick forearm, but his grip was too tight; she wouldn't be able to escape him physically. There was only one thing she could do to stop him.

Kaleena, she whispered in her head. The minute the name escaped her mind, the weight of gravity sent her body crashing to the floor. She tried to cough but couldn't find the power to do so. She tried to scream, but nothing escaped. Instead, all she could do was use what little strength she had left in her legs and push away from Cephis, who stood absolutely still, soaking in the air around him. He didn't seem to notice or care that she was inching away from him, but it didn't matter one bit. Trishen was focused on drawing air into her lungs through a pathway that seemed to have shrunk to the size of a needle. She held her hand to her throat, desperately coaxing her esophagus to expand, to no avail. Every breath was hard and unbearable.

As Trishen reached the opposite end of the window, a new figure walked in. Could that be him? Her love? Her savior?

Where are they? the new man asked.

They've escaped.

How is that possible?

Trishen felt the rage as Cephis turned to his counterpart. *They are of no concern*, he growled.

But, Lord —

I said they are of no concern.

Does Evestylyn know this?

Cephis pushed past the other man and stormed to the door. *They are of no concern*, he said again. *They will find their deaths waiting for them. Kaleena's all Evestylyn desires. Now go back to her. She's waiting.* As he left, Cephis somehow formed into the shadows of the corridors.

The second man turned to Trishen and slowly walked up to her. Though she wanted to turn away from him, unsure of his intentions, she just couldn't.

His soft touch on her chin was mesmerizing and held her in a daze that she was unable to control.

The answer to your question, dear one, is yes. The man set his cold lips to hers. "Now hush, my child. You're on your way to delivering a most powerful gift, and when that happens, your love for Cephis will blossom as well."

The man walked from the room without another word. As the doors closed with an echoing *clang*, Trishen couldn't help but let out a long, piercing scream in her mind, hoping to God that it would eventually be let out through her torn, and as far as she could tell, non-existent vocal chords. When it finally subsided, knowing without a doubt that she'd never speak again, she curled up, hoping to find warmth in her tears.

Atlantis – Hallways – 10 hours 23 minutes after arrival

"Did you hear that?"

Thomas had been walking through the corridors of the city alongside Lauren, enjoying the lush plants and occasionally the views of the city through the giant glass hallways, chatting about the experiences they had had since arriving in Atlantis. Matthew and Kaleena walked a few yards behind, remaining mostly silent. Kaleena listened intently to their conversations, hoping to hear anything that would give her the slightest bit of comfort in knowing she made the right decision. So far, there wasn't any. Matthew seemed to enjoy the stories, which must have been accurate, as she knew he would've stepped in and corrected him had Thomas veered from the truth in any way. Kaleena would have done the same to Lauren's story, and though there were a few gaps between what each of them had witnessed, Lauren seemed to be explaining their time here accurately as well. They had no need to interject, and Kaleena was happy for that; she wasn't sure if she was ready to talk about it just yet.

Gydressina kept pace between the two groups, and neither her stature nor her expression seemed to change at all during the tales being told. The only time she'd stop them from their conversation was to guide them in a new direction, continuing their long journey through the seemingly endless trail.

"Hear what?" Lauren said, cutting off her story of when the Atlanteans brought her Evey as a baby — without once mentioning Henry's involvement. She wasn't sure why, perhaps because it would cause too much anger, or too many questions she wasn't really prepared to answer, but she wasn't ready to let anyone know he was one of them.

"Listen." Thomas held up his hands to everyone, listening to a noise that didn't exist. "You can't hear that?" The group looked at Thomas like he was going insane.

"We can't hear anything," Lauren said, placing her hands on his shoulders.

"No," he said, shrugging her off. "That's impossible."

"Thomas, what is it?" Matthew asked.

"Screaming. A constant screaming."

"Who's screaming?" Kaleena asked.

Thomas stood silent until the screams stopped, leaving nothing but a soft, cry. "Trishen…" he whispered.

"Trishen?"

Thomas's eyes filled with anguish. "She's hurt. We need to help her."

"She's not in danger," Gydressina said.

"You heard it," Thomas said forcefully, pointing his finger at the old woman. "I know you did." He swept Gydressina's frail blouse into his hands. "You heard it."

"Yes," Gydressina said, calmly and without a hint of fear. "But there's nothing we can do for her now. She is protected."

"I don't believe that. We have to find her."

"We're almost to our destination. You must come with us."

"What is wrong with you?" Thomas turned to Matthew. "Come on. Help me out here."

Matthew turned his eyes from Thomas. He couldn't look at him as he said, "I have to trust Gydressina. If she says she's okay…" His voice trailed off. It was evident he didn't quite believe what he was saying.

"Shit," Thomas scolded. "Shit."

"Calm down, Thomas." Lauren again tried to touch him, but he pushed her away.

"You're all insane. Trishen's hurt. She's scared. We need to help her. *I* need to help her."

"I don't agree, but you must do as you need," Gydressina said quietly. "But think before you decide. I will take you to Trishen as soon as we complete my resurrection."

"How do you know it won't be too late by then?" Everyone could see that Thomas truly believed it would be. "Do what you need. I have to find her."

Thomas ran off down the corridor back the way they had come, ignoring Lauren's call for him to stay. She started to go after him, but Gydressina pressed her hand against her stomach.

"Let him be," she said. Lauren felt the woman's determination as she looked at the deep recesses of her eye sockets. "We must let him go."

Lauren hated having to leave Thomas to wander the city alone, but something in Gydressina's touch told Lauren that she was extremely important to her. If she left, all would be lost. Gydressina lowered her arm as Lauren nodded and turned to Matthew and Kaleena. "We're almost there. Come."

Gydressina took the lead. Matthew walked up to Lauren, who was still slightly stunned by the situation. "He'll be all right. They both will." Lauren took Matthew's hand and smiled sweetly, giving it a light kiss. *Thank you.*

Kaleena still wasn't sold on Gydressina's intentions, but her faith in her honesty was promising. She could have forced Thomas to stay, but instead, allowed him to do as he wished. It was always his decision, as was Kaleena's choice to follow her. She was still unsure of what she'd do once they arrived at the undisclosed destination, but she believed her questions would be answered when they did. Suddenly, a sharp pain pinched Kaleena's mind. She grabbed her forehead and fell to her knees. It was possible Matthew and Lauren were there, asking if she was all right and what they could do to help, but Kaleena was in no state of mind to know for sure. As she tried desperately to hiss the pain away, she thought her brain might explode if she wasn't able to control it. Then —

All of the pain was gone. She felt liberated.

When she opened her eyes, she was happy to be back in her apartment. She was wearing a normal set of clothes and her hair lay gently against her shoulders. Usually, there was a constant stream of cars passing by, or the soft hum of the radio from the tenant upstairs who sometimes left his stereo on even when he wasn't home, having gone out to try his hand at scoring a record deal from some overblown producer who just happened to be at the rundown club in nowheres-ville, Connecticut, or scoring the next hooker on the street, but she didn't seem to notice the eerie calm and absolute quiet that surrounded her. There wasn't even a bird chirp or a pigeon warble. It didn't matter. She was back home. Had it all been a dream?

"Are you okay?" The voice was familiar and sent an awkward chill through Kaleena. She turned around as Kyla stepped into the apartment. She looked more beautiful then Kaleena remembered. Her appearance was gentle, her steps light, yet confident.

"What are you doing here?"

"Why didn't you stop it?" she asked.

"Stop what?"

"Why didn't you stop it?"

"Kyla? I don't know what you're talking about."

"Why didn't you stop it?" Kyla sauntered around Kaleena in a steady circle, robotically repeating the question over and over. Kaleena tried hard to remember what she was talking about. When she was unable to find an answer to the question, she grabbed Kyla's shoulders and forced her to look at her.

"Why didn't you stop it?" Kyla screamed.

That's when she saw it. That original pain and regret, the reddening tears and the sickened depression of a girl that had gone through the darkest moment of a life that would be forever changed. She saw in those dark eyes a shadow of a man

smelling the body of a young girl about to become a piece of meat. In those eyes, Kaleena became weak and brittle. Tears spread across her eyes. Kyla stood rather still, lacking any semblance of emotion.

"I'm sorry, Kyla, I am," Kaleena said with a shaky voice. "But I didn't know."

"You didn't know," Kyla said. "You didn't know, and I hurt. I hurt for you."

"You what?"

"I hurt for you."

"What… what are you talking about?"

"Do you not see?" Another voice. It sounded familiar as well, but Kaleena couldn't place it. She turned around and saw a young woman, most likely sixteen or so, with bright blond hair streaming down to her waist with light silver tips and crystal clear periwinkle eyes that sparkled as if the apartment was full of light.

"Evey?" She somehow knew the name that jumped off her lips without ever registering that specific piece of knowledge.

Evey's smile washed the sadness from Kaleena, who had to squeeze away the dryness from her once moist eyes.

"What are you doing here?"

"How do you not understand?" Evey asked gently, without a note of condescension. "Your friend risked her soul for you."

"She what?" Kaleena turned back to Kyla, whose body was devoid of life — shut down, waiting for a recharge. She waved her hand in front of Kyla's deadened eyes, hoping to get a response, but they no longer registered anything. "What is this? What's going on?"

"I need you to realize a truth. One that's led to the abandonment of a person who loved you so deeply, she was willing to do whatever it took to keep you safe."

Kaleena looked to Evey, growing slightly angry. "Would you stop being so cryptic? Just tell me what the hell is going on."

"I can't do that, Kaleena. The truth can't be given. It must be realized."

"What truth? What happened to Kyla?"

"You know what happened to her. The question is…"

"Why?" Kaleena looked over the statue behind her and then said, "Are you trying to tell me that she went through hell and back that night because of me?"

"Not *because* of you."

"For me? Is that it? She let that bastard rape her instead of me?" Evey's smile of recognition didn't help. "What are you smiling about?"

"I'm sorry, and I'm very sorry for your friend, but you need to understand what happened that night."

"Who was it?"

"You already know."

"Gydressina."

"Not directly, but yes."

"Why? Why would she do something like that? Why not just come after me?"

"Because, Kaleena. She needs you."

"For what?"

"That I cannot tell you."

Kaleena's frustration level hit maximum overload. "Fuck you."

"Look," Evey said, reaching up to touch Kaleena's cheek. Kaleena swatted her hand away like a gnat. Evey continued without anger. "You have to trust me. Gydressina is very conniving and manipulative. She needed you to travel to Atlantis, and for that to happen, she needed to make sure that nothing, or anyone, would keep you from doing so."

A fresh light of understanding floated to Kaleena's eyes. "So Gydressina had Kyla attacked to break up our friendship?" Evey nodded. Kaleena took a moment to process the new information. "Did she know?" she finally asked.

"What do you believe?"

Kaleena was sure, deep down, that Kyla knew precisely what she was getting into. She still didn't know the circumstances of that night, or who was sent to do the most sickening act a person could do, but she now understood that Kyla gave herself willingly, and she did it for Kaleena's protection.

"Your heart serves you," Evey said. "Now allow it to serve me." Evey raised

her hand to Kaleena's cheek. The softness of her touch brought the tears back out. Kaleena placed her hand on top of Evey's and caressed it lightly with her forefinger. "Don't allow her memory to be corrupted. She was a treasure. She sacrificed her own well-being for you. You must not let that be in vain."

"What do I do?"

"Gydressina will try and manipulate you into believing something that will lead to your death. You can't allow that to happen."

"What does she plan to do?"

"I don't know the answer to that, but you must not allow her to convince you. If she asks for your hand, she will push you to your death, and that would be detrimental to life itself."

"What should I do?"

"Send her into the light." Evey's voice was cold and stern. Kaleena looked at Evey with distress.

"Send her... what?"

"You must do whatever it takes to send Gydressina into the light. She is frail and her body will not be able to protect her from its power."

"You mean kill her?" Kaleena stepped away from Evey. "I... I can't do that."

"You must."

"No. I can't just kill someone." Kaleena sat down on the couch to try and control her breathing.

"If you don't, you will die. As will your father and your mother."

"But —"

"Stop, Kaleena. Do you not understand what's going on here? Gydressina killed your best friend's spirit. She helped destroy your family. She will stop at nothing until you help her, and when you do, everything will die."

Thoughts swarmed so quickly and fluidly, it was dizzying. If Evey was telling the truth, then not only had Gydressina corrupted her friend, but she was also instrumental in driving her mother away. How could she trust her? But how could she kill her? No matter how much she tried to convince herself she could,

she couldn't justify taking someone's life. It would be then that she would become just like Gydressina.

"I can't just murder someone, Evey. I can't." Kaleena stood up and looked to Evey, her eyes stern. "I won't."

"Why?" Her voice was deep and dry.

"There's no turning back from something like that. I won't lower myself to it."

"Even if it costs your family their lives?"

"I guess I'll just have to take that risk."

"You don't know what you're about to do."

"Yeah? What's new?"

Evey took a deep breath, which felt as if she was attempting to pull Kaleena's soul from her body. Kaleena fought the sharp pain in her chest, sending her back to her knees. "Let me go," she screamed, and once again, all of her pain was gone — just like that. She jumped in fright at feeling Matthew's hands on her arms.

"Kaleena, it's me," Matthew assured. "Are you okay?"

Kaleena backed up, unaware of where she was. Then it all came flooding back. She looked to Matthew and then Lauren and calmed her breathing. "Yeah, yeah," she said. "I'm fine." She looked past Matthew to Gydressina, feeling quite indifferent toward her. Could she be trusted? It was time to find out.

"Come on," she said, standing. "What are we waiting for?" She brushed past Matthew and stopped next to Gydressina. Part of the old woman knew she'd seen everything that had just happened. "Let's get going."

Matthew chuckled oddly, wrapped his arm around Kaleena's shoulders and gave her a squeeze, which Kaleena took with the gratitude of a child. Lauren held back, unsure of what she should do. Matthew turned to her. "Lauren?"

Hearing her name in that tone made her feel light. She licked her lips and bit the lower one as she looked down to her feet like a teen waiting for her first crush to ask her to the homecoming dance. Kaleena couldn't help but crack her own loving smile. This was the first time she saw the true friendship between the two. It calmed her and put a little more vibrancy in her step.

Atlantis – Incubation Room – 10 hours 31 minutes after arrival

"Shit!"

Evey's mind fell back into her body. The disappointment and rage was over-whelming. She quickly stood from where she'd been lying on the floor and walked to the console. Her brain churned through translations and equations with light-ning speed as she swiped her fingers across the screen to bring life back to the line of tubes behind her. When she began to run a series of sample tests, Adamus stepped from the ladder and ran to her with urgency.

What are you doing?

I'm speeding up the process, Evey said, determined.

No. You can't do that.

Evey turned her eyes on Adamus. The piercing black holes with a hint of red blasted their way through his soul, forcing him to shy away.

Evestylyn. Please...

I already know your concern, Adamus, but I cannot guarantee Kaleena's help. She's about to do something dangerous, I can feel it.

Then stop her.

I won't get to her in time. This needs to be done. Now.

Even if it costs you your life?

Evey turned to Adamus, this time with love, and placed her hand to his cheek. *I love you. That will need to be enough.* She sent a magnetic kiss upon his mind, producing a soothing numbness across his body. Adamus stood motionless as she stepped from the console. Upon her disappearance into the side cavern, he regained his strength and slowly followed her. The sound of light water dripping through the crevices of the rock and the sweet smell of moist dirt calmed his mind.

At first, he couldn't see Evey in the dark, quiet room, but a hint of blue light radiating from the walls finally lit her up in a soft hue that made her skin seem even softer than he knew it to be. He watched her like a voyeur as she removed her gown and climbed like a cat onto a long table that stretched from inside the far wall and bent at a thirty-degree angle until it touched the ground. Attached

to the sides of the table were thin wires that snaked upwards to a series of pipes running along the ceiling. Evey rolled onto her back and held her arms along the sides of her body, palms up. She finally registered Adamus's presence and gave a sheepish grin, her eyes halfway closed in exotic torture. She waited patiently for him to come to her, inhaling the sweet pleasure around her and of her.

With a deep breath to help control his desire, Adamus inched his way to the head of the table. He slid his fingers along her leg with the slightest touch, just enough to give Evey a tickle of stimulation. As he reached her thigh, he shifted his hand to hers and wrapped his fingers around hers for a brief second, then let go to continue tracing his fingers along her arm and up to her neck. He eventually wrapped his fingers around her chin and leaned in close.

Beauty walks the halls of the gentle soul, he said.

And with beauty comes the desire for pleasure.

Are you sure you're ready?

I am quite aware. She paused and looked directly into his eyes. *Of all that which you question.*

Adamus lowered his nose to her cheek and took in her scent, knowing full well she was speaking of much more than just the process, or even the escape of their captives. After a soft kiss with the corner of his mouth, he grabbed a few stray wires from above her head and carefully wrapped them around her forehead. He then brushed his hands over her eyes. Instantly, Evey was asleep, and Adamus couldn't help giving her one last kiss.

Do you trust me? he asked before walking to her hand. He pulled a few more wires from underneath the table, wrapped two around her wrists and injected two of them into her skin — one under the fingernail on her middle finger, the other into her wrist, where it immediately attached itself to the vein. He held her hand for a moment, absorbing the smooth texture, then walked around the table and did the same to Evey's other wrist, again with the final act of holding her hand. After giving her knuckles a light kiss, he went to her feet and pulled four wires from each side of the table. He used four of them to strap her feet to the table and injected two into the balls of her feet. The final two, which were longer than all the rest, were pulled up to her stomach. Without taking any further action, the wires slid between her legs and into her body until there was no more slack. Adamus lowered his head and rubbed his eyes, knowing full well what Evey was about to go through and what he was about to feel in conjunction. He watched her chest rise and fall, slowly and methodically, her ribs playing peek-a-boo with her slightly concave stomach. She was so beautiful, so peaceful — so vulnerable.

Adamus finally found the strength to leave Evey to lie in a slumber she would soon be forced to awaken from with a pain that would cause anyone else to give their life up in an instant. But Evey, even in sleep, was expecting the unbearable torment. And when it came, her teeth came together like bricks. Adamus's skin tightened in its own unwanted, but much subtler version of the pain. He didn't know how she could handle such agony, but beyond the scouring of pain that coursed her body, he knew her acceptance for it all was because of the life she was giving up, the spirit she was showering among the hundreds of bodies waiting to be reanimated. It was the simple joy of conceiving her very own children and gifting their flawed, scarred souls with the purity of her own flesh and blood.

For several minutes, Evey fought the intense urge to scream. But even her threshold had a limit, and when that breaking point had been reached, she let out a wail so loud, it carried itself throughout the city, vibrating the walls of every corridor, building and tower. Adamus gritted his teeth as his bones shook to the point of cracking. But he had to push the pain to the back of his mind in order to regulate the transfer of Evey's blood into the tubes, which now swirled the purple substance into a heated red. When there was nothing but a flurry of red liquid across the cavern, covered only by a growing thick layer a steam across the floor, Adamus focused his mind and energy into every last spirit surrounding the air, collected in the walls and plastered to the tubes, and pushed them as hard as he could into the cells of the bodies.

For Evey, the presence of her new family, hundreds of hearts beginning to beat

together rapidly, their minds opening to a new world of existence, helped initiate the final stages of growth, accelerating the blossoming of her maturity by several inches in all areas of her fruitful body.

Once all of the new spirits had entered their new avatars, Adamus stroked a few lines across the keypad and then opened his hand up as full as it would go, sending a bright flash of light at the tubes. Each and every one of them exploded in unison, releasing the substance to pour out along the floor, extinguishing the fog. The bodies came with it, falling to the floor in a massive pile of comatose corpses. Adamus didn't notice right away, but as his breaths came under control, he realized his pain had disappeared, as had the screams of his purity. He swiped his hand over the console again, shutting off the piping of liquid into the tubes, and left the bodies to their task of reconnecting their souls to the minds of their requisite shell. As he entered the bleeding room, the table was empty. Adamus looked around, but Evey was nowhere to be found. He couldn't sense her life either. Had she crawled to an unknown dark corner of the cavern to die? Had she evaporated into the tubes?

Just before succumbing to his loss, a woman stepped from the shadow, her eyes locking on Adamus with a fire of intrigue and sensual aggression. Her body looked pure and supple, free of any marks, and her hair touched the tip of her ankles. She was natural; she was free. She was his.

Without hesitation, she wrapped her fingers into his hair and looked deep into his eyes. *You wished to know if you could trust me?*

Adamus felt foolish, but answered honestly. *I did.*

Evey's eyes sparkled silver. *What does this tell you?* She pressed her lips to his. The taste of this gentle woman was beyond the accent of the mind, and her touch was all Adamus really needed to satisfy his sexual needs. But she needed more of him, and he was happy to reciprocate with slow, pristine motions and a kiss that turned her skin to air. As the two became one, pressing their bodies together on the table as if they had never before been separated, the never ending embrace lasted a new lifetime, unable to reach the apex it so much deserved. Instead the

sensation continued into infinity, over and over, until they shared one breath and beat with one heart.

Atlantis – Tower of Youth – 10 hours 39 minutes after arrival

As Kaleena stepped onto the lower cylindrical catwalk, she finally understood the meaning behind what Evey had said —

Send her into the light.

The room she'd just entered rose nearly twenty stories high, and from what she could tell, dropped another six stories below them. Circling the vine-covered walls was a spiral staircase made entirely of a smooth, glossed metal that looked almost like mirrors. The stairs stopped about halfway up the tower, leading to several other catwalks spaced at about two story intervals, each one on the opposite side of the round wall as the previous one below it. In the center of it all was a large beam of white light that stretched from the floor to the ceiling. It glittered and streamed like water, pulsing every few seconds, splashes of stray flickering light falling back to the pool of light that made up the ground floor.

"Do you like it?" Gydressina asked as she stepped up behind her. She looked quite confident and aware.

"What is it?" Kaleena asked with a mask of hesitation.

"It's the one and only source of pure life. It's what will help me regain my youth."

"A tower of light," Matthew whispered as he stepped into the room alongside Lauren. "A light of life. A life of youth." He paused as he grew more astounded. "It can't be."

Lauren smiled bright. She knew exactly what Matthew was thinking.

"Hold on, there, guys," Kaleena said, her mind catching up to his words. "You don't think this is the actual fountain of youth, do you?"

Matthew just winked. He couldn't do much else.

"Holy shit," she said. "You guys are insane. What's next? Are we gonna get to

meet the infamous Sasquatch?"

Gydressina giggled. It was the first time anyone had ever heard anything like that from her.

"My god, Kaleena," Matthew said, grabbing the moment and running with it. "When are you going to start accepting that you've been wrong about everything?" Even though he was absolutely right, she still wasn't about to admit it. So she gave her father a daggered stare and then turned away.

"Come," Gydressina said. No one noticed her composure return. "We must move to the top level." As she made her way up the stairwell, her steps remained slow, hardly able to lift her legs high enough to step up. Matthew and Lauren just chuckled as they continued to admire the beam of light. Kaleena, frustrated, turned back to Matthew and noticed that, blooming just above them, were small white berries encompassed within horseshoe-shaped leaves and a pair of roses on either side.

Matthew and Lauren looked so harmonious together, wrapped in the greenery and awash with the tenderness of the sun that for the moment, Evey's request was just a dream. She needed to believe that she wouldn't actually have to go as far as the child demanded. Kaleena was at peace; she wasn't about to let anyone hinder that feeling.

"Go ahead. Kiss and make up," Kaleena giggled.

Matthew was clearly confused. Kaleena nodded, urging them to look above them. Lauren turned away quickly, almost blushing. Matthew simply said, "Can't mess with tradition, I guess."

Lauren chuckled lightly. "I guess not." She leaned in and gave Matthew a sweet, friendly kiss on the corner of his mouth before he stepped through the doorway. Lauren held back, a slight flutter in her stomach causing a hint of laughter.

"Come. Quickly." Amazingly, Gydressina had already made it halfway up the stairwell. Kaleena wrapped her arms around Matthew to help his weakened body climb the stairs (and give him a brace in case his knees gave out). She hid her growing fear over what was about to happen, unwilling to screw with his happiness.

By the time they caught up to Gydressina, she was standing in the dead center of the topmost catwalk. Lauren reached the top just after Matthew and Kaleena and simply wanted to admire the grandness of it all. The ray of light looked quite majestic at this level, the spray of stray light dissipating (if not being sucked back up into the light) before hitting the pool, which from here, looked about a mile away and completely welcoming. At the far edge of the catwalk, there was a long ledge that stretched from the wall to the center of the light.

"Now do I get my answers?" Kaleena asked, a bit out of breath.

"I do not lie. But first, I must explain to you what your purpose here must be."

"My purpose?"

Send her into the light. Do not let her actions be in vain.

"I'm afraid, Kaleena, that for the light of life to restore my youth, you must sacrifice yourself to it."

"What? No!" Matthew screamed louder than he was capable. He pulled Kaleena into his chest as the words vibrated among the walls. Lauren stood motionless, her hand covering her mouth in shock.

"You lied to me," Kaleena said with force.

"I did no such thing."

"You said you would take me to my mother."

Gydressina stood strong, piercing Kaleena's sharp glare with her own cold stare. "You wouldn't have come otherwise."

"What else have you been lying to us about?" Matthew added. It was a good question. Kaleena wanted to know that exact same thing.

"I have not lied to you, Matthew. Not once."

"How do I know that? Hell, is Jaime even still alive? Is Trishen?" Matthew turned his eyes down and whispered, "My god, Thomas."

"Kaleena, I must insist that you hear me."

"This is bullshit."

"Please," Gydressina said.

"No," Kaleena screamed, adding in a light whisper, "Goddamn, son of a bitch."

"An act of pure sacrifice is all that will allow life to be given to those of your choosing."

"I've got news for you." Kyla's pain and Jaime's sorrow came rushing to her as she uttered her next words. "There's no such thing." They were said with authority, but to Lauren, they felt like a soft whisper.

"You're wrong. And I can prove it to you."

"Yeah? How?"

"Come to me." Gydressina held out her hand and waited. Kaleena's nostrils flared with every breath. She stared at those bony fingers like they were a set of dentist's drills. She wasn't about to touch her lying, decrepit fingers.

"How do I know you won't just throw me in that damn thing?"

"Because it has to be a selfless sacrifice. Anything else would be a waste. I have no reason to lie to you, Kaleena. I only wish to share with you the truth."

"You're gonna show me the truth? Answer all of my questions?"

Gydressina nodded. "As long as you trust," she said and then looked around at the others. "All of you have to trust that when I show her, no one will try and stop it."

"What does that mean?" Kaleena scorned.

"Take my hand."

Kaleena pursed her lips and looked to Matthew. Although she didn't want to do it, this was most likely her only choice. At least Matthew was there to stop Gydressina if she did anything to her. That or avenge her death. Without another word, Kaleena placed the tips of her fingers to the tips of Gydressina's. The urge to grab Gydressina's wrist and hurl her into the light, to do Evey's bidding, weighed heavy on her mind. But before she could even think about going through with it, Gydressina curled her fingers around Kaleena's wrist and pulled her in close enough for her to ingest the smell of rotting flesh.

"Don't stop me," Gydressina said in a clearer voice than Matthew had ever heard. She slid Kaleena's wrist below her stomach, pulled her head hard into her chest, and lowered her forehead to Kaleena's.

In that moment, Kaleena let out a piercing scream. A blast of light burst from the center of the beam, knocking Matthew and Lauren to the ground. Seconds later, Gydressina lifted her head and allowed Kaleena to slump to the ground. Her breaths were heavier than concrete and her panting was full of frightful, terrified squeaks. She looked at Gydressina, who fell to her knees in exhaustion, with a rare, pure understanding that now linked the two of them as one.

"Fuck," was all that escaped Kaleena's dry lips.

"Now you understand," Gydressina croaked. "Now you know the truth."

Kaleena turned to Matthew, who was slowly sitting up. She couldn't tell if what she had seen had passed through him as well, but she hoped it hadn't, figuring Gydressina had chosen her because her mind was strong enough to handle it all. Every image that permeated her mind — the love, the jealousy, the hatred, the deception, the remorse and the lust — it all became extremely maddening. Not only had it led Kaleena to the truth of the past, but to millions of questions as well. There was one that stood out among all the others, though; one that would no doubt answer a lot of them all at once. She turned back to Gydressina, relaxed her breathing, and asked,

"Was it all a lie?"

"Not lies, Kaleena. Manipulation of truth."

Kaleena felt a burst of tears paint her eyes, but held them firm. She still had more to discover. "What did Evey mean I needed to give her a sister?"

"Cephis was going to use your womb as his vessel for a child that would resemble Evestylyn down to the lust in her eyes."

"Was going to? Why didn't he?"

"Because I made sure you would be cleansed before he had the chance."

"What does that mean? Cleansed?"

"I sped up your reproduction cycle. Over a matter of hours, your body went through a lifetime of menstrual cycles."

"I went through menopause?" Kaleena's breathing was becoming stronger. Gydressina's was growing weaker. Lauren had been able to sit up and listened

intently to the confusing conversation.

"No. This was quite different."

"Why me? Why did Cephis need me?"

"Because you are of the blood."

"What blood?"

"The blood of life. What I just showed you was the beginning of the past. Follow your heart to the moment of true sacrifice."

"I'm a descendant?"

"A descendant of nobility, humbleness and purity. She was chosen, just as you have been, for those specific reasons. And now, you're faced with the ultimate choice." Gydressina coughed softly and tried hard to collect her breath.

"To give my life for the sins of others?"

Gydressina nodded. Matthew's heart stopped.

"I don't know if I can," Kaleena said, looking at the floor, trying hard to believe.

Gydressina collected herself enough to sit and pushed Kaleena's head back up. "Do not doubt yourself, child." She slid her hand to the side of Kaleena's head and watched as tears welled up at the base of her lower eyelid. "This can lead you to your destruction," she said and then lowered her hand to Kaleena's heart. "This will save your life."

Kaleena grasped Gydressina's hand. "And what is this?"

"Compassion. Honor. Trust. You must give yourself to the love before you can vanquish your failures."

A tear dropped from Kaleena's eye and traced the contours of her cheek.

"You must find the strength. Allow yourself to give to the life."

Kaleena again lowered her head. Matthew's sadness welled as she read his thoughts. Though she tried to ignore them, they started to cloud her mind. But she had to control it; she had to believe in what was right, not what she believed was best for her or her father.

"I'll do it," she whispered through the tears. She looked up to Gydressina and saw a hint of a smile form along the transparent arch of skin. "I'll do it."

"No, Kaleena." Matthew's voice was soft and hardly there. Kaleena let a couple of tears drop to the ground before letting go of Gydressina and crawling slowly to her father.

She looked into his reddening eyes. "Dad, you have to let me go."

"Why?" Matthew said without words.

"Because I've seen what they are. They're dangerous." Kaleena turned to Lauren. "All of them." Lauren knew right away who she was speaking of, but didn't want to believe it. She couldn't.

Kaleena turned back to Matthew with more control and authority. "I need to stop them. This is the only way." She picked up his hand and held it gently. "It's what I was brought here to do."

Matthew tried to mask his sadness with a smile, but there was no denying the fact that Kaleena had to do this. He grabbed the back of her head and held her tight.

Kaleena allowed him this moment. The last time she felt this close to him was when she returned home after her resurrection. They sat together on the couch just holding each other. The television was off, there was no radio. There was nothing but the sounds of the traffic outside and the beating of their hearts. Neither of them slept that night and the next morning they only left each other's side to go to the bathroom. The rest of the time was spent talking until they fell asleep. Kaleena wanted nothing more than to fall asleep right here, right now, and wake up from the dream she knew wasn't a dream.

"I love you," Matthew said.

Lauren's eyes were hazy with tears of her own. She absorbed the moment with a hope that something would change; that what she knew in her heart to be true was false; that something would come and stop this madness. How could she possibly allow Kaleena to sacrifice her life when by doing so would devastate the only person that truly cared for her? Without Kaleena, Matthew wouldn't continue to live. He loved her more than the air he breathed, the life he lived. Losing her would end all that; even if he survived for another hundred years, there would be

no true life within him. Lauren knew what it meant to give up a life that couldn't be saved and she didn't wish that pain on anyone.

"Sometimes you have to give up your daughter if it means saving the life of others," she whispered to herself, as Matthew gave Kaleena a gentle kiss on the forehead. This wasn't going to happen. Lauren wouldn't let any of it happen. She strode to Kaleena with confidence and knelt down next to her. "I understand," she said.

"Understand what?"

"All of it. Everything. A mother must protect her child and save herself, even if it means allowing her daughter's death."

"What are you talking about?"

"Don't let me down."

Kaleena didn't want to believe what she knew to be true as she looked into those loving, determined eyes. "No, don't do this."

Lauren gave Kaleena her own kiss on the forehead. "I'll show you true sacrifice." Without hesitation, Lauren ran as fast as she could to the edge of the catwalk. Kaleena was the first to stand and yell out, "No." But nothing she said or did was going to stop Lauren, who was on her way to a special, invigorating new life within death. She felt exhilarated as she turned down the center ledge. Peering directly into the beam of light, she knew exactly what had to be done. She stripped herself of her gown, allowing the breeze of her speed to rip past her bare skin, and as she reached the edge of the catwalk, she took her final step and leapt in flight.

The moment she left the ledge, the beam turned her body into nothing but air. The white light surrounded her, giving her a new perspective on everything she'd ever known. Her mind was washed clear of every bad thing she'd ever thought, had ever done and ever would do. The whisper of the world around her became clear as a crystal chime and she became empowered by the lucidity of the life she now encompassed. After a moment of heavenly bliss, she heard the soft whimper of a baby's cry and a hint of a whisper.

"Hello again, Lauren."

Lauren opened her eyes. She stood on what felt like a cloud. But she wasn't. Her body was gone, but she was alive. Before she could make sense of it all, a woman holding what looked like a newborn baby in her arms appeared. Was she really there? Or was she simply a feeling?

"Janine?"

"Hello, Lauren," Janine said. Her smile was bright. It felt happy; something she never really felt before.

"What are you doing here? What happened to you?"

"I made some mistakes, Lauren. Mistakes that I will always regret for the days of my eternity. But I've been forgiven for those mistakes, as have you." Janine shifted her arms toward Lauren, who accepted the baby into her arms with a gentle smile and a warm heart. "Say hello to your son."

Lauren let out a laugh of joy. The child seemed happy and without judgment. He loved his mother, even if she had killed him. It was true. All of her misdeeds really had been forgiven. Reconnecting with the son she never had was all she could ever have asked for. It was all she would ever desire and all she would live with as the world swallowed her into the corporeal existence of light.

BOOK FOUR

FIGHT OF CONTROL

Atlantis – Tower of Youth – 10 hours 51 minutes after arrival

"Lauren, NO!"

Kaleena was slower than a snail compared to Lauren's lightning speed, which made it seem as if she were the Flash juiced up on a gallon of Red Bull darting to her final act on earth — what would turn out to be her destiny. Kaleena stopped at the edge of the catwalk as Lauren shed the final remnants of the world, leaving in the natural beauty with which she'd once arrived. A tear rolled past Kaleena's lips, a saddened puppy watching what could have been her mother dive into the beam of light without so much as a second thought, a hesitation or remorse. She fell ever so gracefully until the light pulled the remnants of her spirit from the shell that shattered into millions of cells and burned into the pool like the remnants of spray from a giant firework.

"Lauren," Kaleena whimpered, lowering her head in a soft prayer before a new life washed through the tower with hurricane force wind. Kaleena held firm as the fresh smell of enlightenment milked into every pore of her body. Out of the corner of her eye, she saw the beam of light splash across the catwalk and envelop Gydressina in a fresh, milky substance. It picked her up as if she were a precious antique doll. A new outer crust soon formed around her bones, generating new muscles, tearing the tattered rags from her body, and expanding her hair into a soft flowing river of waves and curls. Within a matter of seconds, she had gone from feeble skeleton to mesmerizing exquisiteness with the pure sacrifice she'd been waiting for. Giving up its new doll for the return to its own locked solitude, the light lowered Gydressina to the catwalk and pulled all of its own spirit back unto itself, leaving the room cold, but anew.

Kaleena caught her breath as all motion in the room ceased. Lauren's gown landed gently on the ramp in between her and the beam. After cautiously working her way to her feet, she sauntered to the gown and picked it up with shaky fingertips. She took her time to ingest the smell, hoping to find something that would bring order to the chaos hinted upon in her mind. But as she suspected, she couldn't find anything except for the soft smell of Lauren's body, which Kaleena found comforting nonetheless.

"Thank you," Kaleena said into the gown. No matter how rare it may be, pure sacrifice was now as true to her as everything else she never thought she'd ever believe in. She was grateful for that. "We'll miss you," she finished and then lowered the gown to look into the quiet flow of the light.

Kaleena, Gydressina called out. Kaleena turned and saw two bodies slumped on the ground. Her steps away from the beam started before her conscious mind registered what was happening. When time finally caught back up to her, she was kneeling next to Gydressina. Her hands hovered over the young woman's body, shaking, unsure of what she would do. She didn't want to bruise or inadvertently mangle the untainted freshness of the recently created body, glistening like the ocean under the heat of the sun, reminding her of the beautiful creature she'd encountered in her dreams — if that was what they truly were. She finally lowered her hand to Gydressina's shoulder, which felt warm and smooth, like heated glass.

Kaleena, I need your help.

She reached under Gydressina's neck and pulled it up, balancing the now vibrant shoulder blades on her leg. For a moment, she felt she was looking at the features of a living angel. Gydressina's head fell loosely across her arm, revealing slightly plump lips and a small, rounded nose. Her eyelashes glittered as they encased her closed eyelids. Kaleena couldn't help but move some of the pure white hair from her face and outline the soft curvature of her slightly indented cheekbones.

What do you need me to do? Kaleena finally asked, feeling a rush of splendor wash through her veins.

I need your breath.

My breath?

Quickly. Please.

My breath, Kaleena thought to herself. Finally, unsure if she was doing what was asked of her, Kaleena opened Gydressina's mouth ever so slightly, revealing just a glimpse of what looked like perfectly white baby teeth, and pressed her lips to hers, carefully and tenderly. She exhaled into Gydressina's mouth. A quick tickle in her lips — a movement of sorts — caused Kaleena to lift her head, a bit discomforted. She waited, and when Gydressina still wasn't breathing, she knew she'd have to continue. But as Kaleena came just centimeters from touching Gydressina's lips a second time, feeling the hint of their taste once again, the old woman wretched in a deep breath as if she'd been under water for years. Her eyes sprayed open, and after exhaling long and hard, she sat up and took in a new deep breath, this one more refined and enamored.

She let out a sigh as she exhaled once again and turned to Kaleena with a grateful, majestic smile.

"Thank you," she said, her voice the song of a robin.

"You're welcome," Kaleena said, delight tickling her throat.

Atlantis – Incubation Room – 10 hours 51 minutes after arrival

Lauren, NO!

Evey sat up dramatically, peeling herself away from Adamus. Her eyes burned red and her body was awash with the chill of death. She seethed as Lauren's sacrifice replayed over and over through her mind. She felt ill. Adamus sat up, a bit groggy, and cupped his hands across her tense, cold shoulders.

"You fucking bitch," she whispered under her breath, more as a hiss than a statement. She melted off the table and stormed through the cavern wall. Adamus tried peeking into her mind and hunt for the reason to her sudden burst of outrage and odd fear, but became agitated when his love kept her thoughts walled off from him.

What's wrong? he asked as he stood at the threshold, watching her run her hands across the console. He couldn't help but take in her beautiful curves.

Gydressina's awake.

It took a moment for Adamus to unlatch his delicious thoughts of Evey's smooth skin to register the words. *What? How?*

That bitch mother of mine gave herself to the light.

That can't be possible? he scolded, walking to the console. *How did Gydressina even get into the city?*

I feel the presence of Kaleena's father.

Adamus searched the air of the city and located Matthew. He *was* alive. How could he not have known of his presence before? He should have felt him the moment he stepped into the city, but he hadn't. Gydressina couldn't have been powerful enough to mask anyone other than herself from their minds, so what could have kept him from knowing? He looked over Evey's features and soaked in the new hint of smoldering mint that overwhelmed his mind. *You think he helped her?* he said, his breath heavy.

I know he helped her.

She pushed past Adamus, scraping her hand on his chest. His heart pulled toward her hand like a magnet, sending a soft fire through his veins, once again

hardening his penis, though only until her touch was gone. He sucked in a berated breath to bring the rapid beat of his heart under control as Evey stepped to the nearest incubation tube that once housed a male figure — a fatter than normal white man with a shorter than normal dick. She placed her hand to the man's chest, moving it around the curled, sweaty hair that covered him like a rug.

What are you doing? Even though he couldn't read her thoughts, Adamus knew she was desperately trying to find something within his mind she could connect to, but wanted to hear her say it out loud. She never did answer, though, as she placed her other hand to the fat man's temple. Her eyes rolled slightly back into her head, her eyelids beginning to flutter, her mouth agape.

"My fuck," Adamus said to himself. He quickly slid in close to Evey and lowered his hands to her shoulders. A shock licked his fingertips the moment he touched her skin. He stepped away, the burning beginning to inch into his palms. Adamus concentrated on reducing the pain as the fat man began to convulse and shake, his nipples and penis hardening like daggers. The scent of burning flesh permeated the room as the body of a black female nearing her forties, whose arm had been wrapped around the fat man's back, also began to convulse, spit rolling from her mouth and spilling onto the floor beneath her ear. An Asian female that couldn't have been older than twenty, whose head was lying on the black woman's leg and had her arm wrapped around a white male with a pot belly, whose leg crossed over a man, toned to a degree of nearly popping, who was touching the pregnant women, who kissed the teen with a slightly bad case of acne — they all began to convulse, one after the other, until the entire room was bouncing around like dying fish on the sands of a beach. As each new person in the chain was brought under the spell, it became harder for Evey to sustain her hold on them all. The fat man's connection to his new mind locked into place, but if she didn't end her touch soon, her own mind would be torn beyond repair. Gritting her teeth, her eyes closed tight, Evey finally let go of the fat man and fell back, soft, hazy smoke rising from her hands.

Adamus picked her up and placed his hand under the base of her head. He felt a slight pain in her mind and covered it quickly with a soothing flow of fresh blood. In doing so, he was finally able to walk her mind, waiting for her to encounter him within.

Why would you do that? Adamus asked her as he caught sight of her essence.

I had to.

You should have let the connections develop naturally.

It would have taken too long. Her voice was strict, but very weak. *They would have been destroyed if we waited.*

We could have protected them.

We could have, if all of us fought as one. But Gydressina has Kaleena, and unless I'm able to win her back, no amount of our power will keep this city alive. I'm well aware of your other objections, my love, but with Gydressina back to full health, the veil will soon be drawn around her and anyone she wishes. We will need help locating Kaleena.

But we can't trust these bodies any longer, Adamus continued. Evey had found the strength to regain control over her mind.

Some of our followers will not have a complete connection, I know. But trust me. They are all within the hosts. With enough time, they'll be able to gain full control over their weakened minds. Until then, we'll have to convince them to trust us and do as we say. Evey flowed around Adamus with vivacity. Her warm kiss caressed his entire body. *Take trust in my heart, my love.*

As her spirit slowly consumed his, Adamus was pushed from her mind and returned to the room, the hint of roses fading among the sickening aroma of flesh and hair. He opened his eyes as Evey leaned up and kissed his lips, tasting the bitterness of her actions. She pulled her legs underneath her and then spread them around his waist, allowing his penis to enter her body. As the men and women lining the floor of the room slowly began to lie still once again, Evey made love to Adamus, pushing all doubt and trouble from his mind. She expunged a soft whimper with the power of her climax and then rested her thighs against his goose pimpled flesh, kissing him softly, the touch of her hands along his jaw encasing his mind in a fresh rapture.

Feeling the fat man awakening, Evey rubbed her nose along Adamus's lips and then walked to the console. Adamus pulled his leg up to his chest and rested his elbow on his knee, allowing the flow of his numbing pleasure drift from his pours.

Find them robes and gowns, Evey said as she collected her thoughts and stature. When Adamus didn't immediately oblige, Evey turned to him and said, "Now."

Adamus rose speedily to his feet. Her eyes were reddening, but he didn't question her. He simply nodded and went to the ladder. She watched him leave, a trace of love on her lips.

The fat man watched a blur of Adamus climb up the ladder through the hazy slits of his eyes. "What the hell…?" he groaned as he slid his round torso away from the black woman. Evey turned to him as he rubbed his eyes to get a better look around the room. He then looked up to Evey, who smiled graciously, knowing that the connection had been completed.

"Hello, John," Evey said.

"Evestylyn," the fat man stuttered as he stood up. "It worked?"

For some, he heard her say. John scanned the room.

You mean, not all of us were connected?

Circumstances called for a push, Evey said quickly, driving any other questions he might have had from his mind. He accepted her answer with a nod and looked down at his body.

You couldn't have given me a better body? he said.

Not my choice. Evey winked.

John just rolled his eyes. He stepped closer to Evey as the next few people began to wake. As the black woman (Rose, haven taken the body of Charlotte, a nurse from Alabama) stood and hugged John, Adamus returned with an armful of robes and gowns. The Asian woman took a moment to consider her surroundings when the connection of Hannah took hold, collapsing any and all thoughts of Sun, a college student studying for her doctorate. Adamus left the room again, feeling that as more and more of them woke, the less and less the connections

would take effect, and the more shame, confusion and fright would be a part of their consciousness.

As suspected, men and women alike covered their breasts and genitalia, hoping to hide themselves from the room of nude strangers. Some would vomit in fear, others would simply scream and slink to the walls, lumping themselves into a ball on the floor. Their hearts raced and their nerves tightened as their fear escalated with each passing second. The pile of robes and gowns had grown as Adamus delivered the final garments and stood at the base of the ladder. John nodded a quick hello, as did Rose, her eyes glaring with a hint of come-hither pleasure. Having read the sea of minds among them, Adamus looked at Evey with caution. Other than John, Rose, Hannah and a handful of others (which included all of the children, whose minds didn't need much more than a kick in the pants to connect, and a few others who'd been nearest Evey upon the transfer), no one was going to understand how to use the life swarming around them. Evey glared at him a moment, acknowledging that she didn't much care for his concern. She had her new army, which she knew would lead to the final rise of Ediinis.

"Calm yourselves," Evey said through both mind and voice, enhancing the sound through the room and making sure she didn't scare the already frightened group. *"You are not in any danger. Please."*

The whimpers and cries of terror continued as Evey climbed onto the console and raised her arms into the air. John, Ruth and Hannah stepped in front of her, standing firm with their hands behind their backs. They pierced deep into each of the troubled minds and were able to calm most of their fears, brushing them with a sense of ease and openness. Though a few weren't as easily comforted.

"Everyone, please," Evey said again, her voice sweet and soothing to the ear. *"Calm yourselves and listen to me."*

Everyone, even those that seemed ready to faint or run screaming from the caverns in mindless insanity, felt an odd sense of obligation toward her. As she peered into each of their eyes, displaying her own depth of shamelessness and fortitude, a new calm cleansed the room.

"Many of you don't know who I am. My name is Evestylyn. I am your mother and your protector. You may not understand what's happening to you or where you are right now, but you must find faith in my voice and believe in me and my words. I love you all, and I would not lie to any of you. You are not in any danger. And for those of you who feel discomfort, let me assure you that we will remedy that shortly."

Evey paused to take in the sound of her subjects's calming breaths, which sounded like the gentle roar of the sea. The more she spoke, the more peaceful everyone became. They felt connected to her, willing to do as she asked of them without question. She smiled, her heart beating with adoration.

"My children, you look to me now for leadership. I give to you my full devotion. I am confident that you will heed my guidance and trust my knowledge. There are several demons running throughout our glorious home, or city of redemption, that seek to destroy us and burn you all to the ground. We cannot allow them to succeed. But our only chance at victory relies on you and your dedication to me and my love. I will not lie; destroying these demons will be extremely hard and very dangerous. But if you can find the strength to trust in me, I swear to you that not one of you will be harmed."

Evey felt all of their hearts join hers in faith.

"You are all part of this city, and to keep it alive, you must trust in the man next to you and fight with us. If you find your strength, then the beautiful city of Ediinis will rise from the depths and once again rule the land and the sea as it did centuries ago. Protect your home and help me in my fight to regain control of your beloved lives."

Evey listened to each of their reactions. The half that came from the world of foolishness and lies tried to fight the Ediinis connection, but it was clear they honestly believed they were part of the city. She looked them over again and caught the eyes of a woman with mousy-brown hair standing near the back of the group. A familiar resonance of pleasure sizzled her body.

"My children, I now ask that you join one another in entering the city and begin your journey. Women, take the hearts of the women you see below me as my own and follow them to your destination. Do as they say as if it were my own voice and do not stray. They will take care of you and protect you from any harm. For those women *that are near a female child, please take their hand and keep them safe. They are your children now. Protect them as such. Men, you will wait for their departure and then you will allow these men to guide you in your tasks. The fight begins today."*

Rose stepped forward as Evey climbed down from the console. *"Please grab a gown. After you've clothed yourself, head up the ladder and wait for further instruction."*

As the majority of women took hold of the white gowns like a group of ferocious animals fighting over the remnants of meat on a carcass, those who were next to female children scooped them up and carried them to the gowns, hugged them and kissed them before taking their hands and guiding them to join the group. If they were teenagers, the women talked to their new child in depth before committing them their protection. Adamus watched over everyone carefully, feeling their comfort levels rising, the shame of being nude wearing away as they covered their bodies. Evey grabbed a gown from the pile and paced her way through the crowd, brushing by several of the men (giving each of them a soft erection) until she reached the woman with the mousy-brown hair. She took her arm and escorted her to one of the corners of the cavern. Though she continued to hide the private parts of her body, the woman followed Evey with ease, especially as the young, vibrant woman handed her the gown and situated herself between her and all of the men.

"Go ahead," Evey said. "Put it on. No one's watching."

The woman searched Evey's magnetic eyes, melting into the familiarity of the glistening silver. She took the robe knowing that not one eye would spy on her as she threw the gown over her head and allowed it to slip across her icy skin.

"Feel better?" Evey asked, though she already knew the answer.

The woman nodded and whispered a soft, "Yeah," as she shifted the gown to make it slightly more comfortable. As she tied the belt around her back, she looked past Evey to catch a glimpse of the young man helping a woman onto the ladder. He seemed unbelievably familiar, though she couldn't understand why.

"That's good," Evey smiled. "I need you to keep someone company for me."

The woman nodded slightly, ignoring Evey's original command and accepting

her new assignment. Evey reached out and touched the woman's arm, permeating a warm, sensual smile. Trust between the two had officially been locked in place.

Atlantis – Hallways – 10 hours 54 minutes after arrival

Thomas had lost almost all hope in finding Trishen. The crying that had been leading him in his current direction had faded long ago, but he still felt a presence pulling him toward her, almost as if her breaths were connected to his, able to use it like a compass. The stronger her breath was among his, the more he knew he was going the right way. When it softened, he was moving away from her. But even now, that connection seemed to be slipping no matter which way he traveled. It scared him, as if Trishen was losing her breath entirely — as if she was dying.

But that couldn't be true. He still felt a vibrant, strong connection. She had to be close, possibly right above him. And if she was giving up, he had to get to her quick.

He had to continue to believe.

Climbing the stairs to reach the corridor above him felt like it took days, but when he reached the top, her presence grabbed him and pulled him straight to the wall in front of him. There was no doubt Trishen was on the other side, but he had no idea of how to get in. He slammed his fists against it and called out her name. The sound that came back was hollow and stale. Getting in became bleak as Thomas grew hoarser and more desperate, a light spray of dry tears rising to his aged eyes. Almost out of energy, Thomas rested his forehead on the wall and whispered, "God, Trishen. I'm sorry. I was a coward. I don't want to hide it anymore, but it's impossible. I tried, honestly, I tried. I'm so sorry." He paused to swallow the lump in his throat and finished, "I love you."

As the last words slipped from his tongue, a small light emitted through a crack about five feet to Thomas's left. He looked up, cleared his slightly foggy eyes (though it didn't help all that much, as Thomas knew his eyesight had diminished along with his age), and watched as the crack grew into another room. He cautiously slid toward the middle, making sure no one he wasn't expecting would catch him off guard. Staring directly at a giant picturesque window to the city below the sea, Thomas saw Trishen huddled among a line of pillows, unmoving. Her name echoed around him and his steps were heavy and slow. But at the moment he reached her, his heart burst with joy; she wasn't dead. She was simply asleep (or unconscious — in a coma, maybe?). He grabbed her shoulder and leaned in close to her chest, continuously calling her name, hoping against hope she would wake up for him. To his extreme delight, her eyes opened. A weight of grief and torment lifted off of him. He wrapped his arms around her in a strong, loving embrace. "Trishen, you're all right. Thank God."

What he didn't notice was Trishen's inability to reciprocate the affection. When he let go, her eyes finally warned him of her apprehension. There was distant fear swimming among them and her mouth was open wide, seemingly forcing air into her lungs.

"Trishen," Thomas quickly said, knowing full well why she didn't recognize him. Would he be able to convince her? "It's me. Thomas." Trishen's apprehension transformed into confusion. She shook her head, attempting to push away from him. No sound came from her, not even a whimper or a grunt. Thomas's heart felt about ready to shatter as he watched the fear turn to tears. "Trishen, please. You have to believe me. It's Thomas."

Trishen became more desperate to escape his tightening grip. When he finally let go, she retreated to the corner of the wall and huddled into herself. Thomas fell backward with his fist to his lips, biting back his own set of parched tears and wondering if there was any way he'd be able to prove to her who he was. He thought perhaps his hand might help, but the scars that were so heavy before now just looked like part of his dried, wrinkled skin. His voice had changed slightly, hitting a somewhat lower register than was normal with a hint of mucus-swelled syllables, so that was no help. There was only one possible way he could think of to convince Trishen of the truth. And though Thomas didn't much believe in it, he had no other choice.

Without a word, Thomas lowered his body to the ground and shifted as close as he could to Trishen before she tried to claw her way out of the room. He stopped and simply looked at her with the best puppy-dog eyes he could muster. At first she resisted, shoving her head into her knees. But as Thomas remained quietly motionless, Trishen peeked out and saw his kind, apologetic expression bouncing back to her. As she lifted her head mere millimeters at a time, Thomas raised his hand to her and held it there, waiting patiently for her to react. It took a bit of time, but the more Trishen looked deeper into the old man's eyes, the more she recognized a layer of truth she wasn't sure she was ready to accept. Slowly, her body relaxed and she lowered her legs. In a moment of loving trust, she lifted her hand to his and touched the very ends of his fingers. It was then Trishen saw past the age — past the shell — and saw Thomas's soul. A flush of excitement raced through her. She smiled and took in a few tearful breaths before clasping his hand and wrapping her arms around him. As he held her tight, her tears fell upon his back.

When she let go, she held his face in her hands. Thomas could see the question she so wanted to speak aloud rolling through her mind. He looked away shyly. She pulled him back, gave him a rich smile and set his arm around her shoulder. He didn't fight it; he simply pulled his legs out from underneath him and rested his back against the wall, grasping Trishen's shoulder in comfort and allowing her to rest her head on his chest. The moment was perfect. Even with all of the whispered voices continuing to try and force her to go mad, Trishen was finally at ease. She wanted nothing more than to stay in this embrace forever.

Atlantis – Tower of Youth – 10 hours 56 minutes after arrival

For several minutes, Gydressina kept Kaleena mesmerized, flexing her fingers along the curves of her newborn thighs, legs and chest. There was nothing else around Kaleena but the aura of her… friend? Mentor? Her mother. "Mother?" she whispered without realizing it. Gydressina rested her hand on Kaleena's knee and flashed a tender, affectionate smile.

"Don't worry, my child," she said, softly. "I am safe."

Jaime glistened through the outline of Gydressina's presence. "I know," Kaleena said. "And I'm going to keep you that way."

"Don't stray," Jaime said lightly. "Listen to Gydressina."

"Okay." And with that, Jaime was gone. "Mom," Kaleena called out. *Mom!*

Calm your heart. Gydressina pulled Kaleena to her breast. She could hear the steady rhythm of Gydressina's heartbeat, shifting her mind back to the sacrifice of the light. "Lauren!" she called out, rising to her knees.

It's okay, Gydressina said, raising the tips of her fingers to her lips. *Lauren is quite happy. She's found the true love she once lost.* Kaleena saw a bright, energetic sparkle in Gydressina's eye. *And now, we must find yours.*

My mom. The thought filled Kaleena's body like a warm breeze. That is until Gydressina's features turned distant. *What's wrong?*

I'm afraid I must find your mother alone.

What? The tenderness and warmth was now gone.

Gydressina, knowing full well what possessed Kaleena's heart, took her cheek and drilled deep into her eyes. *Some things are about to occur that are out of my control. It's imperative, for the lives of both you and your father, that you do exactly as I say.*

Kaleena wanted desperately to object, fight to go with her, but Gydressina's touch revealed a weird acceptance.

You need to trust that I'm protecting you. I will find your mother and I will unite you. I promise.

Unable to resist Gydressina's plea, Kaleena nodded. *Okay.*

Gydressina still felt a slight resistance, but knew she meant what she said. *Listen to me closely. You must take your father to Spirited Wind as fast as you can. Do you remember how to get there?*

Yes, Kaleena said quietly.

Don't turn back, don't stray from my words. Whatever happens, find your way there and wait for me to return with your mother.

But —

No questions. Get there. Stay protected. That's all I ask.

Kaleena again wanted to object, but couldn't bring herself to do it. "Fine," she huffed.

Okay. Gydressina's smile was soft and sweet. Everything would occur exactly as she perceived it. Kaleena would not let her down. *Thank you.*

The infectious smile grew upon Kaleena's lips as Gydressina collected her into her arms. Just then, Matthew sat up, his head pounding.

"What the hell was that?"

Kaleena turned. To her surprise, Matthew's appearance had returned to normal, his old age having vanished completely. In some ways, he actually looked younger and healthier. "Dad." Her breath was light. She wrapped her arms around him. "I love you," she said without barrier.

"I love you too, kiddo," Matthew said, basking in the moment. It was the first time he had a hug this long and this loving since just after Kaleena's return from the hospital. He would cherish this moment for as long as he was allowed. Gydressina stood honored to be among such love.

When Kaleena finally let go, her cheeks bright and childlike, Matthew noticed his hands. He stood up, feeling as if he could run a three-day marathon without ever taking a break. "What happened?" he said again, hopping around on his fresh legs like a kid on a trampoline. Kaleena laughed, young and energetic.

"Lauren has become one with us," Gydressina said, crossing her wrists above her naval. "In the spirit of life."

Matthew's smile faded as he became hauntingly spellbound in the perfection that stood before him. She appeared to be a goddess, her skin perfectly unblemished. Her smile was real, trusting and pure, her eyes unaffected and kind. Matthew blushed brightly in her wake and lowered his eyes, beaming a gentleman.

Kaleena giggled and swiped Lauren's gown off the ground. She handed it to Gydressina. "Here," she said, keeping her eyes from straying to Gydressina's body as well. "I think you better toss this on. Lauren would've wanted it."

Gydressina took the gown politely and pulled it over her head, allowing it to

flutter down to her rounded toes. She tied the belt in a bow at the small of her back. "Is that better?" Gydressina asked sweetly as she pulled her soft curls out of the dress. They sank to the gown like cotton. Matthew nodded bashfully.

"I have a question," Kaleena said, breaking the sweetness between them.

"Lauren lives within us," Gydressina said, answering her question. "As she was always meant to."

"Always meant to?" The shock was as clear in Matthew as it was in Kaleena's simple recognition.

"It was always meant to be her," Kaleena acknowledged.

"I needed to break her connection to Evey."

"And the only way to do that was to convince me to sacrifice myself."

Gydressina nodded. "I'm sorry for the deception."

Matthew took hold of Kaleena's shoulders and massaged them gently.

"So, what now?"

A roar that forced Kaleena to her knees and turned Matthew to ice echoed through the tower. Kaleena's stomach turned, but she forced her eyes open to peer down at the lower catwalk. She saw who she knew now was Cephis staring back at her with his dark, muscled arms raised to her — a father urging his daughter to jump. His hot breath invaded her thoughts and her teeth began to sting with needles.

Fight it, Gydressina said, hoping Kaleena would be able to defend her mind. When it became apparent that Cephis was too strong for her, she entered the child's mind and pushed Cephis from it. A second roar erupted as Kaleena inhaled a cool refreshing blast of air. She felt Gydressina shielding her mind, but didn't fight it. Instead, she learned from it, taking everything her protector offered her in the way of defense and strength. She finally understood how to allow her heart to control her mind.

Gydressina helped Kaleena to her feet. *Come close,* Gydressina commanded Matthew, who obliged without delay. She grabbed his wrist and pulled both of her subjects under her arms, placing her hands to the center of their stomachs.

Do as I say. Do not hesitate. Though neither one answered, Gydressina felt their acknowledgment in their fear.

Cephis climbed the stairs like a cheetah hunting its prey, embroiled in taking Kaleena as his own. As he reached the upper catwalk, and came face to face with Gydressina, he calmly composed himself and stood as dead as a statue. Even though she couldn't see him, Kaleena sensed a rather intimate conversation being volleyed back and forth between her friend and her foe. She wanted to listen, to know what was being said, but the more she tried to find the vibration of their voices, the more her mind began to pinch closed. She finally gave up, well aware Gydressina was blocking her communication, most likely to hide Kaleena's eventual destination. That is, if they could escape with their lives.

After several minutes of this tense silence, Cephis lowered his hood. The man underneath had extremely dark skin and even darker hair that was greased back and pulled tight into a short ponytail. His jaw line was chiseled into a thick block with a five o'clock shadow stippled along its edges. Kaleena's heart turned to stone and she assumed the same was happening to Matthew. But Gydressina remained as calm as a Spring flower. Without warning, Cephis dropped to his knees and placed his fist to the floor. A shockwave traversed through the metal like an earthquake. Kaleena suddenly felt fright unlike she'd ever felt before. She couldn't be sure what was headed their way, but knew if it reached her, she'd feel the force of a hundred stampeding mustangs ring through her body. A cold sweat formed across her forehead as the force gained ground Gydressina slowly moved her left foot back, almost bracing herself to take on the full impact. Just before the quake reached their toes, Gydressina tossed Kaleena and Matthew across the room and fought the energy by absorbing the magnitude of its power. Kaleena and Matthew hit the ground halfway between Gydressina and Cephis. They rolled a bit to try and relieve the shock of the landing. As they came to a stop, Gydressina arched her fingers in a small ball shape around her palm as if she were holding a pair of softballs, and then pulled them toward her. A strong wind whipped past Kaleena and Matthew. Cephis was lifted off the ground. He landed hard on his knees at Gydressina's feet. As he did, he grabbed Gydressina's ankle. With the twist of his wrist and push of his thumb, he splintered the bone through the skin of the Achilles. Gydressina didn't scream; she simply pulled Cephis's head up. His teeth began to grind into sparks. That was when Kaleena heard Gydressina's voice ring in her head.

Go. Run. Now. Head to Spirited Wind and do not look back.

Kaleena hesitated, watching her push Cephis to a breaking point of his mind.

I said GO!

Kaleena's trance broke and she grabbed Matthew's arm. "Come on, Dad," she said as she helped him up. He was a bit groggy, but followed her down the stairs without question.

Meanwhile, Gydressina continued to ground Cephis's mind into pieces of garbage. *Your time is up, Cephis. Your reign here has ended.*

Your mind is strong, Gydressina. But your faith in your heart is still your clearest weakness.

You're wrong. My faith in my heart is faith in the life, in the light. It's your most formidable enemy.

You never could accept that nothing is stronger than the mind.

At that moment, Gydressina fell to her knee and Cephis threw the butt of his wrist into her jaw, knocking her back. He stood, proving his dominance over her as she lay on the ground at his feet like a slave. *I will win this war, Gydressina. Once and for all, my essence will corrupt the life you believe in so openly. And those you have controlled into the darkness will exist as the light. My fire will dominate the world.* Cephis then picked her up and threw her limp body over the edge of the catwalk.

A swift wash of nausea swept through Kaleena's stomach. As Gydressina fell through the beam, Kaleena wanted to scream out and jump in after her, but an eerie force seemed to push her from doing so. She could do nothing; but she didn't have to. Gydressina shifted her body to point her head at the pool of light below and dropped her arms above her head, hitting the pool like a diver scoring a perfect ten in the Olympics. And then she was gone. Kaleena held back the tears she

wanted to liberate as Matthew mumbled for them to keep going.

Lay down your life now, Kaleena, Cephis burned into her mind. *You cannot beat me.*

The hell I can't, Kaleena replied, looking up to him. She blocked his continued attempts to enter her mind again, which dropped her to her knees. If she stayed any longer, her mind would implode. Matthew, seeing his daughter struggle, sucked up his own weakened body, lifted Kaleena into his arms and carried her the rest of the way down the steps. As they hit the lowest level catwalk and left the tower, Kaleena hissed, attempting to control her screams.

Cephis remained at the top ledge, smelling the air around him, aggravated, but thrilled by the now heightened abilities of Kaleena. Only Gydressina could have given her that much power. He could have caught them, took their lives with the grip of his palm, but what fun would that have been? He was ready for the fight that was about to come and looked forward to the sport of the hunt.

Let the game begin, Love.

*   *   *

Matthew ran as far as he could until the burn in his legs got the better of him. Crippling to the ground, he did his best to lower Kaleena before he dropped her. As her head slapped the metal floor, the sharp pain that had already been swarming her head was knocked free, replaced by the pain of the bump on the back of her head. Matthew massaged his calves forcefully as Kaleena sat up, rubbing the pain away. She still felt Cephis attempting to trail her with his mind, but it seemed the farther they got from him, the easier it was to block his intrusion.

"Where are we?" she asked, looking at the sterile walls. No plants were present and it seemed like they had traveled into a psych ward or some strange starship she might have seen once on *Star Trek*. Any minute now, some alien creatures would chase down a couple of guys in red shirts who would be gunned down — a diversion to help Captain Kirk escape with Spock and some green alien hottie

by his side. She couldn't help but chuckle at the thought.

"I don't know," Matthew said, agitated. Part of him wanted to hear a thank you for saving her life.

"Thank you," Kaleena said with a wink. Matthew didn't know if he should be frightened or laugh.

Kaleena brushed a couple more rubs past the back of her head and stood up. She searched the memories she had acquired — *downloaded?* — from Gydressina, hoping to figure out where they were. Finding her way to Spirited Wind wouldn't be a problem, but she'd have to know her position within the city first. She stepped up to the wall and pressed her hands to them, believing it would help her figure out the location. What she felt against her fingertips was Evey's heartbeat. It felt so odd, so loving, yet so dangerous. She pulled away from the wall as if she'd just been bitten. Matthew heard her squeak in fright and stood up.

"What happened?"

Kaleena calmed herself quickly for his benefit. "Nothing," she said, the pitch in her voice a bit higher than normal. "Nothing, it's just..." Her mind began to interpret the heartbeat, trying hard to locate the mind behind it. As she peeled away all the layers, she found what she was looking for. The tubes she'd seen when scouring the city had been opened, and the men and women inside were now filling Evey's mind. She was prepping them for — what? Kaleena couldn't tell, not with what little touch she had been given. The only thing she knew for certain was that Evey wasn't tracking her. She had Cephis for that. Evey was tracking someone else, someone very important to Kaleena and the only leverage she'd have to hold over her.

"Mom," she let out under her breath.

Get to Spirited Wind and stay protected. Gydressina's voice was loud and clear. But how could she hide when Gydressina had fallen to what she could only assume was her death to the light? She couldn't take the chance that Gydressina would come back from that fall, which would allow Jaime to collapse into Evey's deceptions. It was time to take a stand against her fears and become the leader of her

own destiny. It was her only chance to get both of her parents out of the city. She remained hopeful that Gydressina was still alive, but until she knew for sure, she'd do everything in her power to save the ones she loved — even if it meant going against Gydressina's wishes? Kaleena made a decision.

"We need to find mom," she said.

"Do you know where she is?"

"No. But Evey's prepping an army. She's not safe anymore."

"An army?" Matthew didn't know how Kaleena could know that, but he no longer felt the need to question her. Never again. "Damn it."

"Don't worry. I'll figure it out." She could tell Matthew doubted she'd be able to track her down, and she herself had little faith in her abilities. But as she tried to imagine the simplest and most obvious place they may be holding Jaime, she caught sight of a memory of Adamus creating a child in Evey's womb as she lay on her silk pillow, smiling up at him, feeling the creation of her new child's life coming to fruition. It all made sense for her. "The conception room. Firelight."

"What?"

Kaleena decided to forgo explanation in favor of time. She gently rested her fingertips on the wall again and felt for Evey, hoping the child wouldn't sense her in return. She searched until she felt Evey's eyes glance her way. The second she removed her hands, she searched her mind, hoping Evey hadn't found her way in. When she was certain she'd only gotten a slight glimpse, it was time to act. Evey was on the move.

"This way," Kaleena said, heading back the way they had come. It was a risk, Kaleena knew, as she could feel Cephis growing closer, but this was the only way she knew of to get to Firelight.

"Wait," Matthew said as he limped quickly after her. "How do you know she'll be there?"

I don't, she thought. But she had to be. There could only be one reason why Cephis would rescue Jaime and the rest of the women. He needed them to create new generations of Ediinis. And if she was right (though she would never tell

Matthew this, in fear of getting his hopes up) they might just end up finding Thomas there as well. It all felt right. She would be there.

She will be there.

Atlantis – Hallways – 11 hours 18 minutes after arrival

"Where the *fuck* are we?" Patricia yelled as loud as she could, hoping someone would hear her so she could punch them, if only it would take away the shake in her hands. Patricia had been following Jaime through the endless halls for what felt like hours, ascending and descending staircases, walking past doors and plants that all looked exactly the same. For the last half hour, she'd been convinced they were going in circles, but hadn't mentioned it in favor of trying to fight her restless withdrawals by telling Kara stories about her daughter, some of the mindless pranks she used to pull on her college roommate and the trouble she used to get into as a kid. But the more they walked, and the less interested Kara seemed to be in the inane antics of an overgrown child, the more maddening it became to deal with. And she just had to let it out. "Please, God. Help us out here, will ya'? With such a highly evolved race of idiots, you'd think we'd get at least one directional sign, or arrow — 'This way to your freedom'."

"Calm down," Jaime snapped. She continued to examine her surroundings carefully, hoping to find something to help guide her through the indistinguishable maze she'd gotten them all into.

"Yeah," Kara said quickly, hoping to lighten the mood a little. She hadn't said anything in about five minutes. "Don't want to get that fire bolt sent up your ass."

Patricia slumped her features in annoyance. "It was a lightning bolt," she said, her voice low and irritated. "And shut the hell up."

"Look, you're not doing us any favors by screaming at the fucking walls," Jaime said, her frustration beginning to match Patricia's.

"What? You afraid your new boyfriend'll find us? You afraid he'll strip you down and lick all your skin off?"

Trying to ignore her idiocy: "I'd just rather stay under the radar until we know where the hell we are, okay?" Jaime paused, a lack of air tightening her lungs. She placed her hand to her chest. "Shit," she breathed as she put her hand to the wall, hoping to calm her growing irritability.

"Under the radar," Patricia mumbled under her breath. "I'll put your mouth under the radar."

That's it! Jaime heard herself scream, her cheeks beaming bright red. She turned to Patricia, seething. "What do you want me to do, huh? I'm just trying to get us the fuck out of this place without getting us fucked over. Or at the very least, killed."

"Well, you're not doing a very good job at it, my fearless leader." The sarcasm burned through Jaime's reddening eyes. "It's not hard to cluelessly send us in circles."

"You think your fat ass could do better?"

"My fat ass could find a toilet in a porcelain shithole."

"Hey," Kara screamed at the top of her lungs, to absolutely no avail.

"What?" Jaime said as she looked at Patricia as if she'd gone completely insane.

"At least I don't fall in even when the seat's down, you skinny bitch." Patricia pushed Jaime, hoping it would end the conversation. Jaime fell back a few steps, but caught her balance quickly. Her eyes glowed with anger. Patricia hoped she'd attack; she was more than ready to lay her out.

Jaime smiled devilishly. "Oh, you're in it now." Keeping her body low, she sprinted toward Patricia, who knew what was coming. She tucked her arms in close to her body and caught Jaime's shoulders. Twisting her around, Patricia wrapped her thick arms around Jaime's neck. She felt a pinch, but it didn't stop her from grabbing Patricia's hair and pulling it down toward her as hard as she could. Patricia screamed and her grip loosened. Jaime slipped out of her grasp and turned back around. She pushed Patricia to the wall and kneed her in the gut.

At this point, Kara finally got into the act. She grabbed Jaime's arms before she could land a right hook to Patricia's nose. Jaime turned to throw Kara off, allowing Patricia to slide from the wall and push them both away. Kara slipped on Jaime's

foot. Before either knew it, their legs got tangled together, sending them both to the floor. As they landed, Jaime's elbow hit Kara's jawbone and swiped across her nose, pounding Kara's head to the floor.

"Mother fudge bucket," Kara yelled as Jaime rolled off of her. Kara could already taste the freshness of blood beginning to curdle in her mouth. She spit some out and grabbed her nose.

"Damn, Reeses. I'm sorry."

"What the hell is wrong with you two?" Kara roared. She could hardly see any of them through the mist in her eyes. Curling up a sitting position, she sat by herself spitting blood onto the floor.

Jaime turned away from Kara, unable to look at her. She couldn't remember ever being angry enough to draw blood before. She suddenly felt her own stress grow in her eyes. She tried to hold back the tears, stay strong —

you are their leader

— but all she could think about was Kaleena's words — *You can't stop acting like a teenager with a tree up their ass. I'm just so frightened that you've forgotten everything we went through. I can't stand being around you knowing who you really are.* She hadn't seen it before, couldn't understand where it had come from until just now. Kaleena wasn't only smarter than she could ever be; she was far more grown-up as well. If everything else Jaime had done hadn't already proved she was unwilling to accept that she was falling apart, arguing like a ten-year old sure did. What would Kaleena think of her if she'd seen that unforgivable invective?

Patricia kept her eyes on Kara. She wanted to help her, but her guilt kept her from doing so. She'd been acting like an ass, that's for sure, and it may have just cost her a friend — *two friends?* — because of it. Though she'd never gone as far as throwing a punch, Jaime sure had taken a lot of abuse — if only verbal — from her over the years, especially after dealing with shit from her husband or trying to get bills paid with toilet paper and Oreos. Much like siblings, they always seemed to let it go once the steam died down. Her fear was that Kara wouldn't be so open to this forgiveness. They didn't know each other that well, and this may have left a more negative impact than Patricia ever wanted. She just had to suck it up and do something. She kneeled next to Kara and rested her hand on her back. "Let me see."

Kara quickly threw her hand at Patricia and pushed her away. "Stop," she said and then stood. Upon looking the two of them over, there seemed to be a lot of regret, but Kara couldn't take it right now. She raised her hand up, prepared to say something she might never be able to take back, and chose instead to turn and walk away. What she truly needed now was room to breathe.

"Reeses," Patricia said.

Kara turned around. "Don't," she said forcefully. "Don't call me that." And then she sprinted away.

Patricia wanted to call for her to come back, but all she could do was turn to Jaime, who watched Kara until she disappeared around the corner. She finally shifted her eyes to meet Patricia's and shook her head, wondering how they had reached this point. Would she ever be able to leave behind the person she had become and prove to Kaleena — and more so, herself — that she was better than this? Jaime lowered her head to her knees and shook slightly.

"I'm going after her," Patricia finally said.

You should let her go, a soft voice said before Patricia could slide herself to her feet.

Patricia turned to Jaime. "Did you say something?"

Jaime eyed Patricia. "No," she drew out.

"Are you sure?"

"Uh… I think I'd know if I said anything."

"That's so weird. I swear —"

You did.

This time Jaime heard it too. Her first thought was Cephis had returned. But that was completely bogus; the voice was too sparkly. "What was that?" she asked.

"You heard it that time," Patricia confirmed, happy she wasn't going insane.

Looking all around them, Jaime said, "I think we better get out of here."

"What about Kara?"

"She's smart," Jaime said. "She'll find her way out of here."

Patricia hesitated. She wanted to make sure Kara was okay, but Jaime was probably just making sure they all stayed safe. If they went after Kara now, they might all be caught, and then what? Would they be probed? Interrogated? Killed? "You're probably right," she said. "We probably should have been following her to begin with, huh?"

Jaime dropped her brow, a confused resentment scouring her face. But as she absorbed Patricia's smarmy smirk, she couldn't help crack her own smile. It was true. "Come on," she said and walked to Patricia, offering her hand. Patricia accepted graciously and Jamie pulled her to her feet.

"Which way, fearless leader?"

"I have no porcelain shithole of an idea."

Patricia shook her finger at Jaime, scowling like Robert DeNiro. "You," she said. "You."

Jaime slapped Patricia on the back, flipping her eyebrows up in recognition. Patricia's calm smile faded as she looked past Jaime to see an incredibly thin woman step around the corner, flanked by two larger-sized men in dark robes.

"What the hell?" Patricia said, taking a step back.

Jaime turned around, her own smile disappearing. She let go of Patricia and stood straight, hiding any fear that swarmed through her blood.

"Hello to you, too, Patricia," the woman said. She walked closer. The two men stayed just a step behind her, seemingly ready to pull out a couple of Uzis at any sign of trouble.

"Whoa, there, miss pretty," Patricia said, acknowledging the woman's natural beauty. "Who are you and how the hell do you know my name?"

"I know many things about you. In fact, I'd say I know you better than even your own husband."

"I wouldn't be surprised about that," Patricia said, continuing to slowly pace backwards. She reached her arm out to touch Jaime's back, almost pushing her to keep her in front as a shield, and at the same time, pulling her to follow. "But

how do you know anything?"

"I know because I've walked your mind."

"Ah, hell."

"You don't believe me?"

"Hey. I'm standing in the halls of Atlantis. I'm right near believing I'm about to see a miniature pig buzz my head any minute."

"Good. So why so frightened?"

"Well… First impressions from this underwater bazaar you call home haven't been so spectacular."

"Okay." The woman held her arms out slightly, stopping the men behind her. They stood silent, staring at Patricia and Jaime. "So query."

"Say what now?" Patricia stopped but retained Jaime at arm's length. Jaime wasn't sure if she should interject or continue to keep guard over the men as she had been doing the whole time. If they made one false move, she would bolt, but hoped she wouldn't have to. For some reason, the woman felt very comfortable to be around. A part of her just wanted to sit and start up a conversation, a couple of friends in their pajamas and sleeping bags, lying around in the living room discussing nothing at the same time they try and keep themselves awake until the sun rises for no other reason than to see if they could do it.

"What will help me repair the negative first impression you hold of my home?"

Patricia looked at the two men before spitting out, "Show me the exit?"

The woman closed her eyes peacefully with enjoyment, as if she was pulling the question in to digest it and compute the correct answer.

"You are quite humorous, Patricia."

"Most would say astonishingly annoying. But thanks, I guess."

The woman nodded, her eye contact sharp.

"What do you want?" Jaime finally spoke. She was tired of listening to the inane back-and-forth that was getting them nowhere.

"All I want is your help," the woman said, without acknowledging the change of speaker.

"With what?"

"Nothing at all, really. Simple, yet necessary."

Jaime paused. Patricia stared at the woman, pushing her for more information with her contorted expressions.

"I need you to help me locate and apprehend Kaleena Stevens."

"Kaleena," Jaime said. She took a step closer to the woman. Patricia wasn't sure if she should move with her or stay put. "She's alive?" Jaime's excitement warmed the woman's mind.

"Very much so. And quite well, I must say."

A fresh smile rose to Jaime's lips. Deep down she already knew Kaleena was okay, but receiving confirmation filled her with something she hadn't felt for a very long time, if ever at all. For a second, she wondered if the woman was simply lying to get them to go with her, but for whatever reason, she had to believe she was telling the truth. Without it, Jaime wasn't sure how much farther she could go.

"But you don't know where she is?"

"I know where she is," the woman sang softly.

"So why do you need us to catch her for you?" Patricia said, acknowledging what she really wanted. "Like a damn fish?"

Jamie finally put the pieces together. "What are you going to do to her?"

A menacing vibe flowed through Jaime's blood as the woman turned cold. "That is none of your concern."

"The hell it is. She's my daughter."

"That is irrelevant."

"Irrelevant?" Jaime stepped foolishly close to the woman, her eyes burning with sudden aggravation.

"But of course." Instead of cowering away (as Jaime irrationally hoped would happen), the woman stepped in extremely close, her nose almost rubbing against Jaime's. "You may have given birth to her, but with everything you've done to her since, you've proven to me that she's nothing more than a biological extremity."

Before the last two words left the woman's lips, Jaime's anger had risen to the guise of fury and her hand had rolled into a fist. Attempting to punch the woman with her whole body, Jamie found herself slower than she expected. Or was it that the woman was just too quick for her? Either way, the woman caught Jaime's fist in her hand as if she knew it was coming. Behind her, Patricia opted to stay neutral for the time being, unable to find even an ounce of bravery.

"Your love has broken, Jaime. She's as much your daughter as I am her sister, and I need her to complete my body. If you will not willingly help me capture her, I will have to force my hand."

"Fuck you, you bitch," Jaime said. A tiny amount of spit escaped her lips, landing on the woman's mouth and dripping down her chin. The woman seemed to enjoy the taste of Jaime's saliva.

"Very good," she said, grabbing Jaime's neck and shoving her up against the wall. Patricia finally made a move toward her, but the woman's bodyguards were on her like lightning. They grabbed her arms and pushed her against the wall several yards from Jaime.

"Get the hell off me, you fucks," she screamed.

Vines started growing around her, collecting her arms and legs tight against the wall. The harder Patricia struggled, the tighter they grew. The plants around Jaime also worked their way around her. The woman continued to stare fiercely into Jaime's eyes, as the plants finished cocooning both of her foes, softly constraining their chests with even the slightest of movements. Only their heads remained free. The woman's attention then deviated slightly. Her lapse in concentration was met with a slight smirk.

"In time, Jaime, I will convince your faulty mind that I am not only to be trusted, but revered." The woman leaned in close, the two men standing guard over Patricia, staring at her like she was a painting.

"My name is Evestylyn. And you will soon bow to me as your god."

* * *

The blood that had dripped down Kara's neck was drying as she stormed swiftly down the hall, hoping she wasn't being followed. She needed to be alone, get away and get her mind straight. Then again, a small piece of her wanted to see Jaime and Patricia race up behind her, if for no other reason than to feel she was wanted. Had they chased after her, it would have proven she was a welcome acquaintance, if not their friend, and showed her that they did, in fact, feel sorry for what happened, wanting to make amends for their boorish behavior. Conflicted anger and a sense of loneliness set in when it became apparent they weren't following her. *What am I going to do?* She had just abandoned the only two people she knew in this godforsaken city. Without them, she believed she'd never find her way out.

She was doing what she felt was right.

Diana had chosen to leave everything she knew behind because it would supposedly make her stronger and prove she wasn't a little girl anymore, that she could be independent and find her way back home only when she found her true self. Kara was envious of that pure confidence. But then, as she pulled her old gray Hatchback into one of the parking stalls near the Southwest gate of the airport, it never occurred to her that Diana would never find her way home. Even though Kara wouldn't have seen her all that much had Diana not gone to Europe, what with trying to expedite her master's degree by taking classes in the summer and going into the field to get some hands on experience, she was still very excited and eager to hear all about the trip. She would never claim living vicariously through her little sister, but she wanted to know everything that happened, everything she encountered, and everyone she met — a schoolgirl joy that evaporated as she stepped into the airport.

The air seemed stale and serene. The flourish of moving bodies was absent, replaced by a calm Kara had never encountered at any of the dozens of airports she'd been in. All around her, people were standing quiet in front of the televisions, sitting slumped in the various chairs lining the walkways, some of them dumbfounded by something beyond their reasoning, others crying over disbelief, and

yet others staring into space as if some creature had just taken over their minds and left them drones of their former selves. Kara stepped soberly up to one of the monitors and watched the news broadcast painted all over the airport atmosphere. She listened to the ramblings of the female reporter spouting something about past crashes over shots of the ocean. The volume on the television had been set low, but it sounded as if Kara was in a movie theater.

Turning to a tall, lean man wearing a business suit and clutching a briefcase that was turning his knuckles red, Kara asked, "What's going on?"

"I don't know," he said. "I just got here myself. But from what I can tell, a plane just disappeared."

"What?" Kara looked back to the television and listened more intently. Her worst fear instantly rushed through her mind. "Which flight?"

"Not sure. But it's making me think twice about taking my trip." The man turned to Kara and felt horrible. "Oh my god," he whispered. "I'm sorry... was...?"

Kara relaxed her features and shook her head. "I don't know."

"He's not coming," a woman said as she passed by them. The woman was holding the hand of a little four-year-old girl.

"Why?" the little girl asked, matching the tears of her mother.

The woman lifted the little girl into her arms and said softly (though Kara could swear it sounded as if she had shouted it), "Because Daddy's plane disappeared, sweetie."

"But I want to see Daddy," the little girl bawled.

"I know, sweetie." The mother tried to calm her daughter, but how could she when she herself was about ready to break down in hysterics. "I'm sure he's fine, but you'll have to be brave okay? Can you be brave for me?"

The little girl rubbed snot from her nose and nodded. The mother wiped some excess saliva from the girl's mouth. "Good. That's good." She carried the little girl out of the airport.

Kara's tumultuous thoughts were pulled back to the voice on the television. "... rescue boats have been dispatched, but there's still no word on whether or not they've found anything. Again, for those of you just joining us, flight eight-fifteen from France to New York has disappeared over the Atlantic."

Kara watched the reporter's lips continue to flap about, but didn't hear any of what she said, as all she could hear were the words, *Flight eight-fifteen has disappeared.* She raised her hand to her mouth and slumped away from the television. After rushing to the flight schedule monitor, she looked it over frantically, growing slightly dizzy with the combination of her recycled breath and the fog of her thoughts. Finally, she saw her sister's flight number. It was listed: Delayed.

"Delayed?" she screamed without realizing. "Delayed?" Kara kicked the counter next to her and slipped to the ground, her toes pounding in pain, her stomach churning. She wanted to vomit but was too perplexed to figure out how.

This can't be happening, she thought. *Could it?* Could it be possible that she was in her own accident and was lying on the side of the road, dripping in her own blood, her car burning to a crisp as she tried to move legs that had been bent the wrong way? She didn't feel like she was alive right now, her body a rock of anguish.

No. No, this can't be, she tried to convince herself. She finally found enough strength to walk to the nearest information desk. As she stepped up, the cheerful attendant behind the counter, with her freshly braided blonde hair and her far too gleeful blue eyes, asked, "How may I help you?"

"Is it true?" Kara said, her glare frozen.

"I'm sorry?"

"The flight. The flight," she repeated, unable to get anything else out. She tried to be calm.

"I'm not sure what you're asking." The attendant began to grow slightly fearful, evident in the lowering of the corners of her smile.

"Flight eight-fifteen!" Kara yelled. "Eight-fifteen. Eight-fifteen. Is it gone?"

"Gone..." Was the attendant really this dense?

"God, damn it."

Though she tried to keep her peppy smile adorned on her lips, the attendant

finally realized what Kara was talking about and felt horrible. "I'm sorry," she said regretfully. "I truly am…"

Kara held up her hand, stopping the flight attendant from finishing her sentence. She knew what words would be let free and didn't want it confirmed. Not now, or ever, though in the back of her mind she knew she'd have to face it eventually. For the moment, Kara wanted to pretend it was a dream, that the flight was in fact, as seen on the boards, only delayed and would arrive within minutes, if not an hour from now. Diana's lovely smile would encase Kara and relieve her of her fear. Kara went and sat down on the floor in baggage claim, her back pressed up against the large view window. She stared at the conveyors delivering hundreds of bags to passengers of flights that weren't delayed —

Crashed!

Girlfriends and boyfriends, mothers and sons, daughters and uncles, fathers and grandparents. All of them came and went, smiling and happy (with the exception of a few overly stressed commuters yelling and seething into their cell phones, complaining about the turbulence and the rubbery food or the kid that threw up and the sick guy that wouldn't cover his mouth when he coughed) and not one of them noticed Kara, or, if they did make eye contact, hardly made an effort to acknowledge her. And through them all, not one of them was Diana. As the day rolled over into the next, she didn't move a muscle; she hardly even blinked. She was tired, fatigued and had to go to the bathroom ever since she arrived. But she wasn't willing to leave, fearing that once she moved, or even closed her eyes for a fraction of a second, Diana would show up and leave without a word. As a new batch of people gathered around the conveyors, having just departed from the red eye from Denver, Kara saw her.

Her heart fluttered to her stomach as she stood, her knees aching and brittle. She ignored it all as she rushed over to Diana, who was grabbing a large black bag from the belt. As she lowered it to the ground, Kara took hold of her shoulder and spun her around.

"Diana," she said with a misplaced euphoria.

"Pardon me." The woman had to be about forty. She looked quizzically at Kara, who turned slightly green with embarrassment. "Can I help you?"

Kara started backing away. "I'm sorry, I thought…" She quickly turned and rushed to the bathroom, slamming into the nearest stall and vomiting her intestines into the toilet. She sat for several more minutes, gagging and dry heaving until she finally brought herself to reality. Diana wasn't coming. This was not a dream. Diana was gone. Kara forced herself to her feet and walked to the sink. A drip of puke hung from her chin. She saw in her puffed eyes a need to cry, to accept her sister's demise, but she couldn't; she could only turn on the water and brush some over her face. After a moment of feeling like she would faint, she dried off, hoping somehow it would wash everything away. But that too was a dream; nothing could wash this pain away. All she had left was the job of telling her parents — if they hadn't already heard.

It took about a half hour to drag herself back to her car and another hour to finally turn the key in the ignition, having barely the strength to just sit and hold the wheel as she figured out how she would break the news. When the car finally turned over, the radio blared, but not with music.

"Rescue crews have begun scouring the area where they believe the crash occurred, though they're skeptical that any remains will be found. No survivors have been recovered in the current fifty-mile radius they've set up. Our hearts and prayers go out to the friends and families of the unfortunate victims of Southwest flight eight-fifteen."

Tears followed, without restraint.

Kara dropped to her knees as the intense weight of stress finally caught up to her. She raised her hand to her mouth and let all of her fears flood from her body. She cried for leaving Patricia and Jaime; cried for being alone in an unfamiliar place; cried for the sister she was unable to let go of; and cried for Matthew and Thomas, Gavin and Benjamin, Kaleena and Trishen, all of whom, for all she knew, had become nothing more than loving memories as well. It was just too much for her to accept all at once. She had nothing left to do but hope someone would come for her, support her, wrap their arms around her and console her. She felt Matthew's tenderness holding her, allowing her openness to wash over him; she felt Thomas's smile, his joy of the expedition and his love for all that he had. But it was Kaleena's thoughts she felt the most; her presence was close. She heard the words of the page roll through her mind. The belief that nothing extraordinary actually existed or ever happened, and the validation that those beliefs were now being tested somehow calmed her. If Kaleena believed so much, and had so much conviction that Atlantis didn't exist, only to learn that it did (though knowing that she may never have learned that fact made her a bit sick to her stomach), did that mean Diana could possibly still be alive, off somewhere on a little tropical island in the middle of nowhere? It was extremely implausible, but as of now, no longer impossible.

Kara wiped some fresh blood from under her nose. The back of her hand whisked by the first stages of hardening on the cut of her lip. She took several breaths to help melt the anguish away (almost forcing her tears to vanish) and used the plants for support as she stood. It was pointless to pity herself, hiding from the real fear she'd been running from all these years. Diana's drive and love of life, which Kara now knew she blamed for Diana's death, washed through her. She couldn't dishonor her sister's memory by fearing her own life. Kara needed to be strong, if not to help Patricia and Jaime, then to help herself truly remember Diana's final gift to Kara.

With a light resurgence of energy, Kara sprinted back down the hall. As she turned the corner, she stopped and retreated back a few steps, plastering herself to the wall. She took a few quick breaths and knelt low to the ground. Peeking around the corner, she saw Jaime standing literally nose-to-nose with a beautiful woman who was holding Jaime's fist and saying something she couldn't quite make out. After another brief second, the woman pushed Jaime against the wall. The the two large men with her nearly tackled Patricia to do the same. The plants then seemed to devour her friends. Kara jumped away when the plants touching her arm vibrated softly. For a moment, she was in clear view of the mysterious woman, who she felt looking at her, even though the woman hadn't turned her head away from Jaime. Kara immediately retreated back down the hall as fast as she could, hoping to heaven the woman hadn't sent her henchman after her like a couple of bull dogs in a trash dump. She ran for probably a half a mile when she finally caught sight of an open room and bolted inside.

Sliding to the opposite side of the door, she peaked out and waited to see if anyone was coming. After several minutes passed (at least it felt like minutes; for all she knew only seconds had passed), Kara peeled away from the wall and struggled to push the door closed. (*Where's the WD-40 when you really need it?*) She eventually gave up, sliding to the ground, using the door to remain hidden. As she calmed the adrenaline whipping through her like a wind in a hurricane, she noticed several leather books lining the walls. The fright that had been pounding at her heart transformed into meek curiosity. Kara peeked into the hall, then waddled past the opening to the other side of the room. One of the books lay on the floor near what looked to be a chair, but could have been some weird ergonomic bed. It reminded Kara of the diary she used to have as a kid, writing down her inner most thoughts on the gross things boys did in art class or the strange words they used, and the mean things her sister would do to get her in trouble with her parents. Diana was only four, but she had a cruel streak about her, always finding ways to go against her authority figure. Whenever she was caught, she'd blame it on Kara. She hated her for doing it, but over time, found respect in her capability to be so conniving.

She picked up the diary and looked it over. There were no writings, creases or marks of any kind on the soft cover of the book. A satin ribbon dangled down from the binding. She wondered what page the ribbon had been marking and how it had been misplaced. Had someone been here recently? She set the question aside and opened the book. A sense of awe raced through her as she recognized the symbols — they matched the writings on the tablets — and instantly started reading.

"It's been confirmed," it read. "I have been rewarded with [*Kara pondered the next few words, but couldn't quite make them out*]. I am so excited. I have chosen

Adamus to be my paramour [*a word she translated loosely — it definitely could have been something much different, but that was as close as she understood it to be*]. I know his touch will bring to me a child of love and I have already chosen a name. [*She couldn't make out the next part, though she considered the name being used within was Abelis or Abeline.*] A son will be perfect as my first child and I do hope, should I be blessed enough to receive the gratification of a second, to deliver another son — a brother that will love and care deeply for the other. If all happens as I wish, I would hope to request a girl, but as delivering three children into

[*Here, Kara had trouble. She could tell the author was saying the name of the city, but was having a hard time connecting it with Atlantis. Of course, she realized Atlantis wasn't the true name, but something in her hoped it was. She couldn't make it out otherwise.*]

"But that will not stop me from trying. And I do hope Adamus will be the paramour for all of them, no matter how many I am blessed. I wouldn't want any other to create the lives and the souls within me than he."

Kara smiled lightly, the true love this woman felt for this man was evident in her hand. She flipped a few pages and continued reading:

"I can feel the miracle becoming within me. Adamus was sweet and calming and his touch was incredible. I cannot explain it all in words. He was certainly the right choice of paramour and I have already asked that he create my next spirit, whenever that miracle may be bequeathed upon my love. He did wonder why I would ask before I've even seen the child he has bestowed within me, but I just know that he will be of perfection, just as I have dreamt. It is quite a miracle and in just a few short moons, I will be a [*Kara wanted to say mother, but somehow, the symbols again didn't quite match.*]

Kara flipped pages once again when she froze with a simple word from a voice that was extremely haunting.

"Kara?"

The pages bent upon themselves as Kara dropped the book to the floor. She stood petrified, taking in the echo of the dream.

"Kara, is that you?" The voice quivered slightly, feeling much like Kara's heart fluttering in her chest. She didn't want to turn around, believing the instant she did, the illusion would be gone as quickly as it had come. But she had to know. She wouldn't be disappointed if she were simply hallucinating. Slowly, Kara turned her head. To her amazement, standing there, looking just as she had when she left, eighteen and full of spirit for a new life, was...

"Diana?"

Atlantis – Hallways – 11 hours 18 minutes after arrival

Kaleena felt as if she were running a treadmill — she was running, but didn't seem to be going anywhere. She was lost in her own mind, searching for any signs of Jaime, keeping herself hidden from Cephis (whom she could no longer feel hunting her mind) and waiting for Evey to tear her down to her knees. She was so enclosed within herself that she hadn't even realized she lost one important piece — her father.

After coming to a halt, Kaleena went back the way she had come, but realized she had no idea which way that had been. So mesmerized with her goals and allowing the city to guide her, she'd blurred her vision to everything. Each part of the city became less important as she moved through it. She couldn't even recall when Matthew might have lost track of her. Had he called out for her to stop? Had Evey somehow masked her thoughts from his in order to take him captive? That couldn't be the case, since she hadn't once felt Evey trespass within her, but then again, she still knew very little as to the powers her new capability could induce. Evey was much stronger, as was Cephis, and either one of them could be controlling her right now like their own little marionette. Deep down, though, she knew she wasn't being controlled. She had simply been far too focused on Jaime and let Matthew fall to the wayside. But what if Evey had tracked him down, dispelling his thoughts, leaving him in an awakened coma, seeing and hearing everything around him, but paralyzed in speech, body and mind.

She could hear him screaming out for her, felt him reaching desperately for her help. He was crying out —

Kaleena!

But he wasn't in pain. He didn't seem in duress —

Kaleena!

Matthew was simply searching for the daughter that had accidentally left him behind.

"Dad," she called out, but the ringing silence that returned told her one simple thing. He wasn't close —

Kaleena!

— but his voice was. In her fear of his pain, she had connected with him — through him. He was searching for her, as if she was right there with him.

Kaleena closed her eyes and diverted all of her concentration to his voice — *Kaleena!* — as he continued to call out for her. This act might very well expose her mind to those she didn't want walking around it, but this was the only way she knew to locate Matthew. She searched every hall, corridor and plant of the city until she found a soft, rapid beat flushing blood through a nervous, chilled body. To make sure it was Matthew, she allowed herself to flow through the heart of the being and push her way into its mind. What she found was a young man, excited, vulnerable and intrigued. He was frightened, but his fear was laced in love and admiration. Looking in the mirror, he pulled his bow tie just a little bit tighter (even though it was already as tight as it could get without completely cutting off the flow of oxygen). Kaleena had a peculiar urge to run to the bathroom and let out one last bit of nervous retching. But it was too late. Sammy — *how did she know him? His name was so clear* — leaned into the room and said,

"Let's roll. The chain awaits."

Oddly, as the man nodded, Kaleena felt her own head bob up and down. Her lungs took in the breath that the man in the mirror sucked down to ease his stomach from running over itself. With the thoughts of the event about to happen and the anticipation at seeing her lovely future become her present, Kaleena didn't register much of her nervous ride in the halfway decent luxury of the jet-black town car. When she arrived at the church (which looked ominously large today, unlike what she could ever remember of it previously), Kaleena blindly walked in. It was thoroughly decorated in white lilies and roses. She didn't know quite how to act as she greeted many well-wishers — shaking their hands, avoiding a hug here and there and robotically repeating a thank you to everyone who wished her well — but she finally made it to the front of the sanctuary. She was met with gracious smiles from a man she knew quite well and his wife, who was already holding a handkerchief in her hand. She didn't get two words out when Sammy was on her back, slapping her along the shoulder, spouting out something along the lines of, "Time to get the party started."

Kaleena nodded, took in a deep breath, which she saw the man in front of her acknowledge with his own, and took her place next to Sammy by the altar. As a concession of music began to play, everyone in the church rose. Several unrecognizable altar servers in excruciatingly plain, white albs walked down the aisle with crucifixes and candles, roses and dresses. Even as the priest took his place in front of the altar, his white ceremonial cope with gold panels blanketing the stole, all of her focus was at the back of the church, waiting — hopeful.

Then, as the music that filled the air as if it were lighter than a dream became a familiar song of love, the patrons turned to the center aisle to catch a glimpse of what Kaleena had been waiting all this time to see. The large, elegantly crafted doors at the end of the sanctuary opened to reveal a flurry of white fabric and lace. Kaleena couldn't see who it was, as all features were hidden behind the light veil, but a soft bow of brown hair curled and draped down the back of the full dress like a soft flow of a cloud. It was enough to send Kaleena's heart aflutter. The woman under it all walked slowly toward Kaleena, her hands wrapped upon a dozen white roses that gracefully enhanced the cut of her dress. The woman's bright, fluttered smile was evident beneath the veil and Kaleena quickly became all too eager to take the woman's hand in hers and escort her the rest of the way up the steps to the center of the altar to meet the priest for their welcoming as one body. Before the music faded into the purity of the air, Kaleena lifted the woman's veil, revealing tremendously stunning, crystal-blue eyes that sparkled even brighter under the sunlight beaming through the windows. They were traced in a light black and silver glitter and radiated a true love that was as unquestionable as her devoted smile. She looked tremendously happy, extremely adored, utterly worshiped.

"In the name of the Father, and of the Son, and of the Holy Spirit," the priest started after making the Sign of the Cross, which was followed by a united "Amen" from what had become an invisible group of well-wishers. "Friends and loved ones, we are gathered for this wonderful event of a union between two lives who have come to God's House to manifest their love for one another by exchanging vows of matrimony. In so doing, they will devote their lives to one another, and to God, more profoundly. Let us pray now for their fidelity and purity of love toward their unification under God."

Kaleena and her bride barely registered the priest's opening prayer. The readings of the Gospels could have come from Charlie Brown's teacher for all they knew; the pronunciations of their love for each other were silent in breath, but no less real; and the exchange of their vows and the blessings of the rings was nothing compared with the electricity that glistened between their unrelenting stares. And when the words came —

"I now present to you all, Mister and Missus Matthew Stevens."

— the touch of their lips was magnetic. For them, each was now one and the same; nothing else around them existed. No evil could touch them.

Kaleena's breath dissipated as she felt her mother's lips. She pulled away from Matthew's mind, her legs numb, her body feeling as if it were about to go into a seizure. For a moment, Kaleena felt ashamed having intruded on what had to be Matthew's most cherished memory. Whether he actually remembers any of it as Kaleena had just felt it, she couldn't be sure, but the power of that perfect serenity must still remain within him, as part of him, and as part of all of his actions. It was enough for her to wonder if Jaime had truly felt the same way.

Kaleena? Matthew's voice was lighter, quieter. Had he felt her sneaking around inside his mind?

Dad? she asked, directing her thoughts to that tender image.

Kaleena. Thank God. Where are you?

Where are you? Kaleena asked, more relaxed now.

I don't know, I can't see anything. Are you close by?

I don't think so.

But I can hear you, he said. He must think she was actually speaking to him.

I'm not there, Dad. I'm talking to you in your mind.

You're what?

Just listen to me. Focus your thoughts on my voice.

Kaleena, please. This isn't funny.

Kaleena felt fear rise into Matthew's thoughts. *I'm sorry I took off without you.*

Matthew took a moment to respond. *It's okay. You were in the zone.*

Kaleena smiled slightly at the joke. She was happy to know he was still in good spirits.

It wasn't that long ago that I lost you. I should still be somewhat close, I just can't see anything.

Kaleena thought a moment and then: *Put your hand to the nearest wall.*

What for?

Just do it. Trust me.

Okay, he said, followed quickly with: *Okay. I'm touching the wall.*

Hold it there.

Kaleena placed her hand through the ivy and roses to touch the metal underneath. She closed her eyes and traveled through the wall, tracing her way to Matthew's memory, which she now felt much stronger than before. Within seconds, his hand rested against hers. She wanted desperately to wrap her fingers around his. Instead, she soaked up his surroundings and lit the room up. Matthew's bright smile washed through her, causing her lips to curl into a child's grin. Kaleena didn't want to let go, but it wasn't long before he left her, causing her smile to fade slightly.

How did you do that? Matthew said.

You wouldn't understand. She waited a moment, but then continued. *Follow the lights I lit up for you. They'll lead you to me.*

Are you sure? he said.

Wait, Kaleena whispered. She couldn't shake the presence of two men, but couldn't quite figure out if they were near her or were coming up on Matthew.

What is it? Matthew asked. His heart beat faster.

Quiet, Kaleena said, raising her finger gently to her lips out of habit. She focused harder on the men's minds and listened carefully to their steps. They seemed to be growing closer, for sure, but the more she changed her focus from around her to Matthew, the men's essences faded. When she pulled it back to her surroundings, they became louder. It was clear now that they were with her, and would see her in mere seconds.

Dad, get moving, she said quickly. *Stay on the path and don't say or think anything until I tell you, okay?*

Kaleena, what's wrong?

Just do it.

Without any more thought, Kaleena looked to the ceiling and pressed her hand to the wall a little harder than she expected. The lights flashed out and for a moment, the room was dark. But as she focused her thoughts, she was able to use the vibrations in her steps, the shimmer of the plants and the smell of the walls to visualize her entire environment. It was mesmerizing; so much so that she had almost forgotten about the men, whose steps had grown more vibrant in the darkness. She fell from her trance in time to skirt away into a small opening in the wall. A soft blue hue highlighted the room through the large picture window on the far side, touching the large plants and plush seats that lined the walls. It almost looked like a waiting room in a doctor's office, but the smell was much sweeter. As she walked farther inside, she saw several shelves in the center of the room with what looked and felt like leather-bound books, or manuscripts of some kind. Could it be some type of library, or perhaps a classroom, where the young

residents of the city would learn and create? Once again, the men became secondary to Kaleena's captivation. She stepped up to the window and looked out onto the city. She was about six stories up overlooking the courtyard. But none of that mattered. She took in the glorious sight of the city, this time with the knowledge of having been here before. She now knew the name of each building, as well as each road and walkway surrounding them. The water surrounding it all was haunting. She felt its life, running through the city, playing with other kids, working the fields just outside the boundaries, smelling the air coming from the lake, feeling the hot sun and soaking it in before returning back to her quarters to cook a meal for fifty of her closest companions, and maybe a cake for the man she wished to ask to implant her womb with life. If nothing else, the sight of the city being so dark and deserted tightened Kaleena's heart. She lowered her head to the window, dreaming of returning to a time before the flood and living the serenity. Her mind went completely blank with desire.

That is until movement in one of the walkways a couple of stories down captured her attention, snapping her back to the present. Kaleena cautiously stepped away from the window (almost as if it was about to snap a bite out of her hand if she continued to touch it) and then focused on the bounty of women and girls from ages near about four to fifty walking toward her tower like a caravan. Their spirits were scared, but at the same time enthralled by what they were looking at. She tried to connect more deeply with them until the eyes of the lead woman darted up to her. Kaleena ducked down and slid herself out of view of the window, her heart racing. Had they seen her?

It didn't matter; she had a more pressing concern. The men she'd initially been trying to hide from had arrived and stood like statues just outside the door. Closing her mind as if she were a robot powering off for the evening, Kaleena slinked even closer to the ground and slid in close to one of the nearby plants. She kept her eyes focused on the men as they stared down the hall, seemingly unclear as to where they should go. But Kaleena knew better; the men knew she was there; they were searching the air for their prey. Their touch attempted to break down her

barriers, but she held strong, hoping they would take the bait of her non-existence and search anew somewhere else.

Kaleena...

Her eyes abruptly flashed open as a bead of sweat formed in the center of her forehead. She instantly subdued the cry, but as the call rang out again, this time louder than before, Kaleena knew that at least one of the men had intercepted it. Kaleena's presence had become vulnerable. As the man closest to her turned his gaze into the room, she attempted to push her spirit away from her, much like a ventriloquist throwing his voice. After a long, tense minute looking into the man's frozen gaze, he whipped his head forward again and waited. The second man nodded and then they raced away from the room as if they had just been summoned, or scared away by some oversized insect. Kaleena sighed in relief. She relaxed her muscles but kept her mind strong, unwilling to allow the men to feel her before they were far enough away. The last thing she wanted was for them to come back to her, the bite of the Venus ending her naiveté.

Kaleena, where are you? Matthew's voice was weak and in pain. For a moment, she held steady, hidden behind the plant.

It could be a trick, she thought to herself.

I need your help, Matthew groaned. *Please...*

She couldn't take the chance. If Matthew really was in danger, she couldn't sit by and let him die. If it were a trap, she would deal with it when the time came.

I'm coming, Kaleena roared, hoping Matthew heard her. She rose to her feet and took one last look at the city. The women were gone. But they were of no concern as she sprinted away from the window to peer down the dark hallway. There was no movement and she hoped the men weren't able to mask her vision of them.

Hurry, Matthew groaned. She couldn't wait any longer. Matthew's life was fading, burning within itself. Hopefully, she wouldn't be too late.

* * *

Matthew followed the lit hallways as instructed, keeping his hands close to the walls in case Kaleena needed him to touch them again. He hadn't heard her voice since she turned on the lights, leaving his mind to wander through thoughts of what may have happened to her. She sounded panicked when she ordered him to be quiet, so he was afraid she might have been caught, or maybe knocked unconscious. And though she'd expressly asked him to keep his mind clear, he couldn't help but whisper her name over and over, even if it was only to hear her tell him to shut the hell up. At least then he'd know she was alive and still coming back for him. Her silence only haunted him.

Just stop, he told himself. *She's fine. Trust in that. Always trust in that.* She had spent the majority of the last three years alone and was far more capable of protecting herself than most people twice her age. He had to believe she was fighting for not only her safety, but his as well. As long as he kept that faith and followed her instructions, he'd find his way back to her.

Then he was coated in darkness.

Matthew stopped just before heading up a stairwell and waited until he could make out objects again. When nothing became visible, he tried feeling his way around, but nothing felt familiar — nothing felt right. Though the air around him was cold, sweat began to form on his brow.

Kaleena, he called out louder. He was worried that doing so would be bad for her, but needed to get her attention. When she didn't respond, he said her name again, this time much stronger (or at least he thought it was stronger). *Kaleena!*

His breaths were dry and stale as he waited for her to scold him, but something in him told him a response wasn't going to come. He was alone and was going to need to find his way through this maze without her. But the more he tried to focus, the more the room seemed to grow darker.

Kaleena, where are you? He finally found the edge of the wall and held his palm against it. The vines were dry and as he touched them, they curled slightly before almost shattering, dropping dust to the ground at his feet as if in an attempt to escape from the forces that built around him. He wasn't sure how he felt it,

but there was an eerie sense of foreboding swarming through them. *Kaleena*, he yelled again. But the voice that came back in response, though very familiar, was not the one he was hoping for.

I am disappointed, Matthew.

Ice formed on the edges of Matthew's lungs. If he could see, he would swear his hand had been frozen to the railing of the stairwell, his other having become part of the plants (or the wall). Stuttering, more from the confusion and slight shake in his body than by the cold, Matthew said, "Henry?"

The lights blinded Matthew. He removed his hand from the wall, taking a bit of vine dust with him, and covered his eyes with his elbow, rubbing them gently as he slowly adjusted to his new vision. As he looked to the top of the stairwell, the thin shape of a figure took small, slow steps down to him, the light washing around him like water.

"I am disappointed. How could it be that the great Matthew Stevens is seeking help from a fragile fourteen-year-old girl? A young woman he so casually abandoned for his own quest of self-fulfillment. It's quite a sad day to see my mentor so weak, so simple-minded, so desperate for help."

"Henry, how did you get here?"

"It doesn't matter how I arrived. The simple fact of it is — I'm here."

"I need to find Kaleena," Matthew said. He could now make out the rich black robe that carried the faded head of his student.

"She's not coming back for you," Henry said quietly. "And even if she was, she'd be far too late."

"What?"

"Kaleena's a very special child, Matthew. Her heart is full of dreams, her mind strong with fight. She is wanted here; she is needed here." Henry was right above Matthew now, staring down on him with cold, black eyes. "You are not."

"Henry!" Matthew shouted as Henry grabbed his wrist. A shock burned Matthew's skin and blazed through his veins, striking his heart within seconds.

"It's a damn shame, Matthew. I truly did find your intellect, your ingenuity and your drive to be quite compelling. I'm sorry to have to witness your death."

Matthew clenched his teeth to the point of breaking as Henry continued to fuel the fire burning through his body. There was only one thing he could think to do as the seething pain scoured each and every cell. He opened his mind and spoke through it as best he could. *Kaleena, I need your help!*

He fell weaker when Kaleena once again failed to respond. Henry was right; she wasn't coming back for him. He was alone in this fight and there was no possible way he was going to best the madman sending him reeling through a poisonous cloud of torture. His mind faded and became the darkness when he heard a soft echo surround him, summoning new strength into his heart. *I'm coming*, it said. Matthew became determined to hold on until she did, if only to prove his protégé wrong.

Henry's eyes became a soft red in response to Matthew's newfound vigor at the sound of Kaleena's distant voice. He pinched Matthew's wrist harder and leaned in extremely close, nearly touching Matthew's nose with his own. "Kaleena cannot save you, Matthew. After all she's gone through, after all she's needed from you and which you were not there to help with, what makes you think she'll help you now?"

Matthew's skin cracked around his knuckles and his knees. The most tender spots of his calves, neck and forearms began to blister. His head itched, about to burst into flames, but he couldn't stop fighting. He may not have been there for Kaleena when she really needed him, but he knew Kaleena had something he'd never have.

"Dad." Matthew thought he was dreaming the call. His eyes were closed tight, straining from the burn. But when she spoke again, he knew it was real.

Kaleena had wrapped around the corner of the stairwell, sliding to a stop to see Matthew held stiff at the bottom. Part of the skin on his neck was beginning to peel away and it seemed his eyebrows had been burnt away completely. She wanted to tackle the man holding onto Matthew's wrist and start beating the living daylights out of him, but that would ignite a flow of stupid decisions based solely on temptation and emotion rather than logic and planning. Matthew was fighting

and she knew he could hold on for, at the very least, several more minutes. So she started to consider her options when a familiar presence pushed to destroy Matthew before her eyes. She knew the thoughts, knew the nuance, knew the name.

"Adamus?"

Adamus turned, his own face burned slightly in rage. Upon seeing Kaleena, he let go of Matthew, who fell to the floor, whimpering in the tenderness of his now melting skin. His clothes cut into him like razors with every small move he made and he barely heard any of the conversation between the man trying to kill him and the young woman trying to save him.

"What the hell are you doing?" Kaleena said, her brow squeezed tightly together between her eyes and the top of her nose. Matthew's anguish swarmed her body and she had to take hold of the rail to support herself.

Adamus sucked in a few breaths as his composure returned, closing his eyes as if he were fixing himself before responding. When he looked back, Kaleena once again saw the kind, collected features of the man that had introduced her to the city.

Hello, Kaleena, Adamus said calmly. *It's good to see you awake.*

Shut the hell up. I don't want to hear it.

This is not your fight, Kaleena.

The hell it isn't.

Please. For your own protection, return to your room.

Fuck you.

Adamus winced and shook his head slightly. Kaleena knew right away it wasn't because he didn't like the word; it was because of her indignation. *Such simple-minded language for such a complex mind.*

I don't want to hear it, Adamus. You can't manipulate me anymore.

Kaleena —

Stop. Kaleena held out her hand. Adamus, who had been inching his way up the steps, stopped and raised his own hands slightly above his hips to try and ease her mind. *Just stop.*

I don't want to harm you, Adamus said, almost politely.

Just my dad? Kaleena said strongly, trying to keep her mind above his.

Your dad is an unfortunate survivor of a destruction that should have killed him, Adamus said honestly. *If he is kept alive, it will only help to distract you from your purpose.*

Distract me?

Adamus nodded.

Is that why you lied to me?

I did not lie. Matthew was to have died in the sea. His return to life was unforeseen.

You are so full of shit, Kaleena roared.

And I'm so disappointed in your lack of trust.

How in the hell can I trust you when you're trying to kill my father?

He's not your father anymore.

Oh, really, Kaleena said. *So who is?*

You already know.

Kaleena took a minute to think — a minute more than she needed to figure out the name of the man Adamus was referring.

Your instincts are quite exceptional, Kaleena.

No. No, I will not accept that. He is not my father.

The sooner you accept your purpose, the easier it will be to accept your fate.

Kaleena lowered her head, continuing to fight Adamus's attempt to control her. This was definitely not the Adamus she'd seen in Gydressina's history, and was not the man she'd thought him to be. As she raised her eyes back to his, the fruit of her determination had blossomed.

Fuck...you, she said softly, but with force. *I have only one father.*

Disappointed, Adamus returned: *I'm afraid he cannot live.*

And I can't let you kill him.

That is truly unfortunate. Adamus grabbed the rail, sending a surge of red heat flashing through it. Before it could reach Kaleena's hand, she became one with the rail, learned to understand its chemistry, to feel its life and its pieces. She reached

deep within her soul to push the elements of the rail into ice, and sent the frost down the railing until it collided with the heat generated by Adamus.

The fusion of the two elements instantly linked their spirits, locking their minds together and flooding Kaleena with all of his memories, as if she had become him. His body was warm as it lay comfortably next to Lauren. She was sound asleep, dreamless and serene, but that didn't stop Kaleena from gently caressing the edge of Lauren's buttocks with her fingertips. Reaching around to her naval, she felt a surge of sperm swimming inside of her, frantically searching for their rightful home. She found one of them, strong and fertile, and guided it through Lauren's fallopian tubes until it reached an egg sitting comfortably, waiting for a connection. She helped the sperm break through the shell and then felt the spark of connectivity of Lauren's body generating a process that seemed familiar, but forgotten.

As Lauren's body lit up with its new life, Kaleena kissed Lauren's smooth shoulder and slid off the bed, making sure she didn't wake. She walked straight to the door. The overwhelming presence of Cephis stood sharp and domineering behind it.

She is primed, Kaleena reported drolly.

Cephis walked into the room without so much as a nod and sat next to Lauren. He set his hand on her stomach and lifted his head to the sky, a firm smile forming on his lips. *Leave me with her.*

Yes, sir. Before leaving, Kaleena watched Cephis grope at the air above Lauren as if he were grabbing several pieces of trash out of the water. The hand on Lauren's stomach glowed a soft white as he escorted the air into his mouth, gyrating his body slightly as he did. Unable to watch any longer, Kaleena walked out. She sat next to the door, pulled her knees up to her chin and waited patiently for Cephis to complete the process. All she could think about was how close Evestylyn's return was to fruition, now that their plan was in effect. Kaleena's heart beat for and around Evestylyn, her life surrounding her soul. Although her spirit was still being created, just the knowledge that she would once again be able to love her, to taste her, to

feel her breath and her touch, and to hear her voice again stiffened her erection and weakened her mind. The door opened before she was able to relieve her lust.

It's complete. You've done well, my son. Kaleena stood straight and solid as Cephis walked down the hall, almost disappearing into the shadows of the night. With a bit of anxious tension, Kaleena walked back into the room and slid onto the bed. She placed her hand on Lauren's stomach, taking in the odor of the fresh creation. The warmth of the life she so wanted to take overwhelmed her, forcing her to her back. She closed her eyes and pictured Evestylyn's smile, smelled the aroma of cherries between her legs and the splendor of her body on top of hers.

"Time for payment," a rather deep voice said. Kaleena opened her eyes and saw the brunette hooker she'd hired for the week standing at the foot of the bed strapping on her leather bodice and adjusting her larger than real breasts to fit comfortably within, but still show enough cleavage to arouse even the gayest of men.

"How much?" Kaleena asked, knowing full well what she had agreed upon.

"Fifteen for the week," the hooker said, "and an extra thousand for the double dose of a daily blow."

Kaleena slid off the bed and groggily stomped over to the hooker. "It was quite something, wasn't it?" She placed her hand behind the hooker's neck and kissed her. The hooker accepted, though it was clearly out of courtesy, wanting nothing more than to get paid and get on to the next job. Just before she was about to pull away and charge Kaleena another hundred bucks for the goodbye, she sent a shock through the hooker's body, paralyzing her. She wrapped her arm around the hooker's waist to hold her up as she finished her kiss of death. When the convulsions ceased, Kaleena lifted her lips from the hooker's now bluish-purple lips and let her fall to the ground. Without a second thought, she got dressed, grabbed a book of matches from the nightstand and left the room. She spent the next hour walking the beach, listening to the water lap across itself, the cool wind of his love ready to be born. A whisper soared through the wind and caressed her ear, stopping her enamored walk.

Time is now, the wind said. Kaleena ushered in a soothing breath and walked away from the ocean without turning around. She felt Evestylyn's touch upon her, but knew it was just a trick of her mind. Within minutes, she was at the dig site Matthew and his team had abandoned just a week before.

She picked up the shovel she'd placed out there a couple days before and started digging, strenuously tossing dirt away until she reached a large piece of plywood. After scraping some excess dirt away, she pulled the piece of wood up. The wind pushed at the board, helping Kaleena shove the remainder of the dirt away and let the board slide down the small mound of dirt she'd built on the side of the hole. It was almost as if Evestylyn was helping her uncover the blue substance that still sat, waiting.

Do it now, the wind whispered. Without another hesitation, Kaleena pulled the matchbook from her pocket, ripped one of the matches from its placement and struck it swiftly across the back of the cardboard. The match lit up, and though the wind seemed to be blowing harder than it had been earlier that night, the flame only grew stronger. Watching the fire dance upon the thin, soft stick, Kaleena knelt down and held the match over the hole. When she loosened her fingers, the match fell to the substance like a feather. For a moment after landing, it simply sat, burning brightly, highlighting the blue color into an almost loving purple. But then, as Kaleena closed her eyes in concentration, the substance enveloped the match. Kaleena felt an excitement blossom between her legs. She wanted to have sex right then with whomever or whatever she could find, but washed the thought from her mind and took a few gentle steps away from the hole. As the fire built more pressure up within the substance, Kaleena moved away more rapidly. She was nearly twenty feet away when the liquid erupted hundreds of stories high, starting a reaction that would send a wall of flame burning southwest away from Bermuda. Kaleena closed her eyes and felt the flames burn within her, a relaxing comfort that melted her mind with fascination. Her love was as close as she could remember her ever being and as she opened her eyes, she saw Evestylyn, caressing her fingers through Kaleena's brother's hair. Her face and exquisite body were hidden behind his, but she knew her love's lips were locked with his, her exposed breasts swiping across his chest, tantalizing her brother's groin.

How could it be possible? Kaleena thought through a layer of rich jealousy and anger. She turned to avoid the sickening sight of her brother's betrayal, of her lover's adultery. It had to be a mistake. Evestylyn would never do that to him. She loved her. Kaleena looked up from behind the grate in time to witness Evestylyn slap her brother hard. She pulled her robe closed, hiding her body from the exposure of her shame. *Bastard*, she whispered, her eyes seething with rage. *If you ever set even a toe near me again, if you ever look in my direction, I will grind your dick into fertilizer.*

Kaleena couldn't see what her brother was saying — or doing, for that matter — but he stared at Evestylyn, his hand glued to his cheek.

Get out of my sight. Evestylyn turned her back to him and took a few steps away. Kaleena turned away as well, fading into the shadows as her brother left Evestylyn's side without a word of objection. She felt his burning regret, but couldn't pinpoint the incident in his mind amidst the swarming chaos. Kaleena held firm as he evaporated into the halls and then turned back to her love.

He tried to take me, Evestylyn said before facing Kaleena. As she looked into those soft blue eyes, Evestylyn's love for her was beyond passionate; and not just a companion's love but a paternal bond — with her complete soul. Kaleena came out from behind her hideaway and walked to Evestylyn, who appeared frightened, holding her arms tight against her body. Kaleena cupped the back of Evestylyn's head into her hand, pulling her close.

Her mother began to cry.

He tried to take me from you, she said. Hatred toward her brother burned through Kaleena. All she could think about were the dozens of things she wanted to do to him for trying to steal her away from her. Not even after her soul was stripped from her body and sent to the darkest pit of life would she see her mother forced into bedding another man, not even in lust.

Kaleena held Evestylyn's shoulders in her hands, trying to get a good look into

her eyes. She kept them turned away, still ashamed of the act that had transpired. *Look at me*, Kaleena said, lowering her eye level to match Evestylyn's. When she finally did, her sadness and fear was evident in the reddening sparks cracking the whites of her eyes.

I will not let him get away with this, Kaleena said.

Evestylyn forced a smile and then kissed her, pushing her tongue to reach the back of her throat. But Kaleena didn't gag; exhilaration urged her to drop her mother to the ground and pound away until she tripled in climaxes. But Evestylyn pulled away and rested her hands on Kaleena's cheeks.

I want you to take care of this right now, she said.

Yes, my love. Kaleena kissed her love again. Pulling away was hard, but her heart was filled with need, desire, and hatred.

And lust.

Evestylyn kept Kaleena's exit hard as she allowed Kaleena's hand to slide down her arm as if she didn't want her to go. When their fingertips touched, they curled upon one another and held tight for a few seconds. Kaleena wasn't sure who let go first, but with the break, Kaleena found enough courage to turn away. Suddenly, all of her sexual energy became fueled in hatred. The sooner she found her brother, the sooner she'd be able to get back to her mother.

Storming from the room, Kaleena stood above him in a flash. He sat cowering on the ground as her nostrils flared delicately.

Please, brother, he said, childishly. *You have no idea what transpired.*

I know enough, brother, she said as she circled him like a buzzard waiting for their next meal to expire. *You tried to take her.* Kaleena knelt down to meet his eyes. *Of all the females in the city you could have lain, you chose to take the keeper of our wombs. My lover; my life.*

You are demented, her brother squealed. *Demented*, he repeated, a bit quieter.

Kaleena leaned closer and carefully gathered all of his thoughts and fears.

Cephis has stolen your mind, he said, the fear within him dissipating. *He has stolen your mind and corrupted your heart.*

My heart is at a place it has never been before, Kaleena said, enjoying the taste of her brother's mind. *It is open now, shed of the barrier it was once trapped upon. And unless you open your mind to these same possibilities, you will never understand the true freedom of the life.*

You are lost, my brother, and so is our keeper. I did not do anything to her. She tried to turn me.

You lie, Kaleena yelled as she stood and turned from him.

She has manipulated you, he screamed. Rage boiled in Kaleena's blood. Her body heated up as she clenched her hands tight into fists. *She has taken you down the path of the imp, and has only done so to control you through your own fear and desire. She was the first, brother. You know that. She was the first, and she will stop at nothing to control all of man.*

Kaleena wanted to yell for him to stop, but couldn't find it in her to do so. If she tried, she was afraid she'd do something much worse. When Kaleena didn't respond:

You know it as truth. You have to know. She does not love you. Many men and woman have fallen to the hand of Cephis. You are just one of her subjects, nothing more. It is not you she loves, brother. How could she? It is Cephis she loves, because he gave her the first taste.

Stop your lies, Kaleena screamed, pounding her fist to his jaw. *You do not know her. You cannot know her.*

Her brother sat back up quickly, blood streaming from both his mouth and nose. *You see what you have become because of her? You see what Cephis has made you?*

Kaleena responded with another punch to his face, dropping her brother to the floor. He lay still, holding his face tight against the cold metal.

I have seen it, brother, he said, stronger than ever. *I have seen them lie together like the disciples they have turned.*

No, you cannot have seen that. Kaleena fell on top of her brother. She wrapped her hands around his neck. *You are a fucking liar, Abeline, and you will die for your blasphemy.*

Go ahead, he said. *Go ahead and send me my death. But I will die with an honor that has been lost upon you and be given to the life.*

Kaleena pressed against Abeline's neck even tighter. He was losing breath quickly, but his mind remained strong.

Gydressina has foreseen it, and she will not let this be the end. Abeline coughed lightly, his final breaths ending. *A war is coming, brother,* he said, this time more as a whisper. And as he fell lifeless among Kaleena's arms, she heard the whisper fade into the air around her. *A war is coming...*

Kaleena couldn't let go of Abeline's neck as anger and fire continued to burn strong within her. She only pressed harder until her fingertips were inside Abeline's neck. Finally, she hid his words in the depths of her mind and found a resurgence of life flow through her. She felt good — free. She felt...

Letting go of the rail, Kaleena fell to her knees and coughed dramatically. Adamus was on the stairwell, his back pressed against the wall as he tried catching his own breath. Kaleena had walked his mind and it was clear now that he was a liar and a murderer. His hunger was his lust, his greed, his rage, and the only way to feed that hunger was with his desire. She carefully rose to her knees and sucked up a final cough as Adamus convulsed in what felt like terror. It could only be assumed he had walked her mind as well, and though there was no way to know what he had seen, whatever it was, it affected him much more than his thoughts had her. She tried to listen to him, understand what was happening inside his mind, but all she saw was a darkness feeding away on itself. Compassionate, Kaleena fell down to him and pulled his head up. His eyes were vacant, unaware.

"I know who you really are," she said, his eyes darting around her as if he was collecting every inch of her to reconstruct in his mind. "Sweet dreams, Caistepher." Kaleena lowered his head and the convulsions got worse. Even after everything he'd put her through, she still had the urge to do something to help him, keep him from being tortured into a slow, painful death. But if she tried to pull him back, there was a chance she'd end up lost as well. She had been there before and didn't want to go back. He'd have to fight his own way

through this madness, whatever it took. For now, she had to take care of a much
more important person.

"Dad." She ran down to him. His eyes were bloodied and dark. "Dad, come
on. You have to get up."

Matthew shook his head, small pieces of skin flying off his neck with each
movement. Kaleena felt his spirit fading into her. "No, please, Dad. Hold on…"
Tears formed at the base of her eyes as she tried desperately to understand the body.
With the fear of losing him trying to take control of her, it was hard, but she was
able to find what she needed and lowered his head. "I need your hand," she said.
Matthew didn't want to move it away from his body, but her eyes convinced him.
She only wanted to help, and if it meant enduring a little more pain, he would
hang on for as long as it took. He winced and groaned as he moved his arm, the
blisters boiling over with puss. Kaleena gently set her fingertips into his hand and
instantly felt the scorch within her. She gritted her teeth and pushed the sensation
as far back in her mind as she could before raising her other hand to the back of
Matthew's neck. He let out a soft whimper. He probably would have cried had
his tear ducts not been destroyed.

"Stay strong," Kaleena whispered before connecting her body to each and every
cell Matthew. She sent them all swarming about, helping them grow and cool.
The more cells she cleaned and rebuilt, the weaker Kaleena's own body became.
But she couldn't stop, not until every last blister, every last cut and every last piece
of skin was healed. As the heat was driven away from Matthew's skin, he slowly
sat up, able to take in fresh, clean breaths of air and watch the last of his blisters
sink back into his skin. When the last one disappeared, Kaleena let her hands die
around him and slumped to the ground.

"Kaleena," he called out and reached for her throat. He felt a pulse. It was
light, but it was there. *What now?* he thought as he pressed her hand between his.
As he pulled it to his mouth to kiss it, he suddenly knew the answer. He lifted
Kaleena into his arms and climbed the stairs as fast as he could, following Kaleena's unknowing guidance.

Atlantis – Women's Quarters – 11 hours 22 minutes after arrival

Trishen squeaked like a mouse as she abruptly woke from her slumber. She couldn't remember falling asleep or even dreaming. All she could remember were the whispers, which had now gotten louder since she first started hearing them. Attempting to ignore them, she wiped her eyes free of the remaining sleep that struck her as fast as her awareness had and focused on Thomas, who slept against the wall, his arm draped around her back. Her hand was pressed against his warm chest and there was a small red impression of what she figured was her hair stamped across it. She would have liked to have joined him in slumber for a bit longer, but the voices wouldn't allow her to. So she groggily rose to her feet and stretched. It was a little surreal to feel so flexible, especially after having slept on the floor for who knows how long. She wasn't quite sure how Thomas, in his new condition, was taking to it so well, although looking at him in these circumstances just enhanced his already distinguished features. Now that he appeared to be nearing eighty, she couldn't help see him in a different light; one not of repulsion, but in a handsome maturity, much how she perceived Tom Hanks or Robert Redford. His outer appearance didn't matter to her in the least; he was still the same, kind, gentle soul within, and proved that when he helped her relieve the anxiety that had been building in her for some time. She was happy she hadn't scared him away with her foolishness, figuring he knew she didn't recognize him behind his seemingly non-existent fluff of white hair and wrinkled skin. But those eyes hadn't, and she knew quite well, would never change.

Attempting to focus her attention away from the voices that rattled on in a language and speed she couldn't make out, Trishen stepped to the window to take in the life of the city, pinpointing aspects to escape into. It didn't work, as the noise grew quicker, fiercer and more intense. It wasn't as if the voices were overwhelming her mind by any means; they were simply persistent — a background hum of static on the television or the buzz of a gnat that won't get the hint after swatting it away a zillion times. On some level, she wished she could understand it all, to know exactly what was being whispered, discussed and talked about. It almost made her feel as if she were back in high school, listening to the popular clicks whispering in the back of class, most likely discussing the party over the weekend, the make-out session down by the creek with the star football player, or the new gadget or high-tech accessory that the unknowingly anointed leader of all those that looked up to her for whatever reason had bought, to which all the rest of her herd would have by the end of the week, to which the leader would then have something brand new in response. It wasn't like she dreamed of ever being part of that group; all they ever did was laugh at her because her parents wouldn't give her everything she asked for and wasn't willing to blow her cash on just any and every 'cool' thing because she had to actually earn what she had. At the same time, she had no true friends to hang out with or crash parties with, or go to the latest Tom Cruise action flick with. Looking back upon it, being shunned from the popular crowds had proved to be one of the better things to happen to her. Her superficial desire to be one of them taught her to be independent. All things considered, her life was better than all of the sheep she once idolized and resented because she had what a lot of them probably didn't, and would never have—truth, honor and integrity. She loved her job, loved the friends she had, and loved being here, at this very moment, looking out onto a city that was deemed a fantasy, non-existent. If she ever had the chance, she'd thank them for that in a heartbeat.

A low grumble seeped through her thoughts. At first she thought it was a new addition to the voices, but then realized it was Thomas shifting slightly and rubbing his eyes. He looked around, apparently for her, and all attempts at saying something to catch his attention failed, as she figured they would — her throat still felt like it was jammed with a ball of socks. So she waited for him to look her direction before moving, partly because she didn't want to leave the view, but mostly to keep from frightening him. Who knew how deep his new age actually went; she didn't want to accidentally give him a heart attack.

Thomas first caught sight of her legs and quickly looked up to meet her gaze with fervor. He wanted to bolt upright and take her in his arms, but failed as his legs almost cracked underneath him. He held out his hand, stopping Trishen

from catching his fall, and then slowly forced his almost arthritic knees to stand.

"I guess I'm truly not as young as I used to be," he said as he stumbled toward her. Hearing his voice, though extremely muffled by the sea of others, was immensely satisfying. She gave him a gentle squeeze, really taking in his new skin. The last time she could remember experiencing that texture and that odd smell was when she hugged her grandparents. A tear rolled from her eye as she thought of them, their death a few years before still a bit painful to think about. They were her best friends; letting them go was awfully hard. "What's wrong?" Thomas asked, wiping the stray tear away with his thumb.

Trishen rubbed her eyes as she looked away, shaking her head. Thomas could only smile with empathy as she was apparently trying to hide her remorse for something. "Hey," he said, turning her back around. He touched his fingers to her chin and raised it up, the water in her eyes making them sparkle intensely. "You don't have to be ashamed."

The two held one another in ecstasy and love beyond mortality. It was the only real passion a human could ever experience — the connection between a man and a woman that rose above all emotion and physicality. A feeling Trishen believed only a handful of people in the history of life had ever felt — if any at all. She wished she and Thomas were the first to truly experience spiritual, sexual, physical, and emotional enlightenment, compacted into one look, one stare; one hidden touch. They didn't have to feel the tenderness of a kiss, or the passion of sex to send their minds and their love to their fruitful climax. All they needed were their eyes.

"So what now," Thomas said after several minutes of serenity that would be felt only once more over the course of time. Trishen lowered her gaze and shrugged. For a moment, she thought of Jaime and Patricia, hoping they had gotten to safety. There was still a lingering confusion for why she stayed behind. She needed to be here, but for what purpose? To wait for Thomas? If that were the case, could she now leave with him? Her eyes darted. "I think we should try and find Matthew," he finally posited. The calm in Trishen's eyes spun to confusion.

"Matthew's alive. So is Lauren." He paused a moment, then, as if as an after-thought: "And Kaleena."

Trishen nodded wildly, excited. She pointed to the door and then down to the room. Small squeaks jumped from her lips as she tried to explain. At first Thomas was a bit confused.

"I'm not sure... what, you?"

Trishen shook her head and pointed to Thomas.

"Me?"

She rolled her finger, asking for more.

"Me...? Matthew?"

Trishen nodded and pointed at Thomas. "Matthew," he acknowledged. "What about him?" She then continued to roll her hands, point and twirl (sometimes even roll her eyes in frustration) as Thomas put all the pieces together. "Me and Matthew? You and Matthew? No... Matthew and Kaleena? Not Kaleena. Jaime? Matthew and Jaime." With the last affirmation, Trishen nodded and moved her fingers and pushed them in the direction of the door.

"Jaime's alive?"

Trishen happily slapped her hands together and hopped in the air with glee.

"She's alive and she left. Alone?"

She ecstatically shook her head and grabbed Thomas's forearms. Her smile was like a child who was about to unwrap that new toy they had been waiting to get for years.

"She left with others? How many others?"

Trishen held up two fingers.

"Patricia?"

Yes.

"And who else?" Thomas's memory was still a bit hazy with sleep, but the realization of who was missing was quick enough. "And Kara? Kara and Patricia are alive, too?"

Trishen nodded emphatically and gave Thomas a great big bear hug.

"Well we better go find 'em," Thomas said, a new excitement rising in his blood. Everyone was alive and somewhere in the city. He just hoped they'd be able to find them before that status changed for the worse.

Trishen slid her hands to his and took hold of them. The magic that ignited the tips of their fingers was as electrifying as her spirit. She kissed him quickly and pulled him to the door. It was time to leave.

You're not going anywhere.

Thomas pulled Trishen behind him as a young Asian woman walked through the door. A somewhat pretty African-American woman stepped in behind her, followed by a river of other women and children. Trishen finally understood where the flood of whispers had originated as they reached their apex in her mind. Somehow she had become connected to all of them — not quite *to* them, but spirits *within* them. She peered around the room, hoping to make a reverse connection to just one of them.

Thomas didn't take notice that all of the kids were also female, but his sights held strong on the two women standing at the door. "Who are you?" he finally asked.

It is of no matter to you, Thomas.

"How do you know my name?"

Again, it is of no matter.

Trishen found her focus on a young girl, about six. She tried to pull away from Thomas, but he was unwilling to let her go. That is until he felt a confidence he hadn't seen since they first met. Without turning back, Trishen walked to the girl, who now sat on an older woman's lap. The woman's hair was graying but hadn't fully gone gray (though Trishen thought it could have been dyed) and she was clearly distraught. Trishen knelt down and offered a reassuring smile. The woman flashed a nervous one in return.

"Who are you?" the woman whispered, pulling the child closer, protecting her as her own. Trishen knew they were not related; the child was Hispanic, not Irish, as the woman's accent clearly defined.

She rested her hand on the woman's arm, hoping to comfort her without words, and looked at the child, who seemed oddly mature. She put all of her energy into focusing on the child's thoughts, when finally, through all of the other clutter of noise, she located the sweet, clear whisper within.

Hello, it said.

Hello? Trishen thought and the little girl smiled. *You can hear me?*

I can, the girl said. Trishen felt comfortable and noticed that the voices clouding her mind had faded somewhat into more of a background hum to this child's resounding voice.

What's your name?

My name is Destin. What is yours?

Trishen.

It is very nice to meet you, Trishen.

You as well, Trishen said, curiously.

Are you our new mother? the girl asked, somewhat abruptly.

New mother? Trishen thought to herself, though she knew it was impossible.

Yes. Our Father was to choose a new mother upon our return. And you are very pretty.

Trishen cleared her thoughts, giving Destin an odd smile. *I'm a bit confused. Return from where?*

From our darkened slumber, silly.

Your darkened slumber? Trishen asked the question hoping to gather more information.

Yes, of course.

Trishen lowered her head. It hadn't worked. *Can you answer me a question?*

Destin nodded. Trishen comforted the woman with another smile. The woman couldn't hear either of them, so she continued.

Destin. Can you tell me where you are?

You do not know?

I'm just curious.

We are part of Ediinis. Our home.

Ediinis? The name fluttered through her mind as all the other voices echoed the name, each whispering it as if they were trying to connect with it. Trishen turned back to Thomas, who looked as if he were part of some kind of futuristic western, about ready to draw his gun on his opponent. He was surrounded by dozens of women so she couldn't pinpoint his thoughts, but felt an odd sense that he was about to die; that the old, veteran gunslinger was about to meet high noon.

Destin shifted on the woman's lap to lean in closer to Trishen, who kept her eyes on Thomas. *You are home now, Trishen,* she said, her breath burning against her ear. *And your friend, Thomas, is unwanted here.*

Trishen sucked in a deep breath as the African-American woman (who appeared to be the unknowing leader of her new flock) closed the doors with her mind, trapping Thomas for his inevitable sentencing.

Atlantis – Hallways – 11 hours 34 minutes after arrival

Evey paced back and forth between Patricia and Jaime, whose eyes stayed dead-locked on her captor. She wanted to say so much, berate her, tear her mind apart, but couldn't seem to find the power to say anything. Not because she couldn't speak. It was almost as if Evey was coaxing her to say something, turn it against her in order find out more about Kaleena or get her to reveal something she didn't want Evey to know —

I walked your mind

— even if she already did. But Jaime stayed silent because she wasn't about to express weakness. Above all the pain delivered by Evey's intense stares — extreme headaches, pounding cramps in her sides, and the deep needling in her eyes — she had to stay sharp, stay above the level Evey so much wanted to pull her down to. Hopefully Patricia would be able to do the same. She was a mother herself who would no doubt do anything to keep her own daughter protected; Jaime prayed she'd see that's all Jaime was trying to do and keep her mouth shut. For the time being, Patricia stuck with her own defense mechanisms, singing off several tunes with the wrong lyrics.

"I will survive," Patricia sang so way off key, Jaime wasn't sure they were even real notes. She kept repeating the phrase over and over, possibly because by singing the words, she was convincing herself to stay strong. Occasionally, she'd head into the chorus with some choice words that fit their current situation. It had always been in Patricia's nature to help in any way she could, and to help their current state, she had to mask her fear with humor, even if her tolerance was waning quickly.

"I will survive," she continued, "no matter how many vines I've got, I know I will survive. I've got all my pain to give, I've got all my kids disease, but I will survive, hey — HEY." It seemed to be working, as every time she sang new words, or screamed out the word 'Hey!', though cringe-inducing to no end, it lifted Jaime's spirit. "You'll never get my life, you'll never get my brain, I will survive, hey-HEY!"

Evey turned out to be far more impatient than Jaime would have believed. As Patricia once again lifted a chorus of *heys* along the corridor, Evey could no longer take the swelling piercing sting in her ears. Her burning eyes subdued Jaime's laughs before she swung in under Patricia and clawed her nails into her robust jugular. Even though she couldn't turn her head enough to see them, Jaime felt Evey's frustration through the intensification of her own pain.

"Stop this nonsense," Evey hissed as Patricia kept singing, "I will survive," through a clenched jaw. The more she did, the harder Evey pressed her hand together, pumping more and more pain through Patricia's body, slowly shutting it down. Patricia started to cry and the corridor filled with a dense silence. As the song echoed into memory, Evey relaxed. Her anger grew subtle and warm. She pushed Patricia's eyes open and searched them for evidence of subjection. Jaime wanted to yell for her to stop, but couldn't open her lips. All she was left with were a series of grunts and groans. Evey didn't care. Whatever she was searching for, whatever she had found, whatever she was manipulating, was keeping her attention locked on Patricia. It was so intense, Jaime probably could have ripped through her cocoon and ran off without Evey taking any notice whatsoever. But she wouldn't

ever leave Patricia behind to be violated even if she could have escaped. She just wanted to know what Evey was doing in Patricia's head so she could attempt to stop it. Finally, Evey removed her fingers from Patricia's jaw, leaving behind four large red marks that started to bleed lightly. Patricia's head fell limp. What had she done? Boiled her brains? Toasted her liver?

"Bitch," Jaime choked out under her breath, fighting off Evey's hold on her voice.

Evey smiled. "Wake," she said and then waited until Patricia found the power to lift her head. She hadn't died and Jaime, amongst the burning pain she still felt over her entire body, was quite relieved.

"I want to apologize, Patricia," Evey continued. Her voice was sweet, almost motherly. "You do not deserve the pain I've caused you. I understand what you've lost and you're quite opposite of your friend, here. You respect your flesh and blood." Evey bent her head down to force Patricia's eyes to meet hers. "Do you not?"

"Fuck you," Jaime said. The words were left on deaf ears.

"I've seen you with her. You fought for her. When your vile, disrespectful husband wanted to take her away from you, you fought to keep her, even when you thought nothing else could be done, when you thought you had nothing left to give her, when you thought you were going to lose her forever to your husband, you held strong and continued to fight, to change... to live."

Patricia's eyes were watering with thoughts of her daughter's smile.

"That's why it took you so little time to reconnect your mind in the transfer. You have no regrets, do you Patricia? You don't have any fears because you've always fought; you've always received what you most desired because it's not in your nature to turn and run. You've taken everything you've ever wanted and turned everything that's been against you into fuel for that strength. I can't say the same for your friend, Patricia. She is weak and always has been."

"Go to hell," Jaime whispered. It felt like she could use the fire within her to burn her way from the wall, but the vines only grew tighter the more she thought about escape.

"Let me ask you, Patricia. Has Jaime ever told you about her first love?" Evey shifted her eyes to Jaime for a moment, watching as she clenched her teeth, her headache raging like an inferno.

"You see, Jaime had someone in her life that she would have given the world for." Evey turned her gaze back to Patricia, whose own eyes now met hers with the interest Evey had been hoping to garner. "She would have crossed a hundred oceans or died in the sun if only to be with him. But after consuming one another in a fit of undying devotion, she ran from him. She ran from her fear of love, from fear of her parents, from fear of her future. She ran because she was too afraid to fight."

Patricia's tears had transferred to Jaime. They dripped down her cheeks, running the path of the vines across her chin to collapse upon her lips. The taste was bitter. "You have no idea what you're talking about," Jaime said, low and deathly.

"Even now she denies her fear, even when it had her trapped within herself. Who rescued her from that fear? Who fought to bring her back from the dream and return her to a reality she's more afraid of than dying?" Evey rested her hand gently on Patricia's chin and held her eyes deep within hers, as if she were falling in love. "You," she said. The small scars on Patricia's jaw closed up, leaving only the tears of her blood traced upon her neck.

"If it were not for you, the regret she had been buried under would have grown more distorted over time. She would have grown hungrier, more desperate, more tired as her dream slowly eclipsed into horror. You rescued her from her deepest and darkest regret, one that proves a lot of her personal character. She's left many in her walk through life, yet when it came to reconnect her mind with her spirit, the only fight she had was not walking away from her marriage. It wasn't walking away from her daughter. It wasn't even distancing herself from her daughter's own death. It was a fight of lust and passion, of intimacy and despair with a man that held her heart above her own flesh. Tell me, Patricia... what kind of rescue does that egotism deserve?"

Patricia tried to look at Jaime, but the vines wouldn't allow her to.

"What has Jaime ever done for you that was not of a selfish nature? Has she ever given you anything, allowed you to do anything that didn't in some way help her, or work around her own schedule? She's not worth saving, Patricia, yet you do so, at every turn. Why? Your husband was far from in need of respect, and because of that, you didn't show him any. Jaime doesn't deserve it either. She won't protect you; she uses you for her own advancement. She fights with you so her grief won't eat her alive. By simply being in her presence, she will hurt you. So why do you protect her so? What hold does she have over you that you'll follow her to the ends of the earth without ever giving you anything real in return?"

"I need her," Patricia said, though her voice was low and barely audible.

"Why? Because she came to you in a time in your life when you needed to be held? Because when you were at what felt like the end of your life, she offered you security, a shoulder to cry on?"

"She gave me my smile." Patricia's words sent a flood of tears into Jaime's mouth. She spit as much as she could down her chin, dribbling like a newborn baby fighting to keep the disgusting strained peas from touching her lips.

"And you deserved it. But she used your depression against you. She needed someone to help her rebuild her career, rebuild her self-worth. Do you think that once she truly got what she wanted she wouldn't have simply left you in the wings? I guarantee, if she was offered the chance, she would send you to the wolves if it meant reaching a false love. When she was offered the choice to stay with her lover, she ran. When she was offered the choice to protect her daughter, she chose herself. When she was offered the choice to stay with her friend — your friend — she chose to run. When she was offered the choice to forgive, to take back what she left behind, to prove to herself that there was more to life than her own selfish desires, she chose a life alone in favor of admission to her own narcissism. Now, where have those choices gotten you. Tell me that abandoning your own daughter because you weren't able to eat your own words and prove your weakness is worth saving and I will let you both go and drown myself. Tell me that Jaime's actions haven't cost you anything and I'll roast myself like a pig. Tell me that you have

never thought she was imperfect and that her actions will only lead everyone you have ever loved into the ground. Tell me you do not believe me. Tell me."

Evey leaned close to Patricia's ear and whispered, "Tell me."

Patricia took a deep breath through spit covered lips, sniffed some running snot into her nose, and sent a cold knife to Jaime's heart with three simple words.

"Is it true?"

"It is," Evey answered. Patricia sneered with fierce eyes that made Evey glow in joy rather than cower in fear.

"I wasn't talking to you," Patricia said deeply before screaming out, "Is it true?" with strong commitment. Jaime's grief wouldn't allow her to answer, and she didn't want to. Patricia was her friend; she didn't want to hurt her.

"I believe your colleague is asking you a question." Evey walked to Jaime and looked her over. Though Jaime wanted to turn away from everything, the vines still wouldn't let her; they almost pushed her to look at Patricia.

"Yes," Jaime gave in. She couldn't lie, not to someone that meant so much to her, professionally and personally.

Patricia gritted her teeth, but not in bodily pain.

"I'm sorry," Jaime pleaded.

Patricia didn't answer her. She didn't even want to look at her. She just wanted to get back to her family, hug her daughter and start a fresh life — without Jaime, without Atlantis.

"The truth feels nice, now, doesn't it?" Evey asked Jaime. "I'm positive that it's not all you will need to answer for before your stomach stops spinning with misery and your life returns to bliss. But it's a step." Evey took a strong whiff of Jaime's tears, her nose delicately touching Jaime's lips. "Now if only you would admit your own penitence and let the young child you call daughter become what she was meant to become. Only then will you truly be free from all of your mistakes."

Jaime closed her lips. She was growing sick from the taste of cherries coming off Evey's skin. "Go fuck yourself," she said lightly. "You can kill me if you want, but I will never allow you to harm Kaleena. You may not feel it, you may not even understand any of what I truly regret, but I love Kaleena more than anything. If that means sacrificing myself to keep her safe, so be it." Jaime cleared her throat, sucked up a mound of mucus into her mouth, and spit it onto Evey's cheek.

Evey didn't flinch. "Much better, but much too late," she said and stepped away. As she did, the vines around Patricia released her, retracting back into the city. Patricia stumbled to the floor, waiting for the blood to begin circulating into her legs. Evey rested her hand on her head. "I will never use you for my own personal gain, or give you up in favor of my own skin. If you trust in that, I will return you to your smile."

Patricia peered up to her. She looked honest and loving.

"I know you can't trust me, not fully, but Jaime admitted she's been lying to you, using you, and would as much go through life without you if it came to it. I offer you peace, here, Patricia. Peace of mind, heart and soul. I'll return you to your daughter and your family — your life. I'll help you turn it all around, give you whatever it is you will ever need. You will never again have to worry. All I ask for is your help."

Patricia's stiffened muscles loosened as she stood. She still wasn't sure she could trust Evey, not in the least. But she was offering her more than she could possibly give up. Jaime was to be forgotten.

"I have already relieved you of your worst addiction," Evey continued. "Your lungs have been cleansed, and are now as healthy as a newborn babe. You may not feel it, but you'll never again have a desire for nicotine."

Taking a deep breath, she did feel different — better. Her lungs were light and open and her body no longer shook in need of a cigarette, the stress having been abated.

"I know what you're thinking, Patricia, but if you help me, you will never again have to worry about your health or your weight. Help me and I will help you become the woman you so desire."

"What do I need to do?" Patricia said, her confidence rising. She knew what was going to be asked of her and felt slightly guilty about it. But it would all be

worth it in the end. This was all about her daughter. For once, she needed to step away from Jaime, prove her own independence and, in a small way, her own per-colating selfishness.

"Don't do it, Patricia, please," Jaime called out. Patricia winced at the sound of Jaime's voice and wouldn't look at her. "I'm sorry for whatever I've done. But she's manipulating you. Don't let her take Kaleena from me."

"From you?" Patricia finally broke, storming up to her within inches. "How could I take something away from you when it's not even yours to begin with?"

Evey stood back, smiling.

"My daughter is my life," Patricia scolded. "Holding her in my arms that first time, I knew no matter what happened, she came first above anything. All Kaleena is to you is a mistake and a nuisance. You never wanted her —"

"That's not true," Jaime interjected.

"Shut up. You never wanted her because you knew she'd keep you from doing what you wanted to do. If she weren't around, you would've had a career, a life. But the second you found out you were pregnant, you regretted it all. You even considered an abortion before telling your husband the truth."

Jaime could only weep in response. Deep down, even though she tried hard to keep from admitting it, everything Patricia was saying was true.

"Everyone knew it, too" Patricia continued. "Gavin, Trishen... they all knew who you were. But they were all broken, weren't they? They were all at the weakest points in their lives when you came along. We believed in you because we had nothing else to trust in. You used that to get us to do anything and everything you ever wanted. To make us believe anything you told us. Well, I'm finished with that, Jaime. I'm finished. I don't need you to save me any longer. And don't you fucking dare tell me that you wouldn't even bat an eye if Kaleena were killed. Her funeral would just be the end of your trapped existence."

Jaime was hysterical. Her lungs burned as she cried. Her throat was sore as she swallowed her tears, mucus and shame for all of the poor decisions she's made over the years. She wasn't, and would never, live the life she's always wanted, and

in some ways, she no longer felt it mattered. The vines could consume her completely for all she cared. At least it would allow everyone she's ever hurt to be free of her punishments. Patricia lowered her head, a bit guilty. But it had to be said. It was the only way Jaime was going to learn and the only way Patricia would gain enough courage to do what she was about to do.

"What do you need me to do?" Patricia asked again, her head turned away from Evey. She didn't want to look at her as she sent a knife into her friend's back.

"Just make sure that whatever happens, Kaleena stays with me. And do everything in your power to stop the others from taking her back."

"Okay," Patricia said slowly and quietly. "Okay, I'll do it." She turned to Evey. "If you promise me that you'll return me back home once it's all over and never come near me or my daughter. Ever."

"You have my word, as a friend, as a woman and as a mother."

Patricia inhaled (a soothing breath Jaime felt was to help her convince herself she was doing the right thing) and stepped away from Jaime, who couldn't stop letting out cries of sorrow.

"How do we find her?" Patricia asked, her remorse having been washed clean from her body language.

"We no longer have to," Evey said, pointing behind Patricia.

Standing petrified at the end of the hall was Matthew, Kaleena draped across his arms, sleeping — or what Patricia *hoped* was sleeping.

"The ex," Patricia said, trying to keep her voice calm.

He cannot see her, she heard Evey say, quietly, almost pushing her to step forward. *Go to him. Ask to help him with Kaleena.*

Patricia immediately jogged him, hoping he wouldn't move and see Jaime, who was so tired now, her eyes puffed, her throat tightened. She could barely breathe much less call out for Matthew.

"Am I damn glad to see you," Patricia said. "What happened?"

Matthew backed away, unable to take his eyes off of Evey. But he didn't run, allowing Patricia to get to him and pat him hard on the back.

"She saved me," he said, handing Kaleena to Patricia, if nothing more than to relieve him of her weight for just a second. "Who's that?"

Patricia shifted Kaleena into her arms. "She's a friend."

"Where's Jaime?"

"Hell to biscuits if I know." Patricia kept her eyes tight on Kaleena. If she didn't, Matthew would have been able to see through her like a greasy piece of paper. "She wasn't with us."

"We need to find her," Matthew said.

"How do you know she's still alive?" Patricia finally looked to him.

"Kaleena knows," he said. Patricia's eyes turned remorseful. She looked away quickly, brushing some of Kaleena's hair into place.

"We have to get her out of here first," she said. "We need to protect the brain."

"I know. But I'm not leaving here without Jaime."

"Don't fret your balls off," Patricia said, trying to instill hope in Matthew. "We'll find her. But we need to get the kid to safety first. Look at her. She may not have long."

Matthew wasn't sure why Patricia was fighting him so hard on this, but he nodded. Kaleena, especially in her current state, was far more important. "What do you suggest?"

"She can help us." Patricia nodded to Evey, who turned to the men standing behind her. They both nodded and Evey started toward Matthew, her demeanor gracious and respectful. He noticed her eyes shift ever so subtly to the wall and took a step past Patricia, curious as to what the stranger had taken an interest in.

"Matthew," Patricia said, grabbing his shirt. He returned her gesture with a stern gaze.

"What are you doing? Let go." Matthew pulled his shirt free. When he turned back, Evey stood in front of him, keeping him from going any farther.

"She doesn't look well. We must hurry if we're going to help."

"Who are you?"

"Matthew!" The scream was light and hoarse, but Matthew heard it as if it had been shouted through a megaphone. "Matthew. Help!"

"Jaime?" he tried to find her, but all he could see were vines and flower buds. Attempts to step past Evey were met with a hand against his chest, keeping him back.

"Stop," Evey said, her eyes held on Kaleena.

"Let go of me." When Evey wouldn't budge, Matthew called out, "Jaime!"

"Don't make me kill her, Matthew."

Evey's glare was iced with anger. Her cronies stepped up to the wall where Matthew could finally make out a small image of a nose and possibly a chin protruding from under the foliage.

"Don't you touch her," Matthew said through his teeth.

"All I want is Kaleena. Allow me to take her and the both of you may go free. Resist, and I will melt your lungs in seconds, kill your wife and take Kaleena as my own anyway."

Matthew could already feel a flame charring his lungs. All he could think about was his attack at the hands of Henry. Evey must have felt it too. "I know what you were recently subjected to, Matthew. Trust me when I say that what I can do to you is far more painful. Don't make me push you to the depths of hell in life."

He tried hard to control his breathing, which now felt as if he were eating hot coals. But he wasn't about to let this woman force him to choose between his daughter and his wife, even if it meant killing all three of them.

"So be it," Evey said and shifted her head to the men. One set his hands to Jaime's temples. She screamed fiercely.

"No!" Matthew said, wanting desperately to kill the both of them. He found out quickly, he wouldn't have to.

A crackling shock spread through Jaime's forehead, sending the man touching her across the room, his heart charred and left barely beating. The second man looked around a moment, then heard Evey call out to him: *Kill her now!* The man hesitated, but decided it better to do as he was told than face Evey's wrath.

Before he could do anything, one of the vines peeled off the wall and wrapped around the man's wrist. He tried to pull away, even tried to claw it off with his other hand, but the vine was unrelenting. It pulled the man to the wall next to Jaime and consumed him.

Evey's eyes grew wide with fear as she watched him disappear among the wall.

"Gydressina," she whispered and let go of Matthew, who stepped back to Patricia to try and recover Kaleena from her.

Patricia pulled the child tight to her chest and moved even closer to Evey. "I'm sorry, Matthew. I need her to save my family."

"Patricia, don't do this."

She turned her gaze back to Kaleena. The youth of her features looked so innocent and precious, Patricia couldn't help see her own daughter, stretching her tiny arms along the blanket as she yawned for the first time. It finally occurred to her that in attempting to save herself to be with her daughter, she was taking away someone else's daughter; someone else's love. What would her daughter think if she found out her mother had taken away a good man's child in a foolish hope that she would be free of her own guilt. This moment would live with her for the rest of her life, no matter what happened. This wasn't her; this wasn't how she brought up her daughter. This wasn't what she wanted to leave as her legacy.

"Please," Matthew insisted.

Patricia could do nothing but wait for something to release her mind from Evey's grip.

Return Kaleena to her father and allow them to walk away, a familiar voice sang through the halls.

She's mine, Gydressina, Evey called back. *You cannot stop me from my destiny.* Evey suddenly felt a presence within her. She growled fiercely and stepped away from Kaleena, staring out into the nothing of the halls. *What game is this? Why do you attack me in hiding? Are you not daring enough to fight me with a brave hand? Are you too weak to take my life in front of your eyes? Show yourself, Gydressina.*

Let them go, Gydressina said in response. *Or face the consequence.*

Consequence? Evey said, mockingly. *There is nothing you can do to me. You're far too giving, too pure to stop me. That's why you're too afraid to show yourself.*

Evey looked around when only fear came back. Just before Patricia was about to hand Kaleena back to Matthew, Evey grabbed the child by the neck. Matthew went to rip Evey's hand away, but received a shock from her skin instead. For a moment, his fingertips burned; not even shoving them in his mouth could calm the sensation. Patricia was far too frightened to do anything but wait for Evey to say something.

I will snap it, Gydressina. I will kill her and fuck the consequences if you do not show your face this instant.

A wash of light filled the room. Matthew fell to his knees and covered his eyes as Patricia covered Kaleena on the floor. Evey held strong, waiting for the light to end. When it did, Gydressina had appeared in front of Jaime, who felt a sudden warmth of protection.

Release them all, Gydressina said, as she started to mend Jaime's body. Once Jaime's legs had been repaired, the vines around her unfurled.

I will do no such thing. You cannot stop me this time, Gydressina. I have what I need and I will take what is mine.

What is yours? Gydressina turned to Evey. *I gave you this life, Evestylyn. I presented you with freedom, a chance to live and breathe, a chance to prove that you were more than the world itself. But Cephis turned you against your beliefs. You failed. It was Adamus who saved you from death and an eternal rest in the bowels of darkness. You have no claim over any of what I once created and fought to protect.*

Matthew lowered his arms and carefully opened his eyes. He saw Jaime slide down off the wall, almost as if the vines were placing her on the ground.

But I do, dear woman, Evey said, inching toward Gydressina. *Cephis is far more powerful and I am his child. I've walked this world once in blindness, but I see through the lies now. This world is as much mine as it is any other spirit. And with Cephis by my side, I will hold more power over any of it.*

You truly believe that?

I know it.

Then you are truly lost. I can no longer protect you.

Protect me? Evey was within mere feet of Gydressina as the vines left Jaime to rejoin the wall. Jaime was safe for now. There was one other Matthew needed to check on. He crawled over to Patricia and rested his hand on her back. Her head bolted up. When she caught sight of Matthew, her eyes clearly acknowledged her mistake. He rubbed her shoulder gently. "It's okay," he whispered, hoping the woman staring down Gydressina in what could only be a verbal fight of their minds wouldn't hear him. "Stay with her. I'm going to get Jaime."

Patricia nodded and held onto Kaleena. Matthew slid to the wall. He moved ever so slowly toward Jaime, his eyes held steadfast on Gydressina and her opponent the whole way.

You never protected me, Evey continued.

You lived long after all else in Ediinis had been destroyed. I protected you from your own death because I knew Cephis had corrupted you. You were not blind before you learned the truth. You were blind with the corruption of that truth.

I was freed by the knowledge.

You were killed the day he touched you, Evestylyn. And Adamus convinced me that you would learn from that mistake. I took mercy on you.

And what of the rest? You killed them all, including the sheep that weren't willing to believe the truth. It didn't matter to you. Where was your mercy for them? You had your chance at living the life, but now, it's my turn.

Evey squeezed Gydressina's neck, sending a blaze of electric fire through her skin, pushing her to her knees. Gydressina wasn't fazed. Her eyes remained wide open, concentrating on absorbing the heat. Evey pumped more and more fire into her body, trying everything in her power to push Gydressina to a threshold that couldn't be fought. But Gydressina easily absorbed every ounce of pain to the point it seemed she was bored to death of this silly little game. It eventually occurred to Evey that if she truly wanted to destroy Gydressina, she'd have to attack her soul, not her physical body. She focused her mind in finding Gydressina's true being, but the harder she looked, the more lost she became.

Matthew, meanwhile, had finally reached Jaime. He knelt next to her and lifted her into a sitting position against his chest. She was alive, as expected, and awake, though he wasn't quite sure if she was all there. "Jaime?" he said quietly.

She looked to him and raised her hand. "I'm okay," she said.

Relief filled Matthew's throat with a lump. He folded his arms around her waist and hugged her. Jaime wasn't sure how to react, but in appreciation, she wrapped her arm around the back of his head and gave a light squeeze, thankful for his help — thankful for his absolute love.

"Thank you," she whispered, hoping he'd accept it as an apology. Her eyes had grown more alive. Matthew nodded, pushing a slight curl to Jaime's lips. It didn't last long. As a slight remnant of pain attacked her stomach, Jaime turned to Evey, whose burning features seemed to form small scales around the contours of her cheekbones, contrasting greatly from Gydressina's calm, untouched smoothness. The two appeared to be sisters — twins broken in half, each having collected the opposite of the other. Evey held Gydressina with a hatred so unmasked, it felt affected by truth; Gydressina took her place as subservient, but stronger and more willed with purity and admiration.

Matthew broke Jaime's mesmerized stare by urging her away from them with a gentle push on her shoulder. Jaime accepted, rising to her feet and shifting across the wall without even realizing it. A steady wind had started to blow through the halls. The plants began a slow, unwanted decay, some shriveling to dust, others catching a spark and igniting into flame.

As the couple reached Kaleena, the rest of Jaime's attention shifted from the duel to the daughter she assumed had died, but believed was far from it. Sitting next to her, petting her hair as if she were a small kitten, was the traitor. An ire swelled within her, prompting her to push Patricia away from Kaleena. Even before Patricia's fat ass hit the floor, Jaime had collected her daughter into her arms.

"You stay away from her," she seethed.

Patricia, her eyes watering, could only find strength enough to whimper, "I'm sorry."

"I don't want to hear it." Jaime pulled Kaleena close to her chest and kissed her forehead. "I'm sorry," she whispered. "I'm so sorry." She didn't seem to care why Kaleena was unconscious; she only cared that she was alive, and that they were once again together. Matthew knelt down and placed his arm around Jaime's back, leaning in and kissing her softly on the cheek. To his surprise, she never pulled away, leaving Matthew wanting nothing more than to stay right here with his family for the rest of eternity.

Unable to stomach the quiet, loving reunion, Patricia turned away. The guilt over what she had almost done shredded her heart. Even if they weren't in the same place they had been just a few years ago, there were no regrets between them because there was no reason for regret. Life had forced them down separate paths, which had led them all back here for this very moment — ultimately, the final moment. She was far above wanting it, or desiring to have such a moment, but she now knew for sure a reunion of this capacity in her own life would always be impossible. Protecting the ones she cared about the most was all she had, and right now, this was the most important family to protect.

The wind in the room blew much stronger as Patricia turned to Evey. For a brief second, she thought she saw a small pair of horns in the shadow displayed on the wall by the growing fire, an illusion of the crackling flames. It wasn't until Gydressina's soothing tranquility melted the cold malevolence from her mind that she was able to believe in Evey's hidden truth. She had been manipulated; had gone against her better judgment because of something she thought she'd never get back. Even through all of her past mistakes, Jaime had only been kind to her. She was her best friend. It was time to repay that favor. It was time to take control — damn the consequences. Her daughter would understand.

"That's it, you crazy demon bitch," she whispered. "You've fucked your last apple pie." Patricia pushed her way through the pounding wind, wrapped her thick arm around Evey's neck and squeezed with all of her spinach-induced might. In

one quick motion, Evey wrapped her arm around Patricia and ignited a soft electric shock through her spine. Patricia winced as her arms locked up and then went completely numb. When the tension dissipated, Evey threw Patricia across the room. Her burly body stopped against the man whose heart had almost pounded its last beat.

"Patricia," Matthew yelled. He started to rise, but Jaime pulled him back down.

"Don't go," she exclaimed over the increasing wind.

"I have to see if she's all right." Matthew gave Jaime a quick kiss on the corner of her mouth. "I'll be safe. Don't worry."

It didn't matter if Matthew would be all right. Jaime didn't want him to protect Patricia after what she'd done. Then again, it was the right thing to do. She nodded and pulled Kaleena closer.

Matthew used every ounce of reserve strength to slide through the gale-force winds, making sure to avoid any eye contact with either Evey or Gydressina, who now looked worn, old, but nevertheless, much more powerful in a slightly yellow (or maybe it was goldish) hue. Evey, meanwhile, became more desperate to locate the heart of Gydressina's spirit. She felt her fading, felt the body eroding within, felt the light filling her mind, but she couldn't find that one precious piece of Gydressina — the one memory that made life what it was for her, for the secret behind her every love, her every fear, her every act, her every failure — that she needed to destroy her. Among everything Gydressina had become, not one moment proved to be her vitality.

You will never locate my truth, Evestylyn, because you truly do not want to see it.

Evey scowled and pushed Gydressina to the ground until her back was nearly touching it, her arms lying loosely on the floor.

I do not need your secret to destroy your body. You may still have power over it all, but without that, you're bound to the life and I will have complete mastery over you.

Go ahead and destroy my body, Evestylyn, for I am the life.

Matthew had finally reached Patricia and rolled her over, placing his hand to her neck like they always do on television. Relief washed through him as he felt a

light pulse. But before he could do anything else, the fire forming along the walls blew across the hall, consuming both Evey and Gydressina. Matthew fell on top of Patricia, covering her from the remnants of the flash.

When the flames were licked clean by the blasting wind, a rumble echoed through the walls. Matthew looked past Gydressina and Evey, both of whom remained locked together in perfect formation as if the fire had never touched them, and made eye contact with Jaime. She looked both frightened for her own life, but brave enough to protect her daughter from what was about to happen.

You will not live to see my death, mother.

And I cannot allow you to live under the fruit of your father.

Evey's eyes grew wide and terrified as Gydressina entered her mind. She'd once held Cephis there, had always allowed Caistepher to walk within and Adamus to love, but she'd never felt the presence of a body so intensely as with Gydressina, who ripped through her soul like a knife. Evey fought hard to push her out, but the old woman was far too strong. A friction grew between their living bodies, causing light full of sparks to form around them. It grew brighter and larger, eventually creating a wall between Jaime and Matthew that neither was unable to look into.

Now you see the truth, Gydressina said, which ignited an explosion that ripped through the corridor, sending a shockwave across the entire floor. The building rocked intensely, as if a magnitude ten earthquake had hit. The walls bent like butter. The floor beneath Jaime and Kaleena cracked like ice under their weight. Before she could get to her feet, it collapsed. Jaime was knocked unconscious after striking her head against a large piece of the debris. The two were immediately left in darkness as the light from above faded and left nothing behind but a quiet, calm sleep.

Atlantis – Lauren's Quarters – 11 hours 45 minutes after arrival

It took Kara a long time to accept Diana's presence. Even when she started moving toward her, Kara could only step away, keeping a minimum safe distance between them. Part of her wanted to give her a big hug, but she was afraid she'd vanish as soon as she touched her, a figment of her imagination that had manifested through the pages of the book she used to wish her back to life. On the other hand, the whole thing might be one elaborate ruse; some type of mind game that the woman holding Jaime and Patricia was playing to keep her occupied. Why else would her sister appear no older than eighteen? But with the look in her eyes… Diana seemed to be as frightened about the whole situation as she was. Kara was sure Diana would have had a different air about her when she returned from her exploration — an aura of adulthood, of maturity. But this woman looked childish, a scared little girl who secretly watched a scary movie before bed and had a bad dream about getting chopped by razor sharp fingernails, or had her brains eaten by some slow motion zombies. The idea Diana had of coming home and going to school, of graduating and finding a job, settling down with a couple of bratty boys that would get into more trouble than her daughter, one ending up in juvenile detention, the other taking his chances in the army to be wounded in a war that made no sense, to come home and be forgotten as a soldier, had all been clearly stripped from her because of a plane crash she had no memory of, and a sister who aged nearly thirteen years in just a few months.

"Is it really you?" Diana asked.

"How did you get here?"

Diana shrugged. "I don't know. I don't even know where here is. Where are we? What happened to you?"

"Diana…" Kara paused a second, wondering if she should even tell her. "You're dead," she finally stuttered.

"Dead?" Diana looked quizzically at Kara. "How… What do you mean 'dead'?"

"I mean… we laid you to rest thirteen years ago, dead."

"Thirteen years… what the fuck are you talking about?"

"Diana. You died in a plane crash thirteen years ago."

Diana held her hand over her mouth, her eyes glazed. As she considered the idea, she rested her other hand over the first. She could hardly breathe. Feeling light-headed, she sat down on the bed and stared at the floor.

"The flight you were on disappeared over the Atlantic," Kara explained. "You don't remember?" She felt a little stupid afterward. "Of course you don't."

Diana shook her head and finally lowered her hands. "All I remember is getting on the plane in France, and then…" Diana's stomach twisted and churned.

"What?"

She looked to Kara. "Nothing. I woke up here, stripped fucking naked with a bunch of people I didn't know."

Kara thought a moment, and then: "When?"

"What?"

"When did you wake up?"

"I don't know… an hour ago, I guess. What does that matter?"

"An hour ago? You sure about that?"

"Has it really been thirteen years?" Diana looked away, her head hurting. Kara finally took a step toward her. It was clear something was different about her, but it couldn't have been because it was a trick or a figment of her imagination. If that were the case, or even if it *was* a mind game, Diana would have come across spunky and fun as ever, as Kara last remembered her. The girl in front of her clearly didn't know what was happening and needed comfort, a familiar touch to calm her down.

Kara sat next to her sister and wrapped her arm around her shoulders. Upon touching her, Diana leaned in and wrapped her own arms around Kara, needing her warmth. In her mind, she hadn't seen Kara in three months. But now, as she held her, she could tell that it had truly been many years. Her mind didn't feel it, but her body did.

"My god, Kara. What happened?"

"I don't know, sweetie," Kara said, trying hard not to sound like a mother, but like the sister Diana remembered.

She looked Kara over. "What are you now, then, fifty?"

Kara backed away. "Do I really look that old?"

"No," Diana said quickly. "No, I didn't mean it like that, I…" Diana turned away, somewhat embarrassed.

"Hey, it's okay." Kara waited for Diana to turn back to her. "Running around the world playing in dirt your whole life can take a toll."

Diana's smile warmed Kara's heart as if she had just stepped out into the sun. "If there's a silver lining, at least *you* still look great," Kara said.

"Well of course I do." Diana gave Kara a little wink. She chuckled and the two sat together a minute longer, unable to speak, neither of them really knowing what to say to the other.

"How was my funeral?" Diana finally asked, breaking the awkwardness.

Kara wasn't quite sure how to answer, but she gave it a shot. "Beautiful… I guess."

Diana smirked devilishly. "I am so glad it wasn't ugly."

"I'm sorry."

"What for. Black is beautiful. Maybe a few daisy petals thrown on top of the fancy box for good measure."

Kara couldn't help but laugh. "Well, I can't say the coffin was very fancy. I mean…it *was* empty."

"True." Diana combed a bit of her hair behind her ear. "Who was there?"

"All your friends, from what I can remember. Ryan was there… poor boy looked about ready to jump in after you."

Diana's smile faded slightly. Remembering Ryan was hard, as what she remembered was bittersweet. She'd been dating him for nearly three years and had been pressuring him to have sex for two of them. But he always held off, claiming he wanted to wait until marriage. She always said it was because he wasn't sure if he'd be a good lay and wanted to wait until the contract was signed before he proved it. It was a joke, he knew that; and she knew he loved her, which made that night before she left even more unforgiving. Diana had already made the decision to explore her sexuality while she was gone, but she couldn't find the nerve to break that resolution to Ryan. She loved him, but wasn't sure she wanted to spend the rest of her life with

him. The only thing she knew for sure was she wanted him to take her youth before she left. Maybe it was because she wanted to have at least one experience before heading overseas so she wasn't a virgin to all areas of her life, or maybe she needed a comparison for all the rest she would certainly bed before her trip was over. At least then it would give her a chance to know how it all felt, what it would mean to her as a woman, and whether Ryan truly was the one she would live forever.

She snuck out that night and spent over a half hour riding over three miles on her bike past the highway to his house. It would have taken her about five minutes by car, but she didn't want her parents to know she'd left. Ryan was surprised and gracious to see her. Even before he invited her in, she was kissing him, as if her death awaited. Within minutes, they had worked their way to his bedroom and his shirt had come off. It wasn't the first time Ryan had seen Diana's breasts, having once explored them in the hot tub when his parents were in Fiji, but something told him this time was different. He was hard and he was ready, but he'd made a promise he wasn't ready to break.

"I can't do this," he said.

"Shut up," Diana said through tapping kisses. "This is my last night. I want to be with you." She pulled his hand between her legs. Ryan was shocked to feel she didn't have on any underwear. "Please, Ryan," she said. "Don't just touch me tonight."

Ryan quickly gave in and the two of them found themselves staring at the ceiling next to each other, breathing heavily as they tried to understand what just happened. It was quicker than Diana had expected it to be, but it was no less enthralling. She felt she could still continue, but Ryan had clearly ejaculated into the condom Diana made sure she kept with her at all times. He grabbed a Kleenex from the box he kept by his bed (claiming it was because he had a lot of allergies, for which Diana joked about his extra-curricular wanking). He removed the used plastic from around his penis and wrapped it in the Kleenex. As he tossed it away in the trashcan by the desk across the room, Diana slid off the edge of the bed and started getting dressed.

"What are you doing?" he asked.

"I have to get back home," Diana said, her excitement faded.

"Will you call me before you take off?"

Diana dropped her shirt over her head and looked at Ryan, saddened. His heart dropped. "No," he said. "Don't you dare."

She crawled across the bed. "I'm sorry," she said and tried to finish the apology with a kiss. He backed off, sick to his stomach, and sat down on the chair at the desk. "Ryan, please."

"Just…get out."

"Ryan, you have to understand —"

"Get out!" Ryan stared at the floor as Diana folded her eyes with regret. For some reason she thought breaking up with him would have been a lot easier to do. Her first notion was to kiss him, tell him it would all be all right, but that clearly hadn't worked. So she left without another word, or another look. When she got back home, she called Kara, and through a waterfall of tears, told her about the break-up, leaving out the part of her sexual experience. Kara would understand the break-up; Diana wasn't sure if she'd respect her if she knew what happened before it. She was back to her old self the next day, knowing full well that she no longer had any ties to her past and that a bright future awaited. But she could never admit, not even to herself, that a small part of her needed to hold onto Ryan and never let him go.

"Did you talk to him at all?" Diana asked Kara.

"I don't think he wanted to talk to any of us. I think he was there to say goodbye and let you go for good. He didn't need me to keep him attached to you."

"That's good. I'm glad he had a chance to move on."

Kara nodded. "I think he went on to become a lawyer."

"Good," Diana said. "What about Jenny? And Susan?"

"Oh, they were both there," Kara said, acknowledging Diana's need to change the subject. "So were Kate and Louise and Harry and Tim and Tyra. You had a lot of friends, there, squirt."

"Hey, if popularity was an Olympic sport…"

"You would win the gold," Kara said, recalling what their family always used to say. "Mom actually used that in her speech at the burial."

"Mom?" Diana's eyes grew wide, once again empowering the child within. "How is she? And Dad? How did they react to, you know…?"

"How do you think they reacted?"

"Devastated," they said simultaneously and then started laughing. Kara's hand had secretly taken a hold of Diana's.

"It took them years to fully recover from it," Kara continued as the laughter died away. "I don't even think Mom really has. If she saw you now, she'd probably have a heart attack."

"So they're still alive?"

"Yeah, of course." Kara felt Diana's pure happiness.

"And what about you," Diana said. "You score a good man yet? Do I have any nieces or nephews?"

"Sorry to disappoint, but nothing's come my way."

"Not one guy? Come on, there has to been at least one."

"After you died, I pretty much went head long into my work. I had no time for frivolities like dating."

"Man, what a waste," Diana said mockingly.

"A waste?" Kara pushed Diana playfully.

"Yeah I mean, check you out. You were gorgeous, last I remember."

"Gee, thanks."

"I'm just sayin'. You used up all your youth with work. With what you had," Diana grabbed her breasts and jiggled them up and down, "it's a complete waste."

"Well, thank you."

"I didn't mean anything by it," Diana said, trying to make up for her sarcasm.

"I know," Kara assured.

"Good. So, tell me this, at least. With you choosing old artifacts over using your assets, did you at least find something worth the looks."

"Diana," Kara said, leaning in close. "You're sittin' in it."

"What? Why? Where are we?"

"You, my dear sister, prepare to be awed. For whatever reason, and however you got here, you are currently part of the lost city of Atlantis."

"No shit?" Diana stood to get a better look at the room.

Kara smiled like a seven-year-old with a new puppy.

"No fucking way. Atlantis. You're serious?" Diana turned back to Kara, who nodded with authority. After a moment, Diana's awe suddenly faded.

"What's wrong?" Kara said, walking to her.

"I don't know. I just got this strange feeling like I already knew that."

"A little déjà vu for the crash victim, huh?"

Diana chuckled. "I guess. But it seems more than that…"

Suddenly, a flash of light filled the room and a stroke of wind knocked them both to the ground. Diana felt an odd serenity in the elements; her mind filled with memories that were not hers. The woman she saw walked the halls of Atlantis, lived life with a passivity and a joy of simply being, and then fought alongside the man she loved in hopes that she would love him for eternity and beyond, his hand warm in hers, her heart filled with childlike fervor. Atlantis was her home; the man was her existence.

An explosion, distant but close, blew the light and the wind away. The room shook, cracking the walls slightly. A few small pieces of the ceiling fell to the ground around them. As the echoes of the debris dissipated, Kara crawled to Diana and shook her arms away from her face.

"Diana, are you okay?"

Diana looked up, lost and seemingly alone.

"Diana?"

Diana finally realized who Kara was and shook her head. "Yeah," she whimpered. "Yeah, sorry. I'm okay. What was that?"

"I have no idea. But we should get out of here."

Diana nodded and stood up, wiping a bit of dust from her gown. Kara quickly

went and picked up the diary and then escorted Diana to the door. She looked out into the corridor. In one direction, debris filled the halls and the plants were all either dead or burned. In the other, it seemed untouched and alive.

"This way," Kara suggested, pointing down the clear path. Diana nodded and followed her out of the room.

"Where are we going?"

"I don't know."

"I think I might know where we can go to be safe," Diana said.

Kara wasn't sure she should trust her, but what other choice did she have? "Lead the way." *Anywhere is probably better than here.*

Atlantis – Women's Quarters – 11 hours 45 minutes after arrival

The two women circled Thomas like vultures waiting to devour their prey. Yet to Trishen, their fear was evident. They knowingly kept their distance and wouldn't get more than just a few feet from him. And from what she could tell through the dozens of other women surrounding him, Thomas saw it too. Every so often he'd take a small step toward one of them to test the waters of their dedication to his capture, only to have them subtlety step back so as to appear it was part of her flow, hidden under her steps. Thomas knew better. If he really wanted, he probably could have walked right up to the door and out of the room. But Trishen was well aware of why he didn't. They never would have allowed him to take her with him, no matter how frightened they were.

Standing a few feet from Destin, Trishen waited patiently for the moment when she could break through the female barrier and hold Thomas's hand, maybe even attempt an escape. But every time that window opened, she felt the women staring at her through her mind, advising her to stay put, even as their eyes never left Thomas.

What do you want? Trishen finally asked, throwing it out in hopes one of them would catch it. Destin was the only one who seemed to hear it, though. She

jumped off her new mother's lap and joined Trishen at her side.

Would you like me to try? Destin asked. Trishen flashed a hint of a smile and nodded. Destin turned her focus to the women. For a moment, Trishen couldn't hear anything. But then a soft voice rang in her ear. *They say you've caused them enough trouble by bringing this plague upon our people. It's Lord Cephis who's kept you alive.*

Trishen stared into Destin's darkened eyes. *What do they mean plague? Where is Cephis? I want to talk to him.*

Destin turned her attention back to the women. After a moment, she said, *They won't answer me.*

Make them, Trishen said.

I will do no such thing.

Why not?

I will not help you rescue this man. He's far too dangerous. He must be destroyed.

Trishen was stunned. She wanted to slap the little brat, but if she did, every woman in the room would probably have attacked her. Then what good would she have been?

It would be wise of you to give up on him now and kill him yourself, Destin said, *than to wait and force Lord Cephis to do so.*

I'm not going to kill him.

Don't delude yourself, Trishen. Either you kill him now, or be forced to kill him later. Either way, he will die, and it will be because of you.

Shut up.

I will not. Kill him. Let it be on your *terms.*

No.

Do it, you fucking bitch.

Trishen did slap her then. The woman pretending to be her mother immediately grabbed Trishen's arm. "What did you do that for?" she roared.

Destin held her cheek with a devilish grin. Before Trishen had a chance to answer for her outrage, the door shifted open. Destin and all of the other children (as well as a handful of adults) dropped to their knee and lowered their heads. Cephis waited motionless for the doors to fully open. He stared at the ground, his hood lowered inches below the curvature of his forehead. As the doors came to a loud halt, Rose and Hannah broke their link to Thomas and walked to either side of Cephis. They remained a few feet in front of him with their arms crossed just below their stomachs, like a pair of noble statues.

"*Lord Cephis Satina is now among you, within you and of you,*" they said in unison. "*Kneel before him, and bow in respect to his grace.*"

The women who had yet to join the others on the floor knelt down as if in prayer. Trishen wasn't sure if it was fear of his dark and almost menacing stature or because the spirits that were slowly connecting their minds to their new hosts were beginning to dominate, but it all seemed to be controlled by respect. Trishen and Thomas were the last to remain standing, each taking a gander at the sea of devotees before returning their attention to Cephis.

You do not kneel, he growled, the air heavy with the bass of his voice.

You don't frighten me, Cephis, Trishen responded before Thomas could say anything, hoping to protect him for as long as possible by fighting the subtle fear growing inside.

You have grown, Cephis said, no doubt referring to the frightened child he first encountered.

I just decided there wasn't much to be afraid of anymore.

And what brought you to that absurd notion?

Perhaps because I now know I'm not alone.

And perhaps you are unwise to believe in a false notion of protection.

A false notion of protection?

I can see your fear, young child. Your bravery is false because it's connected to a hope you know nothing about.

I know enough, Cephis.

Do you?

Cephis lowered his hood gently, revealing his slick jet-black hair. The sea of women shifted, sensing the tension. Something bad was about to happen. Trishen's heart pounded, raising her fear from her gut to her mind. She started to sweat. Thomas stood stone cold in the center of the room, the lump in his throat growing, making it hard to swallow (even though there was hardly a drop of saliva to swallow) and even breathe. When Cephis finally looked up, Thomas's lungs closed. He grabbed his chest and dropped to one knee, lowering his head as if he was bowing.

Thomas! Trishen tried to yell it out, but all that escaped was a small squeal. Cephis turned to her. His eyes were yellow drops of fire among the hot red coals of his pupils. He remained steadfast, though, as Thomas struggled to fight the increasing pain in his chest, one that absorbed all of his thoughts. That is until he saw an image of Trishen hiding inside a small crack in his mind. It sent a flash of ice through his chest, soothing the pain for that instant her image had been a part of him. He quickly tried to find her again, to hold onto her for as long as he could. It was hard to locate her at first, as if Cephis was attempting to keep her from him, but once he cleared the fog away, and heard her heart beat in his chest, the pain Cephis had induced faded. Cephis fought back, driving Trishen into the shadows. But the harder he pushed, the easier it became for Thomas to find Trishen. Eventually, he rose to his feet again. It was still hard to breathe, but his strength, both mentally and physically, was evident in his confidence. He slid in between Trishen and Cephis, slightly uncomfortable but nevertheless unafraid. Rose and Hannah stayed true to their flank, yet there was a strong terror swarming among them. They had never seen someone fight the mind of Cephis — not a mortal anyway. And even the one they had witnessed fight him this confidently and this fiercely before never had the conviction they saw so vigorously in Thomas. They had no idea where it was coming from. And as he looked directly into Cephis's eyes, Rose and Hannah were shocked to witness Cephis take a step back and sneer with a slight pain of his own. So shocked they were, they almost broke their stance.

Suddenly, a soft, distant rumble echoed through the walls. Trishen figured it was Cephis growling in defeat, but as it grew, it became apparent it was something

different. Everyone else heard it as well. The entirety of the room, some with just their eyes, some with their heads and full bodies, looked around at one another, wondering what and where the noise was coming from. As the sound neared its apex, Thomas broke his grip on Cephis, who slipped backward a step upon his release.

Thomas didn't hesitate. He drifted back to Trishen and pulled her to the ground, delicately covering her as the entire room shook. Unlike all of the other women, who screamed as they slid and fell around the room, Trishen didn't feel the need to do so. Thomas's comforting touch was all she needed to feel protected. As parts of the floor collapsed around them, a couple of the voices in Trishen's head dissipated and whispered into nothing. The pain of their deaths — one broke her neck and a couple of others hit the ground to slowly bleed out — were felt in their last, desperate breaths.

Rose and Hannah slid to the floor to balance themselves, knowing they were in no danger where they stood. The shaking was at its peak when Cephis walked toward Thomas as if nothing was happening. Thomas knew he was coming. Upon the arrival of darkness, he reached his hand out to grab him. Cephis countered, unconcerned, taking hold of Thomas before the old man could reach his throat. Each experienced a chill run their spines. Thomas felt as if his brain was melting; Cephis as if his heart was about to explode.

You cannot win this, Thomas, Cephis said, surprisingly respectful.

Thomas stood steadfast, trying hard to pump his love for Trishen through Cephis as the rumbling slowly ceased, but his defeat intensified. Cephis was aware of it as well. His lips curled around his teeth and he threw Thomas across the room. He smashed into the wall, knocking Rose to the ground outside of the room, and landing on top of Hannah, sending her into a whirlwind of screams and fits. She pulled at her hair until it ripped from her head. Pushing Thomas away was futile. The strength in her arms and legs had been severely diminished by the growing numbness of ice burning her body. Her soul melted away as the screams around the room faded into her own. Before long, Hannah's head fell to the ground, her eyes and mouth held wide open as she ceased to exist.

As Thomas tried to bring his dizziness under control, Cephis grabbed a hold of Trishen's hair and pulled her to her feet.

Why must you defy me, Cephis said, glowering. His malevolent presence collected in her thoughts. It wouldn't take long for him to find the true love she held for Thomas, if he hadn't already, but she didn't want to say anything. She wasn't willing to lower herself to his servantry. A low growl soon rolled through her thoughts, weakening her knees. Her eyes grew heavy, about ready to spin back into her head, but she fought him the best she could.

Thomas, she said, strong and hopeful. *Help me, Thomas.*

Thomas will die protecting you. Are you willing to accept that?

No, she said, her mind's voice much stronger than any part of her body. *Thomas is my strength. As long as I'm alive, he'll never die.*

So naïve, my child. His death will haunt you, yes, but your mind will not be able to accept his sacrifice. It will have been in vain as you forget his existence in becoming my love.

I will never love you, Cephis.

You will have no choice. Cephis grabbed hold of Thomas's neck just as he leapt at the monster in a vain attempt to overpower him. "Just as you will have no choice in death," he finished, heat rising in his hand. He let the swell of fire grow for some time, then flung the limp body back across the room. Thomas again hit the wall flush with his back. Had his spine been snapped? He lay on the floor, watching Cephis push Trishen to the ground and place his hand on the floor. The monster collected the heat flaming through his hand into his fingertips and sent a long strip of fire lengthwise across the room, blocking Thomas from his love. Several women and children who were unable to get out of the way erupted into flames. A few tried to roll the fire out, but it burned strong, rising to the ceiling. Thomas stayed glued to his position as the flames consumed Rebecca, a young girl no more than ten.

Help me, she cried out under the screams of the other victims.

Thomas wrapped his scarred hand close to his body as he stared at the child, her desperation leaping through her eyes. She was lonely and scared, needing Thomas to bring her back to the life she once knew. But he couldn't do anything as the little girl — his friend, his first crush — lowered her head and allowed the fire to melt her body to ash. Warm tears rolled down his cheeks as he tried to recapture the beauty he once remembered before Jacob ripped his life to pieces. That day had killed her just as much as it had killed him, and the screams floating among the air made him want to throw-up and die with Rebecca in his arms, whispering blessings into her ear, tasting the kiss he'd never have the pleasure of accepting. But one scream in particular pulled him from it all. One scream pushed the fear away and replaced it with confidence and determination. He wasn't that little kid anymore. The memory that had changed not only his life, but that of a young girl looking to be protected, that had shaped them both, turned them each into what they had become, no longer hurt him. He would always possess her memory, but he now knew that he needed to embrace it, use it to help him guide his strength. He didn't know what had truly happened to Rebecca, but that moment led him to Caitlyn, who led him to grow up, which led him to Matthew, who led him to —

"Trishen," he said aloud, looking past the blackening body of the young girl. Through the licks of flames, he saw her, plastered to the floor, fighting Cephis's power — his control. She didn't look well; he consumed her with his own inner fire. Just as Rebecca had once been burned, Trishen was now burning, and she wouldn't be able to hold on much longer.

Thomas stretched out his fingers and then folded them into a fist. He stood, a small blaze growing within him. He couldn't allow himself to be afraid of the fire, of the burn or the pain any longer. Trishen needed him. Gritting his teeth, Thomas ran at the fire as fast as he could, taking a large leap through the thick wall of flame. His hand throbbed as the heat licked his skin, burning his eyes and nostrils. But all of that was secondary. As he landed next to Cephis, he sent a hard fist to the monster's waist. Cephis roared as his body nearly collapsed in on itself, forcing him to let go of Trishen. She slumped to the ground, trying desperately to

take in a deep breath. Thomas stretched his upper body, fighting away the pain of the flames on his chest and waist, and stood strong against his opponent.

"You ready to dance, Cephis?"

"Time to die," Cephis said, even though he knew that if he didn't get away from Thomas soon, his whole body would crumble. He was able to slow down his own inner degeneration enough to strike at Thomas, but it was weak to say the least, allowing Thomas to grab Cephis's arm before his fist struck his jaw. Smoke rose from his hand, imprinting a replica of Thomas's scars into Cephis's skin. Unwilling to back down, Cephis grabbed Thomas and threw him against the base of the window. This time, Thomas was quick to rise to his feet, ignoring the searing pain being covered by the guiding influence of adrenaline. His brain crushed in on itself, but he concentrated on recapturing Trishen's image while seizing Cephis's eyes. Locked together, Cephis's spirit ripped apart. He fought back hard, feverishly pushing the old man from his body. Thomas matched his power, finding it easier to control as Cephis weakened. He moved forward, his legs like tree trunks pulling out roots. But the closer Thomas got, the more pressure built in the air among them.

Suddenly, a loud explosive pulse erupted between them, flinging both men apart from one another. The fire swirled around Cephis as he blew through it, reforming its glow after his passage. He landed near Rose, who was beginning to come to. The weight of the attack kept him glued to the ground for some time. Rose saw his deteriorated state and placed her hands to his chest, hoping to revive him quickly with her returning confidence.

On the opposite side of the room, Thomas smashed up against the window. A web of cracks sprouted through the center, slowly spreading under the weight of the sea. Blood formed around the small scratches on Thomas's back as he attempted to climb to his knees, only to slump back to the floor.

Trishen, barely able to rise to her own knees, crawled to him and rolled his limp body onto her legs. Tears rolled across her cheeks as she relished in his silence. Destin had been right. Thomas had died protecting her. But she would never forget him, not as Cephis had proclaimed. She had never loved the way she had loved with Thomas; had never felt the power of a connection between two minds and spirits as strong as the one she felt for him, and knew that if she ever found her way out of Atlantis, she would never again feel it. Thomas truly did complete her in every sense of the word. Even though it was clear he wanted to, he never once asked to kiss her, never once came on to her the way all other men did. He was content in just holding her in his arms, protecting her, and would die for that and that alone. It was such a perfect thought. Trishen knew of only one thing she could do to help guide Thomas to his new life. She lowered her head, her lips tainted in tears, and kissed him. She kept her lips closed as they rounded against his and held them there for quite some time, tasting the remnants of his saliva as she absorbed the soft warmth of his final breaths.

When she lifted her head, she smiled. His eyes had opened. She pet his hair as she saw past the wrinkles, grayed hair and sagging skin to spy the young father she met on the *Endeavor* that would carry their love beyond the sea and into the air surrounding them.

I love you, she whispered in her mind. Thomas replied back quickly with the heart of cupid.

My love transcends the heavens and will last for the end of days.

Before she could lean in for another kiss, she was pulled up and pressed hard against the glass, causing the cracks to grow even quicker. Cephis raised his hand to Trishen's head. The sting of flames burned behind her eyes, but she couldn't move them.

"No!" Thomas yelled, though he couldn't find the strength to move. His body was coming back to life, but it would take time to find the power of mobility.

The final kiss will now lead to your own forgetfulness, Cephis said. *Prepare yourself for a brand new life.* Cephis charged into Trishen's mind and found the moment her lips touched Thomas. He imprinted it into his own mind and then washed it clean, blackening it out, using it to lead him to all of her other memories, linked together like a web. As he erased them all from existence, Trishen no longer had

control of her body. Vomit foamed around her mouth and excrement poured down her leg. It wasn't long before she passed out, apparently dead.

When Cephis had finished melting away her memories, he pulled her from the glass, allowing her body to limp to the ground. He dragged her through the remaining women, some of whom watched with fervor as the secondary souls finally connected and were now admiring Cephis in his new body, others huddling against each other in fear of the same happening to them. Ignoring them all, he opened a small path through the continuing flames and pulled Trishen to Rose, who stood waiting for him with readiness and approbation.

Take her to the surface.

Rose's admiration waned slightly at his request. *What for?*

Do not ask questions.

She crossed her arms, defiance radiating from her pores. She wasn't ready to leave Ediinis and Cephis knew that. He lifted Trishen off the floor and nearly threw her into Rose's arms. *Do as I say. She is my wife; she will bear my child. Find a home and prepare a past for her. You are her new guardian. Live with her as her sister, help her raise the child and do not let her out of your sight until my return.*

As Rose looked the young woman over, she felt a very familiar connection. The woman in her arms would be her sister, the child growing within, her niece. She looked back to Cephis and nodded. She couldn't fight it. *As you wish.*

Cephis kissed Rose, his tongue hot and rippled with scales. It tasted sweet to her, smoked and roasted. She didn't want him to pull away, but finally accepted it. She didn't smile, she didn't linger. She just turned from him, pulled Trishen closer to her breast, and left the room; left Ediinis; left Cephis behind forever.

Thomas rose to his knees as Trishen disappeared from his life. He wanted to call out for her, but his lungs seemed to have been burnt by the blast. There was a sharp sting biting his back and a nip of needles pricked his entire body. He was dying, he knew that; and there was no way to stop it. The worst thing he could do would be to die in vain. He wasn't about to let Cephis take Trishen, lie to her, kill her slowly through fear and guilt. He had to do something. He had to take

this last moment to protect his love, his child, his wife and the extended family he knew, after connecting to Cephis's mind, were still very much alive. But to destroy Cephis, he would need to destroy Atlantis.

"Time to die," he whispered and stood, taller than he'd ever felt. Before Cephis could stop him, Thomas turned and leapt at the window, smashing it once and for all. Upon impact, he swallowed a gallon of water. The pain of drowning faded from his mind as the last remaining visage of Trishen helped his spirit become one with the water.

Cephis stood his ground, allowing the water pouring into the room to surround him. He closed his eyes as he consumed the sea along with all the souls that were being collected within it. He used those fresh spirits to soothe him, heal his wounds and allow them their final resting place among the darkness of numbness.

Atlantis – Hallways – 12 hours 12 minutes after arrival

Nausea hit Matthew as he rolled onto his back and rubbed his eyes. He couldn't remember what happened and didn't take notice of the water pouring underneath him. If he had a choice, he'd probably just sit as still as a log, maybe even go back to sleep and rest forever. But as his memory filtered back to existence, Kaleena, limp and near death, flashed through his mind. His eyes shot open.

"Kaleena," he said, sitting up. "Jaime."

He tried to get to his feet, but slipped back to his knees as the lightheadedness caught him off guard. He finally registered the water covering his wrist and felt the weight of his clothes freeze his skin. Clearing his thoughts, Matthew rubbed his temples before attempting to rise again. This time, he was able to stand. He looked across the room and saw a pile of debris to his left, the floor (possibly several floors) above him having collapsed.

"Jaime," he cried out again. "Kaleena." Matthew sloshed his way through the rising water as fast as he could. He tried to dig through the massive layers of wood and steel, but his lack of strength couldn't support the weight. He didn't give up, though, fighting and struggling to move just one simple piece, continuing to do so until his fingers were ripped from his body.

Calm yourself, Matthew, a voice whispered through the air before it could get that far. The voice was familiar, warming. Matthew turned, but couldn't see anyone. After a moment, he turned back to the wall to continue his frivolous attempts at rescuing Kaleena.

"It will do you no good. The debris will hold strong."

Matthew turned again. This time, Gydressina stood just a few feet away.

"We have to get to them," he demanded, not caring one bit as to where she'd come from.

"They are well, Matthew. There is nothing to fear."

"I need to help them."

"Rest assured, they do not need your help. Trust me. Listen to my words."

Tears formed around his eyes.

"Kaleena and Jaime are fine, and will find us again."

Matthew sat against the wall with his head in his hands, fighting the urge to vomit. The cold, salty water sifted around his chest as Gydressina slowly walked to him. She rested her hand upon his head. "It's okay, Matthew. Your love for them shines bright. They know you would never let any harm come to them."

Letting a tear fall to the water, Matthew took hold of Gydressina's hand. He kissed it as if she were his wife, and calmed himself, pulling all of the bravery he could muster to the surface. "She knows where to go," he said confidently. "We'll meet 'em there." He looked up to meet Gydressina's gaze. "Won't we?"

"Yes, we will. That is for certain."

Matthew nodded lightly and then stood, keeping Gydressina's hand in his. He needed it for protection — for his own peace of mind. She graciously led him away from the debris. Her love soared through him with kindness, warmth and safety. She helped him float; it felt like heaven.

Suddenly, Matthew tripped on something in the water. A body lay underneath.

At first, his mind instantly thought it might be Jaime or Kaleena, but that was impossible. It must be one of the guys that tried to kill Jaime, but that, too, seemed far-fetched. They wore black robes and were smaller than the body he was currently looking at. Then it came to him.

"Patricia."

Matthew let go of Gydressina and fell to the ground. He picked Patricia's upper body out of the water and examined her faded white features. "She's not breathing," he said, a bit frantic.

Gydressina knelt down on the other side of Patricia. She lowered one hand to Patricia's chest and the other to her forehead. Taking in a deep breath, she appeared to turn to stone in front of Matthew's eyes. He wanted to take control, give Patricia mouth to mouth, ask Gydressina what the hell she was doing. But he knew better than to go against her; simply being alive confirmed that.

All he could do was wait as Gydressina searched for Patricia's spirit among the air around her. It took more time than she expected, but when she finally found her, she guided her back into her body. She then quickly dissolved all the water from Patricia's lungs and coated her mind with oxygen, sparking a few key synapses within before leaning down and transferring all of the air from her lungs into Patricia's mouth. Her chest rose and held strong.

"Well," Matthew said, unsure of what was happening.

"We must wait," Gydressina said, inspecting Patricia's body. "Her spirit must reconnect with her mind."

"How long will that take?"

"It is unknown, if ever."

"No, we can't just wait. We have to do something."

"It's impossible otherwise. If she can't reconnect on her own, she will cease to be."

Matthew knew fighting would be pointless. So he held Patricia in his arms, urging her to wake up, to reconnect, as the water slowly continued to rise, now sitting just below the top of Matthew's shoulders.

"It's too late," Gydressina said, sensing Patricia's spirit failing to become one with the body.

"What do you mean it's too late?" Matthew screamed.

"The water level is rising. Before long, it will devour us both. We can't wait any longer. We must leave now."

"Bullshit," Matthew said, bending Patricia's neck back a bit. He breathed some air into her mouth and then tried pumping her chest with just one hand.

"It will do you no good, Matthew. She's not in need of life. She's in need of her spirit. And I'm afraid her mind has been dead for far too long to accept the spirit home."

Matthew ignored her, blowing more air into her lungs.

"Matthew." Gydressina rested her hand on his shoulder. Matthew stopped, lowering his head to Patricia's forehead.

"I know how you must feel, and I respect your courage and your devotion. But Kaleena and Jaime need you right now. You must let her go."

Matthew tried to remember her the best he could, her spirits high and sarcastic. She brought life to everyone around her. He felt bad for not being able to return the favor. But Gydressina was right. The water was now up to his neck and he could barely hold her head above the water. They would all die if he didn't let her go.

"Goodbye," he said softly and lowered her head, allowing it to gently fall to the floor. He rubbed his temples, attempting to pull his own strength back to his mind. "Let's go."

Gydressina held out her hand, but Matthew was unable to accept it. He was still angry at her for giving up so easily and felt as if he were leaving behind himself, and everything he was living for.

Just before they were about to round the corner of the corridor, a loud cough followed the slush and splash of water. Matthew turned as Gydressina stood still, a light smile rising to her lips.

"Patricia," he called out.

Patricia coughed hard and spit up some water, desperately sucking in a gallon of air. "Where the hell you think you guys are going?" she said, her voice raspy and rough. "You didn't think I was dumb enough to die, did you?"

"She did," Matthew said, waving a thumb at Gydressina.

"Bitch," Patricia said sarcastically, letting out one last cough.

Matthew trudged to her, the ripples of Patricia's weight lapping against his waist. He got to her in time to not help her the rest of the way to her feet.

"Who is that, anyway?"

"That is Gydressina."

"What kind of shit name is that? If I didn't know any better, I would've thought it was that other bitch, Evey. They look almost identical."

"Evey?" Matthew turned to Gydressina. "That was Evey?"

"Yeah," Patricia said before Gydressina could. "And a mother fucker she is too. I hope this one doesn't turn out to be a mega bitch."

"I don't think you have to worry about that. This one doesn't want to kill Kaleena."

Patricia smiled. "That would be a good thing, yeah?"

"Yeah," Matthew said, patting her on the back like a poker buddy.

"Well, what are we waiting for, then," she said, her voice bouncing along the walls of the room. "Let's get the hell out of here before the ocean tries to kill me a third time."

"You don't have to ask me twice."

Matthew and Patricia took the lead into the corridor, ignoring Gydressina's presence. "What happened, anyway?" Matthew asked, curiously.

"What? When I was dead?"

"Yeah."

"I haven't the foggiest. And if I told you I thought I saw God, you'd probably think I was fucking insane."

"No more than usual," Matthew said. They felt good and Gydressina could see it in their steps. She soon fell a few yards behind them, allowing them space,

unwilling to disturb their bliss. She knew what was about to come and Matthew would need to be strong when it did.

Ediinis – Field of Enlightenment
(*23,500 years ago*)

Six men wearing red robes laced in gold carried Kaleena's body along the smooth, dirt path lined with tall, thick trees. Branches swept over the walkway, weaving together to form a living arc above them, shading the entire trail from the sun. Grass and roses lay evenly along the roots of the trees and whispered lightly in the soft breeze. Kaleena lay on a stretcher made of a bamboo-style wood, which felt strong and comfortable against the curvature of her back. Her breath was soft and shallow and her weight didn't seem to affect the men as they marched effortlessly in step together, making certain to keep the stretcher parallel to the ground. If she hadn't opened her eyes to watch the trees wave their farewell, she would have thought she had been stationary. She took in everything as she absorbed a new sense of appreciation, taking in the fresh smell of the land, like the first rain of the season, the world, a springtime lullaby, and the song, a light, familiar harmonic hum that grew louder as she moved closer to her resting home, where all others before her had gone upon their final hours — a circle of twelve perfectly crafted stones that presented the words that would lead her into the afterlife.

The men carried Kaleena through the opening between the sixth and seventh stones and stopped in the center ring. Standing in front of them were six women, wearing robes of gold laced in red. They were huddled together in front of an angelic statue of the magistrate looking down upon her people, holding a spear that sat about a foot above the ground in one hand (meant not to kill but to present her leadership) and pointing to the heavens with the other. The women sang the notes of their spirits, as they held a dozen roses each against their bosoms. After reaching the end of their hymn, the women took their individual places at the foot of six stones, an empty stone separating each one, and lowered the roses to their waists.

The men remained unmoving until the last woman stood straight and still, then lowered Kaleena to the ground at the foot of the statue so that the spear hovered just above the center of her forehead. The men then joined the women in singing the hymn, adding a baritone to the angelic serenity, as they took their places upon the empty stones. They wrapped their hands behind their backs in honor. As the song once again came to a close, Kaleena closed her eyes. The air became alive with the sound of birds chirping in the distance.

Take the minds of those you have loved, Kaleena heard Gydressina say after a few moments of listening to her heart beat for the last time, *and pull together as one to anoint this child's passage of life into the light.*

The man closest to Kaleena and the woman directly opposite him, knelt down on either side of her. The woman rested the roses upon Kaleena's chest and the man delivered her a tender kiss on the lips before taking the woman's hands and raising them above Kaleena.

For those that have lived and those that have believed, the man and woman said together, *now find truth in the face of their existence. One becomes all and all becomes one in the heart of destiny with the spirit of trust and courage.*

The two brought their coupled hands down and pressed them against Kaleena's stomach, igniting a small warm shock that tickled her entire body. They then stood, let go of one another and walked back to their places at the stones. They each took a knee, wrapping one arm behind their backs and resting the other upon their knee, holding their hand in a fist as they rested their head upon it. The second man and woman then repeated the ritual, lowering the flowers, giving Kaleena a kiss and presenting her with more of her spirit:

For those that have lived and those that have believed now find truth in the face of their existence. One becomes all and all becomes one in the heart of destiny with the spirit of honesty and integrity.

Once they took their knee at the stones, they were followed by the presentation of the third group (*...with the spirit of hope and faith*), then the fourth (*...with the spirit of selflessness and sacrifice*) and the fifth (*...with the spirit of compassion and* *loyalty*). After the sixth group finished presenting their gifts (*…with the spirit of honor and love*), Gydressina walked up to Kaleena, gliding like a ghost as her skin glittered upon the touch of the sun's rays. Her silky white gown floated above her feet and her hair flowed gently in the soft breeze. She stopped at Kaleena's feet and raised her arms above her head. The men and women followed suit, raising their arms to their sides and touching one another's fingertips together. The man and woman standing closest to the statue pressed their palms to its waist.

Let all life accept your name and become the power of all the gifts that you have been given, Gydressina said. *Listen to the song, smell the sanctity, taste the purity, feel the touch and see the aura of all that surrounds your spirit and soul, which can now be presented to each of us, and those that have passed before you, to save and protect the race of the spiritual life. Rise up from the ash of the body and be reborn into the spirit of the land.*

Amen Dello Keli, she finished, a phrase that rang in a chorus among the rest of the group.

Gydressina held her head up to the heavens and sang the hymn once again. The rest of the chorus joined in the song of prayer as Gydressina took her place between the sixth and seventh stones. She lowered her arms and touched the fingertips of those that awaited her, completing the connection. A strong wind blew in a circle around the stones as electricity spread through each of their fingertips until it made contact with the statue, where it was guided through the spear and tenderly into the child's forehead.

To Kaleena's surprise, the electricity wasn't painful, but rather calming, like the kiss of a mother upon her child. She was now ready to accept her path to the force that would give her the gift of everything. Her spirit rose from her body and took hold of the air that blew past her. The song of "Amen Dello Keli" rang soft and distant around her. It was exciting and vibrant, frightening yet perfect. She was going home; she was becoming.

Until she felt an oddly cold, wet sensation spill around her back. Her fascination faded as she opened her eyes. Gydressina and her followers remained still as stone, electricity magnetically spilling through them. But it was all wrong. Nothing felt right. Kaleena was forced to close her eyes as her spirit collapsed into her body. Water poured onto her forehead from the spear, consuming her, leaving her in a state of darkness, unable to breathe. But she didn't fear it. She didn't cry out, or beg forgiveness. She didn't seek out help or hide within herself. She embraced the dark, accepted it, took it upon her heart and cared for it, comforted it and became one with the pain of silence. She held no regrets for what she had done, no regrets for what she had been, no regrets for what she had left behind. She simply was, and she wasn't, and the solitude was her spiritual awakening. It seemed like many years of this calm, fighting off the screams of resistance to contain her loneliness without interference, drowning the hollers, ignoring the hatred and seething degradation of her soul. But eventually, through the torture of existing among nothing, Kaleena found her light and the warmth of a new breath. She learned to control it and live through it so as to become it. She yielded to its grace and allowed her solemnity to bear the fruit —

Amen Dello Keli

— pulling her body off the ground to rise above the water, coughing hysterically. She kept her eyes closed as she tried to catch her breath, clasping her chest tight with both of her frigid hands. She sat in a corridor of Ediinis next to a light waterfall that generated a cool stream of water. The weakened light still highlighted the debris around her. She didn't know where she was in relation to the city. The last thing she remembered was healing Matthew —

Dad, she thought. She looked around but couldn't see him anywhere. The waterfall leaked through a wall of what she could only assume had come from the floor above it, and for a moment, she felt he may have been buried by it, or in the very least buried by the flood of water that was now leaking down to her level. But she couldn't think like that. He couldn't have died. She still felt him; felt his heart beat through the image of his wedding. He was near, but where? Kaleena continued to call out for him as she walked around the corridor, moving and shifting whatever debris was light enough. She was about ready to give up, believing he was most likely at least one floor above her, when a fresh light that seemed to radiate from nothing outlined a body lying upon one of the larger pieces of debris, raised up slightly to keep the figures head above the water, which for the time being, remained about ankle deep. She thought maybe it was Matthew, but the body was far too thin for that to be possible. As she inched in closer, she had to question what she thought she saw.

"Mom?" Kaleena's heart sank, leaving her a bit shocked, yet richly excited. She eventually confirmed the possibility as she made out the features of her mother's thin figure under the smattering of scratches and drying blood. "Mom!" She rushed to her and pulled a small piece of debris off her chest. "Mom," she said again, lifting her head and checking to make sure she was still breathing. "Mom."

All of a sudden, Jaime's eyes snapped open. She screamed and pushed Kaleena away, rolling off her perch and falling into the watery floor below. It didn't take long for her to fling her head up and suck in a deep breath while shaking the water out of her hair like a puppy coming in from the rain.

"Mom?" Kaleena said again, this time softer and more cautious. She slid in closer, watching her mother try and decipher where she was. It took a minute, but Jaime finally heard her daughter's voice. She looked up to her with a mesmerized glare, her breaths heavy with anticipation. "Kaleena?"

A gentle smile climbed to Kaleena's lips, but she couldn't move a muscle.

Jaime got to her feet, ignoring the sharp pain in her side and slight twist in her ankle. "I'm so glad you're alive." She kept her distance, even though the only thing she wanted to do was hug her daughter.

"Where's Dad?" Kaleena asked, avoiding the awkward air that spread between them.

Jaime looked up. Kaleena followed her eye line to the massive hole above her. "Last I remember he was with Patricia."

"Patricia?" Kaleena looked back to Jaime. "She's here, too?"

"And Kara," Jaime said, training her eyes back on Kaleena.

Kaleena flashed a smile. "What happened to them?"

"I'm not sure about Kara, but Matthew and Patricia must still be up there."

"Well what are we waiting for? We have to get to them." Kaleena started off down the hall.

"Kaleena, wait."

Kaleena almost slipped as she stopped. "What?"

"How do we know it's not completely flooded up there?"

"We don't," she said quickly. "But how else are we going to find out?"

"Kaleena —"

"Mom, please. We can't just leave them up there."

"I don't think we are."

"What do you mean?"

Jaime turned her eyes to the floor.

"Mom, what happened up there?"

Jaime took a moment to gather her thoughts. "I don't know for sure. But it wasn't pleasant."

Kaleena looked back up at the hole.

"How did it happen?"

"I don't know who she was, but some woman got into it with someone claiming to be Evey."

"Evey was there?"

"So it was her? How is that even possible?"

"Don't ask," Kaleena said. "Who was the other woman?"

"I don't know."

"Mom, think," Kaleena demanded. "I need to know. Anything you remember."

"I —" Jaime paused to try and think of the best way to explain her. "She looked a lot like Evey. Silver hair, extraordinary beauty."

"Did she do anything, say anything to you?"

"She saved my life, if that's what you're asking."

Relief slowly crept to Kaleena's lips. "Gydressina."

"Who's Gydressina?"

"It doesn't matter," Kaleena said quickly, grabbing Jaime's hand. "We have to get out of here." She pulled her forward. Jaime stumbled over her feet and hissed in pain. Kaleena let go as Jaime hopped on her left foot, trying to bounce the tenderness away.

"Kaleena, wait," she seethed through her teeth. "What's going on?"

Kaleena waited for Jaime to rest her foot flat on the ground and stand still. "If you're right, and Gydressina was up there, then I know exactly where they're going."

"Who?"

"Dad and Patricia."

Jaime wanted to say more, continue to ask questions, but Kaleena's razor-sharp determination kept her lips locked. "Okay," she finally said. "Lead the way."

Kaleena flashed a knowing wink and took off running with Jaime limping cautiously after her.

Atlantis – Hallways – 12 hours 12 minutes after arrival

Although he had essentially been rebuilt and was once again in harmony with the entire city, Cephis's steps remained heavy and precise. Water trailed him like a pet cat playfully attacking his ankles, spilling within inches of his feet and then waiting until he stepped farther away before moving after it again. His thoughts remained pointed at the voices he absorbed while submerged under water in the woman's quarters. He had apologized to his children for what happened and promised them his devotion, providing them hope in his ability to return them all to a living body. That was when he felt Evey's soul among them, warning him about the imminent attack on his city. He became aware of her fight with Gydressina and knew the time to take control was finally upon him.

Evey had failed him.

Thrusting her spirit back to her body, Cephis roared a shockwave through the ocean that would end in a small tidal wave off the coast of South America. He swam to the doors that had been pushed closed by the force of the flood. Within seconds, the wall burst open, pouring the water into the hallways. Cephis rode the stream into the tower and rolled and curled down the stairwell as the water dropped heavily through the slats in the stairs. Ignoring the flow of water that would submerge the city in just under an hour, Cephis closed his eyes and searched the halls for those that might destroy him. Matthew and Patricia had been seriously weakened and posed no threat as they sat near death a few levels below him. Jaime was also there, a level below them, but she, too, was also injured. Behind him on the other side of the tower, Kara was with another woman he couldn't read. But he also sensed the presence of someone he once gave knowledge to. She was growing, and when her mind fully connected to her host, Kara would be neutralized. Then again, there was an ominous aura surrounding them that didn't feel quite right. They were his greatest threat right now. Even though Evey would have posted plenty of guards outside of the incubation room, his blood curdled with the sense that it wouldn't be enough. If Gydressina truly wanted it to happen, someone would find their way in. He needed someone with the knowledge to be there to protect his army. His closest ally was a few floors below him, his disjointed heartbeat consumed by flames of Kaleena's love.

It took several minutes to reach Caistepher, the weight of Cephis's drenched robes weighing him down greatly. The burning sensation had calmed some time ago, but Caistepher continued to convulse every few seconds, his body and mind haven been disengaged and broken. When he tried to remember anything, cold electric shocks pulsed through his chest. The echo of the stairs as Cephis walked down to him pierced his ears to the point of bleeding. He wanted to scream, but all he could do was dribble a bit of foaming spit down his chin.

Cephis bent down and took his friend's head in his hand. Knowing he wouldn't be able to fully repair him, he pressed his massive hand to Caistepher's forehead, searching for the images and emotions that were devouring Caistepher's soul. Cephis growled lightly as he pulled the memories Kaleena had left behind, consumed them into his own mind as fuel for his wrath. When all of the memories had been washed away, Cephis repaired Caistepher's mind the best he could

without destroying his soul and then pushed a new fire into him, restoring his motor functions. Caistepher blinked rapidly as Cephis removed his hand, leaving behind a light scar scorched onto his head.

It took a few moments to finally register his savior. *Lord Cephis*, he choked.

I need you to stand.

Caistepher seemed a bit confused, but then took hold of Cephis's arm and pulled his legs beneath him. A few strained seconds later, Caistepher rose to his feet, using the wall to support him as the blood returned to his legs.

You need to go to Callipse Tower.

Callipse... It took some time to recall what he was talking about, but when it clicked, he looked drearily into Cephis's eyes.

Can you comply?

Yes, my Lord.

Someone will arrive there shortly. You must destroy them at once.

How?

Do what you must. Just take their soul, whatever you do.

Caistepher closed his eyes, fighting back a sharp pain in his side that came and went quickly, then enjoyed the sensation of a cool breath. *I will do thy bidding, my Lord*, he said, Cephis's mind beginning to reconnect his.

Cephis saw recognition and fortitude in Caistepher's eyes. He may barely be able to walk, or even breathe, but he was true to his loyalty. He nodded and left the stairwell.

Hurry, he said, as he became the shadows. *Firelight is drowning.* And he was gone.

Caistepher lowered his head to his hand and leaned over the rail to vomit, which helped clear the residual effects of Kaleena's attack. His anger grew wildly as he hoped with all of his soul that Kaleena or Matthew would be the one to show up in Callipse Tower. Just the thought of destroying one or both of them gave him the strength to move swiftly.

It was time for vengeance.

Atlantis – Outside Incubation Room – 12 hours 18 minutes after arrival

Three men stood guard (if you could call it that) around the portal leading to the incubation room. Two of them paced around one another to stay busy, unclear about what they were actually doing there (or most likely still trying to understand where they were and how they got there, and whether or not they should forget the whole thing and band together to fight their way back to their homes). One spoke Russian and one spoke something in the vain of Mandarin, so communicating with each other was simply out of the question. And so they paced. The third looked bored to death and about ready to fall asleep, possibly even ready to slice his wrists open as he listened to the men squabble back and forth (or mutter to themselves, whatever it was they were doing).

Diana and Kara pulled their heads back from around the corner about fifty yards from the men. "I recognize one of them," Diana said. "The other two I'm not sure about."

"What do you mean?"

"I mean, I'm not sure if they came from the same place I did."

"What's down there, anyway?"

"I don't know what it is, exactly," Diana said as she took another glance to the men. "But it's where I woke up."

"Is that why you think it's safe?"

Diana didn't answer; couldn't answer.

"Diana, think about it for a second. There're three rather large men guarding a hole in the ground. That must mean whatever's down there is pretty darn important to them. How do you know someone's not down there waiting to kill us?"

"I just know, okay." Diana was clearly agitated. "I don't know what the hell's going on, but that's where we need to be right now. Just trust me." Just then, she hissed through her teeth and grabbed her forehead. "God…"

"Are you all right?"

Diana didn't answer as she fell into Kara's lap, trying her best to hold back the screams that were welling up in her throat.

"Diana," Kara whispered loudly, hoping the men wouldn't hear her sister's groans. But Diana was oblivious to everything around her as she made love with a man she didn't recognize, but knew well. She was ready to rip his face off as her climax brewed, driving her into another dimension of devotion. After letting out a healthy scream, she collapsed on the man's chest and kissed him tenderly, her body flushed with euphoria. He kissed her back, making sure she didn't pull away from him as he continued to swirl his hips. He wanted more and her hunger for it quickly returned. It wasn't until she felt his release alongside her orgasm that he finally let her go. She fell to the floor next to him, breathing heavy, a frozen smile laced with perspiration. As she slid back up to him and wrapped her arm around his chest, kissing his arms and his neck gently, three men came storming into the room. She tried to grab her gown and hide her body, but she was pulled to her feet before she could, as was her lover. Her mind locked up and her body froze at their touch. The men wrapped her arms around her back and tore into them, fusing the skin on her wrists together, and then forced her to her knees.

"By order of the magistrate," one of the men said, "you are being detained and will be held in solitude under the city of Ediinis until it is deemed prudent for your return to your original bonds."

"For what reason?" Diana asked, unafraid.

"For following the path of Cephis and living for the knowledge he has planted within you."

"You will all die for this," Diana said before her lips were sealed shut. She was pulled to her feet and escorted from the room. At one point, she looked to the window and saw, beyond the people watching her shameful arrest, the reflection of someone else — *Joyais* — her own reflection haunting the stranger's golden brown eyes. Diana closed them, afraid of the image. When she reopened them, she saw Kara's frightened face hovering above her.

"Diana?" Kara said, hopeful.

Diana sat up and waited until she caught her balance.

"Are you okay?"

"Yeah," Diana said softly, unable to speak fully. "Yeah. I'm fine." She flashed a smile, hoping it would calm Kara enough to listen.

"What happened?"

"I don't know, but whatever the fuck it was, it's getting worse. I'm not sure, but there might be some medicine down in that room that can help."

"Is that why it's so important to you?"

Diana nodded, averting her eyes for the slightest of moments.

"Why didn't you just tell me that before?"

"I didn't want you to worry."

"Diana," Kara scolded. "You know better than that."

"I know," Diana said, shying away.

"I know you want to be independent, but you need to know you can ask for my help when you need it. Okay?"

Diana looked lovingly at her older sister. "Yeah."

"Okay," Kara said after thinking about it. "Now how do you suggest we get past the three stooges over there?"

Diana pulled the bottom of her gown up and ripped a small piece off without a struggle. She held the piece to Kara and got to her knees. "Come here." Diana spun Kara around and grabbed a hold of her arm, trying to pull it behind her back.

"What are you doing?"

"Just give me your arms," Diana demanded.

Kara hesitated, then gave in and placed her arms behind her, slowly understanding what Diana was thinking. "I get it. Going with the Wookie plan of attack, huh?" Diana tied the piece of her gown around Kara's wrists. "Do you think it'll even work?"

"I damn well hope so," Diana said, pulling the knot tight.

"Ow." Kara felt her circulation begin to be cut off.

"Sorry." Diana grabbed Kara's arm and pulled her to her feet. "Just follow my lead, okay."

Kara nodded and Diana pulled her around the corner. The moment they

stepped into view, the men all stood at attention, blocking the passage to the room below, each halting them in their own languages.

"I said stop there," the middle one said after getting the others to shut up.

"I have a prisoner," Diana called out. "Evey has ordered her detainment here until she returns." She hardly knew what she was talking about, but she prayed it would work.

"I have no word from Evestylyn on this woman," the middle guard said.

"Are you really going to do this now?" Diana stopped just a few inches from the main guard. "I have my orders."

"And we have ours," the man said, pumping out his thick chest slightly, as if that was really going to push Diana to back down.

"And what orders are those?"

"No one is to enter for any reason."

"Goddamn it. This is a prize for Cephis. Now get out of my fucking way."

Diana reached out to shove the guard to the side, but he was too quick for her. He grabbed her arm and twisted it back, wrapping her body around and pushing her to her knees. He held her wrist tight, bent back as far as it would go before it completely snapped. Kara slipped and fell to the ground away from the guards.

"Don't make me break it," the man said, his eyes strong. Kara couldn't help but think the man had military training, maybe Navy SEALS or Marine Corps.

Diana whimpered, but the light stabbing in her head transferred her attention away from her arm. For some reason, every part of his body floated within her. It was as if she had somehow become him. In some odd way, she knew every thought he ever had. His name was John and his orders were simple: Protect the incubation room at all costs.

"You can't win this Diana," John said into her ear. "Let go, and allow the spirit within to live among us."

Diana began to sweat. John had learned the truth and his lust drove into her. But it wasn't truly lust; it was fresh and mesmerizing, his touch loving and compassionate. He smelled the taste of the woman he loved within her and Diana

now knew who the man was and what he wanted. The urge to rape her in order to draw the soul back to him was strong in his touch. But as he haunted her mind with his sexual fantasies, Diana found his weaknesses. Her mind was stronger than his; if she focused enough, she'd be able to control him, do as she pleased without any repercussions whatsoever. Without any further hesitation, Diana located the muscles in his arms and bent one of them so far forward it snapped his elbow, pushing the bone through the skin. John yelled hysterically and fell to his knees. Diana quickly spun to her feet and grabbed his hair.

"How do you like them fucking apples?" she said and then kneed him in the face, ramming his nose into his head. John fell lifeless. Kara did everything she could to suppress a maddening scream.

Diana turned to the other two men, who found no reason to stick around.

"What the heck did you do?" Kara yelled, after they had disappeared.

Diana answered by yanking Kara to her feet.

"Hey, careful," she said, thinking Diana would untie her. Instead, she walked her to the portal. "What are you doing? Diana!" She pushed her big sister into the hole. Kara landed square on her back, losing her ability to breathe and just missing breaking her clavicle.

"You can tell Evestylyn to go fuck herself if she doesn't like it," Diana screamed. She then stepped down the ladder as Kara passed out.

Atlantis – Hallways – 12 hours 26 minutes after arrival

Kaleena and Jaime walked in silence for some time, neither of them knowing quite what to say to the other. Jaime was unsure of how to speak to her own daughter, having seen her for barely five minutes in the last three years. She had a lot of questions, and if she had had it in her, she would have just started talking, learning as much as she could about Kaleena's life, how school was going, how her friends were, what she was working on outside of work, if anything, and possibly talk about her book and go into detail on who she was as a person after her near-death experience. But part of Jaime was afraid Kaleena would feed her guilt in return. It was better to let her daughter take the lead in anything said between them, which for now entailed nothing but whispers of 'quiet' and 'move' as they evaded foot soldiers combing the city for them (or for her). What she didn't realize was that Kaleena felt almost the same way toward Jaime. She still felt a bit awkward about the last thing she'd said to her mother, and deep down was still upset with her. But she was more worried about opening up old wounds that Jaime wouldn't want to talk about, which could very well send her into a fit of silent anger. They were at a standstill.

"I need to rest," Jaime finally admitted after walking the last half a mile (or so it felt) with a sharp pain attacking her back. She'd been continually stretching to coax it away, but that wasn't working anymore.

Kaleena turned to her as she sat down against the closest wall. "We have to keep moving," she said, pacing back and forth, afraid that if she stayed in one place for too long, they'd easily be caught.

"I know, but my back is killing me." It was evident she was in pain. Unable to sense any dangers nearby, Kaleena figured they were in the clear for now. It was probably best if she rested, too. Her head felt a little light and achy; a short break might do her some good. She sat down across from Jaime and raised her knees up so as to rest her head between them.

Jaime stretched her back and rubbed it gently. After a moment, Kaleena looked up. "You okay?" It was innocent enough.

"I'll be fine," Jaime said. "Just a little tender, I think, from the fall."

Kaleena nodded and turned away, unable to say anything more.

"Who's Gydressina?" Jaime said after a few more minutes of silence. Kaleena turned back, the corner of her mouth showing a spark of amusement.

"You wouldn't believe the half of it," she said. "But the short answer... she was magistrate of Ediinis before its demise."

"Ediinis?"

Kaleena chuckled. "Yeah, sorry. That's Atlantis's real name."

"Oh," Jaime said. "It's nice."

"Yeah. I guess."

"And she's helped you?"

"She's protected me," Kaleena said, remembering Lauren. But she didn't want to get into all of that right now. Instead she finished, "Protected Dad. Rescued him, actually."

"Sounds like our guardian angel," Jaime said coyly.

"Yeah," Kaleena chuffed. "I sure could use one right now."

Jaime wondered if she should search for more and decided, how could it hurt? "Why's that?"

Kaleena looked down the hallway. No one was coming, but she wanted to make believe someone was so she could figure out the best way to answer the query. "Nothing," she finally muttered, hoping to avoid the question altogether.

"Kaleena," Jaime said in a tone she hadn't used since she left. "Tell me." Her voice was caring — motherly.

Kaleena saw real love radiating back at her. "I've just been going through some major shit these last few weeks is all."

Jaime didn't want to push it any further, but felt Kaleena needed to talk. "What happened?" she said, cautiously.

The silence and pain that coursed Kaleena's features frightened Jaime a bit, and for a moment, made her want to retract the question. Before she could, Kaleena took a breath to relax her nerves and said, "I was nearly raped a few days ago."

Jaime's hand was plastered to her mouth before Kaleena finished her statement. It was accompanied by a large gasp. "My god, Kaleena. Are you — what happened?"

"Don't worry," Kaleena urged. "I'm fine." When it was clear Jaime wasn't buying it, she added, "Really. It's okay."

Jaime believed her sincerity but needed to know more, if only to be able to kick the shit out of the bastard if she ever got the chance. "Do you know who it was?"

Kaleena nodded. "One of my professors."

Jaime's eyes grew wide in shock. "My god."

"I was stupid and blind," Kaleena said.

"No," Jaime commanded. "It wasn't your fault. Don't you fucking believe for one minute that it was your fault."

"I'm not," Kaleena said, defensive. "Far from it. The sick and perverted bastard did it on his own volition. All I'm saying is I knew something was a little off with him and I let my guard down. He was one of my favorite professors and he fooled me, like he's probably fooled a lot of other girls. I just feel if I would've been more attentive, I might have seen it coming and been able to do something about it."

"What makes you think he's done it before?"

"Nothing. It's just the way he seemed to have it all planned out, the way he spoke to me. It all felt too rehearsed, too coordinated for it to have been a first attempt. And I know his wife knew it, too."

"His wife."

"Yeah. She came up to me at the hospital." Kaleena raised her hand to her cheek. "She gave me a pretty good slap, too. But I could read it in her eyes. She knew. I'm just the first one that had the balls to stand up to him."

"How did you get away?"

"Honestly, I don't know. Before he could do anything, some guy came in and stopped him —

You must give him what he needs and do as he asks

"— and then just took off."

"So you do have a guardian angel," Jaime said, smiling lightly.

Kaleena matched her smile —

Don't let him leave you behind

— and pressed her head against the wall, filtering through her thoughts.

"What happened to him?"

Kaleena's smile faded. "He's locked up for now, I guess," she said, clearly leaving something out.

"Kaleena?"

She lowered her head. "I really thought he was one of the good ones, mom. A nice family, a good reputation, and smart, you know. I could talk to him in a way I couldn't talk to either you or Dad. He understood me when I rambled on about some off-the-wall theory or hypothesis. I'd stay back after class with him on occasion to run some new idea by him and see what he thought, see if he could help collaborate with me on it." Kaleena chuckled. "We always joked that we should present my ideas to the class and make bets on how many of them would even understand the basic principles behind them. This one time, I threw out this wild hypothesis that intrigued him enough to claim the whole thing was full of shit. It led to days of discussions and fights over the validity of the argument. I still believe it's when I used his kids as an example after he invited me to his house for dinner one night that I finally proved my point, but he kept pretending to be skeptical just to keep me fighting for it, keep my convictions strong. He was a good teacher; a good friend." Kaleena paused to catch her breath. Jaime could see the beginning of a few tears. "Or so I thought. Now I know he only did it to persuade me into fucking his lying ass."

"I'm so sorry," Jaime whispered. "I should have been there."

Kaleena wiped her eyes clean. "It wouldn't have helped. Dad wasn't there either."

"I still should have been there. As a mother. Your father was just too unpredictable to rely on for something like that." Jaime could tell she hit a nerve she didn't want to touch as Kaleena turned away again. "I didn't mean it like that," Jaime tried to apologize.

"Don't," Kaleena said. "It's okay. I just... don't want to get into it right now."

Jaime nodded and then, hoping to change the subject a bit:

"What was the hypothesis?"

Kaleena looked a bit confused. "What?"

"The hypothesis... the theory you fought over for so long?"

Kaleena chuckled, unsure if Jamie was really interested or simply being a mother. "You wouldn't understand," she said.

"You're probably right," she laughed. "But I've read your book, and I understand…" Jaime paused a moment and then cracked a huge smile. "…Some of it."

Kaleena let loose with a strong laugh, one she really needed. When Jaime joined her, she finally felt bonded to her mother like she was before she left. After a few minutes, Kaleena sat in silence, wanting nothing more than to enjoy the spirit of their love. Jaime needed to do the same. Finally, she decided to give her what she wanted, even if it flew so far over her head, she wouldn't be able to see it with a telescope.

"My idea was in relation to how people view the world and how it correlates with the nature of your first few days on earth." Kaleena paused to see if Jaime was still with her. Whether she was or not, she continued. "I theorized that a person's personality, the way they would always view the world, and everything that they would ever do in life, was developed within the first seven days after their birth."

"Seven *days?*"

"Days," Kaleena reiterated.

"Wow," Jaime said. "Okay."

"I hypothesized that within those first seven days, everything that happened to them, everything they witnessed, everything they touched, everything they heard, everything they tasted shaped them into who they would become, and that nothing that happened after would ever change the way they viewed the world. Not a change in the way they were raised; not a change in their environment; nothing. Their personality traits would be set during that first week of life, end of story." Kaleena waited a moment for it to sink in and then continued. "Take for example a child that's born naturally, with a stick shoved down his throat and given the requisite slap on the ass before he's cleaned, wrapped up and returned to the warmth of the womb, held to his mother's bosom and talked to sweetly, gently and lovingly. He's taken home after a couple of days of living around several other children, nurses and doctors, who all speak kindly and take good care of him. Over the next few days, he's loved, nurtured, allowed to suckle his mother, is read to at night, held when he's awake, sang to as he sleeps. His parents are

always kind to one another, they don't watch much television and the toys he's given are soft and warm."

"Sounds like a momma's boy."

"Hang on," Kaleena said, holding out her hand. "Now take a second child, born through cesarean, pulled abruptly from the womb before he was ready and taken away from his mother for constant testing and probes and who knows what else. The nurses and doctors are constantly stressed out over his incessant crying. After a few days, his mother's finally given permission to take him home. He gets fed normally, and his diaper is changed when needed, but he gets yelled at whenever he won't stop crying. His father is barely around, and when he is, his parents are screaming at one another, fighting about money, or complaining about their jobs, or the mess the house is in, or about the possible affair he's having with his secretary. When she's home alone with the baby, he's usually in his playpen in front of the television, watching some court show or some action film with a lot of swearing and sex playing with a stuffed animal his mom just happened to throw in there to try and keep him occupied. You could imagine the first child, like you said, would grow up to be somewhat of a momma's boy, but he would also grow up to be a nice young man, smarter and more sensitive to those around him. He understands what it means to put others before himself and would never take advantage of anyone because he knows the difference between right and wrong. He cares, he loves. The other grows up exactly opposite, needy and always mad at someone. All of the bad things that happened to him, whether he put them on himself or not, are always someone else's fault. He looks out for no one but himself — screw everyone else, so-to-speak — is in and out of relationships and drinks himself to sleep most nights when he's not fucking the newest girl he picked up at the club. He swears without regard to others and loses his temper with the simplest of triggers."

"It makes sense, but doesn't that just have to do with the way they were raised?"

"Yeah, but what if, after that first week, the babies were switched, and the first baby was then brought up the rest of his life in the second babies home and

environment, and vice versa. My theory is that the first boy would still grow up to be kind, gentle and caring, and the second would grow up to land in prison or found dead in his own vomit. Why? Because it's the initial events in a child's life that shape a child's mind, and that mind is set after those first seven days."

"But how can you prove that?" Jaime said.

"That's why I used his kids as an example. They were born and raised in the exact same manner. Nothing changed. They watched the same things on television, they were read the same stories at night, listened to the exact same music, they heard the same conversations and the marriage was solid for each of them. Their mother cared for them in exactly the same way; their father was around each of them for the same amount of time. Because of that, you could conclude that they should have the same personality and the same interests, right?"

"Yeah... I guess."

"So why don't they? Why is one more of a rebel than the other?"

Jaime shrugged, completely overlooking the entire point of the argument.

"Because of those first seven days," Kaleena said, a bit annoyed. "You see, even though they were both born with the aid of an epidural, and they spent the same amount of time in the same hospital, something was different. Something happened in those three years that separated them. After prying a bit, I found out that his wife had suffered the loss of a parent just before their little boy was born. Over the next few weeks, they were quieter than they normally were, and spent more time apart. He wasn't around his son as often in that first week as his wife was. Because of that, the baby learned the melancholy of existence. When their daughter was born, their lives were much different, much more blissful and fun. In that first week, they played with her a lot, were around her equally and constantly talked to her, cracking jokes and laughing. Not to mention she had a brother that kept his distance but wanted to take care of her. She grew up to be a bit wild, going against the normal perception that boys are more rambunctious than girls. Which mind you, helps my theory. That's when I knew I had him, but he kept at me. And, well, you know me, I had to be thorough. So I did some research and found out that the hospital staff had had some changes in between the births as well, which also could have had an effect on the differences between them."

Jaime contemplated the idea, eventually coming up with something that seemed to go against what she understood of the argument. "Okay, so what about incidents that completely alter your life later on, like a horrible break-up or... a near death experience?"

Kaleena couldn't stop herself from laughing.

"What did I say?"

"Nothing..." Kaleena said, bringing her laughter under control. "It's just... that was one of his early arguments as well. But I truly don't think it matters, because no matter how hard you try to change yourself because of some traumatizing event that forces you to rethink how you've led your life, something is going to force you to revert back to those initial ideas and perceptions you were implanted with in those first seven days. The near death experience or bad break-up may change what you do in the short term, but in the long run, you're still that same person, with those same personality traits. The change is simply based in your youth."

"I don't —"

"Take the rebel for instance. What if in those first seven days, for whatever reason, he developed a grudge against his father? I don't know, maybe he hit him once, or yelled at him or something. It doesn't matter. Whenever the baby looks at him, he gets sick to his stomach. No matter what the father tries to do to help his son, no matter what he said to him in any number of daily conversations, the son would still hold the grudge, reinforcing his father's initial event. When he's finally able to move away, start his own life, he does, without once ever calling his father, leaving him in the past and forgetting about him. Not even when his father has a minor heart attack does the son try and reconcile."

"Then, the son gets shot and almost dies."

Kaleena smiled. "Okay, let's say he does. Let's say it helps him find a new respect for life. He has an awakening and needs to reconcile all of his past mistakes, clear

the air with those he loves. He knows he's now mortal and wants to make up with those that he's been wrong to."

"Like his father."

"Exactly. So he goes to his father to make amends, and let's say they do. His father forgives him and the relationship has finally been mended. A few weeks later, he begins to wonder why his father didn't even go to the hospital after his shooting. He now feels sorry for himself and goes to his father for answers. No excuse is good enough and their talk turns into a massive fight. The son tells his father that he wishes he were dead and walks out of his life for the last time. Why? Because no matter what circumstances change in a man's life, the human mind will always seek to make sure that those initial memories, thoughts, feelings and emotions are always present, no matter how much we want to fight them, or change them."

Jaime was silent as she tried to come up with the best response she could. "You were right," she said. "I didn't understand one word of that."

Kaleena huffed a bit of laughter as Jaime let out her own tittered laugh.

"What brought you to even consider all of this anyway?" Jaime said after silence returned to the air.

"To be honest…" Kaleena started and then peered at Jaime with the eyes of a baby. "It was because of you."

"Me?"

"Yeah. Back when I was still trying to understand why you left me."

"Kaleena, I didn't leave *you*. I left Matthew."

"Same difference, mom. Any way you try and spin it, you still left."

Jaime turned from Kaleena this time, but knew she was right. "Yeah," she said under her breath.

Kaleena was no longer sure she wanted to continue, but did anyway. Jaime needed to hear this. "When I was trying to understand the reasons behind it, I started to look at some old pictures you left behind in your closet. I found this one of a little boy holding you on his lap."

Jaime promptly looked back to Kaleena, her eyes wide. She hadn't thought about that little boy for a long time, and doing so now sent a piercing sting through her heart. Kaleena didn't notice her reaction.

"So I called grandma to find out who it was. She told me he was your brother and that he passed away shortly after the picture was taken."

Jaime's eyes were watering. "What else did she tell you?"

"That when you were about a week old, she had to run to the store for a dozen eggs and some sugar because she'd forgotten about her friend's birthday and wanted to make a cake for her. She packed you and your brother up, but instead of fussing with you and your car seat, she asked your brother to watch you as she went into the store for a couple of minutes. When she got back, he was tickling you, trying to make you laugh, which apparently you refused to do. He kept your attention as grandma started off back home, bouncing stuffed animals on your stomach, playing peek-a-boo with your little blanket. Grandma said she was having more fun watching him than you seemed to be of his antics. She wasn't paying attention to the road and ran a red light, smashing into another car." Kaleena was unable to say the next words louder than a whisper. "Your brother was thrown through the windshield and died instantly."

Jaime was in tears. She didn't remember anything about the accident except what her mom had told her when she, like Kaleena, accidentally stumbled upon that picture. Since then, it's always been in the back of her mind, but she always tried to hide from it, keep it at a distance as if he wasn't really her brother. But she knew better, and now it seemed to have become the most important thing that ever happened to her.

"It was then I concluded it was the loss of your brother that made you run away."

"Kaleena —"

"Just hear me out, mom. Because he was playing with you when the accident happened, you instantly associated love with misery... affection with loss. After that day, you never saw him again, but you knew something was missing.

Something you loved, and that loved you back, had vanished, just like that. You became the lone sibling, without anyone to play with. It became instilled in you that if you ever attached yourself to something that cared for you, that made you happy, that you had fun being with, that they would eventually disappear and leave you alone. To avoid having to deal with that pain again, whenever you became close to making a loving attachment, you chose to leave rather than watch them evaporate without explanation. It's in your nature, and no matter how much you want to avoid it, or spin it, it has to be that way."

"But, Kaleena, I don't even remember the accident."

"It doesn't matter. Your brain was still capturing every word, every event that happened to you. Whether you remember it or not, you still experienced it and because it happened within the first seven days of your life, it became a part of you."

Jaime wiped away the tears that had turned her eyes red and puffy and made her cheeks flush. "I'm so sorry, Kaleena."

"I'm not mad at you for that, mom. I never was. I was more confused about the reason behind it than anything else. After I knew what happened, I understood why you couldn't stay. I will admit, I *was* a little upset you didn't come back after I came home from the hospital, but even then, I understood. I'm more upset with what you've become since then than I ever was with your leaving."

"I never stopped loving you, Kaleena."

"I know," Kaleena said quickly.

"I just wanted you to hear it."

"We never stopped loving you, either. We would have accepted you back at any time. All you had to do was ask."

Jaime nodded, more tears swarming. "I know."

"So why didn't you?" The question had been on Kaleena's mind for three years, and it now came out like a lightning strike.

"I don't know," Jaime said, holding back a little bit of the truth. It might be better if Kaleena didn't know everything. Not now, anyway. "I guess I just thought I was protecting you."

"Protecting us from what?"

Jaime sucked in some air under her sobs before mouthing under her breath, "From me."

It was clear from Kaleena's expression that her answer wasn't clear. Jaime sniffed up some running mucus and calmed down enough to translate. "I think I just felt that you were better off without me. *I* chose to leave. *I* committed adultery. *I* was destructive. I don't think I could have been the same mother to you, or the same wife to Matthew, after all the shit I put you through."

"You underestimated us," Kaleena said. "We would've forgiven you. All you had to do was talk to us."

"I tried."

"No. You argued. You did everything you could to push him away. You never once discussed any of it with me."

Jaime didn't have a response.

"Dad would have forgiven you," Kaleena finished. "He *has* forgiven you."

"I know he has," she said, pressing her hand to the corner of her lips, feeling the tenderness of his last kiss. In that moment, her tears changed from that of pain to that of love.

Kaleena smiled sheepishly. She didn't know what it was or what had happened to make her believe in Matthew's love, but she didn't want to interrupt it. She looked happy. That was enough for Kaleena.

The kiss of a lost hope.

Both Kaleena and Jaime looked around as Evey's voice echoed through the room. Kaleena stood frantically as her footsteps were heard in the distance.

"Shit," she said, looking back and forth down every hallway.

Jaime followed Kaleena to her feet, the memory of Matthew's kiss washed away in fear. "What is it?"

"Shit," Kaleena hissed again. "I let my goddamn guard down."

"What are talking about?"

Just then, several men in white robes spun around the corners of the hallways, flanking Kaleena and Jaime, blocking off any possible escape. Kaleena instantly searched for their minds, but couldn't locate any one of them. She couldn't even hear their heartbeats.

Such a shame, Evey said as she stepped past the guards, her eyes fixed on Jaime. "It was a nice attempt," she continued, using her voice instead of her mind, "but your escape seems to have faltered." Evey wrapped her fingers under Jaime's chin. "Quite brave, but quite reckless."

"Mom," Kaleena called out. Evey immediately grabbed Kaleena's neck and shoved her away, causing her to tumble over herself. As she got back to her knees, Kaleena felt Evey's mind. Gydressina had done something to her that had weakened her greatly.

"Let her go," Kaleena screamed, rising to her feet.

Evey hissed at her. "Do not make me kill her."

Kaleena tried to take advantage of Evey's weakened state, but couldn't find a way through her vulnerability. She had to accept the stalemate. "Okay," she said, surrendering. "I'll do whatever you want."

"No, don't," Jaime seethed, then let out a scream as her head folded in on itself.

"Stop, Evey. Just stop."

"Come with me."

"Okay," Kaleena said without thought. "Okay. Let her go, and I'll go with you, peacefully." Evey tried to enter her mind to seek the truth behind the words, but Kaleena wouldn't allow it. If Evey was going to trust her, she was going to have to do it on faith.

Jaime looked about ready to die. Kaleena did her best to comfort her.

"You do all that I say," Evey demanded. "Or she will die."

"Without question," Kaleena said, looking directly into Evey's eyes.

Evey let go of Jaime, who fell to the ground, the pain in her head beginning to relax. Kaleena went to her as Evey stepped away, hoping to find a way into her mind.

"Mom. Are you okay?" She picked Jaime's head up.

"Yeah," Jaime said through gritted teeth.

"Don't lie. Tell me the truth."

"I'm okay," she said again, looking up to Kaleena with kind eyes.

"I'm sorry I got you into this," Kaleena whispered into her ear. "I was selfish."

"Don't apologize," Jaime returned. "I was selfish. You were only trying to rebuild a family." Jaime pulled Kaleena close and caressed the edge of her ear with her lips. "And I'm grateful for that."

Kaleena felt a smile she hadn't felt in a long time rise to her lips. No matter what Jaime had done, she was her mother and Kaleena would protect her. She pulled away and used what little energy she had left to check Jaime's mind.

You need to find Dad and Gydressina, Kaleena whispered, pushing Evey's attempts at capturing her voice away. *I've given you a map. Can you see it?*

Jaime was surprised to see a map of the city as clear as any memory she's ever had. She nodded lightly.

Follow it. Find them. They will protect you.

Okay, Jaime thought, taking her cue from Kaleena.

I'll be okay, Kaleena assured, answering her quizzical gaze. *Trust me.*

Jaime nodded again and then hugged her long and tight.

"I love you," Kaleena whispered out loud.

"I love you, too, sweetheart. Remember me as I was."

"Always as you are," Kaleena said.

Evey then waved her finger and two of the men grabbed Kaleena around the arms, pulling her away from Jaime, who tried to resist until Kaleena let go. She followed her lead and watched them drag her daughter up to Evey.

"I said I would go peacefully," Kaleena said, but didn't fight their cold grip.

"Call it a precaution," Evey said. The men then pushed Kaleena down the hall, a prisoner being escorted down the green mile for something she didn't do. The rest of the men followed, hiding Kaleena once and for all in a sea of white.

Evey held back a moment. "I hope it was worth it," she said.

Jaime pressed the butt of her hand to her forehead as Evey left. Her first instinct was to go after them, fight for Kaleena, rescue her. But she knew the only way to

save Kaleena was to do as she was asked. She would follow the map, find Matthew. Then and only then would she be able to rescue her family.

Atlantis – Incubation Room – 12 hours 42 minutes after arrival

A slicing pain shot through Kara's back, stiffening her body and forcing her awake. Hissing and groaning, she rolled around the muddy floor to find a position that would subdue the tension. That is until she realized her movement was only compounding the problem. She eventually rolled to her side and stayed perfectly still, tilted on her elbows to relax her bound arms as best she could. It worked, as within a minute or so, the pain drifted away, though fighting the residual aches took a lot out of her. The sweat and aroma of the mud didn't help, mixing into an amalgamation of stale blood and mucus. It took some time for her to contemplate shifting her body again once a level of comfort had settled in. Even the slightest of movements might cause it all to return. But her fears subsided as she pulled her knee up to her chest and rolled on top of it. When no pain was evident, she cautiously brought her other leg underneath. A soft pinch in the small of her back forced her to fall motionless. It drifted away as quickly as it had come, which gave Kara the confidence to lift herself into a full sitting position. The mud latched to her face was beginning to itch her skin. She tried scraping it off, but her shoulder only added to the amount of mud plastered on her face. Attempting to pull her hands apart were met with futility; the gown had been tied far too tight — and much too well? — for her to break free of it on her own. She looked around for anything that might help her escape her bonds (which she didn't really think she'd find) and was eerily awe-struck at the cylindrical objects littered along the floor that looked like large, empty cookie tins. They seemed to be made of gold, but could have been a material that only appeared to be gold in this low-level illumination. Above them, several more cylinders hung above their counterparts, attached to one another by small, thin tubes. Judging by the shards of glass that made up most of the floor and Diana's

claim that she woke up in this room, Kara could only assume some sort of test tube (or something having to do with cryogenics) had once been housed between each pair of cylinders.

Kara carefully slid across the floor to get a better look at what made the machines tick. Just before reaching the nearest cylinder, she caught something moving in the shadows. She looked to the far corner of the room but couldn't make anything out. For a second, she thought it may have been her imagination, her eyes playing tricks on her in the soft light. But then it happened again. The darkness shifted. She held her breath as she waited for it happen a third time. When it didn't, Kara had to make sure she wasn't going crazy.

"Diana?" she said cautiously, with a small amount of sympathy thrown in for good measure. If it was Diana, she didn't want her to believe she was upset at her for tossing her down the hole (or keeping her tied up, for that matter), even though she clearly was.

"I slept with him," Diana's voice came back, sad and with a hush that made Kara wonder if Diana even wanted her to hear it.

"What?"

Diana shifted again. Kara finally saw the outline of her features. She was still too far away, but Kara had the distinct feeling she'd been crying. "I slept with him," she said louder.

"Slept with who?" Kara climbed to her feet, the sound of glass singing along with her movements.

"Ryan," she said after a short pause, lowering her head back into the shadow.

"Diana, can you please untie this thing so we can talk?"

It took some time, but Diana finally lifted her head again, resting it on the wall. "The night before I left for Europe," she said quietly, "when I told you I broke up with him. I did much more than that."

Kara stopped. Tears streamed down Diana's cheeks. Her mouth sat agape in minor shock, afraid anything she might say would come off as scolding her. Diana took the silence as just that.

"It was never my intention to break up with him," she said, defending herself for no reason. "The only reason I went over there was to talk him into sex. It wasn't until after that I made the decision to call it off."

"And that's supposed to make it better? Wasn't he saving himself for marriage?"

"He could have stopped me at any time, you know." Now she was making excuses. "He could have said no."

"You should have known better."

"I know," Diana said, and then in a softer voice: "Mom and Dad were right."

"What?" Kara moved even slower across the room, trying hard to avoid slipping on the glass or even the mud, its viscosity much more pliable around the cylinders than on the outside edge of the room.

"Nothing," Diana mumbled.

"Diana, don't do this."

Diana rolled her head to the side to look directly at Kara. "I don't want to fight."

"I'm not fighting."

"Yeah," Diana said, rolling her head away again. "Yeah."

"What was it that made you decide to break up with him?" Kara asked after several awkward steps. In some way she wanted to understand what she had been thinking so she wouldn't judge her — much like their parents would have — and yet, mostly, she just liked hearing that tender voice. For a moment, she wasn't sure Diana was even going to answer, but then she heard her soft voice over the glitter of the glass.

"A couple of days before I was about to leave, I decided I didn't want to just explore Europe. I wanted to explore myself, too. I don't know why, I just wanted to be able to let myself go. No inhibitions, no regrets. Then I started thinking about how it was going to feel and if I would even be able to go through with it. I thought, maybe, if I was able to have sex just once, feel what it was like, it would help me get over my anxiety."

"Sweetie…" Kara began.

"Don't say it. I already know how stupid it was. What can I say? I was insecure and never thought he'd fall in love with me. But I could feel it. I could see it in him. Maybe I felt it a little myself, I don't know anymore. The bottom line is, I had just used him as a test crash dummy and I felt like shit about it. He believed we were going to be together forever; I couldn't offer him that promise. But I wasn't about to tell him I was going to cheat on him in Europe. He deserved more than that. So I broke up with him to spare him the lies and the pain. I betrayed him, Kara. I betrayed the only person who's ever loved me."

Diana sat cold as stone, clearly fighting her regret. Kara couldn't quite understand how she could have done something like that. This wasn't the sister she remembered at all. She'd kept Diana in such high esteem after her death, but now she wondered if it was because she didn't want to taint the memory of her pure, innocent baby sister. Kara had led herself to believe Diana told her everything, no matter how small or life-changing it was, but now, all she could think about was how many other secrets she was hiding from her.

As she knelt down in front of her, Kara was finally able to examine her gentle, still very youthful, face. What she saw was just that — a kid. She had only just turned eighteen, after all; still young, still very immature. She was going to make mistakes. She was going to keep secrets. Kara was that age once. Who was she to judge?

"Why are you telling me this now?" she asked, hoping her sister would look at her.

Instead, Diana laughed. It began slow, but quickly became more rapid and uncontrolled. It frightened Kara.

When Diana was calm enough to speak again:

"I remember it now. The crash. I can see it all, clear as day. I remember how I felt; how I knew I wasn't going to make it back home; how I would never be able to see Mom or Dad again, or apologize for how I treated them; how I was never going to know what it felt like to have my heart broken, or what a cherry-flavored chicken smoothie would actually taste like."

Kara chuckled at the last statement, recalling the day she told Diana to grind

up a raw chicken with a can of cherries because she was mad their mom wouldn't take them to Jamba Juice. It had been a joke, but Diana had taken it seriously. Their mom stopped her before she was about to take a drink, but because it was Kara's idea, she received the punishment. Diana got off scot-free.

"But mainly, I thought about you," Diana continued, shifting her head so she could see Kara, "and how I would never see you again, talk to you about boys or go shopping and just shoot the shit like a couple of sex-crazed teenagers. I thought about how we would never get to go hiking, or skiing, or how I would never be able to get you into trouble again." Diana chuckled. "Now that I think about it, I was angry at you for not being there to protect me. But what the hell? Just before we hit the water, I prayed for you. I prayed that someday I'd be able to see you again before I died. And that was it."

Kara was now flush with sadness.

"Then I woke up here, as if only a day had gone by. I was surrounded by hundreds of people I didn't know, naked and freaked the fuck out. I didn't know where I was, or how I got here. But I didn't care. All I wanted to do was find you. I had this feeling you were there, searching for me, trying to get to me and take me home. I looked and I looked, but like the plane, you weren't there for me." She paused, then added more for herself than for Kara:

"She must have known that."

"Who?"

Diana remained silent a moment, then snapped out of her daze. "Huh? Oh, I don't know," she said, shaking her head. "There was this woman who spoke to us like she was our mother. She made us all feel safe, like we'd finally returned home from some long trip or something. I think she told the women to follow a couple of others somewhere, I don't know 'cause when she stopped talking, she came up to me like she knew me. She handed me this robe and told me there was someone I needed to keep an eye on, someone that was in trouble. Even though I could barely speak, I asked her who it was. She just said it was someone I knew and I needed to bring her back here until she returned.

"I didn't know it was you, Kara," Diana finished, making a plea for forgiveness that she didn't have to make. "I swear I didn't."

"It's not your fault, Diana," Kara said. "You were scared. And you were probably manipulated. What else were you supposed to do?"

"That's just it, though. When I saw you standing there in that room, I may have been a little weirded out by the whole age thing, but it *was* you, and I wasn't scared anymore. I didn't care about what I was told to do; I was just happy to finally see you again."

"So then why did you bring me back here? Why'd you dump me down that hole?"

"I don't know. There's something happening to me. It feels like someone's growing inside me, like they're trying to take over my body or something. I've been seeing things, these… memories of this woman… of this place. It's starting to really fuck me up. I've been trying to stop it, but I feel…"

Kara waited for Diana to fight the sudden headache that nearly crippled her to the floor. "I feel like it's her guiding me, like she's forcing me to do this stuff. I'm not sure if I'll be able to fight it much longer. What am I supposed to do? I'm losing myself, Kara. I'm dying all over again."

She started crying. Kara wanted to comfort her, but she couldn't move, frozen stiff by what she could only imagine Diana was going through. The best she could do was lay her forehead to Diana's. As she did, Diana wrapped her arms around her and buried her face in Kara's shoulder.

"I'm sorry," she said. "I'm sorry for all the lies, all the schemes, the betrayal. I'm sorry I led you here, I'm sorry I hurt you. I'm sorry…"

Kara let Diana weep. She rested her head on top of Diana's. "You have nothing to be sorry about."

Diana looked to Kara with a smile she knew well. "You forgive me?"

"You're my sister."

Diana gave Kara another quick hug. "You're right," she said and untied Kara's hands. "Get out of here."

"Without you? Hell no."

"Kara, listen to me. Even if I *was* able to get out of here, I wouldn't be the same person anymore. This other woman is taking control and I can't stop it from happening."

"Fuck that," Kara said, swearing for the first time Diana could remember. "Fuck that. I'm sure there's something we can do. There's gotta be someone that can help stop this from happening."

"Kara, please. The only one I know who can stop this is the one that wants it all to happen."

"Then we make her stop it. Together."

"It won't work."

"I don't give a shit."

"Kara!" Diana gripped Kara's shoulders tight, staring into her watery eyes. She didn't have to say another word.

"I lost you once," Kara said.

"I know. And it's killing me to have to lose you again. But I'm already supposed to be dead, right?"

Kara tried to fight her pain with a smile.

"Then let me return things back to normal."

"What are you going to do?"

"Don't even worry about that. Just let me do it."

Kara didn't want to fight anymore. The determination and sense of responsibility in Diana's eyes was fierce. She *had* become the woman she sought to become. It made Kara extremely proud. She hugged her again.

"Say goodbye to Mom and Dad for me, okay?" Diana said.

"Okay," Kara said, pulling away, her tears fading into acceptance.

"Tell them I'm in a better place."

"I will." Kara wiped the remaining water from her eyes. "Take care of yourself."

"Get your ass out of here, sis," Diana said playfully, shoving Kara's head and pushing her away. "Run as fast and as far as you can."

Kara did as she was told, pounding the glass into the drying mud as she sprinted to the ladder, where she turned back to Diana one last time. She was going to remember her, not as the conniving little kid sister, or the beautiful, rebellious teenager, but as the confident, courageous woman that had been reborn to help Kara reach a closure she'd never been able to attain before. Kara had never been allowed to truly say goodbye, and now she could finally move forward to become the person Diana always hoped she would be.

She blew Diana a kiss and waited for her to swipe at the air and hold her closed fist to her heart like they used to when they were kids. Then she climbed up the ladder, leaving behind her sister's ghost.

Atlantis – Spirit Tower – 12 hours 42 minutes after arrival

Gydressina had led Matthew and Patricia through a series of rooms and hallways and stairwells, occasionally seeming to backtrack their way through different levels of different towers. Matthew felt it odd that she would be taking them on such a diversionary path, when it felt like all they had to do was walk a straight line to get to where they were going. But he assumed she had her purpose, and at one point, after Patricia's hundredth attempt to ask where the hell they were going, Matthew spotted the shadows of a group of men. He couldn't quite make out how many there were, but he guessed there may have been a few dozen, all marching together. Gydressina had paused to look around the small room they had entered, which looked to have at least three additional exits, all urging Matthew to take the opportunity and check them out. He tapped Patricia on the shoulder and pointed over to the shadows, holding his finger to his lips to keep her quiet. The two then cautiously stepped to the wall next to one of the exits as the shadows grew closer.

"You think that's why miss pretty here's been taking us on this damned detour?" Patricia asked as quietly as she could (which wasn't all that quiet).

Matthew nodded, but before the men came into full view, Gydressina pulled

them away from the open exit and up against the wall. *You will get us all killed,* she said loudly in their heads. It wasn't out of anger; it was out of protection. *We must move quickly. We're close.*

"Who are they?" Matthew whispered, showing Patricia how it's done.

Cephis's followers. And they'll do everything in their power to do his bidding. Most of them are still weak, though. Still human.

Matthew wasn't quite sure what to make of those last few words, but he didn't want to waste any more time with a bunch of questions he didn't really need answers to. He just hoped Patricia would show the same candor.

But that number's diminishing quickly. As they acquire their original knowledge, their humanity fades. Do not stray.

Matthew nodded. Patricia took Matthew's cue and simply followed suit, hoping to avoid the same type of situation she had with Jaime and Kara.

Gydressina read them carefully and then let them go. *This way*, she said and led them down another glass hallway. As they entered another grand hall filled with a jungle of plant life, she held out her arm to stop them cold.

"What is it?" Patricia asked.

Quiet.

Patricia held her tongue. Matthew tried not to breathe as he heard a rustling in the plants. *What is it?* he asked, hoping Gydressina would hear him so he wouldn't have to say it out loud.

Nothing to be feared, she replied just before Jaime stumbled from the brush and onto the small clear path they were on. She jumped in fright at the sight of Gydressina, but then calmed as she realized who was with her.

"Oh, thank god," she said, nearly tripping over herself to wrap her arms around Matthew. She appeared to be almost in tears.

Patricia smiled bright. She thought about saying something a little off-color or a bit obnoxious to see if she could get a laugh out of her, possibly join in with a great big bear hug, but wasn't sure if Jaime was ready to accept it. Not after what she had done.

Matthew couldn't find any words either. He simply wanted to take in Jaime's breath, her touch — her spirit. He comforted her until she was finally ready to let go.

"I'm so glad to see you," he said when she did.

"I thought I'd never find you." Jaime was overwhelmed and tried hard to fight back a few tears. "There're so many of them. I thought they'd kill me."

"Who?"

"Them," Jaime said.

Matthew was confused, then realized someone was missing from this reunion; the someone those tears were most likely for.

"Where's Kaleena?" he said, a bit frantic.

Jamie looked away, unable to answer.

Matthew grabbed her shoulders and forced her to look at him. "Jaime, where is she?"

"She went with Evey," she said under her breath, terrified of the words.

"She what?"

"I'm sorry. I tried to stop her."

"Why the hell didn't you?"

"Because then I'd be dead." She consciously left out the word 'asshole,' even though she really wanted to say it. This wasn't the time to fight. Not over this. "She did it to protect me."

"Protect you?"

"Evey was going to kill me if she didn't go with her. I had to let her do it."

Matthew wanted to scream a slew of obscenities.

"She must have done it for a reason," Patricia interjected. Matthew was ready to slap her for taking Jaime's side, but let her continue. "I mean, she is a genius, right?"

The group stood in silence as Matthew pulled himself under control. Thinking back over it all, he knew they were right. Kaleena would do anything to protect her family, even if that meant dying. But she also wouldn't do anything without thinking it through completely, making sure every angle was covered and tested.

"She must know something we don't," he whispered.

Jaime wasn't sure how to respond except to gently touch his elbow. "She told me to trust her," she said, turning from them all. "I had to trust her."

Patricia shook her head in Jaime's direction, urging Matthew to reassure her. He looked at the ground, listening to the soft hint of Jaime's guilt hidden under the silence. He projected the guilt of his own inability to protect Kaleena onto Jaime, which he never wanted to do. If he would have been there instead of her, he probably would have done the exact same thing. Because of that, he knew how Jaime must be feeling, having been the one to let it happen. She needed comfort, not a lecture.

He pressed his hand to her back. She turned her head slightly to seize a glimpse of Matthew's face out of the corner of her eye. The gesture urged him to move closer, helping to guide her into another embrace, this one needing no words of apology. It erased all of the mistakes that had been made in the past and rekindled the affectionate connection between them. There were no more lies, no more anger, no more regret. They simply shared the friendship, the companionship, the respect and the honor they had vowed to provide one another nearly fifteen years ago. They were one soul, united under the trust and protection and courage of a daughter that would bind their hearts together forever.

When Jaime let go, she felt freer than she had in a long time. Her reddened face and soft eyes clearly defined it. Gydressina took in a breath, feeding off their faith.

"We must go," she finally said, breaking the rapture that held Matthew and Jaime together. They both nodded in unison and followed her down the path. Patricia kept pace a few feet behind, watching as they walked shoulder-to-shoulder, their hands cupped together. Jaime lowered her head to Matthew's shoulder and he kissed the top of it gently. Patricia simply wished she would someday feel that young and that in love again.

It felt as if they had walked about a mile when Gydressina turned and walked into the brush. Everyone was a bit confused, but followed without objection, knowing they would be protected as long as they were with her. They walked a

few more yards before they reached another small clearing. At their feet was a small puddle of water that appeared to be much deeper than that, as if it were the smallest lake in the world.

"I need someone's help," Gydressina said before any of them could speak.

Matthew pulled Jaime in tight. "Help to do what?"

"To destroy the city," Gydressina said bluntly.

"What?" Jaime said. "Why?"

"You can't do that," Matthew said, loosening his grip on Jaime. "What about Kaleena? Thomas? Kara? They're all still out there somewhere. You just want to kill them?"

"Thomas has already begun the burial," Gydressina said.

"He's done what?"

"He sacrificed himself to protect Trishen. I'm very sorry."

"And when exactly were you going to tell me this?" Matthew yelled, ignoring Jaime's pleas for him to stop.

"I didn't think it prudent," Gydressina said. "You didn't need to know."

"That's just terrific."

Matthew turned away, but whipped back when Jaime's soft touch tickled his chest. He knew right away he needed to apologize.

"Trishen is safe," Gydressina said. "Thomas is a hero. Never forget that."

Matthew nodded, but kept his eyes averted. He needed time to settle his anger.

"What about the others?" Jaime said for him.

"Don't worry about them. Kaleena and Kara are exactly where they need to be."

"I have a question," Patricia said. "If the city is already flooding because of Thomas, why do you need us to destroy it? Isn't that what he's already done?"

"Drowning the city will guarantee that Cephis won't be able to build his army. But as long as the city remains standing, Cephis will find the power to live on, even after the death of his own body."

Jaime suddenly felt Cephis inside her. It turned her stomach sideways.

"So then what crazy ass plan you got up your sleeve for us?" Patricia said.

"There's one point in the city that if it were to fall, it would cause a chain reaction throughout, burying everything once and for all."

"Why can't you do it?" Matthew asked. "Why use one of us?"

"Because it's impossible for me to do such a thing."

"Why?"

"As I've already told you, Matthew, the city was built with my life. Once it falls, I will cease to exist as you know me."

"You're connected to the city?" Jaime said, a bit confused.

"I think she *is* the city," Patricia corrected. "And you aren't about to commit suicide, are you?"

"In a manner of speaking," Gydressina said sweetly.

"Then again, if that's true, you're basically asking us to kill you. Isn't that like, assisted suicide or some shit?"

Jaime turned to Patricia, slightly appalled.

"It must be done."

"I won't do it," Matthew said. "There has to be a way to stop Cephis without having to kill you."

"There is. But it wouldn't be permanent."

"But you *can* stop him?" Matthew tried to confirm.

"We can destroy his living body, yes."

"Then why destroy the city at all?" Jaime asked sincerely.

"Because it's better I'm destroyed than allow Cephis to live in spirit."

"Why?" Jaime was still confused.

"A body is easily destroyed, Jaime, and a mind can be haunted. But unless the spirit's connection is severed from existence, it will always have the chance to resurrect itself. Whether it's tomorrow or another twenty thousand years from now, if we don't completely destroy him, he will rise, and when that happens —"

"We become Revelations," Patricia said.

Gydressina nodded acknowledgment.

"So you're saying if we don't destroy the city," Matthew confirmed, "and you along with it, his soul will remain alive because the city is still alive?"

"Because you're still alive," Jaime added softly.

Gydressina nodded again and Jaime turned to Matthew. He clearly saw what she was thinking. It sent a deep weight to his gut. "Don't you dare," he said, water beginning to swallow his eyes.

"I have to," she whispered, fighting back her fears.

"Jaime, please."

"Matthew, don't do this." She pulled her hand free of his and stepped away slightly. "Of everything I've done to you and to Kaleena... to Benjamin and my parents. This place... this place has given me — has given us all — a second chance."

"A second chance for what?" Matthew said.

Jaime pressed her hand to his cheek and looked deep into his eyes. "To love." She smiled slightly, feeling his need for her, his devotion. She looked away, running through her memories. "Evey told me a little while ago that my only regret was running from Benjamin in Australia. But that's not true. My only real regret was never believing that the choices I made were always the right ones." She looked back to Matthew. "I can't keep running."

She turned back to Gydressina. "I'll do it," she said with confidence. "Just tell me what I have to do?"

Gydressina flashed a supportive, kind smile and then pulled her close. She placed one hand around the back of her head, her fingers spread as wide as they would go, and her other hand at the top of her back, her middle finger pressed hard against the base of her neck. She lowered her head so that her lips were touching Jaime's ear and whispered, "Amen Dello Keli."

A rush of heat blasted Jaime's mind. She saw everything she needed to know: the best path to the birthing room in Callipse Tower, what she needed to do to destroy the city, and how to find her way to Spirited Wind to join everyone in their escape. There was also a surge in her lungs — a relief, in a way — that left behind a weird texture to her breaths. It was exhilarating and frightening

all at the same time. If she didn't know any better, it almost felt more satisfying than an orgasm.

When Gydressina let go, Jaime's muscles relaxed. She shook, a march of goose bumps covering her body. Closing her eyes was all she could do to help stabilize her wobbling legs.

"Need a smoke?" Patricia asked, causing Jaime to laugh giddily.

"What did she do?" Matthew said. Patricia responded with a wink.

As her body came down from the high that Gydressina had pushed upon her, Jaime felt a fresh, new life enter her lungs. There was much more to her task than what she was willing to reveal to Matthew. Jaime fluttered a smile of thanks and appreciation, nonetheless. Then she went to Patricia and pulled her in for a tight squeeze. "I forgive you."

"I'm sorry," Patricia said.

Jaime patted her on the back like a child needing to burp and squeezed her shoulder tight. "You're a great friend, Patricia, and an even better person. Never forget that." She then slapped Patricia lightly on the cheek, flashing her own spirited wink.

Patricia returned it with a light slap of her own. "You be careful, okay. Listen to the city and get your ass back to us, Speedy Gonzalez-style."

"You got it. My ass'll move so fast it'll be on fire."

"That's what I like to hear." Patricia said as she lightly slapped Jaime's ass. Jaime's playful chuckle didn't last. She stepped to Matthew as if she were in slow motion. Setting the fingertips of her right hand on the small of his back and her left hand around the back of his head, she pulled him in for a kiss — the first real, passionate kiss she had shared with him since the night of their wedding. She held him close afterward, making sure he knew she was doing this for him; for Kaleena —

For the world.

Her lips lingered close to his and her eyes remained closed. "I love you, Matthew."

Matthew couldn't find the words behind his pain, but he didn't need to. Jaime felt them in his touch. He lowered his forehead to hers and she couldn't resist giving him another light, loving kiss before stepping away. She slid her hand down his arm and grasped his hand once more, giving it a light squeeze. She then turned back to Gydressina and started unbuttoning her shirt.

"Whoa, there, Starlight," Patricia said. "What are you doing?"

"That water's probably near freezing," Jaime said, tossing her shirt off. She felt warm as her bare skin hit the fresh air. "I'm at least going to try to keep from getting hypothermia." She quickly shoved her arms into the top half of the wetsuit still dangling around her waist and pulled it up around her shoulders.

"Besides, that shirt would've just weighed me down." She peered over her shoulder to Matthew like a teenager waiting for her handsome knight to sweep her off her feet. "Can I get a little help?" she said.

Matthew didn't say anything. He just zipped up the back of her suit, making sure it locked in tight. Jaime lowered her hair over the top and gave him another quick kiss ("Thank you") before stepping up to the pond so that her feet were right on the edge, there was a slight hesitation.

"Take a rich, deep breath," Gydressina said, "and you should have enough air to reach the tower."

"Great," Jaime said, and turned back to Matthew one last time. "Take care of Kaleena." She then took the deepest breath she had ever taken and jumped into the pond, disappearing beneath the dark blue surface.

Dizzy and a bit nauseous, Matthew knelt down a few feet from the pond. Patricia watched the water a moment longer, waiting for Jaime to pop her head back up, aborting the mission. When she didn't, Patricia kissed her fingertips and waved them at the pond.

"She'll be back," she said, her voice less than comforting. Matthew forced a smile, knowing that the kiss Jaime had gifted him would be their last. He wanted nothing more than to cherish it for as long as he could before it became just another memory alongside all of her other loving kisses.

*   *   *

The water wasn't as cold as Jaime expected. It felt quite warm, actually, as if she'd jumped into her grand mum's old pool. She remembered always wanting to go swimming when she visited, even if it was snowing outside (which was usually the case, as they would almost always reserve their trips to Thanksgiving or Christmas; sometimes they went on July fourth when they weren't at Disneyland or a nice, summer resort) because the pool was always so warm.

It didn't take very long to kick and stroke her way out of the building and into the vast openness of the city. At first, she was surrounded by a wall of dirt and rock, the buildings towering above her, hidden in the water as if they were hiding something. She knew she didn't have a whole lot of time, but she needed to see it, be part of it; become one with it. So she swam up until she reached what would have been the surface of the lake in another time and was mesmerized by the grandness and utter perfection of it all. She could imagine people living among it, walking the streets on their way to the harvest, or possibly down to the weekly dance, where the teens would mingle, the women would gossip and the men would gloat. If she had gills, she would have traveled the city simply to ingest its beauty. But it was obvious she didn't. Even as her lungs pulled oxygen in through the pores of her skin, making her whole body glitter with sensitivity and vibrancy, they wouldn't be able to continue to breathe like this forever.

As she spun to locate where she was supposed to go, she suddenly felt an odd sensation of solitude. She hadn't noticed it looking out onto the city from the room in the tower, but the entirety of the city was completely baron. There wasn't one plant, not one fish, not one amoeba to look at, to study, to appreciate. Of all the dives Jamie had ever been on, not once had she ever seen the ocean so devoid of life. She thought maybe it was because of the temperature, but then that didn't make any sense. There were plenty of warm water fish that could have lived quite nicely here. So why was the ocean so lifeless? Perhaps it was because the city —

Gydressina is *the city*

— kept all life from nearing its boundaries. But why would it need to scare so much life away from its borders? Was it protection? A way to make sure that when the moment came, no ocean life would have to suffer the consequences?

Jaime gave up trying to understand it as her skin dried under her wetsuit. Her ability to breathe under these conditions was waning. Glancing over the city one last time, it occurred to her that this whole thing would make the perfect documentary. And not just a short two-hour film, either, but a major production, one that could appear as a series on the Discovery channel, pushing the limits by exploring the deeper meaning of the city. The mystery angle would be enough to entice producers to greenlight the idea. The connection to Atlantis would just be a bonus. And there was no doubt in her mind that if it happened, Patricia would be a major part of it. It sent a spark of excitement up her spine as she swam back down into the lake where she pictured a bunch of kids daring each other to see who could swim the farthest under water, or a young couple enjoying a secret make out session under the stars, the moon glistening off light ripples.

As she neared the second tower, she saw a vent no larger than a sewer drain along the sidewalk of a housing complex. She was glad Patricia hadn't talked everyone into letting her go along because it was obvious even Jaime's thinner than average frame would barely be able to squeeze through it. She didn't want to believe it as Gydressina held her, but it was absolutely clear now that it was always meant to be her that went on this mission. She had been chosen, probably even before she stepped foot on the *Endeavor*; probably even before she got Kaleena's first phone call. Gydressina made it seem as if it had been her decision, a way to redeem herself and live up to her capability (and prove Kaleena wrong about being able to change her character), but none of that was true. It had all been planned — every word, every act, every decision.

But how was that even possible?

It was becoming harder and harder to breathe as Jamie slid into the vent and pulled her way through. It became hard to focus, and she wondered why she spent so much time daydreaming about the city. That one small act may have just cost her not only her life, but that of everyone she cared for and then some. Her mind had grown so foggy, she almost didn't notice the wall in front of her. When it clicked that she was in a room, Jaime skirted her way up (or at least, what she thought was up) to the surface of another wading pool. The taste of fresh air was rich and rewarding. Her head quickly dropped back into the pool for a second of relaxation and then it was back up again, inhaling another beat of air. It took a few seconds to get her bearings, but once she had, she brushed the hair out of her eyes and looked around the room. She couldn't help but admire the architecture of the statues towering over her. The reality of the women, especially the depth and earnestness of their eyes as they relished in the different stages of birth, was incredibly tantalizing. For a moment, she thought she felt Lauren (and possibly Evey) swimming among her in the water. It was a little eerie, but nonetheless thrilling. She would have stayed there forever if she could, but she couldn't waste any more time.

Jaime located the only doors in the entire windowless room, which stood nearly three stories high and partially cracked open. She climbed out of the pool, her lips brimming with the annoying taste of salt, and slid up against the wall next to the open archway. Peering out into the glass hallway, she saw another large metal door that led into the third tower. She couldn't see any apparent danger awaiting her, but something wasn't right. She looked back to the pool. Lauren sat naked within it, holding a small child and waving at her. Freaked out, she closed her eyes tight, sweat forming across her brow. When she opened them, Lauren was gone, but the feeling that she had been there, had died giving birth to Evey, lingered in the air.

"Bye, Lauren," she whispered. "Live well." She then cautiously stepped from the room, crouching as best she could while trotting swiftly along the walkway. She would get through this; she was going to be able to hold Kaleena in her arms again, kiss Matthew and make love to him as she never had before. She felt it in her soul.

It was all she had left to believe in as the door in front of her opened, pushing

her back a step or two. A trio of men stormed into the breezeway and had no trouble subduing her, grabbing her arms and pushing her to her knees. At that moment, she knew, as Gydressina had warned her, that this was truly the end.

Atlantis – Below the city – 12 hours 42 minutes after arrival

The stairwell spiraled down deep into the earth as if it led into a vampire's lair. The steps weren't made of stone, or wood, or steel. There was instead a soft texture of mud between Kaleena's toes — the same element of soft clay that made up the large pillar connecting the steps to the walls… a primitive structure created under a highly developed city — as she was escorted into the depths behind Evey. Both remained quiet as they continued to break through the barriers of each other's minds. Kaleena figured if she tried to speak, it would help Evey in her pursuit of whatever it was she was looking for. She knew Evey would eventually break through; there was no doubt in her mind about that. But if she allowed her to do so before she had the chance to do the same would possibly hurt her chance to locate and exploit the weakness Kaleena sensed within her.

Oddly, the two men gripping Kaleena's arms winced as they entered the darkening stairwell. There was a second soul haunting them, each trying desperately to connect with their minds. It was only a matter of time before that connection was solidified, overtaking their hosts. When that happened, it would be much harder for Kaleena to do what she needed to do. Her time was running out; if she didn't reach out to Evey now, she may not get the chance. It was a risk, but she felt strong enough to begin her interrogation before they reached the bottom of the stairwell, however far that might be.

What are you going to do to me? Kaleena asked, unafraid.

Evey didn't respond. Kaleena was sure it was because the young woman was afraid of her own vulnerability.

Are you going to kill me? Torture me? Take my essence? I'll find out soon enough, Evey. I've learned a lot.

What you've learned is nothing to what I am.

It may have only been for a split second, but Kaleena felt Evey's mind open. What she saw in that time led Kaleena into her next query.

She saved you, didn't she?

Evey once again refused to answer. Kaleena felt her anger percolating.

I've seen it. You defied her law, and yet she protected you. She sent you away from the city to live with Adamus in the great mountains. She kept you safe when the flood came.

Evey's heart beat faster, colder.

She could have chosen anyone to rebuild the population, to begin life anew in a new world, with renewed hope. She had her pick of hundreds of women who had not succumbed to the knowledge, who had not tasted the fruit. Yet she chose you. Why?

Kaleena paused, hoping to read what effect her next words would take.

She loved you —

Evey whipped around, grabbed each man's throat and ripped them out, throwing their bodies down the stairwell. She then dug her sharpened fingertips into Kaleena's jugular and drew her in within an eyelash of her face. Kaleena smelled the fire on her breath.

She was a fool, Evey growled. *I died before I ever left this city. I died the moment she took my freedom and placed her trust in my loyalty. I was never loyal to her. Cephis was my lord, and she was foolish to ever believe that would change. She didn't love me. I was ready to die for him. All she wanted was to punish me for what I had done.*

That's not true. A mother never loses her love for her child.

Evey dug her fingers deeper into Kaleena's skin. *She was not my mother.*

Don't be a fool, Evestylyn, Kaleena said. *You know better than anyone. Gydressina is everyone's mother.* Kaleena prepared herself to have her throat ripped apart. Instead, Evey slipped her fingers out of her jaw and grabbed the back of her hair, nearly dragging her down the remaining set of steps. Kaleena smelled the men's festering blood as they passed over them.

When they reached the bottom, torches sitting loosely on the walls lit up and sprinkled a small array of light throughout the small cavern. Evey dragged Kaleena to the wall and pulled her up to her knees. She then grabbed her throat again to push her chin upward.

Kill me, Kaleena hissed. *But believe when I say that you will be doing so in vain.*

Evey stared at her for a long time and then peered down to Kaleena's chest. She slowly cupped the small necklace into her hand. As she admired it, her anger faded into something much more — a deep reverence for the object that held her love. She never knew why Caistepher had given this child the necklace until now. Evey was Kaleena's sister, not in life, but in spirit. They were connected, not only to each other, but to him, and this necklace was proof that they would always be bonded through the blood of the sacrifice.

I don't wish to kill you, Kaleena, Evey said, calm and subdued. She lowered the necklace to Kaleena's chest and sat on her knees. A heat of sexual electricity flashed over Kaleena. She'd never felt like making love to anyone like this before. *But Gydressina has left me no choice,* Evey continued. *I was to protect you, to guide you and love you as my own child, as my sister and my lover. But the fruit of my desire has been corrupted. I can no longer feel your breath. I can no longer sustain a true bond between our minds. But what you hold within you is still very important to me, because the acquisition of my needs will no doubt destroy you. Your death is on her hands.*

Prepare to become the child of my soul.

Evey leaned in and kissed Kaleena softly, using her breath to slip into her sister's body and take control of her mind. Kaleena didn't fight her; it could take Evey the rest of her life to locate what she was looking for. Instead, she drew the breath in and leapt into Evey. It wouldn't take her near as long to find what she needed, and what she found would give her the opportunity to finish what Gydressina had put into motion. She sifted through several memories of Evey's life in Ediinis — her hidden love of Adamus, the attack on Gydressina's quarters to take control of the city, and the moments of her death in Ediinis and rebirth in the Mountains of Hannah, none of which was as important as when Cephis returned to Ediinis

after spending several years on a pilgrimage that had sent him around the globe and into the bowels of hell within his own mind. Upon his return, everything had changed.

Kaleena lay on her sleeping cube, her latest diary resting on her lap. She had only recently had the clean pages bound in the leather cover and it usually took some time for it to dry before she could touch it, afraid it would fall apart if she didn't. But because so much excitement surrounded the events of the morning, she couldn't wait. It had been generations since the man known as Cephis had chosen to leave Ediinis on his own volition to discover the world and, to everyone's thoughts, vanish into the life. When she saw his visage step over the hill, with nothing more than an animal skin draped over his shoulders to keep him warm, Kaleena, as well as the rest of the city who knew him and had yet to seek the ritual of enlightenment, felt a wave of astonishment and anticipation. She wanted to know everything he'd seen, but was afraid to say anything, or even be close to him. Cephis held something within her that he didn't hold with anyone else, and since his departure, Kaleena had moved on, becoming a woman and a keeper of child. What would he say to that? How would he feel to see the little girl he nearly raised so grown and fruitful? She wrote all of it down in her diary with the fine point of the quill. As she contemplated the perfect way to describe Cephis, she rubbed the end of the rare peacock feather she'd found on one of her usual morning walks with Cephis around her nose. She liked the relaxing tickle it gave her; it reminded her of all that Cephis had done for her, all that he had led her to believe and to become. It all made her feel rather sweet and melancholy.

As Kaleena scratched a new fable among her thoughts, a knock was raised upon her door. She slipped the quill into the diary and rested it on the cube. The knock returned as Kaleena glided for the door, her thin gold robe whisping slightly open as she did. She hoped she'd see Adamus waiting for her, as she hadn't seen him since he took Caistepher out to the grain fields to help him with the harvest. The ceremony of the Wolf moon was upon them, and she hoped he would be inviting to escort her to the acceptance of good news from the magistrate.

When she opened the door, she jumped back slightly in fright, chirping a small, "Oh," and then covering her mouth as she smiled lightly in embarrassment. *Cephis*, she said, her girlish charm emanating around her eyes. *Welcome back.* She wanted to give him a hug, but his sight was too overpowering and demonstrative.

Thank you, he said, bowing his head so as to be able to look over the delicate body peeking through the creases of her robe, attempting to taste the suppleness of her breasts and the odor of her vagina.

Please, she said, flowing her arm gently around the room, guiding him to enter. *Will you come in?*

He bowed slightly again and entered, his steps light and smooth. *I was saddened that you didn't come to my return banquet*, he said, looking over the room, carefully ingesting the sweet nectar of the fresh fruit that grew on her walls.

Oh, no, she said as she closed the door. *My apologies, but I... had other matters to attend to.* Her stutter was frantic — a child's lie.

Other matters, Cephis repeated, somewhat coldly. He looked over the scores of diaries lining the far wall, then grabbed one of the fruits off its vine and rolled it around in his hand. *Such as tending to your garden...* He paused and looked to her sleeping cube. *Or writing in your book.*

Ah, yes, she said sweetly, hopping to the cube and picking the diary off the bed. *This is my alone time, and I must always take it. I'm sorry for missing your banquet. I'm sure it was quite the feast.* Kaleena took the quill from the diary and walked the book to the wall, placing it face down on the ledge of the shelf.

It was, he replied, stepping to her. *But no apologies are necessary. Having returned from my years in solitude, I can certainly understand the need for time for one's own thoughts.*

Kaleena smiled and set the quill down on top of the book. Cephis looked handsome in his thick beard and long hair, which was pulled back into a ponytail that hung to just above his waist. She returned his tender smile with a girlish charm of her own and looked into his eyes with an adoration she hadn't felt since he left.

You look quite beautiful, Evestylyn. From the young child I left behind to the grace of the woman that now stands before me, the splendor of your fruit is overwhelming.

Thank you, she said, combing a line of stray hair behind her ear to help show off her softened cheekbone. *You look much the same as I remember you.*

A good thing, I hope, Cephis returned, feeling the lie of her lips.

Of course.

Cephis took a bite of the fruit. Kaleena shied away to her bed, folding her legs atop one another as she sat. She didn't know quite what was happening to her at the moment, but it felt right; she needed to keep it fresh. From the distance, she saw more than she had ever seen before, and in any man since. She felt somewhat guilty, as if she was betraying Adamus. He had been the only man she ever wanted to have see her bodily truth and create life within her. But now, with Cephis's return, she was open to exposing her treasures to him without question, wanting nothing more than to learn of his, and of his travels. It scared her a bit, but excited her even more.

Juice rolled down Cephis's chin as he took another scintillating bite from the fruit. Kaleena's hands were smooth and delicate as they seemingly hovered above her rounded knee. He licked his lips as he swayed toward her, a gentleman with eager tendencies.

I've heard you were granted the privilege of bearing a son in my absence, he said.

Two sons, to be precise, Kaleena corrected.

Two sons. My, that is a great honor.

Yes, indeed. Quite exciting, I must say.

But of course. Cephis slid behind her and sat on the edge of her bed. She watched him until she floated out of view without turning her head. *And quite the accomplishment. I believe I've met the eldest. Caistepher, is it not?*

Younger, to say truth.

Younger? My, he is becoming quite the man.

He is.

He certainly has quite the fire within him.

He has been a handful to lead, Kaleena said, smiling. *But not so much more than I must have been for you.*

No, my dear. You never caused me any distress. You were near perfect in your youth, which I can see has been granted to you in your womanhood as well.

Kaleena closed her eyes and stretched her arms, a wash of tenderness and exhilaration pouring through her veins.

Don't worry for him, Cephis continued. *He'll grow into a strong leader, I'm sure.*

As am I, Kaleena said, cracking her eyes open.

May I ask you something that may be rather personal?

Please do. Cephis took another bite from the fruit. *My mind is open to all who seek its power.*

I would just like to know what it was like.

What, my dear?

Kaleena shifted her head to peer gently over her shoulder. *Your journey.*

Cephis chuckled. *And why do you ask of such a query?*

You're the first to ever have returned from such an adventure. I just wish to know the power of its grace.

It is quite something, my beautiful Evestylyn. An exploration that changes lives.

And did it change yours?

Beyond your understanding, child.

What did you see?

I saw the touch of the hand of life. I climbed the highest of mountains, swam the deepest of oceans, ate of the land and drank of its soul. Across the land there is life beyond your imagination and a wind that carries the light of the moon. To experience it is to breathe it. There are no words that could ever describe the majestic nature of its spirit.

And what of the dangers?

Sweet child, danger exists only in the fear you bring with you. Of all the many who have left to travel the land, I am the first to have chosen it. My fear rested deep within the walls of this city.

But you left many behind that wished you safety.

I left one behind, Cephis said, leaning closer to Kaleena. He rested his hand on her shoulder, sending a nip of fire through her heart. *And I did so only because the wealth of my knowledge had ended, and I needed more.*

Why?

Because there's no truth without knowledge.

And what knowledge did you find?

Cephis removed his hand from her shoulder and caressed her back as he stood. *I'm afraid I can't reveal that truth to you.*

Kaleena finally turned to him. *Why not?* she asked sweetly.

You're not ready to know the touch of the hand of life.

But I am ready, she pleaded.

I trust that no soul will ever truly be ready to accept what I have learned.

But how do you know if you don't trust them to know?

Cephis turned to her and pet her chin. His eyes were dark and hauntingly seductive. *You're too afraid.*

I am not afraid, she said as Cephis walked back to the diaries. *I wish to know what you learned, live what you lived.*

What I know will scar your heart forever, my child.

I'm willing to be scarred.

What I've learned will hurt you in ways you'll never be able to rectify.

I'm ready to be hurt.

Cephis turned to her. *What I've learned will go against all that you've come to be.*

Kaleena hesitated, then stood confident. *I'm ready to give away who I am.*

Cephis inhaled, then moaned as he let out a soothing breath. *I feel your eagerness, child, and I believe your words to be veritable. I'm willing to show you what I've learned.*

Show me, my heart, Kaleena said, taking a few steps toward Cephis.

What you will learn will never be forgotten, but it will change the way you understand the world and your soul.

Show me, my soul. She continued to inch ever closer.

What you're asking will help you live a love you've never felt.

I want to feel you, my love. Kaleena stopped about a foot from Cephis. He raised his hand to her. *If you're ready, take my hand.*

Kaleena licked her drying lips in anticipation. What she saw in Cephis was a deep affection for her and a love that was different than any man she'd ever looked upon, including the love that filled the heart of Adamus. She didn't understand it, but the aura of his mind captivated her beyond her own resistance. She truly wanted to know what he knew; wanted to feel what he had felt. This was her chance to live the world without living outside of her comfortable home. He would take her to a new level of understanding and she would accept it with faith and gratitude. Whatever it was, Cephis looked the better for it, and it was hers to revere.

With a hesitant breath, Kaleena placed her hand in his. Cephis pulled her tight against his chest and swayed her back and forth. As she soaked in the blissfulness of the dance, his heart started beating faster and something pressed against her navel. She backed away, troubled by the sensation. Cephis's penis was propped out from beneath his robe, hard and straight. Her eyes darted as she peered back to his eyes. She was no longer ready to believe in his truth.

Your fear is natural, my dear, but do not pull away.

No, she said, trying to pull her arm from his grip. *I was false in my veneration. I do not wish to feel the touch of life's hand anymore.*

Cephis pulled her back to his chest, her resistance apparent. Her eyes were beginning to well up with tears. Her heart beat much faster than his. *I can't allow you resistance, my child. You've chosen this path and now you must accept it.*

No, please. I don't wish to know.

There is no turning back. He brushed her hair, which calmed her body. She fell almost limp against him, crying her opposition as he danced with her.

Just listen to my words, child. Let my voice relax you. Let my touch relinquish you from the lies that you've been living.

Please, stop, she whispered.

Cephis continued to sway her back and forth, relaxing her even further. *You've been led to believe in a life of deceit and false desire,* he said and then took another bite from the fruit, waiting for her heart to reach a calm of comfort.

The fruit you keep has been raised to produce the seed of reproduction and bear the juice of its body. They are sweet and enriching. Without tender love and care, they would simply rot and perish under the touch of decay. But the nectar within a fruit is never as sweet as the nectar found within one's own body.

Cephis slid his hand down Kaleena's back and rested it on the lower curvature of her buttocks. He then slid his forefinger underneath and caressed the supple muscle she held tight between her legs. Kaleena's body shook with discomfort and mild stimulation as he removed his hand and combed her hair behind her ear. He blew a soft brush of air upon it. Kaleena's jaw vibrated, mixing her tearful fear with a new, rapturous tingle. He then slid the tip of his forefinger down the edge of her breast and pulled the tie of the robe loose. It slid open, exposing her full body to the air around her. He rubbed her stomach lightly as Adamus once did when presenting her with life.

You have not been cared for, Evestylyn. Not as well as you need to be. You have not been freed to know the true taste of the fruit your body bears; the flowers with which you've been accustomed have yet to blossom as they were always meant to. Tell me you don't want to feel your soul bloom unto the sun of your hidden knowledge.

Upon his word, Cephis inched his finger ever so slowly between her legs, to where her sons had once been given the fruit of life. He vibrated his fingers back and forth against her vulva.

The fruit of your womb has been living in the dark because you've been shielded from the reality of the world and the ecstasy the body is simply waiting to provide.

Kaleena's tears turned to elation as he dug deeper into her body. Her breaths became heavier as his fingers moved quicker and more resiliently. She dropped her head back, groaning softly as his touch invigorated both her mind and her body.

Can you taste it, Evestylyn? Can you taste the nectar of your soul? Kaleena groaned deeper, more impassioned. *Do not be afraid of it. Take it. Enjoy the*

sweet smell, the biting gratification, the breathless power for which the blooming of passion is born.

Kaleena was nearing her apex, an elated sensation she'd never imagined in her deepest of dreams, when Cephis stopped his act of gratification and stepped away from her. She wobbled slightly, trying to reach the peak of euphoria. But as she fell to one knee, her robe floating back around her body, the sensation melted away. Kaleena looked at Cephis, angry and disappointed.

Why did you stop? Her breath heaved in a mixture of irritation and delight.

You must be ready to know the full knowledge before you can truly appreciate its fruit. You must not be afraid to defy your freedom. You must be ready to fight for what has always been yours. I can take you there; I can show you the perfection of your womanly flower. But you must be completely willing and desire the defiance of all you've been taught to believe.

Cephis walked to the door. Before he left he turned back to Kaleena and said, *Let me take you to your heavenly garden.*

He left her alone to ingest his words, trying to recapture that moment, that feeling — that immaculate breath of transcendence. Every step she took seemed to rub her genitalia in such a way that left her needing the taste of more knowledge. She wondered what the full taste would bring to her soul and what it would feel like to begin life anew within the splendor of this brand new truth. Where would it lead? What other emotions would she find in the depths of her body? What would happen if she defied the law of her city; defied the law of her mind; defied the law of her heart? Would Adamus accept her newfound knowledge as she would? Would the fruit of her womb understand her fresh existence? It took several minutes to contemplate stealing this new knowledge, all the while rubbing her legs together, embracing her breasts, hoping and dreaming to reach that place of rapture once more. But she couldn't do it alone. She needed the ultimate truth and only Cephis could provide her with that.

Before she understood what was happening, Kaleena was racing down the halls of the tower. Within seconds of her acceptance, she reached the room Cephis

had been assigned upon his return. She knocked, but when Cephis didn't answer, she grew somewhat scared. Was he not there?

Impossible.

He was there, waiting for her, but he wasn't going to make it easy for her. If she truly wanted the release, she would need to prove her acceptance by exposing her defiance. Without hesitation, and without checking to make sure no one was watching her break into another citizen's room, she opened the door and slid in like a thief about to find a majestic treasure. As she closed the door silently behind her, she heard water running in the purifying chamber. Its sound was almost sensual and expected. Cephis had been out among the land for so long without the capability of a natural cleansing. It was the perfect place to present herself to him. They could complete their refinement together as one.

She walked to the purifier slowly and watched as he stood with one hand pressed hard against the stone in front of him, allowing the water to brush over his muscled body like a waterfall. His other hand lay below his waist, moving swiftly back and forth along his penis. Kaleena smiled slightly, which was enough for Cephis to stop.

She inched back a step as he turned to her with an approving smile, once again holding out his hand. Kaleena took a breath, readying herself for what was to come. She let her robe slide down to the floor and took his hand. Cephis guided her into the chamber with respect and honor. The water felt soft and elegant as it sprayed across her skin. She placed her hands to his chest and pressed her genitalia up against his. He guided her chin up to look into her eyes.

This, my love, is the fruit of being. Never forget the taste. He leaned in then and pressed his lips to hers. The taste was sweet and moist. When his tongue invaded her mouth, she simply returned the favor, enjoying the texture of his gums and teeth. Cephis wrapped his hands along her back and then dropped them to her buttocks. She quickly used the support of his hands to wrap her legs around his waist. And as her body was lowered gently to allow his penis to penetrate her body, Kaleena's thoughts sank into a fog. She felt drunk with a rapture that rivaled the taste of a first breath.

Kaleena pulled in that first breath and backed slowly away from the memory. The power of Evey's soul now felt more perfect, and she knew within seconds that Evey had yet to find what she so desperately needed within her. So she swarmed Evey's anger, her trepidation, her lust and her desire and moved deep into the black of her subconscious, where she met Evey's spirit, surrounded by nothing but the lone light of their eyes.

You will never find what you're looking for, Evey, Kaleena whispered.

I will search your soul forever if I must, Evey said.

It will do you no good. You're not powerful enough.

I'm far more powerful than you can imagine, Kaleena.

But your understanding of that power has been weakened under the breath of Gydressina.

Don't speak of her name upon my mind.

I must, for her love has already begun to burn within you, as it burns within me.

She's blinded you, child. She's not the word of love, as she has so effortlessly proclaimed.

Who's lied, Evey? Gydressina didn't punish you for your crimes. She taught you how to live among the world you so desperately wanted to experience, and yet you still defy her name as truth. Cephis is not your savior. He is your darkness.

And it's with him that I shall ascertain the heart of creation.

In which has been born within me.

Yes.

He led me to it.

Yes.

He helped me discover my own living night.

He did.

Hiding under the guise of my lost mother —

(you must sleep now, sweetheart)

— he chose to implant within me the knowledge you so desperately seek.

Your truth in the light and the key to salvation.

Within the void of nothing, you seek to become everything.

And will do all in my power to do so.

Which includes leading me to my death.

It is necessary.

But you don't wish to kill me. I feel your guilt.

You're everything I am not. You were to bear my daughter among my power. I was to teach you and protect you.

Condemn my spirit to your touch of truth. But Gydressina protected me.

No. She protected herself.

Because she knew you wouldn't kill me. She knew you would have no hesitation in destroying the child I would bear; one who would inherit within her the knowledge that you seek, which in your heart would be used to destroy her.

Only to keep her from lying the blanket of deceit upon my people.

Our people.

Precisely.

Instead, she cleansed me, exiling me to my death.

You can see clearly now. Her selfishness has led you here.

As she has led you.

I follow no one, Evey hissed. *And it's in you that I will prove that. Accept your destiny and give in to the death of your mind.*

I've gone far beyond my own mortality and accepted my path long ago. But you will continue to fail because the life you seek can't be found in the mind or of the heart.

What do you speak of?

I speak only of the love the life creates. And thanks to your serpent of knowledge, I was pushed — persuaded — to accept the hand of death and end the fight, the struggle, the resistance of living among my love. That sin, dear Evey, led me to my darkness.

You lie. You protect the light of the life within you.

I must. How else would you explain my miraculous return to life? But I didn't

live with the spirit of the life in my death. Because I was selfish and died for my own purpose, and not for the purpose of another, I was forced to become the pain of nothing.

That's impossible.

Perhaps. But unless you're willing to accept your *mortality and become the darkness in love with me, the knowledge of true grace will elude you for all time and beyond existence.*

Liar. I will find it.

Not if you're unwilling to let me guide you.

Then guide me, Evey said quickly.

I can't do that until you pay witness to my heart.

I will pay my witness.

I believe you would. But you're not ready.

Don't play games with me.

I'm not playing a game. I simply wish to protect you.

Fuck you. Show me what I want to know.

I can't. You don't truly wish to see it.

I must see what it is I must know.

What you'll witness will scar your heart.

I'm ready to be scarred.

It'll burn your soul.

I'm ready to be burned.

It'll eradicate all life within you, and your soul will be lost to the wind.

I'm ready to be erased from existence. Now, show me.

Kaleena's eyes twisted with devilish excitement and pulled Evey through her life — every moment, every breath, every kiss, every hug, every scar. Evey watched it all with wide, unblinking awareness, her heart peeling away like the layers of an onion.

I've spoken with the life itself, Kaleena whispered, causing Evey's ears to burn. *But I did so only because I nurtured and embraced the dark of the night.*

Evey then found herself lying upon the lap of her mother, Jaime, who sat against a tree on top of a hillside, staring out at the ravishing sunset casting the brilliance of its shadow along the lake below. Dry tears painted Evey's eyes with a fresh pinkness. They were both wearing black dresses and she could feel the loss of a loved one —

A father

— haunting her mind. Jaime hand lay on her small round head, unconsciously combing her fingers through her daughter's soft hair.

"Mom?" Evey said.

"Yeah, sweetie?" Jaime responded.

"Where do you go when you die?"

"Where do you think we go?"

Evey smiled, knowing her answer was only given when she didn't want to answer the question. "The Bible says we go to Heaven or Hell."

"Do you believe that?"

Evey pondered a moment. "No."

"So where do you think we go?"

"I don't think we go anywhere."

"What do you mean? You think we just cease to exist."

"No, not that. I just think we stay where we are."

"Like ghosts?" Jaime playfully tickled her daughter. Evey giggled as she tried to get her to stop. When she did, she sat up.

"Look at the sunset," she said. Jaime smiled, unsure of where Evey was headed. "Just look at it." Jaime chuckled and looked to the light orange sky, dancing now with a soft purple and blue. "Do you see the colors? The rays of the sun through the clouds? The quiet shimmer on the water, about to become the moon?"

"I see it," Jaime said, playing along.

"That's what I feel when I think of dying."

Jaime looked at her child. "Keep looking," Evey demanded. Jaime hesitated, but eventually turned back to the sun.

"I believe that *we* are the sun, and when our life ends, our sun sets, just as

you see now. But when that happens, the day hasn't died. It's only been replaced by the night. It simply transformed into something different, something more, hiding itself away to rise once more as something better. The sun gives itself up to the night so that it can regain its power and return stronger, waking, healing and destroying all life."

"Kaleena." Jaime turned to her, needing to see her eyes. "What are you trying to say?"

"I'm saying the night can bring many horrors, but if you know that the day hasn't truly gone away, it'll return to help life grow."

"Are you talking about reincarnation?"

"Forget it," Evey said. She walked down the hill and sat on the edge of the lake, resting her head in her arms. Jaime waited a minute before following, feeling Evey needed a moment to herself.

"Kaleena. I'm trying to understand."

"You can't understand," she said, disappointed more in her normal brain than she was in her mother herself. "It's too complicated."

"Then dumb it down for me," Jaime said, taking her place next to Evey. "Help me understand."

Evey thought about how she could put it into words that Jaime would understand. "I can't. You have to understand what the night means to even begin to understand what I'm talking about."

"Well, help me. What does the night mean?"

Evey could tell Jaime really wanted to grasp the meaning. She took a breath before reluctantly continuing. "You know how they always say that winter's the season of death, and spring's the season of rebirth?"

"Yeah."

"And you know how they always refer to old age as your twilight years?"

"Yeah, okay. So what you're saying is old age is a person's winter."

"In a way, yeah. But that person needs to understand his winter in order to bloom into his spring. You see, night isn't just a time to rest or go out and party, or

sit around and watch television, or roam the streets looking to rob a liquor store, or throw yourself off a bridge. The night needs to be respected, just as the day is. It needs to be held and comforted. It needs to be seen through the glory of what it brings to all living things."

"And what's that?"

"Hope."

Jaime looked quizzically at Evey.

"The night sends you a message that just because the beauty of the day has passed, it doesn't mean another day isn't dawning — a more beautiful day, a more fruitful day."

"Right, like when they say tomorrow's another day."

"No."

Jaime shifted her body. Evey thought she was starting to get it, but knew she'd barely even chipped away the epidermis from the thick iceberg that was her brain. "I'm sorry, Kaleena," Jaime said sincerely. "Why am I wrong? What don't I understand?"

"What most people don't understand," Evey said. "That the night, the winter, and the end of your life deserves respect."

"You think I don't respect death?"

"I know you don't. No one does. Most people take their lives for granted, turn to the Lord at the very last minute in hopes that they can make a last ditch effort to have their sins washed away and get into heaven. They forget all the good things they've done over their lives in favor of what they did wrong, turning the fruits of their labors into regret over how they didn't try more things or explore new adventures. They feel it's too late for them, that when the end comes, they will have wasted their lives away in an office, or didn't have a child to continue their legacy, or didn't put any real effort into anything and simply slid by and did what was necessary to stay alive one more day.

"It's exactly how they view the night. They feel that it will simply wash the previous day away and allow them to start anew. But because they can't respect the night, they simply fall back into the simplicity of their day and live the mundane comfort of their serenity, only to feel remorse when the sun sets again because they wasted yet another day. What people don't realize is that the night doesn't just cleanse your day away. It's there for you to embrace, to take the time and truly say, 'I am the light. I will guide myself through the night and reach the other side unscathed.' Instead, they simply waste it away in sleep, in front of the television, in getting drunk, in sin. What I'm saying is that if you want to embrace the fruits of the day, you need to feed off the night. You have to actively heal your mind in the winter, so that spring can lead to your growth. And you have to live every day with the knowledge that winter does come for us all, but if we're true believers in the night, then death cannot scare us, or blind us from ourselves. We can live forever within it, and use it to show us the light of the sun and return us to the daylight, helping our souls become more than our thoughts can communicate."

The bottom of Jaime's eyes were wet, not so much by what Evey had said, but because the idea was coming from her seven-year-old daughter. As Jaime's father embraced her soul at that moment, Jaime blinked and a tear rolled down her cheek. Evey saw her grief and sat up on her knees, marking her black tights with fresh grass stains. She wiped the tear away with her thumb and then gave her a kiss on the cheek.

"I'm sure grandpa embraced his night," Evey said.

Jaime wrapped her arms around Evey without a word as the sun disappeared behind the horizon, washing their image into the night.

It's not easily explained, but you can understand, Kaleena informed Evey. *It took my death to understand that the night is part* of *the light, not separate from it. All you have to do is* feel *it.* Feel *what death really is.* Taste *the devotion of the soul's willingness to let go and dream, to bring forth the tenderness of a touch, the gentleness of the child's kiss and her warm embrace. You have to feel it. Not see it, not discover it, not reach for it —* feel *it.* Feel *the light in your soul and use it to guide your mind from the darkness.* Feel *the whisper of its grace, of its love. Are you willing to taste the*

fruit of the light and discover the love of your life?

Evey instantly pulled away from Kaleena's kiss and backed away, tumbling to her knees. "I will not accept it," she screamed, holding her head tight as her brain burned inside her skull. "I can't accept it."

But you must. To understand the light and control it, you must embrace your sin and the darkness that is upon you.

No, she screamed, a high-pitch holler that carried through the caverns and made Kaleena wince with irritation. She fought the nuisance off as she tightened her grip on Evey's impassioned memory, pulling it to become one with her own memory of Jaime, tying them together as if they were the same — the love of a mother and a daughter holding one another in the embrace of night attacking the love of a man and a woman, locked in an embrace of lust and fabricated passion. With each thrust of Evey's hips upon Cephis, Evey felt the kiss of Kaleena's tearful touch. It burned Evey's body with a fire that melted her soul into itself, into Cephis, into Jaime, into Kaleena and into the darkness. Blood poured from her nose, mouth and eyes and seeped from her fingertips and as sweat from her pores. It coated her body and dropped her to her knees. She could do nothing as the blood became her spirit, left to dry and turn Evey's soul to dust, leaving nothing but a body, a mere doll found on the edge of a child's bed to be discarded and forgotten in the twilight of adulthood.

Kaleena's body and mind relaxed as Evey's screams faded into a gentle silence. It took her a few minutes to bring her mind back to normal, collect her thoughts and realize where she was. Once she had, she wiped away the blood dripping from her nose and stood, shaky at first, but nevertheless free.

She walked to Evey's body and knelt down, pulling her blood-drenched hair away from her face. She removed the necklace from around her neck and laid it gently in Evey's hand, covering it with her own.

"Sleep well, Evey," she whispered and then gave her a light kiss on the cheek. Her blood tasted sour, yet fruitful, as if she had just eaten a sour Skittle. She cleaned her lips with her tongue, wanting to take in what was left of a corrupted

soul. Then she slid the eyelids over the body's glass eyes and lowered Evey's head, as if in perpetual prayer.

It was then she finally got a good look around the room. She recognized this place from wandering Evey's thoughts. It was used as a hideout, so-to-speak, for those seeking their sexual freedom from Gydressina. Browsing through Evey's memories, she had witnessed several men and women consummate their desires, sometimes gathering in large groups, an orgy not even Cinemax would air. The room was their sanctuary, not only because it was secret and well hidden, but because it had direct access to the halls of Spirited Wind, occasionally using it to harbor fugitives that were being taken there to be held for sentencing. But there was no path out that Kaleena could see except for the stairwell that led back into the city. Even after scanning every one of Evey's memories, she couldn't find her answer. The only thing she could think to do was turn to the memory of Gydressina collapsing the earth upon itself, hiding them, locking them away for good. Kaleena walked to the wall on her right. She touched it and looked into it — looked through it. On the other side was the tunnel she was looking for. She pressed her other hand to the wall and closed her eyes, breathing her spirit into the earth. Before long, pieces fell away as she grinded her spirit through the dirt and the clay, pushing rock and mud into air until the wall gave way and crumbled at her feet. She opened her eyes with a gentle, excited smile and took off into the darkened tunnel, knowing she was just minutes away from reuniting with her family.

Atlantis – Incubation Room – 12 hours 53 minutes after arrival

Diana stood at the console, staring out at the field of incubators. She had been attempting to remember all of the time she had spent with Kara, all the good things her mother had done for her, what her father had given her. But the more she tried, the more they became simply images of a dream. She was starting to trust the memories of the woman grasping to take control more than her own, feeling them with her heart, accepting them as real. But she continued to fight to

believe in the dreams, take them as a life she once lived, one she wished she could return to. A tear rolled down the edge of her nose in sorrow as she lowered her head, needing to wait as long as she could before she ended both growing reality and faded dreams.

Step away.

The growl was deep and threatening. Diana's head shot up to see a giant man standing at the base of the ladder, watching her, breathing her in. She'd never seen him before, yet could feel his presence within her as if she'd known him for a lifetime.

"Cephis," she whispered, her body suddenly flush with goose bumps. She didn't know if it was her fear that caused them or the rush of unrequited elation, but it gave her an odd sense of needing to be with him, to be part of him. The woman of her future wanted to run to him and kiss him — love him — but Diana held onto the remnants of her past and stood strong. Cephis, she knew, was the cause of her death and wanted to watch him burn, as much as she wanted to lay with him.

I said step away.

"No," she said so light, her voice was stolen by the air just inches away from her lips. But Cephis heard her clearly and was holding her up against the back wall before Diana had time to retract her defiance and fall to his feet to beg forgiveness. She could barely draw in a breath as his thick fingers tightened around her neck. He swarmed her body with his mind, tasting her possessor's soul and turning her blood to ice.

Joyais, he said, closing his eyes and drawing in the smell of Diana's ravishing skin, reaching a peak of gratification. When he opened them again, his eyes were dark with lust. *Speak to me,* he said.

Diana felt Joyais reach out for him, trying to tell him how much she loved him. But she suppressed her efforts, pushing Joyais into a soft anger that weakened the dedication and promise Diana had made to her young mind.

"You can't keep me here," Diana yelled at her mother as she stood to leave the room. They had been fighting for the last hour and a half over whether or not to

let her go to Europe. Diana argued her case for why they should let her go, but parents were gracious with inane excuses, like:

"You're just not ready."

"You're just not ready. You're just not ready," Diana said, mimicking them with the not-so-subtle addition of sarcasm. "I'm tired of listening to this shit."

"Diana," her father scolded.

"Dad. I'll be eighteen in two weeks."

"That doesn't make you mature enough to be on your own," her mother said.

"Mature enough? You don't think I'm *mature* enough?"

"No, I don't."

"I'm not a little girl anymore, mom. I'm an adult and I want to live like one. Can you *not* understand that?"

"I can, Diana, but do you even know what living like an adult means?"

"Yes," Diana screamed, leaving everyone in an unnatural silence. Her mother sat down and lowered her head. "Don't you trust me?" Diana said soberly.

"We trust you," her father said, hoping to clarify her mother's argument the best he could. "We just don't feel you know what you're getting yourself into."

Diana shook her head and walked to the fireplace. "Don't you think I've thought this through?" she asked.

"We don't doubt that you have, but we feel you might still be in a bit of a fantasy world where the reality of what happens isn't going to be what you think it'll be."

"That's what you're afraid of?" Diana said, flashing a look at her mother before turning to her father. "That I'm going to be disappointed?"

Her father lowered his head, slightly defeated. When he looked back to Diana, she was staring at him, waiting for a really good answer. "Doing something like this is exciting, we know. It can also be very dangerous, but not as dangerous as going out there with a fool's hope."

"You think I'm a fool?"

"No, sweetie," her father defended. Diana whipped around, refusing to hear his explanation. She leaned her focus more to the pictures on the mantle than

to that of her parents. "Look, we're not opposed to you going out and exploring, and living life like an adult and all that. We just want to make sure you're not just doing it on a whim or for reasons that have nothing to do with you."

"It's not a whim, Dad. That's the point."

"We just want what's best for you," her mother said, finally rejoining the conversation.

"And what's best for me?" Diana asked calmly, reaching for a picture of her and Kara on the mantle. She was about seven in that picture and Kara had just been accepted into Brown. Her parents had treated her to a fancy dinner to celebrate. When they got home, Kara could tell Diana was a little sad and spent the whole night teasing her about Eddie (the little boy that kept picking on Diana at recess), playing dress-up, and watching movies that Diana wasn't supposed to be watching. They took the picture somewhere in the middle of it all in memory of the occasion.

"To be more like Kara?" she finished.

The silence was enough of an answer. She set the picture down, disappointed. "Well, I'm sorry I let you down." She left the room, mumbling one last testament to her determination. "I'm going on this trip. Live with it."

Her mother tried to stop her as she started up the stairs. She pulled away, but then stopped. Her legs wouldn't move anymore and she felt slightly sick. She closed her eyes and knelt down to relax her stomach. When she was calm enough to open her eyes, Kara was pulling her out of her crib. She wrapped her baby sister in her arms and rocked her up and down. But Diana was stubborn and wouldn't stop crying. There was no reason for it, she just felt like it. Kara never got mad, or frustrated, or stressed. All Diana felt in her touch and her voice was a calm demeanor that did eventually relax and comfort her to the point of serenity.

Once the whimpering had stopped, Kara sat down in the rocking chair that her grandmother had used to rock her mother to sleep when she was fidgety like this, and just held her baby sister. She sang to her, a sweet and loving song. Diana felt much better. With the tune hovering over her, Diana fell back to sleep. Before

she was fully encased in dreamland, Kara stopped singing, and instead, turned to talking to her. Diana wasn't sure what she was talking about — it could have been a story about a princess, or what had happened to her in school that day — but it didn't matter. Diana liked listening to Kara's voice. All she wanted was to stay safe and warm within it.

"Let it come," Kara said sweetly, kissing Diana on the forehead. "Let the sandman take you away into the dreams of your heart. Let peace take you away and allow who you are to rise and become." Kara's voice slowly grew darker and colder as she spoke. It wasn't pleasant, and Diana cried once more with the hand of death on her mind. She opened her eyes and caught the glowing darkness of Cephis. His hand combed through her bangs, yet she felt his need to take her body. But as much as Joyais struggled to erase that final memory, Diana held onto it with a grip stronger than steel, piercing her teeth together to fight until they were all dead.

"I will not let your bitch take control, you dickless motherfucker," she yelled, replaying her dying memory over and over again, watching it flicker away and then flash back to fruition. The grip around her neck grew tighter as she fought. Cephis could take away her final breath for all she cared, just so long as Joyais remained as dead to him as her youth had become to her.

Atlantis – Glass Corridor – 12 hours 53 minutes after arrival

"Let go of me, you fucks." Jaime screamed a series of yelps and grunts until the presence of a man leaning his frail and sweaty body up against the frame of the door silenced her. His eyes were tainted yellow and outlined in thick, red scars. They looked worn and almost dead, but at the same time, quite attentive. His hair was dark and wet, a little bit of dry blood coated throughout. His veins were embossed along most of his skin, the lines of purple painting his features with grotesque paleness.

"Damn you to hell, Jaime," the man said, his voice raspy and barely audible.

"Who the fuck are you?" Jaime demanded, arduously trying to pull away from her captors.

"I go by many names," he said, sliding into the hall. His feet dragged along the floor, unable to lift his knees in fear of snapping them completely. "I am Adamus, I am Henry..."

Henry, Jaime thought. *Could it be the same guy that knocked up Lauren?*

"Very intuitive," he breathed out. "But the name I was given upon my birth from my dear keeper's womb..."

The man dropped to his knee and groped Jaime's chin. His touch froze her body in place. She couldn't feel anything.

"...is Caistepher."

His breath smelled of death and rotten eggs. Squeezing her eyes shut and holding her breath was all she could do to keep from vomiting all over him. "What do you want?" she eked out, staying tough before him.

"You're here to take the life of the city," he said slowly, his eyes looking over her like snakes wrapping around a tree limb. "I've been ordered to stop you."

"Good luck," Jaime said, then spit into his eye.

Caistepher chuckled and huffed at the air, sounding much like a sick old man who can't get that last piece of phlegm out of his throat.

"What's so fucking funny?"

"It's a delight to feel your fire," Caistepher said, "though I'll admit. I had hoped it would be your husband or your daughter standing here in front of me. Nonetheless, I'm going to enjoy devouring your soul."

Caistepher tightened his grip. His rotted smile and his gurgled laughter ended abruptly as he stared into her eyes. Jaime felt herself being pulled from her body. She tried to hold on, resist his kiss, but everything she tried seemed to make it easier for him to take her. Finally, she allowed it to happen, giving him what he sought. She pressed her lips to his and sucked in his breath, tasting the light touch of his tongue. Benjamin was everything she remembered him to be, and her body was ready to have him once again.

They spent over two hours loving one another and an additional hour holding each other. They felt the power of their hearts beat as one. Jaime had just fallen asleep when a song broke through her dream and rapped her back to reality. She snapped upright, pulling her head from Benjamin's chest and waiting a moment to figure out where the noise was coming from. It was the ringtone of her cell phone. The song was abruptly cut off with a loud chime. She rubbed her eyes and looked back to Benjamin. She was about ready to lie back down when the phone rang again. Frustrated, Jaime slid her legs off the bed, the cold night air nipping them with a bite of frost, and grabbed her phone, hoping Benjamin wouldn't wake up. She looked at the caller I.D.: "Matthew." Extreme annoyance set in.

"What is it?" she whispered, sleep beckoning to take her away.

"Where are you?" Matthew said.

"None of your business," Jaime said, ignoring Matthew's low, sad voice.

"We can't do this, Jaime." This time, Jaime did notice a small crack in his voice, as if he'd been crying.

"What's wrong?" she whispered, her heart beginning to beat much faster. The silence on the other end of the phone was frightening. She thought maybe he'd hung up, or the connection had been lost, so she checked her phone. It was still on. She was no longer tired as she feared the worst. When she placed the phone back to her ear, she was about to ask him her question again when she heard him say,

"She's dead…"

Jaime raised her hand to her mouth and stopped breathing. Her first thought was her mother, or his mother, or a good friend of theirs that had accidentally fallen in the shower and cracked her skull open. But Matthew's voice was much sadder than any of those possibilities. She knew exactly who he was talking about, but there was no way she would allow herself to believe it until she heard him say it.

"Who?" she said through a choked cough. "Who's dead?"

"You left her and now she's…"

Matthew's voice trailed off. It wasn't long before she heard the phone click. Her breaths had become erratic as she lowered the phone to see her desktop staring

back at her. He hadn't said her name, but he had said enough. According to Matthew, Kaleena was dead. But how was that possible? What had he done to her?

What had she *done to her?*

Jaime sat sobbing silently for the next fifteen minutes. Not entirely over Kaleena, but also over what her involvement in Kaleena's death may have entailed. It hadn't been three days since she stepped into that cab and now her extremely healthy, eleven-year-old daughter was dead?

You left her, she kept replaying in her head. But Kaleena was far too smart to do something so stupid as to kill herself, especially over something as simple as this. Was that the problem? Had Jaime ignored the complexity of Kaleena's mind and forgotten that she was different? What seemed reasonably simple to Jaime could have become extremely complicated for Kaleena, simply because it was so simple. Could she have allowed herself to waste away because she couldn't understand that she would still be there for her, even if she didn't see her every day? Could Jaime's betrayal of Kaleena's inherent trust erase all of her will to live?

It was devastating for her to even think about. At the same time, it was destroying her to think that Matthew was dealing with all of it alone. He didn't deserve to lose everything he cares about like this. She had left him with Kaleena so it would give him something to remember her; still have someone to care for and to care for him. But somehow she had inadvertently taken his daughter away from him by removing herself from their lives. It hurt her to know that she had done such a thing to someone she still loved, and someone she now could only love in memory. She needed to do something for him. Merely going back to him certainly wouldn't be enough, but perhaps allowing him her love once more would eventually help him find the courage to trust her again, though she highly doubted it. He clearly blamed her for Kaleena's death —

You left her

— but she wasn't willing to let him fall into the same darkness Kaleena had fallen into. Not if she could help it.

Clearing her face of all moisture, Jaime got dressed and quietly packed all of her things. She stood next to Benjamin for several minutes, not wanting to leave him again, but unable to face him with Kaleena's death on her heart. He was a good man, but he was not her love. He couldn't be.

After finally being able to say goodbye, she leaned down and gave him a gentle kiss on the corner of his lips. She then left without once looking back, and without one drop of regret. She was going home, where she belonged.

It could have taken her about a day to get back, but in fear over what she would say to Matthew when she arrived, it took her much longer. She'd constantly pull her rental car over on the highway and think over what Matthew must be going through. Sometimes it was for just a few minutes, hoping to understand what he might say when he saw her, sometimes it was hours of crying over Kaleena and her smile, her joy; her passionate heart. She wouldn't drive at night, but wouldn't sleep either, unable to stop her brain from flourishing with old memories. She hardly ate, as her guilt seemed to shrink her stomach and expel anything she struggled to swallow. But it was the hours she spent with her thumb over the 'Send' button that kept her away from him, even though she knew no matter how slow she went, and how much time she wasted, she was eventually going to arrive.

Four nights after leaving Benjamin, Jaime sat in her car outside of her apartment, again going over possible scenarios of seeing Matthew again. When he opened the door after her gentle knock, he'd instantly bring her into his arms, rejoicing her return with a sense of gratification that he now had someone to talk to, someone to live for and love. Kaleena would never leave their thoughts or their life, but at least they'd have one another to help each other heal. Or else he'd sit and yell at her for leaving the whole time, making her feel guiltier, her tears streaming as she tried over and over to apologize for her mistake —

(*Mistake*, she figured he would say. *You killed your fucking daughter because you were too chickenshit to raise her*)

— and convince him that she never meant for Kaleena to give up her life because of her own personal selfishness.

That was, of course, if Matthew didn't just slam the door in her face the moment he saw her. Each scenario frightened her, keeping her from getting out of the car to face the inevitable. But there was no denying she wanted her husband to be protected and happy. To do that, she had to accept her responsibility; she had to stop running. She had spent too much time fearing her future and had to face the truth of her darkened thoughts — the death of her only child.

Jaime wiped her eyes and her nose with the sleeve of her jacket before finally stepping out of the car. She took a brave breath as she stared at her fate. But before she had the chance to close the car door, a cab pulled up to the building. She retracted herself into the soft shadows surrounding her and watched as Matthew got out of the cab. What was odd was he didn't close the door and head up to his apartment right away. Instead, he reached into the cab to escort a young girl out. She looked extremely frail and tired, and for a moment, Jaime didn't want to believe it. But she couldn't deny her own eyes. The girl turned in Jaime's direction. The dirty yellow glow from the lamplight highlighted her face for Jaime to see. Kaleena was alive and stood just thirty yards away. All she needed to do was scream out for her, get her attention; make everything better with a simple smile.

But she chose silence, allowing Matthew to help Kaleena walk slowly into the building. He treated her with the delicacy of a rare porcelain artifact, taking extra care to make sure she didn't break or fall, or vanish from his sight.

After they disappeared into the building, Jaime fell back into her car and slammed the door shut. She sat for some time, wondering what happened, wondering if Matthew had lied to her about the whole thing to get back at her for leaving him. But that couldn't be; he had been broken — she heard it in his voice. So what did it mean? Had she returned from the brink of death through some incredible miracle in order to keep Matthew from falling into her death?

Whatever had transpired, they appeared to be new, happy. Why else would Matthew have neglected to call her to tell her she was okay? She was sure he would eventually, but why wait unless they had admitted they didn't need her after all? What would they say now if she returned? Could they ever forgive her?

The questions sent fresh new tears across her face for the next hour. When she calmed enough to drive safely, her heart urged her to stay, but her mind told her to leave. Going back now would be the right thing to do until the honeymoon ended and she was right back to where she was before she left — bitter with a need for freedom. There was no guarantee they would accept her even if they did invite her back. And leaving them again was not something she wanted to do — or feel — ever again. She would just have to do what she set out to do in the first place and sever all ties to her past in order to start anew. Not just Matthew, not just her old life, but Benjamin, her parents, and every friend she'd ever known as well. She had to essentially disappear for some time and organize her life before she attempted to rescue what was left of her past.

It was 1:17 in the morning when she left Matthew and Kaleena for the last time. As she drove without sleep for the next thirty-three hours, she believed she would never talk to either Matthew or Kaleena ever again, and didn't — not until she heard her daughter's voice three years later, helping her to make what would become the best decision she had ever made.

Jaime pulled away from Caistepher, finding the strength to tear her spirit from his grasp and reconnect it to both her mind and her heart. She opened her eyes and felt a knife of fear slice through him.

"Fuck you, Caistepher." She slammed him in the nose with her forehead, sending him flailing to the ground. It wasn't clear how, but she suddenly felt the souls of the other men surrounding her and was able to ignite their veins with an electrical shock that burned their skin. The men gripping Jaime let go of her and fell to the ground, trying to stop the pain from coursing their bodies. Upon their release, Jaime raced for the door.

She never made it.

Caistepher tackled her against the wall just inches before, grabbing her neck and growling through his teeth. "Fucking bitch," he said as he stroked his nose across her neck. "You think you can stop me? You think you're better than me?"

Jaime couldn't say anything. It turns out she didn't have to. When Caistepher

tried again to enter her body, she pushed him out with ease. But this time, she was able to attach herself to his weakened mind. She replaced images of death and lust and pain and sexual hunger with thoughts of her and Matthew, her and Benjamin, and everything she could think of that displayed affection, kindness and sacrifice — which included her brother, Steven.

Caistepher screamed as the madness set in. Before he lost all physical power, he slugged Jaime in the face and slammed her hard against the glass, splitting her head open in the process. "You cannot beat me," he yelled over the fading screams of the other men, who either fainted or died due to the pain of the fire within them.

Jaime felt dazed as blood spilled down the glass and around her neck. It traced its way around the collar of her wetsuit and pooled at the base of her throat, eventually dripping down between her breasts. Caistepher licked the stream of cooling blood past her breasts and onto her neck, then pulled away and savored it. After swallowing the sweet nectar, he leaned in again to finish collecting her dying soul.

Past his shoulder, in the glass behind him, Jaime saw reflections of Kaleena and Matthew, Patricia and Trishen, Benjamin and Gavin; each a flash in her mind, each smiling and playful; young and free; loving and perfect. She closed her eyes to draw in as much energy as she could muster. When she opened them with a newfound surge of life, standing on the other side of the glass, smiling and waving at his little sister, was Steven. A tear rolled past her nose as she finally realized she was home. Taking in Steven's spirit, Jaime pressed her palm to the wall.

"Fuck the devil 'til his ass bleeds," she whispered and sent a powerful pulse of vitality into the glass. It instantly shattered and brought the sea in to collect its bounty. At the same time, the still water in the wading pool shot skyward. It struck the ceiling, causing it to crack and bleed with light. It didn't take long for the ceiling to come crashing down. The light of youth flooded the room and poured into the water, collecting it, becoming it. But with nothing to contain it, the light quickly fell back unto itself, burning hotter and hotter. As the ocean began to boil, the light expanded outward and erupted, sending an explosive blast across the tower and a shockwave of destruction throughout the city. Building

upon building collapsed and exploded as the light filled the materials with its uncontained power.

The flames of the ocean burned through Jaime as she gleefully watched the city crumble. But it didn't hurt. Her soul simply lifted from her body as the future presented itself with the past and millions of lives she had just saved became part of her existence. There was nothing left for her now but to slip into slumber with a loving smile and Kaleena's visage implanted within the spirit of the life.

Atlantis – Underground Tunnel – 13 hours 00 minutes after arrival

Kaleena tripped and fell, rolling a few feet and hitting the wall as an explosion ripped through her heart. She pressed her hands to her chest and let out a short scream, trying hard to make the pain stop. When it did, all she felt was Jaime's smile, her love and her sacrifice. Kaleena rolled her legs up tightly to her chest.

"Mom," she whispered and wept.

Remember me, Jaime whispered through the air. *I will always love you.*

Why? Kaleena pleaded.

Because I finally understood the night, she said, the echo of her words sending Kaleena deeper into tears.

I love you, Kaleena said.

Always remember. And Jaime was gone.

Kaleena held herself for another few minutes, letting all of her pain over Jaime's death, Evey's power and Lauren's sacrifice wash from her body. The release of it all gave her a brand new vitality she thought she'd never acquire — true, unadulterated courage. She would miss her mother greatly, but had to be brave enough to fight the pain and finish what she'd started. Matthew was still alive and he was coming for her. She had to stand up; she had to reach him and protect him from the final danger that was currently growing in rage as the life she'd been connected to for so long dissipated, leaving her cold and somewhat alone. There

was no time to mourn. Cephis was vulnerable and she would lose much more if she became the child in the mirror —

I didn't want to live anymore…

I've been running…

I've been tasting…

I've been deep in the dark of…

"My life," she whispered. She stood and took in a deep breath, embracing all that she was and all that she could be. Her mother had started the fall; now it was her mission to complete it.

Atlantis – Incubation Room – 13 hours 00 minutes after arrival

Cephis roared an agonizing shriek, releasing a flash of fire through Diana's body, which forced Joyais to cower in fear within the shadows of her host's fading memory. Diana's mind relaxed as Cephis grabbed his chest and loosened his grip on her. She fell against the wall as he collapsed to his knees.

Diana took a minute to reacquire her senses. Joyais was no longer fighting her, but her essence had taken hold of her body. She knew that once Joyais found the courage to rise back up, she'd be lost to her forever, her own memories having been completely distinguished by Cephis's ejaculation. Diana was still alive, but a shell. The time had come to do what she had set out to do.

As Cephis bent forward, hissing and fighting the crushing weight of his spirit, Diana crawled her way to the console and placed both hands upon it. She then sought out Joyais and used her to connect to the incubators, becoming every inch of the machine and every life that had once lived within them.

"Stay safe, Kara. I'll love you always." With her final breath, Diana ignited the current running through the veins of the device. She felt the spark of the explosion before her soul was permanently extinguished.

Atlantis – Outside Spirited Wind Tunnels – 12 hours 53 minutes after arrival

Mathew hadn't noticed he was running until he saw two large oak trees in front of him. They sat nearly four feet apart and their branches converged between them, forming an archway that led his sights through the gateway from the natural to the manufactured. Gydressina was in front of him, gliding swiftly along until she reached the trees. She slid up to one of them, and if Matthew didn't know any better, seemed to actually become it, camouflaging herself like a giant gecko. Without thinking, Matthew fell against the tree on the opposite side. Patricia joined him, grabbing his shoulder to help stop herself (and in Matthew's mind, to brace her nerve). Gydressina peered ever so slightly around the trunk of the tree to look into the room beyond them. She held her stance for some time without saying a word or moving a muscle. Matthew began to get curious, as did Patricia, who kept trying to look past him into the room. Matthew pushed her back and held up his finger (*"Just a minute"*) to keep her off his back. Once he was satisfied that she'd given up trying to look, Matthew lowered himself to the ground and peered into the room.

The sparse light gave the sterile space a soft, cold blue hue. Marching in two lines in opposite directions were a dozen men, crossing each other in front of a secondary door exactly opposite the opening Matthew was looking through. They paced approximately ten yards before pulling an about face and crossing one another again. The exit the men were guarding looked to be nothing but a deep black hole, but Matthew knew better. There was a stairwell there that led below the city to an area he knew all too well.

"What's so important about that?" Patricia mumbled. Matthew finally felt her leaning on his back, straining to get a good look at the room.

He pushed her off him. "Quiet," he said, flashing a quick look to Gydressina. She was still frozen in place, her eyes motionless; lifeless. "It's where Gydressina was being held," he whispered. "It's probably the safest place in the city, especially when it starts coming down."

"Well how the hell are we supposed to get through that bunch of warthogs?"

"I don't know," Matthew said, a bit annoyed. "Why don't you head on in there and sing 'em a song? It would probably scare the daylights out of 'em!"

Matthew expected a hot temper, but what he got back was a hearty laugh, one Matthew knew the men had heard. He quickly covered her mouth and looked at her as if he was going to rip her head off. When he turned back to the room, what he saw confused and surprised him. The men had dropped to the ground, some to their knees trying to fight off some sudden dizziness, others just outright falling asleep. After the last guard finally couldn't fight it anymore and passed out, Matthew looked to Gydressina. She blinked as if she had finally returned to her own body.

"Can you teach me that?" Patricia said as Gydressina turned to them "I'd love to give my daughter a dose every now and then."

Gydressina smiled — the first genuine smile Matthew could remember ever seeing from her — and then said, "We must hurry. The city's about to come down."

"Is Jaime okay?"

"Go," Gydressina commanded, pushing him into the enormous hall. She did the same to Patricia, then followed after them, taking a moment to ingest and savor the smell of the foliage that had served her well for all of existence. It would live on long after her body had died, but it was the last time she would be able to inhale its life through her human form, a sense she was sad to have to let go. She would have liked to have remained right where she was as she passed over, but she had one last thing to do before she let her body expire.

Matthew had almost reached the black hole when Gydressina stepped from her creation into man's. She got a few yards into the room before she felt Jaime's hand rest upon her heart and send a pulse through her soul that nearly ripped it from her body. She dropped to her knees to brace for the pain. When it hit, she embraced it, pulling her spirit, her life and her death into her heart, which beat quick — *thumpthump-thump-thumpthump-thump* — as her body fell to the ground —

Dead.

Matthew stopped at the edge of the door and reached out for Patricia. He saw Gydressina's head smack the metallic floor near the first of the twelve guards. His eyes nearly bulged from his head, prompting Patricia to turn around.

"Ah, shit," she said and ran to Gydressina as fast as her cramping legs could carry her. "Bitch better not be dead," she mumbled as she labored to her knees. A small score of blood had started to stain the floor. Patricia saw the small cut on her forehead as she pulled the body against her shoulder. She set her ear to Gydressina's chest and heard a gently singing beat. "That'a girl," she said, pulling Gydressina's legs in tight to her body.

Matthew stayed at the door, too stunned to move. His energy returned as a soft kiss was presented to the corner of his mouth. He wasn't sure what it meant, but it gave him a second life. He wasn't willing to break it again. He raced to Patricia as she rose to her feet, Gydressina draped across her arms.

"Thanks for the help, there, muscles," she said, straining a bit.

"Is she dead?" he asked, reaching for her neck to find a pulse.

"She's alive," Patricia huffed. Gydressina's weight felt like she was a two-ton bowling ball, but Patricia could be carrying a feather and complain about having to run with it. "But if this is what I think it is, we're about to be majorly fucked."

Though Matthew looked about ready to throw up, he held his composure and nodded. "And we don't need that to happen, do we?" he said.

"Always better when I can avoid it."

Matthew chuckled and looked up to the ceiling. He gave Jaime a respectful smile, closed his eyes and said a quick prayer that he knew only Jaime could hear.

"She did good, kid," Patricia said softer than she ever had, and ever would again.

"She did," he said, trying hard to remember that final kiss one last time.

"Well, I hate to the Whoopi here, but I already drowned twice today and I always promised myself that would be my limit."

Matthew smiled. "Yeah. I'd like to keep my drowning to a minimum, too. Let's get the hell out of Dodge." He stayed close to Patricia as she stomped and

wobbled her way back toward the stairwell.

"Matthew!"

Matthew and Patricia stopped just before reaching the black hole. Someone ran toward them as best they could. At first, Matthew wasn't sure if it was really her or if it was simply a figment of his imagination. It couldn't be, as it was clear Patricia saw the same thing he did.

"Kara?" he whispered, taking a few cautious steps toward her.

"Matthew," she said again. As she hit the soft haze of the lights, Matthew felt relieved to know it was really her and that she'd made it back to them, if slightly damaged.

"Kara," he said louder, meeting her with an embrace of loving friendship.

"God, I'm glad I found you." She kissed him on the cheek. "Where's Jaime?" His eyes told her everything. "Oh, my god," she said raising her hand to her mouth. "I'm so sorry."

"She's okay," he admitted, taking a knowing peek back to the ceiling. "She's okay." Kara knew exactly what he was talking about.

Suddenly, an explosion rocked the room. Kara grabbed hold of Matthew and pulled him low to the ground. Patricia almost slipped and fell down the stairs, but caught herself, able to hold Gydressina close. She looked past Matthew and Kara to the light glow highlighting the far end of the hallways leading out of the room.

As the echo of the explosion waned, Kara lowered her head into Matthew's shoulder, hiding her tears. "Bye, Diana," she whispered as Matthew squeezed his arms around her, feeling her loss through the shake of her body.

"Hey guys," Patricia finally called out, ripping through the quiet. "Explosion. Water. Drowning. Any of this ringing a bell?"

Matthew pulled Kara to her feet. "We need to move," he said. Kara didn't argue. She wiped her eyes clean and limped for the door, Matthew keeping his hand on her back for support the whole way.

"Hey, Reeses," Patricia said as they met her at the stairwell. "Good to see you

again." Kara saw the remorse in her eyes. She flashed her a quick smile before heading down the stairs, slowly and cautiously.

"Go," Matthew said, urging Patricia to follow her. As she did, a low rumble grew like a rising earthquake, producing a piercing constriction in his chest. Matthew turned around and saw another figure stride through the halls like a shadow, fire consuming him like a torch. Smoke wafted from him like it was running scared. Matthew felt the death of thousands of souls upon his body.

"Ah, shit," he said, his voice weak and cold, then ran into the hole with a pulse that raced even faster. When he reached the bottom of the stairwell, Patricia and Kara were resting against the far wall, waiting for him.

"It's about time," Patricia said as he emerged into the cavern's light.

"No time," he said, pushing Patricia to move. He yanked Kara to her feet. She hissed as she stumbled on her bad ankle.

"What's wrong," Patricia said, almost losing her grip on Gydressina.

"He's coming," Matthew said, trying his damnedest to stay calm and as close to the others as he could.

"Who's coming?"

That's when Kara and Patricia heard the low rumble and felt the heat of their imminent fall into the shadows of life. The halls grew dark and the energy of the city become extremely stale.

"Fuck me," Patricia said for Kara, each one forming a renewed adrenaline to outrun the reaper.

Matthew shot through the halls without looking back, the need to survive outweighing the need to protect. He reached the open gateway of Spirited Wind, believing in his heart he would find Kaleena waiting for him, ready to save him from his penitence. He would hug her as if he were hugging love itself and return her to the family she lost long ago. But when he ran inside, it was as if he had run into his tomb. He fell to his knees, his legs burning, his heart breaking. As he caught his breath and tried to figure out why Gydressina had lied to him, Kara and Patricia returned to the forefront of his thoughts. Their

absence pushed him to stand back up and do what he knew Jaime wouldn't have hesitated to do.

He ran back out into the cavern halls. No one was there. Was he too late? If he was, their death would be on his hands. But he didn't feel their deaths as he had Jaime's. In his gut, he knew they were still running; and so would he. As Matthew was about to start climbing the small hill that kept Spirited Wind hidden even farther from the actual base of the city, Kara hopped and skipped her way over the top. Patricia wasn't too far behind.

"Kara," he yelled. "Patricia. Hurry."

Just before Kara joined Matthew at the bottom, another small explosion at the base of the hill threw both of them to the ground in opposite directions. Patricia dropped to one knee and lowered her upper body to protect Gydressina as best she could from the rising dust and rock that filled the corridor. She started sliding down the hill a bit, but caught herself before she completely turned over to roll down like an out-of-control snowball. She was the first one to look up and see Kaleena step through the wall like the savior she was destined to become.

"Dad," she called out, dropping down to him as he coughed the dust from his lungs.

"Kaleena?" he said. He cleared his eyes. The radiant face of his daughter shone down upon him. His smile grew brighter than the sun as he gave her a long, affectionate hug. "My god, you're okay."

"Was there ever any doubt?" she said, winking before her eyes lit up with dread. She looked up past Patricia to the growing darkness that was now beginning to consume the top of the hill. "Oh, God," she said, feeling Cephis's newborn soul for the first time. She turned back to Matthew, her face white. "We need to get out of here."

She helped Matthew to his feet, who quickly went to Kara and did the same. "Can you keep going?" he asked, about ready to lift her into his arms.

"I'm okay," she said. Matthew wasn't buying it, so he pulled Kara's arm around his neck and become her second leg.

Kaleena waited for Patricia to reach the bottom of the hill and immediately moved some of Gydressina's hair from her face.

"She's alive," Patricia said, a little unsure of her own words.

Kaleena looked at her a moment longer. Patricia was right. Gydressina's presence had faded but still glowed vibrantly within her rapidly beating heart. It was clear she was preserving what life she had left in order to protect them all one last time. "I know," Kaleena said confidently. "Now let's get moving."

"You don't have to tell me twice," Patricia said, taking one last look at the swimming smoke behind her. Cephis's growing need for vengeance and his taste for the blood of the weak turned her stomach. She ran past Kaleena, then stopped. "Hey, genius bar," Patricia called out, breaking her state of hypnosis. "Stop daydreaming and move your ass."

Kaleena shifted backward as the darkness nearly touched her feet. When she reached Patricia, she turned and ran, quickly catching up to Matthew, who wasn't willing to leave them all behind again. Patricia was hot on her heels (or would be if she could run faster than a turtle with a refrigerator on its back). The black fog had nearly reached out to take hold of her as the rest of the group filed through the gateway of Spirited Wind.

"Help me get these closed," Kaleena yelled to Matthew, the low rumble of Cephis beginning to overwhelm their auditory senses. She started pushing one of the doors closed as Matthew let go of Kara — who was too enamored by the walls to even care — and pushed the second door closed along with her. Patricia just barely squeezed through before Kaleena and Matthew fought the pressure of the haunting darkness to lock the doors shut, cutting off a bit of the black mist. Kaleena placed a hand on each door and rested her forehead to the opening between them. The doors started melting together at the seam. When they had been fused into one large piece of wood, Kaleena slid back to Matthew. He wrapped his arm around her shoulder and pulled her closer.

"It's not going to last long," Kaleena said, feeling the fire on the other side.

Suddenly, an explosion rang through the hall, causing bits of dust and small

pieces of rock to fall away from around the doorframe. Everyone ducked in anticipation of something far worse, except Kara, who was far too mesmerized by the inscriptions even hear the explosion. She was so awestruck, in fact, that she didn't even register the black fog inhabiting the air around her. It brushed into her lungs and the chill of acceptance upon her mind.

"What do we do?" Matthew asked Kaleena.

"Whatever it is, can we do it quick?" Patricia said, nearly out of breath. "This chick is killin' me."

Head for the prison.

Kaleena looked to Patricia, who was standing near what used to be a glass doorway. She smiled, knowing what Gydressina had planned.

"This way," she said as another explosion rocked the door. She grabbed Matthew's hand and pulled him to the cavern. Patricia followed them inside but was stopped by Matthew. He was looking around for something. Or someone.

"Kara," he called out, pulling his hand away from Kaleena.

Kara continued to scour the walls with her eyes, running her fingers over the carvings and reading the texts that filled her mind with wonder. Matthew tried to pull her to safety, but she wouldn't budge, instead pushing him away to keep looking at her new love.

"Do you know what this is?" she said under her breath.

"Yeah, but we don't have time for this," Matthew scolded.

"Matthew," she said, reluctantly turning away from the wall. "Have you read this? Those tablets were just the beginning. This is the birth of a new world. I mean, this text alone will make us famous. We can't just leave it."

Another explosion rocked the door, this one much harder and louder.

"I hate to break it to you, but we can't be famous if we're dead."

"Dad, come on," Kaleena called out, staying as close to the cavern as possible.

"We can come back for it." Matthew pulled Kara's arm. She ripped it away and slapped him with every ounce of strength she had.

"No," she screamed. "*I* need this."

It was clear Matthew wasn't getting through to her, but Kaleena knew he wouldn't come back without her. "Do something," she pleaded to her only other ally.

Patricia jumped slightly from the next explosion, appearing frightened as hell. But Kaleena's desperate eyes coaxed her to grow a pair of healthy, hairy balls. She sat Gydressina against the wall and stormed over to Kara, gearing up her hands to slap her around a bit — knock her out if she had to — in order to convince her to leave it alone. She stepped in between her and the wall and forcefully grabbed her arms.

"We don't have time for this, Reeses." An explosion ripped through the air, louder and more intense, lighting a streak of fire through each of them as rocks fell from the ceiling. "You hear that, huh? That's death literally pounding his way in here. I promise you — we will come back to collect all of this shit whenever you want. I'm on board. But we have to go."

"I need to know," Kara said, her eyes beaming in a firm trance.

"Need to know what?"

"This. This. I need it. I need all of it."

Patricia rolled her eyes until you could see just the whites underneath her pupils. "Sorry for this," she finally said and slapped Kara with the might of a sledgehammer. Not once, but twice. She then grabbed a hold of her chin and forced her to look at her. "Snap out of it, Reeses, you hear me. Snap out of it, or swear to God, I will shove my very own lightning bolt up your ass."

Kara stood inert as a louder, more powerful explosion bent the center of the door inward. She blinked. Then flashed a smile. Her indignation had been washed away. Relief poured through Patricia's veins. She took her new friend's arm and escorted her into the cavern. Matthew followed them as a fresh explosion bent the door even farther, dropping larger pieces of debris to the ground. A wind started twisting through the room, collecting dust and rock. Kara and Patricia ran deeper into the cavern as the wind pushed Matthew forward. He grabbed Kaleena and covered her on the ground.

The explosions became more numerous, the wind harder and the rumble louder. That was when Kaleena saw the fingers on Gydressina's right hand begin tapping the floor as if she were playing a grand concerto. The light she still had stored in her heart spilled through her fingertips and melted into the earth. When it had all been consumed, Gydressina's hand stopped cold. Kaleena's eyes watered as her mentor's heart stopped, leaving Gydressina's body — created through Lauren's selfless sacrifice — nothing but a stone among the cave.

Amen Dello Keli, Kaleena whispered before covering her ears to ward off what she could of the final explosion that ripped through the room. Pieces of the door struck the wall in all places like sharpened shrapnel. The wind picked up even harder. Within seconds, the dark fog had seeped into the room to devour Spirited Wind. A hint of fear rose within Kaleena as she peeked out from under Matthew, her chest constricted (as she felt in Matthew as well). What she saw was a small flash of light at the edge of the entry to the prison, rebuilding the glass that had once disappeared from existence. Kaleena felt the molecules from within the wind, dust and the fog being collected as building blocks to create the triple-thick glass. Gydressina was using herself as a shield until the glass had a chance to completely reform, shutting everyone off from the wind, the noise and the darkness.

Everyone stayed deathly still as they tried to find their strength in the now deafening silence. Kaleena was the first to finally move, gently pushing Matthew away. He reluctantly let go and sat against the wall. A flame shot through the fog to rest on the glass, burning hatred and contempt. Kaleena stared hard at the flames and saw a pair of hands within them. They were scarred and bleeding, the fingernails long and yellowed. Cephis attacked her, his hands clawing at her as he tried desperately to rip her spirit apart. Her heart shriveled in upon itself as she started to slip into unconsciousness. She coughed up a bit of blood as the glass cracked at the base of Cephis's palms.

"No!" She pulled a fresh new energy from the earth, from Gydressina, from Jaime and from Lauren to knock Cephis from her body. She coughed again and spit out more blood before going straight for the glass. Matthew reached out for her, but fell back, his strength weakened by Cephis's mind. The moment Kaleena placed her hands on top of Cephis's, she felt Gydressina within the glass and used her spirit to heal the cracks. The dark power that radiated through those small fractures, though, scorched her palms, making it harder to keep Cephis from extending the web outward and infiltrating her increasingly vulnerable mind. He entered her body, mixing his memories with hers. Touching Cephis's true soul — a black fog fueled by the sin of deception, his mind full of nothing but sharp aggression — sent her into a deepening hopelessness. His maddening betrayals ate at her. She couldn't breathe. She was dying in his arms, slowly becoming aware of the pointlessness of it all, ready to give into him, to do as he wanted.

It turns out Kyla had the same experience as she sat on the edge of the bed in just her bathrobe and slippers. Her head was low, her eyes averted from the monster that stood over her petrified body. Kaleena examined every inch of her vulnerability as she brushed a piece of the young girl's just washed hair behind her ear.

"Do not be frightened," Kaleena said, then closed Kyla's bedroom door.

Kyla took the opportunity to comfort herself by tying her arms together tight in front of her. But nothing worked to fight the despair that filled the room.

"You cannot fight it," Kaleena said. "So you might as well accept your fate."

"Fuck you," Kyla said through her teeth, her eyes watering.

"I don't like this tone, Kyla." Kaleena stepped up to her. She ran her finger along her prey's cheek, but Kyla pulled away. Kaleena suppressed a surge of anger and grabbed Kyla's chin, pulling her within an inch of her lips. "If you do not do as I ask, Kaleena is as good as dead. Do you want that? Do you want to see your best friend die?"

Kyla tried pulling away, but Kaleena's grip was too strong for her. "I thought not," she said, then leaned down and kissed her. Kyla desperately tried to keep her mouth closed as the pungent aroma of smoke swarmed her nostrils. When Kaleena let go, she allowed Kyla to scamper up to the head of the bed, as far away as she could get.

Kaleena sat down on the edge next to her. Kyla considered running, but she

knew deep down that if she did, Kaleena was a goner. To protect her friend, there was nothing she could do except what she was asked to do. It was too risky not to give into the nightmare. She remained stiff as Kaleena untied her robe. Her tears were strong, her fear even stronger as she allowed the monster to expose her chilled body and caress her stomach.

"That's good," Kaleena said, taking in the loveliness of her nakedness. "Kaleena will be forever gracious for your protection." She kissed Kyla's tight, dry lips again. Kyla tried to hide herself from the entire encounter, attempting to pretend it was just a dream; that it wasn't really happening. It was the only way she was going to get through it, hoping it wasn't all in vain; praying she would survive the madness that would follow; that Kaleena would remain safe, as she had been promised.

When Kaleena realized she wouldn't be able to penetrate her lips, she began to taste Kyla's neck and touch her breasts. And in her mind, Cephis was laughing.

Kaleena's own tears fell from her chin as she continued to keep the cracks from spreading through the glass. Cephis's laugh, held over Kyla's tender pain, soon became too much for her. She quickly searched for all of those that had sacrificed for her, all of those that were willing to die for her and all of those that had fought for her and protected her, and used their blooming spirits to inherit a brand new strength upon her heart, helping her to keep Cephis from her body. He roared with rage as Kaleena's spirit rose with power flowing throughout her like a wave of life pouring down upon her.

Standing straight up, Kaleena whipped her head back to the glass, her brown eyes washing over in silver. She had found her spirit's ascendancy over Cephis, which allowed her to leap into his mind with the ease of the wind. She traveled his thoughts until she found herself lying in the calm ocean, opening her eyes for the first time, breathing in the air, feeling the water rinse across her nude body as she had never before felt. The sun shone bright above her and the ocean spoke as it crashed in and on itself. The sensation was more than she could have ever imagined, and she was going to use her new senses to find the knowledge that she sought before Gydressina had stripped her of it.

The retreat from his mind was swift, and like a fishhook, stripped his soul into the darkness.

You raped her, you son of a bitch, Kaleena said as his breath burned through her skin.

And your vehemence can only fuel your desire, my dear, Cephis growled sweetly in her ear.

You lied to her, and you raped her. Just so you could tear us apart.

Such a fire can build a legion. Cephis proudly inhaled her anger. Kaleena wrapped her hands around his neck and squeezed with the force of a python.

It's growing within you, Kaleena. You crave the taste of vengeance.

Kaleena seethed as she stared into him, witnessing her life among him.

You yearn for retribution, and have for a very long time. And now you have the chance to take it. Don't hesitate. I am yours. Take me.

She loosened her grip and relaxed her clenched jaw.

Do as you have dreamed of doing from the moment you read her guilt in your eyes. Find your strength, learn your place and take my life in your hands.

She closed her eyes and stepped away as her spirit healed before him.

Take my life, Kaleena, Cephis roared, attempting to reach out for her. But she kept her distance, spinning around him like the arm of a teacup ride. Every inch he moved closer was an inch she became farther away.

Fuel the hunger you so desperately want to quench, child. Do it now, or find your soul consumed by the darkness of the shadows.

Kaleena suddenly stopped, gone from Cephis's mind. He searched for her, but the longer he did, the sicker he became until his own mind began to melt into a light at the center of his soul. He flushed a fire within it, extinguishing it from his presence. But the moment he did, a fresh light opened elsewhere, forcing him to attack that as well. When the third light opened, he saw Kaleena's angelic features, her gloriously silver eyes staring at him like a ghost, highlighting her bright white hair. She floated up to him, smiling, her heart bleeding with heaven.

Kill me, he said in a long, low growl.

I would, Cephis, if my rage couldn't be sustained. But in my wanderings I've learned a great deal and know much of what good you've done.

Cephis seethed. His spirit was weakening.

I once thought Adamus had rescued me from being attacked. But as I watched, I found that it was not he who saved me from the grip of the monster, but in fact, was you. You protected me from a darkness I never would have found my way back from. You rescued my life from a world of remorse and shame. And for that, dear Cephis, I must thank you.

No! Cephis howled.

I don't hate you, Cephis. I don't seek vengeance upon you because you don't deserve vengeance.

A glow of purity sparked a blaze in his soul.

You've made mistakes under the influence of a darkness you couldn't control, but I know now you're still a friend. I realize you've been manipulated by emotion and knowledge that you didn't understand. And for that, I forgive you.

Kaleena then reached up, lightly taking her adversaries cheeks in her hands, and pulled him from the water where he lain. Cephis tried to break free, but couldn't find the power to move under her touch.

I forgive you, Lord Cephis Satina.

And then she kissed him.

Kaleena's lifeless body dropped to the ground as her kiss entrenched Cephis with the light of her spirit. He backed away from the glass, letting loose a scream so deafening, not one human ear could hear it, but whose souls could feel it like a soft, sudden breeze.

The tension on Matthew's chest eased. He was finally able to open his eyes. Kaleena lay face down on the ground. Fright sent a shot of adrenaline through his body. He slid over to her, pulled her into his lap and held her face in his hands hoping she'd wake. But she was gone. It induced a stream of tears to fall upon her.

Meanwhile, the fog swirled into a flurry of tornadoes. When they didn't seem they could spin any faster, a ray of light shot through the darkness, followed by another. And another. Soon, rays were firing in all directions from the center of the room, burning Cephis's soul beyond non-existence to the end of time and filling everything with a brightness the team had to cower from as they were completely enveloped.

Ocean Water – Time Unknown

Wake up, Kaleena, please. Wake up —

Kaleena's eyes opened gently. She lay naked in the cool, calm ocean, staring up at the glowing sun, her arms stretched out to her sides. She felt comfortable as part of the water. She had no fears and no regrets. She was at the beginning of her life, and would savor every sensation with a magnitude of thousands.

Don't do this. Not now. Wake up, please.

The voice was like a song. Kaleena leaned up out of the water and looked around. No one was with her. *Mom?* she called out, but again, nothing came for her.

Kaleena stood. The ocean moved about her, lapping against her legs with ease and reassurance. She tried to understand the meaning of the words, but they had escaped her.

Mom! she called out again. *Where are you? Come back to me!*

A breeze blew past her. With it came a gentle kiss upon her cheek. It was the tenderness of a friend, the love of a mother. She finally understood the meaning behind the song.

Come back to me.

Dad, she whispered. *Dad, I'm here.*

A flurry of memories flooded back into her mind. Her heart became heavy with a need to return to those she had left behind. She looked around, but all she could see was the clear blue ocean and the horizon of the future.

Gydressina, she called. *Gydressina, I need you. I need your help.*

Kaleena grew frightened that she had been left alone, and wasn't sure if she'd ever be able to find her way back. Then, the water shimmered in the distance. She ran for it without question and stopped at the foot of the long light that had laid itself upon the water.

Gydressina, she said, feeling her heart among the ocean. *Can you help me?*

I'm afraid not, the water spoke.

Why not. Please. I can't die. I can't leave my father behind like this.

I know. You haven't died.

Then where am I?

Where do you believe you are?

Kaleena looked around, unsure. The sun beat down on her mind, keeping it blocked from any form of comprehension.

Do not seek without. You must find your answers within.

Kaleena watched the shimmer float upon the water. Like the light hitting a newborn's eyes, she knew.

The beginning, she said.

She felt Gydressina smile her acknowledgment. Life warmed her body once again, pushing a smile to her own lips.

I have one more request before you go, Gydressina sang.

Anything, Kaleena said.

You must finish the burial of Ediinis. Follow the prison cavern until you can walk no more. It will take several weeks to traverse, but the caves will supply you and your family enough sustenance for your travels. When you reach the end, break the rock wall and allow the ocean to pour in.

Okay, Kaleena said. After a moment of reflection: *Will I ever see you again?*

Not within human form. But I will always be with you. Believe in the touch of the light and you will never be left alone.

Thank you. Kaleena bent down and kissed the surface of the water.

Thank you, Gydressina replied, and within the kiss sent a tickle through Kaleena's body to her ovaries. Kaleena held her stomach with a fresh smile.

Your body will heal in time.

A tear fell from Kaleena's eye as she kissed Gydressina once more. *Goodbye, Love.*

Goodbye, my child.

She then lied down on top of the shimmer and allowed the water to drink her body and consume her breath. She faded into it, leaving the ocean the way Gydressina had entered it — with a calm and fervent whisper.

Atlantis – Caverns – 13 hours 20 minutes after arrival

The light held steady as it tore away at the fog, sucking it up into the space at the heart of the light. When it had consumed every inch of it, the light roared and retracted upon itself, leaving behind the orange flicker from the torches perched on the walls. Patricia and Kara opened their eyes and waited.

"Is it over?" Patricia asked.

Her question was answered with an explosion that ripped through the room. It sent a stream of light through the ceiling of Spirited Wind, which was quickly replaced by a rush of water that poured into the room. Shards of Foxlight Fountain fell into the cavern and were quickly washed through the tunnels with the current to finish what Thomas had started.

Kara was the first to stand when the flow of water calmed. She walked cautiously toward the glass, sad and disappointed. The history of Atlantis had been buried, claimed by the entity that owned and protected it. She pressed her hand to the glass knowing this was probably the closest she'd ever be from knowing the truth about the city's origins. But as she grieved, a series of numbers flashed through her head. She pulled away from the glass, shocked and confused. But the numbers remained. It took a few moments of contemplation to realize what they actually were.

"What's the matter, Reeses?" Patricia said, wiping the dirt off her pants.

"I think she just gave me the coordinates of Atlantis," Kara said to herself, peering at the room like a child seeing a foreign animal for the first time.

"Well, that will definitely make it easier to get back here." Patricia slapped her on the back. Kara looked to her, forgiving her with a light smile and nod.

"Better get yourself a double-wide wetsuit," Kara said, slapping Patricia slightly harder on the back.

"Ha," Patricia bellowed. "Don't think they'll ever find enough material for that." She gave Kara a wink then looked to the glass. "You think she might have a message for me?" She reached out, but stopped just shy of touching it when Matthew's voice rang out.

"Kaleena, don't do this. Wake up, Kaleena, please. Wake up."

He rocked his daughter back and forth, his hands wrapped around her head. "Don't do this. Not now. Wake up, please." Matthew's worst fear was becoming real. He'd seen this moment, had lived this moment, most likely exactly where he sat now. But this time, he knew it wasn't an illusion. This time, it was real, and he wasn't ready to let her go.

Kara knelt down next to him, resting her hand on his shoulder in a fool's attempt at calming him. He'd just lost his wife. There wasn't anything she could say that would comfort him or convince him to let his daughter go as well.

"Come back to me."

"Matthew," she finally said as sweet as a cherub. She wanted to tell him about Diana, about her sacrifice, and how both Kaleena and her sister had helped save them. But as Matthew pulled Kaleena in closer and rested his head against her cheeks — letting out a few nonsensical ramblings in the process — Kara knew it wouldn't do any good. The only thing she knew would work was to do as he did on so many occasions and just be here for him when he was ready to let go. Squeezing his shoulder a bit tighter, Kara lowered her head to his.

"She can't be dead. Please don't let her die."

Patricia simply stood in silence. When Kara looked to her, she shrugged.

"Matthew," Kara said again, a bit stricter. She rested her hand on Kaleena's chest and forced him to lower her. She then grabbed his chin. "Matthew, she's gone."

"No, she can't be," Matthew said. "She can't."

"I'm sorry."

Matthew finally looked up to see Kara's gentle, compassionate eyes. "I'm sorry."

Kaleena's head fell against Matthew's lap as he lay his head against the wall and relaxed his arms. He tried desperately to remove himself from all of it, wanting nothing more than to go back in time and hit a dead end in his search for Atlantis instead of finding that ancient bowl.

Kara touched Kaleena's cheek in a final farewell, then walked back to Patricia. "She was a good kid," she said.

"A great mind," Patricia added. Kara nodded and peered back to the historical records, wondering if they would all meet the same fate soon.

And with that thought, Kaleena opened her eyes and sucked in a deep breath. She sat bolt upright and coughed hard.

Matthew's eyes were wide as she rolled off his lap and continued coughing. Shock filled Patricia and Kara with gracious wonder.

"Kaleena?" Matthew said, his hand hovering over her back, unsure if he should touch her. Kaleena took one last deep breath, then turned to Matthew. "Dad," she said softly, her voice a bit hoarse.

"My god," he said pulling her into the greatest embrace they'd ever have. "I thought you were dead."

"Now why would I want to do that?" she said sweetly. "I'm not stupid, you know."

Matthew's tears were replaced with an enormous, albeit annoyed smile. As they hugged again, Patricia did the only thing she could think of and grabbed Kara, giving her one mighty ass squeeze that nearly popped her arms out of her sockets. Kara squeaked from the pinch and grunted as her body squashed up against Patricia's large chest. When she let go, Kara grabbed her arm in slight pain, but smiled graciously nonetheless.

"Sorry to put a damper on the moment," Patricia finally said, breaking the heavy silence, "but how are we supposed to get out of this mess?" She was pointing to the ocean filled room behind her.

Matthew ignored her and kissed Kaleena on the forehead. There was an overwhelming sense that he had just received yet another miracle from Gydressina. Kaleena, on the other hand, saw the room for the first time. The water had settled and sat still and calm on the other side of the glass. She rubbed her mouth gently. "Ready to visit Bimini?" she asked with a luscious smirk tracing her eyes and lips.

"Bimini?" Matthew repeated. He glanced over at Kara, who held the same look of shocked amazement.

When he looked back to her, Kaleena winked. "Just give me one second," she said.

Matthew nodded and playfully shook her head before she crawled to Gydressina's body. She picked up her hand and bequeathed it a gentle kiss. "Love well, live well, forever." She kissed Gydressina's cheek one last time and with a final squeeze, Kaleena set her hand to the ground, stood up and lowered her head in prayer. Kara followed her lead and folded her hands in front of her. Matthew stood and joined the others with a quick prayer of remembrance and thanks. Patricia, after a moment, decided it was probably the right thing to do and lowered her head, not quite sure what to do from there.

"So, what are we waiting for," Kaleena said quickly after Patricia finally got her hands folded like Kara's. Matthew pulled Kaleena in close and gave her another tender kiss on the forehead. She wrapped her arm around him. For the first time (and certainly not the last) Matthew felt Jaime in her touch.

"You lead," he said. They walked together away from the glass wearing a child's grin and a delightful step. Patricia bowed and presented the way to Kara, who nodded and limped after them, Patricia pulling up the rear.

"So how long's this little trip gonna take, anyway, there, mastermind?" Patricia said.

"A couple of weeks, I think," Kaleena said.

"Weeks?" Patricia said, flabbergasted. "What the hell are we supposed to do for food? I'm already starving and I'd hate to have to eat a Reeses."

"I don't think I'd taste the way you remember," Kara joked. Patricia gave her a quick punch on the shoulder.

"Have I ever told you that I like you," Patricia said, rippling a laugh throughout the group. "By the way," she continued as the laughter died away. "Love the new hair. White suites you." Kaleena flashed Patricia a smile, which was returned with a quick wink.

Within no time, Patricia was singing her odd rendition of *On the Road Again*. Kaleena peered up to Matthew with a huge grin, her silver eyes full of faith and warmth, shining bright against the light of the torches. It was discomforting to look into them, yet extraordinarily fascinating.

Amen Dello Keli

(Love well, live well, forever)

ABOUT THE
AUTHOR

Bryan Caron is a multi-talented, award-winning artist and the creative director/owner of Phoenix Moirai, a company based out of Murrieta that serves as the creative genius behind all of your graphic design, writing and videography needs. Believing it was time to move on from the mundane routine of a nine-to-five job, Bryan pooled all of his talents to start the one-stop creative shop in 2014. As a fledging business owner, Bryan dove headfirst into a world he knew almost nothing about and, like any worthwhile endeavor in life, has learned on the fly, failing and succeeding with every new day. Ultimately, Bryan would like Phoenix Moirai to become not only a world-premiere creative agency for everything related to graphic design, writing and video, but a successful publishing company, capable of competing with the big boys while offering artists more creative freedom, giving them a chance where others wouldn't.

On the artistic side, Bryan has published four novels, several short stories and has written, produced and directed several short and feature films. He currently has several novels and screenplays in various stages of development and is always looking for that next big project he can sink his teeth into.

Bryan resides in Riverside County.

publishing.phoenixmoirai.com